These stories seem at times to be stories of a long-lost world when the city of New York was still filled with a river light, when you heard Benny Goodman quartets from a radio in the corner stationery store, and when almost everybody wore a hat. Here is the last of that generation of chain smokers who woke the world in the morning with their coughing, who used to get stoned at cocktail parties and perform obsolete dance steps like "the Cleveland Chicken," sail for Europe on ships, who were truly nostalgic for love and happiness, and whose gods were as ancient as yours and mine, whoever you are.

JOHN CHEEVER,
from the Preface

"As stories go, as compellingly readable narratives of a certain sort of people in a certain time and place—*our* time and place—John Cheever's stories are, simply, the best."
The Washington Post

"Not merely the publishing event of the 'season' but a grand occasion in English literature."
The New York Times

It was that time of year when the woods are still bleak, and mixed with the smells of rotted and changing things is an unaccountable sweetness—a perfume as heavy as roses—although nothing is in flower. The children went on ahead. Will and Maria walked arm and arm. It was nearly dusk. Crows were calling hoarsely to one another in some tall pines. It was that hour of a spring day—or evening—when the dark of the woods and the cold and damp from any nearby pond or brook are suddenly felt, when you realize that the world was lighted, until a minute ago, merely by the sun's fire, and that your clothes are thin.
—from *Just Tell Me Who It Was*

"THE STORIES OF JOHN CHEEVER IS MASTER STORYTELLING!"
The Los Angeles Times

"John Cheever is a magnificent storyteller, and this is a dazzling and powerful book."
The New Republic

"THE STORIES OF JOHN CHEEVER is a book that immediately takes its place on the rather small shelf that houses the classics of American literature, a book that moves Cheever beyond the bestseller lists and into the company of Hawthorne and Fitzgerald, Melville and Faulkner, Crane and James. I think it safe to say that this is a great book."
The Miami Herald

She turned on the stool and held her thin arms toward him, as she had done more than a thousand times. She was no longer young, and more wan, thinner than she might have been. . . . Her smile, her naked shoulders had begun to trouble the indecipherable shapes and symbols that are the touchstones of desire, and the light from the lamp seemed to brighten and give off heat and shed that unaccountable complacency, that benevolence, that the spring sunlight brings to all kinds of fatigue and despair. Desire for her delighted and confused him. Here it was, here it all was, and the shine of the gold seemed to him then to be all around her arms.
—from *The Pot Of Gold*

"GLORIOUS . . . A FABULOUS BOOK!"
St. Louis Post-Dispatch

Also by John Cheever
Published by Ballantine Books

BULLET PARK

FALCONER

OH WHAT A PARADISE IT SEEMS

THE WAPSHOT CHRONICLE

THE WAPSHOT SCANDAL

The Stories of John Cheever

BALLANTINE BOOKS • NEW YORK

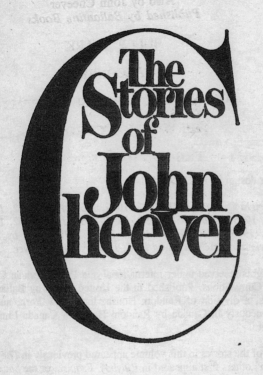

Cover design by R. D. Scudellari

 Published in the United States by Ballantine Books, a division of Random House, Inc., New York, and simultaneously in Canada by Random House of Canada Limited, Toronto.

Most of the stories in this volume appeared previously in *The New Yorker;* others first appeared in *Playboy, Esquire*, or the *Saturday Evening Post*.

Library of Congress Catalog Card Number: 78-160

ISBN 0-345-33567-8

This edition published by arrangement with Alfred A. Knopf, Inc.

Maufactured in the United States of America

First Ballantine Books Edition: March 1980
Ninth Printing: October 1988

CONTENTS

PREFACE

IT WOULD please me if the order in which these stories are published had been reversed and if I appeared first as an elderly man and not as a young one who was truly shocked to discover that genuinely decorous men and women admitted into their affairs erotic bitterness and even greed. The parturition of a writer, I think, unlike that of a painter, does not display any interesting alliances to his masters. In the growth of a writer one finds nothing like the early Jackson Pollock copies of the Sistine Chapel paintings with their interesting cross-references to Thomas Hart Benton. A writer can be seen clumsily learning to walk, to tie his necktie, to make love, and to eat his peas off a fork. He appears much alone and determined to instruct himself. Naïve, provincial in my case, sometimes drunk, sometimes obtuse, almost always clumsy, even a selected display of one's early work will be a naked history of one's struggle to receive an education in economics and love.

These stories date from my Honorable Discharge from the Army at the end of World War II. Their order is, to the best of my memory, chronological and the most embarrassingly immature pieces have been dropped. These stories seem at times to be stories of a long-lost world when the city of New York was still filled with a river light, when you heard the Benny Goodman quartets from a radio in the corner stationery store, and when almost everybody wore a hat. Here is the last of that generation of chain smokers who woke the world in the morning with their coughing, who used to get stoned at cocktail parties and perform obsolete dance steps like "the Cleveland Chicken," sail for Europe on ships, who were truly nostalgic for love and happiness, and whose gods were as ancient as yours and mine, whoever you are. The constants that I look for in this sometimes dated paraphernalia are a love of light and a determination to trace some moral chain of being. Calvin played no part at all in my religious education, but his presence seemed to abide in the barns of my childhood and to have left me with some undue bitterness.

Many of these stories first appeared in *The New Yorker*, where Harold Ross, Gus Lobrano, and William Maxwell gave me the inestimable gifts of a large, discerning, and responsive group of readers and enough money to feed the family and buy a new suit every other year. "This is a family magazine, God damn it," Ross used to yell at any hint at the stirring of erotic drives. He was not himself a decorous man, and when he discovered that I would jump whenever he used the word "fuck" across the lunch table he would frequently say "fuck" and watch me jump. His lack of decorum was, in fact, pronounced and if, for example, he anticipated a dull poker companion, he would go into the bathroom and return with his ears stuffed with toilet paper. This sort of behavior would never, of course, appear in the magazine. But he taught one, I like to think, that decorum is a mode of speech, as profound and connotative as any other, differing not in content but in syntax and imagery. Since the men he encouraged ranged as widely as Irwin Shaw and Vladimir Nabokov, he seems to have done more good than anything else.

Any precise documentation of one's immaturity is embarrassing, and this I find from time to time in the stories, but this embarrassment is redeemed for me by the memories the stories hold for me of the women and men I have loved and the rooms and corridors and beaches where the stories were written. My favorite stories are those that were written in less than a week and that were often composed aloud. I remember exclaiming: "My name is Johnny Hake!" This was in the hallway of a house in Nantucket that we had been able to rent cheaply because of the delayed probating of a will. Coming out of the maid's room in another rented house I shouted to my wife: "This is a night when kings in golden mail ride their elephants over the mountains!" The forbearance of my family has been inestimable. It was under the canopy of a Fifty-ninth Street apartment house that I wrote, aloud, the closing of "Goodbye, My Brother." "Oh, what can you do with a man like that?" I asked, and closed by saying, "I watched the naked women walk out of the sea!" "You're talking to yourself, Mr. Cheever," the doorman said politely, and he too—correct, friendly, and content with his ten-dollar tip at Christmas—seems a figure from the enduring past.

GOODBYE, MY BROTHER

We are a family that has always been very close in spirit. Our father was drowned in a sailing accident when we were young, and our mother had always stressed the fact that our familial relationships have a kind of permanence that we will never meet with again. I don't think about the family much, but when I remember its members and the coast where they lived and the sea salt that I think is in our blood, I am happy to recall that I am a Pommeroy—that I have the nose, the coloring, and the promise of longevity—and that while we are not a distinguished family, we enjoy the illusion, when we are together, that the Pommeroys are unique. I don't say any of this because I'm interested in family history or because this sense of uniqueness is deep or important to me but in order to advance the point that we are loyal to one another in spite of our differences, and that any rupture in this loyalty is a source of confusion and pain.

We are four children; there is my sister Diana and the three men—Chaddy, Lawrence, and myself. Like most families in which the children are out of their twenties, we have been separated by business, marriage, and war. Helen and I live on Long Island now, with our four children. I teach in a secondary school, and I am past the age where I expect to be made headmaster—or principal, as we say—but I respect the work. Chaddy, who has done better than the rest of us, lives in Manhattan, with Odette and their children. Mother lives in Philadelphia, and Diana, since her divorce, has been living in France, but she comes back to the States in the summer to spend a month at Laud's Head. Laud's Head is a summer place on the shore of one of the Massachusetts islands. We used to have a cottage there, and in the twenties our father built the big house. It stands on a cliff above the sea and, excepting St. Tropez and some of the Apennine villages, it is my favorite place in the world. We each have an equity in the place and we contribute some money to help keep it going.

Our youngest brother, Lawrence, who is a lawyer, got a job with a Cleveland firm after the war, and none of us saw him for four years. When he decided to leave Cleveland and go to work for a firm in Albany, he wrote Mother that he would, between jobs, spend ten days at Laud's Head, with his wife and their two children. This was when I had planned to take my vacation—I had been teaching summer school—and Helen and Chaddy and Odette and Diana were all going to be there, so the family would be together. Lawrence is the member of the family with whom the rest of us have least in common. We have never seen a great deal of him, and I suppose that's why we still call him Tifty—a nickname he was given when he was a child, because when he came down the hall toward the dining room for breakfast, his slippers made a noise that sounded like "Tifty, tifty, tifty." That's what Father called him, and so did everyone else. When he grew older, Diana sometimes used to call him Little Jesus, and Mother often called him the Croaker. We had disliked Lawrence, but we looked forward to his return with a mixture of apprehension and loyalty, and with some of the joy and delight of reclaiming a brother.

LAWRENCE crossed over from the mainland on the four-o'clock boat one afternoon late in the summer, and Chaddy and I went down to meet him. The arrivals and departures of the summer ferry have all the outward signs that suggest a voyage—whistles, bells, hand trucks, reunions, and the smell of brine—but it is a voyage of no import, and when I watched the boat come into the blue harbor that afternoon and thought that it was completing a voyage of no import, I realized that I had hit on exactly the kind of observation that Lawrence would have made. We looked for his face behind the windshields as the cars drove off the boat, and we had no trouble in recognizing him. And we ran over and shook his hand and clumsily kissed his wife and the children. "Tifty!" Chaddy shouted. "Tifty!" It is difficult to judge changes in the appearance of a brother, but both Chaddy and I agreed, as we drove back to Laud's Head, that Lawrence still looked very young. He got to the house first, and we took the suitcases out of his car. When I came in, he was standing in the living room, talking with Mother and Diana. They were in their best clothes and all their jewelry, and they were welcoming him extravagantly, but even then, when everyone was endeavoring to seem most affectionate and at a time when these endeavors come easiest, I was aware of a faint tension in the room. Thinking about this as I carried Lawrence's heavy suitcases up the stairs, I realized that our dislikes are as deeply ingrained as our better passions, and I remembered that once, twenty-five years ago, when I had hit Lawrence on the head with a rock, he had picked himself up and gone directly to our father to complain.

I carried the suitcases up to the third floor, where Ruth, Lawrence's wife, had begun to settle her family. She is a thin girl, and she seemed very tired from the journey, but when I asked her if she didn't want me to bring a drink upstairs to her, she said she didn't think she did.

When I got downstairs, Lawrence wasn't around, but the others were all ready for cocktails, and we decided to go ahead. Lawrence is the only member of the family who has never enjoyed drinking. We took our cocktails onto the terrace, so that we could see the bluffs and the sea and the islands in the east, and the return of Lawrence and his wife, their presence in the house, seemed to refresh our responses to the familiar view; it was as if the pleasure they would take in the sweep and the color of that coast, after such a long absence, had been imparted to us. While we were there, Lawrence came up the path from the beach.

"Isn't the beach fabulous, Tifty?" Mother asked. "Isn't it fabulous to be back? Will you have a Martini?"

"I don't care," Lawrence said. "Whiskey, gin—I don't care what I drink. Give me a little rum."

"We don't have any *rum*," Mother said. It was the first note of asperity. She had taught us never to be indecisive, never to reply as Lawrence had. Beyond this, she is deeply concerned with the propriety of her house, and anything irregular by her standards, like drinking straight rum or bringing a beer can to the dinner table, excites in her a conflict that she cannot, even with her capacious sense of humor, surmount. She sensed the asperity and worked to repair it. "Would you like some Irish, Tifty dear?" she said. "Isn't Irish what you've always liked? There's some Irish on the sideboard. Why don't you get yourself some Irish?" Lawrence said that he didn't care. He poured himself a Martini, and then Ruth came down and we went in to dinner.

In spite of the fact that we had, through waiting for Lawrence, drunk too much before dinner, we were all anxious to put our best foot forward and to enjoy a peaceful time. Mother is a small woman whose face is still a striking reminder of how pretty she must have been, and whose conversation is unusually light, but she talked that evening about a soil-reclamation project that is going on up-island. Diana is as pretty as Mother must have been; she is an animated and lovely woman who likes to talk about the dissolute friends that she had made in France, but she talked that night about the school in Switzerland where she had left her two children. I could see that the dinner had been planned to please Lawrence. It was not too rich, and there was nothing to make him worry about extravagance.

After supper, when we went back onto the terrace, the clouds held that kind of light that looks like blood, and I was glad that Lawrence had such a lurid sunset for his homecoming. When we had been out there a few minutes, a man named Edward Chester came to get Diana. She had met him in France, or on the boat home, and he was staying for ten days at the inn in the village. He was introduced to Lawrence and Ruth, and then he and Diana left.

"Is that the one she's sleeping with now?" Lawrence asked.

"What a horrid thing to say!" Helen said.

"You ought to apologize for that, Tifty," Chaddy said.

"I don't know," Mother said tiredly. "I don't know, Tifty. Diana is in a position to do whatever she wants, and I don't ask sordid questions. She's my only daughter. I don't see her often."

"Is she going back to France?"

"She's going back the week after next."

Lawrence and Ruth were sitting at the edge of the terrace, not in the chairs, not in the circle of chairs. With his mouth set, my brother looked to me then like a Puritan cleric. Sometimes, when I try to understand his frame of mind, I think of the beginnings of our family in this country, and his disapproval of Diana and her lover reminded me of this. The branch of the Pommeroys to which we belong was founded by a minister who was eulogized by Cotton Mather for his untiring abjuration of the Devil. The Pommeroys were ministers until the middle of the nineteenth century, and the harshness of their thought—man is full of misery, and all earthly beauty is lustful and corrupt—has been preserved in books and sermons. The temper of our family changed somewhat and became more lighthearted, but when I was of school age, I can remember a cousinage of old men and women who seemed to hark back to the dark days of the ministry and to be animated by perpetual guilt and the deification of the scourge. If you are raised in this atmosphere—and in a sense we were—I think it is a trial of the spirit to reject its habits of guilt, self-denial, taciturnity, and penitence, and it seemed to me to have been a trial of the spirit in which Lawrence had succumbed.

"Is that Cassiopeia?" Odette asked.

"No, dear," Chaddy said. "That isn't Cassiopeia."

"Who was Cassiopeia?" Odette said.

"She was the wife of Cepheus and the mother of Andromeda," I said.

"The cook is a Giants fan," Chaddy said. "She'll give you even money that they win the pennant."

It had grown so dark that we could see the passage of light through the sky from the lighthouse at Cape Heron. In the dark below the cliff, the continual detonations of the surf sounded. And then, as she often does when it is getting dark and she has drunk too much before dinner, Mother began to talk about the improvements and additions that would someday be made on the house, the wings and bathrooms and gardens.

"This house will be in the sea in five years," Lawrence said.

"Tifty the Croaker," Chaddy said.

"Don't call me Tifty," Lawrence said.

"Little Jesus," Chaddy said.

"The sea wall is badly cracked," Lawrence said. "I looked at it this afternoon. You had it repaired four years ago, and it cost eight thousand dollars. You can't do that every four years."

"Please, Tifty," Mother said.

"Facts are facts," Lawrence said, "and it's a damned-fool idea to build a house at the edge of the cliff on a sinking coastline. In my lifetime, half the garden has washed away and there's four feet of water where we used to have a bathhouse."

"Let's have a very *general* conversation," Mother said bitterly. "Let's talk about politics or the boat-club dance."

"As a matter of fact," Lawrence said, "the house is probably in some danger now. If you had an unusually high sea, a hurricane sea, the wall would crumble and the house would go. We could all be drowned."

"I can't *bear* it," Mother said. She went into the pantry and came back with a full glass of gin.

I have grown too old now to think that I can judge the sentiments of others, but I was conscious of the tension between Lawrence and Mother, and I knew some of the history of it. Lawrence couldn't have been more than sixteen years old when he decided that Mother was frivolous, mischievous, destructive, and overly strong. When he had determined this, he decided to separate himself from her. He was at boarding school then, and I remember that he did not come home for Christmas. He spent Christmas with a friend. He came home very seldom after he had made his unfavorable judgment on Mother, and when he did come home, he always tried, in his conversation, to remind her of his estrangement. When he married Ruth, he did not tell Mother. He did not tell her when his children were born. But in spite of these principled and lengthy exertions he seemed, unlike the rest of us, never to have enjoyed any separation, and when they are together, you feel at once a tension, an unclearness.

And it was unfortunate, in a way, that Mother should have picked that night to get drunk. It's her privilege, and she doesn't get drunk often, and fortunately she wasn't bellicose, but we were all conscious of what was happening. As she quietly drank her gin, she seemed sadly to be parting from us; she seemed to be in the throes of travel. Then her mood changed from travel to injury, and the few remarks she made were petulant and irrelevant. When her glass was nearly empty, she stared angrily at the dark air in front of her nose, moving her head a little, like a fighter. I knew that there was not room in her mind then for all the injuries that were crowding into it. Her children were stupid, her husband was drowned, her servants were thieves, and the chair she sat in was uncomfortable. Suddenly she put down her empty glass and interrupted Chaddy, who was talking about baseball. "I know one *thing*," she said hoarsely. "I know that if there is an afterlife, I'm going to have a very different kind of family. I'm going to have nothing but fabulously rich, witty, and enchanting children." She got up and, starting for the door, nearly fell. Chaddy caught her and helped her up the stairs. I could hear their tender good-nights, and then Chaddy came back. I thought that Lawrence by now would be tired from his journey and his return, but he remained on the terrace, as if he were waiting to see the final malfeasance, and the rest of us left him there and went swimming in the dark.

WHEN I WOKE the next morning, or half woke, I could hear the sound of someone rolling the tennis court. It is a fainter and a deeper sound than the iron buoy bells off the point—an unrhythmic iron chiming—that belongs in my mind to the beginnings of a summer day, a good portent. When I went downstairs, Lawrence's two kids were in the living room, dressed in ornate cowboy suits. They are frightened and skinny children. They told me their father was rolling the tennis court but that they did not want to go out because they had seen a snake under the doorstep. I explained to them that their cousins—all the other children—ate breakfast in the kitchen and that they'd better run along in there. At this announcement, the boy began to cry. Then his sister joined him. They cried as if to go in the kitchen and eat would destroy their most precious rights. I told them to sit down with me. Lawrence came in, and I asked him if he wanted to play some tennis. He said no, thanks, although he thought he might play some singles with Chaddy. He was in the right here, because both he and Chaddy play better tennis than I, and he did play some singles with Chaddy after breakfast, but later on, when the others came down to play family doubles, Lawrence disappeared. This made me cross—unreasonably so, I suppose—but we play darned interesting family doubles and he could have played in a set for the sake of courtesy.

Late in the morning, when I came up from the court alone, I saw Tifty on the terrace, prying up a shingle from the wall with his jackknife. "What's the matter, Lawrence?" I said. "Termites?" There are termites in the wood and they've given us a lot of trouble.

He pointed out to me, at the base of each row of shingles, a faint blue line of carpenter's chalk. "This house is about twenty-two years old," he said. "These shingles are about two hundred years old. Dad must have bought shingles from all the farms around here when he built the place, to make it look venerable. You can still see the carpenter's chalk put down where these antiques were nailed into place."

It was true about the shingles, although I had forgotten it. When the house was built, our father, or his architect, had ordered it covered with lichened and weather-beaten shingles. I didn't follow Lawrence's reasons for thinking that this was scandalous.

"And look at these doors," Lawrence said. "Look at these doors and window frames." I followed him over to a big Dutch door that opens onto the terrace and looked at it. It was a relatively new door, but someone had worked hard to conceal its newness. The surface had been deeply scored with some metal implement, and white paint had been rubbed into the incisions to imitate brine, lichen, and weather rot. "Imagine spending thousands of dollars to make a sound house look like a wreck," Lawrence said. "Imagine the frame of mind this implies. Imagine wanting to live so much in the past that you'll pay men carpenters' wages to disfigure your front door." Then I remembered Lawrence's sensitivity to time and his sentiments and opinions about our feelings for the past. I had heard him say, years ago, that we and our friends and our part of the nation, finding ourselves unable to cope with the problems of the present, had, like a wretched adult, turned back to what we supposed was a happier and a simpler time, and that our taste for reconstruction and candlelight was a measure of this irremediable failure. The faint blue line of chalk had reminded him of these ideas, the scarified door had reinforced them, and now clue after clue presented itself to him—the stern light at the door, the bulk of the chimney, the width of the floorboards and the pieces set into them to resemble pegs. While Lawrence was lecturing me on these frailties, the others came up from the court. As soon as Mother saw Lawrence, she responded, and I saw that there was little hope of any rapport between the matriarch and the changeling. She took Chaddy's arm. "Let's go swimming and have Martinis on the beach," she said. "Let's have a *fabulous* morning."

The sea that morning was a solid color, like verd stone. Everyone went to the beach but Tifty and Ruth. "I don't mind *him*," Mother said. She was excited, and she tipped her glass and spilled some gin into the sand. "I don't mind *him*. It doesn't matter to me how *rude* and *horrid* and *gloomy* he is, but what I can't bear are the faces of his wretched little children, those fabulously unhappy little children." With the height of the cliff between us, everyone talked wrathfully about Lawrence; about how he had grown worse instead of better, how unlike the rest of us he was, how he endeavored to spoil every pleasure. We drank our gin; the abuse seemed to reach a crescendo, and then, one by one, we went swimming in the solid green water. But when we came out no one mentioned Lawrence unkindly; the line of abusive conversation had been cut, as if swimming had the cleansing force claimed for baptism. We dried our hands and lighted cigarettes, and if Lawrence was mentioned, it was only to suggest, kindly, something that might please him. Wouldn't he like to sail to Barin's cove, or go fishing?

And now I remember that while Lawrence was visiting us, we went swimming oftener than we usually do, and I think there was a reason for this. When the irritability that accumulated as a result of his company began to lessen our patience, not only with Lawrence but with one another, we would all go swimming and shed our animus in the cold water. I can see the family now, smarting from Lawrence's rebukes as they sat on the sand, and I can see them wading and diving and surface-diving and hear in their voices the restoration of patience and the rediscovery of inexhaustible good will. If Lawrence noticed this change—this illusion of purification—I suppose that he would have found in the vocabulary of psychiatry, or the mythology of the Atlantic, some circumspect name for it, but I don't think he noticed the change. He neglected to name the curative powers of the open sea, but it was one of the few chances for diminution that he missed.

The cook we had that year was a Polish woman named Anna Ostrovick, a summer cook. She was first-rate—a big, fat, hearty, industrious woman who took her work seriously. She liked to cook and to have the food she cooked appreciated and eaten, and whenever we saw her, she always urged us to eat. She cooked hot bread—crescents and brioches—for breakfast two or three times a week, and she would bring these into the dining room herself and say, "Eat, eat, eat!" When the maid took the serving dishes back into the pantry, we could sometimes hear Anna, who was standing there, say, "Good! They eat." She fed the garbage man, the milkman, and the gardener. "Eat!" she told them. "Eat, eat!" On Thursday afternoons, she went to the movies with the maid, but she didn't enjoy the movies, because the actors were all so thin. She would sit in the dark theatre for an hour and a half watching the screen anxiously for the appearance of someone who had enjoyed his food. Bette Davis merely left with Anna the impression of a woman who has not eaten well. "They are all so skinny," she would say when she left the movies. In the evenings, after she had gorged all of us, and washed the pots and pans, she would collect the table scraps and go out to feed the creation. We had a few chickens that year, and although they would have roosted by then, she would dump food into their troughs and urge the sleeping fowl to eat. She fed the songbirds in the orchard and the chipmunks in the yard. Her appearance at the edge of the garden and her urgent voice—we could hear her calling "Eat, eat, eat"—had become, like the sunset gun at the boat club and the passage of light from Cape Heron, attached to that hour. "Eat, eat, eat," we could hear Anna say. "Eat, eat . . ." Then it would be dark.

When Lawrence had been there three days, Anna called me into the kitchen. "You tell your mother," she said, "that *he* doesn't come into my kitchen. If *he* comes into my kitchen all the time, I go. *He* is always coming into my kitchen to tell me what a sad woman I am. He is always telling me that I work too hard and that I don't get paid enough and that I should belong to a union with vacations. Ha! He is so skinny but he is always coming into my kitchen when I am busy to pity me, but I am as good as him, I am as good as *anybody*, and I do not have to have people like that getting into my way all the time and feeling sorry for me. I am a famous and a wonderful cook and I have jobs everywhere and the only reason I come here to work this summer is because I was never before on an island, but I can have other jobs tomorrow, and if he is always coming into my kitchen to pity me, you tell your mother I am going. I am as good as *anybody* and I do not have to have that skinny all the time telling how poor I am."

I was pleased to find that the cook was on our side, but I felt that the situation was delicate. If Mother asked Lawrence to stay out of the kitchen, he would make a grievance out of the request. He could make a grievance out of anything, and it sometimes seemed that as he sat darkly at the dinner table, every word of disparagement, wherever it was aimed, came home to him. I didn't mention the cook's complaint to anyone, but somehow there wasn't any more trouble from that quarter.

The next cause for contention that I had from Lawrence came over our backgammon games.

When we are at Laud's Head, we play a lot of backgammon. At eight o'clock, after we have drunk our coffee, we usually get out the board. In a way, it is one of our pleasantest hours. The lamps in the room are still unlighted, Anna can be seen in the dark garden, and in the sky above her head there are continents of shadow and fire. Mother turns on the light and rattles the dice as a signal. We usually play three games apiece, each with the others. We play for money, and you can win or lose a hundred dollars on a game, but the stakes are usually much lower. I think that Lawrence used to play—I can't remember—but he doesn't play any more. He doesn't gamble. This is not because he is poor or because he has any principles about gambling but because he thinks the game is foolish and a waste of time. He was ready enough, however, to waste his time watching the rest of us play. Night after night, when the game began, he pulled a chair up beside the board, and watched the checkers and the dice. His expression was scornful, and yet he watched carefully. I wondered why he watched us night after night, and, through watching his face, I think that I may have found out.

Lawrence doesn't gamble, so he can't understand the excitement of winning and losing money. He has forgotten how to play the game, I think, so that its complex odds can't interest him. His observations were bound to include the facts that backgammon is an idle game and a game of chance, and that the board, marked with points, was a symbol of our worthlessness. And since he doesn't understand gambling or the odds of the game, I thought that what interested him must be the members of his family. One night when I was playing with Odette—I had won thirty-seven dollars from Mother and Chaddy—I think I saw what was going on in his mind.

Odette has black hair and black eyes. She is careful never to expose her white skin to the sun for long, so the striking contrast of blackness and pallor is not changed in the summer. She needs and deserves admiration—it is the element that contents her—and she will flirt, unseriously, with any man. Her shoulders were bare that night, her dress was cut to show the division of her breasts and to show her breasts when she leaned over the board to play. She kept losing and flirting and making her losses seem like a part of the flirtation. Chaddy was in the other room. She lost three games, and when the third game ended, she fell back on the sofa and, looking at me squarely, said something about going out on the dunes to settle the score. Lawrence heard her. I looked at Lawrence. He seemed shocked and gratified at the same time, as if he had suspected all along that we were not playing for anything so insubstantial as money. I may be wrong, of course, but I think that Lawrence felt that in watching our backgammon he was observing the progress of a mordant tragedy in which the money we won and lost served as a symbol for more vital forfeits. It is like Lawrence to try to read significance and finality into every gesture that we make, and it is certain of Lawrence that when he finds the inner logic to our conduct, it will be sordid.

Chaddy came in to play with me. Chaddy and I have never liked to lose to each other. When we were younger, we used to be forbidden to play games together, because they always ended in a fight. We think we know each other's mettle intimately. I think he is prudent; he thinks I am foolish. There is always bad blood when we play anything—tennis or backgammon or softball or bridge—and it does seem at times as if we were playing for the possession of each other's liberties. When I lose to Chaddy, I can't sleep. All this is only half the truth of our competitive relationship, but it was the half-truth that would be discernible to Lawrence, and his presence at the table made me so self-conscious that I lost two games. I tried not to seem angry when I got up from the board. Lawrence was watching me. I went out onto the terrace to suffer there in the dark the anger I always feel when I lose to Chaddy.

When I came back into the room, Chaddy and Mother were playing. Lawrence was still watching. By his lights, Odette had lost her virtue to me, I had lost my self-esteem to Chaddy, and now I wondered what he saw in the present match. He watched raptly, as if the opaque checkers and the marked board served for an exchange of critical power. How dramatic the board, in its ring of light, and the quiet players and the crash of the sea outside must have seemed to him! Here was spiritual cannibalism made visible; here, under his nose, were the symbols of the rapacious use human beings make of one another.

Mother plays a shrewd, an ardent, and an interfering game. She always has her hands in her opponent's board. When she plays with Chaddy, who is her favorite, she plays intently. Lawrence would have noticed this. Mother is a sentimental woman. Her heart is good and easily moved by tears and frailty, a characteristic that, like her handsome nose, has not been changed at all by age. Grief in another provokes her deeply, and she seems at times to be trying to divine in Chaddy some grief, some loss, that she can succor and redress, and so re-establish the relationship that she enjoyed with him when he was sickly and young. She loves defending the weak and the childlike, and now that we are old, she misses it. The world of debts and business, men and war, hunting and fishing has on her an exacerbating effect. (When Father drowned, she threw away his fly rods and his guns.) She has lectured us all endlessly on self-reliance, but when we come back to her for comfort and for help—particularly Chaddy—she seems to feel most like herself. I suppose Lawrence thought that the old woman and her son were playing for each other's soul.

She lost. "Oh *dear,*" she said. She looked stricken and bereaved, as she always does when she loses. "Get me my glasses, get me my checkbook, get me something to drink." Lawrence got up at last and stretched his legs. He looked at us all bleakly. The wind and the sea had risen, and I thought that if he heard the waves, he must hear them only as a dark answer to all his dark questions; that he would think that the tide had expunged the embers of our picnic fires. The company of a lie is unbearable, and he seemed like the embodiment of a lie. I couldn't explain to him the simple and intense pleasures of playing for money, and it seemed to me hideously wrong that he should have sat at the edge of the board and concluded that we were playing for one another's soul. He walked restlessly around the room two or three times and then, as usual, gave us a parting shot. "I should think you'd go crazy," he said, "cooped up with one another like this, night after night. Come on, Ruth. I'm going to bed."

THAT NIGHT, I dreamed about Lawrence. I saw his plain face magnified into ugliness, and when I woke in the morning, I felt sick, as if I had suffered a great spiritual loss while I slept, like the loss of courage and heart. It was foolish to let myself be troubled by my brother. I needed a vacation. I needed to relax. At school, we live in one of the dormitories, we eat at the house table, and we never get away. I not only teach English winter and summer but I work in the principal's office and fire the pistol at track meets. I needed to get away from this and from every other form of anxiety, and I decided to avoid my brother. Early that day, I took Helen and the children sailing, and we stayed out until suppertime. The next day, we went on a picnic. Then I had to go to New York for a day, and when I got back, there was the costume dance at the boat club. Lawrence wasn't going to this, and it's a party where I always have a wonderful time.

The invitations that year said to come as you wish you were. After several conversations, Helen and I had decided what to wear. The thing she most wanted to be again, she said, was a bride, and so she decided to wear her wedding dress. I thought this was a good choice—sincere, lighthearted, and inexpensive. Her choice influenced mine, and I decided to wear an old football uniform. Mother decided to go as Jenny Lind, because there was an old Jenny Lind costume in the attic. The others decided to rent costumes, and when I went to New York, I got the clothes. Lawrence and Ruth didn't enter into any of this.

Helen was on the dance committee, and she spent most of Friday decorating the club. Diana and Chaddy and I went sailing. Most of the sailing that I do these days is in Manhasset, and I am used to setting a homeward course by the gasoline barge and the tin roofs of the boat shed, and it was a pleasure that afternoon, as we returned, to keep the bow on a white church spire in the village and to find even the inshore water green and clear. At the end of our sail, we stopped at the club to get Helen. The committee had been trying to give a submarine appearance to the ballroom, and the fact that they had nearly succeeded in accomplishing this illusion made Helen very happy. We drove back to Laud's Head. It had been a brilliant afternoon, but on the way home we could smell the east wind—the dark wind, as Lawrence would have said—coming in from the sea.

My wife, Helen, is thirty-eight, and her hair would be gray, I guess, if it were not dyed, but it is dyed an unobtrusive yellow—a faded color—and I think it becomes her. I mixed cocktails that night while she was dressing, and when I took a glass upstairs to her, I saw her for the first time since our marriage in her wedding dress. There would be no point in saying that she looked to me more beautiful than she did on our wedding day, but because I have grown older and have, I think, a greater depth of feeling, and because I could see in her face that night both youth and age, both her devotion to the young woman that she had been and the positions that she had yielded graciously to time, I think I have never been so deeply moved. I had already put on the football uniform, and the weight of it, the heaviness of the pants and the shoulder guards, had worked a change in me, as if in putting on these old clothes I had put off the reasonable anxieties and troubles of my life. It felt as if we had both returned to the years before our marriage, the years before the war.

The Collards had a big dinner party before the dance, and our family—excepting Lawrence and Ruth—went to this. We drove over to the club, through the fog, at about half past nine. The orchestra was playing a waltz. While I was checking my raincoat, someone hit me on the back. It was Chucky Ewing, and the funny thing was that Chucky had on a football uniform. This seemed comical as hell to both of us. We were laughing when we went down the hall to the dance floor. I stopped at the door to look at the party, and it was beautiful. The committee had hung fish nets around the sides and over the high ceiling. The nets on the ceiling were filled with colored balloons. The light was soft and uneven, and the people—our friends and neighbors—dancing in the soft light to "Three O'Clock in the Morning" made a pretty picture. Then I noticed the number of women dressed in white, and I realized that they, like Helen, were wearing wedding dresses. Patsy Hewitt and Mrs. Gear and the Lackland girl waltzed by, dressed as brides. Then Pep Talcott came over to where Chucky and I were standing. He was dressed to be Henry VIII, but he told us that the Auerbach twins and Henry Barrett and Dwight MacGregor were all wearing football uniforms, and that by the last count there were ten brides on the floor.

This coincidence, this funny coincidence, kept everybody laughing, and made this one of the most lighthearted parties we've ever had at the club. At first I thought that the women had planned with one another to wear wedding dresses, but the ones that I danced with said it was a coincidence and I'm sure that Helen had made her decision alone. Everything went smoothly for me until a little before midnight. I saw Ruth standing at the edge of the floor. She was wearing a long red dress. It was all wrong. It wasn't the spirit of the party at all. I danced with her, but no one cut in, and I was darned if I'd spend the rest of the night dancing with her and I asked her where Lawrence was. She said he was out on the dock, and I took her over to the bar and left her and went out to get Lawrence.

The east fog was thick and wet, and he was alone on

the dock. He was not in costume. He had not even bothered to get himself up as a fisherman or a sailor. He looked particularly saturnine. The fog blew around us like a cold smoke. I wished that it had been a clear night, because the easterly fog seemed to play into my misanthropic brother's hands. And I knew that the buoys—the groaners and bells that we could hear then—would sound to him like half-human, half-drowned cries, although every sailor knows that buoys are necessary and reliable fixtures, and I knew that the foghorn at the lighthouse would mean wanderings and losses to him and that he could misconstrue the vivacity of the dance music. "Come on in, Tifty," I said, "and dance with your wife or get her some partners."

"Why should I?" he said. "Why should I?" And he walked to the window and looked in at the party. "Look at it," he said. "Look at that . . ."

Chucky Ewing had got hold of a balloon and was trying to organize a scrimmage line in the middle of the floor. The others were dancing a samba. And I knew that Lawrence was looking bleakly at the party as he had looked at the weather-beaten shingles on our house, as if he saw here an abuse and a distortion of time; as if in wanting to be brides and football players we exposed the fact that, the lights of youth having been put out in us, we had been unable to find other lights to go by and, destitute of faith and principle, had become foolish and sad. And that he was thinking this about so many kind and happy and generous people made me angry, made me feel for him such an unnatural abhorrence that I was ashamed, for he is my brother and a Pommeroy. I put my arm around his shoulders and tried to force him to come in, but he wouldn't.

I got back in time for the Grand March, and after the prizes had been given out for the best costumes, they let the balloons down. The room was hot, and someone opened the big doors onto the dock, and the easterly wind circled the room and went out, carrying across the dock and out onto the water most of the balloons. Chucky Ewing went running out after the balloons, and when he saw them pass the dock and settle on the water, he took off his football uniform and dove in. Then Eric Auerbach dove in and Lew Phillips dove in and I dove in, and you know how it is at a party after midnight when people start jumping into the water. We recovered most of the balloons and dried off and went on dancing, and we didn't get home until morning.

THE NEXT DAY was the day of the flower show. Mother and Helen and Odette all had entries. We had a pickup lunch, and Chaddy drove the women and children over to the show. I took a nap, and in the middle of the afternoon I got some trunks and a towel and, on leaving the house, passed Ruth in the laundry. She was washing clothes. I don't know why she should seem to have so much more work to do than anyone else, but she is always washing or ironing or mending clothes. She may have been taught, when she was young, to spend her time like this, or she may be at the mercy of an expiatory passion. She seems to scrub and iron with a penitential fervor, although I can't imagine what it is that she thinks she's done wrong. Her children were with her in the laundry. I offered to take them to the beach, but they didn't want to go.

It was late in August, and the wild grapes that grow profusely all over the island made the land wind smell of wine. There is a little grove of holly at the end of the path, and then you climb the dunes, where nothing grows but that coarse grass. I could hear the sea, and I remember thinking how Chaddy and I used to talk mystically about the sea. When we were young, we had decided that we could never live in the West because we would miss the sea. "It is very nice here," we used to say politely when we visited people in the mountains, "but we miss the Atlantic." We used to look down our noses at people from Iowa and Colorado who had been denied this revelation, and we scorned the Pacific. Now I could hear the waves, whose heaviness sounded like a reverberation, like a tumult, and it pleased me as it had pleased me when I was young, and it seemed to have a purgative force, as if it had cleared my memory of, among other things, the penitential image of Ruth in the laundry.

But Lawrence was on the beach. There he sat. I went in without speaking. The water was cold, and when I came out, I put on a shirt. I told him that I was going to walk up to Tanners Point, and he said that he would come with me. I tried to walk beside him. His legs are no longer than mine, but he always likes to stay a little ahead of his companion. Walking along behind him, looking at his bent head and his shoulders, I wondered what he could make of that landscape.

There were the dunes and cliffs, and then, where they declined, there were some fields that had begun to turn from green to brown and yellow. The fields were used for pasturing sheep, and I guess Lawrence would have noticed that the soil was eroded and that the sheep would accelerate this decay. Beyond the fields there are a few coastal farms, with square and pleasant buildings, but Lawrence could have pointed out the hard lot of an island farmer. The sea, at our other side, was the open sea. We always tell guests that there, to the east, lies the coast of Portugal, and for Lawrence it would be an easy step from the coast of Portugal to the tyranny in Spain. The waves broke with a noise like a "hurrah, hurrah, hurrah," but to Lawrence they would say "*Vale, vale.*" I suppose it would have occurred to his baleful and incisive mind that the coast was terminal moraine, the edge of the prehistoric world, and it must have occurred to him that we walked along the edge of the known world in spirit as much as in fact. If he should otherwise have overlooked this, there were some Navy planes bombing an uninhabited island to remind him.

That beach is a vast and preternaturally clean and simple landscape. It is like a piece of the moon. The surf had pounded the floor solid, so it was easy walking, and everything left on the sand had been twice changed by the waves. There was the spine of a shell, a broomstick, part of a bottle and part of a brick, both of them milled and broken until they were nearly unrecognizable, and I suppose Lawrence's sad frame of mind—for he kept his head down—went from one broken thing to another. The company of his pessimism began to infuriate me, and I caught up with him and put a hand on his shoulder. "It's only a summer day, Tifty," I said. "It's only a summer day. What's the matter? Don't you like it here?"

"I don't like it here," he said blandly, without raising his eyes. "I'm going to sell my equity in the house to Chaddy.

I didn't expect to have a good time. The only reason I came back was to say goodbye."

I let him get ahead again and I walked behind him, looking at his shoulders and thinking of all the goodbyes he had made. When Father drowned, he went to church and said goodbye to Father. It was only three years later that he concluded that Mother was frivolous and said goodbye to her. In his freshman year at college, he had been very good friends with his roommate, but the man drank too much, and at the beginning of the spring term Lawrence changed roommates and said goodbye to his friend. When he had been in college for two years, he concluded that the atmosphere was too sequestered and he said goodbye to Yale. He enrolled at Columbia and got his law degree there, but he found his first employer dishonest, and at the end of six months he said goodbye to a good job. He married Ruth in City Hall and said goodbye to the Protestant Episcopal Church; they went to live on a back street in Tuckahoe and said goodbye to the middle class. In 1938, he went to Washington to work as a government lawyer, saying goodbye to private enterprise, but after eight months in Washington he concluded that the Roosevelt administration was sentimental and he said goodbye to it. They left Washington for a suburb of Chicago, where he said goodbye to his neighbors, one by one, on counts of drunkenness, boorishness, and stupidity. He said goodbye to Chicago and went to Kansas; he said goodbye to Kansas and went to Cleveland. Now he had said goodbye to Cleveland and come East again, stopping at Laud's Head long enough to say goodbye to the sea.

It was elegiac and it was bigoted and narrow, it mistook circumspection for character, and I wanted to help him. "Come out of it," I said. "Come out of it, Tifty."

"Come out of what?"

"Come out of this gloominess. Come out of it. It's only a summer day. You're spoiling your own good time and you're spoiling everyone else's. We need a vacation, Tifty. I need one. I need to rest. We all do. And you've made everything tense and unpleasant. I only have two weeks in the year. Two weeks. I need to have a good time and so do all the others. We need to rest. You think that your pessimism is an advantage, but it's nothing but an unwillingness to grasp realities."

"What are the realities?" he said. "Diana is a foolish promiscuous woman. So is Odette. Mother is an alcoholic. If she doesn't discipline herself, she'll be in a hospital in a year or two. Chaddy is dishonest. He always has been. The house is going to fall into the sea." He looked at me and added, as an afterthought, "You're a fool."

"You're a gloomy son of a bitch," I said. "You're a gloomy son of a bitch."

"Get your fat face out of mine," he said. He walked along.

Then I picked up a root and, coming at his back—although I have never hit a man from the back before—I swung the root, heavy with sea water, behind me, and the momentum sped my arm and I gave him, my brother, a blow on the head that forced him to his knees on the sand, and I saw the blood come out and begin to darken his hair. Then I wished that he was dead, dead and about to be buried, not buried but about to be buried, because I did not want to be denied ceremony and decorum in putting him away, in putting him out of my consciousness, and I saw the rest of us—Chaddy and Mother and Diana and Helen—in mourning in the house on Belvedere Street that was torn down twenty years ago, greeting our guests and our relatives at the door and answering their mannerly condolences with mannerly grief. Nothing decorous was lacking so that even if he had been murdered on a beach, one would feel before the tiresome ceremony ended that he had come into the winter of his life and that it was a law of nature, and a beautiful one, that Tifty should be buried in the cold, cold ground.

He was still on his knees. I looked up and down. No one had seen us. The naked beach, like a piece of the moon, reached to invisibility. The spill of a wave, in a glancing run, shot up to where he knelt. I would still have liked to end him, but now I had begun to act like two men, the murderer and the Samaritan. With a swift roar, like hollowness made sound, a white wave reached him and encircled him, boiling over his shoulders, and I held him against the undertow. Then I led him to a higher place. The blood had spread all through his hair, so that it looked black. I took off my shirt and tore it to bind up his head. He was conscious, and I didn't think he was badly hurt. He didn't speak. Neither did I. Then I left him there.

I walked a little way down the beach and turned to watch him, and I was thinking of my own skin then. He had got to his feet and he seemed steady. The daylight was still clear, but on the sea wind fumes of brine were blowing in like a light fog, and when I had walked a little way from him, I could hardly see his dark figure in this obscurity. All down the beach I could see the heavy salt air blowing in. Then I turned my back on him, and as I got near the house, I went swimming again, as I seem to have done after every encounter with Lawrence that summer.

When I got to the house, I lay down on the terrace. The others came back. I could hear Mother defaming the flower arrangements that had won prizes. None of ours had won anything. Then the house quieted, as it always does at that hour. The children went into the kitchen to get supper and the others went upstairs to bathe. Then I heard Chaddy making cocktails, and the conversation about the flower show judges was resumed. Then Mother cried, "Tifty! Tifty! Oh, Tifty!"

He stood in the door, looking half dead. He had taken off the bloody bandage and he held it in his hand. "My brother did this," he said. "My brother did it. He hit me with a stone—something—on the beach." His voice broke with self-pity. I thought he was going to cry. No one else spoke. "Where's Ruth?" he cried. "Where's Ruth? Where in hell is Ruth? I want her to start packing. I don't have any more time to waste here. I have important things to do. I have *important* things to do." And he went up the stairs.

THEY LEFT for the mainland the next morning, taking the six-o'clock boat. Mother got up to say goodbye, but she was the only one, and it is a harsh and an easy scene to imagine—the matriarch and the changeling, looking at each other with a dismay that would seem like the powers of love reversed. I heard the children's voices and the car go down the drive, and I got up and went to the window, and what a morning that was! Jesus, what a morning! The wind was northerly. The air was clear. In the early heat, the roses in the garden smelled like strawberry jam. While I was dressing, I heard the boat whistle, first the warning signal and then the double blast, and I could see the good people on the top deck drinking coffee out of fragile paper cups, and Lawrence at the bow, saying to the sea, *"Thalassa, thalassa,"* while his timid and unhappy children watched the creation from the encirclement of their mother's arms. The buoys would toll mournfully for Lawrence, and while the grace of the light would make it an exertion not to throw out your arms and swear exultantly, Lawrence's eyes would trace the black sea as it fell astern; he would think of the bottom, dark and strange, where full fathom five our father lies.

Oh, what can you do with a man like that? What can you do? How can you dissuade his eye in a crowd from seeking out the cheek with acne, the infirm hand; how can you teach him to respond to the inestimable greatness of the race, the harsh surface beauty of life; how can you put his finger for him on the obdurate truths before which fear and horror are powerless? The sea that morning was iridescent and dark. My wife and my sister were swimming—Diana and Helen—and I saw their uncovered heads, black and gold in the dark water. I saw them come out and I saw that they were naked, unshy, beautiful, and full of grace, and I watched the naked women walk out of the sea.

THE COMMON DAY

When Jim woke at seven in the morning, he got up and made a tour of the bedroom windows. He was so accustomed to the noise and congestion of the city that after six days in New Hampshire he still found the beauty of the country morning violent and alien. The hills seemed to come straight out of the northern sky. From the western windows, he saw the strong sun lighting the trees on the mountains, pouring its light onto the flat water of the lake, and striking at the outbuildings of the big, old-fashioned place as commandingly as the ringing of iron bells.

He dressed and softly drew the blinds, so that the light wouldn't wake his wife. Ellen's days in the country, unlike his, were not limited. She had been here all summer and would remain until the first of September, when she would return to the city with the cook, the ice crusher, and the Persian rug.

The first floor of his mother-in-law's big house was still and clean when he went downstairs. Emma Boulanger, the French housemaid, was dusting the hall. He crossed the gloomy dining room and pushed open the pantry door, but another of the servants, Agnes Shay, was there to keep him from going any farther into her preserves. "You just tell me what you want for breakfast, Mr. Brown," she said unpleasantly. "Greta will make it for you."

He wanted to have his breakfast in the kitchen with his five-year-old son, but Agnes had no intention of letting him pass from the front of the house into those quarters that were reserved for servants and children. He told her what he wanted to eat and went back through the dining room and out onto the terrace. The light there was like a blow, and the air smelled as if many wonderful girls had just wandered across the lawn. It was a splendid summer morning and it seemed as if nothing could go wrong. Jim looked at the terrace, at the gardens, at the house, with a fatuous possessiveness. He could hear Mrs. Garrison—his widowed mother-in-law and the rightful owner of everything he saw—talking animatedly to herself in the distant cutting bed.

While Jim was eating his breakfast, Agnes said that Nils Lund wanted to see him. This information flattered Jim. He was in New Hampshire for only ten days and he was there merely as a guest, but he liked to be consulted by the gardener. Nils Lund had worked for Mrs. Garrison for many years. He lived in a cottage on the place and his wife, who was now dead, had worked in the kitchen. Nils resented the fact that none of Mrs. Garrison's sons interested themselves in the place and he often told Jim how happy he was to have a man around with whom he could discuss his problems.

Nils's gardens no longer bore any relationship to the

needs of the house. Each spring he plowed and planted acres of vegetables and flowers. The coming up of the asparagus shoots was the signal for a hopeless race between the vegetables and Mrs. Garrison's table. Nils, embittered by the waste that he himself was the author of, came each evening to the kitchen door to tell the cook that unless they ate more peas, more strawberries, more beans, more lettuce, more cabbages, the magnificent vegetables he had watered with his sweat would rot.

When Jim had finished his breakfast, he went around to the back of the house and Nils told him, with a long face, that something was eating the corn, which had just begun to ripen. They had discussed the pest in the corn patch before. At first they had thought it was deer. Nils had changed his guess that morning to raccoons. He wanted Jim to come with him and view the damage that had been done.

"Those traps in the tool house ought to do the job for us if it's raccoons," Jim said. "And I think there's a rifle around. I'll set the traps tonight."

They walked along a driveway that ran up the hill to the gardens. The fields at the edge of the drive were eroded with moss and spotted with juniper. From the fields came an indescribable perfume, pungent and soporific. "See," Nils said when they reached the corn patch. "See, see . . ." Leaves, silk, and half-eaten ears were strewn and trampled into the dirt. "I plant it," Nils said, like the husband of a shrew recounting instances of unrewarded patience. "Then there's crows after the seed. I cultivate it. Now there's no corn."

They heard Greta, the cook, singing as she came up the drive, bringing garbage to the chickens. They turned to watch her. She was a big, strong woman with a magnificent voice and the breasts of an operatic contralto. A second after they heard Greta, the wind carried Mrs. Garrison's voice to them from the cutting bed. Mrs. Garrison talked to herself continually. Her cultivated and emphatic words sounded across that clear morning like the notes of a trumpet. "Why does he plant this hideous purple verbena every year? He knows I can't use purple. Why *does* he plant this loathsome purple verbena? . . . And I'm going to have him move the arums again. I'm going to have the lilies down by the pool again . . ."

Nils spat in the dirt. "God damn that woman!" he said. "God damn her!" Greta had reminded him of his dead wife and Mrs. Garrison's rich voice had reminded him of that other binding marriage, between mistress and gardener, which would last until death dissolved it. He made no effort to contain his anger, and Jim was caught in the cross fire of his mother-in-law's soliloquy and her gardener's rage. He said he would go and take a look at the traps.

He found the traps in the tool house and a rifle in the cellar. As he was crossing the lawn he met Mrs. Garrison. She was a thin, white-haired woman, and she was dressed in a torn maid's uniform and a broken straw hat. Her arms were full of flowers. She and her son-in-law wished one another good morning, exclaimed on the beauty of the day, and went on in opposite directions. Jim carried the traps and the rifle behind the house. His son, Timmy, was there, playing hospital with Ingrid, the cook's daughter, a pale, skinny girl of eleven. The children watched him briefly and then went back to their game.

Jim oiled the traps and filed their catches so that they slammed shut at the least touch. While he was testing the traps, Agnes Shay came out, leading Carlotta Bronson, another of Mrs. Garrison's grandchildren. Carlotta was four years old. Her mother had gone West to get a divorce that summer, and Agnes had been elevated from the position of housemaid to that of nurse. She was almost sixty and she made an intense nurse. From morning until dark, she gripped Carlotta's hand in hers.

She peered over Jim's shoulder at the traps and said, "You know you shouldn't put out those traps until after the children have gone to bed, Mr. Brown. . . . Don't you go near those traps, Carlotta. Come here."

"I won't put the traps out until late," Jim said.

"Why, one of the children might get caught in one of those traps and break a leg," Agnes said. "And you'll be careful of that gun, too, won't you, Mr. Brown? Guns are made to kill with. I've never seen one yet where there wasn't an accident. . . . Come along, Carlotta, come along. I'll put on your fresh pinafore and then you can play in the sand before you have your fruit juice and your crackers."

The little girl followed her into the house, and together they climbed the back stairs to the nursery. When they were alone, Agnes kissed the child on the top of the head timidly, as if she were afraid of troubling Carlotta with her affection.

"Don't touch me, Agnes," Carlotta said.

"No, dear, I won't."

Agnes Shay had the true spirit of a maid. Moistened with dishwater and mild eau de cologne, reared in narrow and sunless bedrooms, in back passages, back stairs, laundries, linen closets, and in those servants' halls that remind one of a prison, her soul had grown docile and bleak. The ranks of service appeared to her as just and inflexible as the rings of hell. She would no more have yielded Mrs. Garrison a place at the servants' table in the kitchen than Mrs. Garrison would have yielded her one in the gloomy dining room. Agnes loved the ceremonies of a big house. She drew the curtains in the living room at dark, lighted the candles on the table, and struck the dinner chimes like an eager altar boy. On fine evenings, when she sat on the back porch between the garbage pails and the woodbins, she liked to recall the faces of all the cooks she had known. It made her life seem rich.

Agnes had never been as happy as she was that summer. She loved the mountains, the lake, and the sky, and she had fallen in love with Carlotta as a youth falls in love. She worried about her own appearance. She worried about her fingernails, her handwriting, her education. Am I worthy? she wondered. The irascible and unhappy child was her only link with the morning, with the sun, with everything beautiful and exciting. To touch Carlotta, to lay her cheek against the child's warm hair, overpowered her with a sense of recaptured youth. Carlotta's mother would return from Reno in September and Agnes had prepared the speech she would make her: "Let me take care of Carlotta, Mrs. Bronson! While you were away, I read all those articles in the *Daily News* about taking care of children. I love Carlotta. She's used to me. I know what she wants. . . ."

Mrs. Garrison was indifferent to children, and with Mrs.

Bronson in Reno, Agnes had no rivals, but she was in continual torment lest something happen to Carlotta. She would not let her wear a scarf around her neck for fear it would catch on a nail or in some door and strangle the child. Every steep staircase, every deep body of water, the distant barking of every watchdog frightened Agnes. She dreamed at night that the house caught fire and, unable to save Carlotta, she threw herself into the flames. Now, added to her other anxieties, were the steel traps and the rifle. She could see Jim from the nursery window. The traps were not set, but that didn't make them any less dangerous, lying there on the ground where anyone could step on them. He had the rifle apart and was cleaning it with a rag, but Agnes felt as if the rifle were loaded and aimed at Carlotta's heart.

JIM HEARD his wife's voice, and he carried the parts of the rifle around to the terrace, where Ellen was sitting in a deck chair, having her breakfast from a tray. He kissed her, and thought how young, slender, and pretty she looked. They had spent very little of their married life in the country, and to be together on a bright, still morning made them both feel as if they had recaptured the excitement of their first meetings. The warmth of the sun, like a state of continuous and intense desire, blinded them to each other's imperfections.

They had planned to drive up Black Hill and see the Emerson place that morning. Ellen liked to visit abandoned farms with the idea of someday buying a house in the country. Jim humored her in this, although he wasn't really interested; and she, in turn, thought that she was deceiving him and that someday, somewhere, on some dismal hill they would find a farmhouse that would strike directly at his heart.

They drove up Black Hill as soon as Ellen had finished her breakfast. These excursions to abandoned homesteads had taken them over many neglected back roads, but the one up Black Hill was as bad as anything Jim had seen yet. It would be impassable between October and May.

When they reached the Emerson place, Ellen looked from the modest, weathered farmhouse to Jim's face, to see what his reaction would be. Neither of them spoke.

Where she saw charm and security, he saw advanced dilapidation and imprisonment.

The farm lay high on the hill but in a fold of the land, and Jim noticed that while the contour sheltered the house from the lake winds, it also deprived it of any view of the water or the mountains. He noticed, too, that every fair-sized tree within a thousand yards of the granite doorstep had been felled. The sun beat on the tin roof. In one of the front windows, like a talisman, he thought, of the meager rural life he detested, was a faded Red Cross sticker.

They left the car and walked across the dooryard. The grass there was waist high and filled with sweet clover. Briars tore at Jim's pants. The rusted latch came off in his hands when he tried the door. He followed Ellen impatiently through the dark, smelly rooms as he had followed her through rooms in a similar state of dilapidation in Maine, Massachusetts, Connecticut, and Maryland. Ellen was a woman with many inexpressible fears—of traffic, of poverty, and, particularly, of war—and these remote, improbable houses represented safety and security to her.

"Of course, if we bought the place," she said, "we'd have to put at least ten thousand dollars into it. We'd just be buying the land. I realize that."

"Well, I'll admit six thousand is a good price for that much land," he said tactfully. He lit a cigarette and looked through a broken window at a pile of rusted farm machinery.

"You see, we could tear down all these partitions," she said.

"Yes," he said.

"I feel more and more that we've got to get some base away from New York," she said. "If there was a war, we'd be caught like rats. Of course, if we left the city altogether I'm not sure how we could make a living. We could open a deep-freeze locker."

"I don't know much about freezers," he said.

This dialogue was as much a part of his visits to the country, he thought, as the swimming and the drinking; and it would be brief. "Then you don't like the place?" she asked, and when he said no, she sighed and stepped from the dark hallway into the sun. He followed her and closed the door. She looked behind her as if he had closed the door on her salvation, and then she took his arm and walked beside him to the car.

MRS. GARRISON, Ellen, and Jim ate their lunch that day on the terrace. Ingrid and Timmy ate in the kitchen, and Agnes Shay fed Carlotta in the nursery. Then she undressed the child, drew the blinds, and put her to bed. She lay on the floor beside the bed and fell into a sound sleep herself. At three, she woke and roused Carlotta. The child was sweaty and cross.

When Carlotta was dressed, Agnes took her down to the living room. Mrs. Garrison was waiting there. It was one of the rituals of that summer that she should spend an hour with Carlotta each afternoon. Left alone with her grandmother, the child sat stiffly in a chair. Mrs. Garrison and the little girl bored one another.

Mrs. Garrison had led an unusually comfortable life, so well sustained by friends and by all sorts of pleasures that she retained a striking buoyancy. She was impulsive, generous, and very kind. She was also restless. "What shall we do, Carlotta?" she asked.

"I don't know," the child said.

"Shall I make you a necklace of daisies, Carlotta?"

"Yes."

"Well, you wait here, then. Don't touch the candy or the things on my desk, will you?"

Mrs. Garrison went into the hall and got a basket and some shears. The lawn below the terrace ended abruptly in a field that was covered with white-and-yellow daisies. She filled her basket with them. When she returned to the living room, Carlotta was still sitting stiffly in her chair. Mrs. Garrison did not trust the child and she inspected the desk before she settled herself on the sofa. She began to push a threaded needle through the hairy flowers. "I'll make you a necklace and a bracelet and a crown," she said.

"I don't want a daisy necklace," Carlotta said.

"But you told me you wanted one."

"I want a *real* necklace," Carlotta said. "I want a pearl necklace like Aunt Ellen has."

"Oh, dear," Mrs. Garrison said. She put aside her needle and the flowers. She remembered her first pearls.

She had worn them to a party in Baltimore. It had been a wonderful party and the memory excited her for a moment. Then she felt old.

"You're not old enough to have pearls," she told Carlotta. "You're just a little girl." She spoke quietly, for the memory of Baltimore had reminded her of other parties; of the yacht-club party at which she had sprained her ankle and the masquerade she had attended dressed as Sir Walter Raleigh. The day had got very hot. The heat made Mrs. Garrison sleepy and encouraged her to reminisce. She thought about Philadelphia and Bermuda, and became so absorbed in these memories that she was startled when Carlotta spoke again.

"I'm not a little girl," Carlotta said suddenly. "I'm a big girl!" Her voice broke and tears came to her eyes. "I'm bigger than Timmy and Ingrid and everybody!"

"You'll be big enough in time," Mrs. Garrison said. "Stop crying."

"I want to be a big lady. I want to be a big lady like Aunt Ellen and Mummy."

"And when you're as big as your mother, you'll wish you were a child again!" Mrs. Garrison said angrily.

"I want to be a lady," the child cried. "I don't want to be little. I don't want to be a little girl."

"Stop it," Mrs. Garrison called, "stop crying. It's too hot. You don't know what you want. Look at me. I spend half my time wishing I were young enough to dance. It's ridiculous, it's perfectly . . ." She noticed a shadow crossing the lowered awning at the window. She went to the window and saw Nils Lund going down the lawn. He would have overheard everything. This made her intensely uncomfortable. Carlotta was still crying. She hated to hear the child cry. It seemed as if the meaning of that hot afternoon, as if for a second her life, depended upon the little girl's happiness.

"Is there anything you'd like to do, Carlotta?"

"No."

"Would you like a piece of candy?"

"No, thank you."

"Would you like to wear my pearls?"

"No, thank you."

Mrs. Garrison decided to cut the interview short and she rang for Agnes.

IN THE KITCHEN, Greta and Agnes were drinking coffee. The lunch dishes had been washed and the turmoil that attended dinner had not begun. The kitchen was cool and clean and the grounds were still. They met there every afternoon and it was the pleasantest hour of their day.

"Where is *she*?" Greta asked.

"*She's* in there with Carlotta," Agnes said.

"*She* was talking to herself in the garden this morning," Greta said. "Nils heard her. Now she wants him to move some lilies. He won't do anything. He won't even cut the grass."

"Emma cleaned the living room," Agnes said. "Then *she* comes in with all those flowers."

"Next summer I go back to Sweden," Greta said.

"Does it still cost four hundred dollars?" Agnes asked.

"Yes," Greta said. In order to avoid saying *ja*, she hissed the word. "Maybe next year it won't cost so much. But if I don't go next year, Ingrid will be twelve years old and she'll cost full fare. I want to see my mother. She's old."

"You should go," Agnes said.

"I went in 1927, 1935, and 1937," Greta said.

"I went home in 1937," Agnes said. "That was the last time. My father was an old man. I was there all summer. I thought I'll go the year after, but *she* said if I go she fires me, so I didn't go. And that winter my father died. I wanted to see him."

"I want to see my mother," Greta said.

"They talk about the scenery here," Agnes said. "These little mountains! Ireland is like a garden."

"Would I do it again? I ask myself," Greta said. "Now I'm too old. Look at my legs. Varicose veins." She moved one of her legs out from underneath the table for Agnes to see.

"I have nothing to go back for," Agnes said. "My brothers are dead, both my brothers. I have nobody on the other side. I wanted to see my father."

"Oh, that first time I come here," Greta cried. "It was

like a party on that boat. Get rich. Go home. Get rich. Go home."

"Me, too," Agnes said. They heard thunder. Mrs. Garrison rang again impatiently.

A STORM came down from the north then. The wind blew a gale, a green branch fell onto the lawn and the house resounded with cries and the noise of slammed windows. When the rain and the lightning came, Mrs. Garrison watched them from her bedroom window. Carlotta and Agnes hid in a closet. Jim and Ellen and their son were at the beach and they watched the storm from the door of the boathouse. It raged for half an hour and then blew off to the west, leaving the air chill, bitter, and clean; but the afternoon was over.

While the children were having their supper, Jim went up to the corn patch and set and baited his traps. As he started down the hill, he smelled baking cake from the kitchen. The sky had cleared, the light on the mountains was soft, and the house seemed to have all its energies bent toward dinner. He saw Nils by the chicken house and called good evening to him, but Nils didn't reply.

Mrs. Garrison, Jim, and Ellen had cocktails before they went in to dinner, then wine, and when they took their brandy and coffee onto the terrace, they were slightly drunk. The sun was setting.

"I got a letter from Reno," Mrs. Garrison said. "Florrie wants me to bring Carlotta to New York when I go down on the twelfth for the Peyton wedding."

"Shay will die," Ellen said.

"Shay will perish," Mrs. Garrison said.

The sky seemed to be full of fire. They could see the sad, red light through the pines. The odd winds that blow just before dark in the mountains brought, from farther down the lake, the words of a song, sung by some children at a camp there:

"There's a camp for girls
On Bellows Lake.
Camp Massassoit's
Its name.
From the rise of sun

Till the day is done,
There is lots of fun
Down there . . ."

The voices were shrill, bright, and trusting. Then the changing wind extinguished the song and blew some wood smoke down along the slate roof to where the three people sat. There was a rumble of thunder.

"I never hear thunder," Mrs. Garrison said, "without recalling that Enid Clark was struck dead by lightning."

"Who was she?" Ellen said.

"She was an extraordinarily disagreeable woman," Mrs. Garrison said. "She took a bath in front of an open window one afternoon and was struck dead by lightning. Her husband had wrangled with the bishop, so she wasn't buried from the cathedral. They sat her up beside the swimming pool and had the funeral service there, and there wasn't anything to drink. We drove back to New York after the ceremony and your father stopped along the way at a bootlegger's and bought a case of Scotch. It was a Saturday afternoon and there was a football game and a lot of traffic outside Princeton. We had that French-Canadian chauffeur, and his driving had always made me nervous. I spoke to Ralph about it and he said I was a fool, and five minutes later the car was upside down. I was thrown out of the open window into a stony field, and the first thing your father did was to look into the luggage compartment to see what had happened to the Scotch. There I was, bleeding to death, and he was counting bottles."

Mrs. Garrison arranged a steamer rug over her legs and looked narrowly at the lake and the mountains. The noise of footsteps on the gravel drive alarmed her. Guests? She turned and saw that it was Nils Lund. He left the driveway for the lawn and came across the grass toward the terrace, shuffling in shoes that were too big for him. His cowlick, his short, faded hair, his spare figure, and the line of his shoulders reminded Jim of a boy. It was as if Nils's growth, his spirit, had been stopped in some summer of his youth, but he moved warily and without spirit, like a broken-hearted old man. He came to the foot of the terrace and spoke to Mrs. Garrison without looking at her. "I no move the lilies, Mrs. Garrison."

"What, Nils?" she asked, and leaned forward.

"I no move the lilies."

"Why not?"

"I got too much to do." He looked at her and spoke angrily. "All winter I'm here alone. There's snow up to my neck. The wind screams so, I can't sleep. I work for you seventeen years and you never been here once in the bad weather."

"What has the winter got to do with the lilies, Nils?" she asked calmly.

"I got too much to do. Move the lilies. Move the roses. Cut the grass. Every day you want something different. Why is it? Why are you better than me? You don't know how to do anything but kill flowers. I grow the flowers. You kill them. If a fuse burns out, you don't know how to do it. If something leaks, you don't know how to do it. You kill flowers. That's all you know how to do. For seventeen years I wait for you all winter," he shouted. "You write me, 'Is it warm? Are the flowers pretty?' Then you come. You sit here. You drink. God damn you people. You killed my wife. Now you want to kill me. You—"

"Shut up, Nils," Jim said.

Nils turned quickly and retreated across the lawn, so stricken with self-consciousness that he seemed to limp. None of them spoke, for they had the feeling, after he had disappeared behind the hedge, that he might be hiding there, waiting to hear what they would say. Then Ingrid and Greta came up the lawn from their evening walk, overburdened with the stones and wild flowers that they brought back from these excursions to decorate their rooms above the garage. Greta told Jim that something was caught in a trap in the corn patch. She thought it was a cat.

Jim got the rifle and a flashlight and went up the hill to the gardens. As he approached the corn patch, he could hear a wild, thin crying. Then the animal, whatever it was, began to pound the dirt. The stroke was strong, as regular as a heartbeat, and accompanied by the small rattling of the trap chain. When Jim reached the patch, he turned his light into the broken stalks. The animal hissed, sprang in the direction of the light; but it could not escape the chain. It was a fat, humpbacked coon. Now it hid from the light in the ruined corn. Jim waited. Against the starlight he could see the high, ragged stand of corn and when a breeze passed through the leaves they rattled like sticks. The coon, driven by pain, began to strike the ground convulsively and Jim held the light against the barrel of the rifle and fired twice. When the coon was dead, he unstaked the trap and carried it and the carcass out of the garden.

It was an immense, still, and beautiful night. Instead of returning to the drive, he took a short cut through the garden and across a field toward the tool house. The ground was very dark. He moved cautiously and awkwardly. The heavy carcass smelled like a dog. "Mr. Brown, Mr. Brown, oh, Mr. Brown," someone called. It was Agnes. Her voice was breathless and fretful. Agnes and Carlotta were standing in the field. They were in nightgowns. "We heard the noise," Agnes called. "We heard the gun going off. We were afraid there had been an accident. Of course I knew Carlotta was all right. She was right beside me. Weren't you, dear? But we couldn't sleep. We couldn't close our eyes after we heard the noise. Is everything all right?"

"Yes," Jim said. "There was a coon in the garden."

"Where's the coon?" Carlotta asked.

"The coon's gone on a long, long journey, dear," Agnes said. "Come now, come along, sweet. I hope nothing else will wake us up, don't you?" They turned and started back toward the house, warning one another of the sticks and ditches and other perils of the country. Their conversation was filled with diminutives, timidity, and vagueness. He wanted to help them, he wanted urgently to help them, he wanted to offer them his light, but they reached the house without his help and he heard the back door close on their voices.

THE ENORMOUS RADIO

JIM AND IRENE WESTCOTT were the kind of people who seem to strike that satisfactory average of income, endeavor, and respectability that is reached by the statistical reports in college alumni bulletins. They were the parents of two young children, they had been married nine years, they lived on the twelfth floor of an apartment house near Sutton Place, they went to the theatre on an average of 10.3 times a year, and they hoped someday to live in Westchester. Irene Westcott was a pleasant, rather plain girl with soft brown hair and a wide, fine forehead upon which nothing at all had been written, and in the cold weather she wore a coat of fitch skins dyed to resemble mink. You could not say that Jim Westcott looked younger than he was, but you could at least say of him that he seemed to feel younger. He wore his graying hair cut very short, he dressed in the kind of clothes his class had worn at Andover, and his manner was earnest, vehement, and intentionally naïve. The Westcotts differed from their friends, their classmates, and their neighbors only in an interest they shared in serious music. They went to a great many concerts—although they seldom mentioned this to anyone—and they spent a good deal of time listening to music on the radio.

Their radio was an old instrument, sensitive, unpredictable, and beyond repair. Neither of them understood the mechanics of radio—or of any of the other appliances that surrounded them—and when the instrument faltered, Jim would strike the side of the cabinet with his hand. This sometimes helped. One Sunday afternoon, in the middle of a Schubert quartet, the music faded away altogether. Jim struck the cabinet repeatedly, but there was no response; the Schubert was lost to them forever. He promised to buy Irene a new radio, and on Monday when he came home from work he told her that he had got one. He refused to describe it, and said it would be a surprise for her when it came.

The radio was delivered at the kitchen door the following afternoon, and with the assistance of her maid and the handyman Irene uncrated it and brought it into the living room. She was struck at once with the physical ugliness of the large gumwood cabinet. Irene was proud of her living room, she had chosen its furnishings and colors as carefully as she chose her clothes, and now it seemed to her that the new radio stood among her intimate possessions like an aggressive intruder. She was confounded by the number of dials and switches on the instrument panel, and she studied them thoroughly before she put the plug into a wall socket and turned the radio on. The dials flooded with a malevolent green light, and in the distance she heard the music of a piano quintet. The quintet was in the distance for only an instant; it bore down upon her with a speed greater than light and filled the apartment with the noise of music amplified so mightily that it knocked a china ornament from a table to the floor. She rushed to the instrument and reduced the volume. The violent forces that were snared in the ugly gumwood cabinet made her uneasy. Her children came home from school then, and she took them to the Park. It was not until later in the afternoon that she was able to return to the radio.

The maid had given the children their suppers and was supervising their baths when Irene turned on the radio, reduced the volume, and sat down to listen to a Mozart quintet that she knew and enjoyed. The music came through clearly. The new instrument had a much purer tone, she thought, than the old one. She decided that tone was most important and that she could conceal the cabinet behind a sofa. But as soon as she had made her peace with the radio, the interference began. A crackling sound like the noise of a burning powder fuse began to accompany the singing of the strings. Beyond the music, there was a rustling that reminded Irene unpleasantly of the sea, and as the quintet progressed, these noises were joined by many others. She tried all the dials and switches but nothing dimmed the interference, and she sat down, disappointed and bewildered, and tried to trace the flight of the melody. The elevator shaft in her building ran beside the living-room wall, and it was the noise of the elevator that gave her a clue to the character of the static. The rattling of the elevator cables and the opening and closing of the elevator doors were reproduced in her loudspeaker, and, realizing that the radio was sensitive to electrical currents of all sorts, she began to discern through the Mozart the ringing of telephone bells, the dialing of phones, and the lamentation of a vacuum cleaner. By listening more carefully, she was able to distinguish doorbells, elevator bells, electric razors, and Waring mixers, whose sounds had been picked up from the apartments that surrounded hers and transmitted through her loudspeaker. The powerful and ugly instrument, with its mistaken sensitivity to discord, was more than she could hope to master, so she turned the thing off and went into the nursery to see her children.

When Jim Westcott came home that night, he went to the radio confidently and worked the controls. He had the same sort of experience Irene had had. A man was speaking on the station Jim had chosen, and his voice swung instantly from the distance into a force so powerful that it shook the apartment. Jim turned the volume control and reduced the voice. Then, a minute or two later, the interference began. The ringing of telephones and doorbells set in, joined by the rasp of the elevator doors and the whir of cooking appliances. The character of the noise had changed since Irene had tried the radio earlier; the last of the electric razors was being unplugged, the vacuum cleaners had all been returned to their closets, and the static reflected that change in pace that overtakes the city after the sun goes down. He fiddled with the knobs but couldn't get rid of the noises, so he turned the radio off and told Irene that in the morning he'd call the people who had sold it to him and give them hell.

The following afternoon, when Irene returned to the apartment from a luncheon date, the maid told her that a man had come and fixed the radio. Irene went into the living room before she took off her hat or her furs and tried the instrument. From the loudspeaker came a recording of the "Missouri Waltz." It reminded her of the thin, scratchy music from an old-fashioned phonograph that she sometimes heard across the lake where she spent her summers. She waited until the waltz had finished, expecting an explanation of the recording, but there was none. The music was followed by silence, and then the plaintive and scratchy record was repeated. She turned the dial and got a satisfactory burst of Caucasian music—the thump of bare feet in the dust and the rattle of coin jewelry—but in the background she could hear the ringing of bells and a confusion of voices. Her children came home from school then, and she turned off the radio and went to the nursery.

When Jim came home that night, he was tired, and he took a bath and changed his clothes. Then he joined Irene in the living room. He had just turned on the radio when the maid announced dinner, so he left it on, and he and Irene went to the table.

Jim was too tired to make even a pretense of sociability, and there was nothing about the dinner to hold Irene's interest, so her attention wandered from the food to the deposits of silver polish on the candlesticks and from there to the music in the other room. She listened for a few minutes to a Chopin prelude and then was surprised to hear a man's voice break in. "For Christ's sake, Kathy," he said, "do you always have to play the piano when I get home?" The music stopped abruptly. "It's the only chance I have," a woman said. "I'm at the office all day." "So am I," the man said. He added something obscene about an upright piano, and slammed a door. The passionate and melancholy music began again.

"Did you hear that?" Irene asked.

"What?" Jim was eating his dessert.

"The radio. A man said something while the music was still going on—something dirty."

"It's probably a play."

"I don't think it *is* a play," Irene said.

They left the table and took their coffee into the living room. Irene asked Jim to try another station. He turned the knob. "Have you seen my garters?" a man asked. "Button me up," a woman said. "Have you seen my garters?" the man said again. "Just button me up and I'll find your garters," the woman said. Jim shifted to another station. "I wish you wouldn't leave apple cores in the ashtrays," a man said. "I hate the smell."

"This is strange," Jim said.

"Isn't it?" Irene said.

Jim turned the knob again. " 'On the coast of Coromandel where the early pumpkins blow,' " a woman with a pronounced English accent said, " 'in the middle of the woods lived the Yonghy-Bonghy-Bò. Two old chairs, and half a candle, one old jug without a handle . . .' "

"My God!" Irene cried. "That's the Sweeneys' nurse."

" 'These were all his worldly goods,' " the British voice continued.

"Turn that thing off," Irene said. "Maybe they can hear *us.*" Jim switched the radio off. "That was Miss Armstrong, the Sweeneys' nurse," Irene said. "She must be reading to the little girl. They live in 17-B. I've talked with Miss Armstrong in the Park. I know her voice very well. We must be getting other people's apartments."

"That's impossible," Jim said.

"Well, that was the Sweeneys' nurse," Irene said hotly. "I know her voice. I know it very well. I'm wondering if they can hear us."

Jim turned the switch. First from a distance and then nearer, nearer, as if borne on the wind, came the pure accents of the Sweeneys' nurse again: " '*Lady Jingly! Lady Jingly!*' " she said, " '*sitting where the pumpkins blow, will you come and be my wife?* said the Yonghy-Bonghy-Bò . . .' "

Jim went over to the radio and said "Hello" loudly into the speaker.

" '*I am tired of living singly,*' " the nurse went on, " '*on this coast so wild and shingly, I'm a-weary of my life; if you'll come and be my wife, quite serene would be my life . . .*' "

"I guess she can't hear us," Irene said. "Try something else."

Jim turned to another station, and the living room was filled with the uproar of a cocktail party that had overshot its mark. Someone was playing the piano and singing the "Whiffenpoof Song," and the voices that surrounded the piano were vehement and happy. "Eat some more sandwiches," a woman shrieked. There were screams of laughter and a dish of some sort crashed to the floor.

"Those must be the Fullers, in 11-E," Irene said. "I knew they were giving a party this afternoon. I saw her in the liquor store. Isn't this too divine? Try something else. See if you can get those people in 18-C."

The Westcotts overheard that evening a monologue on salmon fishing in Canada, a bridge game, running comments on home movies of what had apparently been a fortnight at Sea Island, and a bitter family quarrel about an overdraft at the bank. They turned off their radio at midnight and went to bed, weak with laughter. Sometime in the night, their son began to call for a glass of water and Irene got one and took it to his room. It was very early. All the lights in the neighborhood were extinguished, and from the boy's window she could see the empty street. She went into the living room and tried the radio. There was some faint coughing, a moan, and then a man spoke. "Are you all right, darling?" he asked. "Yes," a woman said wearily. "Yes, I'm all right, I guess," and then she added with great feeling, "But, you know, Charlie, I don't feel like myself any more. Sometimes there are about fifteen or twenty minutes in the week when I feel like myself. I don't like to go to another doctor, because the doctor's bills are so awful already, but I just don't feel like myself, Charlie. I just never feel like myself." They were not young, Irene thought. She guessed from the timbre of their voices that they were middle-aged. The restrained melancholy of the dialogue and the draft from the bedroom window made her shiver, and she went back to bed.

THE FOLLOWING MORNING, Irene cooked breakfast for the family—the maid didn't come up from her room in the basement until ten—braided her daughter's hair, and waited at the door until her children and her husband had been carried away in the elevator. Then she went into the living room and tried the radio. "I don't want to go to school," a child screamed. "I hate school. I won't go to school. I hate school." "You will go to school," an enraged woman said. "We paid eight hundred dollars to get you into that school and you'll go if it kills you." The next number on the dial produced the worn record of the "Missouri Waltz." Irene shifted the control and invaded the privacy of several breakfast tables. She overheard demonstrations of indigestion, carnal love, abysmal vanity, faith, and despair. Irene's life was nearly as simple and sheltered as it appeared to be, and the forthright and sometimes brutal language that came from the loudspeaker that morning astonished and troubled her. She continued to listen until her maid came in. Then she turned off the radio quickly, since this insight, she realized, was a furtive one.

Irene had a luncheon date with a friend that day, and she left her apartment at a little after twelve. There were a number of women in the elevator when it stopped at her floor. She stared at their handsome and impassive faces, their furs, and the cloth flowers in their hats. Which one of them had been to Sea Island? she wondered. Which one had overdrawn her bank account? The elevator stopped at the tenth floor and a woman with a pair of Skye terriers joined them. Her hair was rigged high on her head and she wore a mink cape. She was humming the "Missouri Waltz."

Irene had two Martinis at lunch, and she looked searchingly at her friend and wondered what her secrets were. They had intended to go shopping after lunch, but Irene excused herself and went home. She told the maid that she was not to be disturbed; then she went into the living room, closed the doors, and switched on the radio. She heard, in the course of the afternoon, the halting conversation of a woman entertaining her aunt, the hysterical conclusion of a luncheon party, and a hostess briefing her maid about some cocktail guests. "Don't give the best Scotch to anyone who hasn't white hair," the hostess said. "See if you can get rid of that liver paste before you pass those hot things, and could you lend me five dollars? I want to tip the elevator man."

As the afternoon waned, the conversations increased in intensity. From where Irene sat, she could see the open sky above the East River. There were hundreds of clouds in the sky, as though the south wind had broken the winter into pieces and were blowing it north, and on her radio she could hear the arrival of cocktail guests and the return of children and businessmen from their schools and offices. "I found a good-sized diamond on the bathroom floor this morning," a woman said. "It must have fallen out of that bracelet Mrs. Dunston was wearing last night." "We'll sell it," a man said. "Take it down to the jeweler on Madison

Avenue and sell it. Mrs. Dunston won't know the difference, and we could use a couple of hundred bucks . . ." "'Oranges and lemons, say the bells of St. Clement's,'" the Sweeneys' nurse sang. "'Halfpence and farthings, say the bells of St. Martin's. When will you pay me? say the bells at old Bailey . . .'" "It's not a hat," a woman cried, and at her back roared a cocktail party. "It's not a hat, it's a love affair. That's what Walter Florell said. He said it's not a hat, it's a love affair," and then, in a lower voice, the same woman added, "Talk to somebody, for Christ's sake, honey, talk to somebody. If she catches you standing here not talking to anybody, she'll take us off her invitation list, and I love these parties."

The Westcotts were going out for dinner that night, and when Jim came home, Irene was dressing. She seemed sad and vague, and he brought her a drink. They were dining with friends in the neighborhood, and they walked to where they were going. The sky was broad and filled with light. It was one of those splendid spring evenings that excite memory and desire, and the air that touched their hands and faces felt very soft. A Salvation Army band was on the corner playing "Jesus Is Sweeter." Irene drew on her husband's arm and held him there for a minute, to hear the music. "They're really such nice people, aren't they?" she said. "They have such nice faces. Actually, they're so much nicer than a lot of the people we know." She took a bill from her purse and walked over and dropped it into the tambourine. There was in her face, when she returned to her husband, a look of radiant melancholy that he was not familiar with. And her conduct at the dinner party that night seemed strange to him, too. She interrupted her hostess rudely and stared at the people across the table from her with an intensity for which she would have punished her children.

It was still mild when they walked home from the party, and Irene looked up at the spring stars. "'How far that little candle throws its beams,'" she exclaimed. "'So shines a good deed in a naughty world.'" She waited that night until Jim had fallen asleep, and then went into the living room and turned on the radio.

JIM CAME HOME at about six the next night. Emma, the

maid, let him in, and he had taken off his hat and was taking off his coat when Irene ran into the hall. Her face was shining with tears and her hair was disordered. "Go up to 16-C, Jim!" she screamed. "Don't take off your coat. Go up to 16-C. Mr. Osborn's beating his wife. They've been quarreling since four o'clock, and now he's hitting her. Go up there and stop him."

From the radio in the living room, Jim heard screams, obscenities, and thuds. "You know you don't have to listen to this sort of thing," he said. He strode into the living room and turned the switch. "It's indecent," he said. "It's like looking in windows. You know you don't have to listen to this sort of thing. You can turn it off."

"Oh, it's so horrible, it's so dreadful," Irene was sobbing. "I've been listening all day, and it's so depressing."

"Well, if it's so depressing, why do you listen to it? I bought this damned radio to give you some pleasure," he said. "I paid a great deal of money for it. I thought it might make you happy. I wanted to make you happy."

"Don't, don't, don't, don't quarrel with me," she moaned, and laid her head on his shoulder. "All the others have been quarreling all day. Everybody's been quarreling. They're all worried about money. Mrs. Hutchinson's mother is dying of cancer in Florida and they don't have enough money to send her to the Mayo Clinic. At least, Mr. Hutchinson says they don't have enough money. And some woman in this building is having an affair with the handyman—with that hideous handyman. It's too disgusting. And Mrs. Melville has heart trouble and Mr. Hendricks is going to lose his job in April and Mrs. Hendricks is horrid about the whole thing and that girl who plays the 'Missouri Waltz' is a whore, a common whore, and the elevator man has tuberculosis and Mr. Osborn has been beating Mrs. Osborn." She wailed, she trembled with grief and checked the stream of tears down her face with the heel of her palm.

"Well, why do you have to listen?" Jim asked again. "Why do you have to listen to this stuff if it makes you so miserable?"

"Oh, don't, don't, don't," she cried. "Life is too terrible, too sordid and awful. But we've never been like that, have we, darling? Have we? I mean, we've always been good and decent and loving to one another, haven't we? And we have two children, two beautiful children. Our lives aren't sordid, are they, darling? Are they?" She flung her arms around his neck and drew his face down to hers. "We're happy, aren't we, darling? We are happy, aren't we?"

"Of course we're happy," he said tiredly. He began to surrender his resentment. "Of course we're happy. I'll have that damned radio fixed or taken away tomorrow." He stroked her soft hair. "My poor girl," he said.

"You love me, don't you?" she asked. "And we're not hypercritical or worried about money or dishonest, are we?"

"No, darling," he said.

A MAN came in the morning and fixed the radio. Irene turned it on cautiously and was happy to hear a California-wine commercial and a recording of Beethoven's Ninth Symphony, including Schiller's "Ode to Joy." She kept the radio on all day and nothing untoward came from the speaker.

A Spanish suite was being played when Jim came home. "Is everything all right?" he asked. His face was pale, she thought. They had some cocktails and went in to dinner to the "Anvil Chorus" from *Il Trovatore*. This was followed by Debussy's "La Mer."

"I paid the bill for the radio today," Jim said. "It cost four hundred dollars. I hope you'll get some enjoyment out of it."

"Oh, I'm sure I will," Irene said.

"Four hundred dollars is a good deal more than I can afford," he went on. "I wanted to get something that you'd enjoy. It's the last extravagance we'll be able to indulge in this year. I see that you haven't paid your clothing bills yet. I saw them on your dressing table." He looked directly at her. "Why did you tell me you'd paid them? Why did you lie to me?"

"I just didn't want you to worry, Jim," she said. She drank some water. "I'll be able to pay my bills out of this month's allowance. There were the slipcovers last month, and that party."

"You've got to learn to handle the money I give you a little more intelligently, Irene," he said. "You've got to understand that we don't have as much money this year as we had last. I had a very sobering talk with Mitchell today. No one is buying anything. We're spending all our time promoting new issues, and you know how long that takes. I'm not getting any younger, you know. I'm thirty-seven. My hair will be gray next year. I haven't done as well as I'd hoped to do. And I don't suppose things will get any better."

"Yes, dear," she said.

"We've got to start cutting down," Jim said. "We've got to think of the children. To be perfectly frank with you, I worry about money a great deal. I'm not at all sure of the future. No one is. If anything should happen to me, there's the insurance, but that wouldn't go very far today. I've worked awfully hard to give you and the children a comfortable life," he said bitterly. "I don't like to see all my energies, all of my youth, wasted in fur coats and radios and slipcovers and—"

"Please, Jim," she said. "Please. They'll hear us."

"*Who'll hear us?* Emma can't hear us."

"The radio."

"Oh, I'm sick!" he shouted. "I'm sick to death of your apprehensiveness. The radio can't hear us. Nobody can hear us. And what if they can hear us? Who cares?"

Irene got up from the table and went into the living room. Jim went to the door and shouted at her from there. "Why are you so Christly all of a sudden? What's turned you overnight into a convent girl? You stole your mother's jewelry before they probated her will. You never gave your sister a cent of that money that was intended for her—not even when she needed it. You made Grace Howland's life miserable, and where was all your piety and your virtue when you went to that abortionist? I'll never forget how cool you were. You packed your bag and went off to have that child murdered as if you were going to Nassau. If you'd had any reasons, if you'd had any good reasons—"

Irene stood for a minute before the hideous cabinet, disgraced and sickened, but she held her hand on the switch before she extinguished the music and the voices, hoping that the instrument might speak to her kindly, that she might hear the Sweeneys' nurse. Jim continued to shout at her from the door. The voice on the radio was suave and noncommital. "An early-morning railroad disaster in Tokyo," the loudspeaker said, "killed twenty-nine people. A fire in a Catholic hospital near Buffalo for the care of blind children was extinguished early this morning by nuns. The temperature is forty-seven. The humidity is eighty-nine."

O CITY OF BROKEN DREAMS

WHEN THE TRAIN from Chicago left Albany and began to pound down the river valley toward New York, the Malloys, who had already experienced many phases of excitement, felt their breathing quicken, as if there were not enough air in the coach. They straightened their backs and raised their heads, searching for oxygen, like the crew of a doomed submarine. Their daughter, Mildred-Rose, took an enviable way out of the agitation. She fell asleep. Evarts Malloy wanted to get the suitcases down from the rack, but Alice, his wife, studied the timetable and said that it was too soon. She stared out of the window and saw the noble Hudson.

"Why do they call it the rind of America?" she asked her husband.

"The Rhine," Evarts said. "Not the rind."

"Oh."

They had left their home in Wentworth, Indiana, the day before, and in spite of the excitements of travel and their brilliant destination, they both wondered, now and then, if they had remembered to turn off the gas and extinguish the rubbish fire behind the barn. They were dressed, like the people you sometimes see in Times Square on Saturday nights, in clothing that had been saved for their flight. His light shoes had perhaps not been out of the back of the closet since his father's funeral or his brother's wedding. She was wearing her new gloves for the first time—the gloves she had been given for Christmas ten years ago. His tarnished collar pin and his initialed tie clip, with its gilt chain, his fancy socks, the rayon handkerchief in his breast pocket, and the carnation made of feathers in his lapel had all been husbanded in the top drawer of his bureau for years in the firm conviction that life would someday call him from Wentworth.

Alice Malloy had dark, stringy hair, and even her husband, who loved her more than he knew, was sometimes reminded by her lean face of a tenement doorway on a rainy day, for her countenance was long, vacant, and weakly lighted, a passage for the gentle transports and miseries of the poor. Evarts Malloy was very thin. He had worked as a bus driver and he stooped a little. Their child slept with her thumb in her mouth. Her hair was dark and her dirty face was lean, like her mother's. When a violent movement of the train roused her, she drew noisily at her thumb until she lost consciousness again. She had been unable to store up as much finery as her parents, since she was only five years old, but she wore a white fur coat. The matching hat and muff had been lost generations before; the skins of the coat were sere and worn, but as she slept, she stroked them, as if they had remarkable properties that assured her that all was well, all was well.

The conductor who came through the car taking tickets after Albany noticed the Malloys, and something about their appearance worried him. As he came back through the car, he stopped at their seat and talked with them, first about Mildred-Rose and then about their destination.

"You people going to New York for the first time?" he asked.

"Yes," Evarts said.

"Going down to see the sights?"

"Oh, no," Alice said. "We're going on business."

"Looking for a job?" the conductor asked.

"Oh, no," Alice said. "Tell him, Evarts."

"Well, it really isn't a job," Evarts said. "I'm not looking for a job, I mean. I mean, I sort of have a job." His manner was friendly and simple and he told his story enthusiastically, for the conductor was the first stranger to ask for it. "I was in the Army, you see, and then, when I got out of the Army, I went back home and began driving the bus again. I'm a night bus driver. But I didn't like it. I kept getting stomach aches, and it hurt my eyes, driving at night, so in my spare time, during the afternoons, I began to write this play. Now, out on Route 7, near Wentworth, where we live, there's this old woman named Mama Finelli, who has a gas station and a snake farm. She's a very salty and haunting old character, and so I decided to write this play about her. She has all these salty and haunting sayings. Well, I wrote this first act—and then Tracey Murchison, the producer, comes out from New York to give a lecture at the Women's Club about the problems of the theatre. Well, Alice went to this lecture, and when he was complaining, when Murchison was complaining about the lack of young playwrights, Alice raises her hand and she tells Murchison that her husband is a young playwright and will he read his play. Didn't you, Alice?"

"Yes," Alice said.

"Well, he hems and haws," Evarts said. "Murchison hems and haws, but Alice pins him down, because all these other people are listening, and when he finishes his lecture, she goes right up on the platform and she gives him the play—she's got it in her pocketbook. Well, then she goes back to his hotel with him and she sits right beside him until he's read the play—the first act, that is. That's all I've written. Well in this play there's a part he wants for his wife, Madge Beatty, right off. I guess you know who Madge Beatty is. So you know what he does then? He sits right down and he writes out a check for thirty-five dollars and he says for me and Alice to come to New York! So we take all our money out of the savings bank and we burn our bridges and here we are."

"Well, I guess there's lots of money in it," the conductor said. Then he wished the Malloys luck and walked away.

Evarts wanted to take the suitcases down at Poughkeepsie and again at Harmon, but Alice checked each place against the timetable and made him wait. Neither of them had seen New York before, and they watched its approaches greedily, for Wentworth was a dismal town and even the slums of Manhattan looked wonderful to them that afternoon. When the train plunged into the darkness beneath Park Avenue, Alice felt that she was surrounded by the inventions of giants and she roused Mildred-Rose and tied the little girl's bonnet with trembling fingers.

As the Malloys stepped from the train, Alice noticed

that the paving, deep in the station, had a frosty glitter, and she wondered if diamonds had been ground into the concrete. She forbade Evarts to ask directions. "If they find out we're green, they'll fleece us," she whispered. They wandered through the marble waiting room, following the noise of traffic and klaxons as if it were the bidding of life. Alice had studied a map of New York, and when they left the station, she knew which direction to take. They walked along Forty-second Street to Fifth Avenue. The faces that passed them seemed purposeful and intent, as if they all belonged to people who were pursuing the destinies of great industries. Evarts had never seen so many beautiful women, so many pleasant, young faces, promising an easy conquest. It was a winter afternoon, and the light in the city was clear and shaded with violet, just like the light on the fields around Wentworth.

Their destination, the Hotel Mentone, was on a side street west of Sixth Avenue. It was a dark place, with malodorous chambers, miserable food, and a lobby ceiling decorated with as much gilt and gesso as the Vatican chapels. It was a popular hotel among the old, it was attractive to the disreputable, and the Malloys had found the way there because the Mentone advertised on railroad-station hoardings all through the West. Many innocents had been there before them, and their sweetness and humility had triumphed over the apparent atmosphere of ruined splendor and petty vice and had left in all the public rooms a humble odor that reminded one of a country feed store on a winter afternoon. A bellboy took them to their room. As soon as he had gone, Alice examined the bath and pulled aside the window curtains. The window looked onto a brick wall, but when she raised it, she could hear the noise of traffic, and it sounded, as it had sounded in the station, like the irresistible and titanic voice of life itself.

THE MALLOYS found their way, that afternoon, to the Broadway Automat. They shouted with pleasure at the magical coffee spigots and the glass doors that sprang open. "Tomorrow, I'm going to have the baked beans," Alice cried, "and the chicken pie the day after that and the fish cakes after that." When they had finished their supper, they went out into the street. Mildred-Rose walked between her parents, holding their callused hands. It was getting dark, and the lights of Broadway answered all their simple prayers. High in the air were large, brightly lighted pictures of bloody heroes, criminal lovers, monsters, and armed desperadoes. The names of movies and soft drinks, restaurants and cigarettes were written in a jumble of light, and in the distance they could see the pitiless winter afterglow beyond the Hudson River. The tall buildings in the east were lighted and seemed to burn, as if fire had fallen onto their dark shapes. The air was full of music, and the light was brighter than day. They drifted with the crowd for hours.

Mildred-Rose got tired and began to cry, so at last her parents took her back to the Mentone. Alice had begun to undress her when someone knocked softly on the door.

"Come in," Evarts called.

A bellboy stood in the doorway. He had the figure of a boy, but his face was gray and lined. "I just wanted to see if you people were all right," he said. "I just wanted to see if maybe you wanted a little ginger ale or some ice water."

"Oh, no, thank you kindly," Alice said. "It was very nice of you to ask, though."

"You people just come to New York for the first time?" the bellboy asked. He closed the door behind him and sat on the arm of a chair.

"Yes," Evarts said. "We left Wentworth—that's in Indiana—yesterday on the nine-fifteen for South Bend. Then we went to Chicago. We had dinner in Chicago."

"I had the chicken pie," Alice said. "It was delicious." She slipped Mildred-Rose's nightgown over her head.

"Then we came to New York," Evarts said.

"What are you doing here?" the bellboy asked. "Anniversary?" He helped himself to a cigarette from a package on the bureau and slipped down into the chair.

"Oh, no," Evarts said. "We hit the jackpot."

"Our ship's come in," Alice said.

"A contest?" the bellboy asked. "Something like that?"

"Oh, no," Evarts said.

"You tell him, Evarts," Alice said.

"Yes," the bellboy said. "Tell me, Evarts."

"Well, you see," Evarts said, "it began like this." He sat

down on the bed and lighted a cigarette. "I was in the Army, you see, and then when I got out of the Army, I went back to Wentworth . . ." He repeated to the bellboy the story he had told the conductor.

"Oh, you lucky, lucky kids!" the bellboy exclaimed when Evarts had finished. "Tracey Murchison! Madge Beatty! You lucky, lucky kids." He looked at the poorly furnished room. Alice was arranging Mildred-Rose on the sofa, where she would sleep. Evarts was sitting on the edge of the bed swinging his legs. "What you need now is a good agent," the bellboy said. He wrote a name and address on a piece of paper and gave it to Evarts. "The Hauser Agency is the biggest agency in the world," he said, "and Charlie Leavitt is the best man in the Hauser Agency. I want you to feel free to take your problems to Charlie, and if he asks you who sent you, tell him Bitsey sent you." He went toward the door. "Good night, you lucky, lucky kids," he said. "Good night. Sweet dreams. Sweet dreams."

The Malloys were the hard-working children of an industrious generation, and they were up at half past six the next morning. They scrubbed their faces and their ears and brushed their teeth with soap. At seven o'clock, they started for the Automat. Evarts had not slept that night. The noise of traffic had kept him awake, and he had spent the small hours sitting at the window. His mouth felt scorched with tobacco smoke, and the loss of sleep had left him nervous. They were all surprised to find New York still sleeping. They were shocked. They had their breakfast and returned to the Mentone. Evarts called Tracey Murchison's office, but no one answered. He telephoned the office several times after that. At ten o'clock, a girl answered the phone. "Mr. Murchison will see you at three," she said. She hung up. Since there was nothing to do but wait, Evarts took his wife and daughter up Fifth Avenue. They stared in the store windows. At eleven o'clock, when the doors of Radio City Music Hall opened, they went there.

This was a happy choice. They prowled the lounges and toilets for an hour before they took their seats, and when, during the stage show, an enormous samovar rose up out of the orchestra pit and debouched forty men in Cossack uniform singing "Dark Eyes," Alice and Mildred-Rose shouted with joy. The stage show, beneath its grandeur, seemed to conceal a simple and familiar intelligence, as if the drafts that stirred the miles of golden curtain had blown straight from Indiana. The performance left Alice and Mildred-Rose distracted with pleasure, and on the way back to the Mentone, Evarts had to lead them along the sidewalk to keep them from walking into hydrants. It was a quarter of three when they got back to the hotel. Evarts kissed his wife and child goodbye and started for Murchison's.

He got lost. He was afraid that he would be late. He began to run. He asked directions of a couple of policemen and finally reached the office building.

The front room of Murchison's office was dingy—intentionally dingy, Evarts hoped—but it was not inglorious, for there were many beautiful men and women there, waiting to see Mr. Murchison. None of them were sitting down, and they chatted together as if delighted by the delay that held them there. The receptionist led Evarts into a further office. This office was also crowded, but the atmosphere was of haste and trouble, as if the place were being besieged. Murchison was there and he greeted Evarts strenuously. "I've got your contracts right here," he said, and he handed Evarts a pen and pushed a stack of contracts toward him. "Now I want you to rush over and see Madge," Murchison said as soon as Evarts had signed the contracts. He looked at Evarts, plucked the feather carnation out of his lapel, and tossed it into a wastebasket. "Hurry, hurry, hurry," he said. "She's at 400 Park Avenue. She's crazy to see you. She's waiting now. I'll see you later tonight—I think Madge has something planned—but hurry."

Evarts rushed into the hall and rang impatiently for the elevator. As soon as he had left the building, he got lost and wandered into the fur district. A policeman directed him back to the Mentone. Alice and Mildred-Rose were waiting in the lobby, and he told them what had happened. "I'm on my way to see Madge Beatty now," he said. "I've got to hurry!" Bitsey, the bellboy, overheard this conversation. He dropped some bags he was carrying and joined the group. He told Evarts how to get to Park

Avenue. Evarts kissed Alice and Mildred-Rose again. They waved goodbye as he ran out the door.

Evarts had seen so many movies of Park Avenue that he observed its breadth and bleakness with a sense of familiarity. He took an elevator to the Murchisons' apartment and was led by a maid into a pretty living room. A fire was burning, and there were flowers on the mantel. He sprang to his feet when Madge Beatty came in. She was frail, animated, and golden, and her hoarse and accomplished voice made him feel naked. "I read your play, Evarts," she said, "and I loved it, I loved it, I loved it." She moved lightly around the room, talking now directly at him, now over her shoulder. She was not as young as she had first appeared to be, and in the light from the windows she looked almost wizened. "You're going to do more with my part when you write the second act, I hope," she said. "You're going to build it up and build it up and build it up."

"I'll do anything you want, Miss Beatty," Evarts said.

She sat down and folded her beautiful hands. Her feet were very big, Evarts noticed. Her shins were thin, and this made her feet seem very big. "Oh, we love your play, Evarts," she said. "We love it, we want it, we need it. Do you know how much we need it? We're in debt, Evarts, we're dreadfully in debt." She laid a hand on her breast and spoke in a whisper. "We owe one million nine hundred and sixty-five thousand dollars." She let the precious light flood her voice again. "But now I'm keeping you from writing your beautiful play," she said. "I'm keeping you from work, and I want you to go back and write and write and write, and I want you and your wife to come here any time after nine tonight and meet a few of our warmest friends."

Evarts asked the doorman how to get back to the Mentone, but he misunderstood the directions and got lost again. He walked around the East Side until he found a policeman, who directed him back to the hotel. It was so late when he returned that Mildred-Rose was crying with hunger. The three of them washed and went to the Automat and walked up and down Broadway until nearly nine. Then they went back to the hotel. Alice put on her evening dress, and she and Evarts kissed Mildred-Rose good night. In the lobby, they met Bitsey and told him where they were going. He promised to keep an eye on Mildred-Rose.

THE WALK OVER to the Murchisons' was longer than Evarts remembered. Alice's wrap was light. She was blue with cold when they reached the apartment building. They could hear in the distance, as they left the elevator, someone playing the piano and a woman singing "A kiss is but a kiss, a sigh is but a sigh . . ." A maid took their wraps, and Mr. Murchison greeted them from a farther door. Alice ruffled and arranged the cloth peony that hung from the front of her dress, and they went in.

The room was crowded, the lights were dim, the singer was ending her song. There was a heady smell of animal skins and astringent perfume in the air. Mr. Murchison introduced the Malloys to a couple who stood near the door, and abandoned them. The couple turned their backs on the Malloys. Evarts was shy and quiet, but Alice was excited and began to speculate, in a whisper, about the identities of the people around the piano. She felt sure that they were all movie stars, and she was right.

The singer finished her song, got up from the piano, and walked away. There was a little applause and then a curious silence. Mr. Murchison asked another woman to sing. "I'm not going to go on after *her*," the woman said. The situation, whatever it was, had stopped conversation. Mr. Murchison asked several people to perform, but they all refused. "Perhaps Mrs. Malloy will sing for us," he said bitterly.

"All right," Alice said. She walked to the center of the room. She took a position and, folding her hands and holding them breast high, began to sing.

Alice's mother had taught her to sing whenever her host asked, and Alice had never violated any of her mother's teachings. As a child, she had taken singing lessons from Mrs. Bachman, an elderly widow who lived in Wentworth. She had sung in grammar-school assemblies and in high-school assemblies. On family holidays, there had always come a time, in the late afternoon, when she would be asked to sing; then she would rise from her place on the hard sofa near the stove or come from the kitchen, where she had been washing dishes, to sing the songs Mrs. Bachman had taught her.

The invitation that night had been so unexpected that Evarts had not had a chance to stop his wife. He had felt the bitterness in Murchison's voice, and he would have stopped her, but as soon as she began to sing, he didn't care. Her voice was well pitched, her figure was stern and touching, and she sang for those people in obedience to her mannerly heart. When he had overcome his own bewilderment, he noticed the respect and attention the Murchisons' guests were giving her music. Many of them had come from towns as small as Wentworth; they were goodhearted people, and the simple air, rendered in Alice's fearless voice, reminded them of their beginnings. None of them were whispering or smiling. Many of them had lowered their heads, and he saw a woman touch her eyes with a handkerchief. Alice had triumphed, he thought, and then he recognized the song as "Annie Laurie."

Years ago, when Mrs. Bachman had taught Alice the song, she had taught her to close it with a piece of business that brought her success as a child, as a girl, as a high-school senior, but that, even in the stuffy living room in Wentworth, with its inexorable smells of poverty and cooking, had begun to tire and worry her family. She had been taught on the closing line, "Lay me doun and dee," to fall in a heap on the floor. She fell less precipitously now that she had got older, but she still fell, and Evarts could see that night, by her serene face, that a fall was in her plans. He considered going to her, embracing her, and whispering to her that the hotel was burning or that Mildred-Rose was sick. Instead, he turned his back.

Alice took a quick breath and attacked the last verse. Evarts had begun to sweat so freely that the brine got into his eyes. "I'll lay me doun and dee," he heard her sing; he heard the loud crash as she hit the floor; he heard the screams of helpless laughter, the tobacco coughs, and the oaths of a woman who laughed so hard she broke her pearl bib. The Murchisons' guests seemed bewitched. They wept, they shook, they stooped, they slapped one another on the back, and walked, like the demented, in circles. When Evarts faced the scene, Alice was sitting on the floor. He helped her to her feet. "Come, darling," he said.

"Come." With his arm around her, he led her into the hall.

"Didn't they like my song?" she asked. She began to cry.

"It doesn't matter, my darling," Evarts said, "it doesn't matter, it doesn't matter." They got their wraps and walked back through the cold to the Mentone.

Bitsey was waiting for them in the corridor outside their room. He wanted to hear all about the party. Evarts sent Alice into the room and talked with the bellboy alone. He didn't feel like describing the party. "I don't think I want to have anything more to do with the Murchisons," he said. "I'm going to get a new producer."

"That's the boy, that's the boy," Bitsey said. "Now you're talking. But, first, I want you to go up to the Hauser Agency and see Charlie Leavitt."

"All right," Evarts said. "All right, I'll go and see Charlie Leavitt."

Alice cried herself to sleep that night. Again, Evarts couldn't sleep. He sat in a chair by the window. He fell into a doze, a little before dawn, but not for long. At seven o'clock, he led his family off to the Automat.

Bitsey came up to the Malloys' room after breakfast. He was very excited. A columnist in one of the four-cent newspapers had reported Evarts' arrival in New York. A cabinet member and a Balkan king were mentioned in the same paragraph. Then the telephone began to ring. First, it was a man who wanted to sell Evarts a secondhand mink coat. Then a lawyer and a dry cleaner called, a dressmaker, a nursery school, several agencies, and a man who said he could get them a good apartment. Evarts said no to all these importunities, but in each case he had to argue before he could hang up. Bitsey had made a noon appointment for him with Charlie Leavitt, and when it was time, he kissed Alice and Mildred-Rose and went down to the street.

The Hauser Agency was located in one of the buildings in Radio City. Now Evarts' business took him through the building's formidable doors as legitimately, he told himself, as anyone else. The Hauser offices were on the twenty-sixth floor. He didn't call his floor until the elevator had begun its ascent. "It's too late now," the operator said.

"You got to tell me the number of the floor when you get in." This branded him as green to all the other people in the car, Evarts knew, and he blushed. He rode to the sixtieth floor and then back to the twenty-sixth. As he left the car, the elevator operator sneered.

At the end of a long corridor, there was a pair of bronze doors, fastened by a bifurcated eagle. Evarts turned the wings of the imperial bird and stepped into a lofty manor hall. The paneling on its walls was worm-pitted and white with rot. In the distance, behind a small glass window, he saw a woman wearing earphones. He walked over to her, told her his business, and was asked to sit down. He sat on a leather sofa and lighted a cigarette. The richness of the hall impressed him profoundly. Then he noticed that the sofa was covered with dust. So were the table, the magazines on it, the lamp, the bronze cast of Rodin's "Le Baiser"—everything in the vast room was covered with dust. He noticed at the same time the peculiar stillness of the hall. All the usual noises of an office were lacking. Into this stillness, from the distant earth, rose the recorded music from the skating rink, where a carillon played "Joy to the World! The Lord Is Come!" The magazines on the table beside the sofa were all five years old.

After a while, the receptionist pointed to a double door at the end of the hall, and Evarts walked there, timidly. The office on the other side of the door was smaller than the room he had just left but dimmer, richer, and more imposing, and in the distance he could still hear the music of the skating rink. A man was sitting at an antique desk. He stood as soon as he saw Evarts. "Welcome, Evarts, welcome to the Hauser Agency!" he shouted. "I hear you've got a hot property there, and Bitsey tells me you're through with Tracey Murchison. I haven't read your play, of course, but if Tracey wants it, I want it, and so does Sam Farley. I've got a producer for you, I've got a star for you, I've got a theatre for you, and I think I've got a pre-production deal lined up. One hundred thou' on a four-hundred-thou' ceiling. Sit down, sit down."

Mr. Leavitt seemed either to be eating something or to be having trouble with his teeth, for at the end of every sentence he worked his lips noisily and thoughtfully, like a gourmet. He might have been eating something, since there were crumbs around his mouth. Or he might have been having trouble with his teeth, because the labial noises continued all through the interview. Mr. Leavitt wore a lot of gold. He had several rings, a gold identification bracelet, and a gold bracelet watch, and he carried a heavy gold cigarette case, set with jewels. The case was empty, and Evarts furnished him with cigarettes as they talked.

"Now, I want you to go back to your hotel, Evarts," Mr. Leavitt shouted, "and I want you to take it easy. Charlie Leavitt is taking care of your property. I want you to promise me you won't worry. Now, I understand that you've signed a contract with Murchison. I'm going to declare that contract null and void, and my lawyer is going to declare that contract null and void, and if Murchison contests it, we'll drag him into court and have the judge declare that contract null and void. Before we go any further, though," he said, softening his voice, "I want you to sign these papers, which will give me authority to represent you." He pressed some papers and a gold fountain pen on Evarts. "Just sign these papers," he said sadly, "and you'll make four hundred thousand dollars. Oh, you authors!" he exclaimed. "You lucky authors!"

As soon as Evarts had signed the papers, Mr. Leavitt's manner changed and he began to shout again. "The producer I've got for you is Sam Farley. The star is Susan Hewitt. Sam Farley is Tom Farley's brother. He's married to Clarissa Douglas and he's George Howland's uncle. Pat Levy's his brother-in-law and Mitch Kababian and Howie Brown are related to him on his mother's side. She was Lottie Mayes. They're a very close family. They're a great little team. When your show opens in Wilmington, Sam Farley, Tom Farley, Clarissa Douglas, George Howland, Pat Levy, Mitch Kababian, and Howie Brown are all right down there in that hotel writing your third act. When your show goes up to Baltimore, Sam Farley, Tom Farley, Clarissa Douglas, George Howland, Pat Levy, Mitch Kababian, and Howie Brown, they go up to Baltimore with it. And when your show opens up on Broadway with a high-class production, who's down there in the front row, rooting for you?" Mr. Leavitt had strained his voice, and he ended in a hoarse whisper, "Sam Farley, Tom Farley, George Howland, Clarissa Douglas, Pat Levy, Mitch Kababian, and Howie Brown.

"Now, I want you to go back to your hotel and have a good time," he shouted after he had cleared his throat. "I'll call you tomorrow and tell you when Sam Farley and Susan Hewitt can see you, and I'll telephone Hollywood now and tell Max Rayburn that he can have it for one hundred thou' on a four-hundred-thou' ceiling, and not one iota less." He patted Evarts on the back and steered him gently toward the door. "Have a good time, Evarts," he said.

As Evarts walked back through the hall, he noticed that the receptionist was eating a sandwich. She beckoned to him.

"You want to take a chance on a new Buick convertible?" she whispered. "Ten cents a chance."

"Oh, no, thank you," Evart said.

"Fresh eggs?" she asked. "I bring them in from Jersey every morning."

"No, thank you," Evarts said.

EVARTS HURRIED BACK through the crowds to the Mentone, where Alice, Mildred-Rose, and Bitsey were waiting. He described his interview with Leavitt to them. "When I get that four hundred thou'," he said, "I'm going to send some money to Mama Finelli." Then Alice remembered a lot of other people in Wentworth who needed money. By way of a celebration, they went to a spaghetti house that night instead of the Automat. After dinner, they went to Radio City Music Hall. Again, that night, Evarts was unable to sleep.

In Wentworth, Alice had been known as the practical member of the family. There was a good deal of jocularity on this score. She drew up the budget and managed the egg money, and it was often said that Evarts would have misplaced his head if it hadn't been for Alice. This businesslike strain in her character led her to remind Evarts on the following day that he had not been working on his play. She took the situation in hand. "You just sit in the room," she said, "and write the play, and Mildred-

Rose and I will walk up and down Fifth Avenue, so you can be alone."

Evarts tried to work, but the telephone began to ring again and he was interrupted regularly by jewelry salesmen, theatrical lawyers, and laundry services. At about eleven, he picked up the phone and heard a familiar and angry voice. It was Murchison. "I brought you from Wentworth," he shouted, "and I made you what you are today. Now they tell me you breached my contract and double-crossed me with Sam Farley. I'm going to break you, I'm going to ruin you, I'm going to sue you, I'm—" Evarts hung up, and when the phone rang a minute later, he didn't answer it. He left a note for Alice, put on his hat, and walked up Fifth Avenue to the Hauser offices.

When he turned the bifurcated eagle of the double doors and stepped into the manor hall that morning, he found Mr. Leavitt there, in his shirt sleeves, sweeping the carpet. "Oh, good morning," Leavitt said. "Occupational therapy." He hid the broom and dustpan behind a velvet drape. "Come in, come in," he said, slipping into his jacket and leading Evarts toward the inner office. "This afternoon, you're going to meet Sam Farley and Susan Hewitt. You're one of the luckiest men in New York. Some men never see Sam Farley. Not even once in a lifetime—never hear his wit, never feel the force of his unique personality. And as for Susan Hewitt . . ." He was speechless for a moment. He said the appointment was for three. "You're going to meet them in Sam Farley's lovely home," he said, and he gave Evarts the address.

Evarts tried to describe the telephone conversation with Murchison, but Leavitt cut him off. "I asked you one thing," he shouted. "I asked you not to worry. Is that too much? I ask you to talk with Sam Farley and take a look at Susan Hewitt and see if you think she's right for the part. Is that too much? Now, have a good time. Take in a newsreel. Go to the zoo. Go see Sam Farley at three o'clock." He patted Evarts on the back and pushed him toward the door.

Evarts ate lunch at the Mentone with Alice and Mildred-Rose. He had a headache. After lunch, they walked up and down Fifth Avenue, and when it got close to three, Alice and Mildred-Rose walked with him to Sam

Farley's house. It was an impressive building, faced with rough stone, like a Spanish prison. He kissed Mildred-Rose and Alice goodbye and rang the bell. A butler opened the door. Evarts could tell he was a butler because he wore striped pants. The butler led him upstairs to a drawing room.

"I'm here to see Mr. Farley," Evarts said.

"I know," the butler said. "You're Evarts Malloy. You've got an appointment. But he won't keep it. He's stuck in a floating crap game in the Acme Garage, at a Hundred and Sixty-fourth Street, and he won't be back until tomorrow. Susan Hewitt's coming, though. You're supposed to see her. Oh, if you only knew what goes on in this place!" He lowered his voice to a whisper and brought his face close to Evarts'. "If these walls could only talk! There hasn't been any heat in this house since we came back from Hollywood and he hasn't paid me since the twenty-first of June. I wouldn't mind so much, but the son of a bitch never learned to let the water out of his bathtub. He takes a bath and leaves the dirty water standing there. To stagnate. On top of everything else, I cut my finger washing dishes yesterday." There was a dirty bandage on the butler's forefinger, and he began, hurriedly, to unwrap layer after layer of bloody gauze. "Look," he said, holding the wound to Evarts' face. "Cut right through to the bone. Yesterday you could see the bone. Blood. Blood all over everything. Took me half an hour to clean up. It's a miracle I didn't get an infection." He shook his head at this miracle. "When the mouse comes, I'll send her up." He wandered out of the room, trailing the length of bloody bandage after him.

Evarts' eyes were burning with fatigue. He was so tired that if he had rested his head against anything, he would have fallen asleep. He heard the doorbell ring and the butler greet Susan Hewitt. She ran up the stairs and into the drawing room.

She was young, and she came into the room as if it were her home and she had just come back from school. She was light, her features were delicate and very small, and her fair hair was brushed simply and had begun to darken, of its own course, and was streaked softly with brown, like the grain in pine wood. "I'm so happy to meet you, Evarts," she said. "I want to tell you that I love your play." How she could have read his play, Evarts did not know, but he was too confused by her beauty to worry or to speak. His mouth was dry. It might have been the antic pace of the last days, it might have been his loss of sleep—he didn't know—but he felt as though he had fallen in love.

"You remind me of a girl I used to know," he said. "She worked in a lunch wagon outside South Bend. Never worked in a lunch wagon outside South Bend, did you?"

"No," she said.

"It isn't only that," he said. "You remind me of all of it. I mean the night drives. I used to be a night bus driver. That's what you remind me of. The stars, I mean, and the grade crossings, and the cattle lined up along the fences. And the girls in the lunch counters. They always looked so pretty. But you never worked in a lunch counter."

"No," she said.

"You can have my play," he said. "I mean, I think you're right for the part. Sam Farley can have the play. Everything."

"Thank you, Evarts," she said.

"Will you do me a favor?" he asked.

"What?"

"Oh, I know it's foolish," he said. He got up and walked around the room. "But there's nobody here, nobody will know about it. I hate to ask you."

"What do you want?"

"Will you let me lift you?" he said. "Just let me lift you. Just let me see how light you are."

"All right," she said. "Do you want me to take off my coat?"

"Yes, yes, yes," he said. "Take off your coat."

She stood. She let her coat fall to the sofa.

"Can I do it now?" he said.

"Yes."

He put his hands under her arms. He raised her off the floor and then put her down gently. "Oh, you're so light!" he shouted. "You're so light, you're so fragile, you don't weigh any more than a suitcase. Why, I could carry you, I could carry you anywhere, I could carry you from one end of New York to the other." He got his hat and coat and ran out of the house.

EVARTS FELT BEWILDERED and exhausted when he returned to the Mentone. Bitsey was in the room with Mildred-Rose and Alice. He kept asking questions about Mama Finelli. He wanted to know where she lived and what her telephone number was. Evarts lost his temper at the bellboy and told him to go away. He lay down on the bed and fell asleep while Alice and Mildred-Rose were asking him questions. When he woke, an hour later, he felt much better. They went to the Automat and then to Radio City Music Hall, and they got to bed early, so that Evarts could work on his play in the morning. He couldn't sleep.

After breakfast, Alice and Mildred-Rose left Evarts alone in the room and he tried to work. He couldn't work, but it wasn't the telephone that troubled him that day. The difficulty that blocked his play was deep, and as he smoked and stared at the brick wall, he recognized it. He was in love with Susan Hewitt. This might have been an incentive to work, but he had left his creative strength in Indiana. He shut his eyes and tried to recall the strong, dissolute voice of Mama Finelli, but before he could realize a word, it would be lost in the noise from the street.

If there had been anything to set his memory free—a train whistle, a moment of silence, the smells of a barn—he might have been inspired. He paced the room, he smoked, he sniffed the sooty window curtains and stuffed his ears with toilet paper, but there seemed to be no way of recalling Indiana at the Mentone. He stayed near the desk all that day. He went without lunch. When his wife and child returned from Radio City Music Hall, where they had spent the afternoon, he told them he was going to take a walk. Oh, he thought as he left the hotel, if I could only hear the noise of a crow!

He strode up Fifth Avenue, holding his head high, trying to divine in the confusion of sound a voice that might lead him. He walked rapidly until he reached Radio City and could hear, in the distance, the music from the skating rink. Something stopped him. He lighted a cigarette. Then he heard someone calling him. "Behold the lordly moose, Evarts," a woman shouted. It was the hoarse, dissolute voice of Mama Finelli, and he thought that desire had deranged him until he turned and saw her, sitting on one of the benches, by a dry pool. "Behold the lordly moose, Evarts," she called, and she put her hands, spaced like antlers, above her head. This was the way she greeted everyone in Wentworth.

"Behold the lordly moose, Mama Finelli," Evarts shouted. He ran to her side and sat down. "Oh, Mama Finelli, I'm so glad to see you," he said. "You won't believe it, but I've been thinking about you all day. I've been wishing all day that I could talk with you." He turned to drink in her vulpine features and her whiskery chin. "How did you ever get to New York, Mama Finelli?"

"Come up on a flying machine," she cried. "Come up on a flying machine today. Have a sandwich." She was eating some sandwiches from a paper bag.

"No, thanks," he said. "What do you think of New York?" he asked. "What do you think of that high building?"

"Well, I don't know," she said, but he could see that she did know and he could see her working her face into shape for a retort. "I guess there's just the one, for if there hada been two, they'd of pollinated and bore!" She whooped with laughter and struck herself on the legs.

"What are you doing in New York, Mama Finelli? How did you happen to come here?"

"Well," she said, "man named Tracey Murchison calls me on the telephone long-distance and says for me to come up to New York and sue you for libel. Says you wrote a play about me and I can sue you for libel and git a lot of money and split it with him, fairly, he says, and then I don't have to run the gas station no more. So he wires me money for the flying-machine ticket and I come up here and I talk with him and I'm going to sue you for libel and split it with him, sixty-forty. That's what I'm going to do," she said.

Later that night, the Malloys returned to the marble waiting room of Grand Central and Evarts began to search for a Chicago train. He found a Chicago train, bought some tickets, and they boarded a coach. It was a rainy night, and the dark, wet paving, deep in the station, did not glitter, but it was still Alice's belief that diamonds had been ground into it, and that was the way she would tell the story. They had picked up the lessons of travel rapidly, and they arranged themselves adroitly over several seats. After the train started, Alice made friends with a plain-spoken couple across the aisle, who were traveling with a baby to Los Angeles. The woman had a brother there, who had written to her enthusiastically about the climate and the opportunities.

"Let's go to Los Angeles," Alice said to Evarts. "We still have a little money and we can buy tickets in Chicago and you can sell your play in Hollywood, where nobody's ever heard of Mama Finelli or any of the others."

Evarts said that he would make his decision in Chicago. He was weary and he fell asleep. Mildred-Rose put her thumb into her mouth, and soon both she and her mother had lost consciousness, too. Mildred-Rose stroked the sere skins of her coat and they told her that all was well, all was well.

THE MALLOYS may have left the train in Chicago and gone back to Wentworth. It is not hard to imagine their homecoming, for they would be welcomed by their friends and relations, although their stories might not be believed. Or they may have changed, at Chicago, for a train to the West, and this, to tell the truth, is easier to imagine. One can see them playing hearts in the lounge car and eating cheese sandwiches in the railroad stations as they traveled through Kansas and Nebraska—over the mountains and on to the Coast.

THE HARTLEYS

MR. AND MRS. HARTLEY and their daughter Anne reached the Pemaquoddy Inn, one winter evening, after dinner and just as the bridge games were getting under way. Mr. Hartley carried the bags across the broad porch and into the lobby, and his wife and daughter followed him. They all three seemed very tired, and they looked around them at the bright, homely room with the gratitude of people who have escaped from tension and danger, for they had been driving in a blinding snowstorm since early morning. They had made the trip from New York, and it had snowed all the way, they said. Mr. Hartley put down the bags and returned to the car to get the skis. Mrs. Hartley sat down in one of the lobby chairs, and her daughter, tired and shy, drew close to her. There was a little snow in the girl's hair, and Mrs. Hartley brushed this away with her fingers. Then Mrs. Butterick, the widow who owned the inn, went out to the porch and called to Mr. Hartley that he needn't put his car up. One of the men would do it, she said. He came back into the lobby and signed the register.

He seemed to be a likable man with an edge to his voice and an intense, polite manner. His wife was a handsome, dark-haired woman who was dazed with fatigue, and his daughter was a girl of about seven. Mrs. Butterick asked Mr. Hartley if he had ever stayed at the Pemaquoddy before. "When I got the reservation," she said, "the name rang a bell."

"Mrs. Hartley and I were here eight years ago February," Mr. Hartley said. "We came on the twenty-third and were here for ten days. I remember the date clearly because we had such a wonderful time." Then they went upstairs. They came down again long enough to make a supper of some leftovers that had been kept warm on the back of the stove. The child was so tired she nearly fell asleep at the table. After supper, they went upstairs again.

In the winter, the life of the Pemaquoddy centered entirely on cold sports. Drinkers and malingerers were not encouraged, and most of the people there were earnest about their skiing. In the morning, they would take a bus across the valley to the mountains, and if the weather was good, they would carry a pack lunch and remain on the slopes until late afternoon. They'd vary this occasionally by skating on a rink near the inn, which had been made by flooding a clothesyard. There was a hill behind the inn that could sometimes be used for skiing when conditions on the mountain were poor. This hill was serviced by a primitive ski tow that had been built by Mrs. Butterick's son. "He bought that motor that pulls the tow when he was a senior at Harvard," Mrs. Butterick always said when she spoke of the tow. "It was in an old Mercer auto, and he drove it up here from Cambridge one night without any license plates!" When she said this, she would put her hand over her heart, as if the dangers of the trip were still vivid.

The Hartleys picked up the Pemaquoddy routine of fresh air and exercise the morning following their arrival.

Mrs. Hartley was an absent-minded woman. She boarded the bus for the mountain that morning, sat down, and was talking to another passenger when she realized that she had forgotten her skis. Her husband went after them while everyone waited. She wore a bright, fur-trimmed parka that had been cut for someone with a younger face, and it made her look tired. Her husband wore some Navy equipment, which was stenciled with his name and rank. Their daughter, Anne, was pretty. Her hair was braided in tight, neat plaits, there was a saddle of freckles across her small nose, and she looked around her with the bleak, rational scrutiny of her age.

Mr. Hartley was a good skier. He was up and down the slope, his skis parallel, his knees bent, his shoulders swinging gracefully in a half circle. His wife was not as clever but she knew what she was doing, and she enjoyed the cold air and the snow. She fell now and then, and when someone offered to help her to her feet, when the cold snow that had been pressed against her face had heightened its color, she looked like a much younger woman.

Anne didn't know how to ski. She stood at the foot of the slope watching her parents. They called to her, but she didn't move, and after a while she began to shiver. Her mother went to her and tried to encourage her, but the child turned away crossly. "I don't want *you* to show me," she said. "I want Daddy to show me." Mrs. Hartley called her husband.

As soon as Mr. Hartley turned his attention to Anne, she lost all of her hesitation. She followed him up and down the hill, and as long as he was with her, she seemed confident and happy. Mr. Hartley stayed with Anne until after lunch, when he turned her over to a professional instructor who was taking a class of beginners out to the slope. Mr. and Mrs. Hartley went with the group to the foot of the slope, where Mr. Hartley took his daughter aside. "Your mother and I are going to ski some trails now," he said, "and I want you to join Mr. Ritter's class and to learn as much from him as you can. If you're ever going to learn to ski, Anne, you'll have to learn without me. We'll be back at around four, and I want you to show me what you've learned when we come back."

"Yes, Daddy," she said.

"Now you go and join the class."

"Yes, Daddy."

Mr. and Mrs. Hartley waited until Anne had climbed the slope and joined the class. Then they went away. Anne watched the instructor for a few minutes, but as soon as she noticed that her parents had gone, she broke from the group and coasted down the hill toward the hut. "Miss," the instructor called after her. "Miss . . ." She didn't answer. She went into the hut, took off her parka and her mittens, spread them neatly on a table to dry, and sat beside the fire, holding her head down so that her face could not be seen. She sat there all afternoon. A little before dark, when her parents returned to the hut, stamping the snow off their boots, she ran to her father. Her face was swollen from crying. "Oh, Daddy, I thought you weren't coming back," she cried. "I thought you weren't ever coming back!" She threw her arms around him and buried her face in his clothes.

"Now, now, now, Anne," he said, and he patted her back and smiled at the people who happened to notice the scene. Anne sat beside him on the bus ride back, holding his arm.

At the inn that evening, the Hartleys came into the bar before dinner and sat at a wall table. Mrs. Hartley and her daughter drank tomato juice, and Mr. Hartley had three Old-Fashioneds. He gave Anne the orange slices and the sweet cherries from his drinks. Everything her father did interested her. She lighted his cigarettes and blew out the matches. She examined his watch and laughed at all his jokes. She had a sharp, pleasant laugh.

The family talked quietly. Mr. and Mrs. Hartley spoke oftener to Anne than to each other, as if they had come to a point in their marriage where there was nothing to say. They discussed haltingly, between themselves, the snow and the mountain, and in the course of this attempt to make conversation Mr. Hartley, for some reason, spoke sharply to his wife. Mrs. Hartley got up from the table quickly. She might have been crying. She hurried through the lobby and went up the stairs.

Mr. Hartley and Anne stayed in the bar. When the dinner bell rang, he asked the desk clerk to send Mrs. Hartley a tray. He ate dinner with his daughter in the dining room. After dinner, he sat in the parlor reading an old copy of *Fortune* while Anne played with some other children who were staying at the inn. They were all a little younger than she, and she handled them easily and affectionately, imitating an adult. She taught them a simple card game and then read them a story. After the younger children were sent to bed, she read a book. Her father took her upstairs at about nine.

He came down by himself later and went into the bar. He drank alone and talked with the bartender about various brands of bourbon. "Dad used to have his bourbon sent up from Kentucky in kegs," Mr. Hartley said. A slight rasp in his voice, and his intense and polite manner, made what he said seem important. "They were small, as I recall. I don't suppose they held more than a gallon. Dad used to have them sent to him twice a year. When Grandmother asked him what they were, he always told her they were full of sweet cider." After discussing bourbons, they discussed the village and the changes in the inn. "We've only been here once before," Mr. Hartley said. "That was eight years ago, eight years ago February." Then he repeated, word for word, what he had said in the lobby the previous night. "We came on the twenty-third and were here for ten days. I remember the date clearly because we had such a wonderful time."

The Hartleys' subsequent days were nearly all like the first. Mr. Hartley spent the early hours instructing his daughter. The girl learned rapidly, and when she was with her father, she was daring and graceful, but as soon as he left her, she would go to the hut and sit by the fire. Each day, after lunch, they would reach the point where he gave her a lecture on self-reliance. "Your mother and I are going away now," he would say, "and I want you to ski by yourself, Anne." She would nod her head and agree with him, but as soon as he had gone, she would return to the hut and wait there. Once—it was the third day—he lost his temper. "Now, listen, Anne," he shouted, "if you're going to learn to ski, you've got to learn by yourself." His loud voice wounded her, but it did not seem to show her the way to independence. She became a familiar figure in the afternoons, sitting beside the fire.

Sometimes Mr. Hartley would modify his discipline. The three of them would return to the inn on the early bus and he would take his daughter to the skating rink and give her a skating lesson. On these occasions, they stayed out late. Mrs. Hartley watched them sometimes from the parlor window. The rink was at the foot of the primitive ski tow that had been built by Mrs. Butterick's son. The terminal posts of the tow looked like gibbets in the twilight, and Mr. Hartley and his daughter looked like figures of contrition and patience. Again and again they would circle the little rink, earnest and serious, as if he were explaining to her something more mysterious than a sport.

Everyone at the inn liked the Hartleys, although they gave the other guests the feeling that they had recently suffered some loss—the loss of money, perhaps, or perhaps Mr. Hartley had lost his job. Mrs. Hartley remained absent-minded, but the other guests got the feeling that this characteristic was the result of some misfortune that had shaken her self-possession. She seemed anxious to be friendly and she plunged, like a lonely woman, into every conversation. Her father had been a doctor, she said. She spoke of him as if he had been a great power, and she spoke with intense pleasure of her childhood. "Mother's living room in Grafton was forty-five feet long," she said. "There were fireplaces at both ends. It was one of those marvelous old Victorian houses." In the china cabinet in the dining room, there was some china like the china Mrs. Hartley's mother had owned. In the lobby there was a paperweight like a paperweight Mrs. Hartley had been given when she was a girl. Mr. Hartley also spoke of his origins now and then. Mrs. Butterick once asked him to carve a leg of lamb, and as he sharpened the carving knife, he said, "I never do this without thinking of Dad." Among the collection of canes in the hallway, there was a blackthorn embossed with silver. "That's exactly like the blackthorn Mr. Wentworth brought Dad from Ireland," Mr. Hartley said.

Anne was devoted to her father but she obviously liked her mother, too. In the evenings, when she was tired, she would sit on the sofa beside Mrs. Hartley and rest her head on her mother's shoulder. It seemed to be only on the mountain, where the environment was strange, that her father would become for her the only person in the world. One evening when the Hartleys were playing bridge—it was quite late and Anne had gone to bed—the child began to call her father. "I'll go, darling," Mrs. Hartley said, and she excused herself and went upstairs. "I want my daddy," those at the bridge table could hear the girl screaming. Mrs. Hartley quieted her and came downstairs again. "Anne had a nightmare," she explained, and went on playing cards.

The next day was windy and warm. In the middle of the afternoon, it began to rain, and all but the most intrepid skiers went back to their hotels. The bar at the Pemaquoddy filled up early. The radio was turned on for weather reports, and one earnest guest picked up the telephone in the lobby and called other resorts. Was it raining in Pico? Was it raining in Stowe? Was it raining in Ste. Agathe? Mr. and Mrs. Hartley were in the bar that afternoon. She was having a drink for the first time since they had been there, but she did not seem to enjoy it. Anne was playing in the parlor with the other children. A little before dinner, Mr. Hartley went into the lobby and asked Mrs. Butterick if they could have their dinner upstairs. Mrs. Butterick said that this could be arranged. When the dinner bell rang, the Hartleys went up, and a maid took them trays. After dinner, Anne went back to the parlor to play with the other children, and after the dining room had been cleared, the maid went up to get the Hartleys' trays.

The transom above the Hartleys' bedroom door was open, and as the maid went down the hall, she could hear Mrs. Hartley's voice, a voice so uncontrolled, so guttural and full of suffering, that she stopped and listened as if the woman's life were in danger. "Why do we have to come back?" Mrs. Hartley was crying. "Why do we have to come back? Why do we have to make these trips back to the places where we thought we were happy? What good is it going to do? What good has it ever done? We go through the telephone book looking for the names of people we knew ten years ago, and we ask them for dinner, and what good does it do? What good has it ever done? We go back to the restaurants, the mountains, we go back to the houses, even the neighborhoods, we walk in the slums, thinking that this will make us happy, and it never does. Why in Christ's name did we ever begin such a wretched thing? Why isn't there an end to it? Why can't we separate again? It was better that way. Wasn't it better that way? It was better for Anne—I don't care what you say, it was better for her than this. I'll take Anne again and you can live in town. Why can't I do that, why can't I, why can't I, why can't I . . ." The frightened maid went back along the corridor. Anne was sitting in the parlor reading to the younger children when the maid went downstairs.

IT CLEARED UP that night and turned cold. Everything froze. In the morning, Mrs. Butterick announced that all the trails on the mountain were closed and that the tramway would not run. Mr. Hartley and some other guests broke the crust on the hill behind the inn, and one of the hired hands started the primitive tow. "My son bought the motor that pulls the tow when he was a senior at Harvard," Mrs. Butterick said when she heard its humble explosions. "It was in an old Mercer auto, and he drove it up here from Cambridge one night without any license plates!" The slope offered the only skiing in the neighborhood, and after lunch a lot of people came here from other hotels. They wore the snow away under the tow to a surface of rough stone, and snow had to be shoveled onto the tracks. The rope was frayed, and Mrs. Butterick's son had planned the tow so poorly that it gave the skiers a strenuous and uneven ride. Mrs. Hartley tried to get Anne to use the tow, but she would not ride it until her father led the way. He showed her how to stand, how to hold the rope, bend her knees, and drag her poles. As soon as he was carried up the hill, she gladly followed. She followed him up and down the hill all afternoon, delighted that for once he was remaining in her sight. When the crust on the slope was broken and packed, it made good running, and that odd, nearly compulsive rhythm of riding and skiing, riding and skiing, established itself.

It was a fine afternoon. There were snow clouds, but a bright and cheerful light beat through them. The country, seen from the top of the hill, was black and white. Its only colors were the colors of spent fire, and this impressed itself upon one—as if the desolation were something more than winter, as if it were the work of a great conflagration. People talk, of course, while they ski, while they wait for their turn to seize the rope, but they can hardly be heard. There is the exhaust of the tow motor and the creak of the iron wheel upon which the tow rope turns, but the skiers themselves seem stricken dumb, lost in the rhythm of riding and coasting. That afternoon was a continuous cycle of movement. There was a single file to the left of the slope, holding the frayed rope and breaking from it, one by one, at the crown of the hill to choose their way down, going again and again over the same surface, like people who, having lost a ring or a key on the beach, search again and again in the same sand. In the stillness, the child Anne began to shriek. Her arm had got caught in the frayed rope; she had been thrown to the ground and was being dragged brutally up the hill toward the iron wheel. "Stop the tow!" her father roared. "Stop the tow! Stop the tow!" And everyone else on the hill began to shout, "Stop the tow! Stop the tow! Stop the tow!" But there was no one there to stop it. Her screams were hoarse and terrible, and the more she struggled to free herself from the rope, the more violently it threw her to the ground. Space and the cold seemed to reduce the voices—even the anguish in the voices—of the people who were calling to stop the tow, but the girl's cries were piercing until her neck was broken on the iron wheel.

The Hartleys left for New York that night after dark. They were going to drive all night behind the local hearse. Several people offered to drive the car down for them, but Mr. Hartley said that he wanted to drive, and his wife seemed to want him to. When everything was ready, the stricken couple walked across the porch, looking around them at the bewildering beauty of the night, for it was very cold and clear and the constellations seemed brighter than the lights of the inn or the village. He helped his wife into the car, and after arranging a blanket over her legs, they started the long, long drive.

THE SUTTON PLACE STORY

DEBORAH TENNYSON waited in her nursery on Sunday morning for a signal from her father that would mean she could enter her parents' bedroom. The signal came late, for her parents had been up the night before with a business friend from Minneapolis and they both had had a good deal to drink, but when Deborah was given the signal she ran clumsily down the dark hall, screaming with pleasure. Her father took her in his arms and kissed her good morning, and then she went to where her mother lay in bed. "Hello, my sweet, my love," her mother said. "Did Ruby give you your breakfast? Did you have a good breakfast?"

"The weather is lovely out," Deborah said. "Weather is divine."

"Be kind to poor Mummy," Robert said. "Mummy has a terrible hangover."

"Mummy has a terrible hangover," Deborah repeated, and she patted her mother's face lightly.

Deborah was not quite three years old. She was a beautiful girl with wonderful, heavy hair that had lights of silver and gold. She was a city child and she knew about cocktails and hangovers. Both her parents worked and she most often saw them in the early evening, when she was brought in to say good night. Katherine and Robert Tennyson would be drinking with friends, and Deborah would be allowed to pass the smoked salmon, and she had naturally come to assume that cocktails were the axis of the adult world. She made Martinis in the sand pile and thought all the illustrations of cups, goblets, and glasses in her nursery books were filled with Old-Fashioneds.

While the Tennysons waited for breakfast that morning, they read the *Times*. Deborah spread the second news section on the floor and began an elaborate fantasy that her parents had seen performed so often they hardly noticed it. She pretended to pick clothing and jewelry from the advertisements in the paper and to dress herself with these things. Her taste, Katherine thought, was avaricious and vulgar, but there was such clarity and innocence in her monologue that it seemed like a wonderful part of the bright summer morning. "Put on the shoes," she said, and pretended to put on shoes. "Put on the mink coat," she said.

"It's too hot for a mink coat, dear," Katherine told her. "Why don't you wear a mink scarf?"

"Put on the mink scarf," Deborah said. Then the cook came into the bedroom with the coffee and orange juice, and said that Mrs. Harley was there. Robert and Katherine kissed Deborah goodbye and told her to enjoy herself in the park.

The Tennysons had no room for a sleep-in nurse, so Mrs. Harley came to the house every morning and took care of Deborah during the day. Mrs. Harley was a widow. She had lived a hearty and comfortable life until her husband's death, but he had left her with no money and she had been reduced to working as a nursemaid. She said that she loved children and had always wanted children herself, but this was not true. Children bored and irritated her. She was a kind and ignorant woman, and this, more than any bitterness, showed in her face when she took Deborah downstairs. She was full of old-country blessings for the elevator man and the doorman. She said that it was a lovely morning, wasn't it, a morning for the gods.

Mrs. Harley and Deborah walked to a little park at the edge of the river. The child's beauty was bright, and the old woman was dressed in black, and they walked hand in hand, like some amiable representation of winter and spring. Many people wished them good morning. "Where did you get that enchanting child?" someone asked. Mrs. Harley enjoyed these compliments. She was sometimes proud of Deborah, but she had been taking care of her for four months, and the little girl and the old woman had established a relationship that was not as simple as it appeared.

They quarreled a good deal when they were alone, and they quarreled like adults, with a cunning knowledge of each other's frailties. The child had never complained about Mrs. Harley; it was as though she already understood the evil importance of appearances. Deborah was taciturn about the way in which she spent her days. She would tell no one where she had been or what she had done. Mrs. Harley had found that she could count on this trait, and so the child and the old woman had come to share a number of secrets.

On several late-winter afternoons when the weather had been bitter and dark and Mrs. Harley had been ordered to keep Deborah out until five, she had taken the child to the movies. Deborah had sat beside her in the dark theatre and never complained or cried. Now and then she craned her neck to look at the screen, but most of the time she just sat quiet, listening to the voices and the music. A second secret—and one much less sinful, in Mrs. Harley's opinion—was that on Sunday mornings, sometimes, and sometimes on weekday afternoons, Mrs. Harley had left the little girl with a friend of the Tennysons. This was a woman named Renée Hall, and there was no harm in it, Mrs. Harley thought. She had never told the Tennysons, but what they didn't know wouldn't hurt them. When Renée took Deborah on Sundays, Mrs. Harley went to the eleven-o'clock Mass, and there was nothing wrong, surely, with an old woman's going into the house of God to pray for her dead.

Mrs. Harley sat down on one of the benches in the park that morning. The sun was hot and it felt good on her old legs. The air was so clear that the perspective of the river seemed to have changed. You could throw a stone onto Welfare Island, it seemed, and a trick of the light made the downtown bridges look much closer to the center of the city. Boats were going up and down the river, and as they cut the water they left in the air a damp and succinct odor, like the smell of fresh earth that follows a plow. Another nurse and child were the only other people in the park. Mrs. Harley told Deborah to go play in the sand. Then Deborah saw the dead pigeon. "The pigeon is sleeping," Deborah said. She stooped down to touch its wings.

"That dirty bird is dead, and don't you dare touch it!" Mrs. Harley shouted.

"The pretty pigeon is sleeping," Deborah said. Her face clouded suddenly and tears came into her eyes. She stood with her hands folded in front of her and her head bowed, an attitude that was a comical imitation of Mrs. Harley's reaction to sorrow, but the grief in her voice and her face came straight from her heart.

"Get away from the dirty bird!" Mrs. Harley shouted, and she got up and kicked the dead bird aside. "Go play in the sand," she told Deborah. "I don't know what's the matter with you. They must have given twenty-five dollars for that doll carriage you have up in your room, but you'd rather play with a dead bird. Go look at the river. Go look at the boats! And don't climb up on that railing, either, for you'll drop in, and with that terrible current that will be the end of you." Deborah walked obediently over to the river. "Here I am," Mrs. Harley said to the other nurse, "here I am, a woman going on sixty who lived forty years in a house of her own, sitting on a park bench like any old bum on a Sunday morning while the baby's parents are up there on the tenth floor sleeping off last night's liquor." The other nurse was a well-bred Scotch woman who was not interested in Mrs. Harley. Mrs. Harley turned her attention to the steps leading down to the park from Sutton Place, to watch for Renée Hall. The arrangement between them had been established for about a month.

Renée Hall had met Mrs. Harley and the child at the Tennysons', where she had frequently been a guest for cocktails that winter. She had been brought there by a business friend of Katherine's. She was pleasant and entertaining, and Katherine had been impressed with her clothes. She lived around the corner and didn't object to late invitations and most men liked her. The Tennysons knew nothing about her other than that she was an attractive guest and did some radio acting.

On the evening when Renée first went to the Tennysons', Deborah had been brought in to say good night, and the actress and the neglected child had sat together on a sofa. There was an odd sympathy between the two, and

Renée let the child play with her jewelry and her furs. Renée was kind to Deborah, for she was at a time in her life when she appreciated kindness herself.

She was about thirty-five years old, dissipated and gentle. She liked to think of the life she was living as an overture to something wonderful, final, and even conventional, that would begin with the next season or the season after that, but she was finding this hope more and more difficult to sustain. She had begun to notice that she always felt tired unless she was drinking. It was just that she didn't have the strength. When she was not drinking she was depressed, and when she was depressed she quarreled with headwaiters and hairdressers, accused people in restaurants of staring at her, and quarreled with some of the men who paid her debts. She knew this instability in her temperament well, and was clever at concealing it—among other things—from casual friends like the Tennysons.

Renée had come to the house again a week later, and when Deborah heard her voice, she escaped from Mrs. Harley and flew down the hall. The child's adoration excited Renée. They sat together again. Renée wore a string of furs and a hat piled with cloth roses, and Deborah thought her the most beautiful lady in the world.

After that, Renée went to the Tennysons' often. It was a standing joke that she came there to see the child and not the Tennysons or their guests. Renée had always wanted children of her own, and now all her regrets seemed centered in Deborah's bright face. She began to feel possessive toward the child. She sent her expensive clothes and toys. "Has she ever been to the dentist?" she asked Katherine. "Are you sure of your doctor? Have you entered her in nursery school?" She made the mistake one night of suggesting that Deborah saw too little of her parents and lacked the sense of security they should give her. "She has eight thousand dollars in the bank in her own name," Katherine said. She was angry. Renée continued to send Deborah elaborate presents. Deborah named all her dolls and her pleasures after Renée, and on several nights she cried for Renée after she had been put to bed. Robert and Katherine thought it would be better if they didn't see Renée any more. They stopped asking her to the house. "After all," Katherine said, "I've always felt that there was something unsavory about that girl." Renée called them twice and asked them for cocktails, and Katherine said no, no thanks, they were all suffering with colds.

Renée knew that Katherine was lying and she determined to forget the Tennysons. She missed the little girl, but she might never have seen her again if it hadn't been for something that happened later that week. One night she left a dull party early in the evening and went home by herself. She was afraid of missing telephone calls and she used a telephone-answering service. They told her that night that a Mrs. Walton had called and left a number.

Walton, Walton, Walton, Renée thought, and then she remembered that she had once had a lover named Walton. That would have been eight or ten years ago. She had once been taken to dinner with his mother, who was visiting from Cleveland. She remembered the evening clearly then. Walton drank too much and his mother had taken Renée aside and told her what a good influence she thought she was, and couldn't she make him stop drinking and go to church oftener? Walton and she had quarreled over his drinking, in the end, Renée remembered, and she had never seen him after that. He might be sick, or drunk, or getting married. She had no idea how old he was, because the thirties were all jumbled in her memory and she could not tell the beginning of the decade from its end. She dialed the number. It was a hotel on the West Side. Mrs. Walton's voice, when she answered, was the small, cracked voice of an old woman. "Billy's dead, Renée," she said. She began to sob. "I'm so glad you called. He's going to be buried tomorrow. I wish you'd come to the funeral. I feel so alone."

Renée put on a black dress the next day and took a cab to the funeral parlor. As soon as she opened the door, she was in the hands of a gloved and obsequious usher, ready to sympathize with a grief more profound and sedate than any grief of hers would ever be. An elevator took her up to the chapel. When she heard the electric organ playing "Oh, What a Beautiful Morning!" she thought she would have to sit down before she had the strength to see Mrs. Walton, and then she saw Mrs. Walton standing by the open door of the chapel. The two women embraced, and Renée was introduced to Mrs. Walton's sister, a Mrs. Henlein. They were the only people there. At the far end of the room, under a meager show of gladioli, lay her dead lover. "He was so alone, Renée dear," Mrs. Walton said. "He was so terribly alone. He died alone, you know, in that furnished room." Mrs. Walton began to cry. Mrs. Henlein cried. A minister came in and the service began. Renée knelt and tried to remember the Lord's Prayer, but she got no further than ". . . on earth as it is in Heaven." She began to cry, but not because she remembered the man tenderly; she had not remembered him for years and it was only by forcing her memory that she could recall that he sometimes brought her breakfast in bed, and that he sewed the buttons on his own shirts. She cried for herself, she cried because she was afraid that she herself might die in the night, because she was alone in the world, because her desperate and empty life was not an overture but an ending, and through it all she could see the rough, brutal shape of a coffin.

The three women left the chapel, helped by the obsequious usher, and rode down in the elevator. Renée said she couldn't go to the cemetery, that she had an appointment. Her hands were shaking with fright. She kissed Mrs. Walton goodbye and took a taxi to Sutton Place. She walked down to the little park where Deborah and Mrs. Harley would be.

Deborah saw Renée first. She called Renée's name and ran toward her, struggling up the steps one at a time. Renée picked her up. "Pretty Renée," the little girl said. "Pretty, pretty Renée." Renée and the child sat down beside Mrs. Harley. "If you want to go shopping," she said, "I'll take Deborah for a few hours."

"Now, I don't know whether I ought to or not," Mrs. Harley said.

"She'll be perfectly safe with me," Renée said. "I'll take her up to my apartment and you can call for her there at five. Mr. and Mrs. Tennyson needn't know."

"Well, maybe I'll do that, now," Mrs. Harley said. In this way, Mrs. Harley had begun an arrangement that gave her a few free hours each week.

WHEN RENÉE hadn't come by half past ten that Sunday, Mrs. Harley knew that she wasn't coming, and she was disappointed because she had counted on going to church that morning. She thought of the Latin and the bells, and the exhilarating sense of having been sanctified and cleansed that she always felt when she got up from her knees. It angered her to think that Renée was lying in bed and that only Renée's laziness was keeping her from prayer. As the morning passed, a lot of children had come to the park, and now she looked for Deborah's yellow coat in the crowd.

The warm sun excited the little girl. She was running with a few children of her age. They were skipping and singing and circling the sand pile with no more purpose than swallows. Deborah tagged a little behind the others, because her coordination was still impulsive and she sometimes threw herself to the ground with her own exertions. Mrs. Harley called to her, and she ran obediently to the old woman and leaned on her knees and began to talk about some lions and little boys. Mrs. Harley asked if she would like to go and see Renée. "I want to go and stay with Renée," the little girl said. Mrs. Harley took her hand and they climbed the steps of the playground and walked to the apartment house where Renée lived. Mrs. Harley called upstairs on the house phone, and Renée answered after a little delay. She sounded sleepy. She said she would be glad to watch the child for an hour if Mrs. Harley would bring her upstairs. Mrs. Harley took Deborah up to the fifteenth floor and said goodbye to her there. Renée was wearing a negligee trimmed with feathers, and her apartment was dark.

Renée closed the door and picked the little girl up in her arms. Deborah's skin and hair were soft and fragrant, and Renée kissed her, tickled her, and blew down her neck until the child nearly suffocated with laughter. Then Renée pulled up the blinds and let some light into the room. The place was dirty and the air was sour. There were whiskey glasses and spilled ashtrays, and some dead roses in a tarnished silver bowl.

Renée had a lunch date, and she explained this to Deborah. "I'm going to the Plaza for lunch," she said. "I'm going to take a bath and dress, and you'll have to be a good girl." She gave Deborah her jewel box and turned on the water in the bathtub. Deborah sat quietly at the dressing table and loaded herself with necklaces and clips. While Renée was drying herself, the doorbell rang, and she put on a wrapper and went out to the living room. Deborah followed her. A man was there.

"I'm driving up to Albany," he told Renée. "Why don't you put some things in a bag and come up with me? I'll drive you back on Wednesday."

"I'd love to, darling," Renée said, "but I can't. I'm having lunch with Helen Foss. She thinks she might be able to get me some work."

"Call off the lunch," the man said. "Come on."

"I can't, darling," Renée said. "I'll see you on Wednesday."

"Who's the kid?" the man asked.

"It's the Tennysons' little girl. I take care of her while the nurse goes to church." The man embraced Renée vigorously and kissed her and left after they had arranged to meet Wednesday night.

"That was your rich Uncle Loathsome," René told the child.

"I have a friend. Her name is Martha," the little girl said.

"Yes, I'm sure you have a friend named Martha," Renée said. She noticed that the child was scowling and that her eyes were full of tears. "What's the matter, darling?" she asked. "What is the matter? Here, here, you sit on the sofa and listen to the radio. I've got to fix my face." She went into the bedroom to arrange her face and brush her hair.

A few minutes later the doorbell rang again. This time it was Mrs. Harley. "Did you enjoy the service?" Renée asked. "I'll put on Deborah's coat." She looked for the hat and coat. They were not where she had left them, and the child was not in the living room. Her heart began to beat fiercely. She went into her bedroom. "It does my soul so much good to go to church," she heard Mrs. Harley say. Renée thought in terror of the open windows. The window in her bedroom was open. She looked out, and fifteen stories below she could see the sidewalk and the canopy and the doorman at the corner whistling for a cab and a blonde walking a poodle. Renée ran back to the living room.

"Where's Deborah?" Mrs. Harley asked.

"I was dressing," Renée said. "She was in here a minute ago. She must have slipped out. She could have opened the door herself."

"You mean you've *lost* the little girl!" Mrs. Harley shouted.

"Please don't get excited," Renée said. "She can't have gone very far. The only way she could get downstairs would be the elevators." She went out the kitchen door and rang for the service elevator. She noticed the perilous service stairs. They were made of iron and concrete, painted a dirty gray, and they fell fifteen stories to the ground. She listened down the stairwell, but all she could hear was the hiss of cooking and someone, way below, singing,

"I'm a soldier, in the army of the Lord,
I'm a soldier,
In the army . . ."

The service elevator was full of stinking garbage. "There was a little girl in my apartment," Renée said to the man who had brought the elevator up. "She's disappeared. Would you look for her?" Then she ran into the front hall and rang for the passenger elevator. "Why, yes," the man said. "I took a little girl down, about ten minutes ago. She had on a yellow coat." Renée smelled whiskey on his breath. She called to Mrs. Harley. Then she went back into the apartment to get some cigarettes. "I'm not going to stay here by myself," Mrs. Harley said. Renée pushed her into a chair. She closed the door and rode down in the elevator. "I thought it was strange, her going down by herself," the elevator man said. "I thought maybe she was going to meet somebody in the lobby." As he spoke, Renée smelled whiskey on his breath again. "You've been drinking," she said. "If you hadn't been drinking, this wouldn't have happened. You ought to know that a child of that age can't be left alone. You ought not to drink while you're working."

When he reached the ground floor, he brought the elevator to a sudden stop and slammed the door open. Renée ran into the lobby. The mirrors, the electric candles, and the doorman's soiled ascot sickened her. "Yes," the doorman said. "It seems to me that I saw a little girl go out. I didn't pay much attention to it. I was out there, trying to get a cab." Renée ran into the street. The child was not there. She ran down to where she could see the river. She felt helpless and feeble, as though she had lost her place in the city in which she had lived for fifteen years. The traffic on the street was heavy. She stood at the corner with her hands cupped to her mouth and screamed, "Deborah! Deborah!"

THE TENNYSONS were going out that afternoon, and they had begun to dress when the telephone rang. Robert answered. Katherine could hear Renée's voice. ". . . I know it's a terrible thing, Bob, I know I should never have done it."

"You mean Mrs. Harley left her with you?"

"Yes, yes. I know it's a terrible thing. I've looked everywhere. Mrs. Harley is here now. Do you want her to come over?"

"No."

"Shall I call the police?"

"No," Robert said. "I'll call the police. Tell me what she was wearing." When Robert had finished talking with Renée, he called the police. "I'll wait here until you come up," he said. "Please come as quickly as you can."

Katherine was standing in the bathroom doorway. She walked over to Robert, and he took her in his arms. He held her firmly, and she began to cry. Then she left his arms and sat on the bed. He went to the open window. Down in the street he could see a truck with COMFORT CARPET COMPANY painted on its roof. There were some tennis courts in the next block, and people were playing tennis. There was a hedge of privet around the tennis courts, and an old woman was cutting some privet with a knife. She wore a round hat and a heavy winter coat that reached to her ankles. He realized that she was stealing the privet. She worked quickly and furtively, and she kept looking over her shoulder to make sure that no one saw her. When she had cut a good bunch of the green branches, she stuffed them into a bag and hurried down the street.

The doorbell rang. A police sergeant and a plainclothesman were there. They took off their hats. "This kind of thing is hard on the ladies," the sergeant said. "Now, if you'd give me the facts again, Mr. Tennyson. We already have men looking for her. You say she went down in the elevator herself. That was about an hour ago." He checked all the facts with Robert. "Now, I don't want to alarm either of you," he said, "but would anyone have any reason to kidnap the child? We have to consider every possibility."

"Yes," Katherine said suddenly and in a strong voice. She got up and began to walk back and forth in the room. "It may be unreasonable, but it's at least worth considering. She may have been kidnapped. I've seen that woman in the neighborhood twice this week and I had a feeling that she was following me. I didn't think anything about it then. And she did write me that letter. I'm not making myself clear. You see, before we had Mrs. Harley to take care of Deborah, we had a woman named Mrs. Emerson. I quarreled with her about Deborah, and she told me, while we were quarreling—I never told you any of this, darling, because I didn't want to worry you and I didn't think any of it was important—but when we quarreled, she said the child would be taken away from me. I tried to forget about it, because I thought she was eccentric. The city is full of strange women like that. Then I saw her on the street twice this week, and I had a sense that she was following me. She lives at the Hotel Princess. It's on the West Side. At least, she used to live there."

"I'll go over," Robert said. "I'll get the car."

"I'll drive you over, Mr. Tennyson," the sergeant said.

"Do you want to come?" Robert asked Katherine.

"No, darling," Katherine said. "I'll be all right."

Robert put on his hat, and he and the sergeant left. The elevator man spoke to Robert. "I'm very sorry, Mr. Tennyson," he said. "We all loved her in this house. I telephoned my wife and she went right over to St. John's and lit a vigil light for the little girl."

There was a police car in front of the house, and Robert and the sergeant got into it and drove west. Robert kept turning his head from side to side, and he did this to avert his eyes from the image of the child's death. He imagined the accident in the clichés of "Drive Safely" posters, badly drawn and in crude colors. He saw a stranger carrying the limp body away from the fenders of a taxi; he saw the look of surprise and horror on a lovely face that had never known any horror; he heard the noise of horns, the shrieking of brakes; he saw a car coming over the rise of a hill. He made a physical effort to force his eyes to look beyond these images into the bright street.

The day had got hot. A few low, swift clouds touched the city with shadow, and he could see the fast darkness traveling from block to block. The streets were crowded. He saw the city only in terms of mortal danger. Each manhole cover, excavation, and flight of stairs dominated the brilliance of the day like the reverse emphasis of a film negative, and he thought the crowds and the green trees in Central Park looked profane. The Hotel Princess was on a dingy street in the West Seventies. The air in the lobby was fetid. The desk clerk became uneasy when he saw the policeman. He looked for Mrs. Emerson's key and said that she was in. There was no telephone in her room. They could go up.

They went up in an elevator cage of gilded iron, driven by an old man. They knocked on the door, and Mrs. Emerson told them to come in. Robert had never known the woman. He had only seen her when she stood in the doorway of the nursery and sent Deborah in to say good night. She was English, he remembered. Her voice had always sounded troubled and refined. "Oh, Mr. Tennyson," she said when she recognized him. The sergeant asked her suddenly where she had been that morning.

"It's all right, Mrs. Emerson," Robert said. He was afraid she would become hysterical and tell them nothing. "Deborah ran away this morning. We thought you might know something about it. Mrs. Tennyson said you wrote her a letter."

"Oh, I'm terribly sorry to hear about Deborah," she said. It was the fine, small voice of someone who knew her place as a lady. "Yes, yes. Of course I wrote that letter to Mrs. Tennyson. It came to me in a dream that you would lose the little girl unless you were very careful. I have a profession, you know. I interpret dreams. I told Mrs. Tennyson when I left her that she should take very good care of the little girl. She was born, after all, under that dreadful new planet, Pluto. I was on the Riviera when they discovered it, in 1938. We knew something dreadful was going to happen then.

"I loved the little girl dearly and I regretted my disagreement with Mrs. Tennyson," she went on. "The little girl was one of the fire people—banked fire. I gave her palm a good deal of study. We were left alone a great deal, of course. She had a long life line and a good sense of balance and a good head. There were signs of imprudence there, but a great deal of that would depend upon you. I saw deep water there and some great danger, some great hazard. That's why I wrote the letter to Mrs. Tennyson. I never charged Mrs. Tennyson for any of my professional services."

"What did you and Mrs. Tennyson fight about?" the sergeant asked.

"We're wasting time," Robert said. "We're wasting so much time. Let's go back." He got up and went out of the room, and the sergeant followed him. It took them a long time to drive back. The Sunday crowds crossing the streets stopped them at every intersection. The plainclothesman was waiting in front of the house. "You'd better go up and see your wife," he told Robert. Neither the doorman nor the elevator man spoke to him. He stepped into his apartment and called to Katherine. She was in their bedroom, sitting by the window. She had a black book in her lap. He saw that it was the Bible. It was a Gideon copy that a drunken friend of theirs had stolen from a hotel. They had used it once or twice as a reference. Beyond the open window, he could see the river, a wide, bright field of light. The room was very still.

"What about Mrs. Emerson?" Katherine asked.

"It was a mistake. It was a mistake to think that she would hurt the child."

"Renée called again. She took Mrs. Harley home. She wants us to telephone her when we find Deborah. I never want to see Renée again."

"I know."

"If anything happens to Deborah," Katherine said, "I

can never forgive myself. I can never forgive myself. I'll feel as though we had sacrificed her. I've been reading about Abraham." She opened the Bible and began to read. " 'And he said, Take now thy son, thine only son Isaac, whom thou lovest and get thee into the land of Moriah; and offer him there for a burnt offering upon one of the mountains which I will tell thee of. And Abraham rose up early in the morning, and saddled his ass, and took two of his young men with him, and Isaac his son, and clave the wood for the burnt offering, and rose up, and went unto the place of which God had told him.' " She closed the book. "The thing I'm afraid of is that I'll go out of my mind. I keep repeating our address and telephone number to myself. That doesn't make any sense, does it?"

Robert put his hand on her forehead and ran it over her hair. Her dark hair was parted on the side and brushed simply, like a child's.

"I'm afraid I'm going out of my mind," Katherine said. "You know what my first impulse was when you left me alone? I wanted to take a knife, a sharp knife, and go into my closet and destroy my clothes. I wanted to cut them to pieces. That's because they're so expensive. That's not a sensible thing to want to do, is it? But I'm not insane, of course. I'm perfectly rational.

"I had a little brother who died. His name was Charles—Charles, junior. He was named after my father and he died of some kind of sickness when he was two and a half years old, about Deborah's age. Of course it was very hard on Mother and Dad, but it wasn't anything as bad as this. You see, I think children mean much more to us than they did to our parents. That's what I've been thinking. I suppose it's because we're not as religious and because the way we live makes us much more vulnerable. I feel filthy with guilt. I feel as though I'd been a rotten mother and a rotten wife and as though this were punishment. I've broken every vow and every promise that I've ever made. I've broken all the good promises. When I was a little girl, I used to make promises on the new moon and the first snow. I've broken everything good. But I'm talking as though we'd lost her, and we haven't lost her, have we? They'll find her, the policeman said they'd find her."

"They'll find her," Robert said.

The room darkened. The low clouds had touched the city. They could hear the rain as it fell against the building and the windows.

"She's lying somewhere in the rain," Katherine cried. She wrenched her body around in the chair and covered her face. "She's lying in the rain."

"They'll find her," Robert said. "Other children get lost. I've read stories about it in the *Times*. This sort of thing happens to everyone who has children. My sister's little girl fell downstairs. She fractured her skull. They didn't think she was going to live."

"It does happen to other people, doesn't it?" Katherine asked. She turned and looked at her husband. The rain had stopped suddenly. It left in the air a smell as powerful as though ammonia had been spilled in the streets. Robert saw the rain clouds darken the bright river. "I mean, there are all the sicknesses and the accidents," Katherine said, "and we've been so lucky. You know, Deborah hasn't had any lunch. She'll be terribly hungry. She hasn't had anything to eat since breakfast."

"I know."

"Darling, you go out," Katherine said. "It will be easier for you than staying here."

"What will you do?"

"I'm going to clean the living room. We left the windows open last night and everything's covered with soot. You go out. I'll be all right." She smiled. Her face was swollen from crying. "You go out. It will be easier for you, and I'll clean the room."

ROBERT WENT DOWN again. The police car was still parked in front of the house. A policeman came up to Robert, and they talked for a while. "I'm going to look around the neighborhood again," the policeman said, "if you want to come with me." Robert said that he would go. He noticed that the policeman carried a flashlight.

Near the apartment house was the ruin of a brewery that had been abandoned during Prohibition. The sidewalk had been inherited by the dogs of the neighborhood and was littered with their filth. The basement windows of a nearby garage were broken, and the policeman flashed his light through a window frame. Robert started when he saw some dirty straw and a piece of yellow paper. It was the color of Deborah's coat. He said nothing and they walked along. In the distance he could hear the vast afternoon noise of the city.

There were some tenements near the brewery. They were squalid, and over the door to one hung a crude sign: "Welcome Home Jerry." The iron gate that led to the steep cellar stairs was open. The policeman flashed his light down the stairs. They were broken. There was nothing there.

An old woman sat on the stoop of the next house, and she watched them suspiciously when they looked down the cellar stairs. "You'll not find my Jimmy there," she screamed, "you—you—" Someone threw open a window and told her to shut up. Robert saw that she was drunk. The policeman paid no attention to her. He looked methodically into the cellar of each house, and then they went around a corner. There were stores, here, along the front of an apartment house. There were no stairs or areaways.

Robert heard a siren. He stopped, and stopped the policeman with him. A police car came around the corner and drew up to the curb where they stood. "Hop in, Mr. Tennyson," the driver said. "We found her. She's down at the station." He started the siren, and they drove east, dodging through the traffic. "We found her down on Third Avenue," the policeman said. "She was sitting out in front of an antique store, eating a piece of bread. Somebody must have given her the bread. She isn't hungry."

She was waiting for him at the station house. He put his hands on her and knelt in front of her and began to laugh. His eyes were burning. "Where have you been, Deborah? Who gave you the bread? Where have you been? Where have you been?"

"The lady gave the bread," she said. "I had to find Martha."

"What lady gave you the bread, Deborah? Where have you been? Who is Martha? Where have you been?" He knew that she would never tell him and that as long as he lived he would never know, and against his palm he could feel the strong beating of her heart, but he went on asking, "Where have you been? Who gave you the bread? Who is Martha?"

THE SUMMER FARMER

THE NOR'EASTER is a train the railroad christened at a moment when its directors were imbued with the mystery of travel. Memory is often more appealing than fact, and a passenger who had long ridden the train might overlook its noise and dirt each time he entered the Grand Central Station and saw there the name of a northerly three-day rain. This, at least, was the case with Paul Hollis, who rode the Nor'easter on nearly every Thursday or Friday night of his summer. He was a bulky man, who suffered in all Pullmans, but in none so much as he did on this ride. As a rule, he stayed in the club car until ten, drinking Scotch. The whiskey ordinarily kept him asleep until they reached the tumultuous delays of Springfield, past midnight. North of Springfield, the train fell into the balky and malingering stride of an old local, and Paul lay in his berth between wakefulness and sleep, like a partially anesthetized patient. The ordeal ended when, after breakfast, he left the Nor'easter, in Meridian Junction, and was met by his gentle wife. There was this to be said about the journey: It made one fully conscious of the terrestrial distance that separated the hot city from the leafy and ingenuous streets of the junction village.

The conversation between Paul and Virginia Hollis during the drive from the Junction to their farm, north of Hiems, was confined to the modest properties and affections they shared; more than this, it seemed to aim at a deliberate inconsequence, as if to mention the checking balance or the wars might ruin the spell of a mild morning and an open car. The drain in the downstairs shower was leaking, Virginia told Paul one morning in July, his sister Ellen was drinking too much, the Marstons had been over for lunch, and the time had come for the children to have a pet. This was a subject to which she had obviously given some thought. No country dog would last in a New York apartment when they returned in the fall, she said, cats were a nuisance, and she had concluded that rabbits were the best they could do. There was a house on the road with a rabbit cage on its lawn, and they could stop there that morning and buy a pair. They would be a present from Paul to the children, and so much the better for that. The purchase would make that weekend the weekend when they had bought the rabbits, and distinguish it from the weekend when they had transplanted the Christmas fern or the weekend when they had removed the dead juniper. They could put the rabbits into the old duck house, Virginia said, and when they went back to the city in the fall, Kasiak could eat them. Kasiak was the hired man.

They were driving upland. From the Junction north, one never quite lost the sense of a gradual climb. Hills blocked off the delicate, the vitiated New Hampshire landscape, with its omnipresence of ruin, but every few miles a tributary of the Merrimack opened a broad valley, with elms, farms, and stone fences. "It's along here," Virginia said. Paul didn't know what she meant until she reminded him of the rabbits. "If you'll slow down here . . . Here, Paul, *here.*" He bumped the car over the shoulder of the road and stopped. On the lawn of a white, neat house, darkened by rock maples, there was a rabbit cage. "Hello," Paul shouted, "hello," and a man in overalls came out of a side door, chewing on something, as if he had been interrupted at a meal. White rabbits were two dollars, he said. Browns and grays were a dollar and a half. He swallowed, and wiped his mouth with his fist. He spoke uneasily, as if he wanted to keep the simple transaction from someone, and after Paul had picked a brown and a gray, he ran to the barn for a box. As Paul turned the car back onto the road, they heard behind them a heartbroken shout. A boy ran from the house to the rabbit cage, and they saw the source of the farmer's uneasiness.

The cash market and the antique store, the Civil War cannon and the post office of Hiems fell behind them, and Paul accelerated the car happily when they escaped from the narrow streets of the village and drove into the fresh lake winds. The road brought them, first, along the unfashionable, or gregarious, end of the lake; then the houses thinned and gave way to pine groves and empty fields as they drove north. The sense of homecoming—of returning to a place where he had summered all his life—became for Paul so violent that the difference between the pace of his imagination and the speed of the car annoyed him until they turned off the road onto grass ruts and saw, literally at the road's end, their farm.

The gentle shadow of a cloud was passing the face of the Hollis house. At the edge of the lawn, there was an upside-down piece of porch furniture that had been abandoned in a thundershower and that seemed to have been drying there since Paul's youth. The light and heat increased and the shade deepened as the moving shadow of the cloud darkened the barn and the clothesyard and vanished into the woods. "Hello, brother." It was Paul's sister Ellen calling to him from one of the open windows. His business suit bound at the shoulders when he left the car, as if he had taken on height, for the place told him that he was ten years younger; the maples, the house, the simple mountains all told him this. His two small children stormed around the edge of the barn and collided against his legs. Taller, browner, healthier, more handsome, more intelligent—they seemed to him to be all these things each weekend when he was reunited with them. A sere branch on a maple caught his eye. That would have to be cut. He stooped down to pick up his little boy and girl in a scalding rush of love, for which he was unarmed and, it seemed, unprepared.

The duck house, where they put the rabbits that morning, had been empty for years, but there was a cage and a shelter, and it would do. "Now, these are your pets, these are your rabbits," Paul told the children. His sternness transfixed them, and the little boy began to suck his thumb. "These are your responsibility, and if you take good care of them, perhaps you can have a dog when we get back to New York. You'll have to feed them and clean their house." His love for the children and his desire to draw for them, even faintly, the mysterious shapes of responsibility reduced him to a fatuity that he was conscious of himself. "I don't want you to expect someone else to help you," he said. "You'll have to give them water twice a day. They're supposed to like lettuce and carrots. Now you can put them in the house yourself. Daddy has to get to work."

Paul Hollis was a summer farmer. He mowed, cultivated, and waxed angry about the price of scratch feed, and at that instant when the plangent winds of Labor Day began to sound he hung up his blunted scythe to rust in the back hall, where the kerosene was kept, and happily shifted his interest to the warm apartments of New York. On that day—the day when he bought the rabbits—he went to his bedroom after he had lectured the children, and changed into a pair of coveralls that were still dimly stenciled with his name, rank, and serial number. Virginia sat on the edge of the bed while he dressed, and talked about his sister Ellen, who was spending a month with them. Ellen needed the rest; Ellen drank too much. But there was no suggestion of correction or change in what Virginia said about Ellen, and when Paul glanced at his wife, he thought how forgiving and comely she was. The room was old and pleasant—it had been his parents' room—and what light reached it reached it through the leaves. They lingered there talking about Ellen, the children, tasting the astringency of their contentment and their worthiness, but not so long as to seem idle. Paul was going to help Kasiak scythe the highest field, and Virginia wanted to pick some flowers.

THE HOLLIS PROPERTY was high, and it was Paul's long-dead father who had called the highest pasture Elysian, because of its unearthly stillness. This pasture was mowed on alternate years to keep the scrub from taking hold. When Paul reached it that morning, Kasiak was there, and Paul judged that he had been working for about three hours; Kasiak was paid by the hour. The two men spoke briefly—the hired man and the vacationist—and picked up the tacit bond of people who happen to be working together. Paul moved below and a little to Kasiak's right. He used a scythe well, but there was no confusing, even at a distance, Kasiak's diligent figure with Paul's.

Kasiak was Russian-born. This and everything else Paul knew about him he had been told while they worked. Kasiak had landed in Boston, worked in a shoe factory, studied English at night, rented, and eventually bought, the farm below the Hollis place. They had been neighbors for twenty years. He was doing the Hollises' work that year for the first time. Up until then, he had been merely a persevering and colorful figure on their landscape. He dressed his deaf wife in salt bags and potato sacks. He was miserly. He was bitter. Even on that summer morning, he cut a figure of chagrin and discontent. He kept his woods clear and stored his hay at precisely the right moment, and his fields, his gardens, his compost heap, and the sour smell of milk in his immaculate kitchen conveyed the sense of security that lies in the power of intelligent husbandry. He mowed, he walked, like a prisoner in a prison yard. From the time he went to the barn, an hour before dawn, until his day ended, there was no hesitation in his thought or in his step, and this flawless link of chores was part of a larger chain of responsibilities and aspirations that had begun with his youth in Russia and that would end, he believed, with the birth of a just and peaceable world, delivered in bloodshed and arson.

Virginia had been amused when Paul told her that Kasiak was a Communist. Kasiak had told Paul himself. Two weeks after he had begun to work for them, he had taken to cutting editorials from a Communist newspaper and handing them to Paul or slipping them under the kitchen door. Reasonableness was Paul's watchword with Kasiak, he liked to think. Twice, in the feed store, when Kasiak's politics had been under discussion, Paul had defended Kasiak's right to draw his own conclusions about the future, and in their conversations he always asked Kasiak lightly when he was going to have his revolution.

That day fell at the end of the haying weather. As it got late in the morning, they could hear dull blasts of thunder. A wind rose in the neighborhood, but there was none to speak of in the field. Kasiak trailed after him a rich blend of citronella and vinegar, and both men were plagued with flies. They did not let the chance of a storm change the pace of their scything. It was as if there were some significance, hidden, surely, to them, in completing that field. Then the wet wind climbed the hill behind them, and Paul, taking one hand off the snath, straightened his back. While they had been working, clouds had blackened the sky from the horizon to above his head, so he was given the illusion of a country divided evenly between the lights of catastrophe and repose. The shade of the storm was traveling as rapidly up the field as a man walks, but the hay it had not touched was yellow, and there was no portent of the storm in the delicate sky ahead of him or in the clouds there or in anything he could see except the green wood, whose color the storm had begun to deepen. Then he felt against his skin a coldness that belonged to no part of that day, and heard at his back the rain begin to drop through the trees.

Paul ran for the woods. Kasiak followed slowly, with the storm at his heels. They sat beside each other on stones in the shelter of the dense foliage, watching the moving curtain of rain. Kasiak took off his hat—for the first time that summer to Paul's knowledge. His hair and forehead were gray. Ruddiness began on his high cheekbones and shaded down to a dark brown that spread from his jaw to his neck.

"How much will you charge me for using your horse to cultivate the garden?" Paul asked.

"Four dollars." Kasiak didn't raise his voice, and Paul couldn't hear him above the noise the rain made crashing into the field.

"How much?"

"Four dollars."

"Let's try it tomorrow morning if it's clear. Shall we?"

"You'll have to do it early. It's too hot for her in the afternoon."

"Six o'clock."

"You want to get up that early?" Kasiak smiled at his gibe at the Hollis family and their disorderly habits. Lightning tipped the woods, so close to them that they could smell the galvanic discharge, and a second later there was an explosion of thunder that sounded as if it had destroyed the county. The front of the storm passed them, the wind died down, and the shower fell around them with the dogged gloom of an autumn rain.

"Have you heard from your family recently, Kasiak?" Paul asked.

"For two years—not for two years."

"Would you like to go back?"

"Yes, yes." There was an intent light in his face. "On my father's farm, there are some big fields. My brothers are still there. I would like to go there in an airplane. I would land the airplane in these big fields, and they would all come running to see who it was and they would see it was me."

"You don't like it here, do you?"

"It's a capitalist country."

"Why did you come, then?"

"I don't know. I think over there they made me work too hard. Over there, we cut the rye at night, when there is some moisture in the air. They put me to work in the fields when I was twelve years old. We get up at three in the morning to cut the rye. My hands are all bleeding, and swollen so I can't sleep. My father beat me like a convict. In Russia, they used to beat convicts. He beat me with a whip for horses until my back was bleeding." Kasiak felt his back, as if the welts still bled. "After that, I decided to go away. I waited six years. That's why I came, I guess—they set me to work in the fields too soon."

"When are you going to have your revolution, Kasiak?"

"When the capitalists make another war."

"What's going to happen to me, Kasiak? What's going to happen to people like me?"

"It depends. If you work on a farm or in a factory, I guess it will be all right. They'll only get rid of useless people."

"All right, Kasiak," Paul said heartily, "I'll work for you," and he slapped the farmer on the back. He frowned at the rain. "I guess I'll go down and get some lunch," he said. "We won't be able to scythe any more today, will we?" He ran down the wet field to the barn. Kasiak followed him a few minutes later, but he did not run. He entered the barn and began to repair a cold frame, as if the thunderstorm fitted precisely into his scheme of things.

BEFORE DINNER that night, Paul's sister Ellen drank too much. She was late coming to the table, and when Paul went into the pantry for a spoon, he found her there, drinking out of the silver cocktail shaker. Seated at the table, high in her firmament of gin, she looked critically at her brother and his wife, remembering some real or imagined injustice of her youth, for with any proximity the constellations of some families generate among themselves as asperity that nothing can sweeten. Ellen was a heavy-featured woman who held her strong blue eyes at a squint. She had had her second divorce that spring. She had wrapped a bright scarf around her head for dinner that night and put on an old dress she had found in one of the attic trunks, and, reminded by her faded clothes of a simpler time of life, she talked uninterruptedly about the past and, particularly, about Father—Father this and Father that. The shabby dress and her reminiscent mood made Paul impatient, and it seemed to him that a vast crack had appeared magically in Ellen's heart the night Father died.

A northwest wind had driven the thundershower out of the county and left in the air a poignant chill, and when they went out on the piazza after dinner to watch the sun go down, there were a hundred clouds in the west—clouds of gold, clouds of silver, clouds like bone and tinder and filth under the bed. "It's so *good* for me to be up here," Ellen said. "It does so much for me." She sat on the rail against the light, and Paul couldn't see her face. "I can't find Father's binoculars," she went on, "and his golf clubs have disappeared." From the open window of the children's room, Paul heard his daughter singing, "How many miles is it to Babylon? Three score miles and ten. Can we get there by candlelight? . . ." Immense tenderness and contentment fell to him with her voice from the open window.

It was so good for them all, as Ellen said; it did so much for them. It was a phrase Paul had heard spoken on that piazza since his memory had become retentive. Ellen was the mote on that perfect evening. There was something wrong, some half-known evil in her worship of the bucolic scene—some measure of her inadequacy and, he supposed, of his.

"Let's have a brandy," Ellen said. They went into the house to drink. In the living room, there was a lot of talk about what they would have—brandy, mint, Cointreau, Scotch. Paul went into the kitchen and put glasses and bottles on a tray. The screen door was shaken by something—the wind, he guessed, until the thumping was repeated and he saw Kasiak standing in the dark. He would offer him a drink. He would settle him in the wing chair and play out that charade of equality between vacationist and hired man that is one of the principal illusions of the leafy months. "Here's something you ought to read," Kasiak said, before Paul could speak, and he passed him a newspaper clipping. Paul recognized the typeface of the Communist paper that was mailed to Kasiak from Indiana. LUXURY LIVING WEAKENS U.S. was the headline, and the story described with traitorous joy the hardy and purposeful soldiers of Russia. Paul's face got warm in anger at Kasiak and at the uprush of chauvinism he felt. "Is that all you want?" His voice broke dryly. Kasiak nodded. "I'll see you tomorrow morning at six," Paul said, master to hired man, and he hooked the screen door and turned his back.

Paul liked to think that his patience with the man was inexhaustible—for, after all, Kasiak not only believed in Bakunin, he believed that stones grow and that thunder curdles milk. In his dealings with Kasiak, he had unconsciously sacrificed some independence, and in order to get to the garden at six the next morning, he got up at five. He made himself some breakfast, and at half past five he heard the rattle of a cart on the road. The puerile race of virtue and industry had begun. Paul was in the garden when Kasiak brought the cart into view. Kasiak was disappointed.

Paul had seen the mare only in pasture, and, aside from the fact that she was costing him four dollars, he was curious about the animal, for, along with a cow and a wife, she made up Kasiak's family. Her coat was dusty, he saw; her belly was swollen; her hoofs were unshod and uncut and had shredded like paper. "What's her name?" he asked, but Kasiak didn't answer. He hitched the mare to the cultivator, and she sighed and labored up the hill. Paul led the mare by the bridle, and Kasiak held down the cultivator.

Halfway along the first row in the garden, a stone stopped them, and when it had been dislodged and rolled away, Kasiak called "Gee-up" to the mare. She didn't move. "Gee-up," he shouted. His voice was harsh, but there was some tenderness hidden in it. "Gee-up, gee-up, gee-up." He slapped her sides lightly with the reins. He looked anxiously at Paul, as if he were ashamed that Paul should notice the mare's extreme decrepitude and reach a mistaken judgment on an animal he loved. When Paul suggested that he might use a whip, Kasiak said no. "Gee-up, gee-up, gee-up," he shouted again, and when she still failed to respond, he struck her rump with the reins. Paul pulled at her bit. They stood for ten minutes in the middle of the row pulling and shouting, and it seemed that the life had gone out of the mare. Then, when they were hoarse and discouraged, she began to stir and gather wind in her lungs. Her carcass worked like a bellows and the wind whistled in her nostrils, and, like the bag Aeolus gave to Ulysses, she seemed to fill with tempests. She shook the flies off her head and pulled the cultivator a few feet forward.

This made for slow work, and by the time they finished, the sun was hot. Paul heard voices from his house as he and Kasiak led the infirm mare back to the cart, and saw his children, still in their nightclothes, feeding their rabbits in the lettuce patch. When Kasiak harnessed the mare to the cart, Paul again asked him her name.

"She has no name," Kasiak said.

"I've never heard of a farm horse without a name."

"To name animals is bourgeois sentimentality," Kasiak said, and he started to drive away.

Paul laughed.

"You never come back!" Kasiak called over his shoulder. It was the only meanness at hand; he knew how deeply Paul loved the hill. His face was dark. "You never come back next year. You wait and see."

THERE IS A MOMENT early on Sunday when the tide of the summer day turns inexorably toward the evening train. You can swim, play tennis, or take a nap or a walk, but it doesn't make much difference. Immediately after lunch, Paul was faced with his unwillingness to leave. This became so strong that he was reminded of the intensity and the apprehensiveness he had felt on furloughs. At six, he put on his tight business suit and had a drink with Virginia in the kitchen. She asked him to buy nail scissors and candy in New York. While they were there, he heard that noise that he lived in dread of above all others—his innocent and gentle children screaming in pain.

He ran out, letting the screen door slam in Virginia's face. Then he turned back and held the door open for her, and she came out and ran up the hill at his side. The children were coming down the road, under the big trees. Lost in their crystalline grief, blinded with tears, they stumbled and ran toward their mother and searched in her dark skirts for a shape to press their heads against. They were howling. But it was nothing serious, after all. Their rabbits were dead.

"There, there, there, there . . ." Virginia drew the children down toward the house. Paul went on up the road and found the limp rabbits in the hutch. He carried them to the edge of the garden and dug a hole. Kasiak came by, carrying water for the chickens, and when he had sized up the situation, he spoke mournfully. "Why you dig a grave?" he asked. "The skunks will dig them up tonight. Throw them in Cavis's pasture. They'll dig them up again. . . ." He went on toward the chicken house. Paul stamped down the grave. Dirt got into his low shoes. He went back to the rabbit house to see if he could find any trace of what had killed them, and in the feeding trough, below some wilted vegetables that the children had uprooted, he saw the crystals of a mortal poison that they used to kill rats in the winter.

Paul made a serious effort to remember whether he could have left the poison there himself. The stifling heat in the hutch raised and sent the sweat rolling down his face. Could Kasiak have done it? Could Kasiak have been so mean, so perverse? Could he, through believing that on some fall evening fires on the mountain would signal the diligent and the reliable to seize power from the hands of those who drank Martinis, have become shrewd enough to put his finger on the only interest in the future Paul had?

Kasiak was in the chicken house. Shadow had begun to cover the ground, and some of the happy and stupid fowl were roosting. "Did you poison the rabbits, Kasiak?" Paul called. "Did you? Did you?" His loud voice maddened the fowl. They spread their heavy wings and cawed. "Did you, Kasiak?" Kasiak didn't speak. Paul put his hands on the man's shoulders and shook him. "Don't you know how strong the poison is? Don't you know that the children might have got into it? Don't you know that it might have killed them?" The fowl involved themselves in the fracas. Signals went from the house to the yard; they pushed one another off the congested gangway and thumped their wings. As if the life in Kasiak hid slyly from violence behind cartilage and bone, there was no apparent resistance in him, and Paul shook him until he creaked. "Did you, Kasiak?" Paul shouted. "Did you? Oh, Kasiak, if you touch my children, if you harm them in any way—in any way—I'll cut your head open." He pushed the man away from him and he sprawled in the dirt.

When Paul got back to the kitchen, there was no one there, and he drank two glasses of water. From the living room he could hear his mourning children, and his sister Ellen, who had no children of her own, struggling awkwardly to distract them with a story about a cat she had once owned. Virginia came into the kitchen and closed the door after her. She asked if the rabbits had been poisoned, and he said yes. She sat in a chair by the kitchen table. "I put it there," she said. "I put it there last fall. I never thought we'd use that house again, and I wanted to keep the rats out of it. I forgot. I never thought we'd use that house again. I completely forgot."

It is true of even the best of us that if an observer can catch us boarding a train at a way station; if he will mark our faces, stripped by anxiety of their self-possession; if he will appraise our luggage, our clothing, and look out of the window to see who has driven us to the station; if he will listen to the harsh or tender things we say if we are with our families, or notice the way we put our suitcase onto the rack, check the position of our wallet, our key ring, and wipe the sweat off the back of our necks; if he can judge sensibly the self-importance, diffidence, or sadness with which we settle ourselves, he will be given a broader view of our lives than most of us would intend.

Paul barely made the train that Sunday night. When he pulled himself up the high steps of the coach, he was short-winded. There was still some straw on his shoes from the violence in the chicken house. The drive had not completely cooled his temper, and his face was red. No harm had been done, he thought. "No harm," he said under his breath as he swung his suitcase onto the rack—a man of forty with signs of mortality in a tremor of his right hand, signs of obsoleteness in his confused frown, a summer farmer with blistered hands, a sunburn, and lame shoulders, so visibly shaken by some recent loss of principle that it would have been noticed by a stranger across the aisle.

TORCH SONG

After Jack Lorey had known Joan Harris in New York for a few years, he began to think of her as the Widow. She always wore black, and he was always given the feeling, by a curious disorder in her apartment, that the undertakers had just left. This impression did not stem from malice on his part, for he was fond of Joan. They came from the same city in Ohio and had reached New York at about the same time in the middle thirties. They were the same age, and during their first summer in the city they used to meet after work and drink Martinis in places like the Brevoort and Charles', and have dinner and play checkers at the Lafayette.

Joan went to a school for models when she settled in the city, but it turned out that she photographed badly, so after spending six weeks learning how to walk with a book on her head she got a job as a hostess in a Longchamps. For the rest of the summer she stood by the hatrack, bathed in an intense pink light and the string music of heartbreak, swinging her mane of dark hair and her black skirt as she moved forward to greet the customers. She was then a big, handsome girl with a wonderful voice, and her face, her whole presence, always seemed infused with a gentle and healthy pleasure at her surroundings, whatever they were. She was innocently and incorrigibly convivial, and would get out of bed and dress at three in the morning if someone called her and asked her to come out for a drink, as Jack often did. In the fall, she got some kind of freshman executive job in a department store. They saw less and less of each other and then for quite a while stopped seeing each other altogether. Jack was living with a girl he had met at a party, and it never occurred to him to wonder what had become of Joan.

Jack's girl had some friends in Pennsylvania, and in the

spring and summer of his second year in town he often went there with her for weekends. All of this—the shared apartment in the Village, the illicit relationship, the Friday-night train to a country house—was what he had imagined life in New York to be, and he was intensely happy. He was returning to New York with his girl one Sunday night on the Lehigh line. It was one of those trains that move slowly across the face of New Jersey, bringing back to the city hundreds of people, like the victims of an immense and strenuous picnic, whose faces are blazing and whose muscles are lame. Jack and his girl, like most of the other passengers, were overburdened with vegetables and flowers. When the train stopped in Pennsylvania Station, they moved with the crowd along the platform, toward the escalator. As they were passing the wide, lighted windows of the diner, Jack turned his head and saw Joan. It was the first time he had seen her since Thanksgiving, or since Christmas. He couldn't remember.

Joan was with a man who had obviously passed out. His head was in his arms on the table, and an overturned highball glass was near one of his elbows. Joan was shaking his shoulders gently and speaking to him. She seemed to be vaguely troubled, vaguely amused. The waiters had cleared off all the other tables and were standing around Joan, waiting for her to resurrect her escort. It troubled Jack to see in these straits a girl who reminded him of the trees and the lawns of his home town, but there was nothing he could do to help. Joan continued to shake the man's shoulders, and the crowd pressed Jack past one after another of the diner's windows, past the malodorous kitchen, and up the escalator.

He saw Joan again, later that summer, when he was having dinner in a Village restaurant. He was with a new girl, a Southerner. There were many Southern girls in the city that year. Jack and his belle had wandered into the restaurant because it was convenient, but the food was terrible and the place was lighted with candles. Halfway through dinner, Jack noticed Joan on the other side of the room, and when he had finished eating, he crossed the room and spoke to her. She was with a tall man who was wearing a monocle. He stood, bowed stiffly from the waist, and said to Jack, "We are very pleased to meet you."

Then he excused himself and headed for the toilet. "He's a count, he's a Swedish count," Joan said. "He's on the radio, Friday afternoons at four-fifteen. Isn't it exciting?" She seemed to be delighted with the count and the terrible restaurant.

Sometime the next winter, Jack moved from the Village to an apartment in the East Thirties. He was crossing Park Avenue one cold morning on his way to the office when he noticed, in the crowd, a woman he had met a few times at Joan's apartment. He spoke to her and asked about his friend. "Haven't you heard?" she said. She pulled a long face. "Perhaps I'd better tell you. Perhaps you can help." She and Jack had breakfast in a drugstore on Madison Avenue and she unburdened herself of the story.

The count had a program called "The Songs of the Fiords," or something like that, and he sang Swedish folk songs. Everyone suspected him of being a fake, but that didn't bother Joan. He had met her at a party and, sensing a soft touch, had moved in with her the following night. About a week later, he complained of pains in his back and said he must have some morphine. Then he needed morphine all the time. If he didn't get morphine, he was abusive and violent. Joan began to deal with those doctors and druggists who peddle dope, and when they wouldn't supply her, she went to the bottom of the city. Her friends were afraid she would be found some morning stuffed in a drain. She got pregnant. She had an abortion. The count left her and moved to a flea bag near Times Square, but she was so impressed by then with his helplessness, so afraid that he would die without her, that she followed him there and shared his room and continued to buy his narcotics. He abandoned her again, and Joan waited a week for him to return before she went back to her place and her friends in the Village.

It shocked Jack to think of the innocent girl from Ohio having lived with a brutal dope addict and traded with criminals, and when he got to his office that morning, he telephoned her and made a date for dinner that night. He met her at Charles'. When she came into the bar, she seemed as wholesome and calm as ever. Her voice was sweet, and reminded him of elms, of lawns, of those glass arrangements that used to be hung from porch ceilings to tinkle in the summer wind. She told him about the count. She spoke of him charitably and with no trace of bitterness, as if her voice, her disposition, were incapable of registering anything beyond simple affection and pleasure. Her walk, when she moved ahead of him toward their table, was light and graceful. She ate a large dinner and talked enthusiastically about her job. They went to a movie and said goodbye in front of her apartment house.

That winter, Jack met a girl he decided to marry. Their engagement was announced in January and they planned to marry in July. In the spring, he received, in his office mail, an invitation to cocktails at Joan's. It was for a Saturday when his fiancée was going to Massachusetts to visit her parents, and when the time came and he had nothing better to do, he took a bus to the Village. Joan had the same apartment. It was a walk-up. You rang the bell above the mailbox in the vestibule and were answered with a death rattle in the lock. Joan lived on the third floor. Her calling card was in a slot in the mailbox, and above her name was written the name Hugh Bascomb.

Jack climbed the two flights of carpeted stairs, and when he reached Joan's apartment, she was standing by the open door in a black dress. After she greeted Jack, she took his arm and guided him across the room. "I want you to meet Hugh, Jack," she said.

Hugh was a big man with a red face and pale-blue eyes. His manner was courtly and his eyes were inflamed with drink. Jack talked with him for a little while and then went over to speak to someone he knew, who was standing by the mantelpiece. He noticed then, for the first time, the indescribable disorder of Joan's apartment. The books were in their shelves and the furniture was reasonably good, but the place was all wrong, somehow. It was as if things had been put in place without thought or real interest, and for the first time, too, he had the impression that there had been a death there recently.

As Jack moved around the room, he felt that he had met the ten or twelve guests at other parties. There was a woman executive with a fancy hat, a man who could imitate Roosevelt, a grim couple whose play was in rehearsal, and a newspaperman who kept turning on the radio for news of the Spanish Civil War. Jack drank Martinis and talked with the woman in the fancy hat. He looked out of the window at the back yards and the ailanthus trees and heard, in the distance, thunder exploding off the cliffs of the Hudson.

Hugh Bascomb got very drunk. He began to spill liquor, as if drinking, for him, were a kind of jolly slaughter and he enjoyed the bloodshed and the mess. He spilled whiskey from a bottle. He spilled a drink on his shirt and then tipped over someone else's drink. The party was not quiet, but Hugh's hoarse voice began to dominate the others. He attacked a photographer who was sitting in a corner explaining camera techniques to a homely woman. "What did you come to the party for if all you wanted to do was to sit there and stare at your shoes?" Hugh shouted. "What did you come for? Why don't you stay at home?"

The photographer didn't know what to say. He was not staring at his shoes. Joan moved lightly to Hugh's side. "Please don't get into a fight now, darling," she said. "Not this afternoon."

"Shut up," he said. "Let me alone. Mind your own business." He lost his balance, and in struggling to steady himself he tipped over a lamp.

"Oh, your lovely lamp, Joan," a woman sighed.

"Lamps!" Hugh roared. He threw his arms into the air and worked them around his head as if he were bludgeoning himself. "Lamps. Glasses. Cigarette boxes. Dishes. They're killing me. They're killing me, for Christ's sake. Let's all go up to the mountains and hunt and fish and live like men, for Christ's sake."

People were scattering as if a rain had begun to fall in the room. It had, as a matter of fact, begun to rain outside. Someone offered Jack a ride uptown, and he jumped at the chance. Joan stood at the door, saying goodbye to her routed friends. Her voice remained soft, and her manner, unlike that of those Christian women who in the face of disaster can summon new and formidable sources of composure, seemed genuinely simple. She appeared to be oblivious of the raging drunk at her back, who was pacing up and down, grinding glass into the rug, and haranguing one of the survivors of the party with a story of how he, Hugh, had once gone without food for three weeks.

IN JULY, Jack was married in an orchard in Duxbury, and he and his wife went to West Chop for a few weeks. When they returned to town, their apartment was cluttered with presents, including a dozen after-dinner coffee cups from Joan. His wife sent her the required note, but they did nothing else.

Late in the summer, Joan telephoned Jack at his office and asked if he wouldn't bring his wife to see her; she named an evening the following week. He felt guilty about not having called her, and accepted the invitation. This made his wife angry. She was an ambitious girl who liked a social life that offered rewards, and she went unwillingly to Joan's Village apartment with him.

Written above Joan's name on the mailbox was the name Franz Denzel. Jack and his wife climbed the stairs and were met by Joan at the open door. They went into her apartment and found themselves among a group of people for whom Jack, at least, was unable to find any bearings.

Franz Denzel was a middle-aged German. His face was pinched with bitterness or illness. He greeted Jack and his wife with that elaborate and clever politeness that is intended to make guests feel that they have come too early or too late. He insisted sharply upon Jack's sitting in the chair in which he himself had been sitting, and then went and sat on a radiator. There were five other Germans sitting around the room, drinking coffee. In a corner was another American couple, who looked uncomfortable. Joan passed Jack and his wife small cups of coffee with whipped cream. "These cups belonged to Franz's mother," she said. "Aren't they lovely? They were the only things he took from Germany when he escaped from the Nazis."

Franz turned to Jack and said, "Perhaps you will give us your opinion on the American educational system. That is what we were discussing when you arrived."

Before Jack could speak, one of the German guests opened an attack on the American educational system. The other Germans joined in, and went on from there to describe every vulgarity that had impressed them in American life and to contrast German and American culture generally. Where, they asked one another passionately, could you find in America anything like the Mitropa dining cars, the Black Forest, the pictures in Munich, the music in Bayreuth? Franz and his friends began speaking in German. Neither Jack nor his wife nor Joan could understand German, and the other American couple had not opened their mouths since they were introduced. Joan went happily around the room, filling everyone's cup with coffee, as if the music of a foreign language were enough to make an evening for her.

Jack drank five cups of coffee. He was desperately uncomfortable. Joan went into the kitchen while the Germans were laughing at their German jokes, and he hoped she would return with some drinks, but when she came back, it was with a tray of ice cream and mulberries.

"Isn't this pleasant?" Franz asked, speaking in English again.

Joan collected the coffee cups, and as she was about to take them back to the kitchen, Franz stopped her.

"Isn't one of those cups chipped?"

"No, darling," Joan said. "I never let the maid touch them. I wash them myself."

"What's that?" he asked, pointing at the rim of one of the cups.

"That's the cup that's always been chipped, darling. It was chipped when you unpacked it. You noticed it then."

"These things were perfect when they arrived in this country," he said.

Joan went into the kitchen and he followed her.

Jack tried to make conversation with the Germans. From the kitchen there was the sound of a blow and a cry. Franz returned and began to eat his mulberries greedily. Joan came back with her dish of ice cream. Her voice was gentle. Her tears, if she had been crying, had dried as quickly as the tears of a child. Jack and his wife finished their ice cream and made their escape. The wasted and unnerving evening enraged Jack's wife, and he supposed that he would never see Joan again.

Jack's wife got pregnant early in the fall, and she seized on all the prerogatives of an expectant mother. She took long naps, ate canned peaches in the middle of the night, and talked about the rudimentary kidney. She chose to see only other couples who were expecting children, and the parties that she and Jack gave were temperate. The baby, a boy, was born in May, and Jack was very proud and happy. The first party he and his wife went to after her convalescence was the wedding of a girl whose family Jack had known in Ohio.

The wedding was at St. James's, and afterward there was a big reception at the River Club. There was an orchestra dressed like Hungarians, and a lot of champagne and Scotch. Toward the end of the afternoon, Jack was walking down a dim corridor when he heard Joan's voice. "Please don't, darling," she was saying. "You'll break my arm. *Please* don't, darling." She was being pressed against the wall by a man who seemed to be twisting her arm. As soon as they saw Jack, the struggle stopped. All three of them were intensely embarrassed. Joan's face was wet and she made an effort to smile through her tears at Jack. He said hello and went on without stopping. When he returned, she and the man had disappeared.

WHEN JACK'S SON was less than two years old, his wife flew with the baby to Nevada to get a divorce. Jack gave her the apartment and all its furnishings and took a room in a hotel near Grand Central. His wife got her decree in due course, and the story was in the newspapers. Jack had a telephone call from Joan a few days later.

"I'm awfully sorry to hear about your divorce, Jack," she said. "She seemed like *such* a nice girl. But that wasn't what I called you about. I want your help, and I wondered if you could come down to my place tonight around six. It's something I don't want to talk about over the phone."

He went obediently to the Village that night and climbed the stairs. Her apartment was a mess. The pictures and the curtains were down and the books were in boxes. "You moving, Joan?" he asked.

"That's what I wanted to see you about, Jack. First, I'll give you a drink." She made two Old-Fashioneds. "I'm being evicted, Jack," she said. "I'm being evicted because I'm an immoral woman. The couple who have the apartment downstairs—they're charming people, I've always thought—have told the real-estate agent that I'm a drunk and a prostitute and all kinds of things. Isn't that fantastic? This real-estate agent has always been so nice to me that I didn't think he'd believe them, but he's canceled my lease, and if I make any trouble, he's threatened to take the matter up with the store, and I don't want to lose my job. This nice real-estate agent won't even talk with me any more. When I go over to the office, the receptionist leers at me as if I were some kind of dreadful woman. Of course, there have been a lot of men here and we sometimes are noisy, but I can't be expected to go to bed at ten every night. Can I? Well, the agent who manages this building has apparently told all the other agents in the neighborhood that I'm an immoral and drunken woman, and none of them will give me an apartment. I went in to talk with one man—he seemed to be such a nice old gentleman—and he made me an indecent proposal. Isn't it fantastic? I have to be out of here on Thursday and I'm literally being turned out into the street."

Joan seemed as serene and innocent as ever while she described this scourge of agents and neighbors. Jack listened carefully for some sign of indignation or bitterness or even urgency in her recital, but there was none. He was reminded of a torch song, of one of those forlorn and touching ballads that had been sung neither for him nor for her but for their older brothers and sisters by Marion Harris. Joan seemed to be singing her wrongs.

"They've made my life miserable," she went on quietly. "If I keep the radio on after ten o'clock, they telephone the agent in the morning and tell him I had some kind of orgy here. One night when Philip—I don't think you've met Philip; he's in the Royal Air Force; he's gone back to England—one night when Philip and some other people were here, they called the police. The police came bursting in the door and talked to me as if I were I don't know what and then looked in the bedroom. If they think there's a man up here after midnight, they call me on the telephone and say all kinds of disgusting things. Of course, I can put my furniture into storage and go to a hotel, I guess. I guess a hotel will take a woman with my kind of reputation, but I thought perhaps you might know of an apartment. I thought—"

It angered Jack to think of this big, splendid girl's being persecuted by her neighbors, and he said he would do what he could. He asked her to have dinner with him, but she said she was busy.

Having nothing better to do, Jack decided to walk uptown to his hotel. It was a hot night. The sky was overcast. On his way, he saw a parade in a dark side street off Broadway near Madison Square. All the buildings in the neighborhood were dark. It was so dark that he could not see the placards the marchers carried until he came to a street light. Their signs urged the entry of the United States into the war, and each platoon represented a nation that had been subjugated by the Axis powers. They marched up Broadway, as he watched, to no music, to no sound but their own steps on the rough cobbles. It was for the most part an army of elderly men and women—Poles, Norwegians, Danes, Jews, Chinese. A few idle people like himself lined the sidewalks, and the marchers passed between them with all the self-consciousness of enemy prisoners. There were children among them dressed in the costumes in which they had, for the newsreels, presented the Mayor with a package of tea, a petition, a protest, a constitution, a check, or a pair of tickets. They hobbled through the darkness of the loft neighborhood like a mortified and destroyed people, toward Greeley Square.

In the morning, Jack put the problem of finding an apartment for Joan up to his secretary. She started phoning real-estate agents, and by afternoon she had found a couple of available apartments in the West Twenties. Joan called Jack the next day to say that she had taken one of the apartments and to thank him.

Jack didn't see Joan again until the following summer. It was a Sunday evening; he had left a cocktail party in a Washington Square apartment and had decided to walk a few blocks up Fifth Avenue before he took a bus. As he was passing the Brevoort, Joan called to him. She was with a man at one of the tables on the sidewalk. She looked cool and fresh, and the man appeared to be respectable. His name, it turned out, was Pete Bristol. He invited Jack to sit down and join in a celebration. Germany had invaded Russia that weekend, and Joan and Pete were drinking champagne to celebrate Russia's changed position in the war. The three of them drank champagne until it got dark. They had dinner and drank champagne with their dinner. They drank more champagne afterward and then went over to the Lafayette and then to two or three other places. Joan had always been tireless in her gentle way. She hated to see the night end, and it was after three o'clock when Jack stumbled into his apartment. The following morning he woke up haggard and sick, and with no recollection of the last hour or so of the previous evening. His suit was soiled and he had lost his hat. He didn't get to his office until eleven. Joan had already called him twice, and she called him again soon after he got in. There was no hoarseness at all in her voice. She said that she had to see him, and he agreed to meet her for lunch in a seafood restaurant in the Fifties.

He was standing at the bar when she breezed in, looking as though she had taken no part in that calamitous night. The advice she wanted concerned selling her jewelry. Her grandmother had left her some jewelry, and she wanted to raise money on it but didn't know where to go. She took some rings and bracelets out of her purse and showed them to Jack. He said that he didn't know anything about jewelry but that he could lend her some money. "Oh, I couldn't borrow money from you, Jack," she said. "You see, I want to get the money for Pete. I want to help him. He wants to open an advertising agency, and he needs quite a lot to begin with." Jack didn't press her to accept his offer of a loan after that, and the project wasn't mentioned again during lunch.

He next heard about Joan from a young doctor who was a friend of theirs. "Have you seen Joan recently?" the doctor asked Jack one evening when they were having dinner together. He said no. "I gave her a checkup last week," the doctor said, "and while she's been through enough to kill the average mortal—and you'll never know what she's been through—she still has the constitution of a virtuous and healthy woman. Did you hear about the last one? She sold her jewelry to put him into some kind of business, and as soon as he got the money, he left her for another girl, who had a car—a convertible."

Jack was drafted into the Army in the spring of 1942. He was kept at Fort Dix for nearly a month, and during this time he came to New York in the evening whenever he could get permission. Those nights had for him the intense keenness of a reprieve, a sensation that was heightened by the fact that on the train in from Trenton women would often press upon him dog-eared copies of *Life* and half-eaten boxes of candy, as though the brown clothes he wore were surely cerements. He telephoned Joan from Pennsylvania Station one night. "Come right over, Jack," she said. "Come right over. I want you to meet Ralph."

She was living in that place in the West Twenties that Jack had found for her. The neighborhood was a slum. Ash cans stood in front of her house, and an old woman was there picking out bits of refuse and garbage and stuffing them into a perambulator. The house in which Joan's apartment was located was shabby, but the apartment itself seemed familiar. The furniture was the same. Joan was the same big, easygoing girl. "I'm so glad you called me," she said. "It's so good to see you. I'll make you a drink. I was having one myself. Ralph ought to be here by now. He promised to take me to dinner." Jack offered to take her to Cavanagh's, but she said that Ralph might come while she was out. "If he doesn't come by nine, I'm going to make myself a sandwich. I'm not really hungry."

Jack talked about the Army. She talked about the store. She had been working in the same place for—how long was it? He didn't know. He had never seen her at her desk and he couldn't imagine what she did. "I'm terribly sorry Ralph isn't here," she said. "I'm sure you'd like him. He's not a young man. He's a heart specialist who loves to play the viola." She turned on some lights, for the summer sky had got dark. "He had this dreadful wife on Riverside Drive and four ungrateful children. He—"

The noise of an air-raid siren, lugubrious and seeming to spring from pain, as if all the misery and indecision in the city had been given a voice, cut her off. Other sirens, in distant neighborhoods, sounded, until the dark air was full of their noise. "Let me fix you another drink before I have to turn out the lights," Joan said, and took his glass. She brought the drink back to him and snapped off the lights. They went to the windows, and, as children watch a thunderstorm, they watched the city darken. All the lights nearby went out but one. Air-raid wardens had begun to sound their whistles in the street. From a distant yard came a hoarse shriek of anger. "Put out your lights, you Fascists!" a woman screamed. "Put out your lights, you

Nazi Fascist Germans. Turn out your lights. Turn out your lights." The last light went off. They went away from the window and sat in the lightless room.

In the darkness, Joan began to talk about her departed lovers, and from what she said Jack gathered that they had all had a hard time. Nils, the suspect count, was dead. Hugh Bascomb, the drunk, had joined the Merchant Marine and was missing in the North Atlantic. Franz, the German, had taken poison the night the Nazis bombed Warsaw. "We listened to the news on the radio," Joan said, "and then he went back to his hotel and took poison. The maid found him dead in the bathroom the next morning." When Jack asked her about the one who was going to open an advertising agency, she seemed at first to have forgotten him. "Oh, Pete," she said after a pause. "Well, he was always very sick, you know. He was supposed to go to Saranac, but he kept putting it off and putting it off and—" She stopped talking when she heard steps on the stairs, hoping, he supposed, that it was Ralph, but whoever it was turned at the landing and continued to the top of the house. "I wish Ralph would come," she said, with a sigh. "I want you to meet him." Jack asked her again to go out, but she refused, and when the all-clear sounded, he said goodbye.

Jack was shipped from Dix to an infantry training camp in the Carolinas and from there to an infantry division stationed in Georgia. He had been in Georgia three months when he married a girl from the Augusta boarding-house aristocracy. A year or so later, he crossed the continent in a day coach and thought sententiously that the last he might see of the country he loved was the desert towns like Barstow, that the last he might hear of it was the ringing of the trolleys on the Bay Bridge. He was sent into the Pacific and returned to the United States twenty months later, uninjured and apparently unchanged. As soon as he received his furlough, he went to Augusta. He presented his wife with the souvenirs he had brought from the islands, quarreled violently with her and all her family, and, after making arrangements for her to get an Arkansas divorce, left for New York.

Jack was discharged from the Army at a camp in the East a few months later. He took a vacation and then went back to the job he had left in 1942. He seemed to have picked up his life at approximately the moment when it had been interrupted by the war. In time, everything came to look and feel the same. He saw most of his old friends. Only two of the men he knew had been killed in the war. He didn't call Joan, but he met her one winter afternoon on a crosstown bus.

Her fresh face, her black clothes, and her soft voice instantly destroyed the sense—if he had ever had such a sense—that anything had changed or intervened since their last meeting, three or four years ago. She asked him up for cocktails and he went to her apartment the next Saturday afternoon. Her room and her guests reminded him of the parties she had given when she had first come to New York. There was a woman with a fancy hat, an elderly doctor, and a man who stayed close to the radio, listening for news from the Balkans. Jack wondered which of the men belonged to Joan and decided on an Englishman who kept coughing into a handkerchief that he pulled out of his sleeve. Jack was right. "Isn't Stephen brilliant?" Joan asked him a little later, when they were alone in a corner. "He knows more about the Polynesians than anyone else in the world."

Jack had returned not only to his old job but to his old salary. Since living costs had doubled and since he was paying alimony to two wives, he had to draw on his savings. He took another job, which promised more money, but it didn't last long and he found himself out of work. This didn't bother him at all. He still had money in the bank, and anyhow it was easy to borrow from friends. His indifference was the consequence not of lassitude or despair but rather of an excess of hope. He had the feeling that he had only recently come to New York from Ohio. The sense that he was very young and that the best years of his life still lay before him was an illusion that he could not seem to escape. There was all the time in the world. He was living in hotels then, moving from one to another every five days.

In the spring, Jack moved to a furnished room in the badlands west of Central Park. He was running out of money. Then, when he began to feel that a job was a desperate necessity, he got sick. At first, he seemed to have only a bad cold, but he was unable to shake it and he began to run a fever and to cough blood. The fever kept him drowsy most of the time, but he roused himself occasionally and went out to a cafeteria for a meal. He felt sure that none of his friends knew where he was, and he was glad of this. He hadn't counted on Joan.

Late one morning, he heard her speaking in the hall with his landlady. A few moments later, she knocked on his door. He was lying on the bed in a pair of pants and a soiled pajama top, and he didn't answer. She knocked again and walked in. "I've been looking everywhere for you, Jack," she said. She spoke softly. "When I found out that you were in a place like this I thought you must be broke or sick. I stopped at the bank and got some money, in case you're broke. I've brought you some Scotch. I thought a little drink wouldn't do you any harm. Want a little drink?"

Joan's dress was black. Her voice was low and serene. She sat in a chair beside his bed as if she had been coming there every day to nurse him. Her features had coarsened, he thought, but there were still very few lines in her face. She was heavier. She was nearly fat. She was wearing black cotton gloves. She got two glasses and poured Scotch into them. He drank his whiskey greedily. "I didn't get to bed until three last night," she said. Her voice had once before reminded him of a gentle and despairing song, but now, perhaps because he was sick, her mildness, the mourning she wore, her stealthy grace, made him uneasy. "It was one of those nights," she said. "We went to the theatre. Afterward, someone asked us up to his place. I don't know who he was. It was one of those places. They're so strange. There were some meat-eating plants and a collection of Chinese snuff bottles. Why do people collect Chinese snuff bottles? We all autographed a lampshade, as I remember, but I can't remember much."

Jack tried to sit up in bed, as if there were some need to defend himself, and then fell back again, against the pillows. "How did you find me, Joan?" he asked.

"It was simple," she said. "I called that hotel. The one you were staying in. They gave me this address. My secretary got the telephone number. Have another little drink."

"You know, you've never come to a place of mine before—never," he said. "Why did you come now?"

"Why did I come, darling?" she asked. "What a question! I've known you for thirty years. You're the oldest friend I have in New York. Remember that night in the Village when it snowed and we stayed up until morning and drank whiskey sours for breakfast? That doesn't seem like twelve years ago. And that night—"

"I don't like to have you see me in a place like this," he said earnestly. He touched his face and felt his beard.

"And all the people who used to imitate Roosevelt," she said, as if she had not heard him, as if she were deaf. "And that place on Staten Island where we all used to go for dinner when Henry had a car. Poor Henry. He bought a place in Connecticut and went out there by himself one weekend. He fell asleep with a lighted cigarette and the house, the barn, everything burned. Ethel took the children out to California." She poured more Scotch into his glass and handed it to him. She lighted a cigarette and put it between his lips. The intimacy of this gesture, which made it seem not only as if he were deathly ill but as if he were her lover, troubled him.

"As soon as I'm better," he said, "I'll take a room at a good hotel. I'll call you then. It was nice of you to come."

"Oh, don't be ashamed of this room, Jack," she said. "Rooms never bother me. It doesn't seem to matter to me where I am. Stanley had a filthy room in Chelsea. At least, other people told me it was filthy. I never noticed it. Rats used to eat the food I brought him. He used to have to hang the food from the ceiling, from the light chain."

"I'll call you as soon as I'm better," Jack said. "I think I can sleep now if I'm left alone. I seem to need a lot of sleep."

"You really *are* sick, darling," she said. "You must have a fever." She sat on the edge of his bed and put a hand on his forehead.

"How is that Englishman, Joan?" he asked. "Do you still see him?"

"What Englishman?" she said.

"You know. I met him at your house. He kept a handkerchief up his sleeve. He coughed all the time. You know the one I mean."

"You must be thinking of someone else," she said. "I haven't had an Englishman at my place since the war. Of course, I can't remember everyone." She turned and, taking one of his hands, linked her fingers in his.

"He's dead, isn't he?" Jack said. "That Englishman's dead." He pushed her off the bed, and got up himself. "Get out," he said.

"You're sick, darling," she said. "I can't leave you alone here."

"Get out," he said again, and when she didn't move, he shouted, "What kind of an obscenity are you that you can smell sickness and death the way you do?"

"You poor darling."

"Does it make you feel young to watch the dying?" he shouted. "Is that the lewdness that keeps you young? Is that why you dress like a crow? Oh, I know there's nothing I can say that will hurt you. I know there's nothing filthy or corrupt or depraved or brutish or base that the others haven't tried, but this time you're wrong. I'm not ready. My life isn't ending. My life's beginning. There are wonderful years ahead of me. There are, there are wonderful, wonderful, wonderful years ahead of me, and when they're over, when it's time, then I'll call you. Then, as an old friend, I'll call you and give you whatever dirty pleasure you take in watching the dying, but until then, you and your ugly and misshapen forms will leave me alone."

She finished her drink and looked at her watch. "I guess I'd better show up at the office," she said. "I'll see you later. I'll come back tonight. You'll feel better then, you poor darling." She closed the door after her, and he heard her light step on the stairs.

Jack emptied the whiskey bottle into the sink. He began to dress. He stuffed his dirty clothes into a bag. He was trembling and crying with sickness and fear. He could see the blue sky from his window, and in his fear it seemed miraculous that the sky should be blue, that the white clouds should remind him of snow, that from the sidewalk he could hear the shrill voices of children shrieking, "I'm the king of the mountain, I'm the king of the mountain, I'm the king of the mountain." He emptied the ashtray containing his nail parings and cigarette butts into the toilet, and swept the floor with a shirt, so that there would be no trace of his life, of his body, when that lewd and searching shape of death came there to find him in the evening.

THE POT OF GOLD

You could not say fairly of Ralph and Laura Whittemore that they had the failings and the characteristics of incorrigible treasure hunters, but you could say truthfully of them that the shimmer and the smell, the peculiar force of money, the promise of it, had an untoward influence on their lives. They were always at the threshold of fortune; they always seemed to have something on the fire. Ralph was a fair young man with a tireless commercial imagination and an evangelical credence in the romance and sorcery of business success, and although he held an obscure job with a clothing manufacturer, this never seemed to him anything more than a point of departure.

The Whittemores were not importunate or overbearing people, and they had an uncompromising loyalty to the gentle manners of the middle class. Laura was a pleasant girl of no particular beauty who had come to New York from Wisconsin at about the same time that Ralph had reached the city from Illinois, but it had taken two years of comings and goings before they had been brought together, late one afternoon, in the lobby of a lower Fifth Avenue office building. So true was Ralph's heart, so well did it serve him then, that the moment he saw Laura's light hair and her pretty and sullen face he was enraptured. He followed her out of the lobby, pushing his way through the crowd, and since she had dropped nothing, since there was no legitimate excuse to speak to her, he shouted after her, *"Louise! Louise! Louise!"* and the urgency in his voice made her stop. He said he'd made a mistake. He said he was sorry. He said she looked just like a girl named Louise Hatcher. It was a January night and the dark air tasted of smoke, and because she was a sensible and a lonely girl, she let him buy her a drink.

This was in the thirties, and their courtship was hasty.

They were married three months later. Laura moved her belongings into a walk-up on Madison Avenue, above a pants presser's and a florist's, where Ralph was living. She worked as a secretary, and her salary, added to what he brought home from the clothing business, was little more than enough to keep them going, but they never seemed touched by the monotony of a saving and gainless life. They ate dinners in drugstores. She hung a reproduction of van Gogh's "Sunflowers" above the sofa she had bought with some of the small sum of money her parents had left her. When their aunts and uncles came to town—their parents were dead—they had dinner at the Ritz and went to the theatre. She sewed curtains and shined his shoes, and on Sundays they stayed in bed until noon. They seemed to be standing at the threshold of plenty, and Laura often told people that she was terribly excited because of this wonderful job that Ralph had lined up.

In the first year of their marriage, Ralph worked nights on a plan that promised him a well-paying job in Texas, but through no fault of his own this promise was never realized. There was an opening in Syracuse a year later, but an older man was decided upon. There were many other profitable but elusive openings and projects between these two. In the third year of their marriage, a firm that was almost identical in size and character with the firm Ralph worked for underwent a change of ownership, and Ralph was approached and asked if he would be interested in joining the overhauled firm. His own job promised only meager security after a series of slow promotions and he was glad of the chance to escape. He met the new owners, and their enthusiasm for him seemed intense. They were prepared to put him in charge of a department and pay him twice what he was getting then. The arrangement was to remain tacit for a month or two, until the new owners had secured their position, but they shook hands warmly and had a drink on the deal, and that night Ralph took Laura out to dinner at an expensive restaurant.

They decided, across the table, to look for a larger apartment, to have a child, and to buy a secondhand car. They faced their good fortune with perfect calm, for it was what they had expected all along. The city seemed to them a generous place, where people were rewarded either by a sudden and deserved development like this or by the capricious bounty of lawsuits, eccentric and peripheral business ventures, unexpected legacies, and other windfalls. After dinner, they walked in Central Park in the moonlight while Ralph smoked a cigar. Later, when Laura had fallen asleep, he sat in the open bedroom window in his pajamas.

The peculiar excitement with which the air of the city seems charged after midnight, when its life falls into the hands of watchmen and drunks, had always pleased him. He knew intimately the sounds of the night street: the bus brakes, the remote sirens, and the sound of water turning high in the air—the sound of water turning a mill wheel—the sum, he supposed, of many echoes, although, often as he had heard the sound, he had never decided on its source. Now he heard all this more keenly because the night seemed to him portentous.

He was twenty-eight years old; poverty and youth were inseparable in his experience, and one was ending with the other. The life they were about to leave had not been hard, and he thought with sentiment of the soiled tablecloth in the Italian restaurant where they usually went for their celebrations, and the high spirits with which Laura on a wet night ran from the subway to the bus stop. But they were drawing away from all this. Shirt sales in department-store basements, lines at meat counters, weak drinks, the roses he brought her up from the subway in the spring, when roses were cheap—these were all unmistakably the souvenirs of the poor, and while they seemed to him good and gentle, he was glad that they would soon be memories.

Laura resigned from her job when she got pregnant. The reorganization and Ralph's new position hung fire, but the Whittemores talked about it freely when they were with friends. "We're *terribly* pleased with the way things are going," Laura would say. "All we need is patience." There were many delays and postponements, and they waited with the patience of people expecting justice. The time came when they both needed clothes, and one evening Ralph suggested that they spend some of the money they had put aside. Laura refused. When he brought up the subject, she didn't answer him and seemed not to hear him. He raised his voice and lost his temper. He shouted. She cried. He thought of all the other girls he could have married—the dark blonde, the worshipful Cuban, the rich and pretty one with a cast in her right eye. All his desires seemed to lie outside the small apartment Laura had arranged. They were still not speaking in the morning, and in order to strengthen his position he telephoned his potential employers. Their secretary told him they were both out. This made him apprehensive. He called several times from the telephone booth in the lobby of the building he worked in and was told that they were busy, they were out, they were in conference with lawyers, or they were talking long-distance. This variety of excuses frightened him. He said nothing to Laura that evening and tried to call them the next day. Late in the afternoon, after many tries, one of them came to the phone. "We gave the job to somebody else, sonny," he said. Like a saddened father, he spoke to Ralph in a hoarse and gentle voice. "Don't try and get us on the telephone any more. We've got other things to do besides answer the telephone. This other fellow seemed better suited, sonny. That's all I can tell you, and don't try to get me on the telephone any more."

Ralph walked the miles from his office to his apartment that night, hoping to free himself in this way from some of the weight of his disappointment. He was so unprepared for the shock that it affected him like vertigo, and he walked with an old, high step, as if the paving were quicksand. He stood downstairs in front of the building he lived in, trying to decide how to describe the disaster to Laura, but when he went in, he told her bluntly. "Oh, I'm sorry, darling," she said softly and kissed him. "I'm terribly sorry." She wandered away from him and began to straighten the sofa cushions. His frustration was so ardent, he was such a prisoner of his schemes and expectations, that he was astonished at the serenity with which she regarded the failure. There was nothing to worry about, she said. She still had a few hundred dollars in the bank, from the money her parents had left her. There was nothing to worry about.

When the child, a girl, was born, they named her Rachel, and a week after the delivery Laura returned to the Madison Avenue walk-up. She took all the care of the baby and continued to do the cooking and the housework.

Ralph's imagination remained resilient and fertile, but he couldn't seem to hit on a scheme that would fit into his lack of time and capital. He and Laura, like the hosts of the poor everywhere, lived a simple life. They still went to the theatre with visiting relatives and occasionally they went to parties, but Laura's only continuous contact with the bright lights that surrounded them was vicarious and came to her through a friend she made in Central Park.

She spent many afternoons on a park bench during the first years of Rachel's life. It was a tyranny and a pleasure. She resented her enchainment but enjoyed the open sky and the air. One winter afternoon, she recognized a woman she had met at a party, and a little before dark, as Laura and the other mothers were gathering their stuffed animals and preparing their children for the cold journey home, the woman came across the playground and spoke to her. She was Alice Holinshed, she said. They had met at the Galvins'. She was pretty and friendly, and walked with Laura to the edge of the Park. She had a boy of about Rachel's age. The two women met again the following day. They became friends.

Mrs. Holinshed was older than Laura, but she had a more youthful and precise beauty. Her hair and her eyes were black, her pale and perfectly oval face was delicately colored, and her voice was pure. She lighted her cigarettes with Stork Club matches and spoke of the inconvenience of living with a child in a hotel. If Laura had any regrets about her life, they were expressed in her friendship for this pretty woman, who moved so freely through expensive stores and restaurants.

It was a friendship circumscribed, with the exception of the Galvins', by the sorry and touching countryside of Central Park. The women talked principally about their husbands, and this was a game that Laura could play with an empty purse. Vaguely, boastfully, the two women discussed the irons their men had in the fire. They sat together with their children through the sooty twilights, when the city to the south burns like a Bessemer furnace, and the air smells of coal, and the wet boulders shine like slag, and the Park itself seems like a strip of woods on the edge of a coal town. Then Mrs. Holinshed would remember that she was late—she was always late for something mysterious and splendid—and the two women would walk together to the edge of the woods. This vicarious contact with comfort pleased Laura, and the pleasure would stay with her as she pushed the baby carriage over to Madison Avenue and then began to cook supper, hearing the thump of the steam iron and smelling the cleaning fluid from the pants presser's below.

ONE NIGHT, when Rachel was about two years old, the frustration of Ralph's search for the goat track that would let him lead his family to a realm of reasonable contentment kept him awake. He needed sleep urgently, and when this blessing eluded him, he got out of bed and sat in the dark. The charm and excitement of the street after midnight escaped him. The explosive brakes of a Madison Avenue bus made him jump. He shut the window, but the noise of traffic continued to pass through it. It seemed to him that the penetrating voice of the city had a mortal effect on the precious lives of the city's inhabitants and that it should be muffled.

He thought of a Venetian blind whose outer surfaces would be treated with a substance that would deflect or absorb sound waves. With such a blind, friends paying a call on a spring evening would not have to shout to be heard above the noise of trucks in the street below. Bedrooms could be silenced that way—bedrooms, above all, for it seemed to him then that sleep was what everyone in the city sought and only half captured. All the harried faces on the streets at dusk, when even the pretty girls talk to themselves, were looking for sleep. Night-club singers and their amiable customers, the people waiting for taxis in front of the Waldorf on a wet night, policemen, cashiers, window washers—sleep eluded them all.

He talked over this Venetian blind with Laura the following night, and the idea seemed sensible to her. He bought a blind that would fit their bedroom window, and experimented with various paint mixtures. At last he stumbled on one that dried to the consistency of felt and was porous. The paint had a sickening smell, which filled their apartment during the four days it took him to coat and recoat the outer surface of the slats. When the paint had dried, he hung the blind, and they opened the window for a test. Silence—a relative silence—charmed their ears. He wrote down his formula, and took it during his lunch hour to a patent attorney. It took the lawyer several weeks to discover that a similar formula had been patented some years earlier. The patent owner—a man named Fellows—had a New York address, and the lawyer suggested that Ralph get in touch with him and try to reach some agreement.

The search for Mr. Fellows began one evening when Ralph had finished work, and took him first to the attic of a Hudson Street rooming house, where the landlady showed Ralph a pair of socks that Mr. Fellows had left behind when he moved out. Ralph went south from there to another rooming house and then west to the neighborhood of ship chandlers and marine boarding houses. The nocturnal search went on for a week. He followed the thread of Mr. Fellows' goings south to the Bowery and then to the upper West Side. He climbed stairs past the open doors of rooms where lessons in Spanish dancing were going on, past whores, past women practicing the "Emperor" Concerto, and one evening he found Mr. Fellows sitting on the edge of his bed in an attic room, rubbing the spots out of his necktie with a rag soaked in gasoline.

Mr. Fellows was greedy. He wanted a hundred dollars in cash and fifty per cent of the royalties. Ralph got him to agree to twenty per cent of the royalties, but he could not get him to reduce the initial payment. The lawyer drew up a paper defining Ralph's and Mr. Fellows' interests, and a few nights later Ralph went over to Brooklyn and got to a Venetian-blind factory after its doors had closed but while the lights of the office were still burning. The manager agreed to manufacture some blinds to Ralph's specifications, but he would not take an order of less than a hundred dollars. Ralph agreed to this and to furnish the compound for the outer surface of the slats. These expenditures had taken more than three-fourths of the Whittemores' capital, and now the problem of money was joined by the element of time. They put a small advertisement in the paper for a housewares salesman, and for a week Ralph interviewed candidates in the living room after supper. He chose a young man who was leaving at the end of the week for the Midwest. He wanted a fifty-dollar advance, and pointed out to them that Pittsburgh and Chicago were just as noisy as New York. A department-store collection agency was threatening to bring them into the small-claims court at this time, and they had come to a place where any illness, any fall, any damage to themselves or to the few clothes they owned would be critical. Their salesman promised to write them from Chicago at the end of the week, and they counted on good news, but there was no news from Chicago at all. Ralph wired the salesman twice, and the wires must have been forwarded, for he replied to them from Pittsburgh: "Can't merchandise blinds. Returning samples express." They put another advertisement for a salesman in the paper and took the first one who rang their bell, an old gentleman with a cornflower in his buttonhole. He had a number of other lines—mirror wastebaskets, orange-juicers—and he said that he knew all the Manhattan housewares buyers intimately. He was garrulous, and when he was unable to sell the blinds, he came to the Whittemores' apartment and discussed their product at length, and with a blend of criticism and charity that we usually reserve for human beings.

Ralph was to borrow money, but neither his salary nor his patent was considered adequate collateral for a loan at anything but ruinous rates, and one day, at his office, he was served a summons by the department-store collection agency. He went out to Brooklyn and offered to sell the Venetian blinds back to the manufacturer. The man gave him sixty dollars for what had cost a hundred, and Ralph was able to pay the collection agency. They hung the samples in their windows and tried to put the venture out of their minds.

Now they were poorer than ever, and they ate lentils for dinner every Monday and sometimes again on Tuesday. Laura washed the dishes after dinner while Ralph read to Rachel. When the girl had fallen asleep, he would go to his desk in the living room and work on one of his projects. There was always something coming. There was a job in Dallas and a job in Peru. There were the plastic arch preserver, the automatic closing device for icebox doors, and the scheme to pirate marine specifications and undersell Jane's. For a month, he was going to buy some fallow acreage in upstate New York and plant Christmas trees on it, and then, with one of his friends, he projected a luxury mail-order business, for which they could never get backing. When the Whittemores met Uncle George and Aunt Helen at the Ritz, they seemed delighted with the way things were going. They were terribly excited, Laura said, about a sales agency in Paris that had been offered to Ralph but that they had decided against, because of the threat of war.

The Whittemores were apart for two years during the war. Laura took a job. She walked Rachel to school in the morning and met her at the end of the day. Working and saving, Laura was able to buy herself and Rachel some clothes. When Ralph returned at the end of the war, their affairs were in good order. The experience seemed to have refreshed him, and while he took up his old job as an anchor to windward, as an ace in the hole, there had never been more talk about jobs—jobs in Venezuela and jobs in Iran. They resumed all their old habits and economies. They remained poor.

Laura gave up her job and returned to the afternoons with Rachel in Central Park. Alice Holinshed was there. The talk was the same. The Holinsheds were living in a hotel. Mr. Holinshed was vice-president of a new firm manufacturing a soft drink, but the dress that Mrs. Holinshed wore day after day was one that Laura recognized from before the war. Her son was thin and bad-tempered. He was dressed in serge, like an English schoolboy, but his serge, like his mother's dress, looked worn and outgrown. One afternoon when Mrs. Holinshed and her son came into the Park, the boy was crying. "I've done a dreadful thing," Mrs. Holinshed told Laura. "We've been to the doctor's and I forgot to bring any money, and I wonder if you could lend me a few dollars, so I can take a taxi back to the hotel." Laura said she would be glad to. She had only a five-dollar bill with her, and she gave Mrs. Holinshed this. The boy continued to cry, and his mother dragged him off toward Fifth Avenue. Laura never saw them in the Park again.

Ralph's life was, as it had always been, dominated by anticipation. In the years directly after the war, the city appeared to be immensely rich. There seemed to be money everywhere, and the Whittemores, who slept under their worn overcoats in the winter to keep themselves warm, seemed separated from their enjoyment of this prosperity by only a little patience, resourcefulness, and luck. On Sunday, when the weather was fine, they walked with the prosperous crowds on upper Fifth Avenue. It seemed to Ralph that it might only be another month, at the most another year, before he found the key to the prosperity they deserved. They would walk on Fifth Avenue until the afternoon was ended and then go home and eat a can of beans for dinner and, in order to balance the meal, an apple for dessert.

They were returning from such a walk one Sunday when, as they climbed the stairs to their apartment, the telephone began to ring. Ralph went on ahead and answered it.

He heard the voice of his Uncle George, a man of the generation that remains conscious of distance, who spoke into the telephone as if he were calling from shore to a passing boat. "This is Uncle George, Ralphie!" he shouted, and Ralph supposed that he and Aunt Helen were paying a surprise visit to the city, until he realized that his uncle was calling from Illinois. "Can you hear me?" Uncle George shouted. "Can you hear me, Ralphie? . . . I'm calling you about a job, Ralphie. Just in case you're looking for a job. Paul Hadaam came through—can you hear me, Ralphie?—Paul Hadaam came through here on his way East last week and he stopped off to pay me a visit. He's got a lot of money, Ralphie—he's rich—and he's starting this business out in the West to manufacture synthetic wool. Can you hear me, Ralphie? . . . I told him about you, and he's staying at the Waldorf, so you go and see him. I saved his life once. I pulled him out of Lake Erie. You go and see him tomorrow at the Waldorf, Ralphie. You know where that is? The Waldorf Hotel. . . . Wait a minute, here's Aunt Helen. She wants to talk with you."

Now the voice was a woman's, and it came to him faintly. All his cousins had been there for dinner, she told him. They had had a turkey for dinner. All the grandchildren were there and they behaved very well. George took them all for a walk after dinner. It was hot, but they sat on the porch, so they didn't feel the heat. She was interrupted in her account of Sunday by her husband, who must have seized the instrument from her to continue his refrain about going to see Mr. Hadaam at the Waldorf. "You go see him tomorrow, Ralphie—the nineteenth—at the Waldorf. He's expecting you. Can you hear me? . . . The Waldorf Hotel. He's a millionaire. I'll say goodbye now."

MR. HADAAM had a parlor and a bedroom in the Waldorf Towers, and when Ralph went to see him, late the next afternoon, on his way home from work, Mr. Hadaam was alone. He seemed to Ralph a very old man, but an obdurate one, and in the way he shook hands, pulled at his earlobes, stretched himself, and padded around the parlor on his bandy legs Ralph recognized a spirit that was unimpaired, independent, and canine. He poured Ralph a strong drink and himself a weak one. He was undertaking the manufacture of synthetic wool on the West Coast, he explained, and had come East to find men who were experienced in merchandising wool. George had given him Ralph's name, and he wanted a man with Ralph's experience. He would find the Whittemores a suitable house, arrange for their transportation, and begin Ralph at a salary of fifteen thousand. It was the size of the salary that made Ralph realize that the proposition was an oblique attempt to repay his uncle for having saved Mr. Hadaam's life, and the old man seemed to sense what he was feeling. "This hasn't got anything to do with your uncle's saving my life," he said roughly. "I'm grateful to him—who wouldn't be?—but this hasn't got anything to do with your uncle, if that's what you're thinking. When you get to be as old and as rich as I am, it's hard to meet people. All my old friends are dead—all of them but George. I'm surrounded by a cordon of associates and relatives that's damned near impenetrable, and if it wasn't for George giving me a name now and then, I'd never get to see a new face. Last year, I got into an automobile accident. It was my fault. I'm a terrible driver. I hit this young fellow's car and I got right out and went over to him and introduced myself. We had to wait about twenty minutes for the wreckers and we got to talking. Well, he's working for me today and he's one of the best friends I've got, and if I hadn't run into him, I'd never have met him. When you get to be as old as me, that's the only way you can meet people—automobile accidents, fires, things like that."

He straightened up against the back of his chair and tasted his drink. His rooms were well above the noise of traffic and it was quiet there. Mr. Hadaam's breath was loud and steady, and it sounded, in a pause, like the heavy breath of someone sleeping. "Well, I don't want to rush you into this," he said. "I'm going back to the Coast the day after tomorrow. You think it over and I'll telephone you." He took out an engagement book and wrote down Ralph's name and telephone number. "I'll call you on Tuesday evening, the twenty-seventh, about nine o'clock—nine o'clock your time. George tells me you've got a nice wife, but I haven't got time to meet her now. I'll see her on the Coast." He started talking about baseball and then brought the conversation back to Uncle George. "He saved my life. My damned boat capsized and then righted herself and sunk right from underneath me. I can still feel her going down under my feet. I couldn't swim. Can't swim today. Well, good-bye." They shook hands, and as soon as the door closed, Ralph heard Mr. Hadaam begin to cough. It was the profane, hammering cough of an old man, full of bitter complaints and distempers, and it hit him pitilessly for all the time that Ralph was waiting in the hallway for the elevator to take him down.

On the walk home, Ralph felt that this might be it, that this preposterous chain of contingencies that had begun with his uncle's pulling a friend out of Lake Erie might be the one that would save them. Nothing in his experience made it seem unlikely. He recognized that the proposition was the vagary of an old man and that it originated in the indebtedness Mr. Hadaam felt to his uncle—an indebtedness that age seemed to have deepened. He gave Laura the details of the interview when he came in, and his own views on Mr. Hadaam's conduct, and, to his mild surprise,

Laura said that it looked to her like the bonanza. They were both remarkably calm, considering the change that confronted them. There was no talk of celebrating, and he helped her wash the dishes. He looked up the site of Mr. Hadaam's factory in an atlas, and the Spanish place name on the coast north of San Francisco gave them a glimpse of a life of reasonable contentment.

Eight days lay between Ralph's interview and the telephone call, and he realized that nothing would be definite until Tuesday, and that there was a possibility that Mr. Hadaam, while crossing the country, might, under the subtle influence of travel, suffer a change of heart. He might be poisoned by a fish sandwich and be taken off the train in Chicago, to die in a nursing home there. Among the people meeting him in San Francisco might be his lawyer, with the news that he was ruined or that his wife had run away. But eventually Ralph was unable to invent any new disasters or to believe in the ones he had invented.

This inability to persevere in doubting his luck showed some weakening of character. There had hardly been a day when he had not been made to feel the power of money, but he found that the force of money was most irresistible when it took the guise of a promise, and that years of resolute self-denial, instead of rewarding him with reserves of fortitude, had left him more than ordinarily susceptible to temptation. Since the change in their lives still depended upon a telephone call, he refrained from talking—from thinking, so far as possible—about the life they might have in California. He would go so far as to say that he would like some white shirts, but he would not go beyond this deliberately contrite wish, and here, where he thought he was exercising restraint and intelligence, he was, instead, beginning to respect the bulk of superstition that is supposed to attend good fortune, and when he wished for white shirts, it was not a genuinely modest wish so much as it was a memory—he could not have put it into words himself—that the gods of fortune are jealous and easily deceived by false modesty. He had never been a superstitious man, but on Tuesday he scooped the money off his coffee table and was elated when he saw a ladybug on the bathroom window sill. He could not remember when he had heard money and this insect associated, but neither could he have explained any of the other portents that he had begun to let govern his movements.

Laura watched this subtle change that anticipation worked on her husband, but there was nothing she could say. He did not mention Mr. Hadaam or California. He was quiet; he was gentle with Rachel; he actually grew pale. He had his hair cut on Wednesday. He wore his best suit. On Saturday, he had his hair cut again and his nails manicured. He took two baths a day, put on a fresh shirt for dinner, and frequently went into the bathroom to wash his hands, brush his teeth, and wet down his cowlick. The preternatural care he gave his body and his appearance reminded her of an adolescent surprised by early love.

The Whittemores were invited to a party for Monday night and Laura insisted that they go. The guests at the party were the survivors of a group that had coalesced ten years before, and if anyone had called the roll of the earliest parties in the same room, like the retreat ceremony of a breached and decimated regiment, "Missing. . . . Missing. . . . Missing" would have been answered for the squad that had gone into Westchester; "Missing. . . . Missing. . . . Missing" would have been spoken for the platoon that divorce, drink, nervous disorders, and adversity had slain or wounded. Because Laura had gone to the party in indifferent spirits, she was conscious of the missing.

She had been at the party less than an hour when she heard some people coming in, and, looking over her shoulder, saw Alice Holinshed and her husband. The room was crowded and she put off speaking to Alice until later. Much later in the evening, Laura went into the toilet, and when she came out of it into the bedroom, she found Alice sitting on the bed. She seemed to be waiting for Laura. Laura sat down at the dressing table to straighten her hair. She looked at the image of her friend in the glass.

"I hear you're going to California," Alice said.

"We hope to. We'll know tomorrow."

"Is it true that Ralph's uncle saved his life?"

"That's true."

"You're lucky."

"I suppose we are."

"You're lucky, all right." Alice got up from the bed and

crossed the room and closed the door, and came back across the room again and sat on the bed. Laura watched her in the glass, but she was not watching Laura. She was stooped. She seemed nervous. "You're lucky," she said. "You're so lucky. Do you know how lucky you are? Let me tell you about this cake of soap," she said. "I have this cake of soap. I mean I had this cake of soap. Somebody gave it to me when I was married, fifteen years ago. I don't know who. Some maid, some music teacher—somebody like that. It was good soap, good English soap, the kind I like, and I decided to save it for the big day when Larry made a killing, when he took me to Bermuda. First, I was going to use it when he got the job in Bound Brook. Then I thought I could use it when we were going to Boston, and then Washington, and then when he got this new job, I thought maybe this is it, maybe *this* is the time when I get to take the boy out of that rotten school and pay the bills and move out of those bum hotels we've been living in. For fifteen years I've been planning to use this cake of soap. Well, last week I was looking through my bureau drawers and I saw this cake of soap. It was all cracked. I threw it out. I threw it out because I knew I was never going to have a chance to use it. Do you realize what that means? Do you know what that feels like? To live for fifteen years on promises and expectations and loans and credits in hotels that aren't fit to live in, never for a single day to be out of debt, and yet to pretend, to feel that every year, every winter, every job, every meeting is going to be the one. To live like this for fifteen years and then to realize that it's never going to end. Do you know what that feels like?" She got up and went over to the dressing table and stood in front of Laura. Tears had risen into her large eyes, and her voice was harsh and loud. "I'm never going to get to Bermuda," she said. "I'm never even going to get to Florida. I'm never going to get out of hock, ever, ever, *ever*. I know that I'm never going to have a decent home and that everything I own that is worn and torn and no good is going to stay that way. I know that for the rest of my life, for the rest of my life, I'm going to wear ragged slips and torn nightgowns and torn underclothes and shoes that hurt me. I know that for the rest of my life nobody is going to come up to me and tell me that

I've got on a pretty dress, because I'm not going to be able to afford that kind of a dress. I know that for the rest of my life every taxi driver and doorman and headwaiter in this town is going to know in a minute that I haven't got five bucks in that black imitation-suede purse that I've been brushing and brushing and brushing and carrying around for ten years. How do you get it? How do you rate it? What's so wonderful about you that you get a break like this?" She ran her fingers down Laura's bare arm. The dress she was wearing smelled of benzine. "Can I rub it off you? Will that make me lucky? I swear to Jesus I'd murder somebody if I thought it would bring us in any money. I'd wring somebody's neck—yours, anybody's—I swear to Jesus I would—"

Someone began knocking on the door. Alice strode to the door, opened it, and went out. A woman came in, a stranger looking for the toilet. Laura lighted a cigarette and waited in the bedroom for about ten minutes before she went back to the party. The Holinsheds had gone. She got a drink and sat down and tried to talk, but she couldn't keep her mind on what she was saying.

The hunt, the search for money that had seemed to her natural, amiable, and fair when they first committed themselves to it, now seemed like a hazardous and piratical voyage. She had thought, earlier in the evening, of the missing. She thought now of the missing again. Adversity and failure accounted for more than half of them, as if beneath the amenities in the pretty room a keen race were in progress, in which the loser's forfeits were extreme. Laura felt cold. She picked the ice out of her drink with her fingers and put it in a flower vase, but the whiskey didn't warm her. She asked Ralph to take her home.

After dinner on Tuesday, Laura washed the dishes and Ralph dried them. He read the paper and she took up some sewing. At a quarter after eight, the telephone, in the bedroom, rang, and he went to it calmly. It was someone with two theatre tickets for a show that was closing. The telephone didn't ring again, and at half past nine he told Laura that he was going to call California. It didn't take long for the connection to be made, and the fresh voice of a young woman spoke to him from Mr. Hadaam's number. "Oh, yes, Mr. Whittemore," she said. "We tried to get you earlier in the evening but your line was busy."

"Could I speak to Mr. Hadaam?"

"No, Mr. Whittemore. This is Mr. Hadaam's secretary. I know he meant to call you, because he had entered this in his engagement book. Mrs. Hadaam has asked me to disappoint as few people as possible, and I've tried to take care of all the calls and appointments in his engagement book. Mr. Hadaam had a stroke on Sunday. We don't expect him to recover. I imagine he made you some kind of promise, but I'm afraid he won't be able to keep it."

"I'm very sorry," Ralph said. He hung up.

Laura had come into the bedroom while the secretary was talking. "Oh, darling!" she said. She put her sewing basket on the bureau and went toward the closet. Then she went back and looked for something in the sewing basket and left the basket on her dressing table. Then she took off her shoes, treed them, slipped her dress over her head and hung it up neatly. Then she went to the bureau, looking for her sewing basket, found it on the dressing table, and took it into the closet, where she put it on a shelf. Then she took her brush and comb into the bathroom and began to run the water for a bath.

The lash of frustration was laid on and the pain stunned Ralph. He sat by the telephone for he did not know how long. He heard Laura come out of the bathroom. He turned when he heard her speak.

"I feel dreadfully about old Mr. Hadaam," she said. "I wish there were something we could do." She was in her nightgown, and she sat down at the dressing table like a skillful and patient woman establishing herself in front of a loom, and she picked up and put down pins and bottles and combs and brushes with the thoughtless dexterity of an experienced weaver, as if the time she spent there were all part of a continuous operation. "It did look like the treasure . . ."

The word surprised him, and for a moment he saw the chimera, the pot of gold, the fleece, the treasure buried in the faint lights of a rainbow, and the primitivism of his hunt struck him. Armed with a sharp spade and a homemade divining rod, he had climbed over hill and dale, through droughts and rain squalls, digging wherever the maps he had drawn himself promised gold. Six paces east of the dead pine, five panels in from the library door, underneath the creaking step, in the roots of the pear tree, beneath the grape arbor lay the bean pot full of doubloons and bullion.

She turned on the stool and held her thin arms toward him, as she had done more than a thousand times. She was no longer young, and more wan, thinner than she might have been if he had found the doubloons to save her anxiety and unremitting work. Her smile, her naked shoulders had begun to trouble the indecipherable shapes and symbols that are the touchstones of desire, and the light from the lamp seemed to brighten and give off heat and shed that unaccountable complacency, that benevolence, that the spring sunlight brings to all kinds of fatigue and despair. Desire for her delighted and confused him. Here it was, here it all was, and the shine of the gold seemed to him then to be all around her arms.

CLANCY IN THE TOWER OF BABEL

JAMES AND NORA CLANCY came from farms near the little town of Newcastle. Newcastle is near Limerick. They had been poor in Ireland and they were not much better off in the new country, but they were cleanly and decent people. Their home farms had been orderly places, long inhabited by the same families, and the Clancys enjoyed the grace of a tradition. Their simple country ways were so deeply ingrained that twenty years in the New World had had little effect on them. Nora went to market with a straw basket under her arm, like a woman going out to a kitchen garden, and Clancy's pleasant face reflected a simple life. They had only one child, a son named John, and they had been able to pass on to him their peaceful and contented views. They were people who centered their lives in half a city block, got down on their knees on the floor to say "Hail Mary, full of grace," and took turns in the bathtub in the kitchen on Saturday night.

When Clancy was still a strong man in his forties, he fell down some stairs in the factory and broke his hip. He was out of work for nearly a year, and while he got compensation for this time, it was not as much as his wages had been and he and his family suffered the pain of indebtedness and need. When Clancy recovered, he was left with a limp and it took him a long time to find another job. He went to church every day, and in the end it was the intercession of a priest that got work for him, running an elevator in one of the big apartment houses on the East Side. Clancy's good manners and his clean and pleasant face pleased the tenants, and with his salary and the tips they gave him he made enough to pay his debts and support his wife and son.

The apartment house was not far from the slum tenement where James and Nora had lived since their marriage, but financially and morally it was another creation, and Clancy at first looked at the tenants as if they were made out of sugar. The ladies wore coats and jewels that cost more than Clancy would make in a lifetime of hard work, and when he came home in the evenings, he would, like a returned traveler, tell Nora what he had seen. The poodles, the cocktail parties, the children and their nursemaids interested him, and he told Nora that it was like the Tower of Babel.

It took Clancy a while to memorize the floor numbers to which his tenants belonged, to pair the husbands and wives, to join the children to their parents, and the servants (who rode on the back elevators) to these families, but he managed at last and was pleased to have everything straight. Among his traits was a passionate sense of loyalty, and he often spoke of the Building as if it were a school or a guild, the product of a community of sentiment and aspiration. "Oh, I wouldn't do anything to harm the Building," he often said. His manner was respectful but he was not humorless, and when 11-A sent his tailcoat out to the dry cleaner's, Clancy put it on and paraded up and down the back hall. Most of the tenants were regarded by Clancy with an indiscriminate benevolence, but there were a few exceptions. There was a drunken wifebeater. He was a bulky, duck-footed lunkhead, in Clancy's eyes, and he did not belong in the Building. Then there was a pretty girl in 11-B who went out in the evenings with a man who was a weak character—Clancy could tell because he had a cleft chin. Clancy warned the girl, but she did not act on his advice. But the tenant about whom he felt most concerned was Mr. Rowantree.

Mr. Rowantree, who was a bachelor, lived in 4-A. He had been in Europe when Clancy first went to work, and he had not returned to New York until winter. When Mr. Rowantree appeared, he seemed to Clancy to be a well-favored man with graying hair who was tired from his long voyage. Clancy waited for him to re-establish himself in the city, for friends and relatives to start telephoning and writing, and for Mr. Rowantree to begin the give-and-take of parties in which most of the tenants were involved.

Clancy had discovered by then that his passengers were not made of sugar. All of them were secured to the world intricately by friends and lovers, dogs and songbirds, debts, inheritances, trusts, and jobs, and he waited for Mr. Rowantree to put out his lines. Nothing happened. Mr. Rowantree went to work at ten in the morning and returned home at six; no visitors appeared. A month passed in which he did not have a single guest. He sometimes went out in the evening, but he always returned alone, and for all Clancy knew he might have continued his friendless state in the movies around the corner. The man's lack of friends amazed and then began to aggravate and trouble Clancy. One night when he was on the evening shift and Mr. Rowantree came down alone, Clancy stopped the car between floors.

"Are you going out for dinner, Mr. Rowantree?" he asked.

"Yes," the man said.

"Well, when you're eating in this neighborhood, Mr. Rowantree," Clancy said, "you'll find that Bill's Clam Bar is the only restaurant worth speaking of. I've been living around here for twenty years and I've seen them come and go. The others have fancy lighting and fancy prices, but you won't get anything to eat that's worth sticking to your ribs excepting at Bill's Clam Bar."

"Thank you, Clancy," Mr. Rowantree said. "I'll keep that in mind."

"Now, Mr. Rowantree," Clancy said, "I don't want to

sound inquisitive, but would you mind telling me what kind of a business you're in?"

"I have a store on Third Avenue," Mr. Rowantree said. "Come over and see it someday."

"I'd like to do that," Clancy said. "But now, Mr. Rowantree, I should think you'd want to have dinner with your friends and not be alone all the time." Clancy knew that he was interfering with the man's privacy, but he was led on by the thought that this soul might need help. "A good-looking man like you must have friends," he said, "and I'd think you'd have your supper with them."

"I'm going to have supper with a friend, Clancy," Mr. Rowantree said.

This reply made Clancy feel easier, and he put the man out of his mind for a while. The Building gave him the day off on St. Patrick's, so that he could march in the parade, and when the parade had disbanded and he was walking home, he decided to look for the store. Mr. Rowantree had told him which block it was in. It was easy to find. Clancy was pleased to see that it was a big store. There were two doors to go in by, separated by a large glass window. Clancy looked through the window to see if Mr. Rowantree was busy with a customer, but there was no one there. Before he went in, he looked at the things in the window. He was disappointed to see that it was not a clothing store or a delicatessen. It looked more like a museum. There were glasses and candlesticks, chairs and tables, all of them old. He opened the door. A bell attached to the door rang and Clancy looked up to see the old-fashioned bell on its string. Mr. Rowantree came out from behind a screen and greeted him cordially.

Clancy did not like the place. He felt that Mr. Rowantree was wasting his time. It troubled him to think of the energy in a man's day being spent in this place. A narrow trail, past tables and desks, urns and statues, led into the store and then branched off in several directions. Clancy had never seen so much junk. Since he couldn't imagine it all being manufactured in any one country, he guessed that it had been brought there from the four corners of the world. It seemed to Clancy a misuse of time to have gathered all these things into a dark store on Third Avenue. But it was more than the confusion and the waste that troubled him; it was the feeling that he was surrounded by the symbols of frustration and that all the china youths and maidens in their attitudes of love were the company of bitterness. It may have been because he had spent his happy life in bare rooms that he associated goodness with ugliness.

He was careful not to say anything that would offend Mr. Rowantree. "Do you have any clerks to help you?" he asked.

"Oh, yes," Mr. Rowantree said. "Miss James is here most of the time. We're partners."

That was it, Clancy thought. Miss James. That was where he went in the evenings. But why, then, wouldn't Miss James marry him? Was it because he was already married? Perhaps he had suffered some terrible human misfortune, like having his wife go crazy or having his children taken away from him.

"Have you a snapshot of Miss James?" Clancy asked.

"No," Mr. Rowantree said.

"Well, I'm glad to have seen your store and thank you very much," Clancy said. The trip had been worth his while, because he took away from the dark store a clear image of Miss James. It was a good name, an Irish name, and now in the evenings when Mr. Rowantree went out, Clancy would ask him how Miss James was.

Clancy's son, John, was a senior in high school. He was captain of the basketball team and a figure in school government, and that spring he entered an essay he had written on democracy in a contest sponsored by a manufacturer in Chicago. There were millions of entries, but John won honorable mention, which entitled him to a trip to Chicago in an airplane and a week's visit there with all expenses paid. The boy was naturally excited by this bonanza and so was his mother, but Clancy was the one who seemed to have won the prize. He told all the tenants in the Building about it and asked them what kind of city Chicago was and if traveling in airplanes was safe. He would get up in the middle of the night and go into John's room to look at the wonderful boy while he slept. The boy's head was crammed with knowledge, Clancy thought. His heart was kind and strong. It was sinful, Clancy knew, to confuse the immortality of the Holy Spirit and earthly love, but when he realized that John was his flesh and blood, that the young man's face was *his* face improved with mobility and thought, and that when he, Clancy, was dead, some habit or taste of his would live on in the young man, he felt that there was no pain in death.

John's plane left for Chicago late one Saturday afternoon. He went to confession and then walked over to the Building to say goodbye to his father. Clancy kept the boy in the lobby as long as he could and introduced him to the tenants who came through. Then it was time for the boy to go. The doorman took the elevator, and Clancy walked John up to the corner. It was a clear, sunny afternoon in Lent. There wasn't a cloud in the sky. The boy had on his best suit and he looked like a million dollars. They shook hands at the corner, and Clancy limped back to the Building. Traffic was slow on the elevator, and he stood at the front door, watching the people on the sidewalk. Most of them were dressed in their best clothes and they were off to enjoy themselves. Clancy's best wishes followed them all. At the far end of the street he saw Mr. Rowantree's head and shoulders and saw that he was with a young man. Clancy waited and opened the door for them.

"Hello, Clancy," Mr. Rowantree said. "I'd like to have you meet my friend Bobbie. He's going to live here now."

Clancy grunted. The young man was not a young man. His hair was cut short and he wore a canary-yellow sweater and a padded coat but he was as old as Mr. Rowantree, he was nearly as old as Clancy. All the qualities and airs of youth, which a good man puts aside gladly when the time comes, had been preserved obscenely in him. He had dope in his eyes to make them shine and he smelled of perfume, and Mr. Rowantree took his arm to help him through the door, as if he were a pretty girl. As soon as Clancy saw what he had to deal with, he took a stand. He stayed at the door. Mr. Rowantree and his friend went through the lobby and got into the elevator. They reached out and rang the bell.

"I'm not taking you up in my car!" Clancy shouted down the lobby.

"Come here, Clancy," Mr. Rowantree said.

"I'm not taking that up in my car," Clancy said.

"I'll have you fired for this," Mr. Rowantree said.

"That's no skin off my nose," Clancy said. "I'm not taking you up in my car."

"Come here, Clancy," Mr. Rowantree said. Clancy didn't answer. Mr. Rowantree put his finger on the bell and held it there. Clancy didn't move. He heard Mr. Rowantree and his friend talking. A moment later, he heard them climb the stairs. All the solicitude he had felt for Mr. Rowantree, the times he had imagined him walking in the Park with Miss James, seemed like money lost in a terrible fraud. He was hurt and bitter. The idea of Bobbie's being in the Building was a painful one for him to take, and he felt as if it contested his own simple view of life. He was curt with everyone for the rest of the day. He even spoke sharply to the children. When he went to the basement to take off his uniform, Mr. Coolidge, the superintendent, called him into his office.

"Rowantree's been trying to get you fired for the last hour, Jim," he said. "He said you wouldn't take him up in your car. I'm not going to fire you, because you're a good, steady man, but I'm warning you now. He knows a lot of rich and influential people, and if you don't mind your own business, it won't be hard for him to get you kicked out." Mr. Coolidge was surrounded by all the treasures he had extricated from the rubbish baskets in the back halls—broken lamps, broken vases, a perambulator with three wheels.

"But he—" Clancy began.

"It's none of your business, Jim," Mr. Coolidge said. "He's been very quiet since he came back from Europe. You're a good, steady man, Clancy, and I don't want to fire you, but you got to remember that you aren't the boss around here."

The next day was Palm Sunday, and, by the grace of God, Clancy did not see Mr. Rowantree. On Monday, Clancy joined his bitterness at having to live in Sodom to the deep and general grief he always felt at the commencement of those events that would end on Golgotha. It was a gloomy day. Clouds and darkness were over the city. Now and then it rained. Clancy took Mr. Rowantree down at ten. He didn't say anything, but he gave the man a scornful look. The ladies began going off for lunch around noon. Mr. Rowantree's friend Bobbie went out then.

About half past two, one of the ladies came back from lunch, smelling of gin. She did a funny thing. When she got into the elevator, she stood with her face to the wall of the car, so that Clancy couldn't see it. He was not a man to look into somebody's face if they wanted to hide it, and this made him angry. He stopped the car. "Turn around," he said. "Turn around. I'm ashamed of you, a woman with three grown children, standing with your face to the wall like a crybaby." She turned around. She was crying about something. Clancy put the car into motion again. "You ought to fast," he mumbled. "You ought to go without cigarettes or meat during Lent. It would give you something to think about." She left the car, and he answered a ring from the first floor. It was Mr. Rowantree. He took him up. Then he took Mrs. DePaul up to 9. She was a nice woman, and he told her about John's trip to Chicago. On the way down, he smelled gas.

For a man who has lived his life in a tenement, gas is the odor of winter, sickness, need, and death. Clancy went up to Mr. Rowantree's floor. That was it. He had the master key and he opened the door and stepped into that hellish breath. It was dark. He could hear the petcocks hissing in the kitchen. He put a rug against the door to keep it open and threw up a window in the hall. He stuck his head out for some air. Then, in terror of being blown into hell himself, and swearing and praying and half closing his eyes as if the poisonous air might blind him, he started for the kitchen and gave himself a cruel bang against the doorframe that made him cold all over with pain. He stumbled into the kitchen and turned off the gas and opened the doors and windows. Mr. Rowantree was on his knees with his head in the oven. He sat up. He was crying. "Bobbie's gone, Clancy," he said. "Bobbie's gone."

Clancy's stomach turned over, his gorge opened and filled up with bitter spit. "Dear Jesus!" he shouted. "Dear Jesus!" He stumbled out of the apartment. He was shaking all over. He took the car down and shouted for the doorman and told him what had happened.

The doorman took the elevator, and Clancy went into the locker room and sat down. He didn't know how long he had been there when the doorman came in and said that he smelled more gas. Clancy went up to Mr. Rowantree's apartment again. The door was shut. He opened it and stood in the hall and heard the petcocks. "Take your God-damned fool head out of that oven, Mr. Rowantree!" he shouted. He went into the kitchen and turned off the gas. Mr. Rowantree was sitting on the floor. "I won't do it again, Clancy," he said. "I promise, I promise."

Clancy went down and got Mr. Coolidge, and they went into the basement together and turned off Mr. Rowantree's gas. He went up again. The door was shut. When he opened it, he heard the hissing of the gas. He yanked the man's head out of the oven. "You're wasting your time, Mr. Rowantree!" he shouted. "We've turned off your gas! You're wasting your time!" Mr. Rowantree scrambled to his feet and ran out of the kitchen. Clancy heard him running through the apartment, slamming doors. He followed him and found him in the bathroom, shaking pills out of a bottle into his mouth. Clancy knocked the pill bottle out of his hand and knocked the man down. Then he called the precinct station on Mr. Rowantree's phone. He waited there until a policeman, a doctor, and a priest came.

Clancy walked home at five. The sky was black. It was raining soot and ashes. Sodom, he thought, the city undeserving of clemency, the unredeemable place, and, raising his eyes to watch the rain and the ashes fall through the air, he felt a great despair for his kind. They had lost the warrants for mercy, there was no movement in the city around him but toward self-destruction and sin. He longed for the simple life of Ireland and the City of God, but he felt that he had been contaminated by the stink of gas.

He told Nora what had happened, and she tried to comfort him. There was no letter or card from John. In the evening, Mr. Coolidge telephoned. He said it was about Mr. Rowantree.

"Is he in the insane asylum?" Clancy asked.

"No," Mr. Coolidge said. "His friend came back and they went out together. But he's been threatening to get you fired again. As soon as he felt all right again, he said he was going to get you fired. I don't want to fire you, but you got to be careful, you got to be careful." This was the twist that Clancy couldn't follow, and he felt sick. He asked Mr. Coolidge to get a man from the union to take his place for a day or so, and he went to bed.

CLANCY stayed in bed the next morning. He got worse. He was cold. Nora lighted a fire in the range, but he shivered as if his heart and his bones were frozen. He doubled his knees up to his chest and snagged the blankets around him, but he couldn't keep warm. Nora finally called the doctor, a man from Limerick. It was after ten before he got there. He said that Clancy should go to the hospital. The doctor left to make the arrangements, and Nora got Clancy's best clothes together and helped him into them. There was still a price tag on his long underwear and there were pins in his shirt. In the end, nobody saw the new underwear and the clean shirt. At the hospital, they drew a curtain around his bed and handed the finery out to Nora. Then he stretched out in bed, and Nora gave him a kiss and went away.

He groaned, he moaned for a while, but he had a fever and this put him to sleep. He did not know or care where he was for the next few days. He slept most of the time. When John came back from Chicago, the boy's company and his story of the trip picked Clancy's spirits up a little. Nora visited him every day, and one day, a couple of weeks after Clancy entered the hospital, she brought Frank Quinn, the doorman, with her. Frank gave Clancy a narrow manila envelope, and when Clancy opened it, asking crossly what it was, he saw that it was full of currency.

"That's from the tenants, Clancy," Frank said.

"Now, why did they do this?" Clancy said. He was smitten. His eyes watered and he couldn't count the money. "Why did they do this?" he asked weakly. "Why did they go to this trouble? I'm nothing but an elevator man."

"It's nearly two hundred dollars," Frank said.

"Who took up the collection?" Clancy said. "Was it you, Frank?"

"It was one of the tenants," Frank said.

"It was Mrs. DePaul," Clancy said. "I'll bet it was that Mrs. DePaul."

"One of the tenants," Frank said.

"It was you, Frank," Clancy said warmly. "You was the one who took up the collection."

"It was Mr. Rowantree," Frank said sadly. He bent his head.

"You're not going to give the money back, Jim?" Nora asked.

"I'm not a God-damned fool!" Clancy shouted. "When I pick up a dollar off the street, I'm not the man to go running down to the lost-and-found department with it!"

"Nobody else could have gotten so much, Jim," Frank said. "He went from floor to floor. They say he was crying."

Clancy had a vision. He saw the church from the open lid of his coffin, before the altar. The sacristan had lighted only a few of the Vaseline-colored lamps, for the only mourners were those few people, all of them poor and old, who had come from Limerick with Clancy on the boat. He heard the priest's youthful voice mingling with the thin music of the bells. Then in the back of the church he saw Mr. Rowantree and Bobbie. They were crying and crying. They were crying harder than Nora. He could see their shoulders rise and fall, and hear their sighs.

"Does he think I'm dying, Frank?" Clancy asked.

"Yes, Jim. He does."

"He thinks I'm dying," Clancy said angrily. "He's got one of them soft heads. Well, I ain't dying. I'm not taking any of his grief. I'm getting out of here." He climbed out of bed. Nora and Frank tried unsuccessfully to push him back. Frank ran out to get a nurse. The nurse pointed a finger at Clancy and commanded him to get back into bed, but he had put on his pants and was tying his shoelaces. She went out and got another nurse, and the two young women tried to hold him down, but he shook them off easily. The first nurse went to get a doctor. The doctor who returned with her was a young man, much smaller than Clancy. He said that Clancy could go home. Frank and Nora took him back in a taxi, and as soon as he got into the tenement, he telephoned Mr. Coolidge and said that he was coming back to work in the morning. He felt a lot better, surrounded by the smells and lights of his own place. Nora cooked him a nice supper and he ate it in the kitchen.

After supper, he sat by the window in his shirtsleeves. He thought about going back to work, about the man with the cleft chin, the wife-beater, Mr. Rowantree and Bobbie. Why should a man fall in love with a monster? Why should a man try to kill himself? Why should a man try to get a man fired and then collect money for him with tears in his eyes, and then perhaps, a week later, try to get him fired again? He would not return the money, he would not thank Mr. Rowantree, but he wondered what kind of judgment he should pass on the pervert. He began to pick the words he would say to Mr. Rowantree when they met. "It's my suggestion, Mr. Rowantree," he would say, "that the next time you want to kill yourself, you get a rope or a gun. It's my suggestion, Mr. Rowantree," he would say, "that you go to a good doctor and get your head examined."

The spring wind, the south wind that in the city smells of drains, was blowing. Clancy's window looked onto an expanse of clotheslines and ailanthus trees, yards that were used as dumps, and the naked backs of tenements, with their lighted and unlighted windows. The symmetry, the reality of the scene heartened Clancy, as if it conformed to something good in himself. Men with common minds like his had built these houses. Nora brought him a glass of beer and sat near the window. He put an arm around her waist. She was in her slip, because of the heat. Her hair was held down with pins. She appeared to Clancy to be one of the glorious beauties of his day, but a stranger, he guessed, might notice the tear in her slip and that her body was bent and heavy. A picture of John hung on the wall. Clancy was struck with the strength and intelligence of his son's face, but he guessed that a stranger might notice the boy's glasses and his bad complexion. And then, thinking of Nora and John and that this half blindness was all that he knew himself of mortal love, he decided not to say anything to Mr. Rowantree. They would pass in silence.

CHRISTMAS IS A SAD SEASON FOR THE POOR

CHRISTMAS is a sad season. The phrase came to Charlie an instant after the alarm clock had waked him, and named for him an amorphous depression that had troubled him all the previous evening. The sky outside his window was black. He sat up in bed and pulled the light chain that hung in front of his nose. Christmas is a very sad day of the year, he thought. Of all the millions of people in New York, I am practically the only one who has to get up in the cold black of 6 A.M. on Christmas Day in the morning; I am practically the only one.

He dressed, and when he went downstairs from the top floor of the rooming house in which he lived, the only sounds he heard were the coarse sounds of sleep; the only lights burning were lights that had been forgotten. Charlie ate some breakfast in an all-night lunchwagon and took an Elevated train uptown. From Third Avenue, he walked over to Sutton Place. The neighborhood was dark. House after house put into the shine of the street lights a wall of black windows. Millions and millions were sleeping, and this general loss of consciousness generated an impression of abandonment, as if this were the fall of the city, the end of time. He opened the iron-and-glass doors of the apartment building where he had been working for six months as an elevator operator, and went through the elegant lobby to a locker room at the back. He put on a striped vest with brass buttons, a false ascot, a pair of pants with a light-blue stripe on the seam, and a coat. The night elevator man was dozing on the little bench in the car. Charlie woke him. The night elevator man told him thickly that the day doorman had been taken sick and wouldn't be in that day. With the doorman sick, Charlie wouldn't have any relief for lunch, and a lot of people would expect him to whistle for cabs.

CHARLIE had been on duty a few minutes when 14 rang

—a Mrs. Hewing, who, he happened to know, was kind of immoral. Mrs. Hewing hadn't been to bed yet, and she got into the elevator wearing a long dress under her fur coat. She was followed by her two funny-looking dogs. He took her down and watched her go out into the dark and take her dogs to the curb. She was outside for only a few minutes. Then she came in and he took her up to 14 again. When she got off the elevator, she said, "Merry Christmas, Charlie."

"Well, it isn't much of a holiday for me, Mrs. Hewing," he said. "I think Christmas is a very sad season of the year. It isn't that people around here ain't generous—I mean, I got plenty of tips—but, you see, I live alone in a furnished room and I don't have any family or anything, and Christmas isn't much of a holiday for me."

"I'm sorry, Charlie," Mrs. Hewing said. "I don't have any family myself. It is kind of sad when you're alone, isn't it?" She called her dogs and followed them into her apartment. He went down.

It was quiet then, and Charlie lighted a cigarette. The heating plant in the basement encompassed the building at that hour in a regular and profound vibration, and the sullen noises of arriving steam heat began to resound, first in the lobby and then to reverberate up through all the sixteen stories, but this was a mechanical awakening, and it didn't lighten his loneliness or his petulance. The black air outside the glass doors had begun to turn blue, but the blue light seemed to have no source; it appeared in the middle of the air. It was a tearful light, and as it picked out the empty street he wanted to cry. Then a cab drove up, and the Walsers got out, drunk and dressed in evening clothes, and he took them up to their penthouse. The Walsers got him to brooding about the difference between his life in a furnished room and the lives of the people overhead. It was terrible.

Then the early churchgoers began to ring, but there were only three of these that morning. A few more went off to church at eight o'clock, but the majority of the building remained unconscious, although the smell of bacon and coffee had begun to drift into the elevator shaft.

At a little after nine, a nursemaid came down with a

child. Both the nursemaid and the child had a deep tan and had just returned, he knew, from Bermuda. He had never been to Bermuda. He, Charlie, was a prisoner, confined eight hours a day to a six-by-eight elevator cage, which was confined, in turn, to a sixteen-story shaft. In one building or another, he had made his living as an elevator operator for ten years. He estimated the average trip at about an eighth of a mile, and when he thought of the thousands of miles he had traveled, when he thought that he might have driven the car through the mists above the Caribbean and set it down on some coral beach in Bermuda, he held the narrowness of his travels against his passengers, as if it were not the nature of the elevator but the pressure of their lives that confined him, as if they had clipped his wings.

He was thinking about this when the DePauls, on 9, rang. They wished him a merry Christmas.

"Well, it's nice of you to think of me," he said as they descended, "but it isn't much of a holiday for me. Christmas is a sad season when you're poor. I live alone in a furnished room. I don't have any family."

"Who do you have dinner with, Charlie?" Mrs. DePaul asked.

"I don't have any Christmas dinner," Charlie said. "I just get a sandwich."

"Oh, Charlie!" Mrs. DePaul was a stout woman with an impulsive heart, and Charlie's plaint struck at her holiday mood as if she had been caught in a cloudburst. "I do wish we could share our Christmas dinner with you, you know," she said. "I come from Vermont, you know, and when I was a child, you know, we always used to have a great many people at our table. The mailman, you know, and the schoolteacher, and just anybody who didn't have any family of their own, you know, and I wish we could share our dinner with you the way we used to, you know, and I don't see any reason why we can't. We can't have you at the table, you know, because you couldn't leave the elevator—could you?—but just as soon as Mr. DePaul has carved the goose, I'll give you a ring, and I'll arrange a tray for you, you know, and I want you to come up and at least share our Christmas dinner."

Charlie thanked them, and their generosity surprised

him, but he wondered if, with the arrival of friends and relatives, they wouldn't forget their offer.

Then old Mrs. Gadshill rang, and when she wished him a merry Christmas, he hung his head.

"It isn't much of a holiday for me, Mrs. Gadshill," he said. "Christmas is a sad season if you're poor. You see, I don't have any family. I live alone in a furnished room."

"I don't have any family either, Charlie," Mrs. Gadshill said. She spoke with a pointed lack of petulance, but her grace was forced. "That is, I don't have any children with me today. I have three children and seven grandchildren, but none of them can see their way to coming East for Christmas with me. Of course, I understand their problems. I know that it's difficult to travel with children during the holidays, although I always seemed to manage it when I was their age, but people feel differently, and we mustn't condemn them for the things we can't understand. But I know how you feel, Charlie. I haven't any family either. I'm just as lonely as you."

Mrs. Gadshill's speech didn't move him. Maybe she was lonely, but she had a ten-room apartment and three servants and bucks and bucks and diamonds and diamonds, and there were plenty of poor kids in the slums who would be happy at a chance at the food her cook threw away. Then he thought about poor kids. He sat down on a chair in the lobby and thought about them.

They got the worst of it. Beginning in the fall, there was all this excitement about Christmas and how it was a day for them. After Thanksgiving, they couldn't miss it. It was fixed so they couldn't miss it. The wreaths and decorations everywhere, and bells ringing, and trees in the park, and Santa Clauses on every corner, and pictures in the magazines and newspapers and on every wall and window in the city told them that if they were good, they would get what they wanted. Even if they couldn't read, they couldn't miss it. They couldn't miss it even if they were blind. It got into the air the poor kids inhaled. Every time they took a walk, they'd see all the expensive toys in the store windows, and they'd write letters to Santa Claus, and their mothers and fathers would promise to mail them, and after the kids had gone to sleep, they'd burn the letters in the stove. And when it came Christmas morning, how could you explain it, how could you tell them that Santa Claus only visited the rich, that he didn't know about the good? How could you face them when all you had to give them was a balloon or a lollipop?

On the way home from work a few nights earlier, Charlie had seen a woman and a little girl going down Fifty-ninth Street. The little girl was crying. He guessed she was crying, he knew she was crying, because she'd seen all the things in the toy-store windows and couldn't understand why none of them were for her. Her mother did housework, he guessed, or maybe was a waitress, and he saw them going back to a room like his, with green walls and no heat, on Christmas Eve, to eat a can of soup. And he saw the little girl hang up her ragged stocking and fall asleep, and he saw the mother looking through her purse for something to put into the stocking— This reverie was interrupted by a bell on 11. He went up, and Mr. and Mrs. Fuller were waiting. When they wished him a merry Christmas, he said, "Well, it isn't much of a holiday for me, Mrs. Fuller. Christmas is a sad season when you're poor."

"Do you have any children, Charlie?" Mrs. Fuller asked.

"Four living," he said. "Two in the grave." The majesty of his lie overwhelmed him. "Mrs. Leary's a cripple," he added.

"How sad, Charlie," Mrs. Fuller said. She started out of the elevator when it reached the lobby, and then she turned. "I want to give your children some presents, Charlie," she said. "Mr. Fuller and I are going to pay a call now, but when we come back, I want to give you some things for your children."

He thanked her. Then the bell rang on 4, and he went up to get the Westons.

"It isn't much of a holiday for me," he told them when they wished him a merry Christmas. "Christmas is a sad season when you're poor. You see, I live alone in a furnished room."

"Poor Charlie," Mrs. Weston said. "I know just how you feel. During the war, when Mr. Weston was away, I was alone at Christmas. I didn't have any Christmas dinner or a tree or anything. I just scrambled myself some eggs and sat there and cried." Mr. Weston, who had gone into the lobby, called impatiently to his wife. "I know just how you feel, Charlie," Mrs. Weston said.

By noon, the climate in the elevator shaft had changed from bacon and coffee to poultry and game, and the house, like an enormous and complex homestead, was absorbed in the preparations for a domestic feast. The children and their nursemaids had all returned from the Park. Grandmothers and aunts were arriving in limousines. Most of the people who came through the lobby were carrying packages wrapped in colored paper, and were wearing their best furs and new clothes. Charlie continued to complain to most of the tenants when they wished him a merry Christmas, changing his story from the lonely bachelor to the poor father, and back again, as his mood changed, but this outpouring of melancholy, and the sympathy it aroused, didn't make him feel any better.

At half past one, 9 rang, and when he went up, Mr. DePaul was standing in the door of their apartment holding a cocktail shaker and a glass. "Here's a little Christmas cheer, Charlie," he said, and he poured Charlie a drink. Then a maid appeared with a tray of covered dishes, and Mrs. DePaul came out of the living room. "Merry Christmas, Charlie," she said. "I had Mr. DePaul carve the goose early, so that you could have some, you know. I didn't want to put the dessert on the tray, because I was afraid it would melt, you know, so when we have our dessert, we'll call you."

"And what is Christmas without presents?" Mr. DePaul said, and he brought a large, flat box from the hall and laid it on top of the covered dishes.

"You people make it seem like a real Christmas to me," Charlie said. Tears started into his eyes. "Thank you, thank you."

"Merry Christmas! Merry Christmas!" they called, and they watched him carry his dinner and his present into the elevator. He took the tray and the box into the locker room when he got down. On the tray, there was a soup, some kind of creamed fish, and a serving of goose. The bell rang again, but before he answered it, he tore open the DePauls' box and saw that it held a dressing gown. Their generosity and their cocktail had begun to work on his brain, and he went jubilantly up to 12. Mrs. Gadshill's maid was standing in the door with a tray, and Mrs. Gadshill stood behind her. "Merry Christmas, Charlie!" she said. He thanked her, and tears came into his eyes again. On the way down, he drank off the glass of sherry on Mrs. Gadshill's tray. Mrs. Gadshill's contribution was a mixed grill. He ate the lamb chop with his fingers. The bell was ringing again, and he wiped his face with a paper towel and went up to 11. "Merry Christmas, Charlie," Mrs. Fuller said, and she was standing in the door with her arms full of packages wrapped in silver paper, just like a picture in an advertisement, and Mr. Fuller was beside her with an arm around her, and they both looked as if they were going to cry. "Here are some things I want you to take home to your children," Mrs. Fuller said. "And here's something for Mrs. Leary and here's something for you. And if you want to take these things out to the elevator, we'll have your dinner ready for you in a minute." He carried the things into the elevator and came back for the tray. "Merry Christmas, Charlie!" both of the Fullers called after him as he closed the door. He took their dinner and their presents into the locker room and tore open the box that was marked for him. There was an alligator wallet in it, with Mr. Fuller's initials in the corner. Their dinner was also goose, and he ate a piece of the meat with his fingers and was washing it down with a cocktail when the bell rang. He went up again. This time it was the Westons. "Merry Christmas, Charlie!" they said, and they gave him a cup of eggnog, a turkey dinner, and a present. Their gift was also a dressing gown. Then 7 rang, and when he went up, there was another dinner and some more toys. Then 14 rang, and when he went up, Mrs. Hewing was standing in the hall, in a kind of negligee, holding a pair of riding boots in one hand and some neckties in the other. She had been crying and drinking. "Merry Christmas, Charlie," she said tenderly. "I wanted to give you something, and I've been thinking about you all morning, and I've been all over the apartment, and these are the only things I could find that a man might want. These are the only things that Mr. Brewer left. I don't suppose you'd have any use for the riding boots, but wouldn't you like the neckties?" Charlie took the neckties and thanked her and hurried back to the car, for the elevator bell had rung three times.

By THREE O'CLOCK, Charlie had fourteen dinners spread on the table and the floor of the locker room, and the bell kept ringing. Just as he started to eat one, he would have to go up and get another, and he was in the middle of the Parsons' roast beef when he had to go up and get the DePauls' dessert. He kept the door of the locker room closed, for he sensed that the quality of charity is exclusive and that his friends would have been disappointed to find that they were not the only ones to try to lessen his loneliness. There were goose, turkey, chicken, pheasant, grouse, and pigeon. There were trout and salmon, creamed scallops and oysters, lobster, crab meat, whitebait, and clams. There were plum puddings, mince pies, mousses, puddles of melted ice cream, layer cakes, *Torten*, éclairs, and two slices of Bavarian cream. He had dressing gowns, neckties, cuff links, socks, and handkerchiefs, and one of the tenants had asked for his neck size and then given him three green shirts. There were a glass teapot filled, the label said, with jasmine honey, four bottles of after-shave lotion, some alabaster bookends, and a dozen steak knives. The avalanche of charity he had precipitated filled the locker room and made him hesitant, now and then, as if he had touched some wellspring in the female heart that would bury him alive in food and dressing gowns. He had made almost no headway on the food, for all the servings were preternaturally large, as if loneliness had been counted on to generate in him a brutish appetite. Nor had he opened any of the presents that had been given to him for his imaginary children, but he had drunk everything they sent down, and around him were the dregs of Martinis, Manhattans, Old-Fashioneds, champagne-and-raspberry-shrub cocktails, eggnogs, Bronxes, and Side Cars.

His face was blazing. He loved the world, and the world loved him. When he thought back over his life, it appeared to him in a rich and wonderful light, full of astonishing experiences and unusual friends. He thought that his job as an elevator operator—cruising up and down through hundreds of feet of perilous space—demanded the nerve and the intellect of a birdman. All the constraints of his life—the green walls of his room and the months of unemployment—dissolved. No one was ringing, but he got into the elevator and shot it at full speed up to the penthouse and down again, up and down, to test his wonderful mastery of space.

A bell rang on 12 while he was cruising, and he stopped in his flight long enough to pick up Mrs. Gadshill. As the car started to fall, he took his hands off the controls in a paroxysm of joy and shouted, "Strap on your safety belt, Mrs. Gadshill! We're going to make a loop-the-loop!" Mrs. Gadshill shrieked. Then, for some reason, she sat down on the floor of the elevator. Why was her face so pale, he wondered; why was she sitting on the floor? She shrieked again. He grounded the car gently, and cleverly, he thought, and opened the door. "I'm sorry if I scared you, Mrs. Gadshill," he said meekly. "I was only fooling." She shrieked again. Then she ran out into the lobby, screaming for the superintendent.

The superintendent fired Charlie and took over the elevator himself. The news that he was out of work stung Charlie for a minute. It was his first contact with human meanness that day. He sat down in the locker room and gnawed on a drumstick. His drinks were beginning to let him down, and while it had not reached him yet, he felt a miserable soberness in the offing. The excess of food and presents around him began to make him feel guilty and unworthy. He regretted bitterly the lie he had told about his children. He was a single man with simple needs. He had abused the goodness of the people upstairs. He was unworthy.

Then up through this drunken train of thought surged the sharp figure of his landlady and her three skinny children. He thought of them sitting in their basement room. The cheer of Christmas had passed them by. This image got him to his feet. The realization that he was in a position to give, that he could bring happiness easily to someone else, sobered him. He took a big burlap sack, which was used for collecting waste, and began to stuff it, first with his presents and then with the presents for his imaginary children. He worked with the haste of a man whose train is approaching the station, for he could hardly wait to see those long faces light up when he came in the door. He changed his clothes, and, fired by a wonderful and unfamiliar sense of power, he slung his bag over his shoulder like a regular Santa Claus, went out the back way, and took a taxi to the Lower East Side.

The landlady and her children had just finished off a turkey, which had been sent to them by the local Democratic Club, and they were stuffed and uncomfortable when Charlie began pounding on the door, shouting "Merry Christmas!" He dragged the bag in after him and dumped the presents for the children onto the floor. There were dolls and musical toys, blocks, sewing kits, an Indian suit, and a loom, and it appeared to him that, as he had hoped, his arrival in the basement dispelled its gloom. When half the presents had been opened, he gave the landlady a bathrobe and went upstairs to look over the things he had been given for himself.

Now, the landlady's children had already received so many presents by the time Charlie arrived that they were confused with receiving, and it was only the landlady's intuitive grasp of the nature of charity that made her allow the children to open some of the presents while Charlie was still in the room, but as soon as he had gone, she stood between the children and the presents that were still unopened. "Now, you kids have had enough already," she said. "You kids have got your share. Just look at the things you got there. Why, you ain't even played with the half of them. Mary Anne, you ain't even looked at that doll the Fire Department give you. Now, a nice thing to do would be to take all this stuff that's left over to those poor people on Hudson Street—them Deckkers. They ain't got nothing." A beatific light came into her face when she realized that she could give, that she could bring cheer, that she could put a healing finger on a case needier than hers, and—like Mrs. DePaul and Mrs. Weston, like Charlie himself and like Mrs. Deckker, when Mrs. Deckker was to think, subsequently, of the poor Shannons—first love, then charity, and then a sense of power drove her. "Now, you kids help me get all this stuff together. Hurry, hurry, hurry," she said, for it was dark then, and she knew that we are bound, one to another, in licentious benevolence for only a single day, and that day was nearly over. She was tired, but she couldn't rest, she couldn't rest.

THE SEASON OF DIVORCE

MY WIFE has brown hair, dark eyes, and a gentle disposition. Because of her gentle disposition, I sometimes think that she spoils the children. She can't refuse them anything. They always get around her. Ethel and I have been married for ten years. We both come from Morristown, New Jersey, and I can't even remember when I first met her. Our marriage has always seemed happy and resourceful to me. We live in a walk-up in the East Fifties. Our son, Carl, who is six, goes to a good private school, and our daughter, who is four, won't go to school until next year. We often find fault with the way we were educated, but we seem to be struggling to raise our children along the same lines, and when the time comes, I suppose they'll go to the same school and colleges that we went to.

Ethel graduated from a women's college in the East, and then went for a year to the University of Grenoble. She worked for a year in New York after returning from France, and then we were married. She once hung her diploma above the kitchen sink, but it was a short-lived joke and I don't know where the diploma is now. Ethel is cheerful and adaptable, as well as gentle, and we both come from that enormous stratum of the middle class that is distinguished by its ability to recall better times. Lost money is so much a part of our lives that I am sometimes reminded of expatriates, of a group who have adapted themselves energetically to some alien soil but who are reminded, now and then, of the escarpments of their native coast. Because our lives are confined by my modest salary, the surface of Ethel's life is easy to describe.

She gets up at seven and turns the radio on. After she is dressed, she rouses the children and cooks the breakfast. Our son has to be walked to the school bus at eight o'clock. When Ethel returns from this trip, Carol's hair has to be braided. I leave the house at eight-thirty, but I know that every move that Ethel makes for the rest of the day will be determined by the housework, the cooking, the shopping, and the demands of the children. I know that on Tuesdays and Thursdays she will be at the A & P between eleven and noon, that on every clear afternoon she will be on a certain bench in a playground from three until five, that she cleans the house on Mondays, Wednesdays, and Fridays, and polishes the silver when it rains. When I return at six, she is usually cleaning the vegetables or making some other preparation for dinner. Then when the children have been fed and bathed, when the dinner is ready, when the table in the living room is set with food and china, she stands in the middle of the room as if she has lost or forgotten something, and this moment of reflection is so deep that she will not hear me if I speak to her, or the children if they call. Then it is over. She lights the four white candles in their silver sticks, and we sit down to a supper of corned-beef hash or some other modest fare.

We go out once or twice a week and entertain about once a month. Because of practical considerations, most of the people we see live in our neighborhood. We often go around the corner to the parties given by a generous couple named Newsome. The Newsomes' parties are large and confusing, and the arbitrary impulses of friendship are given a free play.

We became attached at the Newsomes' one evening, for reasons that I've never understood, to a couple named Dr. and Mrs. Trencher. I think that Mrs. Trencher was the aggressor in this friendship, and after our first meeting she telephoned Ethel three or four times. We went to their house for dinner, and they came to our house, and sometimes in the evening when Dr. Trencher was walking their old dachshund, he would come up for a short visit. He seemed like a pleasant man to have around. I've heard other doctors say that he's a good physician. The Trenchers are about thirty; at least he is. She is older.

I'd say that Mrs. Trencher is a plain woman, but her plainness is difficult to specify. She is small, she has a good figure and regular features, and I suppose that the impression of plainness arises from some inner modesty, some needlessly narrow view of her chances. Dr. Trencher doesn't smoke or drink, and I don't know whether there's any connection or not, but the coloring in his slender face is fresh—his cheeks are pink, and his blue eyes are clear and strong. He has the singular optimism of a well-adjusted physician—the feeling that death is a chance misfortune and that the physical world is merely a field for conquest. In the same way that his wife seems plain, he seems young.

The Trenchers live in a comfortable and unpretentious private house in our neighborhood. The house is old-fashioned; its living rooms are large, its halls are gloomy, and the Trenchers don't seem to generate enough human warmth to animate the place, so that you sometimes take away from them, at the end of an evening, an impression of many empty rooms. Mrs. Trencher is noticeably attached to her possessions—her clothes, her jewels, and the ornaments she's bought for the house—and to Fräulein, the old dachshund. She feeds Fräulein scraps from the table, furtively, as if she has been forbidden to do this, and after dinner Fräulein lies beside her on the sofa. With the play of green light from a television set on her drawn features and her thin hands stroking Fräulein, Mrs. Trencher looked to me one evening like a good-hearted and miserable soul.

Mrs. Trencher began to call Ethel in the mornings for a talk or to ask her for lunch or a matinee. Ethel can't go out in the day and she claims to dislike long telephone conversations. She complained that Mrs. Trencher was a tireless and aggressive gossip. Then late one afternoon Dr. Trencher appeared at the playground where Ethel takes our two children. He was walking by, and he saw her and sat with her until it was time to take the children home. He came again a few days later, and then his visits with Ethel in the playground, she told me, became a regular thing. Ethel thought that perhaps he didn't have many patients and that with nothing to do he was happy to talk with anyone. Then, when we were washing dishes one night, Ethel said thoughtfully that Trencher's attitude toward her seemed strange. "He stares at me," she said. "He sighs and stares at me." I know what my wife looks like in the playground. She wears an old tweed coat, overshoes, and Army gloves, and a scarf is tied under her chin. The playground is a fenced and paved lot between a slum and the river. The picture of the well-dressed, pink-cheeked doctor losing his heart to Ethel in this environment was hard to take seriously. She didn't mention him then for several days, and I guessed that he had stopped his visits. Ethel's birthday came at the end of the month, and I forgot about it, but when I came home that evening, there were a lot of roses in the living room. They were a birthday present from Trencher, she told me. I was cross at myself for having forgotten her birthday, and Trencher's roses made me angry. I asked her if she'd seen him recently.

"Oh, yes," she said, "he still comes to the playground nearly every afternoon. I haven't told you, have I? He's made his declaration. He loves me. He can't live without me. He'd walk through fire to hear the notes of my voice." She laughed. "That's what he said."

"When did he say this?"

"At the playground. And walking home. Yesterday."

"How long has he known?"

"That's the funny part about it," she said. "He knew before he met me at the Newsomes' that night. He saw me waiting for a crosstown bus about three weeks before that. He just saw me and he said that he knew then, the minute he saw me. Of course, he's crazy."

I was tired that night and worried about taxes and bills, and I could think of Trencher's declaration only as a comical mistake. I felt that he was a captive of financial and sentimental commitments, like every other man I know, and that he was no more free to fall in love with a strange woman he saw on a street corner than he was to take a walking trip through French Guiana or to recommence his life in Chicago under an assumed name. His declaration, the scene in the playground, seemed to me to be like those chance meetings that are a part of the life of any large city. A blind man asks you to help him across the street, and as you are about to leave, he seizes your arm and regales you with a passionate account of his cruel and ungrateful children; or the elevator man who is taking you up to a party turns to you suddenly and says that his grandson has infantile paralysis. The city is full of accidental revelation, half-heard cries for help, and strangers who will tell you everything at the first suspicion of sympathy, and Trencher seemed to me like the blind man or the elevator operator. His declaration had no more bearing on the business of our lives than these interruptions.

Mrs. Trencher's telephone conversations had stopped, and we had stopped visiting the Trenchers, but sometimes I would see him in the morning on the crosstown bus when I was late going to work. He seemed understandably embarrassed whenever he saw me, but the bus was always crowded at that time of day, and it was no effort to avoid one another. Also, at about that time I made a mistake in business and lost several thousand dollars for the firm I work for. There was not much chance of my losing my job, but the possibility was always at the back of my mind, and under this and under the continuous urgency of making more money the memory of the eccentric doctor was buried. Three weeks passed without Ethel's mentioning him, and then one evening, when I was reading, I noticed Ethel standing at the window looking down into the street.

"He's really there," she said.

"Who?"

"Trencher. Come here and see."

I went to the window. There were only three people on the sidewalk across the street. It was dark and it would have been difficult to recognize anyone, but because one of them, walking toward the corner, had a dachshund on a leash, it could have been Trencher.

"Well, what about it?" I said. "He's just walking the dog."

"But he wasn't walking the dog when I first looked out of the window. He was just standing there, staring up at this building. That's what he says he does. He says that he comes over here and stares up at our lighted windows."

"When did he say this?"

"At the playground."

"I thought you went to another playground."

"Oh, I do, I do, but he followed me. He's crazy, darling. I know he's crazy, but I feel so sorry for him. He says that he spends night after night looking up at our windows. He says that he sees me everywhere—the back of my head, my eyebrows—that he hears my voice. He says that he's never compromised in his life and that he isn't going to compromise about this. I feel so sorry for him, darling. I can't help but feel sorry for him."

For the first time then, the situation seemed serious to me, for in his helplessness I knew that he might have touched an inestimable and wayward passion that Ethel shares with some other women—an inability to refuse any cry for help, to refuse any voice that sounds pitiable. It is not a reasonable passion, and I would almost rather have had her desire him than pity him. When we were getting ready for bed that night, the telephone rang, and when I picked it up and said hello, no one answered. Fifteen minutes later, the telephone rang again, and when there was no answer this time, I began to shout and swear at Trencher, but he didn't reply—there wasn't even the click of a closed circuit—and I felt like a fool. Because I felt like a fool, I accused Ethel of having led him on, of having encouraged him, but these accusations didn't affect her, and when I finished them, I felt worse, because I knew that she was innocent, and that she had to go out on the street to buy groceries and air the children, and that there was no force of law that could keep Trencher from waiting for her there, or from staring up at our lights.

We went to the Newsomes' one night the next week, and while we were taking off our coats, I heard Trencher's voice. He left a few minutes after we arrived, but his manner—the sad glance he gave Ethel, the way he sidestepped me, the sorrowful way that he refused the Newsomes when they asked him to stay longer, and the gallant attentions he showed his miserable wife—made me angry. Then I happened to notice Ethel and saw that her color was high, that her eyes were bright, and that while she was praising Mrs. Newsome's new shoes, her mind was not on what she was saying. When we came home that night, the baby-sitter told us crossly that neither of the children had slept. Ethel took their temperatures. Carol was all right, but the boy had a fever of a hundred and four. Neither of us got much sleep that night, and in the morning Ethel called me at the office to say that Carl had bronchitis. Three days later, his sister came down with it.

For the next two weeks, the sick children took up most of our time. They had to be given medicine at eleven in the evening and again at three in the morning, and we lost a lot of sleep. It was impossible to ventilate or clean the house, and when I came in, after walking through the cold from the bus stop, it stank of cough syrups and tobacco, fruit cores and sickbeds. There were blankets and pillows, ashtrays, and medicine glasses everywhere. We divided the work of sickness reasonably and took turns at getting up in the night, but I often fell asleep at my desk during the day, and after dinner Ethel would fall asleep in a chair in the living room. Fatigue seems to differ for adults and children only in that adults recognize it and so are not overwhelmed by something they can't name; but even with a name for it they are overwhelmed, and when we were tired, we were unreasonable, cross, and the victims of transcendent depressions. One evening after the worst of the sickness was over, I came home and found some roses in the living room. Ethel said that Trencher had brought them. She hadn't let him in. She had closed the door in his face. I took the roses and threw them out. We didn't quarrel. The children went to sleep at nine, and a few minutes after nine I went to bed. Sometime later, something woke me.

A light was burning in the hall. I got up. The children's room and the living room were dark. I found Ethel in the kitchen sitting at the table, drinking coffee.

"I've made some fresh coffee," she said. "Carol felt croupy again, so I steamed her. They're both asleep now."

"How long have you been up?"

"Since half past twelve," she said. "What time is it?"

"Two."

I poured myself a cup of coffee and sat down. She got up from the table and rinsed her cup and looked at herself in a mirror that hangs over the sink. It was a windy night. A dog was wailing somewhere in an apartment below ours, and a loose radio antenna was brushing against the kitchen window.

"It sounds like a branch," she said.

In the bare kitchen light, meant for peeling potatoes and washing dishes, she looked very tired.

"Will the children be able to go out tomorrow?"

"Oh, I hope so," she said. "Do you realize that I haven't been out of this apartment in over two weeks?" She spoke bitterly and this startled me.

"It hasn't been quite two weeks."

"It's been over two weeks," she said.

"Well, let's figure it out," I said. "The children were taken sick on a Saturday night. That was the fourth. Today is the—"

"Stop it, stop it," she said. "I know how long it's been. I haven't had my shoes on in two weeks."

"You make it sound pretty bad."

"It is. I haven't had on a decent dress or fixed my hair."

"It could be worse."

"My mother's cooks had a better life."

"I doubt that."

"My mother's cooks had a better life," she said loudly.

"You'll wake the children."

"My mother's cooks had a better life. They had pleasant rooms. No one could come into the kitchen without their permission." She knocked the coffee grounds into the garbage and began to wash the pot.

"How long was Trencher here this afternoon?"

"A minute. I've told you."

"I don't believe it. He was in here."

"He was not. I didn't let him in. I didn't let him in because I looked so badly. I didn't want to discourage him."

"Why not?"

"I don't know. He may be a fool. He may be insane but the things he's told me have made me feel marvelously, he's made me feel marvelously."

"Do you want to go?"

"Go? Where would I go?" She reached for the purse that is kept in the kitchen to pay for groceries and counted out of it two dollars and thirty-five cents. "Ossining? Montclair?"

"I mean with Trencher."

"I don't know, I don't know," she said, "but who can say that I shouldn't? What harm would it do? What good would it do? Who knows. I love the children but that isn't enough, that isn't nearly enough. I wouldn't hurt them, but would I hurt them so much if I left you? Is divorce so dreadful and of all the things that hold a marriage together how many of them are good?" She sat down at the table.

"In Grenoble," she said, "I wrote a long paper on

Charles Stuart in French. A professor at the University of Chicago wrote me a letter. I couldn't read a French newspaper without a dictionary today, I don't have the time to follow any newspaper, and I am ashamed of my incompetence, ashamed of the way I look. Oh, I guess I love you, I do love the children, but I love myself, I love my life, it has some value and some promise for me and Trencher's roses make me feel that I'm losing this, that I'm losing my self-respect. Do you know what I mean, do you understand what I mean?"

"He's crazy," I said.

"Do you know what I mean? Do you understand what I mean?"

"No," I said. "No."

Carl woke up then and called for his mother. I told Ethel to go to bed. I turned out the kitchen light and went into the children's room.

THE CHILDREN felt better the next day, and since it was Sunday, I took them for a walk. The afternoon sun was clement and pure, and only the colored shadows made me remember that it was midwinter, that the cruise ships were returning, and that in another week jonquils would be twenty-five cents a bunch. Walking down Lexington Avenue, we heard the drone bass of a church organ sound from the sky, and we and the others on the sidewalk looked up in piety and bewilderment, like a devout and stupid congregation, and saw a formation of heavy bombers heading for the sea. As it got late, it got cold and clear and still, and on the stillness the waste from the smokestacks along the East River seemed to articulate, as legibly as the Pepsi-Cola plane, whole words and sentences. Halcyon. Disaster. They were hard to make out. It seemed the ebb of the year—an evil day for gastritis, sinus, and respiratory disease—and remembering other winters, the markings of the light convinced me that it was the season of divorce. It was a long afternoon, and I brought the children in before dark.

I think that the seriousness of the day affected the children, and when they returned to the house, they were quiet. The seriousness of it kept coming to me with the feeling that this change, like a phenomenon of speed, was affecting our watches as well as our hearts. I tried to remember the willingness with which Ethel had followed my regiment during the war, from West Virginia to the Carolinas and Oklahoma, and the day coaches and rooms she had lived in, and the street in San Francisco where I said goodbye to her before I left the country, but I could not put any of this into words, and neither of us found anything to say. Sometime after dark, the children were bathed and put to bed, and we sat down to our supper. At about nine o'clock, the doorbell rang, and when I answered it and recognized Trencher's voice on the speaking tube, I asked him to come up.

He seemed distraught and exhilarated when he appeared. He stumbled on the edge of the carpet. "I know that I'm not welcome here," he said in a hard voice, as if I were deaf. "I know that you don't like me here. I respect your feelings. This is your home. I respect a man's feelings about his home. I don't usually go to a man's home unless he asks me. I respect your home. I respect your marriage. I respect your children. I think everything ought to be aboveboard. I've come here to tell you that I love your wife."

"Get out," I said.

"You've got to listen to me," he said. "I love your wife. I can't live without her. I've tried and I can't. I've even thought of going away—of moving to the West Coast—but I know that it wouldn't make any difference. I want to marry her. I'm not romantic. I'm matter-of-fact. I'm very matter-of-fact. I know that you have two children and that you don't have much money. I know that there are problems of custody and property and things like that to be settled. I'm not romantic. I'm hardheaded. I've talked this all over with Mrs. Trencher, and she's agreed to give me a divorce. I'm not underhanded. Your wife can tell you that. I realize all the practical aspects that have to be considered—custody, property, and so forth. I have plenty of money. I can give Ethel everything she needs, but there are the children. You'll have to decide about them between yourselves. I have a check here. It's made out to Ethel. I want her to take it and go to Nevada. I'm a practical man and I realize that nothing can be decided until she gets her divorce."

"Get out of here!" I said. "Get the hell out of here!"

He started for the door. There was a potted geranium on the mantelpiece, and I threw this across the room at him. It got him in the small of the back and nearly knocked him down. The pot broke on the floor. Ethel screamed. Trencher was still on his way out. Following him, I picked up a candlestick and aimed it at his head, but it missed and bounced off the wall. "Get the hell out of here!" I yelled, and he slammed the door. I went back into the living room. Ethel was pale but she wasn't crying. There was a loud rapping on the radiator, a signal from the people upstairs for decorum and silence—urgent and expressive, like the communications that prisoners send to one another through the plumbing in a penitentiary. Then everything was still.

We went to bed, and I woke sometime during the night. I couldn't see the clock on the dresser, so I don't know what time it was. There was no sound from the children's room. The neighborhood was perfectly still. There were no lighted windows anywhere. Then I knew that Ethel had wakened me. She was lying on her side of the bed. She was crying.

"Why are you crying?" I asked.

"Why am I crying?" she said. "Why am I crying?" And to hear my voice and to speak set her off again, and she began to sob cruelly. She sat up and slipped her arms into the sleeves of a wrapper and felt along the table for a package of cigarettes. I saw her wet face when she lighted a cigarette. I heard her moving around in the dark.

"Why do you cry?"

"Why do I cry? Why do I cry?" she asked impatiently. "I cry because I saw an old woman cuffing a little boy on Third Avenue. She was drunk. I can't get it out of my mind." She pulled the quilt off the foot of our bed and wandered with it toward the door. "I cry because my father died when I was twelve and because my mother married a man I detested or thought that I detested. I cry because I had to wear an ugly dress—a hand-me-down dress—to a party twenty years ago, and I didn't have a good time. I cry because of some unkindness that I can't remember. I cry because I'm tired—because I'm tired and I can't sleep." I heard her arrange herself on the sofa and then everything was quiet.

I LIKE TO THINK that the Trenchers have gone away, but I still see Trencher now and then on a crosstown bus when I'm late going to work. I've also seen his wife, going into the neighborhood lending library with Fräulein. She looks old. I'm not good at judging ages, but I wouldn't be surprised to find that Mrs. Trencher is fifteen years older than her husband. Now when I come home in the evenings, Ethel is still sitting on the stool by the sink cleaning vegetables. I go with her into the children's room. The light there is bright. The children have built something out of an orange crate, something preposterous and ascendant, and their sweetness, their compulsion to build, the brightness of the light are reflected perfectly and increased in Ethel's face. Then she feeds them, bathes them, and sets the table, and stands for a moment in the middle of the room, trying to make some connection between the evening and the day. Then it is over. She lights the four candles, and we sit down to our supper.

THE CHASTE CLARISSA

THE EVENING BOAT for Vineyard Haven was loading freight. In a little while, the warning whistle would separate the sheep from the goats—that's the way Baxter thought of it—the islanders from the tourists wandering through the streets of Woods Hole. His car, like all the others ticketed for the ferry, was parked near the wharf. He sat on the front bumper, smoking. The noise and movement of the small port seemed to signify that the spring had ended and that the shores of West Chop, across the Sound, were the shores of summer, but the implications of the hour and the voyage made no impression on Baxter at all. The delay bored and irritated him. When someone called his name, he got to his feet with relief.

It was old Mrs. Ryan. She called to him from a dusty station wagon, and he went over to speak to her. "I knew it," she said. "I knew that I'd see someone here from

Holly Cove. I had that feeling in my bones. We've been traveling since nine this morning. We had trouble with the brakes outside Worcester. Now I'm wondering if Mrs. Talbot will have cleaned the house. She wanted seventy-five dollars for opening it last summer and I told her I wouldn't pay her that again, and I wouldn't be surprised if she's thrown all my letters away. Oh, I hate to have a journey end in a dirty house, but if worse comes to worst, we can clean it ourselves. Can't we, Clarissa?" she asked, turning to a young woman who sat beside her on the front seat. "Oh, excuse me, Baxter!" she exclaimed. "You haven't met Clarissa, have you? This is Bob's wife, Clarissa Ryan."

Baxter's first thought was that a girl like that shouldn't have to ride in a dusty station wagon; she should have done much better. She was young. He guessed that she was about twenty-five. Red-headed, deep-breasted, slender, and indolent, she seemed to belong to a different species from old Mrs. Ryan and her large-boned, forthright daughters. " 'The Cape Cod girls, they have no combs. They comb their hair with codfish bones,' " he said to himself but Clarissa's hair was well groomed. Her bare arms were perfectly white. Woods Hole and the activity on the wharf seemed to bore her and she was not interested in Mrs. Ryan's insular gossip. She lighted a cigarette.

At a pause in the old lady's monologue, Baxter spoke to her daughter-in-law. "When is Bob coming down, Mrs. Ryan?" he asked.

"He isn't coming at all," the beautiful Clarissa said. "He's in France. He's—"

"He's gone there for the government," old Mrs. Ryan interrupted, as if her daughter-in-law could not be entrusted with this simple explanation. "He's working on this terribly interesting project. He won't be back until autumn. I'm going abroad myself. I'm leaving Clarissa alone. Of course," she added forcefully, "I expect that she will *love* the island. Everyone does. I expect that she will be kept very busy. I expect that she—"

The warning signal from the ferry cut her off. Baxter said goodbye. One by one, the cars drove aboard, and the boat started to cross the shoal water from the mainland to the resort. Baxter drank a beer in the cabin and watched

Clarissa and old Mrs. Ryan, who were sitting on deck. Since he had never seen Clarissa before, he supposed that Bob Ryan must have married her during the past winter. He did not understand how this beauty had ended up with the Ryans. They were a family of passionate amateur geologists and bird-watchers. "We're all terribly keen about birds and rocks," they said when they were introduced to strangers. Their cottage was a couple of miles from any other and had, as Mrs. Ryan often said, "been thrown together out of a barn in 1922." They sailed, hiked, swam in the surf, and organized expeditions to Cuttyhunk and Tarpaulin Cove. They were people who emphasized *corpore sano* unduly, Baxter thought, and they shouldn't leave Clarissa alone in the cottage. The wind had blown a strand of her flame-colored hair across her cheek. Her long legs were crossed. As the ferry entered the harbor, she stood up and made her way down the deck against the light salt wind, and Baxter, who had returned to the island indifferently, felt that the summer had begun.

BAXTER KNEW that in trying to get some information about Clarissa Ryan he had to be careful. He was accepted in Holly Cove because he had summered there all his life. He could be pleasant and he was a good-looking man, but his two divorces, his promiscuity, his stinginess, and his Latin complexion had left with his neighbors a vague feeling that he was unsavory. He learned that Clarissa had married Bob Ryan in November and that she was from Chicago. He heard people say that she was beautiful and stupid. That was all he did find out about her.

He looked for Clarissa on the tennis courts and the beaches. He didn't see her. He went several times to the beach nearest the Ryans' cottage. She wasn't there. When he had been on the island only a short time, he received from Mrs. Ryan, in the mail, an invitation to tea. It was an invitation that he would not ordinarily have accepted, but he drove eargerly that afternoon over to the Ryans' cottage. He was late. The cars of most of his friends and neighbors were parked in Mrs. Ryan's field. Their voices drifted out of the open windows into the garden, where Mrs. Ryan's climbing roses were in bloom. "Welcome aboard!" Mrs. Ryan shouted when he crossed the porch.

"This is my farewell party. I'm going to Norway." She led him into a crowded room.

Clarissa sat behind the teacups. Against the wall at her back was a glass cabinet that held the Ryans' geological specimens. Her arms were bare. Baxter watched them while she poured his tea. "Hot? . . . Cold? Lemon? . . . Cream?" seemed to be all she had to say, but her red hair and her white arms dominated that end of the room. Baxter ate a sandwich. He hung around the table.

"Have you ever been to the island before, Clarissa?" he asked.

"Yes."

"Do you swim at the beach at Holly Cove?"

"It's too far away."

"When your mother-in-law leaves," Baxter said, "you must let me drive you there in the mornings. I go down at eleven."

"Well, thank you." Clarissa lowered her green eyes. She seemed uncomfortable, and the thought that she might be susceptible crossed Baxter's mind exuberantly. "Well, thank you," she repeated, "but I have a car of my own and—well, I don't know, I don't—"

"What are *you* two talking about?" Mrs. Ryan asked, coming between them and smiling wildly in an effort to conceal some of the force of her interference. "I know it isn't geology," she went on, "and I know that it isn't birds, and I know that it can't be books or music, because those are all things that Clarissa doesn't like, aren't they, Clarissa? Come with me, Baxter," and she led him to the other side of the room and talked to him about sheep raising. When the conversation had ended, the party itself was nearly over. Clarissa's chair was empty. She was not in the room. Stopping at the door to thank Mrs. Ryan and say goodbye, Baxter said that he hoped she wasn't leaving for Europe immediately.

"Oh, but I am," Mrs. Ryan said. "I'm going to the mainland on the six-o'clock boat and sailing from Boston at noon tomorrow."

AT HALF PAST TEN the next morning, Baxter drove up to the Ryans' cottage. Mrs. Talbot, the local woman who helped the Ryans with their housework, answered the door. She said that young Mrs. Ryan was home, and let him in. Clarissa came downstairs. She looked more beautiful than ever, although she seemed put out at finding him there. She accepted his invitation to go swimming, but she accepted it unenthusiastically. "Oh, all right," she said.

When she came downstairs again, she had on a bathrobe over her bathing suit, and a broad-brimmed hat. On the drive to Holly Cove, he asked her plans for the summer. She was noncommittal. She seemed preoccupied and unwilling to talk. They parked the car and walked side by side over the dunes to the beach, where she lay in the sand with her eyes closed. A few of Baxter's friends and neighbors stopped to pass the time, but they didn't stop for long, Baxter noticed. Clarissa's unresponsiveness made it difficult to talk. He didn't care.

He went swimming. Clarissa remained on the sand, bundled in her wrap. When he came out of the water, he lay down near her. He watched his neighbors and their children. The weather had been fair. The women were tanned. They were all married women and, unlike Clarissa, women with children, but the rigors of marriage and childbirth had left them all pretty, agile, and contented. While he was admiring them, Clarissa stood up and took off her bathrobe.

Here was something else, and it took his breath away. Some of the inescapable power of her beauty lay in the whiteness of her skin, some of it in the fact that, unlike the other women, who were at ease in bathing suits, Clarissa seemed humiliated and ashamed to find herself wearing so little. She walked down toward the water as if she were naked. When she first felt the water, she stopped short, for, again unlike the others, who were sporting around the pier like seals, Clarissa didn't like the cold. Then, caught for a second between nakedness and the cold, Clarissa waded in and swam a few feet. She came out of the water, hastily wrapped herself in the robe, and lay down in the sand. Then she spoke, for the first time that morning—for the first time in Baxter's experience—with warmth and feeling.

"You know, those stones on the point have grown a lot since I was here last," she said.

"What?" Baxter said.

"Those stones on the point," Clarissa said. "They've grown a lot."

"Stones don't grow," Baxter said.

"Oh yes they do," Clarissa said. "Didn't you know that? Stones grow. There's a stone in Mother's rose garden that's grown a foot in the last few years."

"I didn't know that stones grew," Baxter said.

"Well, they do," Clarissa said. She yawned; she shut her eyes. She seemed to fall asleep. When she opened her eyes again, she asked Baxter the time.

"Twelve o'clock," he said.

"I have to go home," she said. "I'm expecting guests."

Baxter could not contest this. He drove her home. She was unresponsive on the ride, and when he asked her if he could drive her to the beach again, she said no. It was a hot, fair day and most of the doors on the island stood open, but when Clarissa said goodbye to Baxter, she closed the door in his face.

Baxter got Clarissa's mail and newspapers from the post office the next day, but when he called with them at the cottage, Mrs. Talbot said that Mrs. Ryan was busy. He went that week to two large parties that she might have attended, but she was not at either. On Saturday night, he went to a barn dance, and late in the evening—they were dancing "Lady of the Lake"—he noticed Clarissa, sitting against the wall.

She was a striking wallflower. She was much more beautiful than any other woman there, but her beauty seemed to have intimidated the men. Baxter dropped out of the dance when he could and went to her. She was sitting on a packing case. It was the first thing she complained about. "There isn't even anything to sit on," she said.

"Don't you want to dance?" Baxter asked.

"Oh, I love to dance," she said. "I could dance all night, but I don't think *that's* dancing." She winced at the music of the fiddle and the piano. "I came with the Hortons. They just told me there was going to be a dance. They didn't tell me it was going to be this kind of a dance. I don't like all that skipping and hopping."

"Have your guests left?" Baxter asked.

"What guests?" Clarissa said.

"You told me you were expecting guests on Tuesday. When we were at the beach."

"I didn't say they were coming on Tuesday, did I?" Clarissa asked. "They're coming tomorrow."

"Can't I take you home?" Baxter asked.

"All right."

He brought the car around to the barn and turned on the radio. She got in and slammed the door with spirit. He raced the car over the back roads, and when he brought it up to the Ryans' cottage, he turned off the lights. He watched her hands. She folded them on her purse. "Well, thank you very much," she said. "I was having an awful time and you saved my life. I just don't understand this place, I guess. I've always had plenty of partners, but I sat on that hard box for nearly an hour and nobody even spoke to me. You saved my life."

"You're lovely, Clarissa," Baxter said.

"Well," Clarissa said, and she sighed. "That's just my outward self. Nobody knows the real me."

That was it, Baxter thought, and if he could only adjust his flattery to what she believed herself to be, her scruples would dissolve. Did she think of herself as an actress, he wondered, a Channel swimmer, an heiress? The intimations of susceptibility that came from her in the summer night were so powerful, so heady, that they convinced Baxter that here was a woman whose chastity hung by a thread.

"I think I know the real you," Baxter said.

"Oh no you don't," Clarissa said. "Nobody does."

The radio played some lovelorn music from a Boston hotel. By the calendar, it was still early in the summer, but it seemed, from the stillness and the hugeness of the dark trees, to be much later. Baxter put his arms around Clarissa and planted a kiss on her lips.

She pushed him away violently and reached for the door. "Oh, now you've spoiled everything," she said as she got out of the car. "Now you've spoiled everything. I know what you've been thinking. I know you've been thinking it all along." She slammed the door and spoke to him across the window. "Well, you needn't come around here any more, Baxter," she said. "My girl friends are coming down from New York tomorrow on the morning plane and I'll be too busy to see you for the rest of the summer. Good night."

BAXTER WAS AWARE that he had only himself to blame; he had moved too quickly. He knew better. He went to bed feeling angry and sad, and slept poorly. He was depressed when he woke, and his depression was deepened by the noise of a sea rain, blowing in from the northeast. He lay in bed listening to the rain and the surf. The storm would metamorphose the island. The beaches would be empty. Drawers would stick. Suddenly he got out of bed, went to the telephone, called the airport. The New York plane had been unable to land, they told him, and no more planes were expected that day. The storm seemed to be playing directly into his hands. At noon, he drove in to the village and bought a Sunday paper and a box of candy. The candy was for Clarissa, but he was in no hurry to give it to her.

She would have stocked the icebox, put out the towels, and planned the picnic, but now the arrival of her friends had been postponed, and the lively day that she had anticipated had turned out to be rainy and idle. There were ways, of course, for her to overcome her disappointment, but on the evidence of the barn dance he felt that she was lost without her husband or her mother-in-law, and that there were few, if any, people on the island who would pay her a chance call or ask her over for a drink. It was likely that she would spend the day listening to the radio and the rain and that by the end of it she would be ready to welcome anyone, including Baxter. But as long as the forces of loneliness and idleness were working on his side, it was shrewder, Baxter knew, to wait. It would be best to come just before dark, and he waited until then. He drove to the Ryans' with his box of candy. The windows were lighted. Clarissa opened the door.

"I wanted to welcome your friends to the island," Baxter said. "I—"

"They didn't come," Clarissa said. "The plane couldn't land. They went back to New York. They telephoned me. I had planned such a nice visit. Now everything's changed."

"I'm sorry, Clarissa," Baxter said. "I've brought you a present."

"Oh!" She took the box of candy. "What a beautiful box! What a lovely present! What—" Her face and her voice were, for a minute, ingenuous and yielding, and then he saw the force of resistance transform them. "You shouldn't have done it," she said.

"May I come in?" Baxter asked.

"Well, I don't know," she said. "You can't come in if you're just going to sit around."

"We could play cards," Baxter said.

"I don't know how," she said.

"I'll teach you," Baxter said.

"No," she said. "No, Baxter, you'll have to go. You just don't understand the kind of a woman I am. I spent all day writing a letter to Bob. I wrote and told him that you kissed me last night. I can't let you come in." She closed the door.

From the look on Clarissa's face when he gave her the box of candy, Baxter judged that she liked to get presents. An inexpensive gold bracelet or even a bunch of flowers might do it, he knew, but Baxter was an extremely stingy man, and while he saw the usefulness of a present, he could not bring himself to buy one. He decided to wait.

The storm blew all Monday and Tuesday. It cleared on Tuesday night, and by Wednesday afternoon the tennis courts were dry and Baxter played. He played until late. Then, when he had bathed and changed his clothes, he stopped at a cocktail party to pick up a drink. Here one of his neighbors, a married woman with four children, sat down beside him and began a general discussion of the nature of married love.

It was a conversation, with its glances and innuendoes, that Baxter had been through many times, and he knew roughly what it promised. His neighbor was one of the pretty mothers that Baxter had admired on the beach. Her hair was brown. Her arms were thin and tanned. Her teeth were sound. But while he appeared to be deeply concerned with her opinions on love, the white image of Clarissa loomed up in his mind, and he broke off the conversation and left the party. He drove to the Ryans'.

From a distance, the cottage looked shut. The house

and the garden were perfectly still. He knocked and then rang. Clarissa spoke to him from an upstairs window.

"Oh, hello, Baxter," she said.

"I've come to say goodbye, Clarissa," Baxter said. He couldn't think of anything better.

"Oh, dear," Clarissa said. "Well, wait just a minute. I'll be down."

"I'm going away, Clarissa," Baxter said when she opened the door. "I've come to say goodbye."

"Where are you going?"

"I don't know." He said this sadly.

"Well, come in, then," she said hesitantly. "Come in for a minute. This is the last time that I'll see you, I guess, isn't it? Please excuse the way the place looks. Mr. Talbot got sick on Monday and Mrs. Talbot had to take him to the hospital on the mainland, and I haven't had anybody to help me. I've been all alone."

He followed her into the living room and sat down. She was more beautiful than ever. She talked about the problems that had been presented by Mrs. Talbot's departure. The fire in the stove that heated the water had died. There was a mouse in the kitchen. The bathtub wouldn't drain. She hadn't been able to get the car started.

In the quiet house, Baxter heard the sound of a leaky water tap and a clock pendulum. The sheet of glass that protected the Ryans' geological specimens reflected the fading sky outside the window. The cottage was near the water, and he could hear the surf. He noted these details dispassionately and for what they were worth. When Clarissa finished her remarks about Mrs. Talbot, he waited a full minute before he spoke.

"The sun is in your hair," he said.

"What?"

"The sun is in your hair. It's a beautiful color."

"Well, it isn't as pretty as it used to be," she said. "Hair like mine gets dark. But I'm not going to dye it. I don't think that women should dye their hair."

"You're so intelligent," he murmured.

"You don't mean that?"

"Mean what?"

"Mean that I'm intelligent."

"Oh, but I do," he said. "You're intelligent. You're

beautiful. I'll never forget that night I met you at the boat. I hadn't wanted to come to the island. I'd made plans to go out West."

"I can't be intelligent," Clarissa said miserably. "I must be stupid. Mother Ryan says that I'm stupid, and Bob says that I'm stupid, and even Mrs. Talbot says that I'm stupid, and—" She began to cry. She went to a mirror and dried her eyes. Baxter followed. He put his arms around her. "Don't put your arms around me," she said, more in despair than in anger. "Nobody ever takes me seriously until they get their arms around me." She sat down again and Baxter sat near her. "But you're not stupid, Clarissa," he said. "You have a wonderful intelligence, a wonderful mind. I've often thought so. I've often felt that you must have a lot of very interesting opinions."

"Well, that's funny," she said, "because I do have a lot of opinions. Of course, I never dare say them to anyone, and Bob and Mother Ryan don't ever let me speak. They always interrupt me, as if they were ashamed of me. But I do have these opinions. I mean, I think we're like cogs in a wheel. I've concluded that we're like cogs in a wheel. Do you think we're like cogs in a wheel?"

"Oh, yes," he said. "Oh, yes, I do!"

"I think we're like cogs in a wheel," she said. "For instance, do you think that women should work? I've given that a lot of thought. My opinion is that I don't think married women should work. I mean, unless they have a lot of money, of course, but even then I think it's a full-time job to take care of a man. Or do you think that women should work?"

"What do you think?" he asked. "I'm terribly interested in knowing what you think."

"Well, my opinion is," she said timidly, "that you just have to hoe your row. I don't think that working or joining the church is going to change everything, or special diets, either. I don't put much stock in fancy diets. We have a friend who eats a quarter of a pound of meat at every meal. He has a scales right on the table and he weighs the meat. It makes the table look awful and I don't see what good it's going to do him. I buy what's reasonable. If ham is reasonable, I buy ham. If lamb is reasonable, I buy lamb. Don't you think that's intelligent?"

"I think that's very intelligent."

"And progressive education," she said. "I don't have a good opinion of progressive education. When we go to the Howards' for dinner, the children ride their tricycles around the table all the time, and it's my opinion that they get this way from progressive schools, and that children ought to be told what's nice and what isn't."

The sun that had lighted her hair was gone, but there was still enough light in the room for Baxter to see that as she aired her opinions, her face suffused with color and her pupils dilated. Baxter listened patiently, for he knew by then that she merely wanted to be taken for something that she was not—that the poor girl was lost. "You're very intelligent," he said, now and then. "You're so intelligent."

It was as simple as that.

THE CURE

THIS HAPPENED in the summer. I remember that the weather was very hot, both in New York and in the suburb where we live. My wife and I had a quarrel, and Rachel took the children and drove off in the station wagon. Tom didn't appear—or I wasn't conscious of him—until they had been gone for about two weeks, but her departure and his arrival seemed connected. Rachel's departure was meant to be final. She had left me twice before—the second time, we divorced and then remarried—and I watched her go each time with a feeling that was far from happy, but also with that renewal of self-respect, of nerve, that seems to be the reward for accepting a painful truth. As I say, it was summer, and I was glad, in a way, that she had picked this time to quarrel. It seemed to spare us both the immediate necessity of legalizing our separation. We had lived together—on and off—for thirteen years: we had three children and some involved finances. I guessed that she was content, as I was, to let things ride until September or October.

I was glad that the separation took place in the summer because my job is most exacting at that time of year and I'm usually too tired to think of anything else at night, and because I'd noticed that summer was for me the easiest season of the year to live through alone. I also expected that Rachel would get the house when our affairs were settled, and I like our house and thought of those days as the last I would spend there. There were a few minor symptoms of domestic disorder. First the dog and then the cat ran away. Then I came home one night and found Maureen, the maid, dead drunk. She told me that her husband, when he was with the Army of Occupation in Germany, had fallen in love with another woman. She wept. She got down on her knees. That scene, with the two of us alone in a house unnaturally empty of women and children on a summer evening, was grotesque, and it is this kind of grotesqueness, I know, that can destroy your resolution. I made her some coffee and gave her two weeks' wages and drove her home, and when we said goodbye she seemed composed and sober, and I felt that the grotesqueness could be forgotten. After this, I planned a simple schedule that I hoped to follow until autumn.

You cure yourself of a romantic, carnal, and disastrous marriage, I decided, and, like any addict in the throes of a cure, you must be exaggeratedly careful of every step you take. I decided not to answer the telephone, because I knew that Rachel might repent, and I knew, by then, the size and the nature of the things that could bring us together. If it rained for five days, if one of the children had a passing fever, if she got some sad news in a letter—anything like this might be enough to put her on the telephone, and I did not want to be tempted to resume a relationship that had been so miserable. The first months will be like a cure, I thought, and I scheduled my time with this in mind. I took the eight-ten train into town in the morning and returned on the six-thirty. I knew enough to avoid the empty house in the summer dusk, and I drove directly from the station parking lot to a good restaurant called Orpheo's. There was usually someone there to talk with, and I'd drink a couple of Martinis and eat a steak. Afterward I'd drive over to the Stonybrook Drive-In Theatre and sit through a double feature. All this—the Martinis and the steak and the movie—was intended to induce a kind of anesthesia, and it worked. I didn't want to see anyone outside the people in my office.

But I don't sleep very well in an empty bed, and presently I had the problem of sleeplessness to cope with. When I got home from the movies, I would fall asleep, but only for a couple of hours. I tried to make the best of insomnia. If it was raining, I listened to the rain and the thunder. If it wasn't raining, I listened to the distant noise of trucks on the turnpike, a sound that reminded me of the Depression, when I spent some time on the road. The trucks came gunning down the turnpike—loaded with chickens or canned goods or soap powder or furniture. The sound meant darkness to me, darkness and headlights—and youth, I suppose, since it seemed to be a pleasant sound. Sometimes the noise of the rain or the traffic or something like that would distract me, and I would be able to go to sleep again, but one night nothing at all worked, and at three in the morning I decided to go downstairs and read.

I turned on a light in the living room and looked at Rachel's books. I chose one by an author named Lin Yutang and sat down on a sofa under a lamp. Our living room is comfortable. The book seemed interesting. I was in a neighborhood where most of the front doors were unlocked, and on a street that is very quiet on a summer night. All the animals are domesticated, and the only night birds that I've ever heard are some owls way down by the railroad track. So it was very quiet. I heard the Barstows' dog bark, briefly, as if he had been waked by a nightmare, and then the barking stopped. Everything was quiet again. Then I heard, very close to me, a footstep and a cough.

I felt my flesh get hard—you know that feeling—but I didn't look up from my book, although I felt that I was being watched. Intuition and all that sort of thing may exist, but I am happier if I discount it, and yet, without lifting my eyes from the book, I knew not only that I was being watched but that I was being watched from the picture window at the end of the living room by someone whose intent was to watch me and to violate my privacy. Sitting under a bright lamp, surrounded by the dark, made me feel defenseless. I turned a page and pretended to go on reading. Then a fear, much worse than the fear of the fool outside the window, distracted me. I was afraid that the cough and the step and the feeling that I was being watched had come from my imagination. I looked up.

I saw him, all right, and I think he meant me to; he was grinning. I turned off the light, but it was too dark outside and my eyes were too accustomed to the bright reading light for me to pick out any shape against the glass. I ran into the hallway and switched on some carriage lamps by the front door (the light they gave was not very bright but it was enough for me to see anyone crossing the lawn), but when I got back to the window, the lawn was empty and I could see that there was no one where he had been standing. There were plenty of places where he could have hidden. There is a big clump of syringa at the foot of the walk that would conceal a man, and there is the lilac and the cut-leaved maple. I wasn't going to get the old samurai sword out and chase him. Not me. I turned out the carriage lights then, and stood in the dark wondering who it could have been.

I had never had anything to do with night people, but I know that they exist, and I guessed that he was probably some cracked old man from the row of shanties by the railroad tracks, and perhaps because of my determination, my need, to put a pleasant, or at least a calm, face on everything, I even managed to think compassionately of the old man who was driven, in senescence, to leave his home and wander at night in a strange neighborhood, at the mercy of dogs and policemen, only to be rewarded in the end by the sight of a man reading Lin Yutang or a woman feeding pills to a sick child or somebody eating chili con carne out of the icebox. As I climbed the dark stairs, I heard thunder, and a second later a flux of summer rain inundated the county, and I thought of the poor prowler and his long walk home through the storm.

It was after four then, and I lay in the dark, listening to the rain and to the morning trains coming through. They came from Buffalo and Chicago and the Far West, through Albany and down along the river in the early morning, and at one time or another I've traveled on most of them, and I lay in the dark thinking about the polar air in the Pullman cars and the smell of nightclothes and the taste of dining-car water and the way it feels to end a day in Cleveland or Chicago and begin another in New York, particularly after you've been away for a couple of years, and particularly in the summer. I lay in the dark imagining the dark cars in the rain, and the tables set for breakfast, and the smells.

I was very sleepy the next day, but I got my work done and dozed on the train coming home. I might have been able to go to sleep then, but I didn't want to take any chances, and I followed the routine of going to Orpheo's and then to the movies. I saw a terrible double feature. The pictures stupefied me, and I did go to sleep as soon as I got into bed, but then the telephone woke me. It was two o'clock. I lay in bed until the phone stopped ringing. I knew I was too wakeful then for any night sounds—the wind or the traffic—to make me sleepy, and I went downstairs. I didn't expect that the Peeping Tom would return, but my reading light was conspicuous in the dark neighborhood, so I turned on the carriage lamps by the door and sat down again with the book by Lin Yutang. When I heard the Barstows' dog bark, I put down my book and watched the picture window to assure myself that the Peeping Tom was not coming or, if he should come, to see him before he saw me.

I didn't see anything, anything at all, but after a few minutes I experienced that terrible hardening of the flesh, that certainty that I was being watched. I picked up my book again, not because I intended to read but because I wanted to show him that I was indifferent to the fact that he had returned. Of course, there are many other windows in the room, and I wondered for a minute which one he had taken up his stand at this night. Then I knew, and the fact that he was behind me, that he was at my back, frightened and exasperated me, and I jumped up without turning off the lamp and saw his face in the narrow window above the piano. "Get the hell away from here!" I yelled. "She's gone! Rachel's gone! There's nothing to see! Leave me alone!" I ran to the window, but he had gone. And then, because I had been shouting at the top of my lungs in an empty house, I thought that perhaps I was going crazy. I thought, again, that I might have imagined the face in the window, and I got the flashlight and went outside.

There is a flower bed under the narrow window. I looked at this with the flashlight, and he had been there, all right. There were footprints in the dirt, and he'd stepped on some of the flowers. I followed his tracks out of the flower bed to the edge of the lawn, where I found a man's patent-leather bedroom slipper. It was a little cracked and worn, and I thought it might have belonged to an old man, but I knew it didn't belong to any servant. I guessed that Tom was one of my neighbors. I heaved the slipper over my hedge towards where the Barstows have a compost heap, and went back to the house and turned off the lights and went upstairs.

DURING the next day, I thought once or twice of calling the police, but I couldn't make up my mind. I thought about it again that night while I was standing at the bar at Orpheo's, waiting for them to cook my steak. The situation, on the surface, was ridiculous, and I could see that, but the dread of seeing his face in the window again was real and cumulative, and I didn't see why I should have to endure it, particularly at a time when I was trying to overhaul my whole way of living. It was getting dark outside. I went to the public telephone then and called the police. Stanley Madison, who sometimes directs traffic at the station, answered. He said "Oh" when I told him that I wanted to report a prowler. He asked me if Rachel was at home. Then he said that the village, since its incorporation in 1916, had never had such a complaint registered. He spoke with that understandable pride that we all take in the neighborhood. I had anticipated putting myself at a disadvantage, but Stanley spoke as if I were deliberately trying to damage real-estate values. He went on to say that a five-man police force was inadequate, that they were underpaid and overworked, and that if I wanted a guard put around my house, I should move to enlarge the police force at the next meeting of the civic-improvement association. He tried not to seem unfriendly and ended the conversation by asking about Rachel and the children, but when I left the telephone booth, I felt that I had made a mistake.

That night, a big thunderstorm broke right in the middle of the movie, and it rained until morning. I guess the storm kept Tom at home, because I didn't see him or hear him. But he was back the next night. I heard him come at about three and leave about an hour later, but I didn't look up from my book. I reasoned that he was probably a harmless nuisance, and that if I only knew who he was—that if I only knew his name—his ability to irritate me would be lost and I could peacefully resume the schedule of my cure. I went upstairs with the question of his identity still on my mind. I was pretty sure that he came from the neighborhood. I wondered if any of my friends or neighbors had a cracked relative staying with them for the summer. I went over the names of everyone I knew, trying to associate with them some eccentric uncle or grandfather. I thought that if I could disengage the stranger from the night, from the dark, everything would be all right.

In the morning, when I went down to the station, I walked through the crowd on the platform looking for some stranger who might be the culprit. Even though I had only seen the face dimly, I thought that I would recognize it. Then I saw my man. It was as simple as that. He was waiting on the platform for the eight-ten with the rest of us, but he wasn't any stranger.

It was Herbert Marston, who lives in the big yellow house on Blenhollow Road. If there had been any question in my mind, it would have been answered by the way he looked when he saw that I recognized him. He looked frightened and guilty. I started across the platform to speak to him. "I don't mind you looking in my windows at night, Mr. Marston," I was going to say, in a voice loud enough to embarrass him, "but I wish that you wouldn't trample on my wife's flowers." Then I stopped, because I saw that he was not alone. He was with his wife and his daughter. I walked behind them and stood at the corner of the waiting room, looking at this family.

There was nothing irregular in Mr. Marston's features or—when he saw that I was going to leave him alone—in his manner. He's a gray-haired man, a little over medium height, with a bony face that must have been handsome when he was younger. The belief that a crooked heart is betrayed by palsies, tics, and other infirmities dies hard. I felt the loss of it that morning when I searched his face for some mark. He looked solvent, rested, and moral—much more so than Chucky Ewing, who was job hunting, or Larry Spencer, whose son had polio, or any of a dozen other men on the platform waiting for the train. Then I looked at his daughter, Lydia. Lydia is one of the prettiest girls in our neighborhood. I'd ridden in on the train with her once or twice and I knew that she was doing voluntary secretarial work for the Red Cross. She had on a blue dress that morning, and her arms were bare, and she looked so fresh and pretty and sweet that I wouldn't have embarrassed or hurt her for anything in the world. Then I looked at Mrs. Marston, and if the mark was anywhere, it was on *her* face, although I don't understand why she should be afflicted for her husband's waywardness. It was very hot, but Mrs. Marston had on a brown suit and a worn fur piece. Her face was sallow and plain, but it was wreathed, even while she watched for the morning train, in an impermeable smile. It was a face that must have seemed, long ago, cut out for violent, even malevolent, passion. But years of prayer and abstinence had expunged the inclination to violence, I thought, leaving only a few ugly lines at the mouth and the eyes and rewarding Mrs. Marston with an air of adamant and fetid sweetness. She must pray for him, I thought, while he wanders around the back yards in his bathrobe. I had wanted to know who Tom was, but now that I knew, I didn't feel any better. The graying man and the beautiful girl and the woman, standing together, made me feel worse.

That night, I decided to stay in town and go to a cocktail party. It was in an apartment in one of the tower hotels—way, way, way up. As soon as I got there, I went out onto the terrace, looking around for someone to take to dinner. What I wanted was a pretty girl in new shoes, but it looked as if all the pretty girls had stayed at the shore. There was a gray-haired woman out there, and a woman with a floppy hat, and Grace Harris, this actress I've met a couple of times. Grace Harris is a beauty, a faded one, and we've never had much to say to one another, but that night she gave me a very cordial smile. It was cordial but it was very sad, and the first thing I thought of was that she must have learned that Rachel had left me. I smiled right back at her and went in to the bar, where I found Harry Purcell. I had some drinks and talked with him. I looked around the room a couple of times, and each time I saw Grace Harris giving me this sad, sad look. I wondered about it, and then I thought she had probably mistaken me for somebody else. A lot of those ageless beauties with violet eyes are half blind, I know, and I thought that perhaps she couldn't see across the room. It got late, but there weren't any claims on my time, and I went on drinking. Then Harry went to the bathroom, and I stood alone at the bar for a couple of minutes, but that was too long. Grace Harris, who was with some people at the other end of the room, came over to me. She came right up to me and put her snow-white hand on my arm. "You poor boy," she murmured, "you poor boy."

I'm not a boy, and I'm not poor, and I wished the hell she would get away. She has a clever face, but I felt in it, that night, the force of great sadness and great malice. "I see a rope around your neck," she said sadly. Then she lifted her hand off my coat sleeve and went out of the room, and I guess she must have gone home, because I didn't see her again. Harry came back, and I didn't tell him what had happened, and I tried not to think much about it myself. I stayed at the party too long and got a late train home.

I remember that I took a bath and put on pajamas and lay down. As soon as I shut my eyes, I saw this rope. It had a hangman's noose at the end of it, but I'd known all along what Grace Harris had been talking about; she'd had a premonition that I would hang myself. The rope seemed to come down slowly into my consciousness. I opened my eyes and thought about the work I had to do in the morning, but when I shut my eyes again, there was a momentary blankness into which the rope—as if it had been pushed off a beam—fell, and swung through space. I opened my eyes and thought some more about the office, but when I shut them, there was the rope, still swinging. Whenever I closed my eyes that night and tried to go to sleep, it felt as though sleep had taken on the anguish of blindness. And with the visible world gone, there was nothing to keep the arbitrary rope from occupying the dark. I got out of bed and went downstairs and opened the Lin Yutang. I had only been reading for a few minutes when I heard Mr. Marston in the flower garden. I thought I knew, at last, what he was waiting to see. This frightened me. I turned off the light and stood up. It was dark outside the window and I couldn't see him. I wondered if there was any rope in the house. Then I remembered the painter on my son's dinghy in the cellar. I went into the cellar. The dory was on sawhorses, and there was a long painter on it, long enough for a man to hang himself by. I went upstairs to the kitchen and got a knife and hacked the painter off the boat. Then I got some newspapers and put them into the furnace and opened the drafts and burned up the rope. Then I went upstairs and got into bed. I felt saved.

I don't know how long it had been since I had had a good night's rest. But I felt queer in the morning, and although I could see from the window that it was a bright day, I didn't feel up to it. The sky and the light and everything else seemed dim and remote, as if I saw it all from a great distance. The thought of seeing the Marston family again revolted me, so I skipped the eight-ten and took a later train. The image of the rope was still at the back of my mind, and I saw it once or twice on the trip. I got through the morning, but when I left the office at noon, I told my secretary that I wouldn't be back. I had a lunch date with Nathan Shea, at the University Club, and I went there early and drank a Martini at the bar. I stood beside an old gentleman who was describing to a friend the regularity of his habits, and I had a strong impulse to crown him with a bowl of popcorn, but I drank my drink and stared at the bartender's wristwatch, which was hanging on a long-necked bottle of white crème de menthe. When Shea came in, I had two more drinks with him. Anesthetized by gin, I got through the lunch.

We said goodbye on Park Avenue. There my Martinis forsook me and I saw the rope again. It was about two o'clock on a sunny afternoon but it seemed dark to me. I went to the Corn Exchange Bank and cashed a check for five hundred dollars. Then I went to Brooks Brothers and bought some neckties and a box of cigars and went upstairs to look at suits. There were only a few customers in the store, and among them I noticed this girl or young woman who seemed to be alone. I guess she was looking over the stock for her husband. She had fair hair and the kind of white skin that looks like thin paper. It was a very hot day but she looked cool, as if she had been able to preserve, through the train ride in from Rye or Greenwich, the freshness of her bath. Her arms and her legs were beautiful, but the look on her face was sensible, humorous, even housewifely, and this sensible air seemed to accentuate the beauty of her arms and legs. She walked over and rang for the elevator. I walked over and stood beside her. We rode down together, and I followed her out of the store onto Madison Avenue. The sidewalk was crowded, and I walked beside her. She looked at me once, and she knew that I was following her, but I felt sure she was the kind of woman who would not readily call for help. She waited at the corner for the light to change. I waited beside her. It was all I could do to keep from saying to her, very, very softly, "Madame, will you please let me put my hand around your ankle? That's all I want to do, madame. It will save my life." She didn't look around again, but I could see that she was frightened. She crossed the street and I stayed at her side, and all the time a voice inside my head was pleading, "Please let me put my hand around your ankle. It will save my life. I just want to put my hand around your ankle. I'll be very happy to pay you." I took out my wallet and pulled out some bills. Then I heard someone behind me calling my name. I recognized the hearty voice of an advertising salesman who is in and out of our office. I put the wallet back in my pocket, crossed the street, and tried to lose myself in the crowd.

I walked over to Park Avenue, and then to Lexington, and went into a movie theatre. A stale, cold wind blew down on me from the ventilating machine, like the air in those Pullmans I had listened to coming down the river in the morning from Chicago and the Far West. The lobby was empty, and I felt as if I had stepped into a palace or a basilica. I took a narrow staircase that went up and then turned abruptly, separating itself from the splendor. The landings were dirty and the walls were bare. This stairway brought me into the balcony, and I sat there in the dark, thinking that nothing now was going to save me, that no pretty girl with new shoes was going to cross my path in time.

I took a train home, but I was too tired to go to Orpheo's and then sit through a movie. I drove from the station to the house and put the car in the garage. From there I heard the telephone ringing, and I waited in the garden until the ringing had stopped. As soon as I stepped into the living room, I noticed on the wall some dirty handprints that had been made by the children before they went away. They were near the baseboard and I had to get down on my knees to kiss them.

Then I sat in the living room for a long time. I fell asleep, and when I woke it was late; all the other houses were dark. I turned on a light. Peeping Tom would be putting on his slippers and his bathrobe, I thought, to begin his prowl through the back yards and gardens. Mrs. Marston would be on her knees, praying. I got down the Lin Yutang and began to read. I heard the Barstows' dog barking. The telephone began to ring.

"Oh, my darling!" I shouted when I heard Rachel's voice. "Oh, my darling! Oh, my darling!" She was crying. She was at Seal Harbor. It had rained for a week, and Tobey had a temperature of a hundred and four. "I'll leave now," I said. "I'll drive all night. I'll be there tomorrow. I'll get there in the morning. Oh, my darling!"

That was all. It was all over. I packed a bag and turned off the icebox and drove all night. We've been happy ever since. So far as I know, Mr. Marston has never stood outside our house in the dark, although I've seen him often enough on the station platform and at the country club. His daughter Lydia is going to be married next month, and his sallow wife was recently cited by one of the national charities for her good works. Everyone here is well.

THE SUPERINTENDENT

THE ALARM began ringing at six in the morning. It sounded faintly in the first-floor apartment that Chester Coolidge was given as part wages of an apartment-house superintendent, but it woke him at once, for he slept with the percussive noises of the building machinery on his consciousness, as if they were linked to his own well-being. In the dark, he dressed quickly and ran through the lobby to the back stairs, where his path was obstructed by a peach basket full of dead roses and carnations. He kicked this aside and ran lightly down the iron stairs to the basement and along a hall whose brick walls, encrusted with paint, looked like a passage in some catacomb. The ringing of the bell grew louder as he approached the room where the pump machinery was. The alarm signified that the water tank on the roof was nearly empty and that the mechanism that regulated the water supply wasn't working. In the pump room, Chester turned on the auxiliary pump.

The basement was still. Far up the back elevator shaft he could hear the car moving down, floor by floor, attended by the rattle of milk bottles. It would take an hour for the auxiliary to fill the roof tank, and Chester decided to keep an eye on the gauge himself, and let the handyman sleep. He went upstairs again, and shaved and washed while his wife cooked breakfast. It was a moving day, and before he sat down to breakfast, he saw that the barometer had fallen and, looking out of the window and up eighteen stories, he found the sky as good as black. Chester liked a moving day to be dry and fair, and in the past, when everyone moved on the first of October, the chances for good weather had been favorable; but now all this had been changed for the worse, and they moved in the snow and the rain. The Bestwicks (9-E) were moving out and the Neguses (1-A) were moving up. That was all. While Chester drank his first cup of coffee, his wife talked about the Bestwicks, whose departure excited in her some memories and misgivings. Chester did not answer her questions, nor did she expect him to that early in the day. She talked loosely and, as she put it herself, to hear the sound of her own voice.

Mrs. Coolidge had come with her husband twenty years earlier from Massachusetts. The move had been her idea. Ailing and childless, she had decided that she would be happier in a big city than in New Bedford. Entrenched in a superintendent's apartment in the East Fifties, she was perfectly content. She spent her days in the movies and the stores, and she had seen the Shah of Persia with her own eyes. The only part of city life that troubled her was the inhibitions that it put on her native generosity.

"That poor Mrs. Bestwick," she said. "Oh, that poor woman! You told me they sent the children out to stay with their grandmother, didn't you, until they get settled? I wish there was something I could do to help her. Now, if this was in New Bedford, we could ask her to dinner or give her a basket with a nice dinner in it. You know, I'm reminded by her of those people in New Bedford—the Fenners. The two sisters, they were. They had diamonds as big as filberts, just like Mrs. Bestwick, and no electricity in the house. They used to have to go over to Georgiana Butler's to take a bath."

Chester did not look at his wife, but her mere presence was heartening and wonderful, for he was convinced that she was an extraordinary woman. He felt that there was a touch of genius in her cooking, that her housework was marked with genius, that she had a geniuslike memory, and that her ability to accept the world as she found it was stamped with genius. She had made johnnycake for breakfast, and he ate it with an appreciation that verged on awe. He knew for a fact that no one else in the world could make johnnycake like his wife and that no one else in Manhattan that morning would have tried.

When he had finished breakfast, he lighted a cigar and sat thinking about the Bestwicks. Chester had seen the apartment building through many lives, and it seemed that another was commencing. He had, since 1943, divided the tenants into two groups, the "permanents" and the "ceilings." A rent increase had been granted the management, and he knew that that would weed out a number of the "ceilings." The Bestwicks were the first to go under these conditions, and like his wife, he was sorry to see them leave. Mr. Bestwick worked downtown. Mrs. Bestwick was a conscientious citizen and she had been building captain for the Red Cross, the March of Dimes, and the Girl Scouts. Whatever Mr. Bestwick made, it was not enough—not for that neighborhood. The liquor store knew. The butcher knew. The doorman and the window washer knew, and it had been known for a year to Retail Credit and the Corn Exchange Bank. The Bestwicks had been the last people in the neighborhood to face the facts. Mr. Bestwick wore a high-crowned felt hat, suit coats that were cut full around the waist, tight pants, and a white raincoat. He duck-footed off to work at eight every morning in a pair of English shoes that seemed to pinch him. The Bestwicks had been used to more money than they now had, and while Mrs. Bestwick's tweed suits were worn, her diamonds, as Mrs. Coolidge had noticed, were as big as filberts. The Bestwicks had two daughters and never gave Chester any trouble.

Mrs. Bestwick had called Chester late one afternoon about a month before and asked him if he would come upstairs. It was not urgent, she explained in her pleasant voice, but if it was not inconvenient, she would like to see him. She let him in graciously, as she did everything. She was a slender woman—a too slender woman with a magnificent bust and a graceful way of moving. He followed her that afternoon into the living room, where an older woman was sitting on a sofa. "This is my mother, Mrs. Doubleday, Chester," Mrs. Bestwick said. "Mother, this is Chester Coolidge, our superintendent." Mrs. Doubleday said she was pleased to meet him, and Chester accepted her invitation to sit down. From one of the bedrooms Chester heard the older Bestwick girl singing a song. "Up with Chapin,/Down with Spence," she sang. "Hang Miss Hewitt/To a back-yard fence."

Chester knew every living room in the building, and by his standards the Bestwicks' was as pleasant as any of them. It was his feeling that all the apartments in his building were intrinsically ugly and inconvenient. Watching his self-important tenants walk through the lobby, he sometimes thought that they were a species of the poor. They were poor in space, poor in light, poor in quiet, poor in repose, and poor in the atmosphere of privacy—poor in everything that makes a man's home his castle. He knew the pains they took to overcome these deficiencies: the fans, for instance, to take away the smells of cooking. A six-room apartment is not a house, and if you cook onions in one end of it, you'll likely smell them in the other, but they all installed kitchen exhausts and kept them running, as if ventilating machinery would make an apartment smell like a house in the woods. All the living rooms were, to his mind, too high-ceilinged and too narrow, too noisy and too dark, and he knew how tirelessly the women spent their time and money in the furniture stores, thinking that another kind of carpeting, another set of end tables, another pair of lamps would make the place conform at last to their visions of a secure home. Mrs. Bestwick had done better than most, he thought, or perhaps it was because he liked her that he liked her room.

"Do you know about the new rents, Chester?" Mrs. Bestwick said.

"I never know about rents or leases," Chester said untruthfully. "They handle all of that at the office."

"Our rent's been raised," Mrs. Bestwick said, "and we don't want to pay that much. I thought you might know if there was a less expensive apartment vacant in the building."

"I'm sorry, Mrs. Bestwick," Chester said. "There isn't a thing."

"I see," Mrs. Bestwick said.

He saw that she had something in mind; probably she hoped that he would offer to speak to the management and persuade them that the Bestwicks, as old and very desirable tenants, should be allowed to stay on at their present rental. But apparently she wasn't going to put herself in the embarrassing position of asking for his help, and he refrained, out of tact, from telling her that there was no way of his bringing pressure to bear on the situation.

"Isn't this building managed by the Marshall Cavises?" Mrs. Doubleday asked.

"Yes," Chester said.

"I went to Farmington with Mrs. Cavis," Mrs. Doubleday said to her daughter. "Do you think it would help if I spoke with her?"

"Mrs. Cavis isn't around here very much," Chester said. "During the fifteen years I worked here, I never laid eyes on either of them."

"But they do manage the building?" Mrs. Doubleday said to him.

"The Marshall Cavis Corporation manages it," Chester said.

"Maude Cavis was engaged to Benton Towler," Mrs. Doubleday said.

"I don't expect they have much to do with it personally," Chester said. "I don't know, but it seems to me I heard they don't even live in New York."

"Thank you very much, Chester," Mrs. Bestwick said. "I just thought there might be a vacancy."

WHEN THE ALARM BEGAN ringing again, this time to signify that the tank on the roof was full, Chester lit out through the lobby and down the iron stairs and turned off the pump. Stanley, the handyman, was awake and moving around in his room by then, and Chester told him he thought the float switch on the roof that controlled the pump was broken and to keep an eye on the gauge. The day in the basement had begun. The milk and the newspapers had been delivered; Delaney, the porter, had emptied the waste cans in the back halls; and now the sleep-out cooks and maids were coming to work. Chester could hear them greeting Ferarri, the back-elevator man, and their clear "Good mornings" confirmed his feeling that the level of courtesy was a grade higher in the basement than in the lobby upstairs.

At a little before nine, Chester telephoned the office management. A secretary whose voice he did not recognize took the message. "The float switch on the water tank is busted," he told her, "and we're working the auxiliary manually now. You tell the maintenance crew to get over here this morning."

"The maintenance crew is at one of the other buildings," the unfamiliar voice said, "and we don't expect them back until four o'clock."

"This is an emergency, God damn it!" Chester shouted. "I got over two hundred bathrooms here. This building's just as important as those buildings over on Park Avenue. If my bathrooms run dry, you can come over here and take the complaints yourself. It's a moving day, and the handyman and me have got too much to do to be sitting beside the auxiliary all the time." His face got red. His voice echoed through the basement. When he hung up, he felt uncomfortable and his cigar burned his mouth. Then Ferarri came in with a piece of bad news. The Bestwicks' move would be delayed. They had arranged for a small moving company to move them to Pelham, and the truck had broken down in the night, bringing a load south from Boston.

Ferarri took Chester up to 9-E in the service car. One

of the cheap, part-time maids that Mrs. Bestwick had been hiring recently had thumbtacked a sign onto the back door. "To Whom It May Concern," she had printed. "I never play the numbers and I never will play the numbers and I never played the numbers." Chester put the sign in the waste can and rang the back bell. Mrs. Bestwick opened the door. She was holding a cracked cup full of coffee in one hand, and Chester noticed that her hand was trembling. "I'm terribly sorry about the moving truck, Chester," she said. "I don't quite know what to do. Everything's ready," she said, gesturing toward the china barrels that nearly filled the kitchen. She led Chester across the hall into the living room, where the walls, windows, and floors were bare. "Everything's ready," she repeated. "Mr. Bestwick has gone up to Pelham to wait for me. Mother took the children."

"I wish you'd asked my advice about moving companies," Chester said. "It isn't that I get a cut from them or anything, but I could have put you onto a reliable moving firm that wouldn't cost you any more than the one you got. People try to save money by getting cheap moving companies and in the end they don't save anything. Mrs. Negus—she's in 1-A—she wants to get her things in here this morning."

Mrs. Bestwick didn't answer. "Oh, I'll miss you, Mrs. Bestwick," Chester said, feeling that he might have spoken unkindly. "There's no question about that. I'll miss you and Mr. Bestwick and the girls. You've been good tenants. During the eight years you've been here, I don't believe there's been a complaint from any of you. But things are changing, Mrs. Bestwick. Something's happening. The high cost of living. Oh, I can remember times when most of the tenants in this building wasn't rich nor poor. Now there's none but the rich. And, oh, the things they complain about, Mrs. Bestwick. You wouldn't believe me. The day before yesterday, that grass widow in 7-F called up, and you know what she was complaining about? She said the toilet seats in the apartment wasn't big enough."

Mrs. Bestwick didn't laugh at his joke. She smiled, but her mind seemed to be on something else.

"Well, I'll go down and tell Mrs. Negus that they'll be a delay," Chester said.

Mrs. Negus, who was replacing Mrs. Bestwick, took piano lessons. Her apartment had an entrance off the lobby, and in the afternoon she could be heard practicing her scales. The piano was a difficult instrument for her and she had mastered only a few jingles. Piano lessons were a new undertaking for Mrs. Negus. When she first moved into the building, during the war, her name had been Mary Toms, and she had lived with Mrs. Lasser and Mrs. Dobree. Chester suspected that Mrs. Lasser and Mrs. Dobree were loose women, and when Mary Toms joined them, Chester had worried about her, because she was so young and so pretty. His anxiety was misplaced—the loose life didn't depress or coarsen her at all. Coming in there as a poor girl in a cloth coat, she had at the end of the year more furs than anybody else and she seemed to be as happy as a lark. It was in the second winter that Mr. Negus began to call. He went there by chance, Chester guessed, and the visit changed his whole life. He was a tough-looking middle-aged man, and Chester remembered him because when he came through the lobby on his way to 1-A, he used to bury his nose in the collar of his coat and pull his hat brim down over his eyes.

As soon as Mr. Negus began to visit Mary Toms regularly, she eliminated all her other friends. One of them, a French naval officer, made some trouble, and it took a doorman and a cop to get him out. After this, Mr. Negus pointed out the door to Mrs. Lasser and Mrs. Dobree. It was nothing against Mary Toms, and she tried hard to get her friends another apartment in the building. Mr. Negus was stubborn, and the two older women packed their trunks and moved to an apartment on West Fifty-eighth Street. After they had gone, a decorator came in and overhauled the place. He was followed by the grand piano, the poodles, the Book-of-the-Month Club membership, and the crusty Irish maid. That winter, Mary Toms and Mr. Negus went down to Miami and got married there, but even after his marriage Mr. Negus still skulked through the lobby as if he was acting against his better judgment. Now the Neguses were going to move the whole caboodle up to 9-E. Chester didn't care one way or the other, but he didn't think the move was going to be permanent. Mrs. Negus was on the move. After a year or two in 9-E, he figured she'd ascend to one of the penthouses. From there, she'd probably take off for one of the fancier buildings on upper Fifth.

WHEN CHESTER RANG the bell that morning, Mrs. Negus let him in. She was still as pretty as a picture. "Hi, Chet," she said. "Come on in. I thought you didn't want me to start moving until eleven."

"Well, there may be a delay," Chester said. "The other lady's moving truck hasn't come."

"I got to get this stuff upstairs, Chet."

"Well, if her men don't come by eleven," Chester said, "I'll have Max and Delaney move the stuff down."

"Hi, Chet," Mr. Negus said.

"What's that on the seat of your pants, honey?" Mrs. Negus said.

"There's nothing on my pants," Mr. Negus said.

"Yes, there is, too," Mrs. Negus said. "There's a spot on your pants."

"Look," Mr. Negus said, "these pants just come back from the dry cleaner's."

"Well, if you had marmalade for breakfast," Mrs. Negus said, "you could have sat in that. I mean, you could have got marmalade on them."

"I didn't have marmalade," he said.

"Well, butter, then," she said. "It's awfully conspicuous."

"I'll telephone you," Chester said.

"You get her stuff out of there, Chet," Mrs. Negus said, "and I'll give you ten dollars. That's been my apartment since midnight. I want to get my things in there." Then she turned to her husband and began to rub his pants with a napkin. Chester let himself out.

In Chester's basement office, the telephone was ringing. He picked up the receiver and a maid spoke to him and said that a bathroom in 5-A was overflowing. The telephone rang repeatedly during the time that he was in the office, and he took down several complaints of mechanical failures reported by maids or tenants—a stuck window, a jammed door, a leaky faucet, and a clogged drain. Chester got the toolbox and made the repairs himself. Most of the tenants were respectful and pleasant, but the grass widow in 7-F called him into the dining room and spoke to him curtly.

"You are the janitor?" she asked.

"I'm the superintendent," Chester said. "The handy-man's busy."

"Well, I want to talk with you about the back halls," she said. "I don't think this building is as clean as it should be. The maid thinks that she's seen roaches in the kitchen. We've never had roaches."

"It's a clean building," Chester said. "It's one of the cleanest buildings in New York. Delaney washes the back stairs every second day and we have them painted whenever we get the chance. Sometime when you don't have anything better to do, you might come down cellar and see my basement. I take just as much pains with my basement as I do with my lobby."

"I'm not talking about the basement," the woman said. "I'm talking about the back halls."

Chester left for his office before he lost his temper. Ferarri told him that the maintenance crew had come and were up on the roof with Stanley. Chester wished that they had reported to him, for since he was the superintendent and carried the full burden of the place on his shoulders, he felt he should have been consulted before they went to work on his domain. He went up to Penthouse F and climbed the stairs from the back hall to the roof. A north wind was howling in the television antennas, and there was a little snow left on the roofs and terraces. Tarpaulins covered the porch furniture, and hanging on the wall of one of the terraces was a large straw hat, covered with ice. Chester went to the water tank and saw two men in overalls way up the iron ladder, working on the switch. Stanley stood a few rungs below them, passing up tools. Chester climbed the iron ladder and gave them his advice. They took it respectfully, but as he was going down the ladder, he heard one of the maintenance men ask Stanley, "Who's that—the janitor?"

Hurt for the second time that day, Chester went to the edge of the roof and looked out over the city. On his right was the river. He saw a ship coming down it, a freighter pressing forward on the tide, her deck and porthole lights burning in the overcast. She was off to sea, but her lights and her quietness made her look to Chester as warmed and contained as a farmhouse in a meadow. Down the tide she came like a voyaging farmhouse. Compared to his own domain, Chester thought, a ship was nothing. At his feet, there were thousands of arteries hammering with steam; there were hundreds of toilets, miles of drainpipe, and a passenger list of over a hundred people, any one of whom might at that minute be contemplating suicide, theft, arson, or mayhem. It was a huge responsibility, and Chester thought with commiseration of the relatively paltry responsibilities of a ship's captain taking his freighter out to sea.

When he got back to the basement, Mrs. Negus was on the telephone to ask him if Mrs. Bestwick had gone. He said he would call her back, and hung up. Mrs. Negus's ten dollars seemed to commit Chester to building a fire under Mrs. Bestwick, but he didn't want to add to her troubles, and he thought with regret of what a good tenant she had been. The overcast day, the thought of Mrs. Bestwick and the people who had called him janitor convinced Chester that he needed to be cheered up, and he decided to get his shoes shined.

But the shoeshine parlor that morning was still and empty, and Bronco, the shoeshine man, bent mournfully over Chester's shoes. "I'm sixty-two years old, Chester," Bronco said, "and I got a dirty mind. You think it's because I'm around shoes all the time? You think it has something to do with the way the polish smells?" He lathered Chester's shoes and rubbed in the polish with a coarse brush. "That's what my old lady thinks," Bronco said. "She thinks it's got something to do with being around shoes all the time. All I think about," Bronco said sadly, "is love, love, love. It's disgusting. I see in the paper a picture of a young couple eating supper. For all I know, they're nice young clean-minded people, but I've got different thoughts. A lady comes in to have a pair of heels put on her shoes. 'Yes, madam. No, madam. They'll be ready for you tomorrow, madam,' I'm saying to her, but what's going through my mind I'd be ashamed to tell you. But if it's from being around shoes all the time, how can I help myself? It's the only way I got to make a living. For a job like yours, you got to be a carpenter, a painter, a politician, a regular nursemaid. Oh, that must be some job you got, Chester! A window gets stuck. A fuse burns out. They tell you to come up and fix it. The lady of the house, she opens the door. She's all alone. She's got on her nightgown. She—" Bronco broke off and applied the shoe rag vigorously.

When Chester returned to the building, Mrs. Bestwick's moving truck still hadn't come, and he went directly to 9-E and rang the back bell. There was no answer. There was no sound. He rang and rang, and then he opened the door with the pass key, just as Mrs. Bestwick came into the kitchen. "I didn't hear the bell," she said. "I'm so upset by this delay that I didn't hear the bell. I was in the other room." She sat down at the kitchen table. She looked pale and troubled.

"Cheer up, Mrs. Bestwick," Chester said. "You'll like it in Pelham. Isn't Pelham where you're moving to? Trees, birds. The children'll put on weight. You'll have a nice house."

"It's a small house, Chester," Mrs. Bestwick said.

"Well, I'm going to tell the porters to take your stuff—your things—out now and put them in the alley," Chester said. "They'll be just as safe there as they will be in here, and if it rains, I'll see that everything's covered and kept dry. Why don't you go up to Pelham now, Mrs. Bestwick?" he asked. "I'll take care of everything. Why don't you just get onto a train and go up to Pelham?"

"I think I'll wait, thank you, Chester," Mrs. Bestwick said.

Somewhere a factory whistle blew twelve o'clock. Chester went downstairs and inspected the lobby. The rugs and the floor were clean, and the glass on the hunting prints was shining. He stood under the canopy long enough to see that the brass stanchions were polished, that the rubber doormat was scrubbed, and that his canopy was a good canopy and, unlike some others, had withstood the winter storms. "Good morning," someone said to him elegantly while he was standing there, and he said, "Good morning, Mrs. Wardsworth," before he realized that it was Katie Shay, Mrs. Wardsworth's elderly maid. It was an understandable mistake, for Katie was wearing a hat and a coat that had been discarded by Mrs. Wardsworth and she wore the dregs of a bottle of Mrs. Wardsworth's perfume. In the eclipsed light, the old woman looked like the specter of her employer.

Then a moving van, Mrs. Bestwick's moving van, backed up to the curb. This improved Chester's spirits, and he went in to lunch with a good appetite.

Mrs. Coolidge did not sit down at the table with Chester, and because she was wearing her purple dress, Chester guessed that she was going to the movies.

"That woman up in 7-F asked me if I was the janitor today," Chester said.

"Well, don't you let it worry you, Chester," Mrs. Coolidge said. "When I think of all the things you have on your mind, Chester—of all the things you have to do—it seems to me that you have more to do than almost anybody I ever knew. Why, this place might catch fire in the middle of the night, and there's nobody here knows where the hoses are but you and Stanley. There's the elevator machines and the electricity and the gas and the furnace. How much oil did you say that furnace burned last winter, Chester?"

"Over a hundred thousand gallons," Chester said.

"Just think of that," Mrs. Coolidge said.

THE MOVING was proceeding in an orderly way when Chester got downstairs again. The moving men told him that Mrs. Bestwick was still in the apartment. He lighted a cigar, sat down at his desk, and heard someone singing, "Did you ever see a dream walking?" The song, attended with laughing and clapping, came from the far end of the basement, and Chester followed the voice down the dark hall, to the laundry. The laundry was a brightly lighted room that smelled of the gas dryer. Banana peels and sandwich papers were spread over the ironing boards, and none of the six laundresses were working. In the center of the room, one of them, dressed in a negligee that someone had sent down to have washed, was waltzing with a second, dressed in a tablecloth. The others were clapping and laughing. Chester was wondering whether or not to interfere with the dance when the telephone in his office rang again. It was Mrs. Negus. "Get that bitch out of there,

Chester," she said. "That's been my apartment since midnight. I'm going up there now."

Chester asked Mrs. Negus to wait for him in the lobby. He found her there wearing a short fur coat and dark glasses. They went up to 9-E together and he rang Mrs. Bestwick's front bell. He introduced the two women, but Mrs. Negus overlooked the introduction in her interest in a piece of furniture that the moving men were carrying across the hall.

"That's a lovely piece," she said.

"Thank you," Mrs. Bestwick said.

"You wouldn't want to sell it?" Mrs. Negus said.

"I'm afraid I can't," Mrs. Bestwick said. "I'm sorry that I'm leaving the place in such a mess," she went on. "There wasn't time to have someone come in and clean it up."

"Oh, that doesn't matter," Mrs. Negus said. "I'm going to have the whole thing painted and redecorated anyhow. I just wanted to get my things in here."

"Why don't you go up to Pelham now, Mrs. Bestwick?" Chester said. "Your truck's here, and I'll see that all the stuff is loaded."

"I will in a minute, Chester," Mrs. Bestwick said.

"You've got some lovely stones there," Mrs. Negus said, looking at Mrs. Bestwick's rings.

"Thank you," Mrs. Bestwick said.

"Now, you come down with me, Mrs. Bestwick," Chester said, "and I'll get you a taxi and I'll see that everything gets into the moving van all right."

Mrs. Bestwick put on her hat and coat. "I suppose there are some things I ought to tell you about the apartment," she said to Mrs. Negus, "but I can't seem to remember any of them. It was very nice to meet you. I hope you'll enjoy the apartment as much as we have." Chester opened the door and she went into the hall ahead of him. "Wait just a minute, Chester," she said. "Wait just a minute, please." Chester was afraid then that she was going to cry, but she opened her purse and went through its contents carefully.

Her unhappiness at that moment, Chester knew, was more than the unhappiness of leaving a place that seemed familiar for one that seemed strange; it was the pain of leaving the place where her accent and her looks, her worn suit and her diamond rings could still command a trace of respect; it was the pain of parting from one class and going into another, and it was doubly painful because it was a parting that would never be completed. Somewhere in Pelham she would find a neighbor who had been to Farmingdale or wherever it was; she would find a friend with diamonds as big as filberts and holes in her gloves.

In the foyer, she said goodbye to the elevator man and the doorman. Chester went outside with her, expecting that she would say goodbye to him under the canopy, and he was prepared again to extol her as a tenant, but she turned her back on him without speaking and walked quickly to the corner. Her neglect surprised and wounded him, and he was looking after her with indignation when she turned suddenly and came back. "But I forgot to say goodbye to you, Chester, didn't I?" she said. "Goodbye, and thank you, and say goodbye to Mrs. Coolidge for me. Give Mrs. Coolidge my best regards." Then she was gone.

"WELL, it looks as though it was trying to clear up, doesn't it?" Katie Shay said as she came out the door a few minutes later. She was carrying a paper bag full of grain. As soon as Katie crossed the street, the pigeons that roost on the Queensboro Bridge recognized her, but she did not raise her head to see them, a hundred of them, leave their roost and fly loosely in a circle, as if they were windborne. She heard the roar of their wings pass overhead and saw their shadows darken the puddles of water in the street, but she seemed unconscious of the birds. Her approach was firm and gentle, like that of a nursemaid with importunate children, and when the pigeons landed on the sidewalk and crowded up to her feet, she kept them waiting. Then she began to scatter the yellow grain, first to the old and the sick, at the edges of the flock, and then to the others.

A workman getting off a bus at the corner noticed the flock of birds and the old woman. He opened his lunch pail and dumped onto the sidewalk the crusts from his meal. Katie was at his side in a minute. "I'd rather you didn't feed them," she said sharply. "I'd just as soon you didn't feed them. You see, I live in that house over there, and I can keep an eye on them, and I see that they have everything they need. I give them fresh grain twice a day. Corn in the winter. It costs me nine dollars a month. I see that they have everything they need and I don't like to have strangers feed them." As she spoke, she kicked the stranger's crusts into the gutter. "I change their water twice a day, and in the winter I always see that the ice is broken on it. But I'd just as soon that strangers didn't feed them. I know you'll understand." She turned her back on the workman and dumped the last of the feed out of her bag. She was queer, Chester thought, she was as queer as the Chinese language. But who was queerer—she, for feeding the birds, or he, for watching her?

What Katie had said about the sky was true. The clouds were passing, and Chester noticed the light in the sky. The days were getting longer. The light seemed delayed. Chester went out from under the canopy to see it. He clasped his hands behind his back and stared outward and upward. He had been taught, as a child, to think of the clouds as disguising the City of God, and the low clouds still excited in him the curiosity of a child who thought that he was looking off to where the saints and the prophets lived. But it was more than the liturgical habits of thought that he retained from his pious childhood. The day had failed to have any meaning, and the sky seemed to promise a literal explanation.

Why had it failed? Why was it unrewarding? Why did Bronco and the Bestwicks and the Neguses and the grass widow in 7-F and Katie Shay and the stranger add up to nothing? Was it because the Bestwicks and the Neguses and Chester and Bronco had been unable to help one another; because the old maid had not let the stranger help her feed the birds? Was that it? Chester asked, looking at the blue air as if he expected an answer to be written in vapor. But the sky told him only that it was a long day at the end of winter, that it was late and time to go in.

THE CHILDREN

MR. HATHERLY had many old-fashioned tastes. He wore high yellow boots, dined at Lüchow's in order to hear the music, and slept in a woolen nightshirt.

His urge to establish in business a patriarchal liaison with some young man who would serve as his descendant, in the fullest sense of the word, was another of these old-fashioned tastes. Mr. Hatherly picked for his heir a young immigrant named Victor Mackenzie, who had made the crossing from England or Scotland—a winter crossing, I think—when he was sixteen or seventeen. The winter crossing is a guess. He may have worked his way or borrowed passage money or had some relation in this country to help him, but all this was kept in the dark, and his known life began when he went to work for Mr. Hatherly. As an immigrant, Victor may have cherished an obsolete vision of the American businessman. Here and there one saw in Mr. Hatherly a touch of obsolescence. His beginnings were obscure, and, as everyone knows, he got rich enough to be an ambassador. In business, he was known as a harsh and unprincipled trader. He broke wind when he felt like it and relished the ruin of a competitor. He was very short—nearly a dwarf. His legs were spindly and his large belly had pulled his spine out of shape. He decorated his bald skull by combing across it a few threads of gray hair, and he wore an emerald fob on his watch chain. Victor was a tall man, with the kind of handsomeness that is sooner or later disappointing. His square jaw and all his other nicely proportioned features might at first have led you to expect a man of exceptional gifts of character, but you felt in the end that he was merely pleasant, ambitious, and a little ingenuous. For years, this curmudgeon and the young immigrant walked side by side confidently, as if they might have been accepted in the ark.

Of course, it all took a long time; it took years and years. Victor began as an office boy with a hole in his sock. Like the immigrants of an earlier generation, he had released great stores of energy and naïveness through the act of expatriation. He worked cheerfully all day. He stayed cheerfully at night to decorate the showcases in the waiting room. He seemed to have no home to go to. His eagerness reminded Mr. Hatherly, happily, of the apprentices of his own youth. There was little enough in business that did remind him of the past. He kept Victor in his place for a year or two, speaking to him harshly if he spoke to him at all. Then in his crabbed and arbitrary way he began to instruct Victor in the role of an heir. Victor was sent on the road for six months. After this he worked in the Rhode Island mills. He spent a season in the advertising department and another in the sales division. His position in the business was difficult to assess, but his promotions in Mr. Hatherly's esteem were striking. Mr. Hatherly was sensitive about the odd figure he cut, and disliked going anywhere alone. When Victor had worked with him for a few years, he was ordered to get to the old man's apartment, on upper Fifth Avenue, at eight each morning and walk him to work. They never talked much along the way, but then Hatherly was not loquacious. At the close of the business day, Victor either put him into a taxi or walked him home. When the old man went off to Bar Harbor without his eyeglasses, it was Victor who got up in the middle of the night and put the glasses on the early-morning plane. When the old man wanted to send a wedding present, it was Victor who bought it. When the old man was ailing, it was Victor who got him to take his medicine. In the gossip of the trade Victor's position was naturally the target for a lot of jocularity, criticism, and downright jealousy. Much of the criticism was unfair, for he was merely an ambitious young man who expressed his sense of business enterprise by feeding pills to Mr. Hatherly. Running through all his amenability was an altogether charming sense of his own identity. When he felt that he had grounds for complaint, he said so. After working for eight years under Mr. Hatherly's thumb, he went to the old man and said that he thought his salary was inadequate. The old man rallied with a masterful blend of injury, astonishment, and tenderness. He took Victor to his tailor and let him order four suits. A few months later, Victor again complained—this time about the vagueness of his position in the firm. He was hasty, the old man said, in objecting to his lack of responsibility. He was scheduled to make a presentation, in a week or two, before the board of directors. This was more than Victor had expected, and he was content. Indeed, he was grateful. This was America! He worked hard over his presentation. He read it aloud to the old man, and Mr. Hatherly instructed him when to raise and when to lower his voice, whose eye to catch and whose to evade, when to strike the table and when to pour himself a glass of water. They discussed the clothing that he would wear. Five minutes before the directors' meeting began, Mr. Hatherly seized the papers, slammed the door in Victor's face, and made the presentation himself.

He called Victor into his office at the end of that trying day. It was past six, and the secretaries had locked up their teacups and gone home. "I'm sorry about the presentation," the old man mumbled. His voice was heavy. Then Victor saw that he had been crying. The old man slipped off the high desk chair that he used to increase his height and walked around the large office. This was, in itself, a demonstration of intimacy and trust. "But that isn't what I want to talk about," he said. "I want to talk about my family. Oh, there's no misery worse than bad blood in a family! My wife"—he spoke with disgust—"is a stupid woman. The hours of pleasure I've had from my children I can count on the fingers of one hand. It may be my fault," he said, with manifest insincerity. "What I want you to do now is to help me with my boy, Junior. I've brought Junior up to respect money. I made him earn every nickel he got until he was sixteen, so it isn't my fault that he's a damn fool with money, but he is. I just don't have the time to bother with his bad checks any more. I'm a busy man. You know that. What I want you to do is act as Junior's business adviser. I want you to pay his rent, pay his alimony, pay his maid, pay his household expenses, and give him a cash allowance once a week."

For a moment, anyhow, Victor seemed to breathe the freshness of a considerable skepticism. He had been cheated, that afternoon, out of a vital responsibility and was being burdened now with a foolish one. The tears could be hypocritical. The fact that this request was made to him in a building that had been emptied and was unnaturally quiet and at a time of day when the fading light outside the windows might help to bend his decision were all tricks in the old man's hand. But, even seen skeptically, the hold that Hatherly had on him was complete. "Mr. Hatherly told me to tell you," Victor could always say. "I come from Mr. Hatherly." "Mr. Hatherly . . ." Without this coupling of names his own voice would sound powerless. The comfortable and becoming shirt whose cuffs he shot in indecision had been given to him by Mr. Hatherly. Mr. Hatherly had introduced him into the 7th Regiment. Mr. Hatherly was his only business identity, and to separate himself from this source of power might be mortal. He didn't reply.

"I'm sorry about the presentation," the old man repeated. "I'll see that you make one next year. Promise." He gave his shoulders a hitch to show that he was moving on from this subject to another. "Meet me at the Metropolitan Club tomorrow at two," he said briskly. "I have to buy out Worden at lunch. That won't take long. I hope he brings his lawyer with him. Call his lawyer in the morning and make sure that his papers are in order. Give him hell for me. You know how to do it. You'll help me a great deal by taking care of Junior," he said with great feeling. "And take care of yourself, Victor. You're all I have."

After lunch the next day, the old man's lawyer met them at the Metropolitan Club and went with them to an apartment, where Junior was waiting. He was a thickset man a good ten years older than Victor, and he seemed resigned to having his income taken out of his hands. He called Mr. Hatherly Poppa and sadly handed over to his father a bundle of unpaid bills. With Victor and the lawyer, Mr. Hatherly computed Junior's income and his indebtedness, took into consideration his alimony payments, and arrived at a reasonable estimate for his household expenses and the size of his allowance, which he was to get at Victor's office each Monday morning. Junior's goose was cooked in half an hour.

He came around for his allowance every Monday morning and submitted his household bills to Victor. He sometimes hung around the office and talked about his father—uneasily, as if he might be overheard. All the minutiae of Mr. Hatherly's life—that he was sometimes shaved three times a day and that he owned fifty pairs of shoes—interested Victor. It was the old man who cut these interviews short. "Tell him to come in and get his money and go," the old man said. "This is a business office. That's something he's never understood."

Meanwhile, Victor had met Theresa and was thinking of getting married. Her full name was Theresa Mercereau; her parents were French but she had been born in the

United States. Her parents had died when she was young, and her guardian had put her into fourth-string boarding schools. One knows what these places are like. The headmaster resigns over the Christmas holidays. He is replaced by the gymnastics instructor. The heating plant breaks down in February and the water pipes freeze. By this time, most of the parents who are concerned about their children have transferred them to other schools, and by spring there are only twelve or thirteen boarders left. They wander singly or in pairs around the campus, killing time before supper. It has been apparent to them for months that Old Palfrey Academy is dying, but in the first long, bleakly lighted days of spring this fact assumes new poignancy and force. The noise of a quarrel comes from the headmaster's quarters, where the Latin instructor is threatening to sue for back wages. The smell from the kitchen windows indicates that there will be cabbage again. A few jonquils are in bloom, and the lingering light and the new ferns enjoin the stranded children to look ahead, ahead, but at the back of their minds there is a suspicion that the jonquils and the robins and the evening star imperfectly conceal the fact that this hour is horror, naked horror. Then a car roars up the driveway. "I am Mrs. Hubert Jones," a woman exclaims, "and I have come to get my daughter . . ." Theresa was always one of the last to be rescued, and these hours seemed to have left some impression on her. It was the quality of an especial sadness, a delicacy that was never forlorn, a charming air of having been wronged, that one remembered about her.

That winter, Victor went to Florida with Mr. Hatherly to hoist his beach umbrella and play rummy with him, and while they were there he said that he wanted to get married. The old man yelled his objections. Victor stood his ground. When they returned to New York, the old man invited Victor to bring Theresa to his apartment one evening. He greeted the young woman with great cordiality and then introduced her to Mrs. Hatherly—a wasted and nervous woman who kept her hands at her mouth. The old man began to prowl around the edges of the room. Then he disappeared. "It's all right," Mrs. Hatherly whispered. "He's going to give you a present." He returned in a few minutes and hung a string of amethysts around Theresa's beautiful neck. Once the old man had accepted her, he seemed happy about the marriage. He made all the arrangements for the wedding, of course, told them where to go for a honeymoon, and rented and furnished an apartment for them one day between a business lunch and a plane to California. Theresa seemed, like her husband, to be able to accommodate his interference. When her first child was born, she named it Violet—this was her own idea—after Mr. Hatherly's sainted mother.

When the Mackenzies gave a party, in those years, it was usually because Mr. Hatherly had told them to give a party. He would call Victor into his office at the end of the day, tell him to entertain, and set a date. He would order the liquor and the food, and overhaul the guest list with the Mackenzies' business and social welfare in mind. He would rudely refuse an invitation to come to the party himself, but he would appear before any of the guests, carrying a bunch of flowers that was nearly as tall as he was. He would make sure that Theresa put the flowers in the right vase. Then he would go into the nursery and let Violet listen to his watch. He would go through the apartment, moving a lamp here or an ashtray there and giving the curtains a poke. By this time the Mackenzies' guests would have begun to arrive, but Mr. Hatherly would show no signs of going. He was a distinguished old man and everyone liked to talk with him. He would circle the room, making sure that all the glasses were filled, and if Victor told an anecdote the chances were that Mr. Hatherly had drilled him in how to tell it. When the supper was served, the old man would be anxious about the food and the way the maid looked.

He was always the last to go. When the other guests had said good night, he would settle down and all three would have a glass of milk and talk about the evening. Then the old man would seem happy—with a kind of merriment that his enemies would never have believed him capable of. He would laugh until the tears rolled down his cheeks. He sometimes took off his boots. The small room seemed to be the only room in which he was content, but it must always have been at the back of Mr. Hatherly's mind that these young people were in substance nothing to him, and that it was because his own flesh and blood had been such a bitter disappointment that he found himself in so artificial a position. At last he would get up to go. Theresa would straighten the knot in his tie, brush the crumbs off his vest, and bend down to be kissed. Victor would help him into his fur coat. All three of them would be deep in the tenderness of a family parting. "Take good care of yourselves," the old man would mumble. "You're all I have."

One night, after a party at the Mackenzies', Mr. Hatherly died in his sleep. The funeral was in Worcester, where he was born. The family seemed inclined to keep the arrangements from Victor, but he found out what they were easily enough, and went, with Theresa, to the church and the cemetery. Old Mrs. Hatherly and her unhappy children gathered at the edge of the grave. They must have watched the old man's burial with such conflicting feelings that it would be impossible to extricate from the emotional confusion anything that could be named. "Goodbye, goodbye," Mrs. Hatherly called, halfheartedly, across the earth, and her hands flew to her lips—a habit that she had never been able to break, although the dead man had often threatened to strike her for it. If the full taste of grief is a privilege, this was now the privilege of the Mackenzies. They were crushed. Theresa had been too young when her parents died for her to have, as a grown person, any clear memories of grieving for them, and Victor's parents—whoever they were—had died a few years back, in England or Scotland, and it seemed at Hatherly's grave that she and Victor were in the throes of an accrual of grief and that they were burying more than the bones of one old man. The real children cut the Mackenzies.

The Mackenzies were indifferent to the fact that they were not mentioned in Mr. Hatherly's will. A week or so after the funeral, the directors elected Junior to the presidency of the firm, and one of the first things he did was to fire Victor. He had been compared with this industrious immigrant for years, and his resentment was understandable and deep. Victor found another job, but his intimate association with Mr. Hatherly was held against him in the trade. The old man had a host of enemies, and Victor inherited them all. He lost his new job after six or eight months, and found another that he regarded as temporary—an arrangement that would enable him to meet his monthly bills while he looked around for something better. Nothing better turned up. He and Theresa gave up the apartment that Mr. Hatherly had taken for them, sold all their furniture, and moved around from place to place, but all this—the ugly rooms they lived in, the succession of jobs that Victor took—is not worth going into. To put it simply, the Mackenzies had some hard times; the Mackenzies dropped out of sight.

THE SCENE CHANGES to a fund-raising party for the Girl Scouts of America, in a suburb of Pittsburgh. It is a black-tie dance in a large house—Salisbury Hall—that has been picked by the dance committee with the hope that idle curiosity about this edifice will induce a lot of people to buy the twenty-five-dollar tickets. Mrs. Brownlee, the nominal hostess, is the widow of a pioneer steel magnate. Her house is strung for half a mile along the spine of one of the Allegheny hills. Salisbury Hall is a castle, or, rather, a collection of parts of castles and houses. There is a tower, a battlement, and a dungeon, and the postern gate is a reproduction of the gate at Château Gaillard. The stones and timber for the Great Hall and the armory were brought from abroad. Like most houses of its kind, Salisbury Hall presents insuperable problems of maintenance. Touch a suit of chain mail in the armory and your hand comes away black with rust. The copy of a Mantegna fresco in the ballroom is horribly stained with water. But the party is a success. A hundred couples are dancing. The band is playing a rhumba. The Mackenzies are here.

Theresa is dancing. Her hair is still fair—it may be dyed by now—and her arms and her shoulders are still beautiful. The air of sadness, of delicacy, still clings to her. Victor is not on the dance floor. He is in the orangery, where watery drinks are being sold. He pays for four drinks, walks around the edge of the crowded dance floor, and goes through the armory, where a stranger stops to ask him a question. "Why, yes," Victor says courteously, "I do happen to know about it. It's a suit of mail that was made for the coronation of Philip II. Mr. Brownlee had it copied . . ." He continues along another quarter of a mile of halls and parlors, through the Great

Hall, to a small parlor, where Mrs. Brownlee is sitting with some friends. "Here's Vic with our drinks!" she cries. Mrs. Brownlee is an old lady, plucked and painted and with her hair dyed an astonishing shade of pink. Her fingers and her forearms are loaded with rings and bracelets. Her diamond necklace is famous. So, indeed, are most of her jewels—most of them have names. There are the Taphir emeralds, the Bertolotti rubies, and the Demidoff pearls, and, feeling that a look at this miscellany should be included in the price of admission, she has loaded herself unsparingly for the benefit of the Girl Scouts. "Everybody's having a good time, aren't they, Vic?" she asks. "Well, they should be having a good time. My house has always been known for its atmosphere of hospitality as well as for its wealth of artistic treasures. Sit down, Vic," she says. "Sit down. Give yourself a little rest. I don't know what I'd do without you and Theresa." But Victor doesn't have time to sit down. He has to run the raffle. He goes back through the Great Hall, the Venetian Salon, and the armory, to the ballroom. He climbs onto a chair. There is a flourish of music. "Ladies and gentlemen!" he calls through a megaphone. "Ladies and gentlemen, can I have your attention for a few minutes . . ." He raffles off a case of Scotch, a case of bourbon, a Waring mixer, and a power lawn mower. When the raffle is over and the dancing begins again, he goes out onto the terrace for a breath of air, and we follow him and speak to him there.

"Victor?"

"Oh, how nice to see you again," he exclaims. "What in the world are you doing in Pittsburgh?" His hair has grayed along conventionally handsome lines. He must have had some work done on his teeth, because his smile is whiter and more dazzling than ever. The talk is the conversation of acquaintances who have not met for ten or fifteen years—it has been that long—about this and that, then about Theresa, then about Violet. At the mention of Violet, he seems very sad. He sets the megaphone on the stone terrace and leans on its metal rim. He bows his head. "Well, Violet is sixteen now, you know," he says. "She's given me a lot to worry about. She was suspended from school about six weeks ago. Now I've got her into a new school in Connecticut. It took a lot of doing." He sniffs.

"How long have you been in Pittsburgh, Victor?"

"Eight years," he says. He swings the megaphone into the air and peers through it at a star. "Nine, actually," he says.

"What are you doing, Victor?"

"I'm between jobs now." He lets the megaphone fall.

"Where are you living, Victor?"

"Here," he says.

"I know. But where in Pittsburgh?"

"Here," he says. He laughs. "We live here. At Salisbury Hall. Here's the head of the dance committee, and if you'll excuse me, I'll make my report on the raffle. It's been very nice to see you again."

ANYONE—ANYONE, that is, who did not eat peas off a knife—might have been invited to Salisbury Hall when the Mackenzies first went there. They had only just arrived in Pittsburgh, and were living in a hotel. They drove out with some friends for a weekend. There were fourteen or fifteen guests in the party, and Prescott Brownlee, the old lady's eldest son. There was some trouble before dinner. Prescott got drunk at a roadhouse near the estate, and the bartender called Mrs. Brownlee and told her to have him removed before he called the police. The old lady was used to this kind of trouble. Her children were in it most of the time, but that afternoon she did not know where to turn for help. Nils, the houseman, hated Prescott. The gardener had gone home. Ernest, the butler, was too old. Then she remembered Victor's face, although she had only glimpsed it in the hall when they were introduced. She found him in the Great Hall and called him aside. He thought he was going to be asked to mix the cocktails. When she made her request, he said that he would be glad to help. He drove to the roadhouse, where he found Prescott sitting at a table. Someone had given him a bloody nose, and his clothing was splattered with blood, but he was still pugnacious, and when Victor told him to come home, he got up swinging. Victor knocked him down. This subdued Prescott, who began to cry and stumbled obediently out to the car. Victor returned to Salisbury Hall by a service driveway. Then, supporting Prescott, who could not walk, he got him into a side door that opened into the armory. No one saw them. The air in the unheated room was harsh and bitter. Victor pushed the sobbing drunk under the rags of royal battle flags and pennants that hung from the rafters and past a statue of a man on horseback that displayed a suit of equestrian armor. He got Prescott up a marble staircase and put him to bed. Then he brushed the sawdust off his own evening clothes and went down to the Great Hall and made the cocktails.

He didn't mention this incident to anyone—not even to Theresa—and on Sunday afternoon Mrs. Brownlee took him aside again, to thank him. "Oh, bless your heart, Mr. Mackenzie!" she said. "You're a good Samaritan. When that man called me up yesterday, I didn't know where to turn." They heard someone approaching across the Great Hall. It was Prescott. He had shaved, dressed his wounds, and soaked his hair down with water, but he was drunk again. "Going to New York," he mumbled to his mother. "Ernest's going to drive me to the plane. *See* you." He turned and wandered back across the library into the Venetian Salon and out of sight, and his mother set her teeth as she watched him go. Then she seized Victor's hand and said, "I want you and your lovely wife to come and live at Salisbury Hall. I know that you're living in a hotel. My house has always been known for its atmosphere of hospitality as well as for its wealth of artistic treasures. You'll be doing me a favor. That's what it amounts to."

The Mackenzies gracefully declined her offer and returned to Pittsburgh on Sunday night. A few days later, the old lady, hearing that Theresa was sick in bed, sent flowers, and a note repeating her invitation. The Mackenzies discussed it that night. "We must think of it as a business arrangement, if we think of it at all," Victor said. "We must think of it as the practical answer to a practical problem." Theresa had always been frail, and living in the country would be good for her. This was the first thing they thought of. Victor had a job in town, but he could commute from the railroad station nearest Salisbury Hall. They talked with Mrs. Brownlee again and got her to agree to accept from them what they would have paid for rent and food, so that the arrangement would be kept impersonal. Then they moved into a suite of rooms above the Great Hall.

It worked out very well. Their rooms were large and quiet, and the relationship with Mrs. Brownlee was easygoing. Any sense of obligation they may have felt was dispelled by their knowing that they were useful to their hostess in a hundred ways. She needed a man around the place, and who else would want to live in Salisbury Hall? Except for gala occasions, more than half the rooms were shut, and there were not enough servants to intimidate the rats that lived in the basement. Theresa undertook the herculean task of repairing Mrs. Brownlee's needlepoint; there were eighty-six pieces. The tennis court at Salisbury Hall had been neglected since the war, and Victor, on his weekends, weeded and rolled it and got it in shape again. He absorbed a lot of information about Mrs. Brownlee's house and her scattered family, and when she was too tired to take interested guests around the place, he was always happy to. "This hall," he would say, "was removed panel by panel and stone by stone from a Tudor house near the cathedral in Salisbury. . . . The marble floor is part of the lobby floor of the old First National Bank. . . . Mr. Brownlee gave Mrs. Brownlee the Venetian Salon as a birthday present, and these four columns of solid onyx came from the ruins of Herculaneum. They were floated down Lake Erie from Buffalo to Ashtabula. . . ." Victor could also point out the scar on a tree where Spencer Brownlee had wrecked his car, and the rose garden that had been planted for Hester Brownlee when she was so sick. We have seen how helpful he was on occasions like the dance for the Girl Scout fund.

Violet was away in camps and schools. "Why do you live here?" she asked the first time she came to visit her parents in Salisbury Hall. "What a moldy old wreck! What a regular junk heap!" Mrs. Brownlee may have heard Violet laughing at her house. In any event, she took a violent dislike to the Mackenzies' only child, and Violet's visits were infrequent and brief. The only one of Mrs. Brownlee's children who returned from time to time was Prescott. Then, one evening not long after the Girl Scout dance, Mrs. Brownlee got a wire from her daughter Hester, who had been living in Europe for fifteen years. She had arrived in New York and was coming on to Pittsburgh the following day.

Mrs. Brownlee told the Mackenzies the good news at dinner. She was transported. "Oh, you'll love Hester," she said. "You'll both love her! She was always just like Dresden china. She was sickly when she was a child and I guess that's why she's always been my favorite. Oh, I hope she'll stay! I wish there was time to have her rooms painted! You must urge her to stay, Victor. It would make me so happy. You urge her to stay. I think she'll like you."

Mrs. Brownlee's words echoed through a dining room that had the proportions of a gymnasium; their small table was pushed against a window and separated from the rest of the room by a screen, and the Mackenzies liked to have dinner there. The window looked down the lawns and stairways to the ruin of a formal garden. The iron lace on the roof of the broken greenhouses, the noise of the fountains whose basins were disfigured and cracked, the rattle of the dumbwaiter that brought their tasteless dinner up from the basement kitchens, where the rats lived—the Mackenzies regarded all this foolishness with the deepest respect, as if it had some genuine significance. They may have suffered from an indiscriminate sense of the past or from an inability to understand that the past plays no part in our happiness. A few days earlier, Theresa had stumbled into a third-floor bedroom that was full of old bon-voyage baskets—gilded, and looped with dog-eared ribbons—that had been saved from Mrs. Brownlee's many voyages.

While Mrs. Brownlee talked about Hester that evening, she kept her eye on the garden and saw, in the distance, a man climbing over one of the marble walls. Then a girl handed him down a blanket, a picnic hamper, and a bottle, and jumped into his arms. They were followed by two more couples. They settled themselves in the Temple of Love and, gathering a pile of broken latticework, built a little fire.

"Drive them away, Victor," Mrs. Brownlee said.

Victor left the table and crossed the terrace and went down to the garden and told the party to go.

"I happen to be a very good friend of Mrs. Brownlee's," one of the men said.

"That doesn't matter," Victor said. "You'll have to get out."

"Who says so?"

"I say so."

"Who are you?"

Victor didn't answer. He broke up their fire and stamped out the embers. He was outnumbered and outweighed, and he knew that if it came to a fight, he would probably get hurt, but the smoke from the extinguished fire drove the party out of the temple and gave Victor an advantage. He stood on a flight of steps above them and looked at his watch. "I'll give you five minutes to get over the wall and out," he said.

"But I'm a friend of Mrs. Brownlee's!"

"If you're a friend of Mrs. Brownlee's," Victor said, "come in the front way. I give you five minutes." They started down the path toward the wall, and Victor waited until one of the girls—they were all pretty—had been hoisted over it. Then he went back to the table and finished his dinner while Mrs. Brownlee talked on and on about Little Hester.

The next day was Saturday, but Victor spent most of it in Pittsburgh, looking for work. He didn't get out to Salisbury Hall until about four, and he was hot and dirty. When he stepped into the Great Hall, he saw that the doors onto the terrace were open and the florist's men were unloading a truck full of tubbed orange trees. A maid came up to him excitedly. "Nils is sick and can't drive!" she exclaimed. "Mrs. Brownlee wants you to go down to the station and meet Miss Hester. You'd better hurry. She's coming on the four-fifteen. She doesn't want you to take your car. She wants you to take the Rolls-Royce. She says you have permission to take the Rolls-Royce."

The four-fifteen had come and gone by the time Victor arrived at the station. Hester Brownlee was standing in the waiting room, surrounded by her luggage. She was a middle-aged woman who had persevered with her looks, and might at a distance have seemed pretty. "How do you do, Miss Brownlee?" Victor said. "I'm Victor Mackenzie. I'm—"

"Yes, I know," she said. "I've heard all about you from Prescott." She looked past his shoulder. "You're late."

"I'm sorry," Victor said, "but your mother—"

"These are my bags," she said. She walked out to the Rolls-Royce and got into the back seat.

Victor lighted a cigarette and smoked it halfway down. Then he carried her bags out to the car and started home to Salisbury Hall along a back road.

"You're going the wrong way," Miss Brownlee called. "Don't you *even* know the way?"

"I'm not going the usual way," Victor said patiently, "but a few years ago they built a factory down the road, and the traffic is heavy around closing time. It's quicker this way. But I expect that you'll find a good many changes in the neighborhood. How long has it been, Miss Brownlee, since you've seen Salisbury Hall?" There was no answer to his question, and, thinking that she might not have heard him, he asked again, "How long has it been, Miss Brownlee, since you've seen Salisbury Hall?"

They made the rest of the trip in silence. When they got to the house, Victor unloaded her bags and stood them by the door. Miss Brownlee counted them aloud. Then she opened her purse and handed Victor a quarter. "Why, thank you!" Victor said. "Thank you *very* much!" He went down into the garden to walk off his anger. He decided not to tell Theresa about this meeting. Finally, he went upstairs. Theresa was at work on one of the needlepoint stools. The room they used for a parlor was cluttered with half-repaired needlepoint. She embraced Victor tenderly, as she always did when they had been separated for a day. Victor had dressed when a maid knocked on the door. "Mrs. Brownlee wants to see you, both of you," she said. "She's in the office. At once."

Theresa clung to Victor's arm as they went downstairs. The office, a cluttered and dirty room beside the elevator, was brightly lighted. Mrs. Brownlee, in *grande tenue*, sat at her husband's desk. "You're the straw that broke the camel's back—both of you," she said harshly when they came in. "Shut the door. I don't want everybody to hear me. Little Hester has come home for the first time in fifteen years, and the first thing she gets off the train, you have to insult her. For nine years, you've had the privilege of living in this beautiful house—a wonder of the world—and how do you repay me? Oh, it's the straw that breaks the camel's back! Prescott's told me often enough that you weren't any good, either of you, and Hester feels the same way, and gradually I'm beginning to see it myself."

The harried and garishly painted old lady wielded over the Mackenzies the power of angels. Her silver dress glittered like St. Michael's raiment, and thunder and lightning, death and destruction, were in her right hand. "Everybody's been warning me about you for years," she said. "And you may not mean to do wrong—you may just be unlucky—but one of the first things Hester noticed is that half the needlepoint is missing. You're always repairing the chair that I want to sit down in. And you, Victor—you told me that you fixed the tennis court, and, of course, I don't know about that because I can't play tennis, but when I asked the Beardons over to play tennis last week, they told me that the court wasn't fit to play on, and you can imagine how embarrassed I was, and those people you drove out of the garden last night turned out to be the children of a very dear friend of the late Mr. Brownlee's. And you're two weeks behind with your rent."

"I'll send you the rent," Victor said. "We will go."

Theresa had not taken her arm out of his during the interview, and they left the office together. It was raining, and Ernest was putting out pails in the Venetian Salon, where the domed ceiling had sprung a leak. "Could you help me with some suitcases?" Victor asked. The old butler must have overheard the interview, because he didn't answer.

There was in the Mackenzies' rooms an accumulation of sentimental possessions—photographs, pieces of silver, and so forth. Theresa hastily began to gather these up. Victor went down to the basement and got their bags. They packed hurriedly—they did not even stop to smoke a cigarette—but it took them most of the evening. When they had finished, Theresa stripped the bed and put the soiled towels into a hamper, and Victor carried the bags down. He wrote a postcard to Violet's school, saying that his address was no longer Salisbury Hall. He waited for Theresa by the front door. "Oh, my darling, where will we go?" she murmured when she met him there. She waited in the rain for him to bring their car around, and they drove away, and God knows where they did go after that.

GOD KNOWS where they went after that, but for our purposes they next appeared, years later, at a resort on the coast of Maine called Horsetail Beach. Victor had some kind of job in New York, and they had driven to Maine for his vacation. Violet was not with them. She had married and was living in San Francisco. She had a baby. She did not write to her parents, and Victor knew that she thought of him with bitter resentment, although he did not know why. The waywardness of their only child troubled Victor and Theresa, but they could seldom bring themselves to discuss it. Helen Jackson, their hostess at Horsetail Beach, was a spirited young woman with four children. She was divorced. Her house was tracked with sand, and most of the furniture was broken. The Mackenzies arrived there on a stormy evening when the north wind blew straight through the walls of the house. Their hostess was out to dinner, and as soon as they arrived, the cook put on her hat and coat and went off to the movies, leaving them in charge of the children. They carried their bags upstairs, stepping over several wet bathing suits, put the four children to bed, and settled themselves in a cold guest room.

In the morning, their hostess asked them if they minded if she drove into Camden to get her hair washed. She was giving a cocktail party for the Mackenzies that afternoon, although it was the cook's day off. She promised to be back by noon, and when she had not returned by one, Theresa cooked lunch. At three, their hostess telephoned from Camden to say that she had just left the hairdresser's and would Theresa mind getting a head start with the canapés? Theresa made the canapés. Then she swept the sand out of the living room and picked up the wet bathing suits. Helen Jackson finally returned from Camden, and the guests began to arrive at five. It was cold and stormy. Victor shivered in his white silk suit. Most of the guests were young, and they refused cocktails and drank ginger ale, gathered around the piano, and sang. It was not the Mackenzies' idea of a good party. Helen Jackson tried unsuccessfully to draw them into the circle of hearty, if meaningless, smiles, salutations, and handshakes upon which that party, like every other, was rigged. The guests all left at half past six, and the Mackenzies and their hostess made a supper of leftover canapés. "Would you mind dreadfully taking the children to the movies?" Helen Jackson asked Victor. "I promised them they could go to the movies if they were good about the party, and they've been perfect angels, and I hate to disappoint them, and I'm dead myself."

The next morning, it was still raining. Victor could see by his wife's face that the house and the weather were a drain on her strength. Most of us are inured to the inconveniences of a summer house in a cold rain, but Theresa was not. The power that the iron bedsteads and the paper window curtains had on her spirit was out of proportion, as if these were not ugly objects in themselves but threatened to overwhelm her common sense. At breakfast, their hostess suggested that they take a drive in the rain. "I know that it's vile out," she said, "but you could drive to Camden, and it's a way of killing time, isn't it, and you go through a lot of enchanting little villages, and if you did go down to Camden, you could go to the rental library and get *The Silver Chalice*. They've been reserving it for days and days, and I never find the time to get it. The rental library is on Estrella Lane." The Mackenzies drove to Camden and got *The Silver Chalice*. When they returned, there was another chore for Victor. The battery in Helen Jackson's car was dead. He took it to the garage and got a rental battery and installed it. Then, in spite of the weather, he tried to go swimming, but the waves were high and full of gravel, and after diving once he gave up and went back to the house. When he walked into the guest room in his wet bathing trunks, Theresa raised her face and he saw that it was stained with tears. "Oh, my darling," she said, "I'm homesick."

It was, even for Victor, a difficult remark to interpret. Their only home then was a one-room apartment in the city, which, with its kitchenette and studio couch, seemed oddly youthful and transitory for these grandparents. If Theresa was homesick, it could only be for a collection of parts of houses. She must have meant something else.

"Then we'll go," he said. "We'll leave the first thing in the morning." And then, seeing how happy his words had made her, he went on. "We'll get into the car and we'll drive and we'll drive and we'll drive. We'll go to Canada."

When they told Helen Jackson, at dinner, that they were leaving in the morning, she seemed relieved. She got out a road map and marked with a pencil the best route up through the mountains to Ste. Marie and the border. The Mackenzies packed after dinner and left early in the morning. Helen came out to the driveway to say goodbye. She was wearing her wrapper and carrying a silver coffeepot. "It's been perfectly lovely to have you," she said, "even if the weather has been so vile and disagreeable and horrid, and since you've decided to go through Ste. Marie, would you mind terribly stopping for a minute and returning Aunt Marly's silver coffeepot? I borrowed it years ago, and she's been writing me threatening letters and telephoning, and you can just leave it on the doorstep and run. Her name is Mrs. Sauer. The house is near the main road." She gave the Mackenzies some sketchy directions, kissed Theresa, and handed her the coffeepot. "It's been simply wonderful having you," she called as they drove away.

The waves at Horsetail Beach were still high and the wind was cold when the Mackenzies turned their back on the Atlantic Ocean. The noise and the smell of the sea faded. Inland, the sky seemed to be clearing. The wind was westerly and the overcast began to be displaced with light and motion. The Mackenzies came into hilly farmland. It was country they had never seen before, and as the massive clouds broke and the dilated light poured onto it, Theresa felt her spirits rising. She felt as if she were in a house on the Mediterranean, opening doors and windows. It was a house that she had never been in. She had only seen a picture of it, years ago, on a postcard. The saffron walls of the house continued straight down into the blue water, and all the doors and windows were shut. Now she was opening them. It was at the beginning of summer. She was opening doors and windows, and, leaning into the light from one of the highest, she saw a single sail, disappearing in the direction of Africa, carrying the wicked King away. How else could she account for the feeling of perfect contentment that she felt? She sat in the car with her arm and her shoulder against her husband's, as she always did. As they came into the mountains, she noticed that the air seemed cooler and lighter, but the image of opening doors and windows—doors that stuck at the sill, shuttered windows, casement windows, windows with sash weights, and all of them opening onto the water—stayed in her mind until they came down, at dusk, into the little river resort of Ste. Marie.

"God damn that woman," Victor said; Mrs. Sauer's house was not where Helen Jackson had said it would be. If the coffeepot had not looked valuable, he would have thrown it into a ditch and driven on. They turned up a dirt road that ran parallel to the river, and stopped at a gas station and got out of the car to ask directions. "Sure, sure," the man said. "I know where the Sauers' place is. Their landing's right across the road, and the boatman was in here a minute ago." He threw open the screen door and shouted through his hands. "Perley! There's some people here want to get over to the island."

"I want to leave something," Victor said.

"He'll take you over. It makes a pretty ride this time of day. He don't have nothing to do. He's in here talking my ear off most of the time. Perley! Perley!"

The Mackenzies crossed the road with him to where a crooked landing reached into the water. An old man was polishing the brass on a launch. "I'll take you over and bring you right back," he said.

"I'll wait here," Theresa said.

Trees grew down to the banks on both shores; they touched the water in places. The river at this point was wide, and as it curved between the mountains she could see upstream for miles. The breadth of the view pleased her, and she hardly heard Victor and the boatman talking. "Tell the lady to come," the old man said.

"Theresa?"

She turned, and Victor gave her a hand into the boat. The old man put a dirty yachting cap on his head, and they started upstream. The current was strong, and the boat moved against it slowly, and at first they could not make out any islands, but then they saw water and light separate from the mainland what they had thought was a peninsula. They passed through some narrows and, swinging around abruptly—it was all strange and new to them—came up to a landing in a cove. Victor followed a path that led from the landing up to an old-fashioned frame camp stained the color of molasses. The arbor that joined the house to the garden was made of cedar posts, from which the bark hung in strips among the roses. Victor rang the bell. An old servant opened the door and led him through the house and out to the porch, where Mrs. Sauer was sitting with some sewing in her lap. She thanked him for bringing the coffeepot and, as he was about to leave, asked him if he were alone.

"Mrs. Mackenzie is with me," Victor said. "We're driving to Quebec."

"Well, as Talbot used to say, the time has come for the drinking to begin," the old lady said. "If you and your wife would stop long enough to have a cocktail with me, you would be doing me a great favor. That's what it amounts to."

Victor got Theresa, who was waiting in the arbor, and brought her to the porch.

"I know how rushed you children always are," the old lady said. "I know what a kindness it is for you to stop, but Mr. Sauer and I've been quite lonely up here this season. Here I sit, hemming curtains for the cook's room. What a bore!" She held up her sewing and let it fall. "And since you've been kind enough to stay for a cocktail, I'm going to ask another favor. I'm going to ask you to mix the cocktails. Agnes, who let you in, usually makes them, and she waters the gin. You'll find everything in the pantry. Go straight through the dining room."

Navajo rugs covered the floor of the big living room. The fireplace chimney was made of fieldstone, and fixed to it was, of course, a pair of antlers. At the end of the large and cheerless dining room, Victor found the pantry. The old servant brought him the shaker and the bottles.

"Well, I'm glad you're staying," she said. "I knew she was going to ask you. She's been so lonely this season that I'm worried for her. She's a lovely person—oh, she's a lovely person—but she hasn't been like herself. She begins to drink at about eleven in the morning. Sometimes earlier." The shaker was a sailing trophy. The heavy silver tray had been presented to Mr. Sauer by his business associates.

When Victor returned to the porch, Theresa was hemming the curtains. "How good it is to taste gin again," old Mrs. Sauer exclaimed. "I don't know what Agnes thinks she's accomplishing by watering the cocktails. She's a most devoted and useful servant, and I would be helpless without her, but she's growing old, she's growing old. I sometimes think she's lost her mind. She hides the soap chips in the icebox and sleeps at night with a hatchet under her pillow."

"To what good fortune do we owe this charming visitation?" the old gentleman asked when he joined them. He drew off his gardening gloves and slipped his rose shears into the pocket of his checked coat.

"Isn't it generous of these children to stop and have a drink with us?" Mrs. Sauer said, when they had been introduced. The old man did not seem surprised at hearing the Mackenzies described as children. "They've come from Horsetail Beach and they're on their way to Quebec."

"Mrs. Sauer and I have always detested Horsetail Beach," the old gentleman said. "When do you plan to reach Quebec?"

"Tonight," Victor said.

"Tonight?" Mrs. Sauer asked.

"I doubt that you can reach Quebec tonight," the old gentleman said.

"I suppose you can do it," the old lady said, "the way you children drive, but you'll be more dead than alive. Stay for dinner. Stay the night."

"Do stay for dinner," the old man said.

"You will, won't you?" Mrs. Sauer said. "I will not take no for an answer! I am old and privileged, and if you say no, I'll claim to be deaf and pretend not to hear you. And now that you've decided to stay, make another round of these delicious cocktails and tell Agnes that you are to have Talbot's room. Tell her tactfully. She hates guests. Remember that she's very old."

Victor carried the sailing trophy back into the house, which, in spite of its many large windows, seemed in the early dark like a cave. "Mrs. Mackenzie and I are staying for dinner and the night," he told Agnes. "She said that we were to have Talbot's room."

"Well, that's nice. Maybe it will make her happy. She's had a lot of sorrow in her life. I think it's affected her mind. I knew she was going to ask you, and I'm glad you can stay. It makes me happy. It's more dishes to wash and more beds to make, but it's more—it's more—"

"It's more merrier?"

"Oh, that's it, that's it." The old servant shook with laughter. "You remind me a little of Mr. Talbot. He was always making jokes with me when he came out here to mix the cocktails. God have mercy on his soul. It's hard to realize," she said sadly.

Walking back through the cavelike living room, Victor could hear Theresa and Mrs. Sauer discussing the night air, and he noticed that the cold air had begun to come down from the mountains. He felt it in the room. There were flowers somewhere in the dark, and the night air had heightened their smell and the smell of the boulders in the chimney, so the room smelled like a cave with flowers in it. "Everyone says that the view looks like Salzburg," Mrs. Sauer said, "but I'm patriotic and I can't see that views are improved by such comparisons. They do seem to be improved by good company, however. We used to entertain, but now—"

"Yes, yes," the old gentleman said, and sighed. He uncorked a bottle of citronella and rubbed his wrists and the back of his neck.

"There!" Theresa said. "The cook's curtains are done!"

"Oh, how can I thank you!" Mrs. Sauer said. "Now if someone would be kind enough to get my glasses, I could admire your needlework. They're on the mantelpiece."

Victor found her glasses—not on the mantelpiece but on a nearby table. He gave them to her and then walked up and down the porch a few times. He managed to suggest that he was no longer a chance guest but had become a member of the family. He sat down on the steps, and Theresa joined him there. "Look at them," the old lady said to her husband. "Doesn't it do you good to see, for a change, young people who love one another? . . . There goes the sunset gun. My brother George bought that gun for the yacht club. It was his pride and his joy. Isn't it quiet this evening?"

But the tender looks and attitudes that Mrs. Sauer took for pure love were only the attitudes of homeless summer children who had found a respite. Oh, how sweet, how precious the hour seemed to them! Lights burned on another island. Stamped on the twilight was the iron lace of a broken greenhouse roof. What poor magpies. Their ways and airs were innocent; their bones were infirm. Indeed, they impersonated the dead. Come away, come away, sang the wind in the trees and the grass, but it did not sing to the Mackenzies. They turned their heads instead to hear old Mrs. Sauer. "I'm going up to put on my green velvet," she said, "but if you children don't feel like dressing . . ."

Waiting on table that night Agnes thought that she had not seen such a gay dinner in a long time. She heard them go off after dinner to play billiards on the table that had been bought for poor, dead Talbot. A little rain fell, but, unlike the rain at Horsetail Beach, this was a gentle and excursive mountain shower. Mrs. Sauer yawned at eleven, and the game broke up. They said good night in the upstairs hall, by the pictures of Talbot's crew, Talbot's pony, and Talbot's class. "Good night, good night," Mrs. Sauer exclaimed, and then set her face, determined to overstep her manners, and declared, "I am delighted that you agreed to stay. I can't tell you how much it means. I'm—" Tears started from her eyes.

"It's lovely to be here," Theresa said.

"Good night, children," Mrs. Sauer said.

"Good night, good night," Mr. Sauer said.

"Good night," Victor said.

"Good night, good night," Theresa said.

"Sleep well," Mrs. Sauer said. "And pleasant dreams."

Ten days later, the Sauers were expecting some other guests—some young cousins named Wycherly. They had never been to the house before, and they came up the path late in the afternoon. Victor opened the door to them. "I'm Victor Mackenzie," he said cheerfully. He wore tennis shorts and a pullover, but when he bent down to pick up a suitcase, his knees creaked loudly: "The Sauers are out driving with my wife," he explained. "They'll be back by six, when the drinking begins." The cousins followed him across the big living room and up the stairs. "Mrs. Sauer is giving you Uncle George's room," he said, "because it has the best view and the most hot water. It's the only room that's been added to the house since Mr. Sauer's father built the place in 1903. . . ."

The young cousins did not quite know what to make of him. Was he a cousin himself? an uncle, perhaps? a poor relation? But it was a comfortable house and a brilliant day, and in the end they would take Victor for what he appeared to be, and he appeared to be very happy.

THE SORROWS OF GIN

IT WAS SUNDAY AFTERNOON, and from her bedroom Amy could hear the Beardens coming in, followed a little while later by the Farquarsons and the Parminters. She went on reading *Black Beauty* until she felt in her bones that they might be eating something good. Then she closed her book and went down the stairs. The living-room door was shut, but through it she could hear the noise of loud talk and laughter. They must have been gossiping or worse, because they all stopped talking when she entered the room.

"Hi, Amy," Mr. Farquarson said.

"Mr. Farquarson spoke to you, Amy," her father said.

"Hello, Mr. Farquarson," she said. By standing outside the group for a minute, until they had resumed their conversation, and then by slipping past Mrs. Farquarson, she was able to swoop down on the nut dish and take a handful.

"Amy!" Mr. Lawton said.

"I'm sorry, Daddy," she said, retreating out of the circle, toward the piano.

"Put those nuts back," he said.

"I've handled them, Daddy," she said.

"Well, pass the nuts, dear," her mother said sweetly. "Perhaps someone else would like nuts."

Amy filled her mouth with the nuts she had taken, returned to the coffee table, and passed the nut dish.

"Thank you, Amy," they said, taking a peanut or two.

"How do you like your new school, Amy?" Mrs. Bearden asked.

"I like it," Amy said. "I like private schools better than public schools. It isn't so much like a factory."

"What grade are you in?" Mrs. Bearden asked.

"Fourth," she said.

Her father took Mr. Parminter's glass and his own, and got up to go into the dining room and refill them. She fell into the chair he had left vacant.

"Don't sit in your father's chair, Amy," her mother said, not realizing that Amy's legs were worn out from riding a bicycle, while her father had done nothing but sit down all day.

As she walked toward the French doors, she heard her mother beginning to talk about the new cook. It was a good example of the interesting things they found to talk about.

"You'd better put your bicycle in the garage," her father said, returning with the fresh drinks. "It looks like rain."

Amy went out onto the terrace and looked at the sky, but it was not very cloudy, it wouldn't rain, and his advice, like all the advice he gave her, was superfluous. They were always at her. "Put your bicycle away." "Open the door for Grandmother, Amy." "Feed the cat." "Do your homework." "Pass the nuts." "Help Mrs. Bearden with her parcels." "Amy, please try and take more pains with your appearance."

They all stood, and her father came to the door and called her. "We're going over to the Parminters' for supper," he said. "Cook's here, so you won't be alone. Be sure and go to bed at eight like a good girl. And come and kiss me good night."

After their cars had driven off, Amy wandered through the kitchen to the cook's bedroom beyond it and knocked on the door. "Come in," a voice said, and when Amy entered, she found the cook, whose name was Rosemary, in her bathrobe, reading the Bible. Rosemary smiled at Amy. Her smile was sweet and her old eyes were blue. "Your parents have gone out again?" she asked. Amy said that they had, and the old woman invited her to sit down. "They do seem to enjoy themselves, don't they? During the four days I've been here, they've been out every night, or had people in." She put the Bible face down on her lap and smiled, but not at Amy. "Of course, the drinking that goes on here is all sociable, and what your parents do is none of my business, is it? I worry about drink more than most people, because of my poor sister. My poor sister drank too much. For ten years, I went to visit her on Sunday afternoons, and most of the time she was *non compos mentis*. Sometimes I'd find her huddled up on the floor with one or two sherry bottles empty beside her. Sometimes she'd seem sober enough to a stranger, but I could tell in a second by the way she spoke her words that she'd drunk enough not to be herself any more. Now my poor sister is gone, I don't have anyone to visit at all."

"What happened to your sister?" Amy asked.

"She was a lovely person, with a peaches-and-cream complexion and fair hair," Rosemary said. "Gin makes some people gay—it makes them laugh and cry—but with my sister it only made her sullen and withdrawn. When she was drinking, she would retreat into herself. Drink made her contrary. If I'd say the weather was fine, she'd tell me I was wrong. If I'd say it was raining, she'd say it was clearing. She'd correct me about everything I said, however small it was. She died in Bellevue Hospital one summer while I was working in Maine. She was the only family I had."

The directness with which Rosemary spoke had the effect on Amy of making her feel grown, and for once politeness came to her easily. "You must miss your sister a great deal," she said.

"I was just sitting here now thinking about her. She was in service, like me, and it's lonely work. You're always surrounded by a family, and yet you're never a part of it. Your pride is often hurt. The Madams seem condescending and inconsiderate. I'm not blaming the ladies I've worked for. It's just the nature of the relationship. They order chicken salad, and you get up before dawn to get ahead of yourself, and just as you've finished the chicken salad, they change their minds and want crab-meat soup."

"My mother changes her mind all the time," Amy said.

"Sometimes you're in a country place with nobody else in help. You're tired, but not too tired to feel lonely. You go out onto the servants' porch when the pots and pans are done, planning to enjoy God's creation, and although the front of the house may have a fine view of the lake or the mountains, the view from the back is never much. But there is the sky and the trees and the stars and the birds singing and the pleasure of resting your feet. But then you hear them in the front of the house, laughing and talking with their guests and their sons and daughters. If you're new and they whisper, you can be sure they're talking about you. That takes all the pleasure out of the evening."

"Oh," Amy said.

"I've worked all kinds of places—places where there were eight or nine in help and places where I was expected to burn the rubbish myself, on winter nights, and shovel the snow. In a house where there's a lot of help, there's usually some devil among them—some old butler or parlormaid—who tries to make your life miserable from the beginning. 'The Madam doesn't like it this way,' and 'The Madam doesn't like it that way,' and 'I've been with the Madam for twenty years,' they tell you. It takes a diplomat to get along. Then there is the rooms they give you, and every one of them I've ever seen is cheerless. If you have a bottle in your suitcase, it's a terrible temptation in the beginning not to take a drink to raise your spirits. But I have a strong character. It was different with my poor sister. She used to complain about nervousness, but, sitting here thinking about her tonight, I wonder if she suffered from nervousness at all. I wonder if she didn't make it all up. I wonder if she just wasn't meant to be in service. Toward the end, the only work she could get was out in the country, where nobody else would go, and she never lasted much more than a week or two. She'd take a little gin for her nervousness, then a little for her tiredness, and when she'd drunk her own bottle and everything she could steal, they'd hear about it in the front part of the house. There was usually a scene, and my poor sister always liked to have the last word. Oh, if I had had my way, they'd be a law against it! It's not my business to advise you to take anything from your father, but I'd be proud of you if you'd empty his gin bottle into the sink now and then—the filthy stuff! But it's made me feel better to talk with you, sweetheart. It's made me not miss my poor sister so much. Now I'll read a little more in my Bible, and then I'll get you some supper."

THE LAWTONS had had a bad year with cooks—there had been five of them. The arrival of Rosemary had made Marcia Lawton think back to a vague theory of dispensations; she had suffered, and now she was being rewarded. Rosemary was clean, industrious, and cheerful, and her table—as the Lawtons said—was just like the Chambord. On Wednesday night after dinner, she took the train to New York, promising to return on the evening train Thursday. Thursday morning, Marcia went into the cook's room. It was a distasteful but a habitual precaution. The absence of anything personal in the room—a package of cigarettes, a fountain pen, an alarm clock, a radio, or anything else that could tie the old woman to the place—gave her the uneasy feeling that she was being deceived, as she had so often been deceived by cooks in the past. She opened the closet door and saw a single uniform hanging there and, on the closet floor, Rosemary's old suitcase and the white shoes she wore in the kitchen. The suitcase was locked, but when Marcia lifted it, it seemed to be nearly empty.

Mr. Lawton and Amy drove to the station after dinner on Thursday to meet the eight-sixteen train. The top of the car was down, and the brisk air, the starlight, and the company of her father made the little girl feel kindly toward the world. The railroad station in Shady Hill resembled the railroad stations in old movies she had seen on television, where detectives and spies, bluebeards and their trusting victims, were met to be driven off to remote country estates. Amy liked the station, particularly toward dark. She imagined that the people who traveled on the locals were engaged on errands that were more urgent and sinister than commuting. Except when there was a heavy fog or a snowstorm, the club car that her father traveled on seemed to have the gloss and the monotony of the rest of his life. The locals that ran at odd hours belonged to a world of deeper contrasts, where she would like to live.

They were a few minutes early, and Amy got out of the car and stood on the platform. She wondered what the fringe of string that hung above the tracks at either end of the station was for, but she knew enough not to ask her father, because he wouldn't be able to tell her. She could hear the train before it came into view, and the noise excited her and made her happy. When the train drew in to the station and stopped, she looked in the lighted windows for Rosemary and didn't see her. Mr. Lawton got out of the car and joined Amy on the platform. They could see the conductor bending over someone in a seat, and finally the cook arose. She clung to the conductor as he led her out to the platform of the car, and she was crying. "Like peaches and cream," Amy heard her sob. "A lovely, lovely person." The conductor spoke to her kindly, put his arm around her shoulders, and eased her down the steps. Then the train pulled out, and she stood there drying her tears. "Don't say a word, Mr. Lawton," she said, "and I won't say anything." She held out a small paper bag. "Here's a present for you, little girl."

"Thank you, Rosemary," Amy said. She looked into the paper bag and saw that it contained several packets of Japanese water flowers.

Rosemary walked toward the car with the caution of someone who can hardly find her way in the dim light. A sour smell came from her. Her best coat was spotted with mud and ripped in the back. Mr. Lawton told Amy to get in the back seat of the car, and made the cook sit in front, beside him. He slammed the car door shut after her angrily, and then went around to the driver's seat and drove home. Rosemary reached into her handbag and took out a Coca-Cola bottle with a cork stopper and took a drink. Amy could tell by the smell that the Coca-Cola bottle was filled with gin.

"Rosemary!" Mr. Lawton said.

"I'm lonely," the cook said. "I'm lonely, and I'm afraid, and it's all I've got."

He said nothing more until he had turned into their drive and brought the car around to the back door. "Go and get your suitcase, Rosemary," he said. "I'll wait here in the car."

As soon as the cook had staggered into the house, he told Amy to go in by the front door. "Go upstairs to your room and get ready for bed."

Her mother called down the stairs when Amy came in, to ask if Rosemary had returned. Amy didn't answer. She went to the bar, took an open gin bottle, and emptied it into the pantry sink. She was nearly crying when she encountered her mother in the living room, and told her that her father was taking the cook back to the station.

When Amy came home from school the next day, she found a heavy, black-haired woman cleaning the living room. The car Mr. Lawton usually drove to the station was at the garage for a checkup, and Amy drove to the station with her mother to meet him. As he came across the station platform, she could tell by the lack of color in his face that he had had a hard day. He kissed her mother, touched Amy on the head, and got behind the wheel.

"You know," her mother said, "there's something terribly wrong with the guest-room shower."

"Damn it, Marcia," he said, "I wish you wouldn't always greet me with bad news!"

His grating voice oppressed Amy, and she began to fiddle with the button that raised and lowered the window.

"Stop that, Amy!" he said.

"Oh, well, the shower isn't important," her mother said. She laughed weakly.

"When I got back from San Francisco last week," he said, "you couldn't wait to tell me that we need a new oil burner."

"Well, I've got a part-time cook. That's good news."

"Is she a lush?" her father asked.

"Don't be disagreeable, dear. She'll get us some dinner and wash the dishes and take the bus home. We're going to the Farquarsons'."

"I'm really too tired to go anywhere," he said.

"Who's going to take care of me?" Amy asked.

"You always have a good time at the Farquarsons'," her mother said.

"Well, let's leave early," he said.

"Who's going to take care of me?" Amy asked.

"Mrs. Henlein," her mother said.

When they got home, Amy went over to the piano.

Her father washed his hands in the bathroom off the hall and then went to the bar. He came into the living room holding the empty gin bottle. "What's her name?" he asked.

"Ruby," her mother said.

"She's exceptional. She's drunk a quart of gin on her first day."

"Oh dear!" her mother said. "Well, let's not make any trouble now."

"Everybody is drinking my liquor," her father shouted, "and I am God-damned sick and tired of it!"

"There's plenty of gin in the closet," her mother said. "Open another bottle."

"We paid that gardener three dollars an hour and all he did was sneak in here and drink up my Scotch. The sitter we had before we got Mrs. Henlein used to water my bourbon, and I don't have to remind you about Rosemary. The cook before Rosemary not only drank everything in my liquor cabinet but she drank all the rum, kirsch, sherry, and wine that we had in the kitchen for cooking. Then, there's that Polish woman we had last summer. Even that old laundress. *And* the painters. I think they must have put some kind of a mark on my door. I think the agency must have checked me off as an easy touch."

"Well, let's get through dinner, and then you can speak to her."

"The hell with that!" he said. "I'm not going to encourage people to rob me. *Ruby!*" He shouted her name several times, but she didn't answer. Then she appeared in the dining-room doorway anyway, wearing her hat and coat.

"I'm sick," she said. Amy could see that she was frightened.

"I should think that you would be," her father said.

"I'm sick," the cook mumbled, "and I can't find anything around here, and I'm going home."

"Good," he said. "Good! I'm through with paying people to come in here and drink my liquor."

The cook started out the front way, and Marcia Lawton followed her into the front hall to pay her something. Amy had watched this scene from the piano bench, a position that was withdrawn but that still gave her a good view. She saw her father get a fresh bottle of gin and make a shaker of Martinis. He looked very unhappy.

"Well," her mother said when she came back into the room. "You know, she didn't look drunk."

"Please don't argue with me, Marcia," her father said.

He poured two cocktails, said "Cheers," and drank a little. "We can get some dinner at Orpheo's," he said.

"I suppose so," her mother said. "I'll rustle up something for Amy." She went into the kitchen, and Amy opened her music to "Reflets d'Automne." "COUNT," her music teacher had written. "COUNT and lightly, lightly . . ." Amy began to play. Whenever she made a mistake, she said "Darn it!" and started at the beginning again. In the middle of "Reflets d'Automne" it struck her that *she* was the one who had emptied the gin bottle. Her perplexity was so intense that she stopped playing, but her feelings did not go beyond perplexity, although she did not have the strength to continue playing the piano. Her mother relieved her. "Your supper's in the kitchen, dear," she said. "And you can take a popsicle out of the deep freeze for dessert. Just one."

Marcia Lawton held her empty glass toward her husband, who filled it from the shaker. Then she went upstairs. Mr. Lawton remained in the room, and, studying her father closely, Amy saw that his tense look had begun to soften. He did not seem so unhappy any more, and as she passed him on her way to the kitchen, he smiled at her tenderly and patted her on the top of the head.

When Amy had finished her supper, eaten her popsicle, and exploded the bag it came in, she returned to the piano and played "Chopsticks" for a while. Her father came downstairs in his evening clothes, put his drink on the mantelpiece, and went to the French doors to look at his terrace and his garden. Amy noticed that the transformation that had begun with a softening of his features was even more advanced. At last, he seemed happy. Amy wondered if he was drunk, although his walk was not unsteady. If anything, it was more steady.

Her parents never achieved the kind of rolling, swinging gait that she saw impersonated by a tightrope walker in the circus each year while the band struck up "Show Me the Way to Go Home" and that she liked to imitate herself sometimes. She liked to turn round and round and round on the lawn, until, staggering and a little sick, she would whoop, "I'm drunk! I'm a drunken man!" and reel over the grass, righting herself as she was about to fall and finding herself not unhappy at having lost for a second her ability to see the world. But she had never seen her parents like that. She had never seen them hanging on to a lamppost and singing and reeling, but she had seen them fall down. They were never indecorous—they seemed to get more decorous and formal the more they drank—but sometimes her father would get up to fill everybody's glass and he would walk straight enough but his shoes would seem to stick to the carpet. And sometimes, when he got to the dining-room door, he would miss it by a foot or more. Once, she had seen him walk into the wall with such force that he collapsed onto the floor and broke most of the glasses he was carrying. One or two people laughed, but the laughter was not general or hearty, and most of them pretended that he had not fallen down at all. When her father got to his feet, he went right on to the bar as if nothing had happened. Amy had once seen Mrs. Farquarson miss the chair she was about to sit in, by a foot, and thump down onto the floor, but nobody laughed then, and they pretended that Mrs. Farquarson hadn't fallen down at all. They seemed like actors in a play. In the school play, when you knocked over a paper tree you were supposed to pick it up without showing what you were doing, so that you would not spoil the illusion of being in a deep forest, and that was the way *they* were when somebody fell down.

Now her father had that stiff, funny walk that was so different from the way he tramped up and down the station platform in the morning, and she could see that he was looking for something. He was looking for his drink. It was right on the mantelpiece, but he didn't look there. He looked on all the tables in the living room. Then he went out onto the terrace and looked there, and then he came back into the living room and looked on all the tables again. Then he went back onto the terrace, and then back over the living-room tables, looking three times in the same place, although he was always telling her to look intelligently when she lost her sneakers or her raincoat. "Look for it, Amy," he was always saying. "Try and remember where you left it. I can't buy you a new raincoat every time it rains." Finally he gave up and poured himself a cocktail in another glass. "I'm going to get Mrs.

Henlein," he told Amy, as if this were an important piece of information.

Amy's only feeling for Mrs. Henlein was indifference, and when her father returned with the sitter, Amy thought of the nights, stretching into weeks—the years, almost—when she had been cooped up with Mrs. Henlein. Mrs. Henlein was very polite and was always telling Amy what was ladylike and what was not. Mrs. Henlein also wanted to know where Amy's parents were going and what kind of party it was, although it was none of her business. She always sat down on the sofa as if she owned the place, and talked about people she had never even been introduced to, and asked Amy to bring her the newspaper, although she had no authority at all.

When Marcia Lawton came down, Mrs. Henlein wished her good evening. "Have a lovely party," she called after the Lawtons as they went out the door. Then she turned to Amy. "Where are your parents going, sweetheart?

"But you must know, sweetheart. Put on your thinking cap and try and remember. Are they going to the club?"

"No," Amy said.

"I wonder if they could be going to the Trenchers'," Mrs. Henlein said. "The Trenchers' house was lighted up when we came by."

"They're not going to the Trenchers'," Amy said. "They hate the Trenchers."

"Well, where are they going, sweetheart?" Mrs. Henlein asked.

"They're going to the Farquarsons'," Amy said.

"Well, that's all I wanted to know, sweetheart," Mrs. Henlein said. "Now get me the newspaper and hand it to me politely. *Politely*," she said, as Amy approached her with the paper. "It doesn't mean anything when you do things for your elders unless you do them politely." She put on her glasses and began to read the paper.

Amy went upstairs to her room. In a glass on her table were the Japanese flowers that Rosemary had brought her, blooming stalely in water that was colored pink from the dyes. Amy went down the back stairs and through the kitchen into the dining room. Her father's cocktail things were spread over the bar. She emptied the gin bottle into the pantry sink and then put it back where she had found it. It was too late to ride her bicycle and too early to go to bed, and she knew that if she got anything interesting on the television, like a murder, Mrs. Henlein would make her turn it off. Then she remembered that her father had brought her home from his trip West a book about horses, and she ran cheerfully up the back stairs to read her new book.

It was after two when the Lawtons returned. Mrs. Henlein, asleep on the living-room sofa dreaming about a dusty attic, was awakened by their voices in the hall. Marcia Lawton paid her, and thanked her, and asked if anyone had called, and then went upstairs. Mr. Lawton was in the dining room, rattling the bottles around. Mrs. Henlein, anxious to get into her own bed and back to sleep, prayed that he wasn't going to pour himself another drink, as they so often did. She was driven home night after night by drunken gentlemen. He stood in the door of the dining room, holding an empty bottle in his hand. "You must be stinking, Mrs. Henlein," he said.

"Hmm," she said. She didn't understand.

"You drank a full quart of gin," he said.

The lackluster old woman—half between wakefulness and sleep—gathered together her bones and groped for her gray hair. It was in her nature to collect stray cats, pile the bathroom up to the ceiling with interesting and valuable newspapers, rouge, talk to herself, sleep in her underwear in case of fire, quarrel over the price of soup bones, and have it circulated around the neighborhood that when she finally died in her dusty junk heap, the mattress would be full of bankbooks and the pillow stuffed with hundred-dollar bills. She had resisted all these rich temptations in order to appear a lady, and she was repaid by being called a common thief. She began to scream at him.

"You take that back, Mr. Lawton! You take back every one of those words you just said! I never stole anything in my whole life, and nobody in my family ever stole anything, and I don't have to stand here and be insulted by a drunk man. Why, as for drinking, I haven't drunk enough to fill an eyeglass for twenty-five years. Mr. Henlein took me to a place of refreshment twenty-five years ago, and I drank two Manhattan cocktails that made me so sick and dizzy that I've never liked the stuff ever since. How dare you speak to me like this! Calling me a thief and a drunken woman! Oh, you disgust me—you disgust me in your ignorance of all the trouble I've had. Do you know what I had for Christmas dinner last year? I had a bacon sandwich. Son of a bitch!" She began to weep. "I'm glad I said it!" she screamed. "It's the first time I've used a dirty word in my whole life and I'm glad I said it. Son of a bitch!" A sense of liberation, as if she stood at the bow of a great ship, came over her. "I lived in this neighborhood my whole life. I can remember when it was full of good farming people and there was fish in the rivers. My father had four acres of sweet meadowland and a name that was known far and wide, and on my mother's side I'm descended from patroons, Dutch nobility. My mother was the spit and image of Queen Wilhelmina. You think you can get away with insulting me, but you're very, very, very much mistaken." She went to the telephone and, picking up the receiver, screamed, "Police! Police! Police! This is Mrs. Henlein, and I'm over at the Lawtons'. He's drunk, and he's calling me insulting names, and I want you to come over here and arrest him!"

The voices woke Amy, and, lying in her bed, she perceived vaguely the pitiful corruption of the adult world; how crude and frail it was, like a piece of worn burlap, patched with stupidities and mistakes, useless and ugly, and yet they never saw its worthlessness, and when you pointed it out to them, they were indignant. But as the voices went on and she heard the cry "Police! Police!" she was frightened. She did not see how they could arrest her, although they could find her fingerprints on the empty bottle, but it was not her own danger that frightened her but the collapse, in the middle of the night, of her father's house. It was all her fault, and when she heard her father speaking into the extension telephone in the library, she felt sunk in guilt. Her father tried to be good and kind—and, remembering the expensive illustrated book about horses that he had brought her from the West, she had to set her teeth to keep from crying. She covered her head with a pillow and realized miserably that she would have to go away. She had plenty of friends from the time when they used to live in New York, or she could spend the night in the Park or hide in a museum. She would have to go away.

"GOOD MORNING," her father said at breakfast. "Ready for a good day!" Cheered by the swelling light in the sky, by the recollection of the manner in which he had handled Mrs. Henlein and kept the police from coming, refreshed by his sleep, and pleased at the thought of playing golf, Mr. Lawton spoke with feeling, but the words seemed to Amy offensive and fatuous; they took away her appetite, and she slumped over her cereal bowl, stirring it with a spoon. "Don't slump, Amy," he said. Then she remembered the night, the screaming, the resolve to go. His cheerfulness refreshed her memory. Her decision was settled. She had a ballet lesson at ten, and she was going to have lunch with Lillian Towele. Then she would leave.

Children prepare for a sea voyage with a toothbrush and a Teddy bear; they equip themselves for a trip around the world with a pair of odd socks, a conch shell, and a thermometer; books and stones and peacock feathers, candy bars, tennis balls, soiled handkerchiefs, and skeins of old string appear to them to be the necessities of travel, and Amy packed, that afternoon, with the impulsiveness of her kind. She was late coming home from lunch, and her getaway was delayed, but she didn't mind. She could catch one of the late-afternoon locals; one of the cooks' trains. Her father was playing golf and her mother was off somewhere. A part-time worker was cleaning the living room. When Amy had finished packing, she went into her parents' bedroom and flushed the toilet. While the water murmured, she took a twenty-dollar bill from her mother's desk. Then she went downstairs and left the house and walked around Blenhollow Circle and down Alewives Lane to the station. No regrets or goodbyes formed in her mind. She went over the names of the friends she had in the city, in case she decided not to spend the night in a museum. When she opened the door of the waiting room, Mr. Flanagan, the stationmaster, was poking his coal fire.

"I want to buy a ticket to New York," Amy said.

"One-way or round-trip?"

"One-way, please."

Mr. Flanagan went through the door into the ticket office and raised the glass window. "I'm afraid I haven't got a half-fare ticket for you, Amy," he said. "I'll have to write one."

"That's all right," she said. She put the twenty-dollar bill on the counter.

"And in order to change that," he said, "I'll have to go over to the other side. Here's the four-thirty-two coming in now, but you'll be able to get the five-ten." She didn't protest, and went and sat beside her cardboard suitcase, which was printed with European hotel and place names. When the local had come and gone, Mr. Flanagan shut his glass window and walked over the footbridge to the northbound platform and called the Lawtons'. Mr. Lawton had just come in from his game and was mixing himself a cocktail. "I think your daughter's planning to take some kind of a trip," Mr. Flanagan said.

It was dark by the time Mr. Lawton got down to the station. He saw his daughter through the station window. The girl sitting on the bench, the rich names on her paper suitcase, touched him as it was in her power to touch him only when she seemed helpless or when she was very sick. Someone had walked over his grave! He shivered with longing, he felt his skin coarsen as when, driving home late and alone, a shower of leaves on the wind crossed the beam of his headlights, liberating him for a second at the most from the literal symbols of his life—the buttonless shirts, the vouchers and bank statements, the order blanks, and the empty glasses. He seemed to listen—God knows for what. Commands, drums, the crackle of signal fires, the music of the glockenspiel—how sweet it sounds on the Alpine air—singing from a tavern in the pass, the honking of wild swans; he seemed to smell the salt air in the churches of Venice. Then, as it was with the leaves, the power of her figure to trouble him was ended; his gooseflesh vanished. He was himself. Oh, why should she want to run away? Travel—and who knew better than a man who spent three days of every fortnight on the road—was a world of overheated plane cabins and repetitious magazines, where even the coffee, even the champagne, tasted of plastics. How could he teach her that home sweet home was the best place of all?

O YOUTH AND BEAUTY!

AT THE TAG END of nearly every long, large Saturday-night party in the suburb of Shady Hill, when almost everybody who was going to play golf or tennis in the morning had gone home hours ago and the ten or twelve people remaining seemed powerless to bring the evening to an end although the gin and whiskey were running low, and here and there a woman who was sitting out her husband would have begun to drink milk; when everybody had lost track of time, and the baby-sitters who were waiting at home for these diehards would have long since stretched out on the sofa and fallen into a deep sleep, to dream about cooking-contest prizes, ocean voyages, and romance; when the bellicose drunk, the crapshooter, the pianist, and the woman faced with the expiration of her hopes had all expressed themselves; when every proposal—to go to the Farquarsons' for breakfast, to go swimming, to go and wake up the Townsends, to go here and go there—died as soon as it was made, then Trace Bearden would begin to chide Cash Bentley about his age and thinning hair. The chiding was preliminary to moving the living-room furniture. Trace and Cash moved the tables and the chairs, the sofas and the fire screen, the woodbox and the footstool; and when they had finished, you wouldn't know the place. Then if the host had a revolver, he would be asked to produce it. Cash would take off his shoes and assume a starting crouch behind a sofa. Trace would fire the weapon out of an open window, and if you were new to the community and had not understood what the preparations were about, you would then realize that you were watching a hurdle race. Over the sofa went Cash, over the tables, over the fire screen and the woodbox. It was not exactly a race, since Cash ran it alone, but it was extraordinary to see this man of forty surmount so many obstacles so gracefully. There was not a piece of furniture in Shady Hill that Cash could not take in his stride. The race ended with cheers, and presently the party would break up.

Cash was, of course, an old track star, but he was never aggressive or tiresome about his brilliant past. The college where he had spent his youth had offered him a paying job on the alumni council, but he had refused it, realizing that that part of his life was ended. Cash and his wife, Louise, had two children, and they lived in a medium-cost ranch house on Alewives Lane. They belonged to the country club, although they could not afford it, but in the case of the Bentleys nobody ever pointed this out, and Cash was one of the best-liked men in Shady Hill. He was still slender—he was careful about his weight—and he walked to the train in the morning with a light and vigorous step that marked him as an athlete. His hair was thin, and there were mornings when his eyes looked bloodshot, but this did not detract much from a charming quality of stubborn youthfulness.

In business Cash had suffered reverses and disappointments, and the Bentleys had many money worries. They were always late with their tax payments and their mortgage payments, and the drawer of the hall table was stuffed with unpaid bills; it was always touch and go with the Bentleys and the bank. Louise looked pretty enough on Saturday night, but her life was exacting and monotonous. In the pockets of her suits, coats, and dresses there were little wads and scraps of paper on which was written: "Oleomargarine, frozen spinach, Kleenex, dog biscuit, hamburger, pepper, lard . . ." When she was still half awake in the morning, she was putting on the water for coffee and diluting the frozen orange juice. Then she would be wanted by the children. She would crawl under the bureau on her hands and knees to find a sock for Toby. She would lie flat on her belly and wiggle under the bed (getting dust up her nose) to find a shoe for Rachel. Then there were the housework, the laundry, and the cooking, as well as the demands of the children. There always seemed to be shoes to put on and shoes to take off, snowsuits to be zipped and unzipped, bottoms to be wiped, tears to be dried, and when the sun went down (she saw it set from the kitchen window) there was the supper to be cooked, the baths, the bedtime story, and the Lord's

Prayer. With the sonorous words of the Our Father in a darkened room the children's day was over, but the day was far from over for Louise Bentley. There were the darning, the mending, and some ironing to do, and after sixteen years of housework she did not seem able to escape her chores even while she slept. Snowsuits, shoes, baths, and groceries seemed to have permeated her subconscious. Now and then she would speak in her sleep—so loudly that she woke her husband. "I can't *afford* veal cutlets," she said one night. Then she sighed uneasily and was quiet again.

By the standards of Shady Hill, the Bentleys were a happily married couple, but they had their ups and downs. Cash could be very touchy at times. When he came home after a bad day at the office and found that Louise, for some good reason, had not started supper, he would be ugly. "Oh, for Christ sake!" he would say, and go into the kitchen and heat up some frozen food. He drank some whiskey to relax himself during this ordeal, but it never seemed to relax him, and he usually burned the bottom out of a pan, and when they sat down for supper the dining space would be full of smoke. It was only a question of time before they were plunged into a bitter quarrel. Louise would run upstairs, throw herself onto the bed and sob. Cash would grab the whiskey bottle and dose himself. These rows, in spite of the vigor with which Cash and Louise entered into them, were the source of a great deal of pain for both of them. Cash would sleep downstairs on the sofa, but sleep never repaired the damage, once the trouble had begun, and if they met in the morning, they would be at one another's throats in a second. Then Cash would leave for the train, and, as soon as the children had been taken to nursery school, Louise would put on her coat and cross the grass to the Beardens' house. She would cry into a cup of warmed-up coffee and tell Lucy Bearden her troubles. What was the meaning of marriage? What was the meaning of love? Lucy always suggested that Louise get a job. It would give her emotional and financial independence, and that, Lucy said, was what she needed.

The next night, things would get worse. Cash would not come home for dinner at all, but would stumble in at about eleven, and the whole sordid wrangle would be repeated, with Louise going to bed in tears upstairs and

Cash again stretching out on the living-room sofa. After a few days and nights of this, Louise would decide that she was at the end of her rope. She would decide to go and stay with her married sister in Mamaroneck. She usually chose a Saturday, when Cash would be at home, for her departure. She would pack a suitcase and get her War Bonds from the desk. Then she would take a bath and put on her best slip. Cash, passing the bedroom door, would see her. Her slip was transparent, and suddenly he was all repentance, tenderness, charm, wisdom, and love. "Oh, my darling!" he would groan, and when they went downstairs to get a bite to eat about an hour later, they would be sighing and making cow eyes at one another; they would be the happiest married couple in the whole eastern United States. It was usually at about this time that Lucy Bearden turned up with the good news that she had found a job for Louise. Lucy would ring the doorbell, and Cash, wearing a bathrobe, would let her in. She would be brief with Cash, naturally, and hurry into the dining room to tell poor Louise the good news. "Well, that's very nice of you to have looked," Louise would say wanly, "but I don't think that I want a job any more. I don't think that Cash wants me to work, do you, sweetheart?" Then she would turn her big dark eyes on Cash, and you could practically smell smoke. Lucy would excuse herself hurriedly from this scene of depravity, but never left with any hard feelings, because she had been married for nineteen years herself and she knew that every union has its ups and downs. She didn't seem to leave any wiser, either; the next time the Bentleys quarreled, she would be just as intent as ever on getting Louise a job. But these quarrels and reunions, like the hurdle race, didn't seem to lose their interest through repetition.

On a Saturday night in the spring, the Farquarsons gave the Bentleys an anniversary party. It was their seventeenth anniversary. Saturday afternoon, Louise Bentley put herself through preparations nearly as arduous as the Monday wash. She rested for an hour, by the clock, with her feet high in the air, her chin in a sling, and her eyes bathed in some astringent solution. The clay packs, the too tight girdle, and the plucking and curling and painting that went on were all aimed at rejuvenation. Feeling in the end that she had not been entirely successful, she tied a piece of veiling over her eyes—but she was a lovely woman, and all the cosmetics that she had struggled with seemed, like her veil, to be drawn transparently over a face where mature beauty and a capacity for wit and passion were undisguisable. The Farquarsons' party was nifty, and the Bentleys had a wonderful time. The only person who drank too much was Trace Bearden. Late in the party, he began to chide Cash about his thinning hair and Cash good-naturedly began to move the furniture around. Harry Farquarson had a pistol, and Trace went out onto the terrace to fire it up at the sky. Over the sofa went Cash, over the end table, over the arms of the wing chair and the fire screen. It was a piece of carving on a chest that brought him down, and down he came like a ton of bricks.

Louise screamed and ran to where he lay. He had cut a gash in his forehead, and someone made a bandage to stop the flow of blood. When he tried to get up, he stumbled and fell again, and his face turned a terrible green. Harry telephoned Dr. Parminter, Dr. Hopewell, Dr. Altman, and Dr. Barnstable, but it was two in the morning and none of them answered. Finally, a Dr. Yerkes—a total stranger—agreed to come. Yerkes was a young man—he did not seem old enough to be a doctor—and he looked around at the disordered room and the anxious company as if there was something weird about the scene. He got off on the wrong foot with Cash. "What seems to be the matter, old-timer?" he asked.

Cash's leg was broken. The doctor put a splint on it, and Harry and Trace carried the injured man out to the doctor's car. Louise followed them in her own car to the hospital, where Cash was bedded down in a ward. The doctor gave Cash a sedative, and Louise kissed him and drove home in the dawn.

CASH was in the hospital for two weeks, and when he came home he walked with a crutch and his broken leg was in a heavy cast. It was another ten days before he could limp to the morning train. "I won't be able to run the hurdle race any more, sweetheart," he told Louise sadly. She said that it didn't matter, but while it didn't matter to her, it seemed to matter to Cash. He had lost weight in the hospital. His spirits were low. He seemed discontented. He did not himself understand what had happened. He, or everything around him, seemed subtly to have changed for the worse. Even his senses seemed to conspire to damage the ingenuous world that he had enjoyed for so many years. He went into the kitchen late one night to make himself a sandwich, and when he opened the icebox door he noticed a rank smell. He dumped the spoiled meat into the garbage, but the smell clung to his nostrils. A few days later he was in the attic, looking for his varsity sweater. There were no windows in the attic and his flashlight was dim. Kneeling on the floor to unlock a trunk, he broke a spider web with his lips. The frail web covered his mouth as if a hand had been put over it. He wiped it impatiently, but also with the feeling of having been gagged. A few nights later, he was walking down a New York side street in the rain and saw an old whore standing in a doorway. She was so sluttish and ugly that she looked like a cartoon of Death, but before he could appraise her—the instant his eyes took an impression of her crooked figure—his lips swelled, his breathing quickened, and he experienced all the other symptoms of erotic excitement. A few nights later, while he was reading *Time* in the living room, he noticed that the faded roses Louise had brought in from the garden smelled more of earth than of anything else. It was a putrid, compelling smell. He dropped the roses into a wastebasket, but not before they had reminded him of the spoiled meat, the whore, and the spider web.

He had started going to parties again, but without the hurdle race to run, the parties of his friends and neighbors seemed to him interminable and stale. He listened to their dirty jokes with an irritability that was hard for him to conceal. Even their countenances discouraged him, and, slumped in a chair, he would regard their skin and their teeth narrowly, as if he were himself a much younger man.

The brunt of his irritability fell on Louise, and it seemed to her that Cash, in losing the hurdle race, had lost the thing that had preserved his equilibrium. He was rude to his friends when they stopped in for a drink. He was rude and gloomy when he and Louise went out. When Louise asked him what was the matter, he only murmured, "Nothing, nothing, nothing," and poured himself some bourbon. May and June passed, and then the first part of July, without his showing any improvement.

THEN IT IS a summer night, a wonderful summer night. The passengers on the eight-fifteen see Shady Hill—if they notice it at all—in a bath of placid golden light. The noise of the train is muffled in the heavy foliage, and the long car windows look like a string of lighted aquarium tanks before they flicker out of sight. Up on the hill, the ladies say to one another, "Smell the grass! Smell the trees!" The Farquarsons are giving another party, and Harry has hung a sign, WHISKEY GULCH, from the rose arbor, and is wearing a chef's white hat and an apron. His guests are still drinking, and the smoke from his meat fire rises, on this windless evening, straight up into the trees.

In the clubhouse on the hill, the first of the formal dances for the young people begins around nine. On Alewives Lane sprinklers continue to play after dark. You can smell the water. The air seems as fragrant as it is dark—it is a delicious element to walk through—and most of the windows on Alewives Lane are open to it. You can see Mr. and Mrs. Bearden, as you pass, looking at their television. Joe Lockwood, the young lawyer who lives on the corner, is practicing a speech to the jury before his wife. "I intend to show you," he says, "that a man of probity, a man whose reputation for honesty and reliability . . ." He waves his bare arms as he speaks. His wife goes on knitting. Mrs. Carver—Harry Farquarson's mother-in-law—glances up at the sky and asks, "*Where* did all the stars come from?" She is old and foolish, and yet she is right: Last night's stars seem to have drawn to themselves a new range of galaxies, and the night sky is not dark at all, except where there is a tear in the membrane of light. In the unsold house lots near the track a hermit thrush is singing.

The Bentleys are at home. Poor Cash has been so rude and gloomy that the Farquarsons have not asked him to their party. He sits on the sofa beside Louise, who is sewing elastic into the children's underpants. Through the open window he can hear the pleasant sounds of the summer night. There is another party, in the Rogerses' garden, behind the Bentleys'. The music from the dance drifts down the hill. The band is sketchy—saxophone, drums, and piano—and all the selections are twenty years old. The band plays "Valencia," and Cash looks tenderly toward Louise, but Louise, tonight, is a discouraging figure. The lamp picks out the gray in her hair. Her apron is stained. Her face seems colorless and drawn. Suddenly, Cash begins frenziedly to beat his feet in time to the music. He sings some gibberish—Jabajabajabajaba—to the distant saxophone. He sighs and goes into the kitchen.

Here a faint, stale smell of cooking clings to the dark. From the kitchen window Cash can see the lights and figures of the Rogerses' party. It is a young people's party. The Rogers girl has asked some friends in for dinner before the dance, and now they seem to be leaving. Cars are driving away. "I'm covered with grass stains," a girl says. "I hope the old man remembered to buy gasoline," a boy says, and a girl laughs. There is nothing on their minds but the passing summer nights. Taxes and the elastic in underpants—all the unbeautiful facts of life that threaten to crush the breath out of Cash—have not touched a single figure in this garden. Then jealousy seizes him—such savage and bitter jealousy that he feels ill.

He does not understand what separates him from these children in the garden next door. He has been a young man. He has been a hero. He has been adored and happy and full of animal spirits, and now he stands in a dark kitchen, deprived of his athletic prowess, his impetuousness, his good looks—of everything that means anything to him. He feels as if the figures in the next yard are the specters from some party in that past where all his tastes and desires lie, and from which he has been cruelly removed. He feels like a ghost of the summer evening. He is sick with longing. Then he hears voices in the front of the house. Louise turns on the kitchen light. "Oh, here you are," she says. "The Beardens stopped in. I think they'd like a drink."

Cash went to the front of the house to greet the Beardens. They wanted to go up to the club, for one dance. They saw, at a glance, that Cash was at loose ends, and they urged the Bentleys to come. Louise got someone to stay with the children and then went upstairs to change.

When they got to the club, they found a few friends of their age hanging around the bar, but Cash did not stay in the bar. He seemed restless and perhaps drunk. He banged into a table on his way through the lounge to the ballroom. He cut in on a young girl. He seized her too vehemently and jigged her off in an ancient two-step. She signaled openly for help to a boy in the stag line, and Cash was cut out. He walked angrily off the dance floor onto the terrace. Some young couples there withdrew from one another's arms as he pushed open the screen door. He walked to the end of the terrace, where he hoped to be alone, but here he surprised another young couple, who got up from the lawn, where they seemed to have been lying, and walked off in the dark toward the pool.

Louise remained in the bar with the Beardens. "Poor Cash is tight," she said. And then, "He told me this afternoon that he was going to paint the storm windows," she said. "Well, he mixed the paint and washed the brushes and put on some old fatigues and went into the cellar. There was a telephone call for him at around five, and when I went down to tell him, do you know what he was doing? He was just sitting there in the dark with a cocktail shaker. He hadn't touched the storm windows. He was just sitting there in the dark, drinking Martinis."

"Poor Cash," Trace said.

"You ought to get a job," Lucy said. "That would give you emotional and financial independence." As she spoke, they all heard the noise of furniture being moved around in the lounge.

"Oh, my God!" Louise said. "He's going to run the race. Stop him, Trace, stop him! He'll hurt himself. He'll kill himself!"

They all went to the door of the lounge. Louise again asked Trace to interfere, but she could see by Cash's face that he was way beyond remonstrating with. A few couples left the dance floor and stood watching the preparations. Trace didn't try to stop Cash—he helped him. There was no pistol, so he slammed a couple of books together for the start.

Over the sofa went Cash, over the coffee table, the lamp table, the fire screen, and the hassock. All his grace and strength seemed to have returned to him. He cleared the big sofa at the end of the room and instead of stopping there, he turned and started back over the course. His face was strained. His mouth hung open. The tendons of his neck protruded hideously. He made the hassock, the fire screen, the lamp table, and the coffee table. People held their breath when he approached the final sofa, but he cleared it and landed on his feet. There was some applause. Then he groaned and fell. Louise ran to his side. His clothes were soaked with sweat and he gasped for breath. She knelt down beside him and took his head in her lap and stroked his thin hair.

CASH had a terrible hangover on Sunday, and Louise let him sleep until it was nearly time for church. The family went off to Christ Church together at eleven, as they always did. Cash sang, prayed, and got to his knees, but the most he ever felt in church was that he stood outside the realm of God's infinite mercy, and, to tell the truth, he no more believed in the Father, the Son, and the Holy Ghost than does my bull terrier. They returned home at one to eat the overcooked meat and stony potatoes that were their customary Sunday lunch. At around five, the Parminters called up and asked them over for a drink. Louise didn't want to go, so Cash went alone. (Oh, those suburban Sunday nights, those Sunday-night blues! Those departing weekend guests, those stale cocktails, those half-dead flowers, those trips to Harmon to catch the Century, those postmortems and pickup suppers!) It was sultry and overcast. The dog days were beginning. He drank gin with the Parminters for an hour or two and then went over to the Townsends' for a drink. The Farquarsons called up the Townsends and asked them to come over and bring Cash with them, and at the Farquarsons' they had some more drinks and ate the leftover party food. The Farquarsons were glad to see that Cash seemed like himself again. It was half past ten or eleven when he got home. Louise was upstairs, cutting out of the current copy of *Life* those scenes of mayhem, disaster, and violent death that she felt might corrupt her children. She always did this. Cash came upstairs and spoke to her and then went down again. In a little while, she heard him moving the living-room furniture around. Then he called to her, and when she went down, he was standing at the foot of the stairs in his stocking feet, holding the pistol out to her. She had never fired it before, and the directions he gave her were not much help.

"Hurry up," he said, "I can't wait all night."

He had forgotten to tell her about the safety, and when she pulled the trigger nothing happened.

"It's that little lever," he said. "Press that little lever." Then, in his impatience, he hurdled the sofa anyhow.

The pistol went off and Louise got him in midair. She shot him dead.

THE DAY THE PIG FELL INTO THE WELL

IN THE SUMMER, when the Nudd family gathered at Whitebeach Camp, in the Adirondacks, there was always a night when one of them would ask, "Remember the day the pig fell into the well?" Then, as if the opening note of a sextet had been sounded, the others would all rush in to take their familiar parts, like those families who sing Gilbert and Sullivan, and the recital would go on for an hour or more. The perfect days—and there had been hundreds of them—seemed to have passed into their consciousness without a memory, and they returned to this chronicle of small disasters as if it were the genesis of summer.

The famous pig had belonged to Randy Nudd. He had won it at the fair in Lanchester and brought it home, and he was planning to build a pen for it, but Pamela Blaisdell telephoned, and he put the pig in the tool shed and drove over to the Blaisdell place in the old Cadillac. Russell Young was playing tennis with Esther Nudd. An Irishwoman named Nora Quinn was the cook that year. Mrs. Nudd's sister, Aunt Martha, had gone to the village of Macabit to get some cuttings from a friend, and Mr. Nudd was planning to take the launch across to Polett's Landing and bring her back after lunch. A Miss Coolidge was expected for dinner and the weekend. Mrs. Nudd had known her at school in Switzerland thirty years earlier. Miss Coolidge had written Mrs. Nudd to say that she was staying with friends in Glens Falls and could she pay a visit to her old schoolmate? Mrs. Nudd hardly remembered her and did not care about seeing her at all, but she wrote and asked her for the weekend. Though it was the middle of July, from daybreak a blustering northwest wind had been upsetting everything in the house and roaring in the trees like a storm. When you got out of the wind, if you could, the sun was hot.

In these events of the day the pig fell into the well, there was one other principal who was not a member of the family—Russell Young. Russell's father owned the hardware store in Macabit, and the Youngs were a respected native family. Mrs. Young worked as a cleaning woman for a month each spring, opening the summer houses, but her position was not menial. Russell met the Nudds through the boys—Hartley and Randall—and when he was quite young, he began to spend a lot of time at their camp. He was a year or two older than the Nudd boys, and in a way Mrs. Nudd entrusted the care of her sons to him. Russell was the same age as Esther Nudd and a year younger than Joan. Esther Nudd, at the beginning of this friendship, was a very fat girl. Joan was pretty and spent most of her time in front of the mirror. Esther and Joan adored Randy and gave him money from their allowances to buy paint for his boat, but otherwise there was not much rapport between the sexes. Hartley Nudd was disgusted with his sisters. "I saw Esther yesterday in the bathhouse, naked," he would tell anyone, "and she's got these big rolls of fat around her stomach like I don't know what. She's an awful-looking thing. And Joan is dirty. You ought to see her room. I don't see why anyone wants to take a dirty person like that to a dance."

But they were all much older than this on the day they liked to remember. Russell had graduated from the local high school and gone off to college in Albany, and in the summer of his freshman year he had worked for the Nudds, doing odd jobs around the place. The fact that he was paid a salary did not change his relationship to the family, and he remained good friends with Randall and Hartley. In a way, Russell's character and background seemed to be the dominant ones, and the Nudd boys returned to New York imitating his north-country accent. On the other hand, Russell went with the children on all their picnics to Hewitt's Point, he climbed the mountains and went fishing with them, he went to the square dances at the Town Hall with them, and in doing these things he learned from the Nudds an interpretation of the summer months that he would not have known as a native. He had no misgivings about so ingenuous and pleasing an influence, and he drove with the Nudds over the mountain roads in the old Cadillac, and shared with them the feeling that the clear light of July and August was imparting something rare to all their minds and careers. If the Nudds never referred to the difference between Russell's social position and theirs, it was because the very real barriers that they otherwise observed had been let down for the summer months—because the country, with the sky pouring its glare over the mountains onto the lake, seemed a seasonal paradise in which the strong and the weak, the rich and the poor, lived together peaceably.

THE SUMMER the pig fell into the well was also Esther's tennis summer and the summer that she became so thin. Esther had been very fat when she entered college, but during her freshman year she had begun the arduous—and, in her case, successful—struggle to put on a new appearance and a new personality. She went on a strict diet, and played twelve and fourteen sets of tennis a day, and her chaste, athletic, and earnest manner never relaxed. Russell was her tennis partner that summer. Mrs. Nudd had offered Russell a job again that summer, but instead he had taken a job with a dairy farmer, delivering milk. The Nudds supposed that he wanted to be independent, and they understood, for they all had Russell's best interests at heart. They took a familial pride in the fact that he had finished his sophomore year on the Dean's list. As it turned out, the job with the dairy farmer changed nothing. Russell was finished with his milk route at ten in the morning, and he spent most of the summer playing tennis with Esther. He often stayed to supper.

They were playing tennis that afternoon when Nora came running through the garden and told them that the pig had got out of the tool house and fallen into the well. Someone had left the door of the well shed open. Russell and Esther went over to the well and found the animal swimming in six feet of water. Russell made a slipknot in a clothesline and began fishing for the pig. In the meantime, Mrs. Nudd was waiting for Miss Coolidge to arrive, and Mr. Nudd and Aunt Martha were coming back from Polett's Landing in the launch. There were high waves on the lake, and the boat rolled, and some sediment was dislodged from the gas tank and plugged the feed line. The wind blew the disabled boat onto Gull Rock and put a hole in her bow. Mr. Nudd and Aunt Martha put on life jackets and swam the twenty yards or so to shore.

MR. NUDD's part in the narration was restrained (Aunt Martha was dead), and he did not join in until he was asked. "Was Aunt Martha *really* praying?" Joan would ask, and he would clear his throat to say—his manner was extremely dry and deliberate—"She was indeed, Joany. She was saying the Lord's Prayer. She had never, up until then, been a notably religious woman, but I'm sure that she could be heard praying from the shore."

"Was Aunt Martha *really* wearing corsets?" Joan would ask.

"Well, I should say so, Joany," Mr. Nudd would reply. "When she and I came up onto the porch where your mother and Miss Coolidge were having their tea, the water was still pouring from our clothes in bucketfuls, and Aunt Martha had on very little that couldn't be seen."

Mr. Nudd had inherited from his father a wool concern, and he always wore a full woolen suit, as if he were advertising the business. He spent the whole summer in the country the year the pig fell into the well—not because his business was running itself but because of quarrels with his partners. "There's no sense in my going back to New York now," he kept saying. "I'll stay up here until September and give those sons of bitches enough rope to hang themselves." The cupidity of his partners and associates frustrated Mr. Nudd. "You know, Charlie Richmond doesn't have any principles," he would say to Mrs. Nudd desperately and yet hopelessly, as if he did not expect his wife to understand business, or as if the impact of cupidity was indescribable. "He doesn't have any ethics," he would go on, "he doesn't have any code of morals or manners, he doesn't have any principles, he doesn't think about anything but making money." Mrs. Nudd seemed to understand. It was her opinion that people like that killed themselves. She had known a man like that. He had worked day and night making money. He ruined his partners and betrayed his friends and broke the hearts of his sweet wife and adorable children, and then, after making millions and millions of dollars, he went down to his office one Sunday afternoon and jumped out of the window.

HARTLEY'S PART in the story about the pig centered on a large pike he had caught that day, and Randy didn't enter into the narrative until close to its end. Randy had been fired out of college that spring. He and six friends had gone to a lecture on Socialism, and one of them had thrown a grapefruit at the speaker. Randy and the others refused to name the man who had thrown the grapefruit, and they were all expelled. Mr. and Mrs. Nudd were disheartened by this, but they were pleased with the way Randy had behaved. In the end, this experience made Randy feel like a celebrity and increased his already substantial self-respect. The fact that he had been expelled from college, that he was going to work in Boston in the fall, made him feel superior to the others.

The story did not begin to take on weight until a year after the pig incident, and already in this short time alterations had been made in its form. Esther's part changed in Russell's favor. She would interrupt the others to praise Russell. "You were so wonderful, Russell. How did you *ever* learn to make a slipknot? By *Jupiter*, if it hadn't been for Russell, I'll bet that pig would still be in the well." The year before, Esther and Russell had kissed a few times, and had decided that even if they fell in love they could never marry. He would not leave Macabit. She could not live there. They had reached these conclusions during Esther's tennis summer, when her kisses, like everything else, were earnest and chaste. The following summer, she seemed as anxious to lose her virginity as she had been to lose her corpulence. Something—Russell never knew what—had happened in the winter to make her ashamed of her inexperience.

She talked about sex when they were alone. Russell had got the idea that her chastity was of great value, and he was the one who had to be persuaded, but then he lost his head quickly and went up the back stairs to her room. After they had become lovers, they continued to talk about how they could never marry, but the impermanence of their relationship did not seem to matter, as if this, like everything else, had been enlightened by the innocent and transitory season. Esther refused to make love in any place but her own bed, but her room was at the back of the house and could be reached by the kitchen stairs, and Russell never had any trouble in getting there without being seen. Like all the other rooms of the camp, it was unfinished. The pine boards were fragrant and darkened, a reproduction of a Degas and a photograph of Zermatt were tacked to the walls, the bed was lumpy, and on those summer nights, with the June bugs making the screens resound, with the heat of the day still caught in the boards of the old camp, with the parched smell of her light-brown hair, with her goodness and her slenderness in his arms, Russell felt that this happiness was inestimable.

They thought that everyone would find out, and that they were lost. Esther did not regret what she had done, but she didn't know how it would end. They kept waiting for trouble, and when nothing happened, they were perplexed. Then she decided one night that everyone must know about it, but that everyone understood. The thought that her parents were young enough at heart to understand this passion as innocent and natural made Esther cry. "Aren't they *wonderful* people, darling?" she asked Russell. "Did you *ever* know such *wonderful* people. I mean, they were brought up so *strictly*, and all of their friends are *stuffy*, and isn't it wonderful that they *understand?*" Russell agreed. His respect for the Nudds was deepened by the thought that they could overlook convention for something larger. But both Esther and Russell were mistaken, of course. No one spoke to them about their meetings because no one knew about them. It never once occurred to Mr. and Mrs. Nudd that anything like that was going on.

THE FALL BEFORE, Joan had married suddenly, and gone out to Minneapolis to live. The marriage did not last. She was in Reno by April, and had her divorce in time to return to Whitebeach Camp for the summer. She was still a pretty girl, with a long face and fair hair. No one had expected her to return, and the things in her room had been scattered. She kept looking for her pictures and her books, her rugs and her chairs. When she joined the others on the porch after supper, she would ask a lot of questions. "Has anyone a match?" "Is there an ashtray over there?" "Is there any coffee left?" "Are we going to have drinks?" "Is there an extra pillow around?" Hartley was the only one to answer her questions kindly.

Randy and his wife were there for two weeks. Randy still borrowed money from his sisters. Pamela was a slight, dark girl who did not get on with Mrs. Nudd at all. She had been brought up in Chicago, and Mrs. Nudd, who had spent all her life in the East, sometimes thought that this might account for their differences. "I want the *truth*," Pamela often said to Mrs. Nudd, as if she suspected her mother-in-law of telling lies. "Do you think pink looks well on me?" she would ask. "I want the *truth*." She disapproved of Mrs. Nudd's management of Whitebeach Camp, and on one occasion tried to do something about the waste that she saw everywhere. Behind Mrs. Nudd's garden there was a large currant patch, which the hired man mulched and pruned every year, although the Nudds disliked currants and never picked them. One morning, a truck came up the driveway and four men, strangers, went into the patch. The maid told Mrs. Nudd, and she was on the point of asking Randy to drive the strangers away when Pamela came in and explained everything. "The currants are rotting," she said, "so I told the man in the grocery store that he could pick them if he'd pay us fifteen cents a quart. I hate to see waste . . ." This incident troubled Mrs. Nudd and everyone else, although they could not have said why.

BUT AT ITS HEART that summer was like all the others. Russell and "the children" went to Sherill's Falls, where the water is gold; they climbed Macabit Mountain; and they went fishing at Bates's Pond. Because these excursions were yearly, they had begun to seem like rites. After supper, the family would go out onto the open porch. Often there would be pink clouds in the sky. "I just saw the cook throw out a dish of cauliflower," Pamela would say to Mrs. Nudd. "I'm not in a position to correct her, but I hate to see waste. Don't you?" Or Joan would ask, "Has anyone seen my yellow sweater? I'm sure I left it at the bathhouse but I've just been down there and I can't find it. Did anyone bring it back? That's the second sweater I've lost this year." Then for a time no one would speak, as if they had all been unshackled by the evening from the stern laws of conversation, and when the talk began again it would continue to be trifling; it would involve the best ways of caulking a boat, or the difference in comfort between buses and trolley cars, or the shortest ways of driving into Canada. The darkness would come into the soft air as thickly as silt. Then someone, speaking of the sky, would remind Mrs. Nudd of how red the sky had been the night the pig fell into the well.

"You were playing tennis with Esther, weren't you, Russell? That was Esther's tennis summer. Didn't you win the pig at the fair in Lanchester, Randy? You won it at one of those things where you throw baseballs at a target. You were always *such* a good athlete."

The pig, they all knew, had been won in a raffle, but no one corrected Mrs. Nudd for her slight alteration in the narrative. She had recently begun to praise Randy for distinctions that he had never enjoyed. This was not conscious on her part, and she would have been confused if anyone had contradicted her, but now she would often recall how well he had done in German, how popular he had been in boarding school, how important he had been to the football team—all false, good-hearted memories that seemed aimed at Randy, as if they might hearten him. "You were going to build a pen for the pig," she said. "You were always *such* a good carpenter. Remember that bookcase you built? Then Pamela called you up, and you drove over there in the old Cadillac."

MISS COOLIDGE had arrived on that famous day at four, they all remembered. She was a spinster from the Middle West who made a living as a church soloist. There was nothing remarkable about her, but she was, of course, very different from the easygoing family, and it pleased them to think that they excited her disapproval. When she had been settled, Mrs. Nudd took her out onto the porch and Nora Quinn brought them some tea. After Nora served the tea, she took a bottle of Scotch out of the dining room surreptitiously and went up to her attic and began to drink. Hartley returned from the lake with his seven-pound pike in a pail. He put this in the back hall and joined his mother and Miss Coolidge, attracted by the cookies on the table. Miss Coolidge and Mrs. Nudd were recalling school days in Switzerland when Mr. Nudd and Aunt Martha, fully dressed and soaking wet, came up onto the porch and were introduced. The pig had drowned by this time, and Russell didn't get it out of the well until suppertime. Hartley loaned him a razor and a white shirt, and he stayed for supper. The pig was not mentioned in front of Miss Coolidge, but there was a lot of talk at the table about how salty the water tasted. After supper, they all went out on the porch. Aunt Martha had hung her corsets to dry in her bedroom window, and when she went upstairs to see how they were drying, she noticed the sky and called down to the others to look at it. "Look at the sky, everybody, *look* at the sky!" A moment earlier, the clouds had been shut; now they began to discharge worlds of fire. The glare that spread over the lake was blinding. "Oh, look at the sky, Nora!" Mrs. Nudd called upstairs to the cook, but by the time Nora, who was drunk, got to the window, the illusion of fire had gone and the clouds were dull, and, thinking that she might have misunderstood Mrs. Nudd, she went to the head of the stairs to ask if there was something they wanted. She fell down the stairs and upset the pail with the live pike in it.

AT THIS POINT in the story, Joan and Mrs. Nudd laughed until they wept. They all laughed happily except Pamela, who was waiting impatiently for her part in the narrative. It came immediately after the fall downstairs. Randy had stayed at the Blaisdells for supper and had returned to the camp with Pamela while Hartley and Russell were trying to get Nora into bed. They had news for everybody, they said; they had decided to get married. Mrs.

Nudd had never wanted Randy to marry Pamela, and their news made her sad, but she kissed Pamela tenderly and went upstairs to get a diamond ring. "Oh, it's beautiful!" Pamela said when she was given the ring. "But don't you need it? Won't you miss it? Are you *sure* you want me to have it? Tell me the truth . . ." Miss Coolidge, who had been very quiet until then and who must have felt very much a stranger, asked if she could sing.

ALL THE LONG DISCUSSIONS that Russell had had with Esther about the impermanence of their relationship did not help him that autumn when the Nudds went away. He missed the girl and the summer nights in her room painfully. He began to write long letters to Esther when he got back to Albany. He was troubled and lonely as he had never been before. Esther did not answer his letters, but this did not change the way he felt. He decided that they should become engaged. He would stay on at college and get a Master's degree, and with a teaching job they could live in some place like Albany. Esther did not even answer his proposal of marriage, and in desperation Russell telephoned her at college. She was out. He left a message to call him back. When she had not called him by the next evening, he telephoned her again, and when he got her this time, he asked her to marry him. "I can't marry you, Russell," she said impatiently. "I don't *want* to marry you." He hung up miserably and was lovesick for a week. Then he decided that Esther's refusal was not her decision, that her parents had forbidden her to marry him—a conjecture that was strengthened when none of the Nudds returned to Macabit the next summer. But Russell was mistaken. Mr. and Mrs. Nudd took Joan and Esther to California that summer, not to keep Esther away from Russell but because Mrs. Nudd had received a legacy and had decided to spend it on the trip. Hartley took a job in Maine at a summer camp. Randy and Pamela—Randy had lost his job in Boston and had taken one in Worcester—were having a baby in July, and so Whitebeach Camp was not opened at all.

THEN THEY ALL came back. A year later, on a June day when a horse van was bringing the bays up to the Macabit

Riding Stable and there were a lot of motorboats on trailers along the road, the Nudds returned. Hartley had a teaching job, so he was there all summer. Randy took two weeks without pay so that he and Pamela and their baby could be there for a month. Joan had not planned to come back; she had gone into partnership with a woman who owned a tearoom at Lake George, but she quarreled with her partner early in this venture, and in June Mr. Nudd drove to the lake and brought her home. Joan had been to a doctor that winter because she had begun to suffer from depressions, and she talked freely about her unhappiness. "You know, I think the trouble with me," she would say at breakfast, "is that I was so jealous of Hartley when he first went to boarding school. I could have killed him when he came home that year for Christmas, but I repressed all of my animosity . . ." "Remember that nursemaid, O'Brien?" she would ask at lunch. "Well, I think O'Brien warped my whole outlook on sex. She used to get undressed in the closet, and she beat me once for looking at myself in a mirror when I didn't have any clothes on. I think she warped my whole outlook . . ." "I think the trouble with me is that Grandmother was always so strict," she would say at dinner. "I never had the feeling that I gratified her. I mean, I got such bad marks at school, and she always made me feel so guilty. I think it's colored my attitude toward other women . . ." "You know," she would say on the porch after supper, "I think the whole turning point in my life was that awful Trenchard boy who showed me those pictures when I was only ten . . ." These recollections brought her a momentary happiness, but half an hour later she would be biting her fingernails. Surrounded all her life by just and kindly people, she was having a hard time finding the causes of her irresolution, and, one by one, she blamed the members of her family, and their friends, and the servants.

Esther had married Tom Dennison the previous fall, when she returned from California. This match pleased everyone in the family. Tom was pleasant, industrious, and intelligent. He had a freshman job with a firm that manufactured cash registers. His salary was small, and he and Esther began their marriage in a cold-water tenement in the East Sixties. Speaking of this arrangement, people sometimes added, "That Esther Nudd is so *courageous!*" When the summer came around, Tom had only a short vacation, and he and Esther went to Cape Cod in June. Mr. and Mrs. Nudd hoped that Esther would then come to Whitebeach Camp, but Esther said no, she would stick it out in the city with Tom. She changed her mind in August, and Mr. Nudd drove to the junction and met her train. She would only stay for ten days, she said, and this would be her last summer at Whitebeach Camp. Tom and she were going to buy a summer place of their own on Cape Cod. When it was time for her to go, she telephoned Tom, and he told her to stay in the country; the heat was awful. She telephoned him once a week and stayed at Whitebeach Camp until the middle of September.

Mr. Nudd spent two or three days of every week that summer in New York, flying down from Albany. For a change, he was pleased with the way his business was going. He had been made chairman of the board. Pamela had her baby with her, and she complained about the room they were given. Once, Mrs. Nudd overheard her in the kitchen, saying to the cook, "Things will be very different around here when Randy and I run this place, let me tell you . . ." Mrs. Nudd spoke to her husband about this, and they agreed to leave Whitebeach Camp to Hartley. "That ham only came to the table once," Pamela would say, "and I saw her dumping a dish of good shell beans into the garbage last night. I'm not in a position to correct her, but I hate to see waste. Don't you?"

Randy worshipped his thin wife, and she took full advantage of his protection. She came out onto the porch one evening when they were drinking before dinner, and sat down beside Mrs. Nudd. She had the baby in her arms.

"Do you always have supper at seven, Granny?" she asked.

"Yes."

"I'm afraid I can't get to the table at seven," Pamela said. "I hate to be late for meals, but I have to think of the baby first, don't I?"

"I'm afraid I can't ask them to hold dinner," Mrs. Nudd said.

"I don't want you to hold dinner for me," Pamela said, "but that little room we're in is terribly hot, and we're having trouble getting Binxey to sleep. Randy and I love being here, and we want to do everything we can to make it easy for you to have us here, but I do have to think of Binxey, and as long as he finds it hard to get to sleep, I won't be able to be on time for meals. I hope you don't mind. I want to know the truth."

"If you're late, it won't matter," Mrs. Nudd said.

"That's a beautiful dress," Pamela said, to end the conversation pleasantly. "Is it new?"

"Thank you, dear," Mrs. Nudd said. "Yes, it is new."

"It's a beautiful color," Pamela said, and she got up to feel the material, but some sudden movement made by her or by the baby in her arms or by Mrs. Nudd brought Pamela's cigarette against the new dress and burned a hole in it. Mrs. Nudd caught her breath, smiled awkwardly, and said that it didn't matter.

"But it does matter!" Pamela exclaimed. "I feel awfully about it. I feel awfully. It's all my fault, and if you'll give me the dress, I'll send it to Worcester and have it rewoven. I know a place in Worcester where they do wonderful reweaving."

Mrs. Nudd said again that it didn't matter, and tried to change the subject by asking if it hadn't been a beautiful day.

"I insist that you let me have it rewoven," Pamela said. "I want you to take it off after dinner and give it to me." Then she went to the door and turned and held the baby up. "Wave bye-bye to Granny, Binxey," she said. "Wave bye-bye, Binxey do it. Baby do it. Baby wave bye-bye to Granny. Binxey wave bye-bye. Wave bye-bye to Granny. Baby wave bye-bye . . ."

But none of these disturbances changed the rites of summer. Hartley took the maid and the cook to Mass at St. John's early every Sunday morning and waited for them on the front steps of the feed store. Randy froze the ice cream at eleven. It seemed as if the summer were a continent, harmonious and self-sufficient, with a peculiar range of sensation that included the feel of driving the old Cadillac barefoot across a bumpy pasture, and the taste of water that came out of the garden hose near the tennis court, and the pleasure of pulling on a clean woolen sweater in a mountain hut at dawn, and sitting on the porch in the dark, conscious and yet not resentful of a sensation of being caught up in a web of something as tangible and fragile as thread, and the clean feeling after a long swim.

THE NUDDS didn't ask Russell to Whitebeach Camp that year, and they carried on the narration without his help. After his graduation, Russell had married Myra Hewitt, a local girl. He had given up his plans for getting a Master's degree when Esther refused to marry him. He now worked for his father in the hardware store. The Nudds saw him when they bought a steak grill or some fishing line, and they all agreed that he looked poorly. He was pale. His clothes, Esther noticed, smelled of chicken feed and kerosene. They felt that by working in a store Russell had disqualified himself as a figure in their summers. This feeling was not strong, however, and it was largely through indifference and the lack of time that they did not see him. But the next summer they came to hate Russell; they took Russell off their list.

Late that next spring, Russell and his father-in-law had begun to cut and sell the timber on Hewitt's Point and to slash a three-acre clearing along the lake front in preparation for a large tourist-camp development, to be called Young's Bungalow City. Hewitt's Point was across the lake and three miles to the south of Whitebeach Camp, and the development would not affect the Nudds' property, but Hewitt's Point was the place where they had always gone for their picnics, and they did not like to see the grove cut and replaced with tourist hutches. They were all bitterly disappointed in Russell. They had thought of him as a native who loved his hills. They had expected him, as a kind of foster son, to share their summery lack of interest in money and it was a double blow to have him appear mercenary and to have the subject of his transactions the grove on Hewitt's Point, where they had enjoyed so many innocent picnics.

But it is the custom of that country to leave the beauties of nature to women and ministers. The village of Macabit stands on some high land above a pass and looks into the mountains of the north country. The lake is the floor of this pass, and on all but the hottest mornings clouds lie below the front steps of the feed store and the porch of the Federated Church. The weather in the pass is characterized by what is known on the coast as a sea turn. Across the heart of a hot, still day will be drawn a shadow as deep as velvet, and a bitter rain will extinguish the mountains; but this continuous displacement of light and dark, the thunder and the sunsets, the conical lights that sometimes end a storm and that have been linked by religious artists to godly intercession, have only accentuated the indifference of the secular male to his environment. When the Nudds passed Russell on the road without waving to him, he didn't know what he had done that was wrong.

That year, Esther left in September. She and her husband had moved to a suburb, but they had not been able to swing the house on Cape Cod, and she had spent most of the summer at Whitebeach Camp without him. Joan, who was going to take a secretarial course, went back to New York with her sister. Mr. and Mrs. Nudd stayed on until the first of November. Mr. Nudd had been deceived about his success in business. His position as chairman of the board, he discovered much too late, amounted to retirement with a small pension. There was no reason for him to go back, and he and Mrs. Nudd spent the fall taking long walks in the woods. Gasoline rationing had made that summer a trying one, and when they closed the house, they felt that it would be a long time before they opened it again. Shortages of building materials had stopped construction on Young's Bungalow City. After the trees had been cut and the concrete posts set for twenty-five tourist cabins, Russell hadn't been able to get nails or lumber or roofing to build with.

WHEN THE WAR was over, the Nudds returned to Whitebeach Camp for their summers. They had all been active in the war effort; Mrs. Nudd had worked for the Red Cross, Mr. Nudd had been a hospital orderly, Randy had been a mess officer in Georgia, Esther's husband had been a lieutenant in Europe, and Joan had gone to Africa with the Red Cross, but she had quarreled with her superior, and had hastily been sent home on a troopship. But their memories of the war were less lasting than most memories, and, except for Hartley's death (Hartley had drowned in the Pacific), it was easily forgotten. Now Randy took the cook and the maid to Mass at St. John's early on Sunday morning. They played tennis at eleven, went swimming at three, drank gin at six. "The children"—lacking Hartley and Russell—went to Sherill's Falls, climbed Macabit Mountain, fished in Bates's Pond, and drove the old Cadillac barefoot across the pasture.

The new vicar of the Episcopal chapel in Macabit called on the Nudds the first summer after the war and asked them why they hadn't had services read for Hartley. They couldn't say. The vicar pressed the point. Some nights later, Mrs. Nudd dreamed that she saw Hartley as a discontented figure. The vicar stopped her on the street later in the week, and spoke to her again about a memorial service, and this time she agreed to it. Russell was the only person in Macabit she thought she should invite. Russell had also been in the Pacific. When he returned to Macabit, he went back to work in the hardware store. The land on Hewitt's Point had been sold to real-estate developers, who were now putting up one- and two-room summer cottages.

The prayers for Hartley were read on a hot day at the end of the season, three years after he had drowned. To the relatively simple service, the vicar added a verse about death at sea. Mrs. Nudd derived no comfort whatever from the reading of the prayers. She had no more faith in the power of God than she had in the magic of the evening star. Nothing was accomplished by the service so far as she was concerned. When it was over, Mr. Nudd took her arm, and the elderly couple started for the vestry. Mrs. Nudd saw Russell waiting to speak to her outside the church, and thought: Why did it have to be Hartley? Why not Russell?

She had not seen him for years. He was wearing a suit that was too small for him. His face was red. In her shame at having wished a living man dead (for she had never experienced malevolence or bitterness without hurrying to cover it with love, and, among her friends and her family, those who received her warmest generosity were those who excited her impatience and her shame), she went to Russell impulsively and took his hand. Her face shone with tears. "Oh, it was so good of you to come; you were one of his best friends. We've missed you, Russell. Come see us. Can you come tomorrow? We're leaving on Saturday. Come for supper. It will make it seem like old times. Come for supper. We can't ask Myra and the children because we don't have a maid this year, but we'd love to see you. Please come." Russell said that he would.

The next day was windy and clear, with a heartening lightness, a multiplicity of changes in its moods and its lights—a day that belonged half to summer, half to autumn, precisely like the day when the pig had drowned. After lunch, Mrs. Nudd and Pamela went to an auction. The two women had reached a reasonable truce, although Pamela still interfered in the kitchen and looked on Whitebeach Camp impatiently as her just inheritance. Randy, with the best will in the world, had begun to find his wife's body meager and familiar, his desires as keen as ever, and so he had been unfaithful to her once or twice. There had been accusations, a confession, and a reconciliation, and Pamela liked to talk all this over with Mrs. Nudd, searching, as she said, for "the truth" about men.

Randy had been left with the children that afternoon and had taken them to the beach. He was a loving but impatient father, and from the house he could be heard scolding Binxey. "When I speak to you, Binxey, I don't speak to you because I want to hear the sound of my own voice, I speak to you because I want you to do what I say!" As Mrs. Nudd had told Russell, they had no maid that summer. Esther was doing the housework. Whenever anyone suggested getting a cleaning woman, Esther would say, "We can't afford a cleaning woman, and anyhow I don't have anything to do. I don't *mind* doing the housework, only I just wish you all would remember not to track sand into the living room . . ." Esther's husband had spent his vacation at Whitebeach Camp, but he had returned to work long since.

Mr. Nudd was sitting on the porch in the hot sun that afternoon when Joan came out to him with a letter in her hand. She smiled uneasily and began to speak in an affected singsong that always irritated her father. "I've decided that I won't drive down with you tomorrow," she said. "I've decided that I'll stay here for a little while longer, Daddy. After all, there's nothing for me to do in New

York. I have no reason to go down, have I? I wrote to Helen Parker, and she's going to come up and stay with me, so that I won't be alone. I have her letter right here. She says that she'd like to come. I thought we would stay here until Christmas. I've never been here in the winter before in all these years. We're going to write a book for children, Helen and I. She's going to draw the pictures, and I'm going to write the story. Her brother knows a publisher, and he said—"

"Joan, dear, you can't stay here in the winter." Mr. Nudd spoke gently.

"Oh, yes I can, yes I can, Daddy," Joan said. "Helen understands that it isn't comfortable. I've written her all about that. We're willing to rough it. We can get our own groceries in Macabit. We'll take turns walking into the village. I'm going to buy some firewood and a lot of canned goods and some—"

"But, Joan, dear, this house wasn't built to be lived in during the winter. The walls are thin. The water will be turned off."

"Oh, we don't care about the water—we'll get our water out of the lake."

"Now, Joan, dear, listen to me," Mr. Nudd said firmly. "You cannot stay here in the winter. You would last about a week. I would have to come up here and get you, and I don't want to close this house twice." He had spoken with an edge of impatience, but now reason and affection surged into his voice. "Think of how it would be, dear, with no heat and no water and none of your family."

"Daddy, I want to stay!" Joan cried. "I want to stay! Please let me stay! I've planned it for so long."

"You're being ridiculous, Joan," Mr. Nudd cut in. "This is a summer house."

"But, Daddy, I'm not asking very much!" Joan cried. "I'm not a child any more. I'm nearly forty years old. I've never asked you for anything. You've always been so strict. You never let me do what I want."

"Joan, dear, please try to be reasonable, please at least try to be reasonable, please try and imagine—"

"Esther got everything she wanted. She went to Europe twice; she had that car in college; she had that fur coat." Suddenly, Joan got down on her knees, and then sat on the floor. The movement was ugly, and it was meant to enrage her father.

"I want to stay, I want to stay, I want to stay, I want to stay!" she cried.

"Joan, you're acting like a child!" he shouted. "Get up."

"I want to act like a child!" she screamed. "I want to act like a child for a little while! Is there anything so terrible about wanting to act like a child for a little while? I don't have any joy in my life any more. When I'm unhappy, I try to remember a time when I was happy, but I can't remember a time any more."

"Joan, get up. Get up on your feet. Get up on your two feet."

"I can't, I can't, I can't," she sobbed. "It hurts me to stand up—it hurts my legs."

"Get up, Joan." He stooped down, and it was an effort for the old man to raise his daughter to her feet. "Oh, my baby, oh, my poor baby!" he said, and he put his arm around her. "Come into the bathroom and I'll wash your face, you poor baby." She let him wash her face, and then they had a drink and sat down to a game of checkers.

RUSSELL got to Whitebeach Camp at half past six, and they drank some gin on the porch. The liquor made him garrulous, and he began to talk about his war experiences, but the atmosphere was elastic and forgiving, and he knew that nothing he did there that night would be considered wrong. They went outside again after supper, although it was cool. The clouds had not colored. In the glancing light, the hillside shone like a bolt of velvet. Mrs. Nudd covered her legs with a blanket and looked at the scene. It was the most enduring pleasure of these years. There had been the boom, the crash, the depression, the recession, the malaise of imminent war, the war itself, the boom, the inflation, the recession, the slump, and now there was the malaise again, but none of this had changed a stone or a leaf in the view she saw from her porch.

"You know, I'm thirty-seven years old," Randy said. He spoke importantly, as if the passage of time over his head was singular, interesting, and a dirty trick. He cleaned his teeth with his tongue. "If I'd gone back to Cambridge for my reunion this year, it would have been my fifteenth."

"That's nothing," Esther said.

"Did you know that the Teeters have bought the old Henderson place?" Mr. Nudd asked. "*There's* a man who made a fortune in the war." He stood, turned the chair he was sitting in upside down, and pounded at the legs with his fist. His cigarette was wet. When he sat down again, the long ash spilled onto his vest.

"Do I look thirty-seven?" Randy asked.

"Do you know that you've mentioned the fact that you're thirty-seven eight times today?" Esther said. "I've counted them."

"How much does it cost to go to Europe in an airplane?" Mr. Nudd asked.

The conversation went from ocean fares to whether it was pleasanter to come into a strange city in the morning or the evening. Then they recalled odd names among the guests who had been at Whitebeach Camp; there had been Mr. and Mrs. Peppercorn, Mr. and Mrs. Starkweather, Mr. and Mrs. Freestone, the Bloods, the Mudds, and the Parsleys.

That late in the season, the light went quickly. It was sunny one minute and dark the next. Macabit and its mountain range were canted against the afterglow, and for a while it seemed unimaginable that anything could lie beyond the mountains, that this was not the end of the world. The wall of pure and brassy light seemed to beat up from infinity. Then the stars came out, the earth rumbled downward, the illusion of an abyss was lost. Mrs. Nudd looked around her, and the time and the place seemed strangely important. This is not an imitation, she thought, this is not the product of custom, this is the unique place, the unique air, where my children have spent the best of themselves. The realization that none of them had done well made her sink back in her chair. She squinted the tears out of her eyes. What had made the summer always an island, she thought; what had made it such a small island? What mistakes had they made? What had they done wrong? They had loved their neighbors, respected the force of modesty, held honor above gain. Then where had they lost their competence, their freedom, their greatness? Why should these good and gentle people who surrounded her seem like the figures in a tragedy?

"Remember the day the pig fell into the well?" she asked. The sky was discolored. Below the black mountains, the lake ran a rough and deadly gray. "Weren't you playing tennis with Esther, Russell? That was Esther's tennis summer. Didn't you win the pig at the fair in Lanchester, Randy? You won it at one of those things where you throw baseballs at a target. You were always *such* a good athlete."

They all waited graciously for their turn. They recalled the drowned pig, the launch on Gull Rock, Aunt Martha's corsets hanging in the window, the fire in the clouds, and the blustering northwest wind. They laughed helplessly at the place where Nora fell down the stairs. Pamela cut in to recall the announcement of her engagement. After this, they recalled how Miss Coolidge had gone upstairs and returned with a briefcase full of music, and, standing by the open door, so that she could get the light, had performed the standard repertoire of the rural Protestant Church. She had sung for more than an hour. They couldn't stop her. During her recital, Esther and Russell left the porch and went up to the field to bury the drowned pig. It was cool. Esther held a lantern while Russell dug the grave. They had decided then that even if they were in love they could never marry, because he wouldn't leave Macabit and she would never live there. When they got back to the porch, Miss Coolidge was singing her last selection, and then Russell left and they all went to bed.

The story restored Mrs. Nudd and made her feel that all was well. It had exhilarated the rest, and, talking loudly and laughing, they went into the house. Mr. Nudd lighted a fire and sat down to play checkers with Joan. Mrs. Nudd passed a box of stale candy. It had begun to blow outside, and the house creaked gently, like a hull when the wind takes up the sail. The room with the people in it looked enduring and secure, although in the morning they would all be gone.

THE FIVE-FORTY-EIGHT

When Blake stepped out of the elevator, he saw her. A few people, mostly men waiting for girls, stood in the lobby watching the elevator doors. She was among them. As he saw her, her face took on a look of such loathing and purpose that he realized she had been waiting for him. He did not approach her. She had no legitimate business with him. They had nothing to say. He turned and walked toward the glass doors at the end of the lobby, feeling that faint guilt and bewilderment we experience when we bypass some old friend or classmate who seems threadbare, or sick, or miserable in some other way. It was five-eighteen by the clock in the Western Union office. He could catch the express. As he waited his turn at the revolving doors, he saw that it was still raining. It had been raining all day, and he noticed now how much louder the rain made the noises of the street. Outside, he started walking briskly east toward Madison Avenue. Traffic was tied up, and horns were blowing urgently on a crosstown street in the distance. The sidewalk was crowded. He wondered what she had hoped to gain by a glimpse of him coming out of the office building at the end of the day. Then he wondered if she was following him.

Walking in the city, we seldom turn and look back. The habit restrained Blake. He listened for a minute—foolishly—as he walked, as if he could distinguish her footsteps from the worlds of sound in the city at the end of a rainy day. Then he noticed, ahead of him on the other side of the street, a break in the wall of buildings. Something had been torn down; something was being put up, but the steel structure had only just risen above the sidewalk fence and daylight poured through the gap. Blake stopped opposite here and looked into a store window. It was a decorator's or an auctioneer's. The window was arranged like a room in which people live and entertain their friends. There were cups on the coffee table, magazines to read, and flowers in the vases, but the flowers were dead and the cups were empty and the guests had not come. In the plate glass, Blake saw a clear reflection of himself and the crowds that were passing, like shadows, at his back. Then he saw her image—so close to him that it shocked him. She was standing only a foot or two behind him. He could have turned then and asked her what she wanted, but instead of recognizing her, he shied away abruptly from the reflection of her contorted face and went along the street. She might be meaning to do him harm—she might be meaning to kill him.

The suddenness with which he moved when he saw the reflection of her face tipped the water out of his hat brim in such a way that some of it ran down his neck. It felt unpleasantly like the sweat of fear. Then the cold water falling into his face and onto his bare hands, the rancid smell of the wet gutters and paving, the knowledge that his feet were beginning to get wet and that he might catch cold—all the common discomforts of walking in the rain—seemed to heighten the menace of his pursuer and to give him a morbid consciousness of his own physicalness and of the ease with which he could be hurt. He could see ahead of him the corner of Madison Avenue, where the lights were brighter. He felt that if he could get to Madison Avenue he would be all right. At the corner, there was a bakery shop with two entrances, and he went in by the door on the crosstown street, bought a coffee ring, like any other commuter, and went out the Madison Avenue door. As he started down Madison Avenue, he saw her waiting for him by a hut where newspapers were sold.

She was not clever. She would be easy to shake. He could get into a taxi by one door and leave by the other. He could speak to a policeman. He could run—although he was afraid that if he did run, it might precipitate the violence he now felt sure she had planned. He was approaching a part of the city that he knew well and where the maze of street-level and underground passages, elevator banks, and crowded lobbies made it easy for a man to lose a pursuer. The thought of this, and a whiff of sugary warmth from the coffee ring, cheered him. It was absurd to imagine being harmed on a crowded street. She was foolish, misled, lonely perhaps—that was all it could amount to. He was an insignificant man, and there was no point in anyone's following him from his office to the station. He knew no secrets of any consequence. The reports in his briefcase had no bearing on war, peace, the dope traffic, the hydrogen bomb, or any of the other international skulduggeries that he associated with pursuers, men in trench coats, and wet sidewalks. Then he saw ahead of him the door of a men's bar. Oh, it was so simple!

He ordered a Gibson and shouldered his way in between two other men at the bar, so that if she should be watching from the window she would lose sight of him. The place was crowded with commuters putting down a drink before the ride home. They had brought in on their clothes—on their shoes and umbrellas—the rancid smell of the wet dusk outside, but Blake began to relax as soon as he tasted his Gibson and looked around at the common, mostly not-young faces that surrounded him and that were worried, if they were worried at all, about tax rates and who would be put in charge of merchandising. He tried to remember her name—Miss Dent, Miss Bent, Miss Lent—and he was surprised to find that he could not remember it, although he was proud of the retentiveness and reach of his memory and it had only been six months ago.

Personnel had sent her up one afternoon—he was looking for a secretary. He saw a dark woman—in her twenties, perhaps—who was slender and shy. Her dress was simple, her figure was not much, one of her stockings was crooked, but her voice was soft and he had been willing to try her out. After she had been working for him a few days, she told him that she had been in the hospital for eight months and that it had been hard after this for her to find work, and she wanted to thank him for giving her a chance. Her hair was dark, her eyes were dark; she left with him a pleasant impression of darkness. As he got to know her better, he felt that she was oversensitive and, as a consequence, lonely. Once, when she was speaking to him of what she imagined his life to be—full of friendships, money, and a large and loving family—he had thought he recognized a peculiar feeling of deprivation. She seemed to imagine the lives of the rest of the world to be more brilliant than they were. Once, she had put a rose on his desk, and he had dropped it into the wastebasket. "I don't like roses," he told her.

She had been competent, punctual, and a good typist, and he had found only one thing in her that he could object to—her handwriting. He could not associate the crudeness of her handwriting with her appearance. He would have expected her to write a rounded backhand, and in her writing there were intermittent traces of this, mixed with clumsy printing. Her writing gave him the feeling that she had been the victim of some inner—some emotional—conflict that had in its violence broken the continuity of the lines she was able to make on paper. When she had been working for him three weeks—no longer—they stayed late one night and he offered, after work, to buy her a drink. "If you really want a drink," she said, "I have some whiskey at my place."

She lived in a room that seemed to him like a closet. There were suit boxes and hatboxes piled in a corner, and although the room seemed hardly big enough to hold the bed, the dresser, and the chair he sat in, there was an upright piano against one wall, with a book of Beethoven sonatas on the rack. She gave him a drink and said that she was going to put on something more comfortable. He urged her to; that was, after all, what he had come for. If he had any qualms, they would have been practical. Her diffidence, the feeling of deprivation in her point of view, promised to protect him from any consequences. Most of the many women he had known had been picked for their lack of self-esteem.

When he put on his clothes again, an hour or so later, she was weeping. He felt too contented and warm and sleepy to worry much about her tears. As he was dressing, he noticed on the dresser a note she had written to a cleaning woman. The only light came from the bathroom—the door was ajar—and in this half light the hideously scrawled letters again seemed entirely wrong for her, and as if they must be the handwriting of some other and very gross woman. The next day, he did what he felt was the only sensible thing. When she was out for lunch, he called personnel and asked them to fire her. Then he took the afternoon off. A few days later, she came to the office, asking to see him. He told the switchboard girl not to let her in. He had not seen her again until this evening.

BLAKE DRANK a second Gibson and saw by the clock that he had missed the express. He would get the local—the five-forty-eight. When he left the bar the sky was still light; it was still raining. He looked carefully up and down the street and saw that the poor woman had gone. Once or twice, he looked over his shoulder, walking to the station, but he seemed to be safe. He was still not quite himself, he realized, because he had left his coffee ring at the bar, and he was not a man who forgot things. This lapse of memory pained him.

He bought a paper. The local was only half full when he boarded it, and he got a seat on the river side and took off his raincoat. He was a slender man with brown hair—undistinguished in every way, unless you could have divined in his pallor or his gray eyes his unpleasant tastes. He dressed—like the rest of us—as if he admitted the existence of sumptuary laws. His raincoat was the pale buff color of a mushroom. His hat was dark brown; so was his suit. Except for the few bright threads in his necktie, there was a scrupulous lack of color in his clothing that seemed protective.

He looked around the car for neighbors. Mrs. Compton was several seats in front of him, to the right. She smiled, but her smile was fleeting. It died swiftly and horribly. Mr. Watkins was directly in front of Blake. Mr. Watkins needed a haircut, and he had broken the sumptuary laws; he was wearing a corduroy jacket. He and Blake had quarreled, so they did not speak.

The swift death of Mrs. Compton's smile did not affect Blake at all. The Comptons lived in the house next to the Blakes, and Mrs. Compton had never understood the importance of minding her own business. Louise Blake took her troubles to Mrs. Compton, Blake knew, and instead of discouraging her crying jags, Mrs. Compton had come to imagine herself a sort of confessor and had developed a lively curiosity about the Blakes' intimate affairs. She had probably been given an account of their most recent quarrel. Blake had come home one night, overworked and tired, and had found that Louise had done nothing about getting supper. He had gone into the kitchen, followed by Louise, and had pointed out to her that the date was the fifth. He had drawn a circle around the date on the kitchen calendar. "One week is the twelfth," he had said. "Two weeks will be the nineteenth." He drew a circle around the nineteenth. "I'm not going to speak to you for two weeks," he had said. "That will be the nineteenth." She had wept, she had protested, but it had been eight or ten years since she had been able to touch him with her entreaties. Louise had got old. Now the lines in her face were ineradicable, and when she clapped her glasses onto her nose to read the evening paper, she looked to him like an unpleasant stranger. The physical charms that had been her only attraction were gone. It had been nine years since Blake had built a bookshelf in the doorway that connected their rooms and had fitted into the bookshelf wooden doors that could be locked, since he did not want the children to see his books. But their prolonged estrangement didn't seem remarkable to Blake. He had quarreled with his wife, but so did every other man born of woman. It was human nature. In any place where you can hear their voices—a hotel courtyard, an air shaft, a street on a summer evening—you will hear harsh words.

The hard feeling between Blake and Mr. Watkins also had to do with Blake's family, but it was not as serious or as troublesome as what lay behind Mrs. Compton's fleeting smile. The Watkinses rented. Mr. Watkins broke the sumptuary laws day after day—he once went to the eight-fourteen in a pair of sandals—and he made his living as a commercial artist. Blake's oldest son—Charlie was fourteen—had made friends with the Watkins boy. He had spent a lot of time in the sloppy rented house where the Watkinses lived. The friendship had affected his manners and his neatness. Then he had begun to take some meals with the Watkinses, and to spend Saturday nights there. When he had moved most of his possessions over to the Watkinses' and had begun to spend more than half his nights there, Blake had been forced to act. He had spoken not to Charlie but to Mr. Watkins, and had, of necessity, said a number of things that must have sounded critical. Mr. Watkins' long and dirty hair and his corduroy jacket reassured Blake that he had been in the right.

But Mrs. Compton's dying smile and Mr. Watkins' dirty hair did not lessen the pleasure Blake took in setting himself in an uncomfortable seat on the five-forty-eight deep underground. The coach was old and smelled oddly like a bomb shelter in which whole families had spent the night. The light that spread from the ceiling down onto their heads and shoulders was dim. The filth on the window glass was streaked with rain from some other journey, and clouds of rank pipe and cigarette smoke had begun to rise from behind each newspaper, but it was a scene that meant to Blake that he was on a safe path, and after his brush with danger he even felt a little warmth toward Mrs. Compton and Mr. Watkins.

The train traveled up from underground into the weak daylight, and the slums and the city reminded Blake vaguely of the woman who had followed him. To avoid speculation or remorse about her, he turned his attention to the evening paper. Out of the corner of his eye he could see the landscape. It was industrial and, at that hour, sad. There were machine sheds and warehouses, and above these he saw a break in the clouds—a piece of yellow light. "Mr. Blake," someone said. He looked up. It was she. She was standing there holding one hand on the back of the seat to steady herself in the swaying coach. He remembered her name then—Miss Dent. "Hello, Miss Dent," he said.

"Do you mind if I sit here?"

"I guess not."

"Thank you. It's very kind of you. I don't like to inconvenience you like this. I don't want to . . ." He had been frightened when he looked up and saw her, but her timid voice rapidly reassured him. He shifted his hams—that futile and reflexive gesture of hospitality—and she sat down. She sighed. He smelled her wet clothing. She wore a formless black hat with a cheap crest stitched onto it. Her coat was thin cloth, he saw, and she wore gloves and carried a large pocketbook.

"Are you living out in this direction now, Miss Dent?"

"No."

She opened her purse and reached for her handkerchief. She had begun to cry. He turned his head to see if anyone in the car was looking, but no one was. He had sat beside a thousand passengers on the evening train. He had noticed their clothes, the holes in their gloves; and if they fell asleep and mumbled he had wondered what their worries were. He had classified almost all of them briefly before he buried his nose in the paper. He had marked them as rich, poor, brilliant or dull, neighbors or strangers, but no one of the thousand had ever wept. When she opened her purse, he remembered her perfume. It had clung to his skin the night he went to her place for a drink.

"I've been very sick," she said. "This is the first time I've been out of bed in two weeks. I've been terribly sick."

"I'm sorry that you've been sick, Miss Dent," he said in a voice loud enough to be heard by Mr. Watkins and Mrs. Compton. "Where are you working now?"

"What?"

"Where are you working now?"

"Oh, don't make me laugh," she said softly.

"I don't understand."

"You poisoned their minds."

He straightened his neck and braced his shoulders. These wrenching movements expressed a brief—and hopeless—longing to be in some other place. She meant trouble. He took a breath. He looked with deep feeling at the half-filled, half-lighted coach to affirm his sense of actuality, of a world in which there was not very much bad trouble after all. He was conscious of her heavy breathing and the smell of her rain-soaked coat. The train stopped. A nun and a man in overalls got off. When it started again, Blake put on his hat and reached for his raincoat.

"Where are you going?" she said.

"I'm going to the next car."

"Oh, no," she said. "No, no, no." She put her white face so close to his ear that he could feel her warm breath on his cheek. "Don't do that," she whispered. "Don't try and escape me. I have a pistol and I'll have to kill you and I don't want to. All I want to do is to talk with you. Don't move or I'll kill you. Don't, don't, don't!"

Blake sat back abruptly in his seat. If he had wanted to stand and shout for help, he would not have been able to. His tongue had swelled to twice its size, and when he tried to move it, it stuck horribly to the roof of his mouth. His legs were limp. All he could think of to do then was to wait for his heart to stop its hysterical beating, so that he could judge the extent of his danger. She was sitting a little sidewise, and in her pocketbook was the pistol, aimed at his belly.

"You understand me now, don't you?" she said. "You understand that I'm serious?" He tried to speak but he was still mute. He nodded his head. "Now we'll sit quietly for a little while," she said. "I got so excited that my thoughts are all confused. We'll sit quietly for a little while, until I can get my thoughts in order again."

Help would come, Blake thought. It was only a question of minutes. Someone, noticing the look on his face or her peculiar posture, would stop and interfere, and it would all be over. All he had to do was to wait until someone noticed his predicament. Out of the window he saw the river and the sky. The rain clouds were rolling down like a shutter, and while he watched, a streak of orange light on the horizon became brilliant. Its brilliance spread—he could see it move—across the waves until it raked the banks of the river with a dim firelight. Then it was put out. Help would come in a minute, he thought. Help would come before they stopped again; but the train stopped, there were some comings and goings, and Blake still lived on, at the mercy of the woman beside him. The possibility that help might not come was one that he could not face. The possibility that his predicament was not noticeable, that Mrs. Compton would guess that he was taking a poor relation out to dinner at Shady Hill, was something he would think about later. Then the saliva came back into his mouth and he was able to speak.

"Miss Dent?"

"Yes."

"What do you want?"

"I want to talk to you."

"You can come to my office."

"Oh, no. I went there every day for two weeks."

"You could make an appointment."

"No," she said. "I think we can talk here. I wrote you a letter but I've been too sick to go out and mail it. I've put down all my thoughts. I like to travel. I like trains. One of my troubles has always been that I could never afford to travel. I suppose you see this scenery every night and don't notice it any more, but it's nice for someone who's been in bed a long time. They say that He's not in the river and the hills but I think He is. 'Where shall wisdom be found?' it says. 'Where is the place of understanding? The depth saith it is not in me; the sea saith it is not with me. Destruction and death say we have heard the force with our ears.'

"Oh, I know what you're thinking," she said. "You're thinking that I'm crazy, and I have been very sick again but I'm going to be better. It's going to make me better to talk with you. I was in the hospital all the time before I came to work for you but they never tried to cure me, they only wanted to take away my self-respect. I haven't had any work now for three months. Even if I did have to kill you, they wouldn't be able to do anything to me except put me back in the hospital, so you see I'm not afraid. But let's sit quietly for a little while longer. I have to be calm."

The train continued its halting progress up the bank of the river, and Blake tried to force himself to make some plans for escape, but the immediate threat to his life made this difficult, and instead of planning sensibly, he thought of the many ways in which he could have avoided her in the first place. As soon as he had felt these regrets, he realized their futility. It was like regretting his lack of suspicion when she first mentioned her months in the hospital. It was like regretting his failure to have been warned by her shyness, her diffidence, and the handwriting that looked like the marks of a claw. There was no way of rectifying his mistakes, and he felt—for perhaps the first time in his mature life—the full force of regret. Out of the window, he saw some men fishing on the nearly dark river, and then a ramshackle boat club that seemed to have been nailed together out of scraps of wood that had been washed up on the shore.

Mr. Watkins had fallen asleep. He was snoring. Mrs. Compton read her paper. The train creaked, slowed, and halted infirmly at another station. Blake could see the southbound platform, where a few passengers were waiting to go into the city. There was a workman with a lunch pail, a dressed-up woman, and a woman with a suitcase. They stood apart from one another. Some advertisements were posted on the wall behind them. There was a picture of a couple drinking a toast in wine, a picture of a Cat's Paw rubber heel, and a picture of a Hawaiian dancer. Their cheerful intent seemed to go no farther than the puddles of water on the platform and to expire there. The platform and the people on it looked lonely. The train drew away from the station into the scattered lights of a slum and then into the darkness of the country and the river.

"I want you to read my letter before we get to Shady Hill," she said. "It's on the seat. Pick it up. I would have mailed it to you, but I've been too sick to go out. I haven't gone out for two weeks. I haven't had any work for three months. I haven't spoken to anybody but the landlady. Please read my letter."

He picked up the letter from the seat where she had put it. The cheap paper felt abhorrent and filthy to his fingers. It was folded and refolded. "Dear Husband," she had written, in that crazy, wandering hand, "they say that human love leads us to divine love, but is this true? I dream about you every night. I have such terrible desires. I have always had a gift for dreams. I dreamed on Tuesday of a volcano erupting with blood. When I was in the hospital they said they wanted to cure me but they only wanted to take away my self-respect. They only wanted me to dream about sewing and basketwork but I protected my gift for dreams. I'm clairvoyant. I can tell when the telephone is going to ring. I've never had a true friend in my whole life. . . ."

The train stopped again. There was another platform, another picture of the couple drinking a toast, the rubber heel, and the Hawaiian dancer. Suddenly she pressed her face close to Blake's again and whispered in his ear. "I know what you're thinking. I can see it in your face. You're thinking you can get away from me in Shady Hill, aren't you? Oh, I've been planning this for weeks. It's all I've had to think about. I won't harm you if you'll let me talk. I've been thinking about devils. I mean, if there are devils in the world, if there are people in the world who represent evil, is it our duty to exterminate them? I know that you always prey on weak people. I can tell. Oh, sometimes I think I ought to kill you. Sometimes I think you're the only obstacle between me and my happiness. Sometimes . . ."

She touched Blake with the pistol. He felt the muzzle against his belly. The bullet, at that distance, would make a small hole where it entered, but it would rip out of his back a place as big as a soccer ball. He remembered the unburied dead he had seen in the war. The memory came in a rush; entrails, eyes, shattered bone, ordure, and other filth.

"All I've ever wanted in life is a little love," she said. She lightened the pressure of the gun. Mr. Watkins still slept. Mrs. Compton was sitting calmly with her hands folded in her lap. The coach rocked gently, and the coats and mushroom-colored raincoats that hung between the windows swayed a little as the car moved. Blake's elbow was on the window sill and his left shoe was on the guard above the steampipe. The car smelled like some dismal classroom. The passengers seemed asleep and apart, and Blake felt that he might never escape the smell of heat and wet clothing and the dimness of the light. He tried to summon the calculated self-deceptions with which he sometimes cheered himself, but he was left without any energy for hope of self-deception.

The conductor put his head in the door and said, "Shady Hill, next, Shady Hill."

"Now," she said. "Now you get out ahead of me."

Mr. Watkins waked suddenly, put on his coat and hat, and smiled at Mrs. Compton, who was gathering her parcels to her in a series of maternal gestures. They went to the door. Blake joined them, but neither of them spoke to him or seemed to notice the woman at his back. The conductor threw open the door, and Blake saw on the platform of the next car a few other neighbors who had missed the express, waiting patiently and tiredly in the wan light for their trip to end. He raised his head to see through the open door the abandoned mansion out of town, a NO TRESPASSING sign nailed to a tree, and then the oil tanks. The concrete abutments of the bridge passed, so close to the open door that he could have touched them. Then he saw the first of the lampposts on the northbound platform, the sign SHADY HILL in black and gold, and the little lawn and flower bed kept up by the Improvement Association, and then the cab stand and a corner of the old-fashioned depot. It was raining again; it was pouring. He could hear the splash of water and see the lights reflected in puddles and in the shining pavement, and the idle sound of splashing and dripping formed in his mind a conception of shelter, so light and strange that it seemed to belong to a time of his life that he could not remember.

He went down the steps with her at his back. A dozen or so cars were waiting by the station with their motors running. A few people got off from each of the other coaches; he recognized most of them, but none of them offered to give him a ride. They walked separately or in pairs—purposefully out of the rain to the shelter of the platform, where the car horns called to them. It was time to go home, time for a drink, time for love, time for supper, and he could see the lights on the hill—lights by which children were being bathed, meat cooked, dishes washed—shining in the rain. One by one, the cars picked up the heads of families, until there were only four left. Two of the stranded passengers drove off in the only taxi the village had. "I'm sorry, darling," a woman said tenderly to her husband when she drove up a few minutes later. "All our clocks are slow." The last man looked at his watch, looked at the rain, and then walked off into it, and Blake saw him go as if they had some reason to say goodbye—not as we say goodbye to friends after a party but as we say goodbye when we are faced with an inexorable and unwanted parting of the spirit and the heart. The man's footsteps sounded as he crossed the parking lot to the sidewalk, and then they were lost. In the station, a telephone began to ring. The ringing was loud, evenly spaced, and unanswered. Someone wanted to know about the next train to Albany, but Mr. Flanagan, the stationmaster, had gone home an hour ago. He had turned on all his lights before he went away. They burned in the empty waiting room. They burned, tin-shaded, at intervals up and down the platform and with the peculiar sadness of dim and purposeless lights. They lighted the Hawaiian dancer, the couple drinking a toast, the rubber heel.

"I've never been here before," she said. "I thought it would look different. I didn't think it would look so shabby. Let's get out of the light. Go over there."

His legs felt sore. All his strength was gone. "Go on," she said.

North of the station there were a freight house and a coalyard and an inlet where the butcher and the baker and the man who ran the service station moored the dinghies, from which they fished on Sundays, sunk now to the gunwales with the rain. As he walked toward the freight house, he saw a movement on the ground and heard a scraping sound, and then he saw a rat take its head out of a paper bag and regard him. The rat seized the bag in its teeth and dragged it into a culvert.

"Stop," she said. "Turn around. Oh, I ought to feel sorry for you. Look at your poor face. But you don't know what I've been through. I'm afraid to go out in the daylight. I'm afraid the blue sky will fall down on me. I'm like poor Chicken-Licken. I only feel like myself when it begins to get dark. But still and all I'm better than you. I still have good dreams sometimes. I dream about picnics and heaven and the brotherhood of man, and about castles in the moonlight and a river with willow trees all along the edge of it and foreign cities, and after all I know more about love than you."

He heard from off the dark river the drone of an outboard motor, a sound that drew slowly behind it across the dark water such a burden of clear, sweet memories of gone summers and gone pleasures that it made his flesh crawl, and he thought of dark in the mountains and the children singing. "They never wanted to cure me," she said. "They . . ." The noise of a train coming down from the north drowned out her voice, but she went on talking. The noise filled his ears, and the windows where people ate, drank, slept, and read flew past. When the train had passed beyond the bridge, the noise grew distant, and he heard her screaming at him, "*Kneel down!* Kneel down! Do what I say. *Kneel down!*"

He got to his knees. He bent his head. "There," she said. "You see, if you do what I say, I won't harm you, because I really don't want to harm you, I want to help you, but when I see your face it sometimes seems to me that I can't help you. Sometimes it seems to me that if I were good and loving and sane—oh, much better than I am—sometimes it seems to me that if I were all these things and young and beautiful, too, and if I called to show you the right way, you wouldn't heed me. Oh, I'm better than you, I'm better than you, and I shouldn't waste my time or spoil my life like this. Put your face in the dirt. *Put your face in the dirt!* Do what I say. Put your face in the dirt."

He fell forward in the filth. The coal skinned his face. He stretched out on the ground, weeping. "Now I feel better," she said. "Now I can wash my hands of you, I can wash my hands of all this, because you see there is some kindness, some saneness in me that I can find and use. I can wash my hands." Then he heard her footsteps go away from him, over the rubble. He heard the clearer and more distant sound they made on the hard surface of the platform. He heard them diminish. He raised his head. He saw her climb the stairs of the wooden footbridge and cross it and go down to the other platform, where her figure in the dim light looked small, common, and harmless. He raised himself out of the dust—warily at first, until he saw by her attitude, her looks, that she had forgotten him; that she had completed what she had wanted to do, and that he was safe. He got to his feet and picked up his hat from the ground where it had fallen and walked home.

JUST ONE MORE TIME

THERE IS NO SENSE in looking for trouble, but in any big, true picture of the city where we all live there is surely room for one more word on the diehards, the hangers-on, the people who never got along and who never gave up, the insatiables that we have all known at one time or another. I mean the shoestring aristocrats of the upper East Side—the elegant, charming, and shabby men who work for brokerage houses, and their high-flown wives, with their thrift-shop minks and their ash-can fur pieces, their alligator shoes and their snotty ways with doormen and with the cashiers in supermarkets, their gold jewelry and their dregs of Je Reviens and Chanel. I'm thinking of the Beers now—Alfreda and Bob—who lived in the East Side apartment house that Bob's father used to own, surrounded by sailing trophies, autographed photographs of President Hoover, Spanish furniture, and other relics of the golden age. It wasn't much of a place, really—large and dark—but it was more than they could afford; you could tell by the faces of the doormen and the elevator operators when you told them where you were going. I suppose they were always two or three months behind with the rent and had nothing to spare for tips. Of course, Alfreda had been to school in Fiesole. Her father, like Bob's, had lost millions and millions and millions of dollars. All her memories were thickly inlaid with patines of bright gold: yesteryear's high bridge stakes, and how difficult it was to get the Daimler started on a rainy day, and picnics on the Brandywine with the Du Pont girls.

She was a good-looking woman—long-faced and with that New England fairness that seems to state a tenuous racial claim to privilege. She looked imperturbable. When they were on their uppers, she worked—first at the Steuben glass store, on Fifth Avenue, and then she went to Jensen's, where she got into trouble by insisting on her right to smoke. She went from there to Bonwit's, and from Bonwit's to Bendel's. Schwarz's took her on one Christmas, and she was on the street-floor glove counter at Saks the next Easter. She had a couple of children between jobs and she used to leave them in the care of an old Scotchwoman—an old family retainer from the good days—who seemed just as unable as the Beers to make an advantageous adjustment to change.

They were the kind of people that you met continually at railroad stations and cocktail parties. I mean Sunday-night railroad stations; weekend and season's-end places like the junction at Hyannis or Flemington; places like the station at Lake George, or Aiken and Greenville in the early spring; places like Westhampton, the Nantucket steamer, Stonington, and Bar Harbor; or, to go farther afield, places like Paddington Station, Rome, and the Antwerp night boat. "Hello! Hello!" they called across the crowd of travelers, and there he would be, in his white raincoat, with his stick and his Homburg, and there she was, in her mink or her ash-can fur piece. And in some ways the cocktail parties where your paths crossed were not so different, after all, from the depots, junctions, and boat trains where you met. They were the kind of party where the company is never very numerous and the liquor is never very good—parties where, as you drink and talk, you feel a palpable lassitude overtaking any natural social ardor, as if the ties of family, society, school, and place that held the group together were dissolving like the ice in your drink. But the atmosphere is not so much one of social dissolution as of social change, realignment—in effect, the atmosphere of travel. The guests seem to be gathered in a boat shed or at a railroad junction, waiting for the boat or the train to depart. Past the maid who takes the wraps, past the foyer and the fireproof door, there seems to lie a stretch of dark water, stormy water sometimes—the cry of the wind, the creak of iron sign hinges and the lights, the deckhand voices, and the soulful whistling of an approaching Channel boat.

One reason you always saw the Beers at cocktail parties and railroad stations was that they were always looking for somebody. They weren't looking for somebody like you or me—they were looking for the Marchioness of Bath—but any port in a storm. The way they used to come in to a party and stare around them is understandable—we all do it—but the way they used to peer at their fellow travelers on a station platform was something else. In any place where those two had to wait fifteen minutes or longer for a public conveyance they would turn the crowd inside out, peering under hat brims and behind newspapers for somebody they might happen to know.

I'M SPEAKING of the thirties and the forties now, the years before and after the Big War—years when the Beers' financial problems must have been complicated by the fact that their children were old enough to go to expensive schools. They did some unsavory things; they kited checks, and, borrowing someone's car for a weekend, they ran it into a ditch and walked away, washing their hands of the whole thing. These tricks brought some precariousness to their social as well as their economic status, but they continued to operate on a margin of charm and expectation—there was Aunt Margaret in Philadelphia and

Aunt Laura in Boston—and, to tell the truth, they were charming. People were always glad to see them, for, if they were the pathetic grasshoppers of some gorgeous economic summer, they somehow had it in their power to remind one of good things—good places, games, food, and company—and the ardor with which they looked for friends on railroad platforms could perhaps be accounted for by the fact that they were only looking for a world that they understood.

THEN AUNT MARGARET DIED, and this is how I discovered that interesting fact. It was in the spring, and my boss and his wife were sailing for England, and I went down to the boat one morning with a box of cigars and a historical romance. The ship was new, as I recall, with lots of drifters looking at the sets of Edna Ferber under lock and key in the library and admiring the dry swimming pools and the dry bars. The passageways were crowded, and every cabin in first class was full of flowers and of well-wishers drinking champagne at eleven o'clock on a gloomy morning, with the rich green soup of New York Harbor sending its tragic smell up to the clouds. I gave my boss and his wife their presents, and then, looking for the main deck, passed a cabin or suite where I heard Alfreda's boarding-school laugh. The place was jammed, and a waiter was pouring champagne, and when I had greeted my friends, Alfreda took me aside. "Aunt Margaret has departed this life," she said, "and we're *loaded* again. . . ." I had some champagne, and then the all-ashore whistle blew—vehement, deafening, the hoarse summons of life itself, and somehow, like the smell of harbor water, tragic, too; for, watching the party break up, I wondered how long Aunt Margaret's fortune would last those two. Their debts were enormous, and their habits were foolish, and even a hundred thousand wouldn't take them far.

This idea seems to have stayed at the back of my mind, for at a heavyweight fight at Yankee Stadium that fall I thought I saw Bob wandering around with a tray of binoculars to rent. I called his name—I shouted—and it wasn't he, but the resemblance was so striking that I felt as if I *had* seen him, or had at least seen the scope of the vivid social and economic contrasts in store for such a couple.

I WISH I could say that, leaving the theatre one snowy evening, I saw Alfreda selling pencils on Forty-sixth Street and that she would return to some basement on the West Side where Bob lay dying on a pallet, but this would only reflect on the poverty of my imagination.

In saying that the Beers were the kind of people you met at railroad stations and cocktail parties, I overlooked the beaches. They were *very* aquatic. You know how it is. In the summer months, the northeastern coast up from Long Island and deep into Maine, including all the sea islands, seems to be transformed into a vast social clearinghouse, and as you sit on the sand listening to the heavy furniture of the North Atlantic, figures from your social past appear in the surf, as thick as raisins in a cake. A wave takes form, accelerates its ride over the shallows, boils, and breaks, revealing Consuelo Roosevelt and Mr. and Mrs. Dundas Vanderbilt, with the children of both marriages. Then a wave comes in from the right like a cavalry charge, bearing landward on the rubber raft Lathrope Macy with Emerson Crane's second wife, and the Bishop of Pittsburgh in an inner tube. Then a wave breaks at your feet with the noise of a slammed trunk lid and there are the Beers. "How nice to see you, how very *nice* to see you . . ."

So the summer and the sea will be the setting for their last appearance—their last appearance for our purposes here, at any rate. We are in a small town in Maine—let's say—and decide to take the family for a sail and a picnic. The man at the inn tells us where there is a boat livery, and we pack our sandwiches and follow his directions to a wharf. We find an old man in a shack with a catboat to rent, and we make a deposit and sign a dirty paper, noticing that the old man, at ten in the morning, is drunk. He rows us out to the mooring in a skiff, and we say goodbye, and then, seeing how dilapidated his catboat is, we call after him, but he has already headed for the mainland and is out of hearing.

The floor boards are floating, the rudder pin is bent, and one of the bolts in the rudder has rusted away. The blocks are broken, and when we pump her dry and hoist the sail, it is rotted and torn. We get under way at last—urged by the children—and sail out to an island and eat our picnic.

Then we start home. But now the wind has freshened; it has backed around to the southwest; and when we have left the island our port stay snaps, and the wire flies upward and coils itself around the mast. We take down the sail and repair the stay with rope. Then we see that we are on an ebb tide and traveling rapidly out to sea. With the repaired stay we sail for ten minutes before the starboard stay gives. Now we are in trouble. We think of the old man in the shack, who holds the only knowledge of our whereabouts in his drunken head. We try to paddle with the floor boards, but we can make no headway against the sweep of the tide. Who will save us? The Beers!

They come over the horizon at dusk in one of those bulky cabin cruisers, with a banquette on the bridge and shaded lamps and bowls of roses in the cabin. A hired hand is at the helm, and Bob throws us a line. This is more than a chance reunion of old friends—our lives have been saved. We are nearly delirious. The hired hand is settled in the catboat, and ten minutes after we have been snatched from the jaws of death we are drinking Martinis on the bridge. They will take us back to their house, they say. We can spend the night there. And while the background and the appointments are not so different, their relationship to them has been revolutionized. It is *their* house, *their* boat. We wonder how—we gape—and Bob is civil enough to give us an explanation, in a low voice, a mumble, nearly, as if the facts were parenthetical. "We took most of Aunt Margaret's money and all of Aunt Laura's and a little something Uncle Ralph left us and invested it all in the market, you know, and it's more than tripled in the last two years. I've bought back everything Dad lost—everything I wanted, that is. That's my schooner over there. Of course, the house is new. Those are our lights." The afternoon and the ocean, which seemed so menacing in the catboat, now spread out around us with a miraculous tranquillity, and we settle back to enjoy our company, for the Beers are charming—they always were—and now they appear to be smart, for what else was it but smart of them to know that summertime would come again?

THE HOUSEBREAKER OF SHADY HILL

My name is Johnny Hake. I'm thirty-six years old, stand five feet eleven in my socks, weigh one hundred and forty-two pounds stripped, and am, so to speak, naked at the moment and talking into the dark. I was conceived in the Hotel St. Regis, born in the Presbyterian Hospital, raised on Sutton Place, christened and confirmed in St. Bartholomew's, and I drilled with the Knickerbocker Greys, played football and baseball in Central Park, learned to chin myself on the framework of East Side apartment-house canopies, and met my wife (Christina Lewis) at one of those big cotillions at the Waldorf. I served four years in the Navy, have four kids now, and live in a *banlieue* called Shady Hill. We have a nice house with a garden and a place outside for cooking meat, and on summer nights, sitting there with the kids and looking into the front of Christina's dress as she bends over to salt the steaks, or just gazing at the lights in heaven, I am as thrilled as I am thrilled by more hardy and dangerous pursuits, and I guess this is what is meant by the pain and sweetness of life.

I went to work right after the war for a parablendeum manufacturer, and seemed on the way to making this my life. The firm was patriarchal; that is, the old man would start you on one thing and then switch you to another, and he had his finger in every pie—the Jersey mill and the processing plant in Nashville—and behaved as if he had wool-gathered the whole firm during a catnap. I stayed out of the old man's way as nimbly as I could, and behaved in his presence as if he had shaped me out of clay with his own hands and breathed the fire of life into me. He was the kind of despot who needed a front, and this was Gil Bucknam's job. He was the old man's right hand, front, and peacemaker, and he could garnish any deal with the humanity the old man lacked, but he started staying out of the office—at first for a day or two, then for two weeks, and then for longer. When he returned, he would complain about stomach trouble or eyestrain, although anyone could see that he was looped. This was not so strange, since hard drinking was one of the things he had to do for the firm. The old man stood it for a year and then came into my office one morning and told me to get up to Bucknam's apartment and give him the sack.

This was as devious and dirty as sending an office boy to can the chairman of the board. Bucknam was my superior and my senior by many years, a man who condescended to do so whenever he bought me a drink, but this was the way the old man operated, and I knew what I had to do. I called the Bucknam apartment, and Mrs. Bucknam said that I could see Gil that afternoon. I had lunch alone and hung around the office until about three, when I *walked* from our midtown office to the Bucknams' apartment, in the East Seventies. It was early in the fall—the World Series was being played—and a thunderstorm was entering the city. I could hear the noise of big guns and smell the rain when I got to the Bucknams' place. Mrs. Bucknam let me in, and all the troubles of that past year seemed to be in her face, hastily concealed by a thick coat of powder. I've never seen such burned-out eyes, and she was wearing one of those old-fashioned garden-party dresses with big flowers on it. (They had three kids in college, I knew, and a schooner with a hired hand, and many other expenses.) Gil was in bed, and Mrs. Bucknam let me into the bedroom. The storm was about to break now, and everything stood in a gentle half darkness so much like dawn that it seemed as if we should be sleeping and dreaming, and not bringing one another bad news.

Gil was jolly and lovable and condescending, and said that he was *so* glad to see me; he had bought a lot of presents for my children when he was last in Bermuda and had forgotten to mail them. "Would you get those things, darling?" he asked. "Do you remember where we put them?" Then she came back into the room with five or six large and expensive-looking packages and unloaded them into my lap.

I think of my children mostly with delight, and I love to give them presents. I was charmed. It was a ruse, of course—hers, I guessed—and one of many that she must have thought up over the last year to hold their world together. (The wrappings were not fresh, I could see, and when I got home and found in them some old cashmere sweaters that Gil's daughters had not taken to college and a Scotch cap with a soiled sweatband, it only deepened my feeling of sympathy for the Bucknams in their trouble.) With a lap full of presents for my kiddies and sympathy leaking out of every joint, I couldn't give him the ax. We talked about the World Series and about some small matters at the office, and when the rain and the wind began, I helped Mrs. Bucknam shut the windows in the apartment, and then I left and took an early train home through the storm. Five days later, Gil Bucknam went on the wagon for good, and came back to the office to sit again at the right hand of the old man, and my skin was one of the first he went after. It seemed to me that if it had been my destiny to be a Russian ballet dancer, or to make art jewelry, or to paint *Schuhplattler* dancers on bureau drawers and landscapes on clamshells and live in some very low-tide place like Provincetown, I wouldn't have known a queerer bunch of men and women than I knew in the parablendeum industry, and I decided to strike out on my own.

My MOTHER taught me never to speak about money when there was a shirtful, and I've always been very reluctant to speak about it when there was any scarcity, so I cannot paint much of a picture of what ensued in the next six months. I rented office space—a cubicle with a desk and a phone was what it amounted to—and sent out letters, but the letters were seldom answered and the telephone might just as well have been disconnected, and when it came time to borrow money, I had nowhere to turn. My mother hated Christina, and I don't think she can have much money, in any case, because she never bought me an overcoat or a cheese sandwich when I was a kid without telling me that it came out of her principal. I had plenty of friends, but if my life depended on it I couldn't ask a man for a drink and touch him for five hundred—and I needed more. The worst of it was that I hadn't painted anything like an adequate picture to my wife.

I thought about this one night when we were dressing to go to dinner up the road at the Warburtons'. Christina was sitting at her dressing table putting on earrings. She is a pretty woman in the prime of life, and her ignorance of financial necessity is complete. Her neck is graceful, her breasts gleamed as they rose in the cloth of her dress, and, seeing the decent and healthy delight she took in her own image, I could not tell her that we were broke. She had sweetened much of my life, and to watch her seemed to freshen the wellsprings of some clear energy in me that made the room and the pictures on the wall and the moon that I could see outside the window all vivid and cheerful. The truth would make her cry and ruin her make-up and the Warburtons' dinner party for her, and she would sleep in the guest room. There seemed to be as much truth in her beauty and the power she exerted over my senses as there was in the fact that we were overdrawn at the bank.

The Warburtons are rich, but they don't mix; they may not even care. She is an aging mouse, and he is the kind of man that you wouldn't have liked at school. He has a bad skin and rasping voice and a fixed idea—lechery. The Warburtons are always spending money, and that's what you talk about with them. The floor of their front hall is black-and-white marble from the old Ritz, and their cabanas at Sea Island are being winterized, and they are flying to Davos for ten days, and buying a pair of saddle horses, and building a new wing. We were late that night, and the Meserves and the Chesneys were already there, but Carl Warburton hadn't come home, and Sheila was worried. "Carl has to walk through a terrible slum to get to the station," she said, "and he carries thousands of dollars on him, and I'm so afraid he'll be *victimized*. . . ." Then Carl came home and told a dirty story to the mixed company, and we went in to dinner. It was the kind of party where everybody has taken a shower and put on their best clothes, and where some old cook has been peeling mushrooms or picking the meat out of crab shells since daybreak. I wanted to have a good time. That was my wish, but my wishes could not get me off the ground that night. I felt as if I was at some god-awful birthday party of my childhood that my mother had brought me to with threats and promises. The party broke up at about half past eleven, and we went home. I stayed out in the garden finishing one of Carl Warburton's cigars. It was a Thursday night, and my checks wouldn't bounce until

Tuesday, but I had to do something soon. When I went upstairs, Christina was asleep, and I fell asleep myself, but I woke again at about three.

I had been dreaming about wrapping bread in colored parablendeum Filmex. I had dreamed a full-page spread in a national magazine: BRING SOME COLOR INTO YOUR BREADBOX! The page was covered with jewel-toned loaves of bread—turquoise bread, ruby bread, and bread the color of emeralds. In my sleep the idea had seemed to me like a good one; it had cheered me, and it was a letdown to find myself in the dark bedroom. Feeling sad then, I thought about all the loose ends of my life, and this brought me around to my old mother, who lives alone in a hotel in Cleveland. I saw her getting dressed to go down and have dinner in the hotel dining room. She seemed pitiable, as I imagined her—lonely and among strangers. And yet, when she turned her head, I saw that she still had some biting teeth left in her gums.

She sent me through college, arranged for me to spend my vacations in pleasant landscapes, and fired my ambitions, such as they are, but she bitterly opposed my marriage, and our relations have been strained ever since. I've often invited her to come and live with us, but she always refuses, and always with bad feeling. I send her flowers and presents, and write her every week, but these attentions only seem to fortify her conviction that my marriage was a disaster for her and for me. Then I thought about her apron strings, for when I was a kid, she seemed to be a woman whose apron strings were thrown across the Atlantic and the Pacific oceans; they seemed to be looped, like vapor trails, across the very drum of heaven. I thought of her now without rebellion or anxiety—only with sorrow that all our exertions should have been rewarded with so little clear emotion, and that we could not drink a cup of tea together without stirring up all kinds of bitter feeling. I longed to correct this, to re-enact the whole relationship with my mother against a more simple and human background, where the cost of my education would not have come so high in morbid emotion. I wanted to do it all over again in some emotional Arcadia, and have us both behave differently, so that I could think of her at three in the morning without guilt, and so that she would be spared loneliness and neglect in her old age.

I moved a little closer to Christina and, coming into the area of her warmth, suddenly felt all kindly and delighted with everything, but she moved in her sleep, away from me. Then I coughed. I coughed again. I coughed loudly. I couldn't stop coughing, and I got out of bed and went into the dark bathroom and drank a glass of water. I stood at the bathroom window and looked down into the garden. There was a little wind. It seemed to be changing its quarter. It sounded like a dawn wind—the air was filled with a showery sound—and felt good on my face. There were some cigarettes on the back of the toilet, and I lit one in order to get back to sleep. But when I inhaled the smoke, it hurt my lungs, and I was suddenly convinced that I was dying of bronchial cancer.

I have experienced all kinds of foolish melancholy—I've been homesick for countries I've never seen, and longed to be what I couldn't be—but all these moods were trivial compared to my premonition of death. I tossed my cigarette into the toilet (ping) and straightened my back, but the pain in my chest was only sharper, and I was convinced that the corruption had begun. I had friends who would think of me kindly, I knew, and Christina and the children would surely keep alive an affectionate memory. But then I thought about money again, and the Warburtons, and my rubber checks approaching the clearing-house, and it seemed to me that money had it all over love. I had yearned for some women—turned green, in fact—but it seemed to me that I had never yearned for anyone the way I yearned that night for money. I went to the closet in our bedroom and put on some old blue sneakers and a pair of pants and a dark pullover. Then I went downstairs and out of the house. The moon had set, and there were not many stars, but the air above the trees and hedges was full of dim light. I went around the Trenholmes' garden then, gumshoeing over the grass, and down the lawn to the Warburtons' house. I listened for sounds from the open windows, and all I heard was the ticking of a clock. I went up the front steps and opened the screen door and started across the floor from the old Ritz. In the dim night light that came in at the windows, the house looked like a shell, a nautilus, shaped to contain itself.

I heard the noise of a dog's license tag, and Sheila's old cocker came trotting down the hall. I rubbed him behind the ears, and then he went back to wherever his bed was, grunted, and fell asleep. I knew the plan of the Warburtons' house as well as I knew the plan of my own. The staircase was carpeted, but I first put my foot on one of the treads to see if it creaked. Then I started up the stairs. All the bedroom doors stood open, and from Carl and Sheila's bedroom, where I had often left my coat at big cocktail parties, I could hear the sound of deep breathing. I stood in the doorway for a second to take my bearings. In the dimness I could see the bed, and a pair of pants and a jacket hung over the back of a chair. Moving swiftly, I stepped into the room and took a big billfold from the inside pocket of the coat and started back to the hall. The violence of my emotions may have made me clumsy, because Sheila woke. I heard her say, "Did you hear that noise, darling?" "S'wind," he mumbled, and then they were quiet again. I was safe in the hall—safe from everything but myself. I seemed to be having a nervous breakdown out there. All my saliva was gone, the lubricants seemed to drain out of my heart, and whatever the juices were that kept my legs upright were going. It was only by holding on to the wall that I could make any progress at all. I clung to the banister on my way down the stairs, and staggered out of the house.

BACK in my own dark kitchen, I drank three of four glasses of water. I must have stood by the kitchen sink for a half hour or longer before I thought of looking in Carl's wallet. I went into the cellarway and shut the cellar door before I turned the light on. There was a little over nine hundred dollars. I turned the light off and went back into the dark kitchen. Oh, I never knew that a man could be so miserable and that the mind could open up so many chambers and fill them with self-reproach! Where were the trout streams of my youth, and other innocent pleasures? The wet-leather smell of the loud waters and the keen woods after a smashing rain; or at opening day the summer breezes smelling like the grassy breath of Holsteins—your head would swim—and all the brooks full then (or so I imagined, in the dark kitchen) of trout, our sunken treasure. I was crying.

Shady Hill, as I say, a *banlieue* and open to criticism by city planners, adventurers, and lyric poets, but if you work in the city and have children to raise, I can't think of a better place. My neighbors are rich, it is true, but riches in this case mean leisure, and they use their time wisely. They travel around the world, listen to good music, and given a choice of paper books at an airport, will pick Thucydides, and sometimes Aquinas. Urged to build bomb shelters, they plant trees and roses, and their gardens are splendid and bright. Had I looked, the next morning, from my bathroom window into the evil-smelling ruin of some great city, the shock of recalling what I had done might not have been so violent, but the moral bottom had dropped out of my world without changing a mote of sunlight. I dressed stealthily—for what child of darkness would want to hear the merry voices of his family?—and caught an early train. My gabardine suit was meant to express cleanliness and probity, but I was a miserable creature whose footsteps had been mistaken for the noise of the wind. I looked at the paper. There had been a thirty-thousand-dollar payroll robbery in the Bronx. A White Plains matron had come home from a party to find her furs and jewelry gone. Sixty thousand dollars' worth of medicine had been taken from a warehouse in Brooklyn. I felt better at discovering how common the thing I had done was. But only a little better, and only for a short while. Then I was faced once more with the realization that I was a common thief and an impostor, and that I had done something so reprehensible that it violated the tenets of every known religion. I had stolen, and what's more, I had criminally entered the house of a friend and broken all the unwritten laws that held the community together. My conscience worked so on my spirits—like the hard beak of a carnivorous bird—that my left eye began to twitch, and again I seemed on the brink of a general nervous collapse. When the train reached the city, I went to the bank. Leaving the bank, I was nearly hit by a taxi. My anxiety was not for my bones but for the fact that Carl Warburton's wallet might be found in my pocket. When I thought no one was looking, I wiped the wallet on my trousers (to remove the fingerprints) and dropped it into the ash can.

I thought that coffee might make me feel better, and went into a restaurant, and sat down at a table with a stranger. The soiled lace-paper doilies and half-empty glasses of water had not been taken away, and at the stranger's place there was a thirty-five-cent tip, left by an earlier customer. I looked at the menu, but out of the corner of my eye I saw the stranger pocket the thirty-five-cent tip. What a crook! I got up and left the restaurant.

I walked into my cubicle, hung up my hat and coat, sat down at my desk, shot my cuffs, sighed, and looked into space, as if a day full of challenge and decision were about to begin. I hadn't turned on the light. In a little while, the office beside mine was occupied, and I heard my neighbor clear his throat, cough, scratch a match, and settle down to attack the day's business.

The walls were flimsy—part frosted glass and part plywood—and there was no acoustical privacy in these offices. I reached into my pocket for a cigarette with as much stealth as I had exercised at the Warburtons', and waited for the noise of a truck passing on the street outside before I lit a match. The excitement of eavesdropping took hold of me. My neighbor was trying to sell uranium stock over the telephone. His line went like this: First he was courteous. Then he was nasty. "What's the matter, Mr. X? Don't you want to make any money?" Then he was *very* scornful. "I'm sorry to have bothered you, Mr. X. I thought you *had* sixty-five dollars to invest." He called twelve numbers without any takers. I was as quiet as a mouse. Then he telephoned the information desk at Idlewild, checking the arrival of planes from Europe. London was on time. Rome and Paris were late. "No, he ain't in yet," I heard him say to someone over the phone. "It's dark in there." My heart was beating fast. Then my telephone began to ring, and I counted twelve rings before it stopped. "I'm positive, I'm positive," the man in the next office said. "I can hear his telephone ringing, and he ain't answering it, and he's just a lonely son of a bitch looking for a job. Go ahead, go ahead, I tell you. I ain't got time to get over there. Go ahead. . . . Seven, eight, three, five, seven, seven. . . ." When he hung up, I went to the door, opened and closed it, turned the light on, rattled the coat hangers, whistled a tune, sat down heavily at my desk chair, and dialed the first telephone number that came to my mind. It was an old friend—Burt Howe—and he exclaimed when he heard my voice. "Hakie, I been looking for you everywhere! You sure folded up your tents and stole away."

"Yes," I said.

"Stole away," Howe repeated. "Just stole away. But what I wanted to talk with you about is this deal I thought you might be interested in. It's a one-shot, but it won't take you more than three weeks. It's a steal. They're green, and they're dumb, and they're loaded, and it's just like stealing."

"Yes," I said.

"Well, then, can you meet me for lunch at Cardin's at twelve-thirty, and I'll give you the details?" Howe asked.

"O.K.," I said hoarsely. "Thanks a lot, Burt."

"We went out to the shack on Sunday," the man in the next office was saying as I hung up. "Louise got bit by a poisonous spider. The doctor gave her some kind of injection. She'll be all right." He dialed another number and began, "We went out to the shack on Sunday. Louise got bit by a poisonous spider . . ."

It was possible that a man whose wife had been bitten by a spider and who found some time on his hands might call three or four friends and tell them about it, and it was equally possible that the spider might be a code of warning or of assent to some unlawful traffic. What frightened me was that by becoming a thief I seemed to have surrounded myself with thieves and operators. My left eye had begun to twitch again, and the inability of one part of my consciousness to stand up under the reproach that was being heaped into it by another part made me cast around desperately for someone else who could be blamed. I had read often enough in the papers that divorce sometimes led to crime. My parents were divorced when I was about five. This was a good clue and quickly led me on to something better.

My father went to live in France after the divorce, and I didn't see him for ten years. Then he wrote Mother for permission to see me, and she prepared me for this reunion by telling me how drunken, cruel, and lewd the old man was. It was in the summer, and we were on Nantucket, and I took the steamer alone, and went to New York on the train. I met my father at the Plaza early in the evening, but not so early that he hadn't begun to drink. With the long, sensitive nose of an adolescent I smelled the gin on his breath, and I noticed that he bumped into a table and sometimes repeated himself. I realized later that this reunion must have been strenuous for a man of sixty, which he was. We had dinner and then went to see *The Roses of Picardy*. As soon as the chorus came on, Father said that I could have any one of them that I wanted; the arrangements were all made. I could even have one of the specialty dancers. Now, if I'd felt that he had crossed the Atlantic to perform this service for me, it might have been different, but I felt he'd made the trip in order to do a disservice to my mother. I was scared. The show was in one of those old-fashioned theatres that appear to be held together with angels. Brown-gold angels held up the ceiling; they held up the boxes; they even seemed to hold up the balcony with about four hundred people in it. I spent a lot of time looking at those dusty gold angels. If the ceiling of the theatre had fallen on my head, I would have been relieved. After the show, we went back to the hotel to wash before meeting the girls, and the old man stretched out on the bed for a minute and began to snore. I picked his wallet of fifty dollars, spent the night at Grand Central, and took an early morning train to Woods Hole. So the whole thing was explained, including the violence of the emotion I had experienced in the Warburtons' upstairs hall; I had been reliving that scene at the Plaza. It had not been my fault that I had stolen then, and it had not been my fault when I went to the Warburtons'. It was my father's fault! Then I remembered that my father was buried in Fontainebleau fifteen years ago, and could be nothing much more now than dust.

I went into the men's room and washed my hands and face, and combed my hair down with a lot of water. It was time to go out for lunch. I thought anxiously of the lunch ahead of me, and, wondering why, was astonished to realize that it was Burt Howe's free use of the word "steal." I hoped he wouldn't keep on saying it.

Even as the thought floated across my mind in the men's room, the twitching in my eye seemed to spread over my cheek; it seemed as if this verb were embedded in the English language like a poisoned fishhook. I had committed adultery, and the word "adultery" had no force for me; I had been drunk, and the word "drunkenness" had no extraordinary power. It was only "steal" and all its allied nouns, verbs, and adverbs that had the power to tyrannize over my nervous system, as if I had evolved, unconsciously, some doctrine wherein the act of theft took precedence over all the other sins in the Decalogue and was a sign of moral death.

The sky was dark when I came out on the street. Lights were burning everywhere. I looked into the faces of the people that I passed for some encouraging signs of honesty in such a crooked world, and on Third Avenue I saw a young man with a tin cup, holding his eyes shut to impersonate blindness. That seal of blindness, the striking innocence of the upper face, was betrayed by the frown and the crow's-feet of a man who could see his drinks on the bar. There was another blind beggar on Forty-first Street, but I didn't examine his eye sockets, realizing that I couldn't assess the legitimacy of every beggar in the city.

Cardin's is a men's restaurant in the Forties. The stir and bustle in the vestibule only made me feel retiring, and the hat-check girl, noticing, I suppose, the twitch in my eye, gave me a very jaded look.

Burt was at the bar, and when we had ordered our drinks, we got down to business. "For a deal like this, we ought to meet in some back alley," he said, "but a fool and his money *and* so forth. It's three kids. P.J. Burdette is one of them, and they've got a cool million between them to throw away. Somone's bound to steal from them, so it may as well be you." I put my hand over the left side of my face to cover the tic. When I tried to raise my glass to my mouth, I spilled gin all over my suit. "They're all three of them just out of college," Burt said. "And they've all three of them got so much in the kitty that even if you picked them clean they wouldn't feel any pain. Now, in order to participate in this burglary, all you have to do . . ."

The toilet was at the other end of the restaurant, but I got there. Then I drew a basin of cold water and stuck my head and face into it. Burt had followed me to the washroom. As I was drying myself with a paper towel, he said, "You know, Hakie, I wasn't going to mention it, but now that you've been sick, I may as well tell you that you look awful. I mean, from the minute I saw you I knew something was wrong. I just want to tell you that whatever it is—sauce or dope or trouble at home—it's a lot later than you think, and maybe you should be doing something about it. No hard feelings?" I said that I was sick, and waited in the toilet long enough for Burt to make a getaway. Then I got my hat and another jaded look from the hat-check girl, and saw in the afternoon paper on a chair by the checkroom that some bank robbers in Brooklyn had got away with eighteen thousand dollars.

I walked around the streets, wondering how I would shape up as a pickpocket and bag snatcher, and all the arches and spires of St. Patrick's only reminded me of poor boxes. I took the regular train home, looking out of the window at a peaceable landscape and a spring evening, and it seemed to me fishermen and lone bathers and grade-crossing watchmen and sand-lot ball players and lovers unashamed of their sport and the owners of small sailing craft and old men playing pinochle in firehouses were the people who stitched up the big holes in the world that were made by men like me.

Now Christina is the kind of woman who, when she is asked by the alumnae secretary of her college to describe her status, gets dizzy thinking about the variety of her activities and interests. And what, on a given day, stretching a point here and there, does she have to do? Drive me to the train. Have the skis repaired. Book a tennis court. Buy the wine and groceries for the monthly dinner of the Société Gastronomique du Westchester Nord. Look up some definitions in Larousse. Attend a League of Women Voters symposium on sewers. Go to a full-dress lunch for Bobsie Neil's aunt. Weed the garden. Iron a uniform for the part-time maid. Type two and a half pages of her paper on the early novels of Henry James. Empty the wastebaskets. Help Tabitha prepare the children's supper. Give Ronnie some batting practice. Put her hair in pin curls. Get the cook. Meet the train. Bathe. Dress. Greet her guests in French at half past seven. Say *bon soir* at eleven. Lie in my arms until twelve. Eureka! You might say that she is prideful, but I think only that she is a woman enjoying herself in a country that is prosperous and young. Still, when she met me at the train that night, it was difficult for me to rise to all this vitality.

It was my bad luck to have to take the collection at early Communion on Sunday, although I was in no condition. I answered the pious looks of my friends with a very crooked smile and then knelt by a lancet-shaped stained-glass window that seemed to be made from the butts of vermouth and Burgundy bottles. I knelt on an imitation-leather hassock that had been given by some guild or auxiliary to replace one of the old, snuff-colored hassocks, which had begun to split at the seams and show bits of straw, and made the whole place smell like an old manger. The smell of straw and flowers, and the vigil light, and the candles flickering in the rector's breath, and the damp of this poorly heated stone building were all as familiar to me and belonged as much to my early life as the sounds and smells of a kitchen or a nursery, and yet they seemed, that morning, to be so potent that I felt dizzy. Then I heard, in the baseboard on my right, a rat's tooth working like an auger in the hard oak. "Holy, Holy, Holy," I said very loudly, hoping to frighten the rat. "Lord God of hosts, Heaven and earth are FULL of Thy Glory!" The small congregation muttered its amens with a sound like a footstep, and the rat went on scraping away at the baseboard. And then—perhaps because I was absorbed in the noise of the rat's tooth, or because the smell of dampness and straw was soporific—when I looked up from the shelter I had made of my hands, I saw the rector drinking from the chalice and realized that I had missed Communion.

At home, I looked through the Sunday paper for other thefts, and there were plenty. Banks had been looted, hotel safes had been emptied of jewelry, maids and butlers had been tied to kitchen chairs, furs and industrial diamonds had been stolen in job lots, delicatessens, cigar stores, and pawnshops had been broken into, and someone had stolen a painting from the Cleveland Institute of Art. Late in the afternoon, I raked leaves. What could be more contrite than cleaning the lawn of the autumn's dark rubbish under the streaked, pale skies of spring?

While I was raking leaves, my sons walked by. "The Toblers are having a softball game," Ronnie said. "*Everybody's* there."

"Why don't you play?" I asked.

"You can't play unless you've been invited," Ronnie said over his shoulder, and then they were gone. Then I noticed that I could hear the cheering from the softball game to which we had not been invited. The Toblers lived down the block. The spirited voices seemed to sound clearer and clearer as the night came on; I could even hear the noise of ice in glasses, and the voices of the ladies raised in a feeble cheer.

Why hadn't I been asked to play softball at the Toblers'? I wondered. Why had we been excluded from these simple pleasures, this lighthearted gathering, the fading laughter and voices and slammed doors of which seemed to gleam in the darkness as they were withdrawn from my possession? Why wasn't *I* asked to play softball at the Toblers'? Why should social aggrandizement—*climbing,* really—exclude a nice guy like me from a softball game? What kind of a world was that? Why should I be left alone with my dead leaves in the twilight—as I was—feeling so forsaken, lonely, and forlorn that I was chilled?

If there is anybody I detest, it is weak-minded sentimentalists—all those melancholy people who, out of an excess of sympathy for others, miss the thrill of their own essence and drift through life without identity, like a human fog, feeling sorry for everyone. The legless beggar in Times Square with his poor display of pencils, the rouged old lady in the subway who talks to herself, the exhibitionist in the public toilet, the drunk who has dropped on the subway stairs, do more than excite their pity; they are at a glance transformed into these unfortunates. Derelict humanity seems to trample over their unrealized souls, leaving them at twilight in a condition closely resembling the scene of a prison riot. Disappointed in themselves, they are always ready to be disappointed for the rest of us, and they will build whole cities, whole creations, firmaments and principalities, of tear-wet disappointment. Lying in bed at night, they will think tenderly of the big winner who lost his pari-mutuel ticket, of the great novelist whose magnum opus was burned mistakenly for trash, and of Samuel Tilden, who lost the Presidency of the United States through the shenanigans of the electoral college. Detesting this company, then, it was doubly painful for me to find myself in it. And, seeing a bare dogwood tree in the starlight, I thought, How sad everything is!

WEDNESDAY WAS my birthday. I recalled this fact in the middle of the afternoon, at the office, and the thought that

Christina might be planning a surprise party brought me in one second from a sitting to a standing position, breathless. Then I decided that she wouldn't. But just the preparations the children would make presented an emotional problem; I didn't see how I could face it.

I left the office early and had two drinks before I took the train. Christina looked pleased with everything when she met me at the station, and I put a very good face on my anxiety. The children had changed into clean clothes, and wished me a happy birthday so fervently that I felt awful. At the table there was a pile of small presents, mostly things the children had made—cuff links out of buttons, and a memo pad, and so forth. I thought I was very bright, considering the circumstances, and pulled my snapper, put on my silly hat, blew out the candles on the cake, and thanked them all, but then it seemed that there was another present—my *big* present—and after dinner I was made to stay inside while Christina and the children went outside, and then Juney came in and led me outdoors and around in back of the house, where they all were. Leaning against the house was an aluminum extension ladder with a card and a ribbon tied to it, and I said, as if I'd been hit, "What in *hell* is the meaning of this?"

"We thought you'd need it, Daddy," Juney said.

"What would I ever need a ladder for? What do you think I am—a second-story worker?"

"Storm windows," Juney said. "Screens—"

I turned to Christina. "Have I been talking in my sleep?"

"No," Christina said. "You haven't been talking in your sleep."

Juney began to cry.

"You could take the leaves out of the rain gutters," Ronnie said. Both of the boys were looking at me with long faces.

"Well, you must admit it's a very unusual present," I said to Christina.

"God!" Christina said. "Come on, children. Come on." She herded them in at the terrace door.

I kicked around the garden until after dark. The lights went on upstairs. Juney was still crying, and Christina was singing to her. Then she was quiet. I waited until the lights went on in our bedroom, and after a little while I climbed the stairs. Christina was in a nightgown, sitting at her dressing table, and there were heavy tears in her eyes.

"You'll have to try and understand," I said.

"I couldn't possibly. The children have been saving for months to buy you that damned-fool contraption."

"You don't know what I've been through," I said.

"If you'd been through hell, I wouldn't forgive you," she said. "You haven't been through anything that would justify your behavior. They've had it hidden in the garage for a week. They're so *sweet*."

"I haven't felt like myself," I said.

"Don't tell *me* that you haven't felt like yourself," she said. "I've looked forward to having you leave in the morning, and I've dreaded having you come home at night."

"I can't have been all that bad," I said.

"It's been hell," she said. "You've been sharp with the children, nasty to me, rude to your friends, and malicious behind their backs. It's been hideous."

"Would you like me to go?"

"Oh, Lord, would I like you to go! Then I could breathe."

"What about the children?"

"Ask my lawyer."

"I'll go, then."

I went down the hall to the closet where we keep the bags. When I took out my suitcase, I found that the children's puppy had chewed the leather binding loose all along one side. Trying to find another suitcase, I brought the whole pile down on top of me, boxing my ears. I carried my bag with this long strip of leather trailing behind me back into our bedroom. "*Look,*" I said. "Look at this, Christina. The dog has chewed the binding off my suitcase." She didn't even raise her head. "I've poured twenty thousand dollars a year into this establishment for ten years," I shouted, "and when the time comes for me to go, I don't even have a decent suitcase! Everybody else has a suitcase. Even the cat has a nice traveling bag." I threw open my shirt drawer, and there were only four clean shirts. "I don't have enough clean shirts to last a week!" I shouted. Then I got a few things together, clapped my hat on my head, and marched out. I even thought, for a minute, of taking the car, and I went into the garage and looked it over. Then I saw the FOR SALE sign that had been hanging on the house when we bought it long, long ago. I wiped the dirt off the sign and got a nail and a rock and went around to the front of the house and nailed the FOR SALE sign onto a maple tree. Then I walked to the station. It's about a mile. The long strip of leather was trailing along behind me, and I stopped and tried to rip it off the suitcase, but it wouldn't come. When I got down to the station, I found there wasn't another train until four in the morning. I decided I would wait. I sat down on my suitcase and waited five minutes. Then I marched home again. Halfway there I saw Christina coming down the street, in a sweater and a skirt and sneakers—the quickest things to put on, but summery things—and we walked home together and went to bed.

On Saturday, I played golf, and although the game finished late, I wanted to take a swim in the club pool before I went home. There was no one at the pool but Tom Maitland. He is a dark-skinned and nice-looking man, very rich, but quiet. He seems withdrawn. His wife is the fattest woman in Shady Hill, and nobody much likes his children, and I think he is the kind of man whose parties and friendship and affairs in love and business all rest like an intricate superstructure—a tower of matchsticks—on the melancholy of his early youth. A breath could bring the whole thing down. It was nearly dark when I had finished swimming; the clubhouse was lighted and you could hear the sounds of dinner on the porch. Maitland was sitting at the edge of the pool dabbling his feet in the bright-blue water, with its Dead Sea smell of chlorine. I was drying myself off, and as I passed him, I asked if he wasn't going in. "I don't know how to swim," he said. He smiled and looked away from me then to the still, polished water of the pool, in the dark landscape. "We used to have a pool at home," he said, "but I never got a chance to swim in it. I was always studying the violin." There he was, forty-five years old and at least a millionaire, and he couldn't even float, and I don't suppose he had many occasions to speak as honestly as he had just spoken. While I was getting dressed, the idea settled in my head—with no help from me—that the Maitlands would be my next victims.

A few nights later, I woke up at three. I thought over the loose ends in my life—Mother in Cleveland, and parablendeum—and then I went into the bathroom to light a cigarette before I remembered that I was dying of bronchial cancer and leaving my widow and orphans penniless. I put on my blue sneakers and the rest of the outfit, looked in at the open doors of the children's rooms, and then went out. It was cloudy. I walked through back gardens to the corner. Then I crossed the street and turned up the Maitlands' driveway, walking on the grass at the edge of the gravel. The door was open, and I went in, just as excited and frightened as I had been at the Warburtons' and feeling insubstantial in the dim light—a ghost. I followed my nose up the stairs to where I knew their bedroom was, and, hearing heavy breathing and seeing a jacket and some pants on a chair, I reached for the pocket of the jacket, but there wasn't one. It wasn't a suit coat at all; it was one of those bright satin jackets that kids wear. There was no sense in looking for a wallet in *his* trousers. He couldn't make that much cutting the Maitlands' grass. I got out of there in a hurry.

I did not sleep any more that night but sat in the dark thinking about Tom Maitland, and Gracie Maitland, and the Warburtons, and Christina, and my own sordid destiny, and how different Shady Hill looked at night than in the light of day.

But I went out the next night—this time to the Pewters', who were not only rich but booze fighters, and who drank so much that I didn't see how they could hear thunder after the lights were turned out. I left, as usual, a little after three.

I was thinking sadly about my beginnings—about how I was made by a riggish couple in a midtown hotel after a six-course dinner with wines, and my mother had told me so many times that if she hadn't drunk so many Old-Fashioneds before that famous dinner I would still be unborn on a star. And I thought about my old man and that night at the Plaza and the bruised thighs of the peasant women of Picardy and all the brown-gold angels that held the theatre together and my terrible destiny. While I was walking toward the Pewters', there was a harsh stirring in all the trees and gardens, like a draft on a bed of fire, and I wondered what it was until I felt the rain on my hands and face, and then I began to laugh.

I wish I could say that a kindly lion had set me straight,

or an innocent child, or the strains of distant music from some church, but it was no more than the rain on my head—the smell of it flying up to my nose—that showed me the extent of my freedom from the bones in Fontainebleau and the works of a thief. There were ways out of my trouble if I cared to make use of them. I was not trapped. I was here on earth because I chose to be. And it was no skin off my elbow how I had been given the gifts of life so long as I possessed them, and I possessed them then—the tie between the wet grass roots and the hair that grew out of my body, the thrill of my mortality that I had known on summer nights, loving the children, and looking down the front of Christina's dress. I was standing in front of the Pewters' by this time, and I looked up at the dark house and then turned and walked away. I went back to bed and had pleasant dreams. I dreamed I was sailing a boat on the Mediterranean. I saw some worn marble steps leading down into the water, and the water itself—blue, saline, and dirty. I stepped the mast, hoisted the sail, and put my hand on the tiller. But why, I wondered as I sailed away, should I seem to be only seventeen years old? But you can't have everything.

It is not, as somebody once wrote, the smell of corn bread that calls us back from death; it is the lights and signs of love and friendship. Gil Bucknam called me the next day and said that the old man was dying and would I come back to work? I went to see him, and he explained that it was the old man who was after my skin, and, of course, I was glad to come home to parablendeum.

What I did not understand, as I walked down Fifth Avenue that afternoon, was how a world that had seemed so dark could, in a few minutes, become so sweet. The sidewalks seemed to shine, and, going home on the train, I beamed at those foolish girls who advertise girdles on the signboards in the Bronx. I got an advance on my salary the next morning, and, taking some precautions about fingerprints, I put nine hundred dollars into an envelope and walked over to the Warburtons' when the last lights in the neighborhood had been put out. It had been raining, but the rain had let up. The stars were beginning to show. There was no sense in overdoing prudence, and I went around to the back of their house, found the kitchen door open, and put the envelope on a table in the dark room.

As I was walking away from the house, a police car drew up beside me, and a patrolman I know cranked down the window and asked, "What are you doing out at this time of night, Mr. Hake?"

"I'm walking the dog," I said cheerfully. There was no dog in sight, but they didn't look. "Here, Toby! Here, Toby! Here, Toby! *Good* dog!" I called, and off I went, whistling merrily in the dark.

THE BUS TO ST. JAMES'S

THE BUS to St. James's—a Protestant Episcopal School for boys and girls—started its round at eight o'clock in the morning, from a corner of Park Avenue in the Sixties. The earliness of the hour meant that some of the parents who took their children there were sleepy and still without coffee, but with a clear sky the light struck the city at an extreme angle, the air was fresh, and it was an exceptionally cheerful time of day. It was the hour when cooks and doormen walk dogs, and when porters scrub the lobby floor mats with soap and water. Traces of the night—the parents and children once watched a man whose tuxedo was covered with sawdust wander home—were scarce.

When the fall semester began, five children waited for the school bus at this stop, and they all came from the limestone apartment houses of the neighborhood. Two of the children, Louise and Emily Sheridan, were newcomers. The others—the Pruitt boy, Katherine Bruce, and the little Armstrong girl—had met the bus for St. James's the year before.

Mr. Pruitt brought his son to the corner each morning. They had the same tailor and they both tipped their hats to the ladies. Although Katherine Bruce was old enough to walk to the bus stop by herself, she was nearsighted and her father made the trip with her unless he was out of town on business, in which case a maid brought her. Stephen Bruce's first wife, Katherine's mother, had died, and he was more painstakingly attentive to his daughter than fathers usually are. She was a large girl, but he took her hand tenderly and led her across the street and sometimes stood on the corner with his arm around her shoulders. The second Mrs. Bruce had no children. Mrs. Armstrong took her daughter to the bus stop only when her maid or her cook refused. Like Mrs. Armstrong, Mrs. Sheridan shared this chore with a maid, but she was more constant. At least three mornings a week she came to the corner with her daughters and with an old Scotch terrier on a leash.

St. James's was a small school, and the parents, waiting on the street corner until the bus arrived, spoke confidently to one another. Mr. Bruce knew Mr. Pruitt's brother-in-law and was the second cousin of a woman who had roomed with Mrs. Armstrong in boarding school. Mrs. Sheridan and Mr. Pruitt had friends in common. "We saw some friends of yours last night," Mr. Pruitt said one morning. "The Murchisons?" "Oh yes," Mrs. Sheridan said, "*yes.*" She never gave a simple affirmative; she always said, "Oh yes, *yes,*" or "Oh yes, *yes,* yes."

Mrs. Sheridan dressed plainly and her hair was marked with gray. She was not pretty or provocative, and compared to Mrs. Armstrong, whose hair was golden, she seemed plain; but her features were fine and her body was graceful and slender. She was a well-mannered woman of perhaps thirty-five, Mr. Bruce decided, with a well-ordered house and a perfect emotional digestion—one of those women who, through their goodness, can absorb anything. A great deal of authority seemed to underlie her mild manner. She would have been raised by solid people, Mr. Bruce thought, and would respect all the boarding-school virtues; courage, good sportsmanship, chastity, and honor. When he heard her say in the morning, "Oh yes, *yes!*" it seemed to him like a happy combination of manners and spirit.

Mr. Pruitt continued to tell Mrs. Sheridan that he had met her friends, but their paths never seemed to cross directly. Mr. Bruce, eavesdropping on their conversation, behind his newspaper, was gratified by this because he disliked Mr. Pruitt and respected Mrs. Sheridan; but he knew they were bound to meet somewhere other than on the street, and one day Mr. Pruitt took his hat off to Mrs. Sheridan and said, "Wasn't it a delightful party?" "Oh, yes," Mrs. Sheridan said, "yes." Then Mr. Pruitt asked

Mrs. Sheridan when she and her husband had left, and she said they had left at midnight. She did not seem anxious to talk about the party, but she answered all of Mr. Pruitt's questions politely.

Mr. Bruce told himself that Mrs. Sheridan was wasting her time; Pruitt was a fool and she deserved better. His dislike of Pruitt and his respect for Mrs. Sheridan seemed idle, but he was pleased, one morning, to get to the corner and find that Mrs. Sheridan was there with her two daughters and the dog, and that Pruitt wasn't. He wished her a good morning.

"Good morning," she said. "We seem to be early."

Katherine and the older Sheridan girl began to talk together.

"I think I knew Katherine's mother," Mrs. Sheridan said politely. "Wasn't your first wife Martha Chase?"

"Yes."

"I knew her in college. I didn't know her well. She was in the class ahead of me. How old is Katherine now?"

"She was eight last summer," Mr. Bruce said.

"We have a brother," the younger Sheridan girl said, standing beside her mother. "He's eight."

"Yes, dear," Mrs. Sheridan said.

"He was drowned," the little girl said.

"Oh, I'm sorry," Mr. Bruce said.

"He was quite a good swimmer," the little girl went on, "but we think that he must have gotten a cramp. You see, there was a thunderstorm, and we all went into the boathouse and we weren't looking and—"

"That was a long time ago, dear," Mrs. Sheridan said gently.

"It wasn't so long ago," the little girl said. "It was only last summer."

"Yes, dear," her mother said. "Yes, yes."

Mr. Bruce noticed that there was no trace of pain, or of the effort to conceal it, on her face, and her composure seemed to him a feat of intelligence and grace. They continued to stand together, without talking, until the other parents arrived with their children, just as the bus came up the street. Mrs. Sheridan called to the old dog and went down Park Avenue, and Mr. Bruce got into a taxi and went to work.

Toward the end of October, on a rainy Friday night,

Mr. and Mrs. Bruce took a taxi to St. James's School. It was Parents' Night. One of the senior boys ushered them into a pew at the rear of the chapel. The altar was stripped of its mysteries, and the rector stood on the raised floor between the choir stalls, waiting for the laggard parents to be seated. He tucked and pulled nervously at his clericals, and then signaled for silence by clearing his throat.

"On behalf of the faculty and the board of trustees," he said, "I welcome the parents of St. James's here this evening. I regret that we have such inclement weather, but it doesn't seem to have kept any of you at home." This was said archly, as if the full attendance reflected his powers of intimidation. "Let us begin," he said, "with a prayer for the welfare of our school: Almighty Father, Creator of Heaven and earth! . . ." Kneeling, and with their heads bowed, the congregation looked indestructible and as if the permanence of society depended and could always depend on them. And when the prayer ended, the rector spoke to them about their durability. "I have some very interesting statistics for you all tonight," he said. "This year we have sixteen children enrolled in the school whose parents *and* whose grandparents were St. James's children. I think that's a very impressive number. I doubt that any other day school in the city could equal it."

During the brief speech in defense of conservative education that followed, Mr. Bruce noticed that Mrs. Sheridan was seated a few pews in front of him. With her was a tall man—her husband, presumably—with a straight back and black hair. When the talk ended, the meeting was opened for questions. The first question was from a mother who wanted advice on how to restrict her children's use of television. While the rector was answering this question, Mr. Bruce noticed that the Sheridans were having an argument. They were whispering, and their disagreement seemed intense. Suddenly, Mrs. Sheridan separated herself from the argument. She had nothing further to say. Mr. Sheridan's neck got red. He continued, in a whisper, to press his case, bending toward his wife, and shaking his head. Mrs. Sheridan raised her hand.

"Yes, Mrs. Sheridan," the rector said.

Mr. Sheridan picked up his coat and his derby, and, saying "Excuse me, please," "Thank you," "Excuse me," passed in front of the other people in the pew, and left the chapel.

"Yes, Mrs. Sheridan?" the rector repeated.

"I wonder, Dr. Frisbee," Mrs. Sheridan said, "if you and the board of trustees have ever thought of enrolling Negro children in St. James's?"

"That question came up three years ago," the rector said impatiently, "and a report was submitted to the board of trustees on the question. There have been very few requests for it, but if you would like a copy, I will have one sent to you."

"Yes," Mrs. Sheridan said, "I would like to read it."

The rector nodded and Mrs. Sheridan sat down.

"Mrs. Townsend?" the rector asked.

"I have a question about science and religion," Mrs. Townsend said. "It seems to me that the science faculty stresses science to the detriment of religious sentiment, especially concerning the Creation. It seems to me . . ."

Mrs. Sheridan picked up her gloves and, smiling politely and saying "Excuse me," "Thank you," "Please excuse me," she brushed past the others in the pew. Mr. Bruce heard her heels on the paved floor of the hall and, by craning his neck, was able to see her. The noise of traffic and of the rain grew louder as she pushed open one of the heavy doors, and faded as the door swung to.

LATE ONE AFTERNOON the following week, Mr. Bruce was called out of a stockholders' meeting to take a telephone call from his wife. She wanted him to stop at the stable where Katherine took riding lessons and bring her home. It exasperated him to have been called from the meeting to take this message, and when he returned, the meeting itself had fallen into the hands of an old man who had brought with him Robert's Rules of Order. Business that should have been handled directly and simply dragged, and the meeting ended in a tedious and heated argument. Immediately afterward, he took a taxi up to the Nineties, and went through the tack room of the riding stable into the ring. Katherine and some other girls, wearing hunting bowlers and dark clothes, were riding. The ring was cold and damp, its overhead lights burned whitely, the mirrors along the wall were fogged and streaked with moisture, and the riding mistress spoke to her pupils with an elaborate courteousness. Mr. Bruce watched his daughter. Katherine wore glasses, her face was plain, and her light hair was long and stringy. She was a receptive and obedient girl, and her exposure to St. James's had begun faintly to show in her face. When the lesson ended, he went into the tack room. Mrs. Sheridan was there, waiting for her daughters.

"Can I give you a lift home?" Mr. Bruce said.

"You most certainly can," Mrs. Sheridan said. "We were going to take a bus."

The children joined them and they all went out and waited for a cab. It was dark.

"I was interested in the question you asked at the parents' meeting," Mr. Bruce said. This was untrue. He was not interested in the question, and if Negroes had been enrolled in St. James's, he would have removed Katherine.

"I'm glad someone was interested," she said. "The Rector was wild."

"That's principally what interested me," Mr. Bruce said, trying to approach the truth.

A cab came along, and they got into it. He let Mrs. Sheridan off at the door of her apartment house and watched her walk with her two daughters into the lighted lobby.

MRS. SHERIDAN had forgotten her key and a maid let her in. It was late and she had asked people for dinner. The door to her husband's room was shut, and she bathed and dressed without seeing him. While she was combing her hair, she heard him go into the living room and turn on the television set. In company, Charles Sheridan always spoke contemptuously of television. "By Jove," he would say, "I don't see how anyone can look at that trash. It must be a year since I've turned our set on." Now his wife could hear him laughing uproariously.

She left her room and went down the hall to the dining room to check on everything there. Then she went through the pantry into the kitchen. She sensed trouble as soon as the door closed after her. Helen, the waitress, was sitting at a table near the sink. She had been crying. Anna, the cook, put down the pan she had been washing, to be sure of hearing everything that was said.

"What's the matter, Helen?" Mrs. Sheridan asked.

"From my pie he took twelff dollars, Mrs. Seridan," Helen said. She was Austrian.

"What for, Helen?"

"The day I burn myself. You told me to go to the doctor?"

"Yes."

"For that he took from my pie twelff dollars."

"I'll give you a check tomorrow, Helen," Mrs. Sheridan said. "Don't worry."

"Yes, ma'am," Helen said. "Thank you."

Mr. Sheridan came through the pantry into the kitchen. He looked handsome in his dark clothes. "Oh, here you are," he said to his wife. "Let's have a drink before they come." Then, turning to the waitress, he asked, "Have you heard from your family recently?"

"No, Mr. Seridan," Helen said.

"Where is it your family lives?" he asked.

"In Missigan, Mr. Seridan." She giggled, but this joke had been made innumerable times in the past few years and she was tired of it.

"Where?" Mr. Sheridan asked.

"In Missigan, Mr. Seridan," she repeated.

He burst out laughing. "By Jove, I think that's funny!" he said. He put his arm around his wife's waist and they went in to have a drink.

Mr. Bruce returned to a much pleasanter home. His wife, Lois, was a pretty woman, and she greeted him affectionately. He sat down with her for a cocktail. "Marguerite called me this morning," she said, "and told me that Charlie's lost his job. When I heard the phone ring, I sensed trouble; I *sensed* it. Even before I picked up the receiver, I knew that something was wrong. At first, I thought it was going to be poor Helen Luckman. She's had so many misfortunes recently that she's been on my mind a lot of the time. Then I heard Marguerite's voice. She said that poor Charlie had been a wonderful sport about the whole thing and that he was determined to get an even better job. He's traveled all over the United States for that firm and now they're just letting him go. *She* called while I was in bed, and the reason I stayed in bed this morning is because my back's been giving me a little trouble again.

It's nothing serious—it's nothing serious at all—but the pain's excruciating and I'm going to Dr. Parminter tomorrow and see if he can help me."

Lois had been frail when Mr. Bruce first met her. It had been one of her great charms. The extreme pallor and delicacy of her skin could be accounted for partly by a year of her life when, as she said, the doctors had given her up for dead. Her frailness was a fact, a mixture of chance and inheritance, and she could not be blamed for her susceptibility to poison oak, cold germs, and fatigue.

"I'm very sorry to hear about your back, dear," Mr. Bruce said.

"Well, I didn't spend the whole day in bed," she said. "I got up around eleven and had lunch with Betty and then went shopping."

Lois Bruce, like a great many women in New York, spent a formidable amount of time shopping along Fifth Avenue. She read the advertisements in the newspapers more intently than her husband read the financial section. Shopping was her principal occupation. She would get up from a sickbed to go shopping. The atmosphere of the department stores had a restorative effect on her disposition. She would begin her afternoon at Altman's—buy a pair of gloves on the first floor, and then travel up on the escalator and look at andirons. She would buy a purse and some face cream at Lord & Taylor's, and price coffee tables, upholstery fabrics, and cocktail glasses. "Down?" she would ask the elevator operator when the doors rolled open, and if the operator said "Up," Lois would board the car anyhow, deciding suddenly that whatever it was that she wanted might be in the furniture or the linen department. She would buy a pair of shoes and a slip at Saks, send her mother some napkins from Mosse's, buy a bunch of cloth flowers at De Pinna's, some hand lotion at Bonwit's, and a dress at Bendel's. By then, her feet and her head would be pleasantly tired, the porter at Tiffany's would be taking in the flag, the lamps on the carriages by the Plaza would be lighted. She would buy a cake at Dean's, her last stop, and walk home through the early dark like an honest workman, contented and weary.

When they sat down to dinner, Lois watched her husband taste his soup and smiled when she saw that he was pleased. "It is good, isn't it?" she said. "I can't taste it myself—I haven't been able to taste anything for a week—but I don't want to tell Katie, bless her, because it would hurt her feelings, and I didn't want to compliment her if it wasn't right. Katie," she called, through the pantry, "your soup is delicious."

Mrs. Sheridan did not come to the corner all the next week. On Wednesday afternoon, Mr. Bruce stopped by for Katherine at her dancing class, on the way home from his office. The Sheridan girls were in the same class, and he looked for Mrs. Sheridan in the lobby of the Chardin Club, but she wasn't there. He didn't see her again, actually, until he went, on Sunday afternoon, to bring Katherine home from a birthday party.

Because Lois sometimes played cards until seven o'clock, it often fell to Mr. Bruce to call for Katherine at some address at the end of the day, to see her through the stiff thanks and goodbyes that end a children's party. The streets were cold and dark; the hot rooms where the parties were smelled of candy and flowers. Among the friends and relatives there he was often pleased to meet people with whom he had summered or been to school. Some of these parties were elaborate, and he had once gone to get Katherine at an apartment in the Waldorf Towers where six little girls were being entertained by a glass blower.

In the hallway that Sunday afternoon, an Irish maid was taking up peanut shells with a carpet sweeper, lost balloons were bunched on the ceiling above her white head, and Mr. Bruce met a dwarf, dressed as a clown, who had entertained at parties in his own childhood. The old man had not changed his stock of tricks or his patter, and he was proud that he was able to remember the names and faces of most of the generations of children he had entertained. He held Mr. Bruce in the hall until, after several wrong guesses, he came up with his name. In the living room a dozen friends and relatives were drinking cocktails. Now and then, a weary child, holding a candy basket or a balloon, would wander through the crowd of grown people. At the end of the living room, a couple who worked a marionette show were dismantling their stage. The woman's hair was dyed, and she smiled and gesticulated broadly while she worked, like a circus performer, though no one was watching her.

While Mr. Bruce was waiting for Katherine to put her coat on, Mrs. Sheridan came in from the foyer. They shook hands. "Can I take you home?" he asked.

She said, "Yes, *yes,*" and went in search of her older daughter.

Katherine went up to her hostess and dropped a curtsy. "It was nice of you to ask me to your party, Mrs. Howells," she said, without mumbling. "And thank you very much."

"She's such a dear. It's such a joy to have her!" Mrs. Howells said to Mr. Bruce, and laid a hand absent-mindedly on Katherine's head.

Mrs. Sheridan reappeared with her daughter. Louise Sheridan curtsied and recited her thanks, but Mrs. Howells was thinking about something else and did not hear. The little girl repeated her thanks, in a louder voice.

"Why, thank you for coming!" Mrs. Howells exclaimed abruptly.

Mr. Bruce and Mrs. Sheridan and the two children went down in the elevator. It was still light when they came out of the building onto Fifth Avenue.

"Let's walk," Mrs. Sheridan said. "It's only a few blocks."

The children went on ahead. They were in the lower Eighties and their view was broad; it took in the avenue, the Museum, and the Park. As they walked, the double track of lights along the avenue went on with a faint click. There was a haze in the air that made the lamps give off a yellow light, and the colonnades of the Museum, the mansard roof of the Plaza above the trees, and the multitude of yellow lights reminded Stephen Bruce of many pictures of Paris and London ("Winter Afternoon") that had been painted at the turn of the century. This deceptive resemblance pleased him, and his pleasure in what he could see was heightened by the woman he was with. He felt that she saw it all very clearly. They walked along without speaking most of the way. A block or two from the building where she lived, she took her arm out of his.

"I'd like to talk with you someday about St. James's School," Mr. Bruce said. "Won't you have lunch with me? Could you have lunch with me on Tuesday?"

"I'd love to have lunch with you," Mrs. Sheridan said.

THE RESTAURANT WHERE Mrs. Sheridan and Mr. Bruce met for lunch on Tuesday was the kind of place where they were not likely to see anyone they knew. The menu was soiled, and so was the waiter's tuxedo. There are a thousand places like it in the city. When they greeted one another, they could have passed for a couple that had been married fifteen years. She was carrying bundles and an umbrella. She might have come in from the suburbs to get some clothes for the children. She said she had been shopping, she had taken a taxi, she had been rushed, she was hungry. She took off her gloves, rattled the menu, and looked around. He had a whiskey and she asked for a glass of sherry.

"I want to know what you really think about St. James's School," he said, and she began, animatedly, to talk.

They had moved a year earlier from New York to Long Island, she said, because she wanted to send her children to a country school. She had been to country schools herself. The Long Island school had been unsatisfactory, and they had moved back to New York in September. Her husband had gone to St. James's, and that had determined their choice. She spoke excitedly, as Mr. Bruce had known she would, about the education of her daughters, and he guessed that this was something she couldn't discuss with the same satisfaction with her husband. She was excited at finding someone who seemed interested in her opinions, and she put herself at a disadvantage, as he intended she should, by talking too much. The deep joy we take in the company of people with whom we have just recently fallen in love is undisguisable, even to a purblind waiter, and they both looked wonderful. He got her a taxi at the corner. They said goodbye.

"You'll have lunch with me again?"

"Of course," she said, "of course."

She met him for lunch again. Then she met him for dinner—her husband was away. He kissed her in the taxi, and they said good night in front of her apartment house. When he called her a few days later, a nurse or a maid answered the telephone and said that Mrs. Sheridan was ill and could not be disturbed. He was frantic. He called several times during the afternoon, and finally Mrs. Sheridan answered. Her illness was not serious, she said. She would be up in a day or two and she would call him when she was well. She called him early the next week, and they met for lunch at a restaurant in an uptown apartment house. She had been shopping. She took off her gloves, rattled the menu, and looked around another failing restaurant, poorly lighted and with only a few customers. One of her daughters had a mild case of measles, she said, and Mr. Bruce was interested in the symptoms. But he looked, for a man who claimed to be interested in childhood diseases, bilious and vulpine. His color was bad. He scowled and rubbed his forehead as if he suffered from a headache. He repeatedly wet his lips and crossed and recrossed his legs. Presently, his uneasiness seemed to cross the table. During the rest of the time they sat there, the conversation was about commonplace subjects, but an emotion for which they seemed to have no words colored the talk and darkened and enlarged its shapes. She did not finish her dessert. She let her coffee get cold. For a while, neither of them spoke. A stranger, noticing them in the restaurant, might have thought that they were a pair of old friends who had met to discuss a misfortune. His face was gray. Her hands were trembling. Leaning toward her, he said, finally, "The reason I asked you to come here is because the firm I work for has an apartment upstairs."

"Yes," she said. "*Yes.*"

For lovers, touch is metamorphosis. All the parts of their bodies seem to change, and they seem to become something different and better. That part of their experience that is distinct and separate, the totality of the years before they met, is changed, is redirected toward this moment. They feel they have reached an identical point of intensity, an ecstasy of rightness that they command in every part, and any recollection that occurs to them takes on this final clarity, whether it be a sweep hand on an airport clock, a snow owl, a Chicago railroad station on Christmas Eve, or anchoring a yawl in a strange harbor while all along the stormy coast strangers are blowing their horns for the yacht-club tender, or running a ski trail at that hour when, although the sun is still in the sky, the north face of every mountain lies in the dark.

"DO YOU WANT to go downstairs alone?" The elevator men in these buildings—" Stephen Bruce said when they had dressed.

"I don't care about the elevator men in these buildings," she said lightly.

She took his arm, and they went down in the elevator together. When they left the building, they were unwilling to part, and they decided on the Metropolitan Museum as a place where they were not likely to be seen by anyone they knew. The nearly empty rotunda looked, at that hour of the afternoon, like a railroad station past train time. It smelled of burning coal. They looked at stone horses and pieces of cloth. In a dark passage, they found a prodigal representation of the Feast of Love. The god—disguised now as a woodcutter, now as a cowherd, a sailor, a prince—came through every open door. Three spirits waited by a holly grove to lift the armor from his shoulders and undo his buckler. A large company encouraged his paramour. The whole creation was in accord—the civet and the bear, the lion and the unicorn, fire and water.

Coming back through the rotunda, Mr. Bruce and Mrs. Sheridan met a friend of Lois's mother. It was impossible to avoid her and they said How-do-you-do and I'm-happy-to-meet-you, and Stephen promised to remember the friend to his mother-in-law. Mr. Bruce and Mrs. Sheridan walked over to Lexington and said goodbye. He returned to his office and went home at six. Mrs. Bruce had not come in, the maid told him. Katherine was at a party, and he was supposed to bring her home. The maid gave him the address and he went out again without taking off his coat. It was raining. The doorman, in a white raincoat, went out into the storm, and returned riding on the running board of a taxi. The taxi had orange seats, and as it drove uptown, he heard the car radio playing a tango. Another doorman let him out and he went into a lobby that, like the one in the building where he lived, was meant to resemble the hall of a manor house. Upstairs, there were peanut shells on the rug, balloons on the ceiling; friends and relatives were drinking cocktails in the living room, and at the end of the room, the marionette stage was again being dismantled. He drank a Martini and talked with a friend while he waited for Katherine to put her coat on. "Oh yes, *yes*!" he heard Mrs. Sheridan say, and then he saw her come into the room with her daughters.

Katherine came between them before they spoke, and he went, with his daughter, over to the hostess. Katherine dropped her curtsy and said brightly, "It was very nice of you to ask me to your party, Mrs. Bremont, and thank you very much." As Mr. Bruce started for the elevator, the younger Sheridan girl dropped her curtsy and said, "It was a very nice party, Mrs. Bremont. . . ."

He waited downstairs, with Katherine, for Mrs. Sheridan, but something or someone delayed her, and when the elevator had come down twice without bringing her, he left.

MR. BRUCE AND MRS. SHERIDAN met at the apartment a few days later. Then he saw her in a crowd at the Rockefeller Center skating rink, waiting for her children. He saw her again in the lobby of the Chardin Club, among the other parents, nursemaids, and chauffeurs who were waiting for the dancing class to end. He didn't speak to her but he heard her at his back, saying to someone, "Yes, Mother's very well, thank you. Yes, I will give her your love." Then he heard her speaking to someone farther away from him and then her voice fell below the music. That night, he left the city on business and did not return until Sunday, and he went Sunday afternoon to a football game with a friend. The game was slow and the last quarter was played under lights. When he got home, Lois met him at the door of the apartment. The fire in the living room was lighted. She fixed their drinks and then sat across the room from him in a chair near the fire. "I forgot to tell you that Aunt Helen called on Wednesday. She's moving from Gray's Hill to a house nearer the shore."

He tried to find something to say to this item of news and couldn't. After five years of marriage he seemed to have been left with nothing to say. It was like being embarrassed by a shortage of money. He looked desperately back to the football game and the trip to Chicago for something that might please her, and couldn't find a word. Lois felt his struggle and his failure. She stopped talking herself. I haven't had anyone to talk to since Wednesday, she thought, and now he has nothing to say. "While you were away, I strained my back again, reaching for a hatbox," she said. "The pain is excruciating, and Dr. Parminter doesn't seem able to help me, so I'm going to another doctor, named Walsh, who—"

"I'm terribly sorry your back is bothering you," he said. "I hope Dr. Walsh will be able to help."

The lack of genuine concern in his voice hurt her feelings. "Oh, and I forgot to tell you—there's been some *trouble,*" she said crossly. "Katherine spent the afternoon with Helen Woodruff and some other children. There were some boys. When the maid went into the playroom to call them for supper, she found them all undressed. Mrs. Woodruff was very upset and I told her you'd call."

"Where is Katherine?"

"She's in her room. She won't speak to me. I don't like to be the one to say it, but I think you ought to get a psychiatrist for that girl."

"I'll go and speak to her," Mr. Bruce said.

"Well, will you want any supper?" Lois asked.

"Yes," he said, "I would like some supper."

Katherine had a large room on the side of the building. Her furniture had never filled it. When Mr. Bruce went in, he saw her sitting on the edge of her bed, in the dark. The room smelled of a pair of rats that she had in a cage. He turned on the light and gave her a charm bracelet that he had bought at the airport, and she thanked him politely. He did not mention the trouble at the Woodruffs', but when he put his arm around her shoulders, she began to cry bitterly.

"I didn't want to do it this afternoon," she said, "but *she* made me, and she was the hostess, and we always have to do what the hostess says."

"It doesn't matter if you wanted to or not," he said. "You haven't done anything terribly wrong."

He held her until she was quiet, and then left her and went into his bedroom and telephoned Mrs. Woodruff. "This is Katherine Bruce's father," he said. "I understand that there was some difficulty there this afternoon. I just wanted to say that Katherine has been given her lecture, and as far as Mrs. Bruce and I are concerned, the incident has been forgotten."

"Well, it hasn't been forgotten over here," Mrs. Woodruff said. "I don't know who started it, but I've put Helen to bed without any supper. Mr. Woodruff and I haven't decided how we're going to punish her yet, but we're going to punish her severely." He heard Lois calling to him from the living room that his supper was ready. "I suppose you know that immorality is sweeping this country," Mrs. Woodruff went on. "Our child has never heard a dirty word spoken in her life in this household. There is no room for filth here. If it takes fire to fight fire, that's what I'm going to do!"

The ignorant and ill-tempered woman angered him, but he listened helplessly to her until she had finished, and then went back to Katherine.

Lois looked at the clock on the mantelpiece and called to her husband sharply, a second time. She had not felt at all like making his supper. His lack of concern for her feelings and then her having to slave for him in the kitchen had seemed like an eternal human condition. The ghosts of her injured sex thronged to her side when she slammed open the silver drawer and again when she poured his beer. She set the tray elaborately, in order to deepen her displeasure in doing it at all. She heaped cold meat and salad on her husband's plate as if they were poisoned. Then she fixed her lipstick and carried the heavy tray into the dining room herself, in spite of her lame back.

Now, smoking a cigarette and walking around the room, she let five minutes pass. Then she carried the tray back to the kitchen, dumped the beer and coffee down the drain, and put the meat and salad in the icebox. When Mr. Bruce came back from Katherine's room he found her sobbing with anger—not at him but at her own foolishness. "Lois?" he asked, and she ran out of the room and into her bedroom and slammed the door.

During the next two months, Lois Bruce heard from a number of sources that her husband had been seen with a Mrs. Sheridan. She confided to her mother that she was losing him and, at her mother's insistence, employed a private detective. Lois was not vindictive; she didn't want to trap or intimidate her husband; she had, actually, a feeling that this maneuver would somehow be his salvation.

The detective telephoned her one day when she was having lunch at home, and told her that her husband and Mrs. Sheridan had just gone upstairs in a certain hotel. He was telephoning from the lobby, he said. Lois left her lunch unfinished but changed her clothes. She put on a hat with a veil, because her face was strained, and she was able because of the veil to talk calmly with the doorman, who got her a taxi. The detective met her on the sidewalk. He told her the floor and the number of the apartment, and offered to go upstairs with her. She dismissed him officiously then, as if his offer was a reflection on her ability to handle the situation competently. She had never been in the building before, but the feeling that she was acting on her rights kept her from being impressed at all with the building's strangeness.

The elevator man closed the door after her when she got off at the tenth floor, and she found herself alone in a long, windowless hall. The twelve identical doors painted dark red to match the dusty carpet, the dim ceiling lights, and the perfect stillness of the hall made her hesitate for a second, and then she went directly to the door of the apartment, and rang the bell. There was no sound, no answer. She rang the bell several times. Then she spoke to the shut door. "Let me in, Stephen. It's Lois. Let me in. I know you're in there. Let me in."

She waited. She took off her gloves. She put her thumb on the bell and held it there. Then she listened. There was still no sound. She looked at the shut red doors around her. She jabbed the bell. "Stephen!" she called. "Stephen. Let me in there. Let me in. I know you're in there. I saw you go in there. I can hear you. I can hear you moving around. I can hear you whispering. Let me in, Stephen. Let me in. If you don't let me in, I'll tell her husband."

She waited again. The silence of the early afternoon filled the interval. Then she attacked the door handle. She pounded on the door with the frame of her purse. She kicked it. "You let me in there, Stephen Bruce!" she screamed. "You let me in there, do you hear! Let me in, let me in, let me in!"

Another door into the hallway opened, and she turned and saw a man in his shirtsleeves, shaking his head. She ran into the back hall and, crying, started down the fire stairs. Like the stairs in a monument, they seemed to have no beginning and no end, but at last she came down into a dark hall where tricycles and perambulators were stored, and found her way into the lobby.

WHEN Mr. Bruce and Mrs. Sheridan left the hotel, they walked through the Park, which, in the late-winter sunshine, smelled faintly like a wood. Crossing a bridle path, they saw Miss Prince, the children's riding mistress. She was giving a lesson to a fat little girl whose horse was on a lead. "Mrs. Sheridan!" she said. "Mr. Bruce! Isn't this fortunate!" She stopped the horses. "I wanted to speak to both of you," she said. "I'm having a little gymkhana next month, and I want your children to ride in it. I want them all three to ride in the good-hands class. . . . And perhaps the next year," she said, turning to the fat little girl, "you too may ride in the good-hands class."

They promised to allow their children to take part in the gymkhana, and Miss Prince said goodbye and resumed her riding lesson. In the Seventies they heard the roaring of a lion. They walked to the southern edge of the Park. It was then late in the afternoon. From the Plaza he telephoned his office. Among the messages was one from the maid; he was to stop at the Chardin Club and bring Katherine home.

From the sidewalk in front of the dancing school they could hear the clatter of the piano. The Grand March had begun. They moved through the crowd in the vestibule and stood in the door of the ballroom, looking for their children. Through the open door they could see Mrs. Bailey, the dancing teacher, and her two matrons curtsying stiffly as the children came to them in couples. The boys wore white gloves. The girls were simply dressed. Two by two the children bowed, or curtsied, and joined the grown people at the door. Then Mr. Bruce saw Katherine. As he watched his daughter doing obediently what was expected of her, it struck him that he and the company that crowded around him were all cut out of the same cloth. They were bewildered and confused in principle, too selfish or too unlucky to abide by the forms that guarantee the permanence of a society, as their fathers and mothers had done. Instead, they put the burden of order onto their children and filled their days with specious rites and ceremonies.

One of the dancing teachers came up to them and said, "Oh, I'm so glad to see you, Mrs. Sheridan. We were afraid that you'd been taken sick. Very soon after the class began this afternoon, Mr. Sheridan came and got the two girls. He said he was going to take them out to the country, and we wondered if you were ill. He seemed very upset."

The assistant smiled and wandered off.

Mrs. Sheridan's face lost its color and got dark. She looked very old. It was hot in the ballroom, and Mr. Bruce led her out the door into the freshness of a winter evening, holding her, supporting her really, for she might have fallen. "It will be all right," he kept saying, "it will be all right, my darling, it will be all right."

THE WORM IN THE APPLE

THE CRUTCHMANS were so very, very happy and so temperate in all their habits and so pleased with everything that came their way that one was bound to suspect a worm in their rosy apple and that the extraordinary rosiness of the fruit was only meant to conceal the gravity and the depth of the infection. Their house, for instance, on Hill Street with all those big glass windows. Who but someone suffering from a guilt complex would want so much light to pour into their rooms? And all the wall-to-wall carpeting as if an inch of bare floor (there was none) would touch on some deep memory of unrequition and loneliness. And there was a certain necrophilic ardor to their gardening. Why be so intense about digging holes and planting seeds and watching them come up? Why this morbid concern with the earth? She was a pretty woman with that striking pallor you so often find in nymphomaniacs. Larry was a big man who used to garden without a shirt, which may have shown a tendency to infantile exhibitionism.

They moved happily out to Shady Hill after the war. Larry had served in the Navy. They had two happy children: Rachel and Tom. But there were already some clouds on their horizon. Larry's ship had been sunk in the war and he had spent four days on a raft in the Mediterranean and surely this experience would make him skeptical about the comforts and songbirds of Shady Hill and leave him with some racking nightmares. But what was perhaps more serious was the fact that Helen was rich. She was the only daughter of old Charlie Simpson—one of the last of the industrial buccaneers—who had left her with a larger income than Larry would ever take away from his job at Melcher & Thaw. The dangers in this situation are well known. Since Larry did not have to make a living—since he lacked any incentive—he might take it easy, spend too much time on the golf links, and always have a glass in his hand. Helen would confuse financial with emotional independence and damage the delicate balances within their marriage. But Larry seemed to have no nightmares and Helen spread her income among the charities and lived a comfortable but a modest life. Larry went to his job each morning with such enthusiasm that you might think he was trying to escape from something. His participation in the life of the community was so vigorous that he must have been left with almost no time for self-examination. He was everywhere: he was at the communion rail, the fifty-yard line, he played the oboe with the Chamber Music Club, drove the fire truck, served on the school board, and rode the 8:03 into New York every morning. What was the sorrow that drove him?

He may have wanted a larger family. Why did they only have two children? Why not three or four? Was there perhaps some breakdown in their relationship after the birth of Tom? Rachel, the oldest, was terribly fat when she was a girl and quite aggressive in a mercenary way. Every spring she would drag an old dressing table out of the garage and set it up on the sidewalk with a sign saying: FReSH LEMonADE. 15¢. Tom had pneumonia when he was six and nearly died, but he recovered and there were no visible complications. The children may have felt rebellious about the conformity of their parents, for they were exacting conformists. Two cars? Yes. Did they go to church? Every single Sunday they got to their knees and prayed with ardor. Clothing? They couldn't have been more punctilious in their observance of the sumptuary laws. Book clubs, local art and music lover associations, athletics and cards—they were up to their necks in everything. But if the children were rebellious they concealed their rebellion and seemed happily to love their parents and happily to be loved in return, but perhaps there was in this love the ruefulness of some deep disappointment. Perhaps he was impotent. Perhaps she was frigid—but hardly, with that pallor. Everyone in the community with wandering hands had given them both a try but they had all been put off. What was the source of this constancy? Were they frightened? Were they prudish? Were they monogamous? What was at the bottom of this appearance of happiness?

As their children grew one might look to them for the worm in the apple. They would be rich, they would inherit Helen's fortune, and we might see here, moving over them, the shadow that so often falls upon children who can count on a lifetime of financial security. And anyhow Helen loved her son too much. She bought him everything he wanted. Driving him to dancing school in his first blue serge suit she was so entranced by the manly figure he cut as he climbed the stairs that she drove the car straight into an elm tree. Such an infatuation was bound to lead to trouble. And if she favored her son she was bound to discriminate against her daughter. Listen to her. "Rachel's feet," she says, "are immense, simply immense. I can never get shoes for her." Now perhaps we see the worm. Like most beautiful women she is jealous; she is jealous of her own daughter! She cannot brook competition. She will dress the girl in hideous clothing, have her hair curled in some unbecoming way, and keep talking about the size of her feet until the poor girl will refuse to go to the dances or if she is forced to go she will sulk in the ladies' room, staring at her monstrous feet. She will become so wretched and so lonely that in order to express herself she will fall in love with an unstable poet and fly with him to Rome, where they will live out a miserable and a boozy exile. But when the girl enters the room she is pretty and prettily dressed and she smiles at her mother with perfect love. Her feet are quite large, to be sure, but so is her front. Perhaps we should look to the son to find our trouble.

And there is trouble. He fails his junior year in high school and has to repeat and as a result of having to repeat he feels alienated from the members of his class and is put, by chance, at a desk next to Carrie Witchell, who is the most conspicuous dish in Shady Hill. Everyone knows about the Witchells and their pretty, high-spirited daughter. They drink too much and live in one of those frame houses in Maple Dell. The girl is really beautiful and everyone knows how her shrewd old parents are planning to climb out of Maple Dell on the strength of her white, white skin. What a perfect situation! They will know about Helen's wealth. In the darkness of their bedroom they will calculate the settlement they can demand and in the malodorous kitchen where they take all their meals they will tell their pretty daughter to let the boy go as far as he wants. But Tom fell out of love with Carrie as swiftly as he fell into it and after that he fell in love with Karen Strawbridge and Susie Morris and Anna Macken and you might think he was unstable, but in his second year in college he announced his engagement to Elizabeth Trustman and they were married after his graduation and since he then had to serve his time in the Army she followed him to his post in Germany, where they studied and learned the language and befriended the people and were a credit to their country.

Rachel's way was not so easy. When she lost her fat she became very pretty and quite fast. She smoked and drank and probably fornicated and the abyss that opens up before a pretty and an intemperate young woman is unfathomable. What, but chance, was there to keep her from ending up as a hostess at a Times Square dance hall? And what would her poor father think, seeing the face of his daughter, her breasts lightly covered with gauze, gazing mutely at him on a rainy morning from one of those showcases? What she did was to fall in love with the son of the Farquarsons' German gardener. He had come with his family to the United States on the Displaced Persons quota after the war. His name was Eric Reiner and to be fair about it he was an exceptional young man who looked on the United States as a truly New World. The Crutchmans must have been sad about Rachel's choice—not to say heartbroken—but they concealed their feelings. The Reiners did not. This hard-working German couple thought the marriage hopeless and improper. At one point the father beat his son over the head with a stick of firewood. But the young couple continued to see each other and presently they eloped. They had to. Rachel was three months pregnant. Eric was then a freshman at Tufts, where he had a scholarship. Helen's money came in handy here and she was able to rent an apartment in Boston for the young couple and pay their expenses. That their first grandchild was premature did not seem to bother the Crutchmans. When Eric graduated from college he got a fellowship at M.I.T. and took his Ph.D. in physics and was taken on as an associate in the department. He could have gone into industry at a higher salary but he liked to teach and Rachel was happy in Cambridge, where they remained.

With their own dear children gone away the Crutchmans might be expected to suffer the celebrated spiritual destitution of their age and their kind—the worm in the apple would at last be laid bare—although watching this charming couple as they entertained their friends or read the books they enjoyed one might wonder if the worm was not in the eye of the observer who, through timidity or moral cowardice, could not embrace the broad range of their natural enthusiasms and would not grant that, while Larry played neither Bach nor football very well, his pleasure in both was genuine. You might at least expect to see in them the usual destructiveness of time, but either through luck or as a result of their temperate and healthy lives they had lost neither their teeth nor their hair. The touchstone of their euphoria remained potent, and while Larry gave up the fire truck he could still be seen at the communion rail, the fifty-yard line, the 8:03, and the Chamber Music Club, and through the prudence and shrewdness of Helen's broker they got richer and richer and richer and lived happily, happily, happily, happily.

THE TROUBLE OF MARCIE FLINT

THIS IS being written aboard the S.S. *Augustus,* three days at sea. My suitcase is full of peanut butter, and I am a fugitive from the suburbs of all large cities.

What holes! The suburbs, I mean. God preserve me from the lovely ladies taking in their asters and their roses at dusk lest the frost kill them, and from ladies with their heads whirling with civic zeal. I'm off to Torino, where the girls love peanut butter and the world is a man's castle and . . ." There was absolutely nothing wrong with the suburb (Shady Hill) from which Charles Flint was fleeing, his age is immaterial, and he was no stranger to Torino, having been there for three months recently on business.

"God preserve me," he continued, "from women who dress like *toreros* to go to the supermarket, and from cowhide dispatch cases, and from flannels and gabardines. Preserve me from word games and adulterers, from basset hounds and swimming pools and frozen canapés and Bloody Marys and smugness and syringa bushes and P.T.A. meetings." On and on he wrote, while the *Augustus,* traveling at seventeen knots, took a course due east; they would raise the Azores in a day.

Like all bitter men, Flint knew less than half the story and was more interested in unloading his own peppery feelings than in learning the truth. Marcie, the wife from whom he was fleeing, was a dark-haired, dark-eyed woman—not young by any stretch of the imagination but gifted with great stories of feminine sweetness and gallantry. She had not told her neighbors that Charlie had left her; she had not even called her lawyer; but she had fired the cook, and she now took a south-southwest course between the stove and the sink, cooking the children's supper. It was not in her to review the past, as her husband would, or to inspect the forces that could put an ocean between a couple who had been cheerfully married for fifteen years. There had been, she felt, a slight difference in their points of view during his recent absence on business, for while he always wrote that he missed her, he also wrote that he was dining at the Superga six nights a week and having a wonderful time. He had only planned to be away for six weeks, and when this stretched out to three months, she found that it was something to be borne.

Her neighbors had stood by her handsomely during the first weeks, but she knew, herself, that an odd woman can spoil a dinner party, and as Flint continued to stay away, she found that she had more and more lonely nights to get through. Now, there were two aspects to the night life of Shady Hill; there were the parties, of course, and then there was another side—a regular Santa Claus's workshop of madrigal singers, political discussion groups, recorder groups, dancing schools, confirmation classes, committee meetings, and lectures on literature, philosophy, city planning, and pest control. The bright banner of stars in heaven has probably never before been stretched above such a picture of nocturnal industry. Marcie, having a sweet, clear voice, joined a madrigal group that met on Thursdays and a political workshop that met on Mondays. Once she made herself available, she was sought as a committeewoman, although it was hard to say why; she almost never opened her mouth. She finally accepted a position on the Village Council, in the third month of Charlie's absence, mostly to keep herself occupied.

Virtuousness, reason, civic zeal, and loneliness all contributed to poor Marcie's trouble. Charlie, far away in Torino, could imagine her well enough standing in their lighted doorway on the evening of his return, but could he imagine her groping under the bed for the children's shoes or pouring bacon fat into an old soup can? "Daddy has to stay in Italy in order to make the money to buy the things we need," she told the children. But when Charlie called her from abroad, as he did once a week, he always seemed to have been drinking. Regard this sweet woman, then, singing "Hodie Christus Natus Est," studying Karl Marx, and sitting on a hard chair at meetings of the Village Council.

If there was anything really wrong with Shady Hill, anything that you could put your finger on, it was the fact that the village had no public library—no foxed copies of Pascal, smelling of cabbage; no broken sets of Dostoevski and George Eliot; no Galsworthy, even; no Barrie and no Bennett. This was the chief concern of the Village Council during Marcie's term. The library partisans were mostly newcomers to the village; the opposition whip was Mrs. Selfredge, a member of the Council and a very decorous woman, with blue eyes of astonishing brilliance and inexpressiveness. Mrs. Selfredge often spoke of the chosen quietness of their life. "We never go out," she would say, but in such a way that she seemed to be expressing not some choice but a deep vein of loneliness. She was married to a wealthy man much older than herself, and they had no children; indeed, the most indirect mention of sexual fact brought a deep color to Mrs. Selfredge's face. She took the position that a library belonged in that category of public service that might make Shady Hill attractive to a development. This was not blind prejudice. Carsen Park, the next village, had let a development inside its boundaries, with disastrous results to the people already living there. Their taxes had been doubled, their schools had been ruined. That there was any connection between reading and real estate was disputed by the partisans of the library, until a horrible murder—three murders, in fact—took place in one of the cheese-box houses at the Carsen Park development, and the library project was buried with the victims.

From the terraces of the Superga you can see all of Torino and the snow-covered mountains around, and a man drinking wine there might not think of his wife attending a meeting of the Village Council. This was a board of ten men and two women, headed by the Mayor, who screened the projects that came before them. The Council met in the Civic Center, an old mansion that had been picked up for back taxes. The board room had been the parlor. Easter eggs had been hidden here, children had pinned paper tails on paper donkeys, fires had burned on the hearth, and a Christmas tree had stood in the corner, but once the house had become the property of the village, a conscientious effort seems to have been made to exorcise these gentle ghosts. Raphael's self-portrait and the pictures of the Broken Bridge at Avignon and the Avon at Stratford were taken down and the walls were painted a depressing shade of green. The fireplace remained, but the flue was sealed up and the bricks were spread with green paint. A track of fluorescent tubing across the ceiling threw a withering light down into the faces of the Village Council members and made them all look haggard and tired. The room made Marcie uncomfortable. In its harsh light her sweetness was unavailing, and she felt not only bored but somehow painfully estranged.

On this particular night they discussed water taxes and parking meters, and then the Mayor brought up the public library for the last time. "Of course, the issue is closed," he said, "but we've heard everyone all along, on both sides. There's one more man who wants to speak to us, and I think we ought to hear him. He comes from Maple Dell." Then he opened the door from the board room into the corridor and let Noel Mackham in.

Now, the neighborhood of Maple Dell was more like a development than anything else in Shady Hill. It was the kind of place where the houses stand cheek by jowl, all of them white frame, all of them built twenty years ago, and parked beside each was a car that seemed more substantial than the house itself, as if this were a fragment of some nomadic culture. And it was a kind of spawning ground, a place for bearing and raising the young and for nothing else—for who would ever come back to Maple Dell? Who, in the darkest night, would ever think with longing of the three upstairs bedrooms and the leaky toilet and the sour-smelling halls? Who would ever come back to the little living room where you couldn't swing a cat around without knocking down the colored photograph of Mount Rainier? Who would ever come back to the chair that bit you in the bum and the obsolete TV set and the bent ashtray with its pressed-steel statue of a naked woman doing a scarf dance?

"I understand that the business is closed," Mackham said, "but I just wanted to go on record as being in favor of a public library. It's been on my conscience."

He was not much of an advocate for anything. He was tall. His hair had begun an erratic recession, leaving him with some sparse fluff to comb over his bald brow. His features were angular; his skin was bad. There were no deep notes to his voice. Its range seemed confined to a delicate hoarseness—a monotonous and laryngitic sound that aroused in Marcie, as if it had been some kind of Hungarian music, feelings of irritable melancholy. "I just wanted to say a few words in favor of a public library," he rasped. "When I was a kid we were poor. There wasn't much good about the way we lived, but there was this Carnegie Library. I started going there when I was about eight. I guess I went there regularly for ten years. I read everything—philosophy, novels, technical books, poetry, ships' logs. I even read a cookbook. For me, this library amounted to the difference between success and failure. When I remember the thrill I used to get out of cracking a good book, I just hate to think of bringing my kids up in a place where there isn't any library."

"Well, of course, we know what you mean," Mayor Simmons said. "But I don't think that's quite the question. The question is not one of denying books to children. Most of us in Shady Hill have libraries of our own."

Mark Barrett got to his feet. "And *I'd* like to throw in a word about poor boys and reading, if I might," he said, in a voice so full of color and virility that everyone smiled. "I was a poor boy myself," he said cheerfully, "and I'm not ashamed to say so, and I'd just like to throw in—for what it's worth—that I never put my nose inside a public library, except to get out of the rain, or maybe follow a pretty girl. I just don't want anybody to be left with the impression that a public library is the road to success."

"I didn't say that a public library was the road to—"

"Well, you *implied* it!" Barrett shouted, and he seated himself with a big stir. His chair creaked, and by bulging his muscles a little he made his garters, braces, and shoes all sound.

"I only wanted to say—" Mackham began again.

"You *implied* it!" Barrett shouted.

"Just because *you* can't read," Mackham said, "it doesn't follow—"

"Damn it, man, I didn't say that I couldn't read!" Barrett was on his feet again.

"Please, gentlemen. Please! Please!" Mayor Simmons said. "Let's keep our remarks temperate."

"I'm not going to sit here and have someone who lives in Maple Dell tell me the reason he's such a hot rock is because he read a lot of books!" Barrett shouted. "Books have their place. I won't deny it. But no book ever helped me to get where I am, and from where I am I can spit on Maple Dell. As for my kids, I want them out in the fresh air playing ball, not reading cookbooks."

"Please, Mark. Please," the Mayor said. And then he turned to Mrs. Selfredge and asked her to move that the meeting be adjourned.

"MY DAY, my hour, my moment of revelation," Charlie wrote, in his sun-deck cabin on the *Augustus*, "came on a Sunday, when I had been home eight days. Oh God, was I happy! I spent most of the day putting up storm windows, and I like working on my house. Things like putting up storm windows. When the work was done, I put the ladder away and grabbed a towel and my swimming trunks and walked over to the Townsends' swimming pool. They were away, but the pool hadn't been drained. I put on my trunks and dove in and I remember seeing—way, way up in the top of one of the pine trees—a brassiere that I guess the Townsend kids had snitched and heaved up there in midsummer, the screams of dismay from their victim having long since been carried away on the west wind. The water was very cold, and blood pressure or some other medical reason may have accounted for the fact that when I got out of the pool and dressed I was nearly busting with happiness. I walked back to the house, and when I stepped inside it was so quiet that I wondered if anything had gone wrong. It was not an ominous silence—it was just that I wondered why the clock should sound so loud. Then I went upstairs and found Marcie asleep in her bedroom. She was covered with a light wrap that had slipped from her shoulders and breasts. Then I heard Henry and Katie's voices, and I went to the back bedroom window. This looked out onto the garden, where a gravel path that needed weeding went up a little hill. Henry and Katie were there. Katie was scratching in the gravel with a stick—some message of love, I guess. Henry had one of those broad-winged planes—talismanic planes, really—made of balsa wood and propelled by a rubber band. He twisted the band by turning the propeller, and I could see his lips moving as he counted. Then, when the rubber was taut, he set his feet apart in the gravel, like a marksman—Katie watched none of this—and sent the plane up. The wings of the plane were pale in the early dark, and then I saw it climb out of the shade up to where the sun washed it with yellow light. With not much more force than a moth, it soared and circled and meandered and came slowly down again into the shade and crashed on the peony hedge. 'I got it up again!' I heard Henry shout. 'I got it up into the light.' Katie went on writing her message in the dirt. And then, like some trick in the movies, I saw myself as my son, standing in a like garden and sending up out of the dark a plane, an arrow, a tennis ball, a stone—anything—while my sister drew hearts in the gravel. The memory of how deep this impulse to reach into the light had been completely charmed me, and I watched the boy send the plane up again and again.

"Then, still feeling very springy and full of fun, I walked back toward the door, stopping to admire the curve of Marcie's breasts and deciding, in a blaze of charity, to let her sleep. I felt so good that I needed a drink—not to pick me up but to dampen my spirits—a libation, anyhow—and I poured some whiskey in a glass. Then I went into the kitchen to get some ice, and I noticed that ants had got in somehow. This was surprising, because we never had much trouble with ants. Spiders, yes. Before the equinoctial hurricanes—even before the barometer had begun to fall—the house seemed to fill up with spiders, as if they sensed the trouble in the air. There would be spiders in the bathtubs and spiders in the living room and spiders in the kitchen, and, walking down the long upstairs hallway before a storm, you could sometimes feel the thread of a web break against your face. But we had had almost no trouble with ants. Now, on this autumn afternoon, thousands of ants broke out of the kitchen woodwork and threw a double line across the drainboard and into the sink, where there seemed to be something they wanted.

"I found some ant poison at the back of the broom-closet shelf, a little jar of brown stuff that I'd bought from Timmons in the village years ago. I put a generous helping of this into a saucer and put it on the drainboard. Then I took my drink and a piece of the Sunday paper out onto the terrace in front of the house. The house faced west, so I had more light than the children, and I felt so happy that even the news in the papers seemed cheerful. No kings had been assassinated in the rainy black streets of Marseille; no storms were brewing in the Balkans; no clerkly Englishman—the admiration of his landlady and his aunts—had dissolved the remains of a young lady in an acid bath; no jewels, even, had been stolen. And that sometime power of the Sunday paper to evoke an anxious, rain-wet world of fallen crowns and inevitable war seemed gone. Then the sun withdrew from my paper and from the chair where I sat, and I wished I had put on a sweater.

"It was late in the season—the salt of change was in the air—and this tickled me, too. Last Sunday, or the Sunday before, the terrace would have been flooded with light. Then I thought about other places where I would like to be—Nantucket, with only a handful of people left and the sailing fleet depleted and the dunes casting, as they never do in the summer, a dark shadow over the bathing beach. And I thought about the Vineyard and the farina-colored bluffs and the purple autumn sea and that stillness in which you might hear, from way out in the Sound, the rasp of a block on a traveler as a sailboard there came about. I tasted my whiskey and gave my paper a shake, but the view of the golden light on the grass and the trees was more compelling than the news, and now mixed up with my memories of the sea islands was the whiteness of Marcie's thighs.

"Then I was seized by some intoxicating pride in the hour, by the joy and the naturalness of my relationship to the scene, and by the ease with which I could put my hands on what I needed. I thought again of Marcie sleeping and that I would have my way there soon—it would be a way of expressing this pride. And then, listening for the voices of my children and not hearing them, I decided to celebrate the hour as it passed. I put the paper down and ran up the stairs. Marcie was still sleeping and I stripped off my clothes and lay down beside her, waking her from what seemed to be a pleasant dream, for she smiled and drew me to her."

To GET BACK TO Marcie and her trouble: She put on her coat after the meeting was adjourned and said, "Good night. Good night . . . I'm expecting him home next week." She was not easily upset, but she suddenly felt that she had looked straight at stupidity and unfairness. Going down the stairs behind Mackham, she felt a powerful mixture of pity and sympathy for the stranger and some clear anger toward her old friend Mark Barrett. She wanted to apologize, and she stopped Mackham in the door and said that she had some cheerful memories of her own involving a public library.

As it happened, Mrs. Selfredge and Mayor Simmons were the last to leave the board room. The Mayor waited, with his hand on the light switch, for Mrs. Selfredge, who was putting on her white gloves. "I'm glad the library's over and done with," he said. "I have a few misgivings, but right now I'm against anything public, anything that would make this community attractive to a development." He spoke with feeling, and at the word "development" a ridge covered with identical houses rose in his mind. It seemed wrong to him that the houses he imagined should be identical and that they should be built of green wood and false stone. It seemed wrong to him that young couples should begin their lives in an atmosphere that lacked grace, and it seemed wrong to him that the rows of houses could not, for long, preserve their slender claim on propriety and would presently become unsightly tracts. "Of course, it isn't a question of keeping children from books," he repeated. "We all have libraries of our own. There isn't any problem. I suppose you were brought up in a house with a library?"

"Oh yes, yes," said Mrs. Selfredge. The Mayor had turned off the light, and the darkness covered and softened the lie she had told. Her father had been a Brooklyn patrolman, and there had not been a book in his house. He had been an amiable man—not very sweet-smelling—who talked to all the children on his beat. Slovenly and jolly, he had spent the years of his retirement drinking beer in the kitchen in his underwear, to the deep despair and shame of his only child.

The Mayor said good night to Mrs. Selfredge on the sidewalk, and standing there she overheard Marcie speaking to Mackham. "I'm terribly sorry about Mark, about what he said," Marcie said. "We've all had to put up with him at one time or another. But why don't you come back to my house for a drink? Perhaps we could get the library project moving again."

So it wasn't over and done with, Mrs. Selfredge thought indignantly. They wouldn't rest until Shady Hill was nothing but developments from one end to the other. The colorless, hard-pressed people of the Carsen Park project, with their flocks of children, and their monthly interest payments, and their picture windows, and their view of identical houses and treeless, muddy, unpaved streets, seemed to threaten her most cherished concepts—her lawns, her pleasures, her property rights, even her self-esteem.

Mr. Selfredge, an intelligent and elegant old gentleman, was waiting up for his Little Princess and she told him her troubles. Mr. Selfredge had retired from the banking business—mercifully, for whenever he stepped out into the world today he was confronted with the deterioration of those qualities of responsibility and initiative that had made the world of his youth selective, vigorous, and healthy. He knew a great deal about Shady Hill—he even recognized Mackham's name. "The bank holds the mortgage on his house," he said. "I remember when he applied for it. He works for a textbook company in New York that has been accused by at least one Congressional committee of publishing subversive American histories. I wouldn't worry about him, my dear, but if it would put your mind at ease, I could easily write a letter to the paper."

"BUT THE CHILDREN were not as far away as I thought," Charlie wrote, aboard the *Augustus*. "They were still in the garden. And the significance of that hour for them, I guess, was that it was made for stealing food. I have to make up or imagine what took place with them. They may have been drawn into the house by a hunger as keen as mine. Coming into the hall and listening for sounds, they would hear nothing, and they would open the icebox slowly, so that the sound of the heavy latch wouldn't be heard. The icebox must have been disappointing, because Henry wandered over to the sink and began to eat the sodium arsenate. 'Candy,' he said, and Katie joined him, and they had a fight over the remaining poison. They must have stayed in the kitchen for quite a while, because they were still in the kitchen when Henry began to retch. 'Well, don't get it all *over* everything,' Katie said. 'Come on outside.' She was beginning to feel sick herself, and they went outside and hid under a syringa bush, which is where I found them when I dressed and came down.

"They told me what they had eaten, and I woke Marcie up and then ran downstairs again and called Doc Mullens. 'Jesus Christ!' he said. 'I'll be right over.' He asked me to read the label on the jar, but all it said was sodium arsenate; it didn't say the percentage. And when I told him I had bought it from Timmons, he told me to call and ask Timmons who the manufacturer was. The line was busy and so, while Marcie was running back and forth between the two sick children, I jumped into the car and drove to the village. There was a lot of light in the sky, I remember, but it was nearly dark in the streets. Timmons' drugstore was the only place that was lighted, and it was the kind of place that seems to subsist on the crumbs from other tradesmen's tables. This late hour when all the other stores were shut was Timmons' finest. The crazy jumble of displays in his windows—irons, ashtrays, Venus in a truss, ice bags, and perfumes—was continued into the store itself, which seemed like a pharmaceutical curiosity shop or funhouse: a storeroom for cardboard beauties anointing themselves with sun oil; for cardboard mountain ranges in the Alpine glow, advertising pine-scented soap; for bookshelves, and bins filled with card-table covers, and plastic water pistols. The drugstore was a little like a house, too, for Mrs. Timmons stood behind the soda fountain, a neat and anxious-looking woman, with photographs of her three sons (one dead) in uniform arranged against the mirror at her back, and when Timmons himself came to the counter, he was chewing on something and wiped the crumbs of a sandwich off his mouth with the back of his hand. I showed him the jar and said, 'The kids ate some of this about an hour ago. I called Doc Mullens, and he told me to come and see you. It doesn't say what the percentage of arsenate is, and he thought if you could remember where you got it, we could telephone the manufacturer and find out.'

" 'The children are poisoned?' Timmons asked.

" 'Yes!' I said.

" 'You didn't buy this merchandise from me,' he said.

"The clumsiness of his lie and the stillness in that crazy store made me feel hopeless. 'I *did* buy it from you, Mr. Timmons,' I said. 'There's no question about that. My children are deathly sick. I want you to tell me where you got the stuff.'

" 'You didn't buy this merchandise from me,' he said.

"I looked at Mrs. Timmons, but she was mopping the counter; she was deaf. 'God damn it to hell, Timmons!' I shouted, and I reached over the counter and got him by the shirt. 'You look up your records! You look up your God-damned records and tell me where this stuff came from.'

" 'We know what it is to lose a son,' Mrs. Timmons said at my back. There was nothing full to her voice; nothing but the monotonous, the gritty, music of grief and need. 'You don't have to tell us anything about that.'

" 'You didn't buy this merchandise from me,' Timmons

said once more, and I wrenched his shirt until the buttons popped, and then I let him go. Mrs. Timmons went on mopping the counter. Timmons stood with his head so bent in shame that I couldn't see his eyes at all, and I went out of the store.

"When I got back, Doc Mullens was in the upstairs hall, and the worst was over. 'A little more or a little less and you might have lost them,' he said cheerfully. 'But I've used a stomach pump, and I think they'll be all right. Of course, it's a heavy poison, and Marcie will have to keep specimens for a week—it's apt to stay in the kidneys—but I think they'll be all right.' I thanked him and walked out to the car with him, and then I came back to the house and went upstairs to where the children had been put to bed in the same room for company and made some foolish talk with them. Then I heard Marcie weeping in our bedroom, and I went there. 'It's all right, baby,' I said. 'It's all right now. They're all right.' But when I put my arms around her, her wailing and sobbing got louder, and I asked her what she wanted.

" 'I want a divorce,' she sobbed.

" 'What?'

" 'I want a divorce. I can't bear living like this any more. I can't bear it. Every time they have a head cold, every time they're late from school, whenever anything bad happens, I think it's retribution. I can't stand it.'

" 'Retribution for what?'

" 'While you were away, I made a mess of things.'

" 'What do you mean?'

" 'With somebody.'

" 'Who?'

" 'Noel Mackham. You don't know him. He lives in Maple Dell.'

"Then for a long time I didn't say anything—what could I say? And suddenly she turned on me in fury.

" 'Oh, I knew you'd be like this, I knew you'd be like this, I knew you'd blame me!' she said. 'But it wasn't my fault, it just wasn't my fault. I knew you'd blame me, I knew you'd blame me, I knew you'd be like this, and I . . .'

"I didn't hear much else of what she said, because I was packing a suitcase. And then I kissed the kids goodbye, caught a train to the city, and boarded the *Augustus* next morning."

WHAT HAPPENED TO Marcie was this: The evening paper printed Selfredge's letter, the day after the Village Council meeting, and she read it. She called Mackham on the telephone. He said he was going to ask the editor to print an answer he had written, and that he would stop by her house at eight o'clock to show her the carbon copy. She had planned to eat dinner with her children, but just before she sat down, the bell rang, and Mark Barrett dropped in. "Hi, honey," he said. "Make me a drink?" She made him some Martinis, and he took off his hat and topcoat and got down to business. "I understand you had that meatball over here for a drink last night."

"Who told you, Mark? Who in the world told you?"

"Helen Selfredge. It's no secret. She doesn't want the library thing reopened."

"It's like being followed. I hate it."

"Don't let that bother you, sweetie." He held out his glass, and she filled it again. "I'm just here as a neighbor—friend of Charlie's—and what's the use of having friends and neighbors if they can't give you advice? Mackham is a meatball, and Markham is a wolf. With Charlie away, I feel kind of like an older brother—I want to keep an eye on you. I want you to promise me that you won't have that meatball in your house again."

"I can't, Mark. He's coming tonight."

"No, he isn't, sweetie. You're going to call him up and tell him not to come."

"He's human, Mark."

"Now, listen to me, sweetie. You listen to me. I'm about to tell you something. Of course he's human, but so is the garbage man and the cleaning woman. I'm about to tell you something very interesting. When I was in school, there was a meatball just like Mackham. Nobody liked him. Nobody spoke to him. Well, I was a high-spirited kid, Marcie, with plenty of friends, and I began to wonder about this meatball. I began to wonder if it wasn't my responsibility to befriend him and make him feel that he was a member of the group. Well, I spoke to him, and I wouldn't be surprised if I was the first person who did. I took a walk with him. I asked him up to my room. I did everything I could to make him feel accepted.

"It was a terrible mistake. First, he began going around the school telling everybody that he and I were going to do this and he and I were going to do that. Then he went to the Dean's office and had himself moved into my room without consulting me. Then his mother began to send me these lousy cookies, and his sister—I'd never laid eyes on her—began to write me love letters, and he got to be such a leech that I had to tell him to lay off. I spoke frankly to him; I told him the only reason I'd ever spoken to him was because I pitied him. This didn't make any difference. When you're stuck with a meatball, it doesn't matter what you tell them. He kept hanging around, waiting for me after classes, and after football practice he was always down in the locker room. It got so bad that we had to give him the works. We asked him up to Pete Fenton's room for a cup of cocoa, roughed him up, threw his clothes out the window, painted his rear end with iodine, and stuck his head in a pail of water until he damned near drowned."

Mark lighted a cigarette and finished his drink. "But what I mean to say is that if you get mixed up with a meatball you're bound to regret it. Your feelings may be kindly and generous in the beginning, but you'll do more harm than good before you're through. I want you to call up Mackham and tell him not to come. Tell him you're sick. I don't want him in your house."

"Mackham isn't coming here to visit me, Mark. He's coming here to tell me about the letter he wrote for the paper."

"I'm ordering you to call him up."

"I won't, Mark."

"You go to that telephone."

"Please, Mark. Don't shout at me."

"You go to that telephone."

"Please get out of my house, Mark."

"You're an intractable, weak-headed, God-damned fool!" he shouted. "That's the trouble with you!" Then he went.

She ate supper alone, and was not finished when Mackham came. It was raining, and he wore a heavy coat and a shabby hat—saved, she guessed, for storms. The hat made him look like an old man. He seemed heavy-spirited and tired, and he unwound a long yellow woolen scarf from around his neck. He had seen the editor. The editor would not print his answer. Marcie asked him if he would like a drink, and when he didn't reply, she asked him a second time. "Oh, no, thank you," he said heavily, and he looked into her eyes with a smile of such engulfing weariness that she thought he must be sick. Then he came up to her as if he were going to touch her, and she went into the library and sat on the sofa. Halfway across the room he saw that he had forgotten to take off his rubbers.

"Oh, I'm sorry," he said. "I'm afraid I've tracked mud—"

"It doesn't matter."

"It would matter if this were *my* house."

"It doesn't matter here."

He sat in a chair near the door and began to take off his rubbers, and it was the rubbers that did it. Watching him cross his knees and remove the rubber from one foot and then the other so filled Marcie with pity at this clumsy vision of humanity and its touching high purpose in the face of adversity that he must have seen by her pallor or her dilated eyes that she was helpless.

The sea and the decks are dark. Charlie can hear the voices from the bar at the end of the passageway, and he has told his story, but he does not stop writing. They are coming into warmer water and fog, and the foghorn begins to blow at intervals of a minute. He checks it against his watch. And suddenly he wonders what he is doing aboard the *Augustus* with a suitcase full of peanut butter. "Ants, poison, peanut butter, foghorns," he writes, "love, blood pressure, business trips, inscrutability. I know that I will go back." The foghorn blasts again, and in the held note he sees a vision of his family running toward him up some steps—crumbling stone, wild pinks, lizards, and their much-loved faces. "I will catch a plane in Genoa," he writes. "I will see my children grow and take up their lives, and I will gentle Marcie—sweet Marcie, dear Marcie, Marcie my love. I will shelter her with the curve of my body from all the harms of the dark."

THE BELLA LINGUA

WILSON STREETER, like many Americans who live in Rome, was divorced. He worked as a statistican for the F.R.U.P.C. agency, lived alone, and led a diverting social life with other expatriates and those Romans who were drawn into expatriate circles, but he spoke English all day long at his office and the Italians he met socially spoke English so much better than he spoke Italian that he could not bring himself to converse with them in their language. It was his feeling that in order to understand Italy he would have to speak Italian. He did speak it well enough when it was a question of some simple matter of shopping or making arrangements of one kind or another, but he wanted to be able to express his sentiments, to tell jokes, and to follow overheard conversations on trolley cars and buses. He was keenly conscious of the fact that he was making his life in a country that was not his own, but this sense of being an outsider would change, he thought, when he knew the language.

For the tourist, the whole experience of traveling through a strange country is on the verge of the past tense. Even as the days are spent, these *were* the days in Rome, and everything—the sightseeing, souvenirs, photographs, and presents—is commemorative. Even as the traveler lies in bed waiting for sleep, these *were* the nights in Rome. But for the expatriate there is no past tense. It would defeat his purpose to think of this time in another country in relation to some town or countryside that was and might again be his permanent home, and he lives in a continuous and unrelenting present. Instead of accumulating memories, the expatriate is offered the challenge of learning a language and understanding a people. So they catch a glimpse of one another in the Piazza Venezia—the expatriates passing through the square on their way to their Italian lessons, the tourists occupying, by prearrangement, all the tables at a sidewalk café and drinking Campari, which they have been told is a typical Roman *aperitivo*.

Streeter's teacher was an American woman named Kate Dresser, who lived in an old palace near the Piazza Firenze, with an adolescent son. Streeter went there for his lessons on Tuesday and Friday evenings and on Sunday afternoons. He enjoyed the walk in the evening from his office, past the Pantheon, to his Italian lesson. Among the rewards of his expatriation were a heightened awareness of what he saw and an exhilarating sense of freedom. Mixed with the love we hold for our native country is the fact that it is the place where we were raised, and, should anything have gone a little wrong in this process, we will be reminded of this fault, by the scene of the crime, until the day we die. Some such unhappiness may have accounted for Streeter's sense of freedom, and his heightened awareness may have been nothing but what is to be expected of a man with a good appetite walking through the back streets of a city in the autumn. The air was cold and smelled of coffee—sometimes of incense, if the doors to a church stood open—and chrysanthemums were for sale everywhere. The sights were exciting and confusing—the ruins of Republican and Imperial Rome, and the ruins of what the city had been the day before yesterday—but the whole thing would be revealed to him when he could speak Italian.

It was not easy, Streeter knew, for a man his age to learn anything, and he had not been fortunate in his search for a good Italian teacher. He had first gone to the Dante Alighieri Institute, where the classes were so large that he made no progress. Then he had taken private lessons from an old lady. He was supposed to read and translate Collodi's *Pinocchio,* but when he had done a few sentences the teacher would take the book out of his hands and do the reading and translating herself. She loved the story so much that she laughed and cried, and sometimes whole lessons passed in which Streeter did not open his mouth. It disturbed his sense of fitness that he, a man of fifty, should be sitting in a cold flat at the edge of Rome, being read a children's tale by a woman of seventy, and after a dozen lessons he told his teacher that he had to go to Perugia on business. After this he enrolled in the Tauchnitz School and had private lessons. His teacher was an astonishingly pretty young woman who wore the tight-waisted clothes that were in fashion that year, and a wedding ring—a prop, he guessed, because she seemed so openly flirtatious and gay. She wore a sharp perfume, rattled her bracelets, pulled down her jacket, swung her hips when she walked to the blackboard, and gave Streeter, one evening, such a dark look that he took her in his arms. What she did then was to shriek, kick over a little desk, and run through three intervening classrooms to the lobby, screaming that she had been attacked by a beast. After all his months of study, "beast" was the only word in her tirade that Streeter understood. The whole school was alerted, of course, and all he could do was to wipe the sweat off his forehead and start through the classrooms toward the lobby. People stood on chairs to get a better look at him, and he never went back to Tauchnitz.

His next teacher was a very plain woman with gray hair and a lavender shawl that she must have knitted herself, it was so full of knots and tangles. She was an excellent teacher for a month, and then one evening she told him that her life was difficult. She waited to be encouraged to tell him her troubles, and when he did not give her any encouragement, she told them to him anyhow. She had been engaged to be married for twenty years, but the mother of her betrothed disapproved of the match and, whenever the subject was raised, would climb up onto the window sill and threaten to jump into the street. Now her betrothed was sick, he would have to be cut open (she gestured) from the neck to the navel, and if he died she would go to her grave a spinster. Her wicked sisters had got pregnant in order to force their marriages—one of them had walked down the aisle eight months gone (more gestures)—but she would rather (with a hitch at her lavender shawl) solicit men in the street than do that. Streeter listened helplessly to her sorrow, as we will listen to most human troubles, having some of our own, but she was still talking when her next student, a Japanese, came in for his lesson, and Streeter had learned no Italian that night. She had not told Streeter all of the story, and she continued it when he came again. The fault might have been his—he should have discouraged her rudely—but now that she had made him her confidant, he saw that he could not change this relationship. The force he had to cope with was the loneliness that is to be found in any large city, and he invented another trip to Perugia. He had two more teachers, two more trips to Perugia, and then, in the late autumn of his second year in Rome, someone from the Embassy recommended Kate Dresser.

An American woman who teaches Italian in Rome is unusual, but then all arrangements in Rome are so complicated that lucidity and skepticism give way when we try to follow the description of a scene in court, a lease, a lunch, or anything else. Each fact or detail breeds more questions than it answers, and in the end we lose sight of the truth, as we were meant to do. Here comes Cardinal Micara with the True Finger of Doubting Thomas—that much is clear—but is the man beside us in church asleep or dead, and what are all the elephants doing in the Piazza Venezia?

The lessons took place at one end of a huge *sala*, by the fireplace. Streeter spent an hour and sometimes two hours preparing for them. He finished *Pinocchio* and began to read *I Promessi Sposi*. After this would come the *Divine Comedy*. He was as proud as a child of his completed homework, loved to be given tests and dictation, and usually came into Kate's apartment with a big, foolish smile on his face, he was so pleased with himself. She was a very good teacher. She understood his fatuousness, the worn condition of his middle-aged memory, and his desire to learn. She spoke an Italian that he could almost always understand, and by keeping a wristwatch on the table to mark the period, by sending him bills through the mail, and by never speaking of herself, she conducted the lessons in an atmosphere that was practical and impersonal. He thought she was a good-looking woman—intense, restless, overworked, perhaps, but charming.

Among the things that Kate Dresser did not tell him, as they sat in this part of the room that she had staked out for herself with a Chinese screen and some rickety gold chairs, was the fact that she was born and raised in the little town of Krasbie, Iowa. Her father and mother were both dead. In a place where almost everybody worked in the chemical-fertilizer factory, her father had happened to be a trolley conductor. When she was growing up, Kate could never bring herself to admit that her father took fares in a trolley car. She could never even admit that he was her father, although she had inherited his most striking physical feature—a nose that turned up so spectacularly at the tip that she was called Roller Coaster and Pug.

She had gone from Krasbie to Chicago, from Chicago to New York, where she married a man in the Foreign Service. They lived in Washington and then Tangier. Shortly after the war, they moved to Rome, where her husband died of food poisoning, leaving her with a son and very little money. So she made her home in Rome. The only preparation Krasbie had given her for Italy was the curtain in the little movie theatre where she had spent her Saturday afternoons when she was a girl. Skinny then, dressed no better than most rebellious children and smelling no sweeter, her hair in braids, her pockets full of peanuts and candy and her mouth full of chewing gum, she had put down her quarter every Saturday afternoon, rain or shine, and spread herself out in a seat in the front row. There were shouts of "Roller Coaster!" and "Pug!" from all over the theatre, and, what with the high-heeled shoes (her sister's) that she sometimes wore and the five-and-ten-cent-store diamonds on her fingers, it was no wonder that people made fun of her. Boys dropped chewing gum into her hair and shot spitballs at the back of her skinny neck, and, persecuted in body and spirit, she would raise her eyes to the curtain and see a remarkably precise vision of her future. It was painted on canvas, very badly cracked from having been rolled and unrolled so many times—a vision of an Italian garden, with cypress trees, a terrace, a pool and fountain, and a marble balustrade with roses spilling from marble urns. She seemed literally to have risen up from her seat and to have entered the cracked scene, for it was almost exactly like the view from her window into the courtyard of the Palazzo Tarominia, where she lived.

Now, you might ask why a woman who had so little money was living in the Palazzo Tarominia, and there was a Roman answer. The Baronessa Tramonde—the old Duke of Rome's sister—lived in the west wing of the palace, in an apartment that had been built for Pope Andros X and that was reached by a great staircase with painted walls and ceilings. It had pleased the Baronessa, before the war, to stand at the head of this staircase and greet her friends and relations, but things had changed. The Baronessa had grown old, and so had her friends; they could no longer climb the stairs. Oh, they tried. They had straggled up to her card parties like a patrol under machine-gun fire, the gentlemen pushing the ladies and sometimes vice versa, and old marchesas and princesses—the cream of Europe—huffing and puffing and sitting down on the steps in utter exhaustion. There was a lift in the other wing of the palace—the wing Kate lived in—but a lift could not be installed in the west wing, because it would ruin the paintings. The only other way to enter the Baronessa's quarters was to take the lift to Kate's apartment and walk through it and out a service door that led into the other wing. By giving the Duke of Rome, who also had an apartment in the Palazzo, a kind of eminent domain, Kate had a palace apartment at a low rent. The Duke usually passed through twice a day to visit his sister, and on the first Thursday of every month, at five minutes after eight, a splendid and elderly company would troop through Kate's rooms to the Baronessa's card party. Kate did not mind. In fact, when she heard the doorbell ring on Thursdays her heart would begin a grating beat of the deepest excitement. The old Duke always led the procession. His right hand had been chopped off at the wrist by one of Mussolini's public executioners, and now that the old man's enemies were dead, he carried the stump proudly. With him would come Don Fernando Marchetti, the Duke of Treno, the Duke and Duchess Ricotto-Sporci, Count Ambro di Albentiis, Count and Countess Fabrizio Daromeo, Princess Urbana Tessoro, Princess Isabella Tessoro, and Federico Cardinal Baldova. They had all distinguished themselves in one way or another. Don Fernando had driven a car from Paris to Peking, via the Gobi Desert. Duke Ricotto-Sporci had broken most of his bones in a steeplechase accident, and the Countess Daromeo had operated an Allied radio station in the middle of Rome during the German Occupation. The old Duke of Rome would present Kate with a little bouquet of flowers, and then he and his friends would file through the kitchen and go out the service door.

Kate spoke an admirable Italian, and had done some translating and given lessons, and for the past three years she had supported herself and her son by dubbing parts of English dialogue into old Italian movies, which were then shown over British TV. With her cultivated accent, she played mostly dowagers and the like, but there seemed to be plenty of work, and she spent much of her time in a sound studio near the Tiber. With her salary and the money her husband had left her, she had barely enough to get by on. Her elder sister, in Krasbie, wrote her a long lament two or three times a year: "Oh, you lucky, lucky dog, Kate! Oh, how I envy you being away from all the tiresome, nagging, stupid, petty details of life at home." Kate Dresser's life was not lacking in stupid and nagging details, but instead of mentioning such things in her letters, she inflamed her sister's longing to travel by sending home photographs of herself in gondolas, or cards from Florence, where she always spent Easter with friends.

STREETER KNEW that under Kate Dresser's teaching he was making progress with his Italian, and usually when he stepped out of the Palazzo Tarominia into the street after his lesson, he was exhilarated at the thought that in another month—at the end of the season, anyhow—he would understand everything that was going on and being said. But his progress had its ups and downs.

The beauty of Italy is not easy to come by any longer, if it ever was, but, driving to a villa below Anticoli for a weekend with friends, Streeter saw a country of such detail and loveliness that it could not be described. They had reached the villa early on a rainy night. Nightingales sang in the trees, the double doors of the villa stood open, and in all the rooms there were bowls of roses and olivewood fires. It had seemed, with the servants bowing and bringing in candles and wine, like some gigantic and princely homecoming in a movie, and, going out onto the terrace after dinner to hear the nightingales and see the lights of the hill towns, Streeter felt that he had never been put by dark hills and distant lights into a mood of such tenderness. In the morning, when he stepped out onto his bedroom balcony, he saw a barefoot maid in the garden, picking a rose to put in her hair. Then she began to sing. It was like a flamenco—first guttural and then falsetto—and poor Streeter found his Italian still so limited that he couldn't understand the words of the song, and this brought him around to the fact that he couldn't quite understand the landscape, either. His feeling about it was very much what he might have felt about some excellent resort or summer place—a scene where, perhaps as children, we have thrown ourselves into a temporary relationship with beauty and simplicity that will be rudely broken off on Labor Day. It was the evocation of a borrowed, temporary, bittersweet happiness that he rebelled against—but the maid went on singing, and Streeter did not understand a word.

When Streeter took his lessons at Kate's, her son, Charlie, usually passed through the *sala* at least once during the hour. He was a baseball fan, and had a bad complexion and an owlish laugh. He would say hello to Streeter and pass on some sports news from the Rome *Daily American*. Streeter had a son of his own of about the same age, and was enjoined by the divorce settlement from seeing the boy, and he never looked at Charlie without a pang of longing for his own son. Charlie was fifteen, and one of those American boys you see waiting for the school bus up by the Embassy, dressed in black leather jackets and Levi's, and with sideburns or duck-tail haircuts, and fielder's mitts—anything that will stamp them as American. These are the real expatriates. On Saturdays after the movies they go into one of those bars called Harry's or Larry's or Jerry's, where the walls are covered with autographed photographs of unknown electric-guitar players and unknown soubrettes, to eat bacon and eggs and talk baseball and play American records on the jukebox. They are Embassy children, and the children of writers and oil-company and airline employees and divorcées and Fulbright Fellows. Eating bacon and eggs, and listening to the jukebox, they have a sense of being far, far from home that is a much sweeter and headier distillation than their parents ever know. Charlie had spent five years of his life under a ceiling decorated with gold that had been brought from the New World by the first Duke of Rome, and he had seen old marchesas with diamonds as big as acorns slip the cheese parings into their handbags when the lunch was finished. He had ridden in gondolas and played softball on the Palatine. He had seen the Palio at Siena, and had heard the bells of Rome and Florence and Venice and Ravenna and Verona. But it wasn't about these things that he wrote in a letter to his mother's Uncle George in Krasbie toward the middle of March. Instead, he asked the old man to take him home and let him be an American boy. The timing was perfect. Uncle George had just retired from the fertilizer factory and had always wanted to bring Kate and her son home. Within two weeks he was on board a ship bound for Naples.

Streeter, of course, knew nothing of this. But he had suspected that there was some tension between Charlie and his mother. The boy's hoedown American clothes, the poses he took as a rail splitter, pitcher, and cowboy, and his mother's very Italianate manners implied room for sizable disagreement, at least, and, going there one Sunday afternoon, Streeter stepped into a quarrel. Assunta, the maid, let him in, but he stopped at the door of the *sala* when he heard Kate and her son shouting at one another in anger. Streeter could not retreat. Assunta had gone on ahead to say he was there, and all he could do was wait in the vestibule. Kate came out to him then—she was crying—and said, in Italian, that she could not give him a lesson that afternoon. She was sorry. Something had come up, and there had not been time to telephone him. He felt like a fool, confronted with her tears, holding his grammar, his copybook, and *I Promessi Sposi* under one arm. He said it didn't matter about the lesson, it was nothing, and could he come on Tuesday? She said yes, yes, would he come on Tuesday—and would he come on Thursday, not for a lesson but to do her a favor? "My father's brother—my Uncle George—is coming, to try and take Charlie home. I don't know what to do. I don't know what I *can* do. But I would appreciate it if there was a man here; I would feel so much better if I weren't alone. You don't have to say anything or do anything but sit in a chair and have a drink, but I would feel so much better if I weren't alone."

Streeter agreed to come, and went away then, wondering what kind of a life it was she led if she had to count in an emergency on a stranger like him. With his lesson canceled and nothing else that he had to do, he took a walk up the river as far as the Ministry of the Marine, and then came back through a neighborhood that was neither new nor old nor anything else you could specify. Because it was Sunday afternoon, the houses were mostly shut. The streets were deserted. When he passed anyone, it was usually a family group returning from an excursion to the zoo. There were also a few of those lonely men and women carrying pastry boxes that you see everywhere in the world at dusk on Sunday—unmarried aunts and uncles going out to tea with their relations and bringing a little pastry to sweeten the call. But mostly he was alone, mostly there was no sound but his own footsteps and, in the distance, the iron ringing of iron trolley-car wheels on iron tracks—a lonely sound on Sunday afternoons for many Americans; a lonely one for him, anyhow, and reminding him of some friendless, loveless, galling Sunday in his youth. As he came closer to the city, there were more lights and people—flowers and the noise of talk—and under the gate of Santa Maria del Popolo a whore spoke to him. She was a beautiful young woman, but he told her, in his broken Italian, that he had a friend, and walked on.

Crossing the Piazza, he saw a man struck by a car. The noise was loud—that surprising loudness of our bones when they are dealt a mortal blow. The driver of the car slipped out of his seat and ran up the Pincian Hill. The victim lay in a heap on the paving, a shabbily dressed man but with a lot of oil in his black, wavy hair, which must have been his pride. A crowd gathered—not solemn at all, although a few women crossed themselves—and everyone began to talk excitedly. The crowd, garrulous, absorbed in its own opinions and indifferent, it seemed, to the dying man, was so thick that when the police came they had to push and struggle to reach the victim. With the words of the whore still in his ears, Streeter wondered why it was that they regarded a human life as something of such dubious value.

He turned away from the Piazza then, toward the river, and, passing the Tomb of Augustus, he noticed a young man calling to a cat and offering it something to eat. The cat was one of those thousands of millions that live in the ruins of Rome and eat leftover spaghetti, and the man was offering the cat a piece of bread. Then, as the cat approached him, the man took a firecracker out of his pocket, put it into the piece of bread, and lit the fuse. He put the bread on the sidewalk, and just as the cat took it the powder exploded. The animal let out a hellish shriek and leaped into the air, its body all twisted, and then it streaked over the wall and was lost in the darkness of Augustus' Tomb. The man laughed at his trick, and so did several people who had been watching.

Streeter's first instinct was to box the man's ears and teach him not to feed lighted firecrackers to stray cats. But, with such an appreciative audience, this would have amounted to an international incident, and he realized there wasn't anything he could do. The people who had laughed at the prank were good and kind—most of them affectionate parents. You might have seen them earlier in the day on the Palatine, picking violets.

Streeter walked on into a dark street and heard at his back the hoofs and trappings of horses—it sounded like cavalry—and stepped aside to let a hearse and a mourner's carriage pass. The hearse was drawn by two pairs of bays with black plumes. The driver wore funerary livery, with an admiral's hat, and had the brutish red face of a drunken horse thief. The hearse banged, slammed, and rattled over the stones in such a loose-jointed way that the poor soul it carried must have been in a terrible state of disarrangement, and the mourner's carriage that followed was empty. The friends of the dead man had probably been too late or had got the wrong date or had forgotten the whole thing, as was so often the case in Rome. Off the hearse and carriage rattled toward the Servian Gate.

Streeter knew one thing then: He did not want to die in Rome. He was in excellent health and had no reason to think about death; nevertheless, he was afraid. Back at his flat, he poured some whiskey and water into a glass and stepped out onto his balcony. He watched the night fall and the street lights go on with complete bewilderment at his own feelings. He did not want to die in Rome. The power of this idea could only stem from ignorance and stupidity, he told himself—for what could such a fear represent but the inability to respond to the force of life? He reproached himself with arguments and consoled himself with whiskey, but in the middle of the night he was waked by the noise of a carriage and horses' hoofs, and again he sweated with fear. The hearse, the horse thief, and the empty mourner's carriage, he thought, were rattling back, under his balcony. He got up out of bed and went to the window to see, but it was only two empty carriages going back to the stables.

WHEN UNCLE GEORGE LANDED in Naples, on Tuesday, he was exicted and in a good humor. His purpose in coming abroad was twofold—to bring Charlie and Kate home, and to take a vacation, the first in forty-three years. A friend of his in Krasbie who had been to Italy had written an itinerary for him: "Stay at the Royal in Naples. Go to the National Museum. Have a drink in the Galleria Umberto. Eat supper at the California. Good American food. Take the Roncari *auto-pullman* in the morning for Rome. This goes through two interesting villages and stops at Nero's villa. In Rome stay at the Excelsior. Make reservations in advance. . . ."

On Wednesday morning, Uncle George got up early and went down to the hotel dining room. "Orange juice and ham and eggs," he said to the waiter. The waiter brought him orange juice, coffee, and a roll. "Where's my ham and eggs?" Uncle George asked, and then realized, when the waiter bowed and smiled, that the man did not understand English. He got out his phrase book, but there was nothing about ham and eggs. "You gotta no hamma?" he asked loudly. "You gotta no eggsa?" The waiter went on smiling and bowing, and Uncle George gave up. He ate the breakfast he hadn't ordered, gave the waiter a twenty-lira tip, cashed four hundred dollars' worth of traveler's checks at the desk, and checked out. All this money in lire made a bump in his suit jacket, and he held his left hand over his wallet as if he had a pain there. Naples, he knew, was full of thieves. He took a cab to the bus station, which was in a square near the Galleria Umberto. It was early in the morning, the light was slanting, and he enjoyed the smell of coffee and bread and the stir of people hurrying along the streets to work. A fine smell of the sea rose up the streets from the bay. He was early and was shown his seat in the bus by a red-faced gentleman who spoke English with a British accent. This was the guide—one of those who, whatever conveyance you take and wherever you go, make travel among the monuments bizarre. Their command of languages is extraordinary, their knowledge of antiquity is impressive, and their love of beauty is passionate, but when they separate themselves from the party for a moment it is to take a pull from a hip flask or to pinch a young pilgrim. They praise the ancient world in four languages, but their clothes are threadbare, their linen is dirty, and their hands tremble with thirst and lechery. While the guide chatted about the weather with Uncle

George, the whiskey could already be smelled on his breath. Then the guide left Uncle George to greet the rest of the party, now coming across the square.

There were about thirty—they moved in a flock, or mass, understandably timid about the strangeness of their surroundings—and they were mostly old women. As they came into the bus, they cackled (as we all will when we grow old), and made the fussy arrangements of elderly travelers. Then, with the guide singing the praises of ancient Naples, they started on their way.

They first went along the coast. The color of the water reminded Uncle George of postcards he had received from Honolulu, where one of his friends had gone for a vacation. It was green and blue. He had never seen anything like it himself. They passed some resorts only half open and sleepy, where young men sat on rocks in their bathing trunks, waiting patiently for the sun to darken their skins. What did they think about? Uncle George wondered. During all those hours that they sat on rocks, what on earth did they think about? They passed a ramshackle colony of little bathhouses no bigger than privies, and Uncle George remembered—how many years ago—the thrill of undressing in such briny sea chambers as these when he had been taken to the seashore as a boy. As they turned inland, he craned his neck to get a last look at the sea, wondering why it should seem, shining and blue, like something that he remembered in his bones. Then they went into a tunnel and came out in farmland. Uncle George was interested in farming methods and admired the way that vines were trained onto trees. He admired the terracing of the land, and was troubled by the traces of soil erosion that he saw. And he recognized that he was separated only by a pane of glass from a life that was as strange to him as life on the moon.

The bus, with its glass roof and glass windows, was like a fishbowl, and the sunlight and cloud shadows of the day fell among the travelers. Their way was blocked by a flock of sheep. Sheep surrounded the bus, isolated this little island of elderly Americans, and filled the air with dumb, harsh bleating. Beyond the sheep they saw a girl carrying a water jug on her head. A man lay sound asleep in the grass by the side of the road. A woman sat on a doorstep, suckling a child. Within the dome of glass the old ladies discussed the high price of airplane luggage. "Grace got ringworm in Palermo," one of them said. "I don't think she'll ever be cured."

The guide pointed out fragments of old Roman road, Roman towers and bridges. There was a castle on a hill—a sight that delighted Uncle George, and no wonder, for there had been castles painted on his supper plate when he was a boy, and the earliest books that had been read to him and that he had been able to read had been illustrated with castles. They had meant everything that was exciting and strange and wonderful in life, and now, by raising his eyes, he could see one against a sky as blue as the sky in his picture books.

After traveling for an hour or two, they stopped in a village where there were a coffee bar and toilets. Coffee cost one hundred lire a cup, a fact that filled the ladies' conversation for some time after they had started again. Coffee had been sixty lire at the hotel. Forty at the corner. They took pills and read from their guidebooks, and Uncle George looked out of the windows at this strange country, where the spring flowers and the autumn flowers seemed to grow side by side in the grass. It would be miserable weather in Krasbie, but here everything was in bloom—fruit trees, mimosa—and the pastures were white with flowers and the vegetable gardens already yielding crops.

They came into a town or city then—an old place with crooked and narrow streets. He didn't catch the name. The guide explained that there was a *festa*. The bus driver had to blow his horn continuously to make any progress, and two or three times came to a full stop, the crowd was so dense. The people in the streets looked up at this apparition—this fishbowl of elderly Americans—with such incredulity that Uncle George's feelings were hurt. He saw a little girl take a crust of bread out of her mouth to stare at him. Women held their children up in the air to see the strangers. Windows were thrown open, bars were emptied, and people pointed at the curious tourists and laughed. Uncle George would have liked to address them, as he so often addressed the Rotary. "Don't stare," he wanted to say to them. "We are not so queer and rich and strange. Don't stare at us."

The bus turned down a side street, and there was another stop for coffee and toilets. Most of the travelers scattered to buy postcards. Uncle George, seeing an open church across the street, decided to go inside. The air smelled of spice when he pushed the door open. The stone walls inside were bare—it was like an armory—and only a few candles burned in the chapels at the sides. Then Uncle George heard a loud voice and saw a man kneeling in front of one of the chapels, saying his prayers. He carried on in a way that Uncle George had never seen before. His voice was strong, supplicatory, sometimes angry. His face was wet with tears. He was beseeching the Cross for something—an explanation or an indulgence or a life. He waved his hands, he wept, and his voice and his sobs echoed in the barny place. Uncle George went out and got back into his seat on the bus.

They left the city for the country again, and a little before noon they stopped at the gates to Nero's villa, bought their tickets, and went in. It was a large ruin, fanciful, and picked clean of everything but its brick supports. The place had been vast and tall, and now the walls and archways of roofless rooms, the butts of towers, stood in a stretch of green pasture, with nothing leading anywhere any more except to nothing, and all the many staircases mounting and turning stopped in midair. Uncle George left the party and wandered happily through these traces of a palace. The atmosphere seemed to him pleasant and tranquil—a little like the feeling in a forest—and he heard a bird singing and the noise of water. The forms of the ruins, all bristling with plants like the hair in an old man's ears, seemed pleasantly familiar, as if his unremembered dreams had been played out against a scene like this. He found himself then in a place that was darker than the rest. The air was damp, and the senseless brick rooms, opening onto one another, were full of brush. It might have been a dungeon or a guardhouse or a temple where obscene rites were performed, for he was suddenly stirred licentiously by the damp. He turned back, looking for the sun, the water, and the bird, and found a guide standing in his path.

"You wish to see the special place?"

"What do you mean?"

"Very special," the guide said. "For men only. Only for strong men. Such pictures. Very old."

"How much?"

"Two hundred lire."

"All right." Uncle George took two hundred lire out of his change pocket.

"Come," the guide said. "This way." He walked on briskly—so briskly that Uncle George nearly had to run to keep up with him. He saw the guide go through a narrow opening in the wall, a place where the brick had crumbled, but when Uncle George followed him the guide seemed to have disappeared. It was a trap. He felt an arm around his throat, and his head was thrown back so violently that he couldn't call for help. He felt a hand lift the wallet out of his pocket—a touch as light as the nibble of a fish on a line—and then he was thrown brutally to the ground. He lay there dazed for a minute or two. When he sat up, he saw that he had been left his empty wallet and his passport.

Then he roared with anger at the thieves, and hated Italy, with its thieving population of organ grinders and bricklayers. But even during this outburst his anger was not as strong as a feeling of weakness and shame. He was terribly ashamed of himself, and when he picked up his empty wallet and put it in his pocket, he felt as if his heart had been plucked out and broken. Who could he blame? Not the damp ruins. He had asked for something that was by his lights all wrong, and he could only blame himself. The theft might happen every day—some lecherous old fool like him might be picked clean each time the bus stopped. He got to his feet, weary and sick of the old bones that had got him into trouble. He dusted the dirt off his clothes. Then he realized that he might be late. He might have missed the bus and be stranded in the ruins without a cent. He began to walk and run through the rooms, until he came out into a clearing and saw in the distance the flock of old ladies, still clinging to one another.

The guide came out from behind a wall, and they all got in the bus and started off again.

Rome was ugly; at least, the outskirts were: trolley cars and cut-rate furniture stores and torn-up streets and the sort of apartment houses that nobody ever really wants to live in. The old ladies began to gather their guidebooks and put on their coats and hats and gloves. Journey's end is the same everywhere. Then, dressed for their destination, they all sat down again, with their hands folded in their laps, and the bus was still. "Oh, I wish I'd never come," one old lady said to another. "I just wish I'd never left home." She was not the only one.

"Ecco, ecco Roma," the guide said, and so it was.

STREETER WENT to Kate's at seven on Thursday. Assunta let him in, and, for the first time, he walked down the *sala* without his copy of *I Promessi Sposi,* and sat down by the fireplace. Charlie came in then. He had on the usual outfit—the tight Levi's, with cuffs turned up, and a pink shirt. When he moved, he dragged or banged the leather heels of his loafers on the marble floor. He talked about baseball and exercised his owlish laugh, but he didn't mention Uncle George. Neither did Kate, when she came in, nor did she offer Streeter a drink. She seemed to be in the throes of an emotional storm, with all her powers of decision suspended. They talked about the weather. At one point, Charlie came and stood by his mother, and she took both of his hands in one of hers. Then the doorbell rang, and Kate went down the room to meet her uncle. They embraced very tenderly—the members of a family—and when this was over he said, "I was robbed, Katie. I was robbed yesterday of four hundred dollars. Coming up from Naples on the bus."

"Oh, I'm so sorry!" she said. "Wasn't there anything you could do, George? Wasn't there anyone you could speak to?"

"Speak to, Katie? There hasn't been anyone I could speak to since I got off the boat. No speaka da English. If you cut off their hands, they wouldn't be able to say anything. I can afford to lose four hundred dollars—I'm not a poor man—but if I could only have given it to some worthwhile cause."

"I'm terribly sorry."

"You've got quite a place here, Katie."

"And, Charlie, this is Uncle George."

If she had counted on their not getting along, this chance was lost in a second. Charlie forgot his owlish laugh and stood so straight, so in need of what America could do for him that the rapport between the man and the boy was instantaneous, and Kate had to separate them in order to introduce Streeter. Uncle George shook hands with her student and came to a likely but erroneous conclusion.

"Speaka da English?" he asked.

"I'm an American," Streeter said.

"How long is your sentence?"

"This is my second year," Streeter said. "I work at F.R.U.P.C."

"It's an immoral country," Uncle George said, sitting down in one of the golden chairs. "First they rob me of four hundred dollars, and then, walking around the streets here, all I see is statues of men without any clothes on. Nothing."

Kate rang for Assunta, and when the maid came in she ordered whiskey and ice, in very rapid Italian. "It's just another way of looking at things, Uncle George," she said.

"No, it isn't," Uncle George said. "It isn't natural. Not even in locker rooms. There's very few men who'd choose to parade around a locker room stark naked if a towel was handy. It's not natural. Everywhere you look. Up on the roofs. At the main traffic intersections. When I was coming over here, I passed through a little garden—playground, I guess you'd say—and right in the middle of it, right in the middle of all these little children, is one of these men without anything on."

"Will you have some whiskey?"

"Yes, please. . . . The boat sails on Saturday, Katie, and I want you and the boy to come home with me."

"I don't want Charlie to leave," Kate said.

"He wants to leave—don't you, Charlie? He wrote me a nice letter. Nicely worded, and he's got a nice handwriting. That was a nice letter, Charlie. I showed it to the high-school superintendent, and he said you can enter the Krasbie high school whenever you want. And I want you to come, too, Kate. It's your home, and you've only got one. The trouble with you, Katie, is that when you were a kid they used to make fun of you in Krasbie, and you just started running, that's all, and you never stopped."

"If that's true—and it may be," she said quickly, "why should I want to go back to a place where I will seem ridiculous."

"Oh, Katie, you won't seem ridiculous. I'll take care of that."

"I want to go home, Mama," Charlie said. He was sitting on a stool by the fireplace—not so straight-backed any more. "I'm homesick all the time."

"How could you possibly be homesick for America?" Her voice was very sharp. "You've never seen it. This is your home."

"How do you mean?"

"Your home is with your mother."

"There's more to it than that, Mama. I feel strange here all the time. Everybody on the street speaking a different language."

"You've never even tried to learn Italian."

"Even if I had, it wouldn't make any difference. It would still sound strange. I mean, it would still remind me that it wasn't my language. I just don't understand the people, Mama. I like them all right, but I just don't understand them. I never know what they're going to do next."

"Why don't you try and understand them?"

"Oh, I do, but I'm no genius, and you don't understand them, either. I've heard you say so, and sometimes you're homesick, too, I know. I can tell by the way you look."

"Homesickness is nothing," she said angrily. "It is absolutely nothing. Fifty per cent of the people in the world are homesick all the time. But I don't suppose you're old enough to understand. When you're in one place and long to be in another, it isn't as simple as taking a boat. You don't really long for another country. You long for something in yourself that you don't have, or haven't been able to find."

"Oh, I don't mean that, Mama. I just mean if I was with people who spoke my language, people who understood me, I'd be more comfortable."

"If comfort is all you expect to get out of life, God help you."

Then the doorbell rang and Assunta answered it. Kate glanced at her watch and saw that it was five after eight. It was also the first Thursday in the month. Before she could get out an explanation, they had started down the *sala,* with the old Duke of Rome in the lead, holding some flowers in his left hand. A little behind him was the Duchess, his wife—a tall, willowy, gray-haired woman wearing a lot of jewelry that had been given to the family by Francis I. An assortment of nobles brought up the rear, looking like a country circus, gorgeous and travel-worn. The Duke gave Kate her flowers. They all bowed vaguely to her company and went out through the kitchen, with its smell of gas leaks, to the service door.

"Oh, Giuseppe the barber he gotta the cash," Uncle George sang loudly, "He gotta the bigga the blacka mustache." He waited for someone to laugh, and when no one did he asked, "What was that?"

Kate told him, but her eyes were brighter, and he noticed this.

"You like that kind of thing, don't you?" he said.

"Possibly," she said.

"It's crazy, Katie," he said. "It's crazy, it's crazy. You come home with me and Charlie. You and Charlie can live in the other half of my house, and I'll have a nice American kitchen put in for you."

Streeter saw that she was touched by this remark, and he thought she was going to cry. She said quickly, "How in hell do you think America would have been discovered if everybody stayed home in places like Krasbie?"

"You're not discovering anything, Katie."

"I am. I am."

"We'll all be happier, Mama," Charlie said. "We'll all be happier if we have a nice clean house and lots of nice friends and a nice garden and kitchen and stall shower."

She stood with her back to them, by the mantelpiece, and said loudly, "No nice friends, no kitchen, no garden, no shower bath or anything else will keep me from wanting to see the world and the different people who live in it." Then she turned to her son and spoke softly. "You'll miss Italy, Charlie."

The boy laughed his owlish laugh. "I'll miss the black hairs in my food," he said. She didn't make a sound. She didn't even sigh. Then the boy went to her and began to cry. "I'm sorry, Mummy," he said. "I'm sorry. That was a dumb thing to say. It's just an old joke." He kissed her hands and the tears on her cheeks, and Streeter got up and left.

"Tal era ciò che di meno deforme e di men compassionevole si faceva vedere intorno, i sani, gli agiati," Streeter read when he went again for his lesson Sunday. *"Chè, dopo tante immagini di miseria, e pensando a quella ancor più grave, per mezzo alla quale dovrem condurre il lettore,*

no ci fermeremo ora a dir qual fosse lo spettacolo degli appestati che si strascicavano o giacevano per le strade, de' poveri, de' fanciulli, delle donne."

The boy had gone, he could tell—not because she said so but because the place seemed that much bigger. In the middle of his lesson, the old Duke of Rome came through in his bathrobe and slippers, carrying a bowl of soup to his sister, who was sick. Kate looked tired, but then she always did, and when the lesson ended and Streeter stood up, wondering if she would mention Charlie or Uncle George, she complimented him on the progress he had made and urged him to finish *I Promessi Sposi* and to buy a copy of the *Divine Comedy* for next week.

THE WRYSONS

THE WRYSONS WANTED things in the suburb of Shady Hill to remain exactly as they were. Their dread of change—of irregularity of any sort—was acute, and when the Larkin estate was sold for an old people's rest home, the Wrysons went to the Village Council meeting and demanded to know what sort of old people these old people were going to be. The Wrysons' civic activities were confined to upzoning, but they were very active in this field, and if you were invited to their house for cocktails, the chances were that you would be asked to sign an upzoning petition before you got away. This was something more than a natural desire to preserve the character of the community. They seemed to sense that there was a stranger at the gates—unwashed, tirelessly scheming, foreign, the father of disorderly children who would ruin their rose garden and depreciate their real-estate investment, a man with a beard, a garlic breath, and a book. The Wrysons took no part in the intellectual life of the community. There was hardly a book in their house, and, in a place where even cooks were known to have Picasso reproductions hanging above their washstands, the Wrysons' taste in painting stopped at marine sunsets and bowls of flowers. Donald Wryson was a large man with thinning fair hair and the cheerful air of a bully, but he was a bully only in the defense of rectitude, class distinctions, and the orderly appearance of things. Irene Wryson was not a totally unattractive woman, but she was both shy and contentious—especially contentious on the subject of upzoning. They had one child, a little girl named Dolly, and they lived in a pleasant house on Alewives Lane, and they went in for gardening. This was another way of keeping up the appearance of things, and Donald Wryson was very critical of a neighbor who had ragged syringa bushes and a bare spot on her front lawn. They led a limited social life; they seemed to have no ambitions or needs in this direction, although at Christmas each year they sent out about six hundred cards. The preparation and addressing of these must have occupied their evenings for at least two weeks. Donald had a laugh like a jackass, and people who did not like him were careful not to sit in the same train coach with him. The Wrysons were stiff; they were inflexible. They seemed to experience not distaste but alarm when they found quack grass in their lawn or heard of a contemplated divorce among their neighbors. They were odd, of course. They were not as odd as poor, dizzy Flossie Dolmetch, who was caught forging drug prescriptions and was discovered to have been under the influence of morphine for three years. They were not as odd as Caruthers Mason, with his collection of two thousand lewd photographs, or as odd as Mrs. Temon, who, with those two lovely children in the next room— But why go on? They were odd.

Irene Wryson's oddness centered on a dream. She dreamed once or twice a month that someone—some enemy or hapless American pilot—had exploded a hydrogen bomb. In the light of day, her dream was inadmissible, for she could not relate it to her garden, her interest in upzoning, or her comfortable way of life. She could not bring herself to tell her husband at breakfast that she had dreamed about the hydrogen bomb. Faced with the pleasant table and its view of the garden—faced even with rain and snow—she could not find it in herself to explain what had troubled her sleep. The dream cost her much in energy and composure, and often left her deeply depressed. Its sequence of events varied, but it usually went like this.

The dream was set in Shady Hill—she dreamed that she

woke in her own bed. Donald was always gone. She was at once aware of the fact that the bomb had exploded. Mattress stuffing and a trickle of brown water were coming through a big hole in the ceiling. The sky was gray—lightless—although there were in the west a few threads of red light, like those charming vapor trails we see in the air after the sun has set. She didn't know if these were vapor trails or some part of that force that would destroy the marrow in her bones. The gray air seemed final. The sky would never shine with light again. From her window she could see a river, and now, as she watched, boats began to come upstream. At first, there were only two or three. Then there were tens, and then there were hundreds. There were outboards, excursion boats, yachts, schooners with auxiliary motors; there were even rowboats. The number of boats grew until the water was covered with them, and the noise of motors rose to a loud din. The jockeying for position in this retreat up the river became aggressive and then savage. She saw men firing pistols at one another, and a rowboat, in which there was a family with little children, smashed and sunk by a cruiser. She cried, in her dream, to see this inhumanity as the world was ending. She cried, and she went on watching, as if some truth was being revealed to her—as if she had always known this to be the human condition, as if she had always known the world to be dangerous and the comforts of her life in Shady Hill to be the merest palliative.

Then in her dream she turned away from the window and went through the bathroom that connected their room and Dolly's. Her daughter was sleeping sweetly, and she woke her. At this point, her emotions were at their strongest. The force and purity of the love that she felt toward this fragrant child was an agony. She dressed the little girl and put a snowsuit on her and led her into the bathroom. She opened the medicine cabinet, the one place in the house that the Wrysons, in their passion for neatness, had not put in order. It was crowded with leftover medicines from Dolly's trifling illnesses—cough syrups, calamine lotion for poison ivy, aspirin, and physics. And the mild perfume of these remnants and the tenderness she had felt for her daughter when she was ill—as if the door of the medicine cabinet had been a window opening onto some dazzling summer of the emotions—made her cry again.

Among the bottles was one that said "Poison," and she reached for this and unscrewed the top, and shook into her left hand a pill for herself and one for the girl. She told the trusting child some gentle lie, and was about to put the pill between her lips when the ceiling of the bathroom collapsed and they stood knee deep in plaster and dirty water. She groped around in the water for the poison, but it was lost, and the dream usually ended in this way. And how could she lean across the breakfast table and explain her pallor to her husky husband with this detailed vision of the end of the world? He would have laughed his jackass laugh.

Donald Wryson's oddness could be traced easily enough to his childhood. He had been raised in a small town in the Middle West that couldn't have had much to recommend it, and his father, an old-fashioned commercial traveler, with a hothouse rose in his buttonhole and buff-colored spats, had abandoned his wife and his son when the boy was young. Mrs. Wryson had few friends and no family. With her husband gone, she got a job as a clerk in an insurance office, and took up, with her son, a life of unmitigated melancholy and need. She never forgot the horror of her abandonment, and she leaned so heavily for support on her son that she seemed to threaten his animal spirits. Her life was a Calvary, as she often said, and the most she could do was to keep body and soul together.

She had been young and fair and happy once, and the only way she had of evoking these lost times was by giving her son baking lessons. When the nights were long and cold and the wind whistled around the four-family house where they lived, she would light a fire in the kitchen range and drop an apple peel onto the stove lid for the fragrance. Then Donald would put on an apron and scurry around, getting out the necessary bowls and pans, measuring out flour and sugar, separating eggs. He learned the contents of every cupboard. He knew where the spices and the sugar were kept, the nutmeats and the citron, and when the work was done, he enjoyed washing the bowls and pans and putting them back where they belonged. Donald loved these hours himself, mostly because they seemed to dispel the oppression that stood unlifted over those years of his mother's life—and was there any reason why a lonely boy should rebel against the feeling of security that he found in the kitchen on a stormy night? She taught him how to make cookies and muffins and banana bread and, finally, a Lady Baltimore cake. It was sometimes after eleven o'clock when their work was done. "We do have a good time together, don't we, son?" Mrs. Wryson would ask. "We have a lovely time together, don't we, you and me? Oh, hear that wind howling! Think of the poor sailors at sea." Then she would embrace him, she would run her fingers through his light hair, and sometimes, although he was much too big, she would draw him onto her lap.

All of that was long ago. Mrs. Wryson was dead, and when Donald stood at the edge of her grave he had not felt any very great grief. She had been reconciled to dying years before she did die, and her conversation had been full of gallant references to the grave. Years later, when Donald was living alone in New York, he had been overtaken suddenly, one spring evening, by a depression as keen as any in his adolescence. He did not drink, he did not enjoy books or movies or the theatre, and, like his mother, he had few friends. Searching desperately for some way to take himself out of this misery, he hit on the idea of baking a Lady Baltimore cake. He went out and bought the ingredients—deeply ashamed of himself—and sifted the flour and chopped the nuts and citron in the kitchen of the little walk-up apartment where he lived. As he stirred the cake batter, he felt his depression vanish. It was not until he had put the cake in the oven and sat down to wipe his hands on his apron that he realized how successful he had been in summoning the ghost of his mother and the sense of security he had experienced as a child in her kitchen on stormy nights. When the cake was done he iced it, ate a slice, and dumped the rest into the garbage.

The next time he felt troubled, he resisted the temptation to bake a cake, but he was not always able to do this, and during the eight or nine years he had been married to Irene he must have baked eight or nine cakes. He took extraordinary precautions, and she knew nothing of this. She believed him to be a complete stranger to the kitchen. And how could he at the breakfast table—all two hundred and sixteen pounds of him—explain that he looked sleepy because he had been up until three baking a Lady Baltimore cake, which he had hidden in the garage?

GIVEN these unpleasant facts, then, about these not attractive people, we can dispatch them brightly enough, and who but Dolly would ever miss them? Donald Wryson, in his crusading zeal for upzoning, was out in all kinds of weather, and let's say that one night, when he was returning from a referendum in an ice storm, his car skidded down Hill Street, struck the big elm at the corner, and was demolished. Finis. His poor widow, either through love or dependence, was inconsolable. Getting out of bed one morning, a month or so after the loss of her husband, she got her feet caught in the dust ruffle and fell and broke her hip. Weakened by a long convalescence, she contracted pneumonia and departed this life. This leaves us with Dolly to account for, and what a sad tale we can write for this little girl. During the months in which her parents' will is in probate, she lives first on the charity and then on the forbearance of her neighbors. Finally, she is sent to live with her only relative, a cousin of her mother's, who is a schoolteacher in Los Angeles. How many hundreds of nights will she cry herself to sleep in bewilderment and loneliness. How strange and cold the world will seem. There is little to remind her of her parents except at Christmas, when, forwarded from Shady Hill, will come Greetings from Mrs. Sallust Trevor, who has been living in Paris and does not know about the accident; Salutations from the Parkers, who live in Mexico and never did get their lists straight; Season's Greetings from Meyers' Drugstore; Merry Christmas from the Perry Browns; Santissimas from the Oak Tree Italian Restaurant; A Joyeux Noël from Dodie Smith. Year after year, it will be this little girl's responsibility to throw into the wastebasket these cheerful holiday greetings that have followed her parents to and beyond the grave. . . . But this did not happen, and if it had, it would have thrown no light on what we know.

What happened was this: Irene Wryson had her dream one night. When she woke, she saw that her husband was not in bed. The air smelled sweet. Sweating suddenly, the beating of her heart strained with terror, she realized that the end had come. What could that sweetness in the air be but atomic ash? She ran to the window, but the river was empty. Half asleep and feeling cruelly lost as she was, she was kept from waking Dolly only by a healthy curiosity. There was smoke in the hallway, but it was not the smoke of any common fire. The sweetness made her feel sure that this was lethal ash. Led on by the smell, she went on down the stairs and through the dining room into the lighted kitchen. Donald was asleep with his head on the table and the room was full of smoke. "Oh, my darling," she cried, and woke him.

"I burned it," he said when he saw the smoke pouring from the oven. "I burned the damned thing."

"I thought it was the hydrogen bomb," she said.

"It's a cake," he said. "I burned it. What made you think it was the hydrogen bomb?"

"If you wanted something to eat, you should have waked me," she said.

She turned off the oven, and opened the window to let out the smell of smoke and let in the smell of nicotiana and other night flowers. She may have hesitated for a moment, for what would the stranger at the gates—that intruder with his beard and his book—have made of this couple, in their nightclothes, in the smoke-filled kitchen at half past four in the morning? Some comprehension—perhaps momentary—of the complexity of life must have come to them, but it was only momentary. There were no further explanations. He threw the cake, which was burned to a cinder, into the garbage, and they turned out the lights and climbed the stairs, more mystified by life than ever, and more interested than ever in a good appearance.

THE COUNTRY HUSBAND

To begin at the beginning, the airplane from Minneapolis in which Francis Weed was traveling East ran into heavy weather. The sky had been a hazy blue, with the clouds below the plane lying so close together that nothing could be seen of the earth. Then mist began to form outside the windows, and they flew into a white cloud of such density that it reflected the exhaust fires. The color of the cloud darkened to gray, and the plane began to rock. Francis had been in heavy weather before, but he had never been shaken up so much. The man in the seat beside him pulled a flask out of his pocket and took a drink. Francis smiled at his neighbor, but the man looked away; he wasn't sharing his pain killer with anyone. The plane began to drop and flounder wildly. A child was crying. The air in the cabin was overheated and stale, and Francis' left foot went to sleep. He read a little from a paper book that he had bought at the airport, but the violence of the storm divided his attention. It was black outside the ports. The exhaust fires blazed and shed sparks in the dark, and, inside, the shaded lights, the stuffiness, and the window curtains gave the cabin an atmosphere of intense and misplaced domesticity. Then the lights flickered and went out. "You know what I've always wanted to do?" the man beside Francis said suddenly. "I've always wanted to buy a farm in New Hampshire and raise beef cattle." The stewardess announced that they were going to make an emergency landing. All but the children saw in their minds the spreading wings of the Angel of Death. The pilot could be heard singing faintly, "I've got sixpence, jolly, jolly sixpence. I've got sixpence to last me all my life . . ." There was no other sound.

The loud groaning of the hydraulic valves swallowed up the pilot's song, and there was a shrieking high in the air, like automobile brakes, and the plane hit flat on its belly in a cornfield and shook them so violently that an old man up forward howled, "Me kidneys! Me kidneys!" The stewardess flung open the door, and someone opened an emergency door at the back, letting in the sweet noise of their continuing mortality—the idle splash and smell of a heavy rain. Anxious for their lives, they filed out of the doors and scattered over the cornfield in all directions, praying that the thread would hold. It did. Nothing happened. When it was clear that the plane would not burn or explode, the crew and the stewardess gathered the passengers together and led them to the shelter of a barn. They were not far from Philadelphia, and in a little while a string of taxis took them into the city. "It's just like the Marne," someone said, but there was surprisingly little relaxation of that suspiciousness with which many Americans regard their fellow travelers.

In Philadelphia, Francis Weed got a train to New York. At the end of that journey, he crossed the city and caught just as it was about to pull out the commuting train that he took five nights a week to his home in Shady Hill.

He sat with Trace Bearden. "You know, I was in that plane that just crashed outside Philadelphia," he said. "We came down in a field . . ." He had traveled faster than the newspapers or the rain, and the weather in New York was sunny and mild. It was a day in late September, as fragrant and shapely as an apple. Trace listened to the story, but how could he get excited? Francis had no powers that would let him re-create a brush with death—particularly in the atmosphere of a commuting train, journeying through a sunny countryside where already, in the slum gardens, there were signs of harvest. Trace picked up his newspaper, and Francis was left alone with his thoughts. He said good night to Trace on the platform at Shady Hill and drove in his secondhand Volkswagen up to the Blenhollow neighborhood, where he lived.

The Weeds' Dutch Colonial house was larger than it appeared to be from the driveway. The living room was spacious and divided like Gaul into three parts. Around an ell to the left as one entered from the vestibule was the long table, laid for six, with candles and a bowl of fruit in the center. The sounds and smells that came from the open kitchen door were appetizing, for Julia Weed was a good cook. The largest part of the living room centered on a fireplace. On the right were some bookshelves and a piano. The room was polished and tranquil, and from the windows that opened to the west there was some late-summer sunlight, brilliant and as clear as water. Nothing here was neglected; nothing had not been burnished. It was not the kind of household where, after prying open a stuck cigarette box, you would find an old shirt button and a tarnished nickel. The hearth was swept, the roses on the piano were reflected in the polish of the broad top, and there was an album of Schubert waltzes on the rack. Louisa Weed, a pretty girl of nine, was looking out the western windows. Her younger brother Henry was standing beside her. Her still younger brother, Toby, was studying the figures of some tonsured monks drinking beer on the polished brass of the woodbox. Francis, taking off his hat and putting down his paper, was not consciously pleased with the scene; he was not that reflective. It was his element, his creation, and he returned to it with that sense of lightness and strength with which any creature returns to his home. "Hi, everybody," he said. "The plane from Minneapolis . . ."

Nine times out of ten, Francis would be greeted with affection, but tonight the children are absorbed in their own antagonisms. Francis had not finished his sentence about the plane crash before Henry plants a kick in Louisa's behind. Louisa swings around, saying, "*Damn* you!" Francis makes the mistake of scolding Louisa for bad language before he punishes Henry. Now Louisa turns on her father and accuses him of favoritism. Henry is always right; she is persecuted and lonely; her lot is hopeless. Francis turns to his son, but the boy has justification for the kick—she hit him first; she hit him on the ear, which is dangerous. Louisa agrees with this passionately. She hit him on the ear, and she *meant* to hit him on the ear, because he messed up her china collection. Henry says that this is a lie. Little Toby turns away from the woodbox to throw in some evidence for Louisa. Henry claps his hand over little Toby's mouth. Francis separates the two boys but accidentally pushes Toby into the woodbox. Toby begins to cry. Louisa is already crying. Just then, Julia Weed comes into that part of the room where the table is laid. She is a pretty, intelligent woman, and the white in her hair is premature. She does not seem to notice the fracas. "Hello, darling," she says serenely to Francis. "Wash your hands, everyone. Dinner is ready." She strikes a match and lights the six candles in this vale of tears.

This simple announcement, like the war cries of the Scottish chieftains, only refreshes the ferocity of the combatants. Louisa gives Henry a blow on the shoulder. Henry, although he seldom cries, has pitched nine innings and is tired. He bursts into tears. Little Toby discovers a splinter in his hand and begins to howl. Francis says loudly that he has been in a plane crash and that he is tired. Julia appears again from the kitchen and, still ignoring the chaos, asks Francis to go upstairs and tell Helen that everything is ready. Francis is happy to go; it is like getting back to headquarters company. He is planning to tell his oldest daughter about the airplane crash, but Helen is lying on her bed reading a *True Romance* magazine, and the first thing Francis does is to take the magazine from her hand and remind Helen that he has forbidden her to buy it. She did not buy it, Helen replies. It was given to her by her best friend, Bessie Black. Everybody reads *True Romance.* Bessie Black's father reads *True Romance.* There isn't a girl in Helen's class who doesn't read *True Romance.* Francis expresses his detestation of the magazine and then tells her that dinner is ready—although from the sounds downstairs it doesn't seem so. Helen follows him down the stairs. Julia has seated herself in the candlelight and spread a napkin over her lap. Neither Louisa nor Henry has come to the table. Little Toby is still howling, lying face down on the floor. Francis speaks to him gently: "Daddy was in a plane crash this afternoon, Toby. Don't you want to hear about it?" Toby goes on crying. "If you don't come to the table now, Toby," Francis says, "I'll have to send you to bed without any supper." The little boy rises, gives him a cutting look, flies up the stairs to his bedroom, and slams the door. "Oh dear," Julia says, and starts to go after him. Francis says that she will spoil him. Julia says that Toby is ten pounds underweight and has to be encouraged to eat. Winter is coming, and he will spend the cold months in bed unless he has his dinner. Julia goes upstairs. Francis sits down at the table with Helen. Helen is suffering from the dismal feeling of having read too intently on a fine day, and she gives her father and the room a jaded look. She doesn't understand about the plane crash, because there wasn't a drop of rain in Shady Hill.

Julia returns with Toby, and they all sit down and are served. "Do I have to look at that big, fat slob?" Henry says, of Louisa. Everybody but Toby enters into this skirmish, and it rages up and down the table for five minutes. Toward the end, Henry puts his napkin over his head and, trying to eat that way, spills spinach all over his shirt. Francis asks Julia if the children couldn't have their dinner earlier. Julia's guns are loaded for this. She can't cook two dinners and lay two tables. She paints with lightning strokes that panorama of drudgery in which her youth, her beauty, and her wit have been lost. Francis says that he must be understood; he was nearly killed in an airplane crash, and he doesn't like to come home every night to a battlefield. Now Julia is deeply concerned. Her voice trembles. He doesn't come home every night to a battlefield. The accusation is stupid and mean. Everything was tranquil until he arrived. She stops speaking, puts down her knife and fork, and looks into her plate as if it is a gulf. She begins to cry. "Poor Mummy!" Toby says, and when Julia gets up from the table, drying her tears with a napkin, Toby goes to her side. "Poor Mummy," he says. "Poor Mummy!" And they climb the stairs together. The other children drift away from the battlefield, and Francis goes into the back garden for a cigarette and some air.

It was a pleasant garden, with walks and flower beds and places to sit. The sunset had nearly burned out, but there was still plenty of light. Put into a thoughtful mood by the crash and the battle, Francis listened to the evening sounds of Shady Hill. "Varmints! Rascals!" old Mr. Nixon shouted to the squirrels in his bird-feeding station. "Avaunt and quit my sight!" A door slammed. Someone was cutting grass. Then Donald Goslin, who lived at the corner, began to play the "Moonlight Sonata." He did this nearly every night. He threw the tempo out the window and played it *rubato* from beginning to end, like an outpouring of tearful petulance, lonesomeness, and self-pity—of everything it was Beethoven's greatness not to know. The music rang up and down the street beneath the trees like an appeal for love, for tenderness, aimed at some lovely housemaid—some fresh-faced, homesick girl from Galway, looking at old snapshots in her third-floor room. "Here, Jupiter, here, Jupiter," Francis called to the Mercers' retriever. Jupiter crashed through the tomato vines with the remains of a felt hat in his mouth.

Jupiter was an anomaly. His retrieving instincts and his high spirits were out of place in Shady Hill. He was as black as coal, with a long, alert, intelligent, rakehell face. His eyes gleamed with mischief, and he held his head high. It was the fierce, heavily collared dog's head that appears in heraldry, in tapestry, and that used to appear on umbrella handles and walking sticks. Jupiter went where he pleased, ransacking wastebaskets, clotheslines, garbage pails, and shoe bags. He broke up garden parties and tennis matches, and got mixed up in the processional at Christ Church on Sunday, barking at the men in red dresses. He crashed through old Mr. Nixon's rose garden two or three times a day, cutting a wide swath through the Condesa de Sastagos, and as soon as Donald Goslin lighted his barbecue fire on Thursday nights, Jupiter would get the scent. Nothing the Goslins did could drive him away. Sticks and stones and rude commands only moved him to the edge of the terrace, where he remained, with his gallant and heraldic muzzle, waiting for Donald Goslin to turn his back and reach for the salt. Then he would spring onto the terrace, lift the steak lightly off the fire, and run away with the Goslins' dinner. Jupiter's days were numbered. The Wrightsons' German gardener or the Farquarsons' cook would soon poison him. Even old Mr. Nixon might put some arsenic in the garbage that Jupiter loved. "Here, Jupiter, Jupiter!" Francis called, but the dog pranced off, shaking the hat in his white teeth. Looking at the windows of his house, Francis saw that Julia had come down and was blowing out the candles.

Julia and Francis Weed went out a great deal. Julia was well liked and gregarious, and her love of parties sprang from a most natural dread of chaos and loneliness. She went through her morning mail with real anxiety, looking for invitations, and she usually found some, but she was insatiable, and if she had gone out seven nights a week, it would not have cured her of a reflective look—the look of someone who hears distant music—for she would always suppose that there was a more brilliant party somewhere else. Francis limited her to two week-night parties, putting a flexible interpretation on Friday, and rode through the weekend like a dory in a gale. The day after the airplane crash, the Weeds were to have dinner with the Farquarsons.

Francis got home late from town, and Julia got the sitter while he dressed, and then hurried him out of the house. The party was small and pleasant, and Francis settled down to enjoy himself. A new maid passed the drinks. Her hair was dark, and her face was round and pale and seemed familiar to Francis. He had not developed his memory as a sentimental faculty. Wood smoke, lilac, and other such perfumes did not stir him, and his memory was something like his appendix—a vestigial repository. It was not his limitation at all to be unable to escape the past; it was perhaps his limitation that he had escaped it so successfully. He might have seen the maid at other parties, he might have seen her taking a walk on Sunday afternoons, but in either case he would not be searching his memory now. Her face was, in a wonderful way, a moon face—Norman or Irish—but it was not beautiful enough to account for his feeling that he had seen her before, in circumstances that he ought to be able to remember. He asked Nellie Farquarson who she was. Nellie said that the maid had come through an agency, and that her home was Trenon, in Normandy—a small place with a church and a restaurant that Nellie had once visited. While Nellie talked on about her travels abroad, Francis realized where he had seen the woman before. It had been at the end of the war. He had left a replacement depot with some other men and taken a three-day pass in Trenon. On their second day, they had walked out to a crossroads to see the public chastisement of a young woman who had lived with the German commandant during the Occupation.

It was a cool morning in the fall. The sky was overcast, and poured down onto the dirt crossroads a very discouraging light. They were on high land and could see how like one another the shapes of the clouds and the hills were as they stretched off toward the sea. The prisoner arrived sitting on a three-legged stool in a farm cart. She stood by the cart while the Mayor read the accusation and the sentence. Her head was bent and her face was set in that empty half smile behind which the whipped soul is suspended. When the Mayor was finished, she undid her hair and let it fall across her back. A little man with a gray mustache cut off her hair with shears and dropped it on the ground. Then, with a bowl of soapy water and a straight razor, he shaved her skull clean. A woman approached and began to undo the fastenings of her clothes, but the prisoner pushed her aside and undressed herself. When she pulled her chemise over her head and threw it on the ground, she was naked. The women jeered; the men were still. There was no change in the falseness or the plaintiveness of the prisoner's smile. The cold wind made her white skin rough and hardened the nipples of her breasts. The jeering ended gradually, put down by the recognition of their common humanity. One woman spat on her, but some inviolable grandeur in her nakedness lasted through the ordeal. When the crowd was quiet, she turned—she had begun to cry—and, with nothing on but a pair of worn black shoes and stockings, walked down the dirt road alone away from the village. The round white face had aged a little, but there was no question but that the maid who passed his cocktails and later served Francis his dinner was the woman who had been punished at the crossroads.

The war seemed now so distant and that world where the cost of partisanship had been death or torture so long ago. Francis had lost track of the men who had been with him in Vesey. He could not count on Julia's discretion. He could not tell anyone. And if he had told the story now, at the dinner table, it would have been a social as well as a human error. The people in the Farquarsons' living room seemed united in their tacit claim that there had been no past, no war—that there was no danger or trouble in the world. In the recorded history of human arrangements, this extraordinary meeting would have fallen into place, but the atmosphere of Shady Hill made the memory unseemly and impolite. The prisoner withdrew after passing the coffee, but the encounter left Francis feeling languid; it had opened his memory and his senses, and left them dilated. Julia went into the house. Francis stayed in the car to take the sitter home.

Expecting to see Mrs. Henlein, the old lady who usually stayed with the children, he was surprised when a young girl opened the door and came out onto the lighted stoop. She stayed in the light to count her textbooks. She was frowning and beautiful. Now, the world is full of beautiful young girls, but Francis saw here the difference between beauty and perfection. All those endearing flaws, moles, birthmarks, and healed wounds were missing, and he experienced in his consciousness that moment when music breaks glass, and felt a pang of recognition as strange, deep, and wonderful as anything in his life. It hung from her frown, from an impalpable darkness in her face—a look that impressed him as a direct appeal for love. When she had counted her books, she came down the steps and opened the car door. In the light, he saw that her cheeks were wet. She got in and shut the door.

"You're new," Francis said.

"Yes. Mrs. Henlein is sick. I'm Anne Murchison."

"Did the children give you any trouble?"

"Oh, no, no." She turned and smiled at him unhappily in the dim dashboard light. Her light hair caught on the collar of her jacket, and she shook her head to set it loose.

"You've been crying."

"Yes."

"I hope it was nothing that happened in our house."

"No, no, it was nothing that happened in your house." Her voice was bleak. "It's no secret. Everybody in the village knows. Daddy's an alcoholic, and he just called me from some saloon and gave me a piece of his mind. He thinks I'm immoral. He called just before Mrs. Weed came back."

"I'm sorry."

"Oh, *Lord!*" She gasped and began to cry. She turned toward Francis, and he took her in his arms and let her cry on his shoulder. She shook in his embrace, and this movement accentuated his sense of the fineness of her flesh and bone. The layers of their clothing felt thin, and when her shuddering began to diminish, it was so much like a paroxysm of love that Francis lost his head and pulled her roughly against him. She drew away. "I live on Belleview Avenue," she said. "You go down Lansing Street to the railroad bridge."

"All right." He started the car.

"You turn left at that traffic light. . . . Now you turn right here and go straight on toward the tracks."

The road Francis took brought him out of his own neighborhood, across the tracks, and toward the river, to a street where the near-poor lived, in houses whose peaked gables and trimmings of wooden lace conveyed the purest feelings of pride and romance, although the houses themselves could not have offered much privacy or comfort, they were all so small. The street was dark, and, stirred by the grace and beauty of the troubled girl, he seemed, in turning into it, to have come into the deepest part of some submerged memory. In the distance, he saw a porch light burning. It was the only one, and she said that the house with the light was where she lived. When he stopped the car, he could see beyond the porch light into a dimly lighted hallway with an old-fashioned clothes tree. "Well, here we are," he said, conscious that a young man would have said something different.

She did not move her hands from the books, where they were folded, and she turned and faced him. There were tears of lust in his eyes. Determinedly—not sadly—he opened the door on his side and walked around to open hers. He took her free hand, letting his fingers in between hers, climbed at her side the two concrete steps, and went up a narrow walk through a front garden where dahlias, marigolds, and roses—things that had withstood the light frosts—still bloomed, and made a bittersweet smell in the night air. At the steps, she freed her hand and then turned and kissed him swiftly. Then she crossed the porch and shut the door. The porch light went out, then the light in the hall. A second later, a light went on upstairs at the side of the house, shining into a tree that was still covered with leaves. It took her only a few minutes to undress and get into bed, and then the house was dark.

Julia was asleep when Francis got home. He opened a second window and got into bed to shut his eyes on that night, but as soon as they were shut—as soon as he had dropped off to sleep—the girl entered his mind, moving with perfect freedom through its shut doors and filling chamber after chamber with her light, her perfume, and the music of her voice. He was crossing the Atlantic with her on the old *Mauretania* and, later, living with her in Paris. When he woke from his dream, he got up and smoked a cigarette at the open window. Getting back into bed, he cast around in his mind for something he desired to do that would injure no one, and he thought of skiing. Up through the dimness in his mind rose the image of a mountain deep in snow. It was late in the day. Wherever his eyes looked, he saw broad and heartening things. Over his shoulder, there was a snow-filled valley, rising into wooded hills where the trees dimmed the whiteness like a sparse coat of hair. The cold deadened all sound but the loud, iron clanking of the lift machinery. The light on the trails was blue, and it was harder than it had been a minute or two earlier to pick the turns, harder to judge—now that the snow was all deep blue—the crust, the ice, the bare spots, and the deep piles of dry powder. Down the mountain he swung, matching his speed against the contours of a slope that had been formed in the first ice age, seeking with ardor some simplicity of feeling and circumstance. Night fell then, and he drank a Martini with some old friend in a dirty country bar.

In the morning, Francis' snow-covered mountain was gone, and he was left with his vivid memories of Paris and the *Mauretania.* He had been bitten gravely. He washed his body, shaved his jaws, drank his coffee, and missed the seven-thirty-one. The train pulled out just as he brought his car to the station, and the longing he felt for the coaches as they drew stubbornly away from him reminded him of the humors of love. He waited for the eight-two, on what was now an empty platform. It was a clear morning; the morning seemed thrown like a gleaming bridge of light over his mixed affairs. His spirits were feverish and high. The image of the girl seemed to put him into a relationship to the world that was mysterious and enthralling. Cars were beginning to fill up the parking lot, and he noticed that those that had driven down from the high land above Shady Hill were white with hoarfrost. This first clear sign of autumn thrilled him. An express train—a night train from Buffalo or Albany—came down the tracks between the platforms, and he saw that the roofs of the foremost cars were covered with a skin of ice. Struck by the miraculous physicalness of everything, he smiled at the passengers in the dining car, who could be seen eating eggs and wiping their mouths with napkins as they traveled. The sleeping-car compartments, with their soiled bed linen, trailed through the fresh morning like a string of rooming-house windows. Then he saw an extraordinary thing; at one of the bedroom windows sat an unclothed woman of exceptional beauty, combing her golden hair. She passed like an apparition through Shady Hill, combing and combing her hair, and Francis followed her with his eyes until she was out of sight. Then old Mrs. Wrightson joined him on the platform and began to talk.

"Well, I guess you must be surprised to see me here the third morning in a row," she said, "but because of my window curtains I'm becoming a regular commuter. The curtains I bought on Monday I returned on Tuesday, and the curtains I bought Tuesday I'm returning today. On Monday, I got exactly what I wanted—it's a wool tapestry with roses and birds—but when I got them home, I found they were the wrong length. Well, I exchanged them yesterday, and when I got them home, I found they were still the wrong length. Now I'm praying to high heaven that the decorator will have them in the right length, because you know my house, you *know* my living-room windows, and you can imagine what a problem they present. I don't know what to do with them."

"I know what to do with them," Francis said.

"What?"

"Paint them black on the inside, and shut up."

There was a gasp from Mrs. Wrightson, and Francis looked down at her to be sure that she knew he meant to be rude. She turned and walked away from him, so damaged in spirit that she limped. A wonderful feeling enveloped him, as if light were being shaken about him, and he thought again of Venus combing and combing her hair as she drifted through the Bronx. The realization of how many years had passed since he had enjoyed being deliberately impolite sobered him. Among his friends and neighbors, there were brilliant and gifted people—he saw that—but many of them, also, were bores and fools, and he had made the mistake of listening to them all with equal attention. He had confused a lack of discrimination with Christian love, and the confusion seemed general and destructive. He was grateful to the girl for this bracing sensation of independence. Birds were singing—cardinals and the last of the robins. The sky shone like enamel. Even the smell of ink from his morning paper honed his appetite for life, and the world that was spread out around him was plainly a paradise.

If Francis had believed in some hierarchy of love—in spirits armed with hunting bows, in the capriciousness of Venus and Eros—or even in magical potions, philters, and stews, in scapulae and quarters of the moon, it might have explained his susceptibility and his feverish high spirits. The autumnal loves of middle age are well publicized, and he guessed that he was face to face with one of these, but there was not a trace of autumn in what he felt. He wanted to sport in the green woods, scratch where he itched, and drink from the same cup.

His secretary, Miss Rainey, was late that morning—she went to a psychiatrist three mornings a week—and when she came in, Francis wondered what advice a psychiatrist would have for him. But the girl promised to bring back into his life something like the sound of music. The realization that this music might lead him straight to a trial for statutory rape at the county courthouse collapsed his happiness. The photograph of his four children laughing into the camera on the beach at Gay Head reproached him. On the letterhead of his firm there was a drawing of the Laocoön, and the figure of the priest and his sons in the coils of the snake appeared to him to have the deepest meaning.

He had lunch with Pinky Trabert. At a conversational level, the mores of his friends were robust and elastic, but he knew that the moral card house would come down on them all—on Julia and the children as well—if he got caught taking advantage of a baby-sitter. Looking back over the recent history of Shady Hill for some precedent, he found there was none. There was no turpitude; there had not been a divorce since he lived there; there had not even been a breath of scandal. Things seemed arranged with more propriety even than in the Kingdom of Heaven. After leaving Pinky, Francis went to a jeweler's and bought the girl a bracelet. How happy this clandestine purchase made him, how stuffy and comical the jeweler's clerks seemed, how sweet the women who passed at his back smelled! On Fifth Avenue, passing Atlas with his shoulders bent under the weight of the world, Francis thought of the strenuousness of containing his physicalness within the patterns he had chosen.

He did not know when he would see the girl next. He had the bracelet in his inside pocket when he got home. Opening the door of his house, he found her in the hall. Her back was to him, and she turned when she heard the door close. Her smile was open and loving. Her perfection stunned him like a fine day—a day after a thunderstorm. He seized her and covered her lips with his, and she struggled but she did not have to struggle for long, because just then little Gertrude Flannery appeared from somewhere and said, "Oh, Mr. Weed . . ."

Gertrude was a stray. She had been born with a taste for exploration, and she did not have it in her to center her life with her affectionate parents. People who did not know the Flannerys concluded from Gertrude's behavior that she was the child of a bitterly divided family, where drunken quarrels were the rule. This was not true. The fact that little Gertrude's clothing was ragged and thin was her own triumph over her mother's struggle to dress her warmly and neatly. Garrulous, skinny, and unwashed, she drifted from house to house around the Blenhollow neighborhood, forming and breaking alliances based on an attachment to babies, animals, children her own age, adolescents, and sometimes adults. Opening your front door in the morning, you would find Gertrude sitting on your stoop. Going into the bathroom to shave, you would find Gertrude using the toilet. Looking into your son's crib, you would find it empty, and, looking further, you would find that Gertrude had pushed him in his baby carriage into the next village. She was helpful, pervasive, honest, hungry, and loyal. She never went home of her own choice. When the time to go arrived, she was indifferent to all its signs. "Go home, Gertrude," people could be heard saying in one house or another, night after night. "Go home, Gertrude. It's time for you to go home now, Gertrude." "You had better go home and get your supper, Gertrude." "I told you to go home twenty minutes ago, Gertrude." "Your mother will be worrying about you, Gertrude." "Go home, Gertrude, go home."

There are times when the lines around the human eye seem like shelves of eroded stone and when the staring eye itself strikes us with such a wilderness of animal feeling that we are at a loss. The look Francis gave the little girl was ugly and queer, and it frightened her. He reached into his pockets—his hands were shaking—and took out a quarter. "Go home, Gertrude, go home, and don't tell anyone, Gertrude. Don't—" He choked and ran into the living room as Julia called down to him from upstairs to hurry and dress.

The thought that he would drive Anne Murchison home later that night ran like a golden thread through the events of the party that Francis and Julia went to, and he laughed uproariously at dull jokes, dried a tear when Mabel Mercer told him about the death of her kitten, and stretched, yawned, sighed, and grunted like any other man with a rendezvous at the back of his mind. The bracelet was in his pocket. As he sat talking, the smell of grass was in his nose, and he was wondering where he would park the car. Nobody lived in the old Parker mansion, and the driveway was used as a lovers' lane. Townsend Street was a dead end, and he could park there, beyond the last house. The old lane that used to connect Elm Street to the riverbanks was overgrown, but he had walked there with his children, and he could drive his car deep enough into the brushwoods to be concealed.

The Weeds were the last to leave the party, and their host and hostess spoke of their own married happiness while they all four stood in the hallway saying good night. "She's my girl," their host said, squeezing his wife. "She's my blue sky. After sixteen years, I still bite her shoulders. She makes me feel like Hannibal crossing the Alps."

The Weeds drove home in silence. Francis brought the car up the driveway and sat still, with the motor running. "You can put the car in the garage," Julia said as she got out. "I told the Murchison girl she could leave at eleven. Someone drove her home." She shut the door, and Francis sat in the dark. He would be spared nothing then, it seemed, that a fool was not spared: ravening lewdness, jealousy, this hurt to his feelings that put tears in his eyes, even scorn—for he could see clearly the image he now presented, his arms spread over the steering wheel and his head buried in them for love.

FRANCIS had been a dedicated Boy Scout when he was young, and, remembering the precepts of his youth, he left his office early the next afternoon and played some round-robin squash, but, with his body toned up by exercise and a shower, he realized that he might better have stayed at his desk. It was a frosty night when he got home. The air smelled sharply of change. When he stepped into the house, he sensed an unusual stir. The children were in their best clothes, and when Julia came down, she was wearing a lavender dress and her diamond sunburst. She explained the stir: Mr. Hubber was coming at seven to take their photograph for the Christmas card. She had put out Francis' blue suit and a tie with some color in it, because the picture was going to be in color this year. Julia was lighthearted at the thought of being photographed for Christmas. It was the kind of ceremony she enjoyed.

Francis went upstairs to change his clothes. He was

tired from the day's work and tired with longing, and sitting on the edge of the bed had the effect of deepening his weariness. He thought of Anne Murchison, and the physical need to express himself, instead of being restrained by the pink lamps of Julia's dressing table, engulfed him. He went to Julia's desk, took a piece of writing paper, and began to write on it. "Dear Anne, I love you, I love you, I love you . . ." No one would see the letter, and he used no restraint. He used phrases like "heavenly bliss," and "love nest." He salivated, sighed, and trembled. When Julia called him to come down, the abyss between his fantasy and the practical world opened so wide that he felt it affected the muscles of his heart.

Julia and the children were on the stoop, and the photographer and his assistant had set up a double battery of floodlights to show the family and the architectural beauty of the entrance to their house. People who had come home on a late train slowed their cars to see the Weeds being photographed for their Christmas card. A few waved and called to the family. It took half an hour of smiling and wetting their lips before Mr. Hubber was satisfied. The heat of the lights made an unfresh smell in the frosty air, and when they were turned off, they lingered on the retina of Francis' eyes.

Later that night, while Francis and Julia were drinking their coffee in the living room, the doorbell rang. Julia answered the door and let in Clayton Thomas. He had come to pay for some theatre tickets that she had given his mother some time ago, and that Helen Thomas had scrupulously insisted on paying for, though Julia had asked her not to. Julia invited him in to have a cup of coffee. "I won't have any coffee," Clayton said, "but I will come in for a minute." He followed her into the living room, said good evening to Francis, and sat awkwardly in a chair.

Clayton's father had been killed in the war, and the young man's fatherlessness surrounded him like an element. This may have been conspicuous in Shady Hill because the Thomases were the only family that lacked a piece; all the other marriages were intact and productive. Clayton was in his second or third year of college, and he and his mother lived alone in a large house, which she hoped to sell. Clayton had once made some trouble. Years ago, he had stolen some money and run away; he had got to California before they caught up with him. He was tall and homely, wore horn-rimmed glasses, and spoke in a deep voice.

"When do you go back to college, Clayton?" Francis asked.

"I'm not going back," Clayton said. "Mother doesn't have the money, and there's no sense in all this pretense. I'm going to get a job, and if we sell the house, we'll take an apartment in New York."

"Won't you miss Shady Hill?" Julia asked.

"No," Clayton said. "I don't like it."

"Why not?" Francis asked.

"Well, there's a lot here I don't approve of," Clayton said gravely. "Things like the club dances. Last Saturday night, I looked in toward the end and saw Mr. Granner trying to put Mrs. Minot into the trophy case. They were both drunk. I disapprove of so much drinking."

"It was Saturday night," Francis said.

"And all the dovecotes are phony," Clayton said. "And the way people clutter up their lives. I've thought about it a lot, and what seems to me to be really wrong with Shady Hill is that it doesn't have any future. So much energy is spent in perpetuating the place—in keeping out undesirables, and so forth—that the only idea of the future anyone has is just more and more commuting trains and more parties. I don't think that's healthy. I think people ought to be able to dream big dreams about the future. I think people ought to be able to dream great dreams."

"It's too bad you couldn't continue with college," Julia said.

"I wanted to go to divinity school," Clayton said.

"What's your church?" Francis asked.

"Unitarian, Theosophist, Transcendentalist, Humanist," Clayton said.

"Wasn't Emerson a transcendentalist?" Julia asked.

"I mean the English transcendentalists," Clayton said. "All the American transcendentalists were goops."

"What kind of job do you expect to get?" Francis asked.

"Well, I'd like to work for a publisher," Clayton said, "but everyone tells me there's nothing doing. But it's the kind of thing I'm interested in. I'm writing a long verse play about good and evil. Uncle Charlie might get me into a bank, and that would be good for me. I need the discipline. I have a long way to go in forming my character. I have some terrible habits. I talk too much. I think I ought to take vows of silence. I ought to try not to speak for a week, and discipline myself. I've thought of making a retreat at one of the Episcopalian monasteries, but I don't like Trinitarianism."

"Do you have any girl friends?" Francis asked.

"I'm engaged to be married," Clayton said. "Of course, I'm not old enough or rich enough to have my engagement observed or respected or anything, but I bought a simulated emerald for Anne Murchison with the money I made cutting lawns this summer. We're going to be married as soon as she finishes school."

Francis recoiled at the mention of the girl's name. Then a dingy light seemed to emanate from his spirit, showing everything—Julia, the boy, the chairs—in their true colorlessness. It was like a bitter turn of the weather.

"We're going to have a large family," Clayton said. "Her father's a terrible rummy, and I've had my hard times, and we want to have lots of children. Oh, she's wonderful, Mr. and Mrs. Weed, and we have so much in common. We like all the same things. We sent out the same Christmas card last year without planning it, and we both have an allergy to tomatoes, and our eyebrows grow together in the middle. Well, goodnight."

Julia went to the door with him. When she returned, Francis said that Clayton was lazy, irresponsible. affected, and smelly. Julia said that Francis seemed to be getting intolerant; the Thomas boy was young and should be given a chance. Julia had noticed other cases where Francis had been short-tempered. "Mrs. Wrightson has asked everyone in Shady Hill to her anniversary party but us," she said.

"I'm sorry, Julia."

"Do you know why they didn't ask us?"

"Why?"

"Because you insulted Mrs. Wrightson."

"Then you know about it?"

"June Masterson told me. She was standing behind you."

Julia walked in front of the sofa with a small step that expressed, Francis knew, a feeling of anger.

"I did insult Mrs. Wrightson, Julia, and I meant to. I've never liked her parties, and I'm glad she's dropped us."

"What about Helen?"

"How does Helen come into this?"

"Mrs. Wrightson's the one who decides who goes to the assemblies."

"You mean she can keep Helen from going to the dances?"

"Yes."

"I hadn't thought of that."

"Oh. I knew you hadn't thought of it," Julia cried, thrusting hilt-deep into this chink of his armor. "And it makes me furious to see this kind of stupid thoughtlessness wreck everyone's happiness."

"I don't think I've wrecked anyone's happiness."

"Mr. Wrightson runs Shady Hill and has run it for the last forty years. I don't know what makes you think that in a community like this you can indulge every impulse you have to be insulting, vulgar, and offensive."

"I have very good manners," Francis said, trying to give the evening a turn toward the light.

"Damn you, Francis Weed!" Julia cried, and the spit of her words struck him in the face. "I've worked hard for the social position we enjoy in this place, and I won't stand by and see you wreck it. You must have understood when you settled here that you couldn't expect to live like a bear in a cave."

"I've got to express my likes and dislikes."

"You can conceal your dislikes. You don't have to meet everything head on, like a child. Unless you're anxious to be a social leper. It's no accident that we get asked out a great deal! It's no accident that Helen has so many friends. How would you like to spend your Saturday nights at the movies? How would you like to spend your Sundays raking up dead leaves? How would you like it if your daughter spent the assembly nights sitting at her window, listening to the music from the club? How would you like it—" He did something then that was, after all, not so unaccountable, since her words seemed to raise up between them a wall so deadening that he gagged. He struck her full in the face. She staggered and then, a moment later, seemed composed. She went up the stairs to their room. She didn't slam the door. When Francis followed, a few minutes later, he found her packing a suitcase.

"Julia, I'm very sorry."

"It doesn't matter," she said. She was crying.

"Where do you think you're going?"

"I don't know. I just looked at a timetable. There's an eleven-sixteen into New York. I'll take that."

"You can't go, Julia."

"I can't stay. I know that."

"I'm sorry about Mrs. Wrightson, Julia, and I'm—"

"It doesn't matter about Mrs. Wrightson. That isn't the trouble."

"What is the trouble?"

"You don't love me."

"I do love you, Julia."

"No, you don't."

"Julia, I do love you, and I would like to be as we were—sweet and bawdy and dark—but now there are so many people."

"You hate me."

"I don't hate you, Julia."

"You have no idea of how much you hate me. I think it's subconscious. You don't realize the cruel things you've done."

"What cruel things, Julia?"

"The cruel acts your subconscious drives you to in order to express your hatred of me."

"What, Julia?"

"I've never complained."

"Tell me."

"You don't know what you're doing."

"Tell me."

"Your clothes."

"What do you mean?"

"I mean the way you leave your dirty clothes around in order to express your subconscious hatred of me."

"I don't understand."

"I mean your dirty socks and your dirty pajamas and your dirty underwear and your dirty shirts!" She rose from kneeling by the suitcase and faced him, her eyes blazing and her voice ringing with emotion. "I'm talking about the fact that you've never learned to hang up anything. You just leave your clothes all over the floor where they drop, in order to humiliate me. You do it on purpose!" She fell on the bed, sobbing.

"Julia, darling!" he said, but when she felt his hand on her shoulder she got up.

"Leave me alone," she said. "I have to go." She brushed past him to the closet and came back with a dress. "I'm not taking any of the things you've given me," she said. "I'm leaving my pearls and the fur jacket."

"Oh, Julia!" Her figure, so helpless in its self-deceptions, bent over the suitcase made him nearly sick with pity. She did not understand how desolate her life would be without him. She didn't understand the hours that working women have to keep. She didn't understand that most of her friendships existed within the framework of their marriage, and that without this she would find herself alone. She didn't understand about travel, about hotels, about money. "Julia, I can't let you go! What you don't understand, Julia, is that you've come to be dependent on me."

She tossed her head back and covered her face with her hands. "Did you say that *I* was dependent on *you?*" she asked. "Is that what you said? And who is it that tells you what time to get up in the morning and when to go to bed at night? Who is it that prepares your meals and picks up your dirty clothes and invites your friends to dinner? If it weren't for me, your neckties would be greasy and your clothing would be full of moth holes. You were alone when I met you, Francis Weed, and you'll be alone when I leave. When Mother asked you for a list to send out invitations to our wedding, how many names did you have to give her? Fourteen!"

"Cleveland wasn't my home, Julia."

"And how many of your friends came to the church? Two!"

"Cleveland wasn't my home, Julia."

"Since I'm not taking the fur jacket," she said quietly, "you'd better put it back into storage. There's an insurance policy on the pearls that comes due in January. The name of the laundry and the maid's telephone number—all those things are in my desk. I hope you won't drink too much, Francis. I hope that nothing bad will happen to you. If you do get into serious trouble, you can call me."

"Oh, my darling, I can't let you go!" Francis said. "I can't let you go, Julia!" He took her arms.

"I guess I'd better stay and take care of you for a little while longer," she said.

Riding to work in the morning, Francis saw the girl walk down the aisle of the coach. He was surprised; he hadn't realized that the school she went to was in the city, but she was carrying books, she seemed to be going to school. His surprise delayed his reaction, but then he got up clumsily and stepped into the aisle. Several people had come between them, but he could see her ahead of him, waiting for someone to open the car door, and then, as the train swerved, putting out her hand to support herself as she crossed the platform into the next car. He followed her through that car and halfway through another before calling her name—"Anne! Anne!"—but she didn't turn. He followed her into still another car, and she sat down in an aisle seat. Coming up to her, all his feelings warm and bent in her direction, he put his hand on the back of her seat—even this touch warmed him—and leaning down to speak to her, he saw that it was not Anne. It was an older woman wearing glasses. He went on deliberately into another car, his face red with embarrassment and the much deeper feeling of having his good sense challenged; for if he couldn't tell one person from another, what evidence was there that his life with Julia and the children had as much reality as his dreams of iniquity in Paris or the litter, the grass smell, and the cave-shaped trees in Lovers' Lane.

Late that afternoon, Julia called to remind Francis that they were going out for dinner. A few minutes later, Trace Bearden called. "Look, fellar," Trace said. "I'm calling for Mrs. Thomas. You know? Clayton, that boy of hers, doesn't seem able to get a job, and I wondered if you could help. If you'd call Charlie Bell—I know he's indebted to you—and say a good word for the kid, I think Charlie would—"

"Trace, I hate to say this," Francis said, "but I don't feel that I can do anything for that boy. The kid's worthless. I know it's a harsh thing to say, but it's a fact. Any kindness done for him would backfire in everybody's face. He's just a worthless kid, Trace, and there's nothing to be done about it. Even if we got him a job, he wouldn't be able to keep it for a week. I know that to be a fact. It's an awful thing, Trace, and I know it is, but instead of recommending that kid, I'd feel obligated to warn people against him—people who knew his father and would naturally want to step in and do something. I'd feel obliged to warn them. He's a thief . . ."

The moment this conversation was finished, Miss Rainey came in and stood by his desk. "I'm not going to be able to work for you any more, Mr. Weed," she said. "I can stay until the seventeenth if you need me, but I've been offered a whirlwind of a job, and I'd like to leave as soon as possible."

She went out, leaving him to face alone the wickedness of what he had done to the Thomas boy. His children in their photograph laughed and laughed, glazed with all the bright colors of summer, and he remembered that they had met a bagpiper on the beach that day and he had paid the piper a dollar to play them a battle song of the Black Watch. The girl would be at the house when he got home. He would spend another evening among his kind neighbors, picking and choosing dead-end streets, cart tracks, and the driveways of abandoned houses. There was nothing to mitigate his feeling—nothing that laughter or a game of softball with the children would change—and, thinking back over the plane crash, the Farquarsons' new maid, and Anne Murchison's difficulties with her drunken father, he wondered how he could have avoided arriving at just where he was. He was in trouble. He had been lost once in his life, coming back from a trout stream in the north woods, and he had now the same bleak realization that no amount of cheerfulness or hopefulness or valor or perseverance could help him find, in the gathering dark, the path that he'd lost. He smelled the forest. The feeling of bleakness was intolerable, and he saw clearly that he had reached the point where he would have to make a choice.

He could go to a psychiatrist, like Miss Rainey; he could go to church and confess his lusts; he could go to a Danish massage parlor in the West Seventies that had been recommended by a salesman; he could rape the girl or trust that he would somehow be prevented from doing this; or he could get drunk. It was his life, his boat, and, like every other man, he was made to be the father of thousands, and what harm could there be in a tryst that would make them both feel more kindly toward the world? This was the wrong train of thought, and he came back to the first, the psychiatrist. He had the telephone number of Miss Rainey's doctor, and he called and asked for an immediate appointment. He was insistent with the doctor's secretary—it was his manner in business—and when she said that the doctor's schedule was full for the next few weeks, Francis demanded an appointment that day and was told to come at five.

The psychiatrist's office was in a building that was used mostly by doctors and dentists, and the hallways were filled with the candy smell of mouthwash and memories of pain. Francis' character had been formed upon a series of private resolves—resolves about cleanliness, about going off the high diving board or repeating any other feat that challenged his courage, about punctuality, honesty, and virtue. To abdicate the perfect loneliness in which he had made his most vital decisions shattered his concept of character and left him now in a condition that felt like shock. He was stupefied. The scene for his *miserere mei Deus* was, like the waiting room of so many doctor's offices, a crude token gesture toward the sweets of domestic bliss: a place arranged with antiques, coffee tables, potted plants, and etchings of snow-covered bridges and geese in flight, although there were no children, no marriage bed, no stove, even, in this travesty of a house, where no one had ever spent the night and where the curtained windows looked straight onto a dark air shaft. Francis gave his name and address to a secretary and then saw, at the side of the room, a policeman moving toward him. "Hold it, hold it," the policeman said. "Don't move. Keep your hands where they are."

"I think it's all right, Officer," the secretary began. "I think it will be—"

"Let's make sure," the policeman said, and he began to slap Francis' clothes, looking for what—pistols, knives, an icepick? Finding nothing, he went off and the secretary began a nervous apology: "When you called on the telephone, Mr. Weed, you seemed very excited, and one of the doctor's patients has been threatening his life, and we have to be careful. If you want to go in now?" Francis pushed open a door connected to an electrical chime, and in the doctor's lair sat down heavily, blew his nose into a handkerchief, searched in his pockets for cigarettes, for matches, for something, and said hoarsely, with tears in his eyes, "I'm in love, Dr. Herzog."

It is a week or ten days later in Shady Hill. The seven-fourteen has come and gone, and here and there dinner is finished and the dishes are in the dish-washing machine. The village hangs, morally and economically, from a thread; but it hangs by its thread in the evening light. Donald Goslin had begun to worry the "Moonlight Sonata" again. *Marcato ma sempre pianissimo*! He seems to be wringing out a wet bath towel, but the housemaid does not heed him. She is writing a letter to Arthur Godfrey. In the cellar of his house, Francis Weed is building a coffee table. Dr. Herzog recommends woodwork as a therapy, and Francis finds some true consolation in the simple arithmetic involved and in the holy smell of new wood. Francis is happy. Upstairs, little Toby is crying, because he is tired. He puts off his cowboy hat, gloves, and fringed jacket, unbuckles the belt studded with gold and rubies, the silver bullets and holsters, slips off his suspenders, his checked shirt, and Levi's, and sits on the edge of his bed to pull off his high boots. Leaving this equipment in a heap, he goes to the closet and takes his space suit off a nail. It is a struggle for him to get into the long tights, but he succeeds. He loops the magic cape over his shoulders and, climbing onto the footboard of his bed, he spreads his arms and flies the short distance to the floor, landing with a thump that is audible to everyone in the house but himself.

"Go home, Gertrude, go home," Mrs. Masterson says. "I told you to go home an hour ago, Gertrude. It's way past your suppertime, and your mother will be worried. Go home!" A door on the Babcocks' terrace flies open, and out comes Mrs. Babcock without any clothes on, pursued by a naked husband. (Their children are away at boarding school, and their terrace is screened by a hedge.) Over the terrace they go and in at the kitchen door, as passionate and handsome a nymph and satyr as you will find on any wall in Venice. Cutting the last of the roses in her garden, Julia hears old Mr. Nixon shouting at the squirrels in his bird-feeding station. "Rapscallions! Varmints! Avaunt and quit my sight!" A miserable cat wanders into the garden, sunk in spiritual and physical discomfort. Tied to its head is a small straw hat—a doll's hat—and it is securely buttoned into a doll's dress, from the skirts of which protrudes its long, hairy tail. As it walks, it shakes its feet, as if it had fallen into water.

"Here, pussy, pussy, pussy!" Julia calls.

"Here, pussy, here, poor pussy!" But the cat gives her a skeptical look and stumbles away in its skirts. The last to come is Jupiter. He prances through the tomato vines, holding in his generous mouth the remains of an evening slipper. Then it is dark; it is a night where kings in golden suits ride elephants over the mountains.

THE DUCHESS

IF YOU SHOULD happen to be the son of a coal miner or were brought up (as I was) in a small town in Massachusetts, the company of a ranking duchess might excite some of those vulgar sentiments that have no place in fiction, but she was beautiful, after all, and beauty has nothing to do with rank. She was slender, but not thin. And rather tall. Her hair was ash blond, and her fine, clear brow belonged against that grandiose and shabby backdrop of limestone and marble, the Roman palace where she lived. It was hers, and stepping from the shadows of her palace to walk along the river to early Mass, she never quite seemed to leave the grainy light. One would have been surprised but not alarmed to see her join the company of the stone saints and angels on the roof of Sant' Andrea della Valle. This was not the guidebook city but the Rome of today, whose charm is not the Colosseum in the moonlight, or the Spanish Stairs wet by a sudden shower, but the poignance of a great and an ancient city succumbing confusedly to change. We live in a world where the banks of even the most remote trout streams are beaten smooth by the boots of fishermen, and the music that drifts down from the medieval walls into the garden where we sit is an old recording of Vivienne Segal singing "Bewitched, Bothered and Bewildered"; and Donna Carla lived, like you and me, with one foot in the past.

She was Donna Carla Malvolio-Pommodori, Duchess of Vevaqua-Perdere-Giusti, etc. She would have been considered fair anywhere, but in Rome her blue eyes, her pale skin, and her shining hair were extraordinary. She spoke English, French, and Italian with equal style, but Italian was the only language she wrote correctly. She carried on her social correspondence in a kind of English: "Donna Carla thinks you for the flahers," "Donna Carla rekests the honor of your compagnie," etc. The first floor of her palace on the Tiber had been converted into shops, and she lived on the *piano nobile*. The two upper floors had been rented out as apartments. This still left her with something like forty rooms.

Most guidebooks carry the family history, in small print, and you can't travel in Italy without coming on those piles of masonry that Malvolio-Pommodoris have scattered everywhere, from Venice to Calabria. There were the three popes, the doge, and the thirty-six cardinals, as well as many avaricious, bloodthirsty, and dishonest nobles. Don Camillo married the Princess Plèves, and after she had given him three sons he had her excommunicated, on a rigged charge of adultery, and seized all her lands. Don Camillo and his sons were butchered at dinner by assassins who had been hired by their host, Don Camillo's uncle Marcantonio. Marcantonio was strangled by Cosimo's men, and Cosimo was poisoned by his nephew Antonio. The palace in Rome had had an oubliette—a dungeon below a chamber whose floor operated on the principle of a seesaw. If you walked or were pushed beyond the axis, you went howling down for good into the bone pit. All this was long before the nineteenth century, when the upper stories were remodeled into apartments. Donna Carla's grandparents were exemplary Roman nobles. They were even prudish, and had the erotic frescoes in the ballroom rectified. They were commemorated by a marble portrait statue in the smoking room. It was life-size and showed them as they might have appeared for a walk on the Lungo-Tevere—marble hats, marble gloves, a marble walking stick. He even had a marble fur colla on his marble coat. The most corrupt and tasteless par commissioner could not have been bribed to give it space.

Donna Carla was born in the family village of Vevaqua in Tuscany, where her parents lived for many years in kind of exile. Her father was simple in his tastes, bold, pious, just, and the heir to an immense patrimony. Huntin in England as a young man, he had a bad spill. His arm and legs were broken, his skull was fractured, and severa vertebrae were smashed. His parents took what was the the long trip from Rome to England, and waited thre days for their brilliant son to regain consciousness. It wa thought he would never walk again. His recuperative powers were exceptional, but it was two years before he took a step. Then, wasted, leaning on two sticks and half supported by a busty nurse named Winifred-Mae Bolton, he crossed the threshold of the nursing home into the garden. He held his head up, smiled his quick smile, and moved haltingly, as if he were delayed by his pleasure in the garden and the air, and not by his infirmity. It was six months before he could return to Rome, and he returned with the news that he was going to marry Winifred-Mae Bolton. She had given him—literally—his life, and what, as a good nobleman, could he do but give her his? The consternation in Rome, Milan, and Paris was indescribable. His parents wept, but they were up against that single-minded concern for probity that had appeared in his character when he was a boy. His father, who loved him as he loved his own life, said that Winifred-Mae would not enter the gates of Rome so long as he lived, and she did not.

Donna Carla's mother was a large cheerful woman with a coronet of yellow-reddish hair and a very broad manner. The only Italian she ever learned was "*prego*" and "*grazie*," and she pronounced these "*prygo*" and "*gryzia*." During the years in exile in Vevaqua, she worked in the garden. Her taste in formal gardening was colored by the railroad-station gardens of England, and she spelled out her husband's name—Cosimo—in pansies and set it in a heart-shaped bed of artichokes. She liked to fry fish and chips, for which the peasants thought she was crazy. The only evidence that the Duke may have regretted his marriage was an occasional—a charming—look of bewilderment on his handsome face. With his wife he was always loving, courteous, and protective. Donna Carla was twelve years old when her grandparents died. After a period of mourning, she, Winifred-Mae, and the Duke entered Rome by the gate of Santa Maria del Popolo.

Winifred-Mae had probably, by then, seen enough of ducal gigantism not to exclaim over the size of the palace on the Tiber. Their first night in Rome set the pattern for their life there. "Now that we're back in a city again," she said, "with all the shops and all, I'll go out and buy a bit of fresh fish, shall I, ducky, and fry it for you the way I used to when you were in hospital?" Perfect love was in the Duke's smile of assent. In the fish market she squealed at the squid and the eels, but she found a nice piece of sole, and took it home and fried it, with some potatoes, in the kitchen, while the servants watched with tears in their eyes to see the fall of such a great house. After dinner, as had been the custom in Vevaqua, she sang. It was not true that, as her enemies said, she had sung ditties and kicked up her petticoats in English music halls. She had sung in music halls before she became a nurse, but she had sung the "Méditation" from *Thaïs,* and "The Road to Mandalay." Her display of talentlessness was exhaustive; it was stupendous. She seemed to hold her lack of talent up to the light for examination, and to stretch its seams. She flatted and she sharped, and she strummed noisily on the piano, but she did all this with such perfect candor and self-assurance that the performance was refreshing. The Duke beamed at these accomplishments of his wife, and did not seem in any way inclined to compare this entertainment with the days of his youth, when he had stood with his nursemaid on the ballroom balcony and seen a quadrille danced by one emperor, two kings, three queens, and a hundred and thirty-six grand dukes and grand duchesses. Winifred-Mae sang for an hour, and then they turned out the lights and went to bed. In those years, an owl had nested in the palace tower, and they could hear, above the drifting music of fountains, the belling of the owl. It reminded Winifred-Mae of England.

Rome had intended never to make any acknowledgment of Winifred-Mae's existence, but a lovely duchessina who was also a billionairess was too good a thing to pass up, and it seemed that Donna Carla would be the richest woman in Europe. If suitors were to be presented to her, Winifred-Mae had to be considered, and she was called on by the high nobility. She went on cooking, sewing, singing, and knitting; they got her on her own terms. She was a scandal. She asked noble callers into the kitchen while she popped a steak-and-kidney pie into the oven. She made cretonne slip-covers for the furniture in the *salottino*. She complained, in explicit detail, about the old-fashioned plumbing in the palace. She installed a radio. At her insistence, the Duke employed as his secretary a young Englishman named Cecil Smith. Smith was not even liked by the English. Coming down the Spanish Stairs in the morning sun, he could remind you of the industrial Midlands. He smelled of Stoke-on-Trent. He was a tall man with brown curly hair parted and combed across his forehead like a drapery. He wore dark, ill-fitting clothes that were sent to him from England, and as a result of a fear of drafts and a fear of immodesty, he gave one the impression that he was buried in clothing. He wore nightcaps, undervests, mufflers, and rubbers, and the cuff of his long underwear could be seen when he reached out his cup for another spot of tea, which he took with Winifred-Mae. His manners were refined. He wore paper cuffs and an eyeshade in the Duke's office, and he fried sausages and potatoes on a gas ring in his flat.

But the sewing, the singing, the smell of fish and chips, and Cecil Smith had to be overlooked by the needy nobility. The thought of what Donna Carla's grace and her billions could do to lubricate the aristocracy would make your heart thump. Potential suitors began coming up to the palace when she was thirteen or fourteen. She was pleasant to them all. She had even then the kind of inner gracefulness that was to make her so persuasive as a young woman. She was not a solemn girl, but hilarity seemed to lie outside her range, and some countess who had come to display her son remarked afterward that she was like the princess in the fairy tale—the princess who had never laughed. There must have been some truth in the observation, because it stuck; people repeated the remark, and what they meant was an atmosphere of sadness or captivity that one sensed in spite of her clear features and her light coloring.

THIS WAS in the thirties—a decade, in Italy, of marching in the streets, arrests, assassinations, and the loss of familiar lights. Cecil Smith returned to England when the war broke out. Very few suitors came to the palace in those days. The crippled Duke was an implacable anti-Fascist, and he told everyone that Il Duce was an abomination and an infection, but he was never molested or thrown into prison, as were some less outspoken men; this may have been because of his rank, his infirmities, or his popularity with the Romans. But when the war began, the family was forced into a complete retirement. They were thought, wrongly, to be in sympathy with the Allies, and were allowed to leave the palace only once a day, to go to late or early Mass at San Giovanni. They were in bed and asleep on the night of September 10, 1943. The owl was hooting. Luigi, the old butler, woke them and said there was a messenger in the hall. They dressed quickly and went down. The messenger was disguised as a farmer, but the Duke recognized the son of an old friend. He informed the Duke that the Germans were coming down the Via Cassia and were entering the city. The commanding general had put a price of a million lire on the Duke's head; it was the price of his intransigence. They were to go at once, on foot, to an address on the Janiculum. Winifred-Mae could hear the owl hooting in the tower, and she had never been so homesick for England. "I don't want to go, ducky," she said. "If they're going to kill us, let them kill us in our own beds." The Duke smiled kindly and opened the door for her onto one of the most troubled of Roman nights.

There were already German patrols in the streets. It was a long walk up the river, and they were very conspicuous—the weeping Englishwoman, the Duke with his stick, and the graceful daughter. How mysterious life must have seemed at that moment! The Duke moved slowly and had to stop now and then to rest, but though he was in pain, he did not show it. With his head up and a price on it, he looked around alertly, as if he had stopped to observe or admire some change in his old city. They crossed the river by separate bridges and met at a barbershop, where they were taken into a cellar and disguised. Their skin was stained and their hair dyed. They left Rome before dawn, concealed in a load of furniture, and that evening reached a small village in the mountains, where they were hidden in a farmhouse cellar.

The village was shelled twice, but only a few buildings and barns on the outskirts were destroyed. The farmhouse was searched a dozen times, by Germans and Fascists, but the Duke was always warned long in advance. In the village, they were known as Signor and Signora Giusti, and it was Winifred-Mae who chafed at this incognito. She was the Duchess Malvolio-Pommodori, and she wanted it known. Donna Carla liked being Carla Giusti. She went one day, as Carla Giusti, to the washing trough and spent a pleasant morning cleaning her clothes and gossiping with the other women. When she got back to the farm, Winifred-Mae was furious. She was Donna Carla; she must not forget it. A few days later, Winifred-Mae saw Donna Carla being taught by a woman at the fountain how to carry a copper vase on her head, and she called her daughter into the house and gave her another fierce lecture on rank. Donna Carla was always malleable and obedient, but without losing her freshness, and she never tried to carry a *conca* again.

When Rome was liberated, the family returned to the city, to find that the Germans had sacked the palace; and they then retired to an estate in the south and waited there for the war to end. The Duke was invited to help in the formation of a government, but he declined this invitation, claiming to be too old; the fact was that he supported, if not the King, the concept of monarchy. The paintings and the rest of the family treasure were found in a salt mine and returned to the palace. Cecil Smith came back, put on his paper cuffs, and resumed the administration of the family fortune, which had come through the war intact. Suitors began to call on Donna Carla.

In the second year after the war, a hundred and seventeen suitors came to the palace. These were straight and honest men, crooked men, men suffering from hemophilia, and many cousins. It was Donna Carla's prerogative to propose marriage, and she saw them all to the door without hinting at the subject. This was a class of men whose disinheritedness was grandiose. Lying in bed in the Excelsior Hotel, they dreamed of what her wealth could do. The castle roof was repaired. Plumbing was installed at last. The garden bloomed. The saddle horses were fat and sleek. When she saw them to the door without having mentioned the subject of marriage, she offended them and she offended their dreams. She sent them back to a leaky castle and a ruined garden; she turned them out into the stormy weather of impoverished rank. Many of them were angry, but they kept on coming. She turned away so many suitors that she was finally summoned to the Vatican, where the Holy Father refreshed her sense of responsibility toward her family and its ancient name.

Considering that Winifred-Mae had upset the aristocratic applecart, she took a surprisingly fervid interest in the lineage of Donna Carla's suitors, and championed her favorites as they came. There was some hard feeling between the mother and daughter on this score, and—from Winifred-Mae—some hard words. More and more suitors came, and the more persistent and needy returned, but the subject of marriage was still not mentioned. Donna Carla's father-confessor then suggested that she see a psychiatrist, and she was willing. She was never unwilling. He made an appointment for her with a devout and elderly doctor who practiced within the Catholic faith. He had been a friend of Croce's, and a large cabinet photograph of the philosopher hung on one of the dark walls of his office, but this may have been wasted on Donna Carla. He offered the Duchess a chair, and then, after some questioning, invited her to lie down on his couch. This was a massive piece of furniture, covered with worn leather and dating back to the earlier days of Freud. She walked gracefully toward the couch, and then turned and said, "But it is not possible for me to lie down in the presence of a gentleman." The doctor could see her point; it was a true impasse. She seemed to look longingly at the couch, but she could not change the facts of her upbringing, and so they said goodbye.

The Duke was growing old. It was getting more and more difficult for him to walk, but this pain did not change his handsomeness and seemed only to increase his vitality. When people saw him, they thought: How nice it will be to eat a cutlet, take a swim, or climb a mountain; how pleasant, after all, life is. He passed on to Donna Carla his probity, and his ideal of a simple and elegant life. He ate plain fare off fine dishes, wore fine clothes in third-class train carriages, and, on the trip to Vevaqua, ate his simple lunch out of a basket. He kept—at great expense—his paintings cleaned and in good condition, but the dust covers on the chairs and chandeliers in the reception room had not been removed for years. Donna Carla began to interest herself in what she would inherit, and spent some time going over the ledgers in Cecil Smith's office. The impropriety of a beautiful Roman noblewoman's studying ledgers at a desk caused some gossip, and may have been the turning point in her reputation.

THERE WAS a turning point. Her life was not especially solitary, but her shy gracefulness gave this impression, and she had made enemies of enough of her former suitors to be the butt of gossip. It was said that the Duke's probity was miserliness and that the family's simple tastes were lunatic. It was said that the family ate bread crusts and canned sardines, and had only one electric-light bulb in the whole palace. It was said that they had gone crazy—all three of them—and would leave their billions to the dogs. Someone else said Donna Carla had been arrested for shoplifting on the Via Nazionale. Someone had seen her pick up a ten-lira piece on the Corso and put it in her bag. When Luigi, the old butler, collapsed on the street one day and was taken to the hospital in an ambulance, someone said that the doctors at the clinic had found him dying of starvation.

The Communist party got on the band wagon and began to attack Donna Carla as the archetype of dying feudalism. A Communist deputy in the Chamber made a speech saying that the sufferings of Italy would not be over until the Duchessina was dead. The village of Vevaqua voted Communist in the local elections. She went there after the harvest to audit the accounts. Her father was too frail and Smith was busy. She traveled third-class, as she had been taught. The old calash and the shabby coachman were waiting for her at the station. Clouds of dust came from the leather cushions when she sat down. As the carriage was entering an olive grove below the walls of the village, someone threw a rock. It struck Donna Carla on the shoulder. Another stone struck her on the thigh and another on the breast. The coachman's hat was knocked off, and he whipped the horse, but the horse was too used to pulling a plow to change his pace. Then a stone hit the coachman on the forehead and blood spurted out. Blinded with blood, he dropped the reins. The horse moved over to the side of the road and began to eat grass. Donna Carla got out of the calash. The men in the olive grove ran off. She bound up the coachman's head with a scarf, took up the reins, and drove the old carriage up into the village, where "DEATH TO DONNA CARLA! DEATH TO THE DUCHESS!" was written everywhere. The streets were deserted. The servants in the castle were loyal, and they dressed her cuts and bruises, and they brought her tea, and cried. When she began the audit in the morning, the tenants came in, one by one, and she did not mention the incident. With grace and patience she went over the accounts with men she recognized as her assailants. Three days later she drove back through the olive grove and took the train, third-class, to Rome.

But her reputation in Rome was not improved by this incident. Someone said that she had turned a starving child away from her door, that her avarice was pathological. She was smuggling her paintings into England and amassing a fortune there. She was selling the jewels. Noble Roman property owners are expected to be sharp, but stories of unusual dishonesty were fabricated and circulated about Donna Carla. It was also said that she was losing her looks. She was growing old. People disputed about her age. She was twenty-eight. She was thirty-two. She was thirty-six. She was thirty-eight. And she was still a familiar figure on the Lungo-Tevere, as grave and lovely as ever, with her shining hair and her half smile. But what was the truth? What would a German prince, a suitor with a leaky palace, find if he went there for tea?

PRINCE BERNSTRASSER-FALCONBERG went under the massive arch at five one Sunday afternoon, into a garden where there were some tangerine trees and a fountain. He was a man of forty-five, with three illegitimate children, and with a jolly mistress waiting for him at the Grand Hotel. Looking up at the walls of the palace, he could not help thinking of all the good Donna Carla's wealth would do. He would pay his debts. He would buy a bathtub for his old mother. He would fix the roof. An old porter in yellow livery let him in, and Luigi opened a second pair of double doors, into a hall with a marble staircase. Donna Carla was waiting here in the dusk. "Awfully nice of you to come," she said, in English. "Frightfully gloomy, isn't it?" The fragile English music of her voice echoed lightly off the stones. The hall *was* gloomy, he could see, but this was only half the truth, and the Prince sensed at once that he was not supposed to notice that it was also stupendous. The young woman seemed to be appealing to him for some understanding of her embarrassment, of her dilemma at having to greet him in such surroundings, and of her wish to pretend that this was some quite ordinary hall, where two friends might meet on a Sunday afternoon. She gave him her hand, and apologized for her parents' absence, saying that they were unwell. (This was not quite the truth; Winifred-Mae had a cold, but the old Duke had gone off to a double feature.)

The Prince was pleased to see that she was attractive, that she had on a velvet dress and some perfume. He wondered about her age, and saw that her face, that close, seemed quite pale and drawn.

"We have quite a walk ahead of us," she said. "Shall we begin? The *salottino*, the only room where one can sit down, is at the other end of the palace, but one can't use the back door, because then one makes a *brutta figura*. . . ." They stepped from the hall into the cavernous picture gallery. The room was dimly lighted, its hundreds of chairs covered with chamois. The Prince wondered if he should mention the paintings, and tried to take his cue from the Duchess. She seemed to be waiting, but was she waiting for him to join her or waiting for a display of his sensibilities? He took a chance and stopped in front of a Bronzino and praised it. "He looks rather better now that he's been cleaned," she said. The Prince moved from the Bronzino to a Tintoretto. "I say," she said, "shall we go on to someplace more comfortable?"

The next gallery was tapestries, and her one concession to these was to murmur, "Spanish. A frightful care. Moths and all that sort of thing." When the Prince stopped to admire the contents of a cabinet, she joined him and explained the objects, and he caught for the first time a note of ambivalence in her apparent wish to be taken for a simple woman who lived in a flat. "Carved lapis lazuli," she said. "The vase in the center is supposed to be the largest piece of lapis lazuli in the world." Then, as if she sensed and regretted this weakening of her position, she asked, as they stepped into the next room, "Did you ever see so much rubbish?"

Here were the cradles of popes, the crimson sedan chairs of cardinals, the bread-and-butter presents of emperors, kings, and grand dukes piled up to the ceiling, and the Prince was confused by her embarrassment. What tack should he take? Her behavior was not what one would expect of an heiress, but was it, after all, so queer, so unreasonable? What strange attitudes might one not be forced into, saddled with a mile or more of paintings, burdened with the bulky evidence of four consecutive centuries of wealth and power? She might, playing in these icy rooms as a girl, have discovered in herself a considerable disinclination to live in a monument. In any event, she would have had to make a choice, for if she took this treasure seriously, it would mean living moment by moment with the past, as the rest of us live with our appetites and thirsts, and who would want to do that?

Their destination was a dark parlor. The Prince watched her stoop down to the baseboard and plug in a feeble lamp.

"I keep all the lamps unplugged, because the servants sometimes forget, and electricity is frightfully expensive in Rome. *There* we are!" she exclaimed, straightening up and gesturing hospitably to a sofa from which the worn velvet hung in rags. Above this was a portrait by Titian of the first Malvolio-Pommodori pope. "I make my tea on a spirit lamp, because in the time it takes the man to bring tea from the kitchen the water gets quite cold. . . ."

They sat waiting for the kettle to boil. She handed him his tea and smiled, and he was touched, although he didn't know why. But there seemed about this charming woman, as there was about so much that he admired in Rome, the threat of obsolescence. Her pallor was a little faded. Her nose was a little sharp. Her grace, her accent were close to excessive. She was not yet the kind of woman who carries her left hand adrift in midair, the little finger extended, as vulgar people are supposed to hold a teacup; her airs and graces were not yet mistaken, and through them the Prince thought he felt the beating of a healthy and decent heart. But he felt, at the same time, that her days ended inexorably in the damps of a lonely bed, and that much more of this life would transform her into that kind of wasted virgin whose musical voice has upon men the force of complete sexual discouragement.

"My mother regrets that she was unable to come to Rome," the Prince said, "but she asked me to express to you her hope that you will someday visit us in our country."

"How nice," Donna Carla said. "And please thank your mother. I don't believe we've ever met, but I do recall your cousins Otto and Friedrich, when they were in school here, and please remember me to them when you return."

"You should visit my country, Donna Carla."

"Oh, I would adore to, but I can't leave Rome, as things stand now. There is so much to do. There are the twenty shops downstairs and the flats overhead. Drains are forever bursting, and the pigeons nest in the tiles. I have to go to Tuscany for the harvests. There's never a minute."

"We have much in common, Donna Carla."

"Yes?"

"Painting. I love painting. It is the love of my life."

"Is that so?"

"I would love to live as you do, in a great house where one finds—how can I say it?—the true luminousness of art."

"Would you really? I can't say that I like it much myself. Oh, I can see the virtues in a pretty picture of a vase of flowers, but there's nothing like that here. Everywhere I look I see bloody crucifixions, nakedness, and cruelty." She drew her shawl closer. "I really don't like it."

"You know why I am here, Donna Carla?"

"Quite."

"I come from a good family. I am not young, but I am strong. I . . ."

"Quite," she said. "Will you have some more tea."

"Thank you."

Her smile, when she passed him his cup, was an open appeal to keep the conversation general, and he thought of his old mother, the Princess, taking her bath in a pail. But there was some persuasiveness, some triumphant intelligence in her smile that also made him feel, with shame, the stupidity and rudeness of his quest. Why should she want to buy his mother a bathtub? Why should she want to fix his roof? Why had he been told everything about the Duchess but the fact that she was sensible? He could see her point. Indeed, he could see more. He saw how idle the gossip had been. This "swindler," this "miser," this "shoplifter" was no more than a pleasant woman who used her head. He knew the kind of suitors who had preceded him—more often than not with a mistress waiting at the hotel—and why shouldn't they have excited her suspicions? He knew the brilliant society she had neglected; he knew its grim card parties, its elegant and malicious dinners, its tedium, not relieved in any way by butlers in livery and torchlit gardens. How sensible of her to have stayed home. She was a sensible woman—much too sensible to be interested in him—and what lay at the heart of the mystery was her brains. No one would have expected to find blooming in ancient Rome this flower of common sense.

He talked with her for twenty minutes. Then she rang for Luigi and asked him to show the Prince to the door.

It came with a crash, the old Duke's death. Reading Joseph Conrad in the *salottino* one night, he got up to get an ashtray and fell down dead. His cigarette burned in the carpet long after his heart had stopped beating. Luigi found him. Winifred-Mae was hysterical. A cardinal with acolytes rushed to the palace, but it was too late. The Duke was buried in the great Renaissance tomb, surrounded by ruined gardens, on the Appia Antica, and half the aristocracy of Europe went into mourning. Winifred-Mae was shattered. She planned to return to England, but, having packed her bags, she found she was too ill to travel. She drank gin for her indigestion. She railed at the servants, she railed at Donna Carla for not having married, and then, after three months of being a widow, she died.

Every day for thirty days after her mother's death, Donna Carla left the palace in the morning for early Mass and then went out to the family tomb. Sometimes she drove. Sometimes she took a bus. Her mourning veil was so heavy that her features could hardly be seen. She went rain or shine, said her prayers, and was seen wandering in the garden in a thunderstorm. It made one sad to see her on the Lungo-Tevere; there seemed to be such finality to her black clothes. It made everyone sad—the beggars and the women who sold chestnuts. She had loved her parents too well. Something had gone wrong. Now she would spend the rest of her life—how easy this was to imagine—between the palace and the tomb. But at the end of thirty days Donna Carla went to her father-confessor and asked to see His Holiness. A few days later, she went to the Vatican. She did not go bowling through the Piazza San Pietro in a hired limousine, wiping off her lipstick with a piece of Kleenex. She parked her dusty little car near the fountains and went through the gates on foot. She kissed His Holiness's ring, curtsied gracefully to the floor, and said, "I wish to marry Cecil Smith."

Wood smoke, confetti, and the smell of snow and manure spun on the wind on the changeable day when they were married, in Vevaqua. She entered the church as Donna Carla Malvolio-Pommodori, Duchess of Vevaqua-Perdere-Giusti, etc., and came out Mrs. Cecil Smith. She was radiant. They returned to Rome, and she took an office adjoining his, and shared the administration of the estate and the work of distributing her income among convents, hospitals, and the poor. Their first son—Cecil Smith, Jr.—was born a year after their marriage, and a year later they had a daughter, Jocelyn. Donna Carla was cursed in every leaky castle in Europe, but surely shining choirs of angels in heaven will sing of Mrs. Cecil Smith.

THE SCARLET MOVING VAN

GOODBYE to the mortal boredom of distributing a skinny chicken to a family of seven and all the other rites of the hill towns. I don't mean the real hill towns—Assisi or Perugia or Saracinesco, perched on a three-thousand-foot crag, with walls the dispiriting gray of shirt cardboards and mustard lichen blooming on the crooked roofs. The land, in fact, was flat, the houses frame. This was in the eastern United States, and the kind of place where most of us live. It was the unincorporated township of B———, with a population of perhaps two hundred married couples, all of them with dogs and children, and many of them with servants; it resembled a hill town only in a manner of speaking, in that the ailing, the disheartened, and the poor could not ascend the steep moral path that formed its natural defense, and the moment any of the inhabitants became infected with unhappiness or discontent, they sensed the hopelessness of existing on such a high spiritual altitude, and went to live in the plain. Life was unprecedentedly comfortable and tranquil. B——— was exclusively for the felicitous. The housewives kissed their husbands tenderly in the morning and passionately at nightfall. In nearly every house there were love, graciousness, and high hopes. The schools were excellent, the roads were smooth, the drains and other services were ideal, and one spring evening at dusk an immense scarlet moving van with gold lettering on its sides came up the street and stopped in the front of the Marple house, which had been empty then for three months.

The gilt and scarlet of the van, bright even in the twilight, was an inspired attempt to disguise the true sorrowfulness of wandering. "We Carry Loads and Part Loads to All Far-Distant Places," said the gold letters on the sides, and this legend had the effect of a distant train whistle. Martha Folkestone, who lived next door, watched through a window as the portables of her neighbors were carried across the porch. "That looks like real Chippendale," she said, "although it's hard to tell in this light. They have two children. They seem like nice people. Oh, I wish there was something I could bring them to make them feel at home. Do you think they'd like flowers? I suppose we could ask them for a drink. Do you think they'd like a drink? Would you want to go over and ask them if they'd like a drink?"

Later, when the furniture was all indoors and the van had gone, Charlie Folkestone crossed the lawn between the two houses and introduced himself to Peaches and Gee-Gee. This is what he saw. Peaches was peaches—blond and warm, with a low-cut dress and a luminous front. Gee-Gee had been a handsome man, and perhaps still was, although his yellow curls were thin. His face seemed both angelic and menacing. He had never (Charlie learned later) been a boxer, but his eyes were slightly squinted and his square, handsome forehead had the conformation of layers of scar tissue. You might have said that his look was thoughtful until you realized that he was not a thoughtful man. It was the earnest and contained look of those who are a little hard of hearing or a little stupid.

They would be delighted to have a drink. They would be right over. Peaches wanted to put on some lipstick and say good night to the children, and then they would be right over. They came right over, and what seemed to be an unusually pleasant evening began. The Folkestones had been worried about who their new neighbors would be, and to find a couple as sympathetic as Gee-Gee and Peaches made them very high-spirited. Like everyone else, they loved to express an opinion about their neighbors, and Gee-Gee and Peaches were, naturally, interested. It was the beginning of a friendship, and the Folkestones overlooked their usual concern with time and sobriety. It got late—it was past midnight—and Charlie did not notice how much whiskey was being poured or that Gee-Gee seemed to be getting drunk. Gee-Gee became very quiet—he dropped out of the conversation—and then he suddenly interrupted Martha in a flat, unpleasant drawl.

"God, but you're stuffy people," he said.

"Oh, no, Gee-Gee!" Peaches said. "Not on our first night!"

"You've had too much to drink, Gee-Gee," Charlie said.

"Like hell I have," said Gee-Gee. He bent over and began to unlace his shoes. "I haven't had half enough."

"Please, Gee-Gee, please," Peaches said.

"I have to teach them, honey," Gee-Gee said. "They've got to learn."

Then he stood up and with the cunning and dexterity of a drunk, got out of most of his clothing before anyone could stop him.

"Get out of here," Charlie said.

"The pleasure's all mine, neighbor," said Gee-Gee. He kicked over a hammered-brass umbrella stand on his way out the door.

"Oh, I'm frightfully sorry!" Peaches said. "I feel terribly about this!"

"Don't worry, my dear," Martha said. "He's probably very tired, and we've all had too much to drink."

"Oh, no," Peaches said. "It always happens. Everywhere. We've moved eight times in the last eight years, and there's never been anyone to say goodbye to us. Not a soul. Oh, he was a beautiful man when I first knew him! You never saw anyone so fine and strong and generous. They called him the Greek God at college. That's why he's called Gee-Gee. He was All-America twice, but he was never a money player—he always played straight out of his heart. Everybody loved him. Now it's all gone, but I tell myself that I once had the love of a good man. I don't think many women have known that kind of love. Oh, I wish he'd come back. I wish he'd be the way he was. The night before last, when we were packing up the dishes in the old house, he got drunk and I slapped him in the face, and I shouted at him, 'Come back! Come back! Come back to me, Gee-Gee!' But he didn't listen. He didn't hear me. He doesn't hear anyone any more—not even the voices of his children. I ask myself every day what I've done to be punished so cruelly."

"I'm sorry, my dear!" Martha said.

"You won't be around to say goodbye when we go," Peaches said. "We'll last a year. You wait and see. Some people have tender farewell parties, but even the garbage man in the last place was glad to see us go." With a grace and resignation that transcended the ruined evening, she began to gather up the clothing that her husband had scattered on the rug. "Each time we move, I think that the change will be good for him," she said. "When we got here tonight, it all looked so pretty and quiet that I thought he might change. Well you don't have to ask us again. You know what it's like."

A FEW DAYS or perhaps a week later, Charlie saw Gee-Gee on the station platform in the morning and saw how completely personable his neighbor was when he was sober. B——— was not an easy place to conquer, but Gee-Gee seemed already to have won the affectionate respect of his neighbors. Charlie could see, as he watched him standing in the sun among the other commuters, that he would be asked to join everything. Gee-Gee greeted Charlie heartily, and there was no trace of the ugliness he had shown that night. Indeed, it was impossible to believe that this charming and handsome man had been so offensive. In the morning light, and surrounded by new friends, he seemed to challenge the memory. He seemed almost able to transfer the blame onto Charlie.

Arrangements for a social initiation of the new couple were unusually rapid and elaborate, and began with a dinner party at the Watermans'. Charlie was already at the party when Gee-Gee and Peaches came in, and they came in like royalty. Arm in arm, radiant and beautiful, they seemed, at the moment of their entrance, to make the evening. It was a large party, and Charlie hardly saw them until they went in to dinner. He sat close to Peaches, but Gee-Gee was at the other end of the table. They were halfway through dessert when Gee-Gee's flat and unpleasant drawl sounded, like a parade command, over the general conversation.

"What a God-damned bunch of stuffed shirts!" he said. "Let's put a little vitality into the conversation, shall we?" He sprang onto the center of the table and began to sing a dirty song and dance a jig. Women screamed. Dishes were upset and broken. Dresses were ruined. Peaches pled to her wayward husband. The effect of this outrageous performance was to empty the dining room of everyone but Gee-Gee and Charlie.

"Get down off there, Gee-Gee," Charlie said.

"I have to teach them," Gee-Gee said, "I've got to teach them."

"You're not teaching anybody anything but the fact that you're rotten drunk."

"They've got to learn," Gee-Gee said. "I've got to teach them." He got down off the table, breaking a few more dishes, and wandered out into the kitchen, where he embraced the cook, and then went on out into the night.

One might have thought that this was warning enough to a worldly community, but unusual amounts of forgiveness were extended to Gee-Gee. One liked him, and there was always the chance that he might not misbehave. There was always his charming figure in the morning light to confound his enemies, but it began to seem more and more like a lure that would let him into houses where he could break the crockery. Forgiveness was not what he wanted, and if he seemed to have failed at offending the sensibilities of his hostess he would increase and complicate his outrageousness. No one had ever seen anything like it. He undressed at the Bilkers'. At the Levys' he drop-kicked a bowl of soft cheese onto the ceiling. He danced the Highland fling in his underpants, set fire to wastebaskets, and swung on the Townsends' chandelier—that famous chandelier. Inside of six weeks, there was not a house in B——— where he was welcome.

The Folkestones still saw him, of course—saw him in his garden in the evening and talked to him across the hedge. Charlie was greatly troubled at the spectacle of someone falling so swiftly from grace, and he would have liked to help. He and Martha talked with Peaches, but Peaches was without hope. She did not understand what had happened to her Adonis, and that was as far as her intelligence took her. Now and then some innocent stranger from the next town or perhaps some newcomer would be taken with Gee-Gee and ask him to dinner. The performance was always the same, the dishes were always broken. The Folkestones were neighbors—there was this ancient bond—and Charlie may have thought that he could save the man. When Gee-Gee and Peaches quarreled, sometimes she telephoned Charlie and asked his protection. He went there one summer evening after she had telephoned.

The quarrel was over; Peaches was reading a comic book in the living room, and Gee-Gee was sitting at the dining-room table with a drink in his hand. Charlie stood over his friend.

"Gee-Gee."

"Yes."

"Will you go on the wagon?"

"No."

"Will you go on the wagon if I go on the wagon?"

"No."

"Will you go to a psychiatrist?"

"Why? I know myself. I only have to play it out."

"Will you go to a psychiatrist if I go with you?"

"No."

"Will you do anything to help yourself?"

"I have to teach them." Then he threw back his head and sobbed, "Oh, Jesus . . ."

Charlie turned away. It seemed, at that instant, that Gee-Gee had heard, from some wilderness of his own, the noise of a distant horn that prophesied the manner and the hour of his death. There seemed to be some tremendous validity to the drunken man. Folkestone felt an upheaval in his spirit. He felt he understood the drunken man's message; he had always sensed it. It was at the bottom of their friendship. Gee-Gee was an advocate for the lame, the diseased, the poor, for those who through no fault of their own live out their lives in misery and pain. To the happy and the wellborn and the rich he had this to say—that for all their affection, their comforts, and their privileges, they would not be spared the pangs of anger and lust and the agonies of death. He only meant for them to be prepared for the blow when the blow fell. But was it not possible to accept this truth without having him dance a jig in your living room? He spoke from some vision of the suffering in life, but was it necessary to suffer oneself in order to accept his message? It seemed so.

"Gee-Gee?" Charlie asked.

"Yes."

"*What* are you trying to teach them?"

"You'll never know. You're too God-damned stuffy."

THEY didn't even last a year. In November, someone

made them a decent offer for the house and they sold it. The gold-and-scarlet moving van returned, and they crossed the state line, into the town of Y———, where they bought another house. The Folkestones were glad to see them go. A well-behaved young couple took their place, and everything was as it had been. They were seldom remembered. But through a string of friends Charlie learned, the following winter, that Gee-Gee had broken his hip playing football a day or two before Christmas. This fact, for some reason, remained with him, and one Sunday afternoon when he had nothing much better to do he got Gee-Gee's telephone number from Information and called his old neighbor to say that he was coming over for a drink. Gee-Gee roared with enthusiasm and gave Charlie directions for getting to the house.

It was a long drive, and halfway there Charlie wondered why he had undertaken it. Y——— was several cuts below B———. The house was in a development, and the builder had not stopped at mere ugliness; he had constructed a community that looked, with its rectilinear windows, like a penal colony. The streets were named after universities—Princeton Street, Yale Street, Rutgers Street, and so forth. Only a few of the houses had been sold, and Gee-Gee's house was surrounded by empty dwellings. Charlie rang the bell and heard Gee-Gee shouting for him to come in. The house was a mess, and as he was taking his coat off, Gee-Gee came slowly down the hall half riding in a child's wagon, which he propelled by pushing a crutch. His right hip and leg were encased in a massive cast.

"Where's Peaches?" Charlie asked.

"She's in Nassau. She and the children went to Nassau for Christmas."

"And left you alone?"

"I wanted them to go. I made them go. Nothing can be done for me. I get along all right on this wagon. When I'm hungry, I make a sandwich. I wanted them to go. I made them go. Peaches needed a vacation, and I like being alone. Come on into the living room and make me a drink. I can't get the ice trays out—that's about the only thing I can't do. I can shave and get into bed and so forth, but I can't get the ice trays out."

Charlie got some ice. He was glad to have something to

do. The image of Gee-Gee in his wagon shocked him, and he felt a terrifying stillness over the place. Out of the kitchen window he could see row upon row of ugly, empty houses. He felt as if some hideous melodrama were approaching its climax. But in the living room Gee-Gee was his most charming, and his smile and his voice gave the afternoon a momentary equilibrium. Charlie asked if Gee-Gee couldn't get a nurse to stay with him. Couldn't someone be found to stay with him? Couldn't he at least rent a wheelchair? Gee-Gee laughed away all these suggestions. He was contented. Peaches had written him from Nassau. They were having a marvelous time.

Charlie believed that Gee-Gee had made them go. It was this detail, above everything else, that gave the situation its horror. Peaches would have liked, naturally enough, to go to Nassau, but she never would have insisted. She was much too innocent to have any envious dreams of travel. Gee-Gee would have insisted that she go; he would have made the trip so tempting that she could not, in her innocence, resist it. Did he wish to be left alone, drunken and crippled, in an isolated house? Did he need to feel abused? It seemed so. The disorder of the house and the image of his wife and children running, running, running on some coral beach seemed like a successful contrivance—a kind of triumph.

Gee-Gee lit a cigarette and, forgetting about it, lit another, and fumbled so clumsily with the matches that Charlie saw that he might easily burn to death. Hoisting himself from the wagon to the chair, he nearly fell, and, if he were alone and fell, he could easily die of hunger and thirst on his own rug. But there might be some drunken cunning in his clumsiness, his playing with fire. He smiled slyly when he saw the look on Charlie's face. "Don't worry about me," he said. "I'll be all right. I have my guardian angel."

"That's what everybody thinks," Charlie said.

"Oh, but I have."

Outside, it had begun to snow. The winter sky was overcast, and it would soon be dark. Charlie said that he had to go. "Sit down," Gee-Gee said. "Sit down and have another drink." Charlie's conscience held him there a few moments longer. How could he openly abandon a friend—a neighbor, at least—to the peril of death? But he had no choice; his family was waiting and he had to go. "Don't worry about me," Gee-Gee said when Charlie was putting on his coat. "I have my angel."

It was later than Charlie had realized. The snow was heavy now, and he had a two-hour drive, on winding back roads. There was a little rise going out of Y———, and the new snow was so slick that he had trouble making the hill. There were steeper hills ahead of him. Only one of his windshield wipers worked, and the snow quickly covered the glass and left him with one small aperture onto the world. The snow sped into the headlights at a dizzying rate, and at one place where the road was narrow the car slid off onto the shoulder and he had to race the motor for ten minutes in order to get back onto the hard surface. It was a lonely stretch there—miles from any house—and he would have had a sloppy walk in his loafers. The car skidded and weaved up every hill, and it seemed that he reached the top by the thinnest margin of luck.

After driving for two hours, he was still far from home. The snow was so deep that guiding the car was like the trickiest kind of navigation. It took him three hours to get back, and he was tired when he drove into the darkness and peace of his own garage—tired and infinitely grateful. Martha and the children had eaten their supper, and she wanted to go over to the Lissoms' and discuss some school-board business. He told her that the driving was bad, and since it was such a short distance, she decided to walk. He lit a fire and made a drink, and the children sat at the table with him while he ate his supper. After supper on Sunday nights, the Folkestones played, or tried to play, trios. Charlie played the clarinet, his daughter played the piano, and his older son had a tenor recorder. The baby wandered around underfoot. This Sunday night they played simple arrangements of eighteenth-century music in the pleasantest family atmosphere—complimenting themselves when they squeezed through a difficult passage, and extending into the music what was best in their relationship. They were playing a Vivaldi sonata when the telephone rang. Charlie knew immediately who it was.

"Charlie, Charlie," Gee-Gee said. "Jesus. I'm in hot water. Right after you left I fell out of the God-damned wagon. It took me two hours to get to the telephone. You've got to get over. There's nobody else. You're my only friend. You've got to get over here. Charlie? You hear me?"

It must have been the strangeness of the look on Charlie's face that made the baby scream. The little girl picked him up in her arms. and stared, as did the other boy, at their father. They seemed to know the whole picture, every detail of it, and they looked at him calmly, as if they were expecting him to make some decision that had nothing to do with the continuing of a pleasant evening in a snowbound house—but a decision that would have a profound effect on their knowledge of him and on their final happiness. Their looks were, he thought, clear and appealing, and whatever he did would be final.

"You hear me, Charlie? You hear me?" Gee-Gee asked. "It took me damned near two hours to crawl over to the telephone. You've got to help me. No one else will come."

Charlie hung up. Gee-Gee must have heard the sound of his breathing and the baby crying, but Charlie had said nothing. He gave no explanation to the children, and they asked for none. They knew. His daughter went back to the piano, and when the telephone rang again and he did not answer it, no one questioned the ringing of the phone. They seemed happy and relieved when it stopped ringing, and they played Vivaldi until nine o'clock, when he sent them up to bed.

He made a drink to diminish the feeling that some emotional explosion had taken place, that some violence had shaken the air. He did not know what he had done or how to cope with his conscience. He would tell Martha about it when she came in, he thought. That would be a step toward comprehension. But when she returned he said nothing. He was afraid that if she brought her intelligence to the problem it would only confirm his guilt. "But why didn't you telephone me at the Lissoms'?" she might have asked. "I could have come home and you could have gone over." She was too compassionate a woman to accept passively, as he was doing, the thought of a friend, a neighbor, lying in agony. She went on upstairs. He poured some whiskey into his glass. If he had called the Lissoms', if she had returned to care for the children and left him free to help Gee-Gee, would he have been able to make the return trip in the heavy snow? He could have put on chains, but where were the chains? Were they in the car or in the cellar? He didn't know. He hadn't used them that year. But perhaps by now the roads would have been plowed. Perhaps the storm was over. This last, distressing possibility made him feel sick. Had the sky betrayed him? He switched on the outside light and went hesitantly, unwillingly, toward the window.

The clean snow gave off an ingratiating sparkle, and the beam of light shone into empty and peaceful air. The snow must have stopped a few minutes after he had entered the house. But how could he have known? How could he be expected to take into consideration the caprices of the weather? And what about that look the children had given him—so stern, so clear, so like a declaration that his place at that hour was with them, and not with the succoring of drunkards who had forfeited the chance to be taken seriously?

Then the image of Gee-Gee returned, crushing in its misery, and he remembered Peaches standing in the hallway at the Watermans' calling, "Come back! Come back!" She was calling back the youth that Charlie had never known, but it was easy to imagine what Gee-Gee must have been—fair, high-spirited, generous, and strong—and why had it all come to ruin? *Come back! Come back!* She seemed to call after the sweetness of a summer's day—roses in bloom and all the doors and windows open on the garden. It was all there in her voice; it was like the illusion of an abandoned house in the last rays of the sun. A large place, falling to pieces, haunted for children and a headache for the police and fire departments, but, seeing it with its windows blazing in the sunset, one thinks that they have all come back. Cook is in the kitchen rolling pastry. The smell of chicken rises up the back stairs. The front rooms are ready for the children and their many friends. A coal fire burns in the grate. Then as the light goes off the windows, the true ugliness of the place scowls into the dusk with redoubled force, as, when the notes of that long-ago summer left Peaches' voice, one saw the finality and confusion of despair in her innocent face. *Come back! Come back!* He poured himself some more whiskey, and as he raised the glass to his mouth he heard the wind change and saw—the outside light was still on—the snow begin to spin down again, with the vindictive swirl of a blizzard. The road was impassable; he could not have made the trip. The change in the weather had given him sweet absolution, and he watched the snow with a smile of love, but he stayed up until three in the morning with the bottle.

He was red-eyed and shaken the next morning, and ducked out of his office at eleven and drank two Martinis. He had two more before lunch and another at four and two on the train, and came reeling home for supper. The clinical details of heavy drinking are familiar to all of us; it is only the human picture that concerns us here, and Martha was finally driven to speak to him. She spoke most gently.

"You're drinking too much, darling," she said. "You've been drinking too much for three weeks."

"My drinking," he said, "is my own God-damned business. You mind your business and I'll mind mine."

It got worse and worse, and she had to do something. She finally went to their rector—a good-looking young bachelor who practiced both psychology and liturgy—for advice. He listened sympathetically. "I stopped at the rectory this afternoon," she said when she got home that night, "and I talked with Father Hemming. He wonders why you haven't been in church, and he wants to talk to you. He's such a good-looking man," she added, trying to make what she had just said sound less like a planned speech, "that I wonder why he's never married." Charlie—drunk, as usual—went to the telephone and called the rectory. "Look, Father," he said. "My wife tells me that you've been entertaining her in the afternoons. Well, I don't like it. You keep your hands off my wife. You hear me? That damned black suit you wear doesn't cut any ice with me. You keep your hands off my wife or I'll bust your pretty little nose."

In the end, he lost his job, and they had to move, and began their wanderings, like Gee-Gee and Peaches, in the scarlet-and-gold van.

AND WHAT HAPPENED to Gee-Gee—what ever became of him? That boozy guardian angel, her hair disheveled and the strings of her harp broken, still seemed to hover over where he lay. After telephoning Charlie that night, he telephoned the fire department. They were there in eight minutes flat, with bells ringing and sirens blowing. They got him into bed, made him a fresh drink, and one of the firemen, who had nothing better to do, stayed on until Peaches got back from Nassau. They had a fine time, eating all the steaks in the deep freeze and drinking a quart of bourbon every day. Gee-Gee could walk by the time Peaches and the children got back, and he took up that disorderly life for which he seemed so much better equipped than his neighbor, but they had to move at the end of the year, and, like the Folkestones, vanished from the hill towns.

JUST TELL ME WHO IT WAS

WILL PYM was a self-made man; that is, he had started his adult life without a nickel or a connection, other than the general friendliness of man to man, and had risen to a vice-presidency in a rayon-blanket firm. He made a large annual contribution to the Baltimore settlement house that had set his feet upon the right path, and he had a few anecdotes to tell about working as a farmhand long, long ago, but his appearance and demeanor were those of a well-established member of the upper class, with hardly a trace—hardly a trace of the anxieties of a man who had been through a grueling struggle to put some money into the bank. It is true that beggars, old men in rags, thinly dressed men and women eating bad food in the penitential lights of a cafeteria, slums and squalid mill towns, the faces in rooming-house windows—even a hole in his daughter's socks—could remind him of his youth and make him uneasy. He did not ever like to see the signs of poverty. He took a deep pleasure in the Dutch Colonial house where he lived—in its many lighted windows, in the soundness of his roof and his heating plant—in the warmth of his children's clothing, and in the fact that he had been able to make something plausible and coherent in spite of his mean beginnings. He was always conscious and sometimes mildly resentful of the fact that most of his business associates and all of his friends and neighbors had been skylarking on the turf at Groton or Deerfield or some such school while he was taking books on how to improve your grammar and vocabulary out of the public library. But he recognized this dim resentment of people whose development had been along easier lines than his own as some meanness in his character. Considering merely his physical bulk, it was astonishing that he should have preserved an image of himself as a hungry youth standing outside a lighted window in the rain. He was a cheerful, heavy man with a round face that looked exactly like a pudding. Everyone was glad to see him, as one is glad to see, at the end of a meal, the appearance of a bland, fragrant, and nourishing dish made of fresh eggs, nutmeg, and country cream.

Will had not married until he was past forty and had moved to New York. He had not had the money or the time, and the destitution of his youth had not been sweetened by much natural love. His stepmother—wearing a nightgown for comfort and a flowered hat for looks—had spent her days sitting in their parlor window in Baltimore drinking sherry out of a coffee cup. She was not a jolly old toper, and what she had to say was usually bitter. The picture she presented may have left with Will some skepticism about the emotional richness of human involvements. It may have delayed his marriage. When he finally did marry, he picked a woman much younger than he—a sweet-tempered girl with red hair and green eyes. She sometimes called him Daddy. Will was so proud of her and spoke so extravagantly of her beauty and her wit that when people first met her they were always disappointed. But Will had been poor and cold and alone, and when he came home at the end of the day to a lovely and loving woman, when he took off his hat and coat in the front hall, he would literally groan with joy. Every stick of furniture that Maria bought seemed to him to be hallowed by her taste and charm. A footstool or a set of pots would so delight him that he would cover her face and throat with kisses. She was extravagant, but he seemed to want a childish and capricious wife, and the implausible excuses that she made for having bought something needless and expensive aroused in him the deepest tenderness. Maria was not much of a cook, but when she put a plate of canned soup in front of him on the maid's night out, he would get up from his end of the table and embrace her with gratitude.

At first, they had a big apartment in the East Seventies. They went out a good deal. Will disliked parties, but he concealed this distaste for the sake of his young wife. At dinners, he would look across the table at her in the candlelight—laughing, talking, and flashing the rings he had bought her—and sigh deeply. He was always impatient for the party to end, so that they would be alone again, in a taxi or in an empty street where he could kiss her. When Maria first got pregnant, he couldn't describe his happiness. Every development in her condition astonished him. He was captivated by the preparations she made for the baby. When their first child was born, when milk flowed from her breasts, when their daughter excited in her a most natural tenderness, he was amazed.

The Pyms had three girls. When their third child was born, they moved to the suburbs. Will was past fifty then, but he carried Maria over the threshold, lighted a fire in the hearth, and observed all kinds of sentimental and amorous rites in taking possession of the house. To tell the truth, he did seem, once in a while, to talk about Maria too much. He was anxious to have her shine. At parties, he would stop the general conversation and announce, "Maria will now tell us something very funny that happened at the Women's Club this afternoon." Riding into town on the commuting train, he would ring in her opinions on the baseball season or the excise tax. Eating dinner alone in a hotel in Rochester or Toledo—for he often traveled on business—he would show the waitress a picture of Maria. When he served on the grand jury, all the other members of the panel knew about Maria long before the session ended. When he went salmon fishing in Newfoundland, he wondered constantly if Maria was all right.

On a Saturday in the early spring, they celebrated their tenth wedding anniversary with a party at their house in Shady Hill. Twenty-five or thirty people came to drink their health in champagne. Most of the guests were

Maria's age. Will did not like her to be surrounded by young men, and he supervised her comings and goings with a nearly paternal scrutiny. When she wandered out onto the terrace, he was not far behind. But he was a good host, he held in admirable equilibrium the pleasure he took in his guests and the pleasure he took in thinking that they soon would all be gone. He watched Maria talking with Henry Bulstrode across the room. He supposed that ten years of marriage must have left lines on her face and wasted her figure, but he could see only that her beauty had improved. A pretty young woman was talking with him, but his admiration of Maria made him absentminded. "You must get Maria to tell you what happened at the florist's this morning," he said.

Late on Sunday afternoon, the Pyms took a walk with their children, as they usually did when the weather was fair. It was that time of year when the woods are still bleak, and mixed with the smells of rotted and changing things is an unaccountable sweetness—a perfume as heavy as roses—although nothing is in flower. The children went on ahead. Will and Maria walked arm in arm. It was nearly dusk. Crows were calling hoarsely to one another in some tall pines. It was that hour of a spring day—or evening—when the dark of the woods and the cold and damp from any nearby pond or brook are suddenly felt, when you realize that the world was lighted, until a minute ago, merely by the sun's fire, and that your clothes are thin.

Will stopped and took a knife from his pocket and began to cut their initials in the bark of a tree. What sense would there be in pointing out that his hair was thin? He meant to express love. It was Maria's youth and beauty that had informed his sense and left his mind so open that the earth seemed spread out before his eyes like a broad map of reason and sensuality. It was her company that made the singing of the crows so fine to hear. For his children, whose voices sounded down the path, he held out the most practical and abundant hopes. All that he had ever been deprived of was now his.

But Maria was cold and tired and hungry. They had not gone to bed until two, and it had been an effort for her to keep her eyes open while they walked in the woods. When they got home, she would have to fix the supper. Cold cuts or lamb chops, she wondered while she watched Will enclose their initials in the outline of a heart and pierce it with an arrow. "Oh, you're so lovely!" she heard him murmur when he had finished. "You're so young and beautiful!" He groaned; he took her in his arms and kissed her wildly. She went on worrying about the supper.

On a Monday night not long after this, Maria sat in the living room tying paper apple blossoms to branches. She was on the committee in charge of decorations for the Apple Blossom Fete, a costume ball given for charity at the country club each year. Will was reading a magazine while he waited for her to finish her work. He wore bedroom slippers and a red brocade smoking jacket—a present from Maria—which bunched in thick folds around his stomach, making him look portly. Maria's hands moved quickly. When she had covered a branch with blossoms, she would hold it up and say, "Isn't that pretty?" Then she would stand it in a corner where there was the beginning of a forest of flowering branches. Upstairs, the three children slept.

The decorations-committee job was the kind of thing Maria did best. She did not like to go to early-morning meetings on the reform of the primary system, or to poke her nose into dirty hospital kitchens, or to meet with other women in the late afternoons to discuss trends in modern fiction. She had tried being secretary of the Women's Club, but her minutes were so garbled that she had had to be replaced—not without some hard feeling. On the evening of the day when she was relieved of her position, Will had found her in tears, and it had taken him hours to console her. He relished these adversities. She was young and beautiful, and anything that turned her to him for succor only made his position more secure. Later, when Maria was put in charge of the mink-stole raffle to raise some money for the hospital, she had kept such poor records that Will had had to stay home from the office for a day to straighten things out. She cried and he comforted her, where a younger husband might have expressed some impatience. Will did not encourage her inefficiency, but it was a trait that he associated with the fineness of her eyes and her pallor.

While she tied flowers she talked about the fete. There was going to be a twelve-piece orchestra. The decorations had never been so beautiful. They hoped to raise ten thousand dollars. The dressmaker had delivered her costume. Will asked what her costume was, and she said she would go upstairs and put it on. She usually went to the Apple Blossom Fete as a figure from French history, and Will's interest was not intense.

Half an hour later, she came down, and went to the mirror by the piano. She was wearing gold slippers, pink tights, and a light velvet bodice, cut low enough to show the division of her breasts. "Of course, my hair will be all different," she said. "And I haven't decided what jewels to wear."

A terrible sadness came over Will. The tight costume—he had to polish his eyeglasses to see it better—displayed all the beauty he worshipped, and it also expressed her perfect innocence of the wickedness of the world. The sight filled poor Will with lust and dismay. He couldn't bear to disappoint her, and yet he couldn't let her flagrantly provoke his neighbors—a group of men who seemed at that moment, to his unsettled mind, to be voracious, youthful, bestial, and lewd. Watching her pose happily in front of the mirror, he thought that she looked like a child—a maiden, at least—approaching some obscene doom. In her sweet and gentle face and her half-naked bosom he saw all the sadness of life.

"You can't wear that, Mummy," he said.

"What?" She turned away from the mirror.

"Mummy, you'll get pinched to death."

"Everybody else is going to wear tights, Willy. Helen Benson and Grace Heatherstone are going to wear tights."

"They're different, Mummy," he said sadly. "They're very different. They're tough, hardheaded, cynical, worldly women."

"What am I?"

"You're lovely and you're innocent," he said. "You don't understand what a bunch of dogs men are."

"I don't want to be lovely and innocent all the time."

"Oh, Mummy, you don't mean that! You can't mean that! You don't know what you're saying."

"I only want to have a good time."

"Don't you have a good time with me?"

She began to cry. She threw herself on the sofa and buried her face. Her tears ate like acid into Will's resolve as he bent over her slender and miserable form. Years and years ago he had wondered if a young wife would give him trouble. Now, with his eyeglasses steaming and the brocade jacket bunched up around his stomach, he stood face to face with the problem. How—even when they were in grave danger—could he refuse innocence and beauty? "All right, Mummy, all right," he said. He was nearly in tears himself. "You can wear it."

WILL LEFT the next morning for a trip that took him to Cleveland, Chicago, and Topeka. He called Maria on Tuesday and Wednesday nights, and the maid said that she was out. She would be putting up the decorations in the club, he realized. The pancakes he ate for breakfast on Thursday disagreed with him at once, and gave him a stomach ache that none of the many medicines he carried with him in his suitcase could cure. Friday was foggy in Kansas, and his plane was grounded until late that night. At the airport, he ate some chicken pie; it made him feel worse. He arrived in New York on Saturday morning, and had to go directly to his office, and did not get out to Shady Hill until late Saturday afternoon. It was the day of the party, and Maria was still at the club. He spent an hour raking dead leaves from the flower beds at the side of the house. When Maria came home, he thought she looked superb. Her color was high and her eyes were bright.

She showed Will the costume she had rented for him. It was a suit of chain mail with a helmet. Will was pleased with the costume, because it was a disguise. Exhausted and bilious, he felt he needed a disguise for the dance. When he had bathed and shaved, Maria helped him strap himself into his coat of mail. She cut some ostrich plumes off an old hat and stuck them gaily into his helmet. Will went toward a mirror to see himself, but just as he got there, the visor slammed shut, and he couldn't get it to stay open. He went downstairs, holding on to the banister—the chain mail was heavy—and wedged the visor open with a folded timetable and sat down to have a drink. When Maria came down in her pink tights and her gold slippers, Will rose to admire her. She said that she would not be able to leave the dance early, because she was on the committee; if Will wanted to go home, she would get a ride with someone else. He had never gone home from a party without her, and he hated the idea. Maria put on a wrap and kissed the children, and they went off to dinner at the Beardens'.

At the Beardens', the party was large and late. They drank cocktails until after nine. When they went in to dinner, Will sat beside Ethel Worden. She was a pretty young woman, but she had been drinking Martinis for two hours; her face was drawn and her eyes were red. She said that she loved Will, that she always had, but Will was looking down the table at Maria. Even at that distance, he seemed to take in something vital from the play of shadow upon her face. He would have liked to be near enough to hear what she was saying.

Ethel Worden didn't make it any easier. "We're poor, Will," she said sadly. "Did you know that we're poor? Nobody realizes that there are people like us in a community like this. We can't afford eggs for breakfast. We can't afford a cleaning woman. We can't afford a washing machine. We can't afford . . ."

Before dessert was finished, several couples got up to leave for the club. Will saw Trace Bearden handing Maria her wrap, and got up suddenly. He wanted to get to the club in time to have the first dance with her. When he got outside, Trace and Maria had gone. He asked Ethel Worden to drive over with him. She was delighted. As he put the car in the parking lot at the country club, Ethel began to cry. She was poor and lonely and hungry for love. She drew Will to her and wept on his chain-mail shoulder, while he looked out the back windows of the station wagon to see if he could recognize Trace Bearden's car. He wondered if Maria was already in the clubhouse or if she was having trouble in a parked car herself. He dried Ethel's tears and spoke to her tenderly, and they went in.

It was late by then—it was after midnight—and that

dance was always a rhubarb. The floor was crowded, and plumes, crowns, animal heads, and turbans were rocking in the dim light. It was that hour when the band accelerates its beat, when the drums deepen, when the aging dancers utter loud cries of lust and joy, seize their partners by the girdle, and break into all kinds of youthful and wanton specialities—the shimmy, the Charleston, hops, and belly dances. Will danced clumsily in his mail. Now and then, he glimpsed Maria in the distance, but he was never able to catch up with her. Going into the bar for a drink, he saw her at the other end of the room, but the crowd was too dense for him to get to her. She was surrounded by men. He looked for her in the lounge during the next intermission, but he could not find her. When the music started again, he gave the band ten dollars and asked them to play "I Could Write a Book." It was their music. She would hear it through the bedlam. It would remind her of their marrage, and she would leave her partner and find him. He waited alone at the edge of the floor through this song.

Discouraged, then, and tired from his traveling and the weight of his chain mail, he went into the lounge, took off his helmet, and fell asleep. When he woke, a half hour later, he saw Larry Helmsford taking Ethel Worden out the terrace door toward the parking lot. She was staggering. Will wandered back to the ballroom, drawn there by shouts of excitement. Someone had set fire to a feathered headdress. The fire was being put out with champagne. It was after three o'clock. Will put on his helmet, propped the visor open with a folded match paper, and went home.

Maria danced the last dance. She had a drink from the last bottle of wine. It was morning then. The band had gone, but a pianist was still playing and a few couples were dancing in the daylight. Breakfast parties were forming, but she refused these invitations in order to drive home with the Beardens. Will might be worried. After she said goodbye to the Beardens, she stood on her front steps to get some air. She had lost her pocketbook. Her tights had been torn by the scales of a dragon. The smell of spilled wine came from her clothes. The sweetness of the air and the fineness of the light touched her. The party seemed like gibberish. She had had all the partners she wanted, but she had not had all the right ones. The hundreds of apple blossoms that she had tied to branches and that had looked, at a distance, so like real blossoms would soon be swept into the ash can.

The trees of Shady Hill were filled with birds—larks, thrushes, robins, crows—and now the air began to ring with their song. The pristine light and the loud singing reminded her of some ideal—some simple way of life, in which she dried her hands on an apron and Will came home from the sea—that she had betrayed. She did not know where he had failed, but the gentle morning light illuminated her failure pitilessly. She began to cry.

Will was asleep, but he woke when she opened the front door. "Mummy?" he asked as she climbed the stairs. "Mummy? . . . Hello, Mummy. Good morning!" She didn't reply.

He saw her tears, the gash in her tights, and the stains on her front. She sat down at her dressing table, laid her face on the glass, and went on crying. "Oh, don't cry, Mummy!" he said. "Don't cry! I don't care, Mummy. I thought I would but I guess it doesn't really matter. I won't ever mention it, Mummy. Now, come to bed. Come to bed and get some sleep."

Her sobbing got louder. He got up and went to the dressing table and put his arms around her. "I told you what would happen if you wore that costume, didn't I? But it doesn't matter any more. I'll never ask you anything about it. I'll forget the whole thing. But come to bed now and get some sleep."

Her head was swimming, and his voice droned on and on, shutting out the noises of the morning. Then his anxious love, his nagging passion, were more than she could support. "I don't care. I'm willing to forget it," he said.

She got out of his embrace, crossed the room to the hall, and shut the guest-room door in his face.

DOWNSTAIRS, sitting over a cup of coffee, Will realized that his supervision of Maria's life had been anything but thorough. If she had wanted to deceive him, her life couldn't have been planned along more convenient lines. In the summer, she was alone most of the time, except weekends. He was away on business one week out of every month. She went to New York whenever she pleased—sometimes in the evening. Only a week before the dance she had gone into town to have dinner with some old friends. She had planned to come home on a train that reached Shady Hill at eleven. Will drove to the station to meet her. It was a rainy night and he remembered waiting, in a rather gloomy frame of mind, on the station platform. As soon as he saw the distant lights of the train, his mood was changed by the anticipation of greeting her and taking her home. When the train stopped and only Charlie Curtin—half tipsy—got off, Will was disappointed and worried. Soon after he got home, the telephone rang. It was Maria calling to say that she had missed the train and would not be home until two. At two, Will returned to the station. It was still rainy. Maria and Henry Bulstrode were the only passengers. She walked swiftly up the platform in the rain to kiss Will. He remembered that there had been tears in her eyes, but he had not thought anything about it at the time. Now he wondered about her tears.

A few nights before that, she had said, after dinner, that she wanted to go to the movies in the village. Will had offered to take her, although he was tired, but she said she knew how much he disliked movies. It had seemed odd to him at the time that before going off to the nine o'clock show she should take a bath, and when she came downstairs, he heard, under her mink coat, the rustling of a new dress. He fell asleep before she returned, and for all he knew, she might have come in at dawn. It had always seemed generous of her not to insist on his going with her to meetings of the Civic Improvement Association, but how did he know whether she had gone off to discuss the fluorination of water or to meet a lover?

He remembered something that had happened in February. The Women's Club had given a revue for charity. He had known before he went to it that Maria was going to do a dance expressing the views of the Current Events Committee on the tariff. She came onto the stage to the music of "A Pretty Girl Is Like a Melody." She wore a long evening dress, gloves, and a fur piece—the recognizable getup of a striptease artist—and, to his dismay, she was given a rousing reception. Maria walked around the stage and took off her fur piece, to applause, shouts, and some whistling. During the next chorus, she peeled off her gloves. Will pretended to be enjoying himself, but he had begun to sweat. With the third chorus, she took off her belt. This was all, but the uproarious applause she had been given rang again in Will's ears now and made them warm.

A few weeks earlier, Will had gone uptown for lunch—a thing he seldom did. Walking down Madison Avenue, he thought he saw Maria ahead of him, with another man. The dark-red suit, the fur piece, and the hat were hers. He did not recognize the man. Acting impulsively where he might have acted stealthily, he had shouted her name—"Maria! Maria! Maria!" The street was crowded, and there was the distance of half a block between them. Before he could reach the woman, she had disappeared. She might have stepped into a taxi or a store. That evening, when he said to Maria, cheerfully enough, that he thought he saw her on Madison Avenue, she answered crossly, "Well, you didn't." After dinner, she claimed to have a headache. She asked him to sleep in the guest room.

The afternoon of the day after the dance, Will took the children for a walk without Maria. He lectured them, as he always did, on the names of the trees. "That's a ginkgo. . . . That's a weeping beech. . . . That bitter smell comes from the boxwood in the hollow." It may have been because he had received no education himself that he liked to give an educational tone to his time with the children. They recited the states of the Union at the lunch table, discussed geology during some of their walks, and named the stars in the sky if they stayed out after dusk. Will was determined to be cheerful this afternoon, but the figures of his children, walking ahead, saddened him, for they seemed like live symbols of his trouble. He had not actually thought of leaving Maria—he had not let the idea form—but he seemed to breathe the atmosphere of separation. When he passed the tree where he had carved their initials, he thought of the stupendous wickedness of the world.

The house was dark when they came back up the driveway at the end of their walk—dark and cold. Will turned on some lights and heated the coffee he had made at breakfast. The telephone rang, but he did not answer it. He took a cup of coffee up to the guest room, where Maria was. He thought at first she was still sleeping. When he turned on the lights, he saw that she was sitting against the pillows. She smiled, but he responded warily to her charm.

"Here's some coffee, Mummy."

"Thank you. Did you have a nice walk?"

"Yes."

"I feel better," she said. "What time is it?"

"Half past five."

"I don't feel strong enough to go to the Townsends'."

"Then I won't go."

"Oh, I wish you would, Willy. Please go to the party and come home and tell me all about it. Please go."

Now that she urged him, the party seemed like a good idea.

"You must go, Will," Maria said. "There'll be a lot of gossip about the dance, and you can hear it all, and then you can come home and tell me all about it. Please go to the party, darling. It will make me feel guilty if you stay home on my account."

At the Townsends', cars were parked on both sides of the street, and all the windows of the big house were brightly lighted. Will stepped in the lamplight, the firelight, and the cheerful human noises of the gathering with a sincere desire to lose his heaviness of spirit. He went upstairs to leave his coat. Bridget, an old Irishwoman, took it. She was a free-lance maid who worked at most of the big parties in Shady Hill. Her husband was caretaker at the country club. "So your lady isn't with you," she said in her sweet brogue. "Ah, well, I can't say that I blame her." Then she laughed suddenly. She put her hands on her knees and rocked back and forth. "I shouldn't tell you, I know, so help me God, but when Mike was sweeping up the parking lot this morning, he found a pair of gold slippers and a blue lace girdle."

Downstairs, Will spoke with his hostess, and she said she was so sorry that Maria hadn't come. Crossing the living room, he was stopped by Pete Parsons, who drew him over to the fireplace and told him a joke. This was what Will had come for, and his spirits began to improve. But, going from Pete Parsons toward the door of the bar, he found his way blocked by Biff Worden. Ethel's story of their neediness, her tears, and her trip to the parking lot with Larry Helmsford were still fresh in his mind. He did not want to see Biff Worden. He did not like it that Biff could muster a cheerful and open face after his wife had been seduced in the Helmsfords' station wagon.

"Did you hear what Mike Reilly found in the parking lot this morning?" Biff asked. "A pair of slippers and a girdle." Will said that he wanted a drink, and he got past Biff, but the entrance to the passage between the living room and the bar was blocked by the Chesneys.

In almost every suburb there is a charming young couple designated by their gifts to be an ambassadorial pair. They are the ones who meet John Mason Brown at the train and drive him to the auditorium. They are the ones who organize the bumper tennis tournaments, handle the most difficult cases in the fund-raising campaign, and can be counted on by their hostesses to humor the bore, pass the stuffed celery, breathe fire into the dying conversation, and expel the drunk. Their social and family connections are indescribably rich and varied, and physically they are models of attractiveness and fashion—direct, mild, well groomed, their eyes twinkling with trust and friendliness. Such a young couple were the Chesneys.

"So glad to see you," Mark Chesney said, removing his pipe from his mouth and putting a hand on Will's shoulder. "Missed you at the dance last night, although I saw Maria enjoying herself. But what I wanted to speak to you about is something of a higher order. Give me a minute? As you may or may not know, I'm in charge of the adult-education program at the high school this year. We've had a disappointing attendance, and we have a speaker coming on Thursday for whom I'm anxious to rustle up a sizable audience. Her name is Mary Bickwald, and she's going to speak on marriage problems—extramarital affairs, that sort of thing. If you and Maria are free on Thursday, I think you'll find it worth your time." The Chesneys went on into the living room, and Will continued toward the bar.

The bar was full of a noisy and pleasant company, and Will was glad to join it and get a drink. He had begun to feel like himself when the rector of Christ Church bore down on him, shook his hand, and drew him away from the others.

The rector was a large man and, unlike some of his suburban colleagues, not at all wary of clerical black. When he and Will met at cocktail parties, they usually talked about blankets. Will had given many blankets to the church. He had given blankets to its missions and blankets to its shelters. When the shepherds knelt in the straw at Mary's knees in the Nativity play, they were clothed in Will's blankets. Since he expected to be asked for blankets, he was surprised to hear the rector say, "I want you to feel free to come to my study, Will, and talk to me if anything is troubling you." While Will was thanking the rector for this invitation, they were joined by Herbert McGrath.

Herbert McGrath was a banker, a wealthy, irritable man. At the bottom of his thinking there seemed to be an apprehension—a nightmare—that without the kind of order he represented, the world would fly apart. He despised men who raced to catch the morning train. In the "no smoking" car, it was customary for people to light cigarettes as the train approached Grand Central Station, and this infringement so irritated Herbert that he would tap his neighbors on the shoulder and tell them that the smoker was in the rear. Mixed with his insistence on propriety was a curious strain of superstition. When he walked along the station platform in the morning, he looked around him. If he saw a coin, he would shoulder his way past the other commuters and bend down to get it. "Good luck, you know," he would explain as he put the coin in his pocket. "You need both luck *and* brains." Now he wanted to talk about the immorality at the party, and Will decided to go home.

He put his glass on the bar and started thoughtfully through the passage to the living room. His head was down, and he walked straight into Mrs. Walpole, a very plain woman. "I see that your wife hasn't recovered sufficiently to face the public today," she said gaily.

A peculiar fate seems to overtake homely women at the ends of parties—and journeys, too. Their curls and their ribbons come undone, particles of food cling to their teeth, their glasses steam, and the wide smile with which they planned to charm the world lapses into a look of habitual discontent and bitterness. Mrs. Walpole had got herself up bravely for the Townsends' party, but time itself—she was drinking sherry—had destroyed the impression she intended to make. Someone seemed to have sat on her hat, her voice was strident, and the camellia pinned to her shoulder had died.

"But I suppose Maria sent you to see what they're saying about her," she said.

Will got past Mrs. Walpole and went up the stairs to get his coat. Bridget had gone, and Helen Bulstrode was sitting alone in the hall in a red dress. Helen was a lush. She was treated kindly in Shady Hill. Her husband was pleasant, wealthy, and forbearing. Now Helen was very drunk, and whatever she had meant to forget when she first poured herself a drink that day had long since been lost in the clutter. She rolled a little in her chair while Will was putting on his coat, and suddenly she addressed him copiously in French. Will did not understand. Her voice got louder and angrier, and when he got down to the hall, she went to the head of the stairs to call after him. He went off without saying goodbye to anyone.

MARIA was in the living room reading a magazine when Will came in. "Look, Mummy," he said. "Can you tell me this? Did you lose your shoes last night?"

"I lost my pocketbook," Maria said, "but I don't think I lost my shoes."

"Try and remember," he said. "It isn't like a raincoat or an umbrella. People usually remember when they lose their shoes."

"What is the matter with you, Willy?"

"Did you lose your shoes?"

"I don't know."

"Did you wear a girdle?"

"What are you talking about, Will?"

"By Christ, I've got to find out!"

He went upstairs to their room, which was dark. He turned on a light in her closet and opened the chest where she kept her shoes. There were a great many pairs, and among them were gold shoes, silver shoes, bronze shoes, and he was shuffling through the collection when he saw Maria standing in the doorway. "Oh, my God, Mummy, forgive me!" he said. "Forgive me!"

"Oh, Willie!" she exclaimed. "Look what you've done to my shoes."

WILL FELT all right in the morning, and he had a good day in the city. At five, he made the trip uptown on the subway and crossed the station to his train automatically. In the train, he got an aisle seat and scanned the asininities in the evening paper. An old man was suing his young wife for divorce, on the ground of adultery; the fact that this story had no power to disturb Will not only pleased him but left him feeling exceptionally fit and happy. The train traveled north under a sky that was still spread with light.

A little rain had begun to fall when Will stepped onto the platform at Shady Hill. "Hello. Trace," he said. "Hello, Pete. Hello, Herb." Around him, his neighbors were greeting their wives and children. He took the route up Alewives Lane to Shadrock Road, past rows and rows of lighted houses. He put his car in the garage and went around to the front and looked at his tulips, gleaming in the rain and the porch light. He let the fawning cat in out of the wet, and Flora, his youngest daughter, ran through the hall to kiss him. Some deep recess in his spirit seemed to respond to the good child and the light-filled rooms. He had the feeling that there would never be any less to his life than this. Presently, he would be sitting on a folding chair in the June sunlight watching Flora graduate from Smith.

Maria came into the hall wearing a gray silk dress—a cloth and a color that flattered her. Her eyes were bright and wide, and she kissed him tenderly. The telephone began to ring, for it was that hour in the suburbs when the telephone rings steadily with board-meeting announcements, scraps of gossip, fund-raising pleas, and invitations. Maria answered it and he heard her say, "Yes, Edith."

Will went into the living room to make a cocktail, and a few minutes later the doorbell rang. Edith Hastings, a good neighbor and a friendly woman, preceded Maria into the living room, protesting, "I really shouldn't break in on you like this." Still protesting, she sat down and took the glass that Will handed her. He had never seen her color so high or her eyes so bright. "Charlie's in Oregon," she said.

"He'll be gone three weeks this trip. He wanted me to speak to you, Will, about some apple trees. He meant to speak to you before he left, but he didn't have the time. He can get apple trees by the dozen from a nursery in New Jersey, and he wanted to know if you wouldn't like to buy six."

Edith Hastings was one of those women—and there were many of them in Shady Hill—whose husbands were away on business from one to three weeks out of every month. They lived—conjugally—the life of a Grand Banks fisherman's wife, with none of the lore of ships and sailors to draw on. None—or almost none—of these widows could be accused of not having attacked their problems gallantly. They solicited funds for cancer, heart trouble, lameness, deafness, and mental health. They cultivated tropical plants in a capricious climate, wove cloth, made pottery, cared tenderly for their children, and did everything imaginable to make up for the irremediable absence of their men. They remained lonely women with a natural proneness to gossip.

"But of course you don't have to decide this minute," Edith went on when he didn't answer her question. "I don't suppose you really have to decide until Charlie comes back from Oregon. I mean, there isn't any special time for planting apple trees, is there? And, speaking of apple trees, how was the fete?"

Will turned his back and opened a window. Outside, the rain fell steadily, but he doubted than that it was the rain that had heightened Edith's color and made her eyes shine. He heard Maria reply, and then he heard Edith ask, "When did you people leave?" She could not keep the excitement out of her voice. "And I understand that a pair of slippers and a girdle—"

Will swung around. "Is that what you came here to talk about?" he asked sharply.

"What?"

"Is that what you came here to talk about?"

"I really came here to talk about apple trees."

"I gave Charlie a check for those apple trees six months ago."

"Charlie didn't tell me."

"Why should he? It was all settled."

"Well, I guess I'd better go."

"Please do," Will said. "Please go. And if anyone asks how we are, tell them we're getting along fine."

"Oh, Will, Will, Will!" Maria said.

"I seem to have come at the wrong time," Edith said.

"And when you call the Trenchers and the Farquarsons and the Abbotts and the Beardens, tell them that I don't give a good goddamn what happened at the party. Tell them to think up some gossip about someone else. Tell them to imagine some filth about the Fuller Brush man or the chump who delivers eggs on Friday or the Slaters' gardener, but tell them to leave us alone."

She was gone. Maria, crying, looked at him so wantonly that he nearly choked. Then she climbed the stairs in her gray silk dress and shut the door to their room. He followed her and found her lying on their bed in the dark. "Who was it, Mummy?" he asked. "Just tell me who it was and I'll forget about it."

"It wasn't anybody," she said. "There wasn't anybody."

"Now, Mummy," he said heavily. "I know better than that. I don't want to reproach you. That isn't why I asked. I just want to know so I can forget about it."

"Please let me alone!" she cried. "Please let me alone for a little while."

WAKING AT DAWN in the guest room, Will saw the whole thing clearly. He was astonished to realize how the strength of his feeling had obstructed his vision. The villain was Henry Bulstrode. It was Henry who had been with her on the train when she returned that rainy night at two. It was Henry who had whistled when she did her dance at the Women's Club. It was Henry's head and shoulders he had seen on Madison Avenue when he recognized Maria ahead of him. And now he remembered poor Helen Bulstrode's haggard face at the Townsends' party—the face of a woman who was married to a libertine. It was her husband's unregeneracy that she had been trying to forget. The spate of drunken French she had aimed at him must have been about Maria and Henry. Henry Bulstrode's face, grinning with naked and lascivious mockery, appeared in the middle of the guest room. There was only one thing to do.

Will bathed, dressed, and ate his breakfast. Maria slept on. It was still early when he finished his coffee, and he decided to walk to the train. He strode down Shadrock Road with the peculiar briskness of the aging. Only a few people had gathered on the platform for the eight-nineteen when he reached the station. Trace Bearden joined him, and then Biff Worden. And then Henry Bulstrode stepped out of the waiting room, showed his white teeth in a smile, and frowned at his newspaper. Without any warning at all, Will walked over to him and knocked him down. Women screamed, and the scuffle that followed was very confusing. Herbert McGrath, who had missed the action, assumed that Henry had started it and stood over him saying, "No more of this, young man! No more of this!" Trace and Biff pinned Will's arms to his sides and quick-stepped him down to the far end of the platform, asking, "You crazy, Will? Have you gone crazy?" Then the eight-nineteen came around the bend, the fracas was suspended by the search for seats, and when the stationmaster rushed out onto the platform to see what was happening, the train had departed and they were all gone.

The amazing thing was how well Will felt when he boarded the train. Now his fruitful life with Maria would be resumed. They would walk on Sunday afternoon again, and play word games by the open fire again, and weed the roses again, and love one another under the sounds of the rain again, and hear the singing of the crows; and he would buy her a present that afternoon as a signal of love and forgiveness. He would buy her pearls or gold or sapphires—something expensive; emeralds maybe; something no young man could afford.

BRIMMER

NO ONE IS INTERESTED in a character like Brimmer because the facts are indecent and obscene; but come then out of the museums, gardens, and ruins where obscene facts are as numerous as daisies in Nantucket. In the dense population of statuary around the Mediterranean shores there are more satyrs than there are gods and heroes. Their general undesirability in organized society only seems to have whetted their aggressiveness and they are everywhere; they are in Paestum and Syracuse and in the rainy courts and porches north of Florence. They are even in the gardens of the American Embassy. I don't mean those pretty boys with long ears—although Brimmer may have been one of those in the beginning. I mean the older satyrs with lined faces and conspicuous tails. They always carry grapes or pipes, and the heads are up and back in attitudes of glee. Aside from the long ears, the faces are never animal—these are the faces of men, sometimes comely and youthful, but advanced age does not change in any way the lively cant of the head and the look of lewd glee.

I speak of a friend, an acquaintance anyhow—a shipboard acquaintance on a rough crossing from New York to Naples. These were his attitudes in the bar where I mostly saw him. His eyes had a pale, horizontal pupil like a goat's eye. Laughing eyes, you might have said, although they were sometimes very glassy. As for the pipes, he played, so far as I know, no musical instrument; but the grapes could be accounted for by the fact that he almost always had a glass in his hand. Many of the satyrs stand on one leg with the other crossed over in front—toe down, heel up—and that's the way he stood at the bar, his legs crossed, his head up in that look of permanent glee, and the grapes, so to speak, in his right hand. He was lively—witty and courteous and shrewd—but had he been much less I would have been forced to drink and talk with him anyhow. Excepting Mme. Troyan, there was no one else on board I would talk with.

How dull travel really is! How, at noon, when the whistle sounds and the band plays and the confetti has been thrown, we seem to have been deceived into joining something that subsists upon the patronage of the lonely and the lost—the emotionally second-rate of all kinds. The whistle blows again. The gangways and the lines are cleared and the ship begins to move. We see the faces of our dearly beloved friends and relations rubbed out by distance, and going over to the port deck to make profoundly emotional farewell to the New York skyline we find the buildings hidden in rain. Then the chimes sound and we go below to eat a heavy lunch. Obsolescence might explain that chilling unease we experience when we observe the elegance of the lounges and the wilderness of the sea. What will we do between now and tea? Between tea and dinner? Between dinner and the horse races? What will we do between here and landfall?

She was the oldest ship of the line and was making that April her last Atlantic crossing. Many seasoned travelers came down to say goodbye to her famous interiors and to filch an ashtray or two, but they were sentimentalists to a man, and when the go-ashore was sounded they all went ashore, leaving the rest of us, so to speak, alone. It was a cheerless, rainy midday with a swell in the channel and, beyond the channel, gale winds and high seas. Her obsolescence you could see at once was more than a matter of marble fireplaces and grand pianos. She was a tub. It was not possible to sleep on the first night out, and going up on deck in the morning I saw that one of the lifeboats had been damaged in the gale. Below me, in second class, some undiscourageable travelers were trying to play Ping-Pong in the rain. It was a bleak scene to look at and a hopeless prospect for the players and they finally gave up. A few minutes later a miscalculation of the helmsman sent a wall of water up the side of the ship and filled the stern deck with a boiling sea. Up swam the Ping-Pong table and, as I watched, it glided overboard and could be seen bobbing astern in the wake, a reminder of how mysterious the world must seem to a man lost overboard.

Below, all the portable furniture had been corralled and roped together as if this place were for sale. Ropes were strung along all the passageways, and all the potted palm trees had been put into some kind of brig. It was hot—terribly hot and humid—and the elegant lounges, literally abandoned and very much abandoned in their atmosphere, seemed to be made, if possible, even more forlorn by the continuous music of the ship's orchestra. They began to play that morning and they played for the rest of the voyage and they played for no one. They played day and night to those empty rooms where the chairs were screwed to the floor. They played opera. They played old dance music. They played selections from *Show Boat*. Above the crashing of the mountainous seas there was always this wild, tiresome music in the air. And there was really nothing to do. You couldn't write letters, everything tipped so; and if you sat in a chair to read, it would withdraw itself from you and then rush up to press itself against you like some apple-tree swing. You couldn't play cards, you couldn't play chess, you couldn't even play Scrabble. The grayness, the thinly jubilant and continuous music, and the roped-up furniture all made it seem like an unhappy dream, and I wandered around like a dreamer until twelve-thirty, when I went into the bar. The regulars in the bar then were a Southern family—Mother, Father, Sister, and Brother. They were going abroad for a year. Father had retired and this was their first trip. There were also a couple of women whom the bartender identified as a "Roman businesswoman" and her secretary. And there was Brimmer, myself, and presently Mme. Troyan. I had drinks with Brimmer on the second day out. He was a man of about my age, I should say, slender, with well-kept hands that were, for some reason, noticeable, and a light but never monotonous voice and a charming sense of urgency—liveliness—that seemed to have nothing to do with nervousness. We had lunch and dinner together and drank in the bar after dinner. We knew the same places, but none of the same people, and yet he seemed to be an excellent companion. When we went below—he had the cabin next to mine—I was contented to have found someone I could talk with for the next ten days.

Brimmer was in the bar the next day at noon, and while we were there Mme. Troyan looked in. Brimmer invited her to join us and she did. At my ripe age, Mme. Troyan's age meant nothing. A younger man might have placed her in her middle thirties and might have noticed that the lines around her eyes were ineradicable. For me these lines meant only a proven capacity for wit and passion. She was a charming woman who did not mean to be described. Her dark hair, her pallor, her fine arms, her vivacity, her sadness when the bartender told us about his sick son in Genoa, her impersonations of the captain—the impression of a lovely and a brilliant woman who was accustomed to seeming delightful was not the listed sum of her charms.

We three had lunch and dinner together and danced in

the ballroom after dinner—we were the only dancers—but when the music stopped and Brimmer and Mme. Troyan started back to the bar I excused myself and went down to bed. I was pleased with the evening and when I closed my cabin door I thought how pleasant it would have been to have Mme. Troyan's company. This was, of course, impossible, but the memory of her dark hair and her white arms was still strong and cheering when I turned out the light and got into bed. While I waited patiently for sleep it was revealed to me that Mme. Troyan was in Brimmer's cabin.

I was indignant. She had told me that she had a husband and three children in Paris—and what, I thought, about them? She and Brimmer had only met by chance that morning and what carnal anarchy would crack the world if all such chance meetings were consummated! If they had waited a day or two—long enough to give at least the appearance of founding their affair on some romantic or sentimental basis—I think I would have found it more acceptable. To act so quickly seemed to me skeptical and depraved. Listening to the noise of the ship's motors and the faint sounds of tenderness next door, I realized that I had left my way of life a thousand knots astern and that there is no inclination to internationalism in my disposition. They were both, in a sense, Europeans.

But the sounds next door served as a kind of trip wire: I seemed to stumble and fall on my face, skinning and bruising myself here and there and scattering my emotional and intellectual possessions. There was no point in pretending that I had not fallen, for when we are stretched out in the dirt we must pick ourselves up and brush off our clothes. This then, in a sense, is what I did, reviewing my considered opinions of marriage, constancy, man's nature, and the importance of love. When I had picked up my possessions and repaired my appearance, I fell asleep.

It was dark and rainy in the morning—now the wind was cold—and I walked around the upper deck, four laps to the mile, and saw no one. The immorality next door would have changed my relationship to Brimmer and Mme. Troyan, but I had no choice but to look forward to meeting them in the bar at noon. I had no resources to enliven a deserted ship and a stormy sea. My depraved acquaintances were in the bar when I went there at half past twelve, and they had ordered a drink for me. I was content to be with them and thought perhaps they regretted what they had done. We lunched together, amiably, but when I suggested that we find a fourth and play some bridge Brimmer said that he had to send some cables and Mme. Troyan wanted to rest. There was no one in the lounges or on the decks after lunch, and when the orchestra began, dismally, to tune up for their afternoon concert, I went down to my cabin where I discovered that Brimmer's cables and Mme. Troyan's rest were both fabrications, meant, I suppose, to deceive me. She was in his cabin again. I went up and took a long walk around the deck with an Episcopalian clergyman. I found him to be a most interesting man, but he did not change the subject, since he was taking a vacation from a parish were alcoholism and morbid promiscuity were commonplace. I later had a drink with the clergyman in the bar, but Brimmer and Mme. Troyan didn't show up for dinner.

They came into the bar for cocktails before lunch on the next day. I thought they both looked tired. They must have had sandwiches in the bar or made some other arrangement because I didn't see them in the dining room. That evening the sky cleared briefly—it was the first clearing of the voyage—and I watched this from the stern deck with my friend the minister. How much more light we see from an old ship than we see from the summit of a mountain! The cuts in the overcast, filled with colored light, the heights and reaches all reminded me of my dear wife and children and our farm in New Hampshire and the modest pyrotechnics of a sunset there. I found Mme. Troyan and Brimmer in the bar when I went down before dinner, but they didn't know the sky had cleared.

They didn't see the Azores, nor were they around two days later when we sighted Portugal. It was half past four or five in the afternoon. First, there was some slacking off in the ship's roll. She was still rolling, but you could go from one place to another without ending up on your face, and the stewards had begun to take down the ropes and rearrange the furniture. Then on our port side we could see some cliffs and, above them, round hills rising to form a mountain, and on the summit some ruined fort or bastion—low-lying, but beautiful—and behind this a bank of clouds so dense that it was not until we approached the shore that you could distinguish which was cloud and which was mountain. A few gulls picked us up, and then villas could be seen, and there was the immemorial smell of inshore water like my grandfather's bathing shoes. Here was a different sea—catboats and villas and fish nets and sand castles flying flags and people calling in their children off the beach for supper. This was the landfall, and as I went up toward the bow I heard the Sanctus bell in the ballroom, where the priest was saying prayers of thanksgiving over water that has seen, I suppose, a million, million times the bells and candles of the Mass. Everyone was at the bow, as pleased as children to see Portugal. Everyone stayed late to watch the villas take shape, the lights go on, and to smell the shallows. Everyone but Brimmer and Mme. Troyan, who were still in Brimmer's cabin when I went down, and who couldn't have seen anything.

Mme. Troyan left the ship at Gibraltar the next morning, when her husband was to meet her. We got there at dawn—very cold for April—cold and bleak with snow on the African mountains and the smell of snow in the air. I didn't see Brimmer around, although he may have been on another deck. I watched a deckhand put the bags aboard the cutter, and then Mme. Troyan walked swiftly onto the cutter herself, wearing a coat over her shoulders and carrying a scarf. She went to the stern and began to wave her scarf to Brimmer or to me or to the ship's musicians—since we were the only people she had spoken to on the crossing. But the boat moved more swiftly than my emotions and, in the few minutes it took for my stray feelings of tenderness to accumulate, the cutter had moved away from the ship, and the shape, the color of her face was lost.

When we left Gibraltar, the potted palms were retired again, the lines were put up, and the ship's orchestra began to play. It remained rough and dreary. Brimmer was in the bar at half past twelve looking very absent-minded, and I suppose he missed Mme. Troyan. I didn't see him again until after dinner, when he joined me in the bar. Something, sorrow I suppose, was on his mind, and when I began to talk about Nantucket (where we had both spent some summers) his immense reservoirs of courtesy seemed taxed. He excused himself and left; half an hour later I saw that he was drinking in the lounge with the mysterious businesswoman and her secretary.

It was the bartender who had first identified this couple as a "Roman businesswoman" and her secretary. Then, when it appeared that she spoke a crude mixture of Spanish and Italian, the bartender decided that she was a Brazilian—although the purser told me that she was traveling on a Greek passport. The secretary was a hard-faced blonde, and the businesswoman was herself a figure of such astonishing unsavoriness—you might say evil—that no one spoke to her, not even the waiters. Her hair was dyed black, her eyes were made up to look like the eyes of a viper, her voice was guttural, and whatever her business was, it had stripped her of any appeal as a human being. These two were in the bar every night, drinking gin and speaking a jumble of languages. They were never with anyone else until Brimmer joined them that evening.

This new arrangement excited my deepest and my most natural disapproval. I was taking with the Southern family when, perhaps an hour later, the secretary strayed into the bar alone and ordered whiskey. She seemed so distraught that rather than entertain any obscene suspicions about Brimmer, I lit up the whole scene with an artificial optimism and talked intently with the Southerners about real estate. But when I went below I could tell that the businesswoman was in Brimmer's cabin. They made quite a lot of noise, and at one point they seemed to fall out of bed. There was a loud thump. I could have knocked on the door—like Carrie Nation—ordering them to desist, but who would have seemed the most ridiculous?

But I could not sleep. It had been my experience, my observation, that the kind of personality that emerges from this sort of promiscuity embodies an especial degree of human failure. I say observation and experience because I would not want to accept the tenets of any other authority—any preconception that would diminish the feeling of life as a perilous moral adventure. It is difficult to be a man, I think; but the difficulties are not insuperable. Yet if we relax our vigilance for a moment we pay an exorbitant price. I have never seen such a relationship as that between Brimmer and the businesswoman that was not based on bitterness, irresolution, and cowardice—the very opposites of love—and any such indulgence on my part would, I was sure, turn my hair white in a moment, destroy the pigmentation in my eyes, incline me to simper, and leave a hairy tail coiled in my pants. I knew no one who had hit on such a way of life except as an expression of inadequacy—a shocking and repugnant unwillingness to cope with the generous forces of life. Brimmer was my friend and consequently enough of a man to make him deeply ashamed of what he was doing. And with this as my consolation I went to sleep.

He was in the bar at twelve-thirty the next day, but I did not speak to him. I drank my gin with a German businessman who had boarded the ship at Lisbon. It may have been because my German friend was dull that I kept scrutinizing Brimmer for some telling fault—insipidity or bitterness in his voice. But even the full weight of my prejudice, which was immense, could not project, as I would have liked, traces of his human failure. He was just the same. The businesswoman and her secretary rejoined one another after dinner, and Brimmer joined the Southern family, who were either so obtuse or so naïve that they had seen nothing and had no objection to letting Brimmer dance with Sister and walk her around in the rain.

I DID NOT speak to him for the rest of the voyage. We docked at Naples at seven o'clock on a rainy morning, and when I had cleared customs and was leaving the port with my bags, Brimmer called to me. He was with a good-looking, leggy blonde who must have been twenty years younger than he, and he asked if they could drive me up to Rome. Why I accepted, why I arose with such agility over my massive disapproval, seems to have been, in retrospect, a dislike of loneliness. I did not want to take the train alone to Rome. I accepted their offer and drove with them to Rome, stopping in Terracina for lunch. They were driving up to Florence in the morning, and since this was my destination, I went on with them.

Considering Brimmer's winning ways with animals and small children—they were all captivated—and his partiality (as I was to discover later) to the Franciscan forms of prayer, it might be worth recounting what happened that day when we turned off the road and drove up into Assisi for lunch. Portents mean nothing, but the truth is that when we begin a journey in Italy to a clap of thunder and a sky nearly black with swallows we pay more emotional attention to this spectacle than we would at home. The weather had been fair all that morning, but as we turned off toward Assisi a wind began to blow, and even before we reached the gates of the town the sky was dark. We had lunch at an inn near the duomo with a view of the valley and a good view of the storm as it came up the road and struck the holy city. It was darkness, wind, and rain of an unusual suddenness and density. There was an awning over the window where we sat and a palm tree in the garden below us, and while we ate our lunch we saw both the awning and the palm tree picked to pieces by the wind. When we finished lunch it was like night in the streets. A young brother let us into the duomo, but it was too dark to see the Cimabues. Then the brother took us to the sacristy and unlocked the door. The moment Brimmer entered the holy place the windows exploded under the force of the wind, and it was only by some kind of luck that we were not all cut to pieces by the glass that flew against the chest where the relics are stored. For the moment or two that the door was opened, the wind ranged through the church, extinguishing every candle in the place, and it took Brimmer and me and the brother, all pulling, to get the door shut again. Then the brother hurried off for help, and we climbed to the upper church. As we drove out of Assisi the wind fell, and looking back I saw the clouds pass over the town and the place fill up and shine with the light of day.

WE SAID GOODBYE in Florence and I did not see Brimmer again. It was the leggy blonde who wrote to me in July or August, when I had returned to the United States and our farm in New Hampshire. She wrote from a hospital in Zurich, and the letter had been forwarded from my address in Florence. "Poor Brimmer is dying," she wrote. "And if you could get up here to see him I know it would make him very happy. He often speaks of you, and I know you were one of his best friends. I am enclosing some papers that might interest you since you are a writer. The doctors do not think he can live another week. . . ." To refer to me as a friend exposed what must have been the immensity of his loneliness; and it seemed all along that I had known he was going to die, that his promiscuity was a relationship not to life but to death. That was in the afternoon—it was four or five—the light glancing, and that gratifying stillness in the air that falls over the back country with the earliest signs of night. I didn't tell my wife. Why should I? She never knew Brimmer and why introduce death into such a tranquil scene? What I remember feeling was gladness. The letter was six weeks old. He would be dead.

I don't suppose she could have read the papers she sent on. They must have represented a time of life when he had suffered some kind of breakdown. The first was a facetious essay, attacking the modern toilet seat and claiming that the crouched position it enforced was disadvantageous to those muscles and organs that were called into use. This was followed by a passionate prayer for cleanliness of heart. The prayer seemed to have gone unanswered, because the next piece was a very dirty essay on sexual control, followed by a long ballad called *The Ups and Downs of Jeremy Funicular*. This was a disgusting account of Jeremy's erotic adventures, describing many married and unmarried ladies and also one garage mechanic, one wrestler, and one lighthouse keeper. The ballad was long, and each stanza ended with a reprise lamenting the fact that Jeremy had never experienced remorse—excepting when he was mean to children, foolish with money, or overate of bread and meat at table. The last manuscript was the remains of fragments of a journal. "*Gratissimo Signore,*" he wrote, "for the creaking shutter, the love of Mrs. Pigott, the smells of rain, the candor of friends, the fish in the sea, and especially for the smell of bread and coffee, since they mean mornings and newness of life." It went on, pious and lewd, but I read no more.

My wife is lovely, lovely were my children, and lovely that scene, and how dead he and his dirty words seemed in the summer light. I was glad of the news, and his death seemed to have removed the perplexity that he had represented. I could remember with some sadness that he had been able to convey a feeling that the exuberance and the pain of life was a glass against which his nose was pressed: that he seemed able to dramatize the sense of its urgency and its deadly seriousness. I remembered the fineness of his hands, the light voice, and the cast in his eye that made the pupil seem like a goat's; but I wondered why he had failed, and by my lights he had failed horribly. Which one of us is not suspended by a thread above carnal anarchy, and what is that thread but the light of day? The difference between life and death seemed no more than the difference between going up to see the landfall of Lisbon and remaining in bed with Mme. Troyan. I could remember the landfall—the pleasant, brackish smell of inshore water like my grandfather's bathing shoes—distant voices on a beach, villas, sea bells, and Sanctus bells, and the singing of the priest and the faces of the passengers all raised, all smiling in wonder at the sight of land as if nothing like it had ever been seen before.

BUT I WAS WRONG, and set the discovery of my mistake in any place where you can find an old copy of *Europa* or *Epoca*. It is a Monday and I am spearfishing with my son off the rocks near Porto San Stefano. My son and I are not good friends, and it is at our best that we seem to be in disagreement with one another. We seem to want the same place in the sun. But we are great friends under water. I am delighted to see him there like a figure in a movie, head down, feet up, armed with a fishing spear, air streaming from his snorkel—and the rilled sand, where he stirs it, turning up like smoke. Here, in the deep water among the rocks, we seem to escape the tensions that make our relationships in other places vexatious. It is lovely here. With a little chop on the surface, the sun falls to the bottom of the sea in a great net of light. There are starfish in the colors of lipstick, and all the rocks are covered with white flowers. And after a *festa*, a Sunday when the beaches have been crowded, there are other things so many fathoms down—bits of sandwich paper, the crossword-puzzle page from *Il Messaggero*, and waterlogged copies of *Epoca*. It is out of the back pages of one of these that Brimmer looks up to me from the bottom of the sea. He is not dead. He has just married an Italian movie actress. He has his left arm around her slender waist, his right foot crossed in front of his left and in his right hand the full glass. He looks no better and no worse, and I don't know if he has sold his lights and vitals to the devil or only discovered himself. I go up to the surface, shake the water out of my hair, and think that I am worlds away from home.

THE GOLDEN AGE

OUR IDEAS of castles, formed in childhood, are inflexible, and why try to reform them? Why point out that in a real castle thistles grow in the courtyard, and the threshold of the ruined throne room is guarded by a nest of green adders? Here are the keep, the drawbridge, the battlements and towers that we took with our lead soldiers when we were down with the chicken pox. The first castle was English, and this one was built by the King of Spain during an occupation of Tuscany, but the sense of imaginative supremacy—the heightened mystery of nobility—is the same. Nothing is inconsequential here. It is thrilling to drink Martinis on the battlements, it is thrilling to bathe in the fountain, it is even thrilling to climb down the stairs into the village after supper and buy a box of matches. The drawbridge is down, the double doors are open, and early one morning we see a family crossing the moat, carrying the paraphernalia of a picnic.

They are Americans. Nothing they can do will quite conceal the touching ridiculousness, the clumsiness of the traveler. The father is a tall young man, a little stooped, with curly hair and fine white teeth. His wife is pretty, and they have two sons. Both boys are armed with plastic machine guns, which were recently mailed to them by their grandparents. It is Sunday, bells are ringing, and who ever brought the bells into Italy? Not the *vaca* in Florence but the harsh country bells that bing and bang over the olive groves and the cypress alleys in such an alien discord that they might have come in the carts of Attila the Hun. This urgent jangling sounds over the last of the antique fishing villages—really one of the last things of its kind. The stairs of the castle wind down into a place that is lovely and remote. There are no bus or train connections to this place, no *pensioni* or hotels, no art schools, no tourists or souvenirs; there is not even a postcard for sale. The natives wear picturesque costumes, sing at their work, and haul up Greek vases in their fishing nets. It is one of the last places in the world where you can hear shepherds' pipes, where beautiful girls with loose bodices go unphotographed as they carry baskets of fish on their heads, and where serenades are sung after dark. Down the stairs come the Americans into the village.

The women in black, on their way to church, nod and wish them good morning. *"Il poeta,"* they say, to each other. Good morning to the poet, the wife of the poet, and the poet's sons. Their courtesy seems to embarrass the stranger. "Why do they call you a poet?" his older son asks, but Father doesn't reply. In the piazza there is some evidence of the fact that the village is not quite perfect. What has been kept out by its rough roads has come in on the air. The village boys roosting around the fountain have their straw hats canted over their foreheads, and matchsticks in their teeth, and when they walk they swagger as if they had been born in a saddle, although there is not a saddle horse in the place. The blue-green beam of the television set in the café has begun to transform them from sailors into cowboys, from fishermen into gangsters, from shepherds into juvenile delinquents and masters of ceremonies, their bladders awash with Coca-Cola, and this seems very sad to the Americans. *E colpa mia,* thinks Seton, the so-called poet, as he leads his family through the piazza to the quays where their rowboat is moored.

The harbor is as round as a soup plate, the opening lies between two cliffs, and on the outermost, the seaward cliff, stands the castle, with its round towers, that the Setons have rented for the summer. Regarding the nearly perfect scene, Seton throws out his arms and exclaims, "Jesus, what a *spot!*" He raises an umbrella at the stern of the rowboat for his wife, and quarrels with the boys about where they will sit. "You sit where I tell you to sit, Tommy!" he shouts. "And I don't want to hear another word *out* of you." The boys grumble, and there is a burst of machine-gun fire. They put out to sea in a loud but not an angry uproar. The bells are silent now, and they can hear the wheezing of the old church organ, its lungs rotted with sea fog. The inshore water is tepid and extraordinarily dirty, but out past the mole the water is so clear, so finely colored that it seems like a lighter element, and when Seton glimpses the shadow of their hull, drawn over the sand and rocks ten fathoms down, it seems that they float on blue air.

There are thongs for oarlocks, and Seton rows by standing in the waist and putting his weight against the oars. He thinks that he is quite adroit at this—even picturesque—but he would never, even at a great distance, be taken for an Italian. Indeed, there is an air of criminality, of shame about the poor man. The illusion of levitation, the charming tranquillity of the day—crenelated towers against that blueness of sky that seems to be a piece of our consciousness—are not enough to expunge his sense of guilt but only to hold it in suspense. He is a fraud, an impostor, an aesthetic criminal, and, sensing his feelings, his wife says gently, "Don't worry, darling, no one will know, and if they do know, they won't care." He is worried because he is not a poet, and because this perfect day is, in a sense, his day of reckoning. He is not a poet at all, and only hoped to be better understood in Italy if he introduced himself as one. It is a harmless imposture—really an aspiration. He is in Italy only because he wants to lead a more illustrious life, to at least broaden his powers of reflection. He has even thought of writing a poem—something about good and evil.

There are many other boats in the water, rounding the cliff. All the idlers and beach boys are out, bumping gunwales, pinching their girls, and loudly singing phrases of *canzone*. They all salute *il poeta*. Around the cliff the shore is steep, terraced for vineyards, and packed with wild rosemary, and here the sea has beaten into the shore a chain of sandy coves. Seton heads for the largest of these, and his sons dive off the boat as he approaches the beach. He lands, and unloads the umbrella and the other gear.

Everyone speaks to them, everyone waves, and everyone in the village but the few churchgoers is on the beach. The Setons are the only strangers. The sand is a dark-golden color, and the sea shines like the curve of a rainbow—emerald, malachite, sapphire, and indigo. The striking absence of vulgarity and censoriousness in the scene moves Seton so that his chest seems to fill up with some fluid of appreciation. This is simplicity, he thinks, this is beauty, this is the raw grace of human nature! He swims in the fresh and buoyant water, and when he has finished swimming he stretches out in the sun. But now he seems restless, as if he were troubled once more about the fact that he is not a poet. And if he is not a poet, then what is he?

He is a television writer. Lying on the sand of the cove, below the castle, is the form of a television writer. His crime is that he is the author of an odious situation comedy called "The Best Family." When it was revealed to him that in dealing with mediocrity he was dealing not with flesh and blood but with whole principalities and kingdoms of wrongdoing, he threw up his job and fled to Italy. But now "The Best Family" had been leased by Italian television—it is called "La Famiglia Tosta" over here—and the asininities he has written will ascend to the towers of Siena, will be heard in the ancient streets of Florence, and will drift out of the lobby of the Gritti Palace onto the Grand Canal. This Sunday is his début, and his sons, who are proud of him, have spread the word in the village. *Poeta!*

His sons have begun to skirmish with their machine guns. It is a harrowing reminder of his past. The taint of television is on their innocent shoulders. While the children of the village sing, dance, and gather wild flowers, his own sons advance from rock to rock, pretending to kill. It is a mistake, and a trivial one, but it flusters him, although he cannot bring himself to call them to him and try to explain that their adroitness at imitating the cries and the postures of the dying may deepen an international misunderstanding. They are misunderstood, and he can see the women wagging their heads at the thought of a country so barbarous that even little children are given guns as playthings. *Mamma mia!* One has seen it all in the movies. One would not dare to walk on the streets of New York because of gang warfare, and once you step out of New York you are in a wilderness, full of naked savages.

The battle ends, they go swimming again, and Seton,

who has brought along some spearfishing gear, for an hour explores a rocky ledge that sinks off the tip of the cove. He dives, and swims through a school of transparent fish, and farther down, where the water is dark and cold, he sees a large octopus eye him wickedly, gather up its members, and slip into a cave paved with white flowers. There at the edge of the cave he sees a Greek vase, an amphora. He dives for it, feels the rough clay on his fingers, and goes up for air. He dives again and again, and finally brings the vase triumphantly into the light. It is a plump form with a narrow neck and two small handles. The neck is looped with a scarf of darker clay. It is broken nearly in two. Such vases, and vases much finer, are often found along that coast, and if they are of no value they stand on the shelves of the café, the bakery, and the barbershop, but the value of this one to Seton is inestimable—as if the fact that a television writer could reach into the Mediterranean and bring up a Greek vase were a hopeful cultural omen, proof of his own worthiness. He celebrates his find by drinking some wine, and then it is time to eat. He polishes off the bottle of wine with his lunch, and then, like everyone else on the beach, lies down in the shade and goes to sleep.

JUST AFTER SETON had waked and refreshed himself with a swim, he saw the strangers coming around the point in a boat—a Roman family, Seton guessed, who had come up to Tarlonia for the weekend. There were a father, a mother, and a son. Father fumbled clumsily with the oars. The pallor of all three of them, and their attitudes, set them apart from the people of the village. It was as if they had approached the cove from another continent. As they came nearer, the woman could be heard asking her husband to bring the boat up on the beach.

The father's replies were short-tempered and very loud. His patience was exhausted. It was not easy to row a boat, he said. It was not as easy as it looked. It was not easy to land in strange coves where, if a wind came up, the boat could be dashed to pieces and he would have to buy the owner a new boat. Boats were expensive. This tirade seemed to embarrass the mother and tire the son. They were both dressed for bathing and the father was not, and, in his white shirt, he seemed to fit that much less into the halcyon scene. The purple sea and the graceful swimmers only deepened his exasperation, and, red-faced with worry and discomfort, he called out excited and needless warnings to the swimmers, fired questions at the people on the shore (How deep was the water: How safe was the cove?), and finally brought his boat in safely. During this loud performance, the boy smiled slyly at his mother and she smiled slyly back. They had put up with this for so many years! Would it never end? Fuming and grunting, the father dropped anchor in two feet of water, and the mother and the son slipped over the gunwales and swam away.

Seton watched the father, who took a copy of *Il Tempo* out of his pocket and began to read, but the light was too bright. Then he felt anxiously in his pockets to see if the house keys and the car keys had taken wing and flown away. After this, he scraped a little bilge out of the boat with a can. Then he examined the worn oar thongs, looked at his watch, tested the anchor, looked at his watch again, and examined the sky, where there was a single cloud, for signs of a tempest. Finally, he sat down and lit a cigarette, and his worries, flying in from all points of the compass, could be seen to arrive on his brow. They had left the hot-water heater on in Rome! His apartment and all his valuables were perhaps at that very moment being destroyed by the explosion. The left front tire on the car was thin and had probably gone flat, if the car itself had not been stolen by the brigands that you found in these remote fishing villages. The cloud in the west was small, to be sure, but it was the kind of cloud that heralded bad weather, and they would be tossed mercilessly by the high waves on their way back around the point, and would reach the *pensione* (where they had already paid for dinner) after all the best cutlets had been eaten and the wine had been drunk. For all he knew, the President might have been assassinated in his absence, the lira devalued. The government might have fallen. He suddenly got to his feet and began to roar at his wife and son. It was time to go, it was time to go. Night was falling. A storm was coming. They would be late for dinner. They would get caught in the heavy traffic near Fregene. They would miss all the good television programs. . . .

His wife and his son turned and swam back toward the boat, but they took their time. It was not late, they knew. Night was not falling, and there was no sign of a storm. They would not miss dinner at the *pensione*. They knew from experience that they would reach the *pensione* long before the tables were set, but they had no choice. They climbed aboard while the father weighed anchor, shouted warning to the swimmers, and asked advice from the shore. He finally got the boat into the bay, and started around the point.

They had just disappeared when one of the beach boys climbed to the highest rock and waved a red shirt, shouting, *"Pesce cane! Pesce cane!"* All the swimmers turned, howling with excitement and kicking up a heavy surf, and swam for the shore. Over the bar where they had been one could see the fin of a shark. The alarm had been given in time, and the shark seemed surly as he cruised through the malachite-colored water. The bathers lined the shore, pointing out the menace to one another, and a little child stood in the shallows shouting, *"Brutto! Brutto! Brutto!"* Then everyone cheered as down the path came Mario, the best swimmer in the village, carrying a long spear gun. Mario worked as a stonemason, and for some reason—perhaps his industriousness—had never fitted into the scene. His legs were too long or too far apart, his shoulders were too round or too square, his hair was too thin, and that luxuriance of the flesh that had been dealt out so generously to the other bucks had bypassed poor Mario. His nakedness seemed piteous and touching, like a stranger surprised in some intimacy. He was cheered and complimented as he came through the crowd, but he could not even muster a nervous smile, and, setting his thin lips, he strode into the water and swam to the bar. But the shark had gone, and so had most of the sunlight. The disenchantment of a dark beach moved the bathers to gather their things and start for home. No one waited for Mario; no one seemed to care. He stood in the dark water with his spear, ready to take on his shoulders the safety and welfare of the community, but they turned their backs on him and sang as they climbed the cliff.

To hell with "La Famiglia Tosta," Seton thought. To hell with it. This was the loveliest hour of the whole day.

All kinds of pleasure—food, drink, and love—lay ahead of him, and he seemed, by the gathering shadow, gently disengaged from his responsibility for television, from the charge of making sense of his life. Now everything lay in the dark and ample lap of night, and the discourse was suspended.

The stairs they took went past the ramparts they had rented, which were festooned with flowers, and it was on this stretch from here up to the drawbridge and the portal, that the triumph of the King, the architect, and the stonemasons was most imposing, for one was involved in the same breath with military impregnability, princeliness, and beauty. There was no point, no turning, no tower or battlement where these forces seemed separate. All the ramparts were finely corniced, and at every point where the enemy could have been expected to advance, the great, eight-ton crest of the Christian King of Spain proclaimed the blood, the faith, and the good taste of the defender. Over the main portal, the crest had fallen from its fine setting of sea gods with tridents and had crashed into the moat, but it had landed with its blazonings upward, and the quarterings, the cross, and the marble draperies could be seen in the water.

Then on the wall, among the other legends, Seton saw the words *"Americani, go home, go home."* The writing was faint; it might have been there since the war, or its faintness might be accounted for by the fact that it had been done in haste. Neither his wife nor his children saw it, and he stood aside while they crossed the drawbridge into the courtyard, and then he went back to rub the words out with his fingers. Oh, who could have written it? He felt mystified and desolate. He had been invited to come to this strange country. The invitations had been clamorous. Travel agencies, shipping firms, airlines, even the Italian government itself had besought him to give up his comfortable way of life and travel abroad. He had accepted the invitations, he had committed himself to their hospitality, and now he was told, by this ancient wall, that he was not wanted.

He had never before felt unwanted. It had never been said. He had been wanted as a baby, wanted as a young man, wanted as a lover, a husband and father, wanted as a scriptwriter, a raconteur and companion. He had, if anything, been wanted excessively, and his only worry had been to spare himself, to spread his sought-after charms with prudence and discretion, so that they would do the most good. He had been wanted for golf, for tennis, for bridge, for charades, for cocktails, for boards of management—and yet this rude and ancient wall addressed him as if he were a pariah, a nameless beggar, an outcast. He was most deeply wounded.

ICE WAS STORED in the castle dungeon, and Seton took his cocktail shaker there, filled it, made some Martinis, and carried them up to the battlements of the highest tower, where his wife joined him to watch the light ring its changes. Darkness was filling in the honeycombed cliffs of Tarlonia, and while the hills along the shore bore only the most farfetched resemblance to the breasts of women, they calmed Seton's feelings and stirred in him the same deep tenderness.

"I might go down to the café after dinner," his wife said, "just to see what sort of a job they did with the dubbing."

She did not understand the strength of his feelings about writing for television; she had never understood. He said nothing. He supposed that, seen at a distance, on his battlement, he might have been taken for what he was not—a poet, a seasoned traveler, a friend of Elsa Maxwell's, a prince or a duke—but this world lying all about him now did not really have the power to elevate and change him. It was only himself—the author of "The Best Family"—that he had carried at such inconvenience and expense across borders and over the sea. The flowery and massive setting had not changed the fact that he was sunburned, amorous, hungry, and stooped, and that the rock he sat on, set in its place by the great King of Spain, cut into his rump.

At dinner, Clementina, the cook, asked if she might go to the village and see "La Famiglia Tosta." The boys, of course, were going with their mother. After dinner, Seton went back to his tower. The fishing fleet had begun to go out past the mole, their torches lighted. The moon rose and blazed so brightly on the sea that the water seemed to turn, to spin in the light. From the village he could hear the *bel canto* of mothers calling their girls, and from time to time, a squawk from the television set. It would all be over in twenty minutes, but the sense of wrongdoing *in absentia* made itself felt in his bones. Oh, how could one stop the advance of barbarism, vulgarity, and censoriousness? When he saw the lights his family carried coming up the stairs, he went down to the moat to meet them. They were not alone. Who was with them? Who were these figures ascending: The doctor? The Mayor? And a little girl carrying gladioli. It was a delegation—and a friendly one, he could tell by the lightness of their voices. They had come to praise him.

"It was so beautiful, so comical, so true to life!" the doctor said.

The little girl gave him the flowers, and the Mayor embraced him lightly. "Oh, we thought, signore," he said, "that you were merely a poet."

THE LOWBOY

OH I HATE small men and I will write about them no more but in passing I would like to say that's what my brother Richard is: small. He has small hands, small feet, a small waist, small children, a small wife, and when he comes to our cocktail parties he sits in a small chair. If you pick up a book of his, you will find his name, "Richard Norton," on the flyleaf in his very small handwriting. He emanates, in my opinion, a disgusting *aura* of smallness. He is also spoiled, and when you go to his house you eat *his* food from *his* china with *his* silver, and if you observe his capricious and vulgar house rules you may be lucky enough to get some of *his* brandy, just as thirty years ago one went into his room to play with *his* toys at *his* pleasure and to be rewarded with a glass of *his* ginger ale. Some people make less of an adventure than a performance of their passions. They do not seem to fall in love and make friends but to cast, with men, women, children, and dogs, some stirring drama that they were committed to producing at the moment of their birth. This is especially noticeable on the part of those whose casting is limited by a slender emotional budget. The clumsy performances draw our attention to the play. The ingénue is much too old. So is the leading lady. The dog is the wrong breed, the furniture is ill-matched, the costumes are threadbare, and when the coffee is poured there seems to be nothing in the pot. But the drama goes on with as much terror and pity as it does in more magnificent productions. Watching my brother, I feel that he has marshaled a second-rate cast and that he is performing, perhaps for eternity, the role of a spoiled child.

It is traditional in our family to display our greatest emotional powers over heirlooms—to appropriate sets of dishes before the will can be probated, to have tugs-of-war with carpets, and to rupture blood relationships over the subject of a rickety chair. Stories and tales that dwell on some wayward attachment to an object—a soup tureen or a lowboy—seem to narrow down to the texture of the object itself, the glaze on the china or the finish on the wood, and to generate those feelings of frustration that I, for one, experience when I hear harpsichord music. My last encounter with my brother involved a lowboy. Because our mother died unexpectedly and there was an ambiguous clause in her will, certain of the family heirlooms were seized by Cousin Mathilda. No one felt strong enough at the time to contest her claims. She is now in her nineties, and age seems to have cured her rapacity. She wrote to Richard and me saying that if she had anything we wanted she would be happy to let us have it. I wrote to say that I would like the lowboy. I remembered it as a graceful, bowlegged piece of furniture with heavy brasses and a highly polished veneer of the color of cordovan. My request was halfhearted. I did not really care, but it seemed that my brother did. Cousin Mathilda wrote him that she was giving the lowboy to me, and he telephoned to say that he wanted it—that he wanted it so much more than I did that there was no point in even discussing it. He asked if he could visit me on Sunday—we live about fifty miles apart—and, of course, I invited him.

It was not his house or his whiskey that day, but it was his charm that he was dispensing and in which I was entitled to bask, and, noticing some roses in the garden that he had given my wife many years back, he said, "I see *my* roses are doing well." We drank in the garden. It was a spring day—one of those green-gold Sundays that excite our incredulity. Everything was blooming, opening, burgeoning. There was more than one could see—prismatic lights, prismatic smells, something that set one's teeth on edge with pleasure—but it was the shadow that was most mysterious and exciting, the light one could not define. We sat under a big maple, its leaves not yet fully formed but formed enough to hold the light, and it was astounding in its beauty, and seemed not like a single tree but one of a million, a link in a long chain of leafy trees beginning in childhood.

"What about the lowboy?" Richard asked.

"What about it? Cousin Mathilda wrote to ask if I wanted anything, and it was the only thing I wanted."

"You've never cared about those things."

"I wouldn't say that."

"But it's *my* lowboy!"

"Everything has always been yours, Richard."

"Don't quarrel," my wife said, and she was quite right. I had spoken foolishly.

"I'll be happy to buy the lowboy from you," Richard said.

"I don't want your money."

"What do you want?"

"I would like to know why you want the lowboy so much."

"It's hard to say, but I do want it, and I want it terribly!" He spoke with unusual candor and feeling. This seemed more than his well-known possessiveness. "I'm not sure why. I feel that it was the center of our house, the center of our life before Mother died. If I had one solid piece of furniture, one object I could point to, that would remind me of how happy we all were, of how we used to live . . ."

I understood him (who wouldn't?), but I suspected his motives. The lowboy was an elegant piece of furniture, and I wondered if he didn't want it for cachet, as a kind of family crest, something that would vouch for the richness of his past and authenticate his descent from the most aristocratic of the seventeenth-century settlers. I could see him standing proudly beside it with a drink in his hand. *My* lowboy. It would appear in the background of their Christmas card, for it was one of those pieces of cabinetwork that seem to have a countenance of the most exquisite breeding. It would be the final piece in the puzzle of respectability that he had made of his life. We had shared a checkered, troubled, and sometimes sorrowful past, and Richard had risen from this chaos into a dazzling and resplendent respectability, but perhaps this image of himself would be improved by the lowboy; perhaps the image would not be complete without it.

I said that he could have it, then, and his thanks were intense. I wrote to Mathilda, and Mathilda wrote to me. She would send me, as a consolation, Grandmother DeLancey's sewing box, with its interesting contents—the Chinese fan, the sea horse from Venice, and the invitation to Buckingham Palace. There was a problem of delivery. Nice Mr. Osborn was willing to take the lowboy as far as my house but no farther. He would deliver it on Thursday, and then I could take it on to Richard's in my station wagon whenever this was convenient. I called Richard and explained these arrangements to him, and he was, as he had been from the beginning, nervous and intense. Was my station wagon big enough? Was it in good condition? And where would I keep the lowboy between Thursday and Sunday? I mustn't leave it in the garage.

When I came home on Thursday the lowboy was there, and it was in the garage. Richard called in the middle of dinner to see if it had arrived, and spoke revealingly, from the depths of his peculiar feelings.

"Of course you'll let me have the lowboy?" he asked.

"I don't understand."

"You won't *keep* it?"

What was at the bottom of this? I wondered. Why should he endure jealousy as well as love for a stick of wood? I said that I would deliver it to him on Sunday, but he didn't trust me. He would drive up with Wilma, his small wife, on Sunday morning, and accompany me back.

On Saturday my oldest son helped me carry the thing from the garage into the hall, and I had a good look at it. Cousin Mathilda had cared for it tenderly and the ruddy veneer had a polish of great depth, but on the top was a dark ring—it gleamed through the polish like something seen under water—where, for as long as I could remember, an old silver pitcher had stood, filled with apple blossoms or peonies or roses or, as the summer ended, chrysanthemums and colored leaves. I remembered the contents of the drawers, gathered there like a precipitate of our lives: the dog leashes, the ribbons for the Christmas wreaths, golf balls and playing cards, the German angel, the paper knife with which Cousin Timothy had stabbed himself, the crystal inkwell, and the keys to many forgotten doors. It was a powerful souvenir.

Richard and Wilma came on Sunday, bringing a pile of soft blankets to protect the varnish from the crudities of my station wagon. Richard and the lowboy were united like true lovers, and, considering the possibilities of magnificence and pathos in love, it seemed tragic that he should have become infatuated with a chest of drawers. He must have had the same recollections as I when he saw the dark ring gleaming below the polish and looked into the ink-stained drawers. I have seen gardeners attached to their lawns, violinists to their instruments, gamblers to their good-luck pieces, and old ladies to their lace, and it was in this realm of emotion, as unsparing as love, that Richard found himself. He anxiously watched my son and me carry the thing out to the station wagon, wrapped in blankets. It was a little too big. The carved claw feet extended a few inches beyond the tail gate. Richard wrung his hands, but he had no alternative. When the lowboy was tucked in, we started off. He did not urge me to drive carefully, but I knew this was on his mind.

When the accident occurred, I could have been blamed in spirit but not in fact. I don't see how I could have avoided it. We were stopped at a toll station, where I was waiting for my change, when a convertible, full of adolescents, collided with the back of my car and splintered one of the bowed legs.

"Oh, you crazy fools!" Richard howled. "You crazy, thoughtless criminals!" He got out of the car, waving his hands and swearing. The damage did not look too great to me, but Richard was inconsolable. With tears in his eyes, he lectured the bewildered adolescents. The lowboy was of inestimable value. It was over two hundred years old. No amount of money, no amount of insurance could compensate for the damage. Something rare and beautiful had been lost to the world. While he raved, cars piled up behind us, horns began to blow, and the toll collector told us to move. "This is *serious*," Richard said to him. When we had got the name and the registration of the criminal in the driver's seat, we went along, but he was terribly shaken. At his house we carried the injured antique tenderly into the dining room and put it on the floor in its wrappings. His shock seemed to have given way now to a glimmer of hope, and when he fingered the splintered leg you could see that he had begun to think of a future in which the leg would be repaired. He gave me a correct drink, and talked about his garden, as any well-mannered man in the face of a personal tragedy will carry on, but you could feel that his heart was with the victim in the next room.

RICHARD AND I do not see much of one another, and we did not meet for a month or so, and when we did meet it was over dinner in the Boston airport, where we both chanced to be waiting for planes. It was summer—midsummer, I guess, because I was on the way to Nantucket. It was hot. It was getting dark. There was a special menu that night involving flaming swords. The cooked food—shish kebab or calves' liver or half a broiler—was brought to a side table and impaled on a small sword. Then a waiter would put what looked like cotton wool on the tip of the sword, ignite this, and serve the food in a blaze of fire and chivalry. I mention this not because it seemed comical or vulgar but because it was affecting to see, in the summer dusk, how delighted the good and modest people of Boston were with this show. While the flaming swords went to and fro, Richard talked about the lowboy.

What an adventure! What a story! First he had checked all the cabinetmakers in the neighborhood and found a man in Westport who could be relied upon to repair the leg, but when the cabinetmaker saw the lowboy he, too, fell in love. He wanted to buy it, and when Richard refused he wanted to know its history. When the thing was repaired, they had it photographed and sent the picture to an authority on eighteenth-century furniture. It was famous, it was notorious, it was the Barstow lowboy, made by the celebrated Sturbridge cabinetmaker in 1780 and thought to have been lost in a fire. It had belonged to the Pooles (our great-great-grandmother was a Poole) and appeared in their inventories until 1840, when their house was destroyed, but only the knowledge of its whereabouts had been lost. The piece itself had come down, safely enough, to us. And now it had been reclaimed. like a prodigal, by the most highminded antiquarians. A curator at the Metropolitan had urged Richard to let the Museum have it on loan. A collector had offered him ten thousand dollars. He was enjoying the delicious experience of discovering that what he adored and possessed was adored by most of mankind.

I flinched when he mentioned the ten thousand dollars—after all, I could have kept the thing—but I did not want it, I had never really wanted it, and I sensed in the airport dining room that Richard was in some kind of danger. We said goodbye then and flew off in different directions. He called me in the autumn about some business, and he mentioned the lowboy again. Did I remember the rug on which it had stood at home? I did. It was an old Turkey carpet, multicolored and scattered with arcane symbols. Well, he had found very nearly the same rug at a New York dealer's, and now the claw feet rested on the same geometric fields of brown and yellow. You could see that he was putting things together—he was completing the puzzle—and while he never told me what happened next, I could imagine it easily enough. He bought a silver pitcher and filled it with leaves and sat there alone one autumn evening drinking whiskey and admiring his creation.

It would have been raining on the night I imagined; no other sound transports Richard with such velocity backward in time. At last everything was perfect—the pitcher, the polish on the heavy brasses, the carpet. The chest of drawers would seem not to have been lifted into the present but to have moved the past with it into the room. Wasn't that what he wanted? He would admire the dark ring in the varnish and the fragrance of the empty drawers, and under the influence of two liquids—rain and whiskey—the hands of those who had touched the lowboy, polished it, left their drinks on it, arranged the flowers in the pitcher and stuffed odds and ends of string into the drawers would seem to reach out of the dark. As he watched, their dull fingerprints clustered on the polish, as if this were their means of clinging to life. By recalling them, by going a step further, he evoked them, and they came down impetuously into the room—they flew—as if they had been waiting in pain and impatience all those years for his invitation.

First to come back from the dead was Grandmother DeLancey, all dressed in black and smelling of ginger. Handsome, intelligent, victorious, she had broken with the past, and the thrill of this had borne her along with the force of a wave through all the days of her life and, so far as one knew, had washed her up into the very gates of heaven. Her education, she said scornfully, had consisted of learning how to hem a pocket handkerchief and speak a little French, but she had left a world where it was improper for a lady to hold an opinion and come into one where she could express her opinions on a platform, pound the lectern with her fist, walk alone in the dark, and cheer (as she always did) the firemen when the red wagon came helling up the street. Her manner was firm and oracular, for she had traveled as far west as Cleveland lecturing on women's rights. A lady could be anything! A doctor! A lawyer! An engineer! A lady could, like Aunt Louisa, smoke cigars.

Aunt Louisa was smoking a cigar as she flew in to join the gathering. The fringe of a Spanish shawl spread out behind her in the air, and her hoop earrings rocked as she made, as always, a forceful, a pressing entrance, touched the lowboys, and settled on the blue chair. She was an artist. She had studied in Rome. Crudeness, flamboyance, passion, and disaster attended her. She tackled all the big subjects—the Rape of the Sabines, and the Sack of Rome. Naked men and women thronged her huge canvases, but they were always out of drawing, the colors were dim, and even the clouds above her battlefields seemed despondent. Her failure was not revealed to her until it was too late. She poured her ambitions onto her oldest son, Timothy, who walked in sullenly from the grave, carrying a volume of the Beethoven sonatas, his face dark with rancor.

Timothy would be a great pianist. It was her decision. He was put through every suffering, deprivation, and humiliation known to a prodigy. It was a solitary and bitter life. He had his first recital when he was seven. He played with an orchestra when he was twelve. He went on tour the next year. He wore strange clothes, and used grease on his long curls, and killed himself when he was fifteen. His mother had pushed him pitilessly. And why should this passionate and dedicated woman have made such a mistake? She may have meant to heal or avenge a feeling that, through birth or misfortune, she had been kept out of the blessed company of contented men and women. She may have believed that fame would end all this—that if she were a famous painter or he a famous pianist, they would never again taste loneliness or know scorn.

Richard could not have kept Uncle Tom from joining them if he had wanted to. He was powerless. He had been too late in realizing that the fascination of the lowboy was the fascination of pain, and he had committed himself to it. Uncle Tom came in with the grace of an old athlete. He was the amorous one. No one had been able to keep track of his affairs. His girls changed weekly—they sometimes changed in midweek. There were tens, there were hundreds, there may have been thousands. He carried in his arms his youngest son, Peter, whose legs were in braces. Peter had been crippled just before his birth, when, during a quarrel between his parents, Uncle Tom pushed Aunt Louisa down the stairs.

Aunt Mildred came stiffly through the air, drew her blue skirt down over her knees as she settled herself, and looked uneasily at Grandmother. The old lady had passed on to Mildred her emancipation, as if it were a nation secured by treaties and compacts, flags and anthems. Mildred knew that passivity, needlepoint, and housework were not for her. To decline into a contented housewife would have meant handing over to the tyrant those territories that her mother had won for eternity with the sword. She knew well enough what it was that she must not do, but she had never decided what it was that she should do. She wrote pageants. She wrote verse. She worked for six years on a play about Christopher Columbus. Her husband, Uncle Sidney, pushed the perambulator and sometimes the carpet sweeper. She watched him angrily at his housework. He had usurped her rights, her usefulness. She took a lover and, going for the first three or four times to the hotel where they met, she felt that she had found herself. This was not one of the opportunities that her mother had held out to her, but it was better than Christopher Columbus. Furtive love was the contribution she was meant to make. The affair was sordid and came to a sordid end, with disclosures, anonymous letters, and bitter tears. Her lover absconded, and Uncle Sydney began to drink.

Uncle Sidney staggered back from the grave and sat down on the sofa beside Richard, stinking of liquor. He had been drunk ever since he discovered his wife's folly. His face was swollen. His belly was so enlarged that it had burst a shirt button. His mind and his eyes were glazed. In his drunkenness he dripped a lighted cigarette onto the sofa, and the velvet began to smoke. Richard's position seemed confined to observation. He could not speak or move. Then Uncle Sidney noticed the fire and poured the contents of his whiskey glass onto the upholstery. The whiskey and the sofa burst into flame. Grandmother, who was sitting on the old pegged Windsor chair, sprang to her feet, but the pegs caught her clothing and tore the seat of her dress. The dogs began to bark, and Peter, the young cripple, began to sing in a thin voice—obscenely sarcastic—"Joy to the world! the Lord is come. Let Heaven and nature sing," for it was a Christmas dinner that Richard had reconstructed.

At some point—perhaps when he purchased the silver pitcher—Richard committed himself to the horrors of the past, and his life, like so much else in nature, took the form of an arc. There must have been some felicity, some clearness in his feeling for Wilma, but once the lowboy took a commanding position in his house, he seemed driven back upon his wretched childhood. We went there for dinner—it must have been Thanksgiving. The lowboy stood in the dining room, on its carpet of mysterious symbols, and the silver pitcher was full of chrysanthemums. Richard spoke to his wife and children in a tone of vexation that I had forgotten. He quarreled with everyone; he even quarreled with my children. Oh, why is it that life is for some an exquisite privilege and others must pay for their seats at the play with a ransom of cholers, infections, and nightmares? We got away as soon as we could.

When we got home, I took the green glass epergne that belonged to Aunt Mildred off the sideboard and smashed it with a hammer. Then I dumped Grandmother's sewing box into the ash can, burned a big hole in her lace tablecloth, and buried her pewter in the garden. Out they go—the Roman coins, the sea horse from Venice, and the Chinese fan. We can cherish nothing less than our random understanding of death and the earth-shaking love that draws us to one another. Down with the stuffed owl in the upstairs hall and the statue of Hermes on the newel post! Hock the ruby necklace, throw away the invitation to Buckingham Palace, jump up and down on the perfume atomizer from Murano and the Canton fish plates. Dismiss whatever molests us and challenges our purpose, sleeping or waking. Cleanliness and valor will be our watchwords. Nothing less will get us past the armed sentry and over the mountainous border.

THE MUSIC TEACHER

IT ALL SEEMED to have been arranged—Seton sensed this when he opened the door of his house that evening and walked down the hall into the living room. It all seemed to have been set with as much care as, in an earlier period of his life, he had known girls to devote to the flowers, the candles, and the records for the phonograph. This scene was not arranged for his pleasure, nor was it arranged for anything so simple as reproach. "Hello," he said loudly and cheerfully. Sobbing and moaning rent the air. In the middle of the small living room stood an ironing board. One of his shirts was draped over it, and his wife, Jessica, wiped away a tear as she ironed. Near the piano stood Jocelin, the baby. Jocelin was howling. Sitting in a chair near her little sister was Millicent, his oldest daughter, sobbing and holding in her hands the pieces of a broken doll. Phyllis, the middle child, was on her hands and knees, prying the stuffing out of an armchair with a beer-can opener. Clouds of smoke from what smelled like a burning leg of lamb drifted out of the open kitchen door into the living room.

He could not believe that they had passed the day in such disorder. It must all have been planned, arranged—including the conflagration in the oven—for the moment of his homecoming. He even thought he saw a look of inner tranquillity on his wife's harassed face as she glanced around the room and admired the effectiveness of the scene. He felt routed but not despairing and, standing on the threshold, he made a quick estimate of his remaining forces and settled on a kiss as his first move; but as he approached the ironing board his wife waved him away, saying, "Don't come near me. You'll catch my cold. I have a *terrible* cold." He then got Phyllis away from the armchair, promised to mend Millicent's doll, and carried the baby into the bathroom and changed her diapers. From the kitchen came loud oaths as Jessica fought her way through the clouds of smoke and took the meat out of the stove.

It was burned. So was almost everything else—the rolls, the potatoes, and the frozen apple tart. There were cinders in Seton's mouth and a great heaviness in his heart as he looked past the plates of spoiled food to Jessica's face, once gifted with wit and passion but now dark and lost to him. After supper he helped with the dishes and read to the children, and the purity of their interest in what he read and did, the power of trust in their love, seemed to make the taste of burned meat sad as well as bitter. The smell of smoke stayed in the air long after everyone but Seton had gone to bed. He sat alone in the living room, recounting his problems to himself. He had been married ten years, and Jessica still seemed to him to possess an unusual loveliness of person and nature, but in the last year or two something grave and mysterious had come between them. The burned roast was not unusual; it was routine. She burned the chops, she burned the hamburgers, she even burned the turkey at Thanksgiving, and she seemed to burn the food deliberately, as if it was a means of expressing her resentment toward him. It was not rebellion against drudgery. Cleaning women and mechanical appliances—the lightening of her burden—made no difference. It was not, he thought, even resentment. It was like some subterranean sea change, some sexual campaign or revolution stirring—unknown perhaps to her—beneath the shining and common appearance of things.

He did not want to leave Jessica, but how much longer could he cope with the tearful children, the dark looks, the smoky and chaotic house? It was not discord that he resisted but a threat to the most healthy and precious part of his self-esteem. To be long-suffering under the circumstances seemed to him indecent. What could he do? Change, motion, openings seemed to be what he and Jessica needed, and it was perhaps an indication of his limitations that, in trying to devise some way of extending his marriage, the only thing he could think of was to take Jessica to dinner in a restaurant where they had often gone ten years ago, when they were lovers. But even this, he knew, would not be simple. A point-blank invitation would only get him a point-blank, bitter refusal. He would have to be wary. He would have to surprise and disarm her.

This was in the early autumn. The days were clear. The yellow leaves were falling everywhere. From all the windows of the house and through the glass panes in the front door, one saw them coming down. Seton waited for two or three days. He waited for an unusually fine day, and then he called Jessica from his office, in the middle of the morning. There was a cleaning woman at the house, he knew. Millicent and Phyllis would be in school, and Jocelin would be asleep. Jessica would not have too much to do. She might even be idle and reflective. He called her and told her—he did not invite her—to come to town and to have dinner with him. She hesitated; she said it would be difficult to find someone to stay with the children; and finally she succumbed. He even seemed to hear in her voice when she agreed to come a trace of the gentle tenderness he adored.

It was a year since they had done anything like dining together in a restaurant, and when he left his office that night and turned away from the direction of the station he was conscious of the mountainous and deadening accrual of habit that burdened their relationship. Too many circles had been drawn around his life, he though; but how easy it was to overstep them. The restaurant where he went to wait for her was modest and good—polished, starched, smelling of fresh bread and sauces, and in a charming state of readiness when he reached it that evening. The hat-check girl remembered him, and he remembered the exuberance with which he had come down the flight of steps into the bar when he was younger. How wonderful everything smelled. The bartender had just come on duty, freshly shaved and in a white coat. Everything seemed cordial and ceremonious. Every surface was shining, and the light that fell onto his shoulders was the light that had fallen there ten years ago. When the headwaiter stopped to say good evening, Seton asked to have a bottle of wine—*their* wine—iced. The door into the night was the door he used to watch in order to see Jessica come in with snow in her hair, to see her come in with a new dress and new shoes, to see her come in with good news, worries, apologies for being late. He could remember the way she glanced at the bar to see if he was there, the way she stopped to speak with the hat-check girl, and then lightly crossed the floor to put her hand in his and to join lightly and gracefully in his pleasure for the rest of the night.

Then he heard a child crying, He turned toward the door in time to see Jessica enter. She carried the crying baby against her shoulder. Phyllis and Millicent followed in their worn snowsuits. It was still early in the evening, and the restaurant was not crowded. This entrance, this tableau, was not as spectacular as it would have been an hour later, but it was—for Seton, at least—powerful enough. As Jessica stood in the doorway with a sobbing child in her arms and one on each side of her, the sense was not that she had come to meet her husband and through some breakdown in arrangements, had been forced to bring the children; the sense was that she had come to make a public accusation of the man who had wronged her. She did not point her finger at him, but the significance of the group was dramatic and accusatory.

Seton went to them at once. It was not the kind of restaurant one brought children to, but the hat-check girl was kindly and helped Millicent and Phyllis out of their snowsuits. Seton took Jocelin in his arms, and she stopped crying.

"The baby-sitter couldn't come," Jessica said, but she hardly met his eyes, and she turned away when he kissed her. They were taken to a table at the back of the place. Jocelin upset a bowl of olives, and the meal was as gloomy and chaotic as the burned supper at home. The children fell asleep on the drive back, and Seton could see that he had failed—failed or been outwitted again. He wondered, for the first time, if he was dealing not with the shadows and mysteries of Jessica's sex but with plain fractiousness.

He tried again, along the same lines; he asked the Thompsons for cocktails one Saturday afternoon. He could tell that they didn't want to come. They were going to the Carmignoles'—everyone was going to the Carmignoles'—and it was a year or more since the Setons had entertained; their house had suffered a kind of social infamy. The Thompsons came only out of friendship, and they came only for one drink. They were an attractive couple, and Jack Thompson seemed to enjoy a tender mastery over his wife that Seton envied. He had told Jessica the Thompsons were coming. She had said nothing. She was not in the living room when they arrived, but she appeared a few minutes later, carrying a laundry basket full of wash, and when Seton asked her if she wouldn't have a drink, she said that she didn't have time. The Thompsons could see that he was in trouble, but they could not stay to help him—they would be late at the Carmignoles'. But when Lucy Thompson had got into the car, Jack came back to the door and spoke to Seton so forcefully—so clearly out of friendship and sympathy—that Seton hung on his words. He said that he could see what was going on, and that Seton should have a hobby—a specific hobby: he should take piano lessons. There was a lady named Miss Deming and he should see her. She would help. Then he waved goodbye and went down to his car. This advice did not seem in any way strange to Seton. He was desperate and tired, and where was the sense in life? When he returned to the living room, Phyllis was attacking the chair again with the beer-can opener. Her excuse was that she had lost a quarter in the upholstery. Jocelin and

Millicent were crying. Jessica had begun to burn the evening meal.

THEY HAD burned veal on Sunday, burned meat loaf on Monday, and on Tuesday the meat was so burned that Seton couldn't guess what it was. He thought of Miss Deming, and decided she might be a jolly trollop who consoled the men of the neighborhood under the guise of giving music lessons. But when he telephoned, her voice was the voice of a crone. He said that Jack Thompson had given him her name, and she said for him to come the next evening at seven o'clock. As he left his house after supper on Wednesday, he thought that there was at least some therapy in getting out of the place and absorbing himself in something besides his domestic and business worries. Miss Deming lived on Bellevue Avenue, on the other side of town. The house numbers were difficult to see, and Seton parked his car at the curb and walked, looking for the number of her house.

It was an evening in the fall. Bellevue Avenue was one of those back streets of frame houses that are irreproachable in their demeanor, their effect, but that are ornamented, through some caprice, with little minarets and curtains of wooden beading, like a mistaken or at least a mysterious nod to the faraway mosques and harems of bloody Islam. This paradox gave the place its charm. The street was declining, but it was declining gracefully; its decay was luxuriant, and in the back yards roses bloomed in profusion, and cardinals sang in the fir trees. A few householders were still raking their lawns. Seton had been raised on just such a street, and he was charmed to stumble on this fragment of his past. The sun was setting—there was a show of red light at the foot of the street—and at the sight of this he felt a pang in his stomach as keen as hunger, but it was not hunger, it was simple aspiration. Oh to lead an illustrious life!

Miss Deming's house had no porch, and may have needed paint more than the others, although he could not tell for sure, now that the light had begun to fade. A sign on the door said: KNOCK AND COME IN. He stepped into a small hallway, with a staircase and a wooden hatrack. In a farther room he saw a man as old as himself bent over the piano keys. "You're early," Miss Deming called out. "Please sit down and wait."

She spoke with such deep resignation, such weariness, that the tone of her voice seemed to imply to Seton that what he waited for would be disgusting and painful. He sat down on a bench, under the hatrack. He was uncomfortable. His hands sweated, and he felt painfully large for the house, the bench, the situation. How mysterious was this life, he thought, where his wife had hidden her charms and he was planning to study the piano. His discomfort got so intense that he thought for a moment of fleeing. He could step out of the door, into Bellevue Avenue, and never come back again. A memory of the confusion at home kept him where he was. Then the thought of waiting as a mode of eternity attacked him. How much time one spent waiting in dentists' and doctors' anterooms, waiting for trains, for planes, waiting in front of telephone booths and in restaurants. It seemed that he had wasted the best of his life in waiting, and that by contracting to wait for piano lessons he might throw away the few vivid years that were left to him. Again he thought of escaping, but at that moment the lesson in the other room came to an end. "You've not been practicing enough," he heard Miss Deming say crossly. "You have to practice an hour a day, without exception, or else you'll simply be wasting my time." Her pupil came through the little hall with his coat collar turned up so that Seton couldn't see his face. "Next," she said.

The little room with the upright piano in it was more cluttered than the hall. Miss Deming hardly looked up when he came in. She was a small woman. Her brown hair was streaked with gray, braided, and pinned to her head in a sparse coronet. She sat on an inflated cushion, with her hands folded in her lap, and moved her lips now and then with distaste, as if something galled her. Seton blundered onto the little piano stool. "I've never taken piano lessons," he said. "I once took cornet lessons. I rented a cornet when I was in high school—"

"We'll forget about that," she said. She pointed out middle C and asked him to play a scale. His fingers, in the bright light from the music rack, looked enormous and naked. He struggled with his scale. Once or twice, she rapped his knuckles with a pencil; once or twice, she manipulated his fingers with hers, and he had a vision of her life as a nightmare of clean hands, dirty hands, hairy hands, limp and muscular hands, and he decided that this might account for her feeling of distaste. Halfway through the lesson, Seton dropped his hands into his lap. His irresolution only made her impatient, and she placed his hands back on the keys. He wanted to smile, but on the wall above the piano there was a large sign that forbade this. His shirt was wet when the lesson ended.

"Please bring the exact change when you come again. Put the money in the vase on the desk," she said. "Next." Seton and the next pupil passed each other in the doorway, but the stranger averted his face.

The end of the ordeal elated Seton, and as he stepped out into the darkness of Bellevue Avenue he had a pleasant and silly image of himself as a pianist. He wondered if these simple pleasures were what Jack Thompson had meant. The children were in bed when he got home, and he sat down to practice. Miss Deming had given him a two-handed finger drill with a little melody, and he went over this again and again for an hour. He practiced every day, including Sunday, and sincerely hoped when he went for his second lesson that she would compliment him by giving him something more difficult, but she spent the hour criticizing his phrasing and fingering, and told him to practice the drill for another week. He thought that at least after his third lesson he would have a change, but he went home with the same drill.

Jessica neither encouraged him nor complained. She seemed mystified by this turn of events. The music got on her nerves, and he could see where it would. The simple drill, with its melody, impressed itself even onto the memories of his daughters. It seemed to become a part of all their lives, as unwelcome as an infection, and as pestilential. It drifted through Seton's mind all during the business day, and at any sudden turn of feeling—pain or surprise—the melody would swell and come to the front of his consciousness. Seton had never known that this drudgery, this harrying of the mind was a part of mastering the piano. Now in the evening after supper when he sat down to practice, Jessica hastily left the room and went upstairs. She seemed intimidated by the music, or perhaps afraid. His own relationship to the drill was oppressive and unclear. Taking a late train one evening and walking up from the station past the Thompsons', he heard the same pestilential drill coming through the walls of their house. Jack must be practicing. There was nothing very strange about this, but when he passed the Carmignoles' and heard the drill again, he wondered if it was not his own memory that made it ring in his ears. The night was dark, and with his sense of reality thus shaken, he stood on his own doorstep thinking that the world changed more swiftly than one could perceive—died and renewed itself—and that he moved through the events of his life with no more comprehension than a naked swimmer.

Jessica had not burned the meat that night. She had kept a decent supper for him in the oven, and she served it to him with a timidity that made him wonder if she was not about to return to him as his wife. After supper, he read to the children and then rolled back his shirtsleeves and sat down at the piano. As Jessica was preparing to leave the room, she turned and spoke to him. Her manner was pleading, and this made her eyes seem larger and darker, and deepened her natural pallor. "I don't like to interfere," she said softly, "and I know I don't know anything about music, but I wonder if you couldn't ask her—your teacher—if she couldn't give you something else to practice. That exercise is on my mind so. I hear it all day. If she could give you a new piece—"

"I know what you mean," he said. "I'll ask her."

BY HIS FIFTH LESSON, the days had grown much shorter and there was no longer any fiery sunset at the foot of Bellevue Avenue to remind him of his high hopes, his longings. He knocked, and stepped into the little house, and noticed at once the smell of cigarette smoke. He took off his hat and coat and went into the living room, but Miss Deming was not on her cushion. He called her, and she answered from the kitchen and opened the door onto a scene that astonished him. Two young men sat at the kitchen table, smoking and drinking beer. Their dark hair gleamed with oil and was swept back in wings. They wore motorcycle boots and red hunting shirts, and their manners seemed developed, to a fine point, for the expression of lawless youth. "We'll be waiting for you, lover," one of them said loudly as she closed the door after her, and as she came toward Seton he saw a look of pleasure on her face—of lightness and self-esteem—fade, and the return of her habitually galled look.

"My boys," she said, and sighed.

"Are they neighbors?" Seton asked.

"Oh, no. They come from New York. They come up and spend the night sometimes. I help them when I can, poor things. They're like sons to me."

"It must be nice for them," Seton said.

"Please commence," she said. All the feeling had left her voice.

"My wife wanted to know if I couldn't have something different—a new piece."

"They always do," she said wearily.

"Something a little less repetitious," Seton said.

"None of the gentlemen who come here have ever complained about my methods. If you're not satisfied, you don't have to come. Of course, Mr. Purvis went too far. Mrs. Purvis is still in the sanatorium, but I don't think the fault is mine. You want to bring her to her knees, don't you? Isn't that what you're here for? Please commence."

Seton began to play, but with more than his usual clumsiness. The unholy old woman's remarks had stunned him. What had he got into? Was he guilty? Had his instinct to flee when he first entered the house been the one he should have followed? Had he, by condoning the stuffiness of the place, committed himself to some kind of obscenity, some kind of witchcraft? Had he agreed to hold over a lovely woman the subtle threat of madness? The old crone spoke softly now and he thought, wickedly. "Play the melody lightly, lightly, lightly," she said. "That is how it will do its work."

He went on playing, borne along on an unthinking devotion to consecutiveness, for if he protested, as he knew he should, he would only authenticate the nightmare. His head and his fingers worked with perfect independence of his feelings, and while one part of him was full of shock, alarm, and self-reproach, his fingers went on producing the insidious melody. From the kitchen he could hear deep laughter, the pouring of beer, the shuffle of motorcycle boots. Perhaps because she wanted to rejoin her friends—her boys—she cut the lesson short, and Seton's relief was euphoric.

He had to ask himself again and again if she had really said what he thought he heard her say, and it seemed so improbable that he wanted to stop and talk with Jack Thompson about it, until he realized that he could not mention what had happened; he would not be able to put it into words. This darkness where men and women struggled pitilessly for supremacy and withered crones practiced witchcraft was not the world where he made his life. The old lady seemed to inhabit some barrier reef of consciousness, some gray moment after waking that would be demolished by the light of day.

Jessica was in the living room when he got home, and as he put his music on the rack he saw a look of dread in her face. "Did she give you a piece?" she asked. "Did she give you something besides that drill?"

"Not this time," he said. "I guess I'm not ready. Perhaps next time."

"Are you going to practice now?"

"I might."

"Oh, not tonight, darling! Please not tonight! Please, please, *please* not tonight, my love!" and she was on her knees.

THE RESTORATION of Seton's happiness—and it returned to them both with a rush—left him oddly self-righteous about how it had come about, and when he thought of Miss Deming he thought of her with contempt and disgust. Caught up in a whirl of palatable suppers and lovemaking, he didn't go near the piano. He washed his hands of her methods. He had chosen to forget the whole thing. But when Wednesday night came around again, he got up to go there at the usual time and say goodbye. He could have telephoned her. Jessica was uneasy about his going back, but he explained that it was merely to end the arrangement, and kissed her, and went out.

It was a dark night. The Turkish shapes of Bellevue Avenue were dimly lighted. Someone was burning leaves. He knocked on Miss Deming's door and stepped into the little hall. The house was dark. The only light came through the windows from the street. "Miss Deming," he called. "Miss Deming?" He called her name three times. The chair beside the piano bench was empty, but he could feel the old lady's touch on everything in the place. She was not there—that is, she did not answer his voice—but she seemed to be standing in the door to the kitchen, standing on the stairs, standing in the dark at the end of the hall; and a light sound he heard from upstairs seemed to be her footfall.

He went home, and he hadn't been there half an hour when the police came and asked him to come with them. He went outside—he didn't want the children to hear—and he made the natural mistake of protesting, since, after all, was he not a most law-abiding man? Had he not always paid for his morning paper, obeyed the traffic lights, bathed daily, prayed weekly, kept his tax affairs in order, and paid his bills on the tenth of the month? There was not, in the broad landscape of his past, a trace, a hint of illegality. What did the police want with him? They wouldn't say, but they insisted that he come with them, and finally he got into the patrol car with them and drove to the other side of town, across some railroad tracks, to a dead-end place, a dump, where there were some other policemen. It was a scene for violence—bare, ugly, hidden away from any house, and with no one to hear her cries for help. She lay on the crossroads, like a witch. Her neck was broken, and her clothes were still disordered from her struggle with the great powers of death. They asked if he knew her, and he said yes. Had he ever seen any young men around her house, they asked, and he said no. His name and address had been found in a notebook on her desk, and he explained that she had been his piano teacher. They were satisfied with this explanation, and they let him go.

A WOMAN WITHOUT A COUNTRY

I SAW HER that spring between the third and fourth races at Campino with the Conte de Capra—the one with the mustache—drinking Campari at that nice easygoing track, with the mountains in the distance and beyond the mountains a mass of cumulus clouds that at home would have meant a tree-splitting thunderstorm by supper but that amounts to nothing over there. I next saw her at the Tennerhof in Kitzbühel, where a Frenchman was singing American cowboy songs to an audience that included the Queen of the Netherlands, but I never saw her in the mountains, and I don't think she skied, but just went there, like so many others, for the crowds and the excitement. Then I saw her at the Lido, and again in Venice late one morning when I was taking a gondola to the station and was sitting on the terrace of the Gritti, drinking coffee. I saw her at the Passion Play in Erl—not at the Passion Play, actually, but at the inn in the village, where you have lunch during the intermission, and I saw her at the horse show in the Piazza di Siena, and that autumn in Treviso, boarding the plane for London. Blooey.

But it all might have happened. She was one of those tireless wanderers who go to bed night after night to dream of bacon-lettuce-and-tomato sandwiches. Although she came from a small lumber-mill town in the north where they manufactured wooden spoons, the kind of lonely place where international society is spawned, this had nothing to do with her wanderings. Her father was the mill agent, and the mill was owned by the Tonkin family—they owned a great deal, they owned whole counties, and their divorce proceedings were followed by the tabloids—and young Marchand Tonkin, learning the business, spent a month there and fell in love with Anne. She was a plain girl with a sweet and modest disposition—qualities that she never lost—and they were married at the end of a year. Though immensely rich, the Tonkins were poor-mouthed, and the young couple lived modestly in a small town near New York where Marchand worked in the family office. They had one child and lived a contented and uneventful life until one humid morning in the seventh year of their marriage.

Marchand had a meeting in New York, and he had to catch an early train. He planned to have breakfast in the city. It was about seven when he kissed Anne goodbye. She had not dressed and was lying in bed when she heard him grinding the starter on the car that he used to take to the station. Then she heard the front door open and he called up the stairs. The car wouldn't start, and could she drive him to the station in the Buick? There was no time to dress, so she drew a jacket over her shoulders and drove him to the station. What was visible of her was properly clad, but below the jacket her nightgown was transparent. Marchand kissed her goodbye and urged her to get some clothes on, and she drove away from the station, but at the junction of Alewives Lane and Hill Street she ran out of gas.

She was stopped in front of the Beardens', and they would give her some gasoline, she knew, or at least lend her a coat. She blew the horn and blew it and blew it, until she remembered that the Beardens were in Nassau. All she could do then was to wait in the car, virtually naked, until some friendly housewife came by and offered her help. First, Mary Pym drove by, and although Anne waved to her, she did not seem to notice. Then Julia Weed raced by, rushing Francis to the train, but she was going too fast to notice anything. Then Jack Burden, the village rake, who, without being signaled to or appealed to in any way, seemed drawn magnetically to the car. He stopped and asked if he could help. She got into his car—what else could she do—thinking of Lady Godiva and St. Agnes. The worst of it was that she didn't seem able to wake up—to accomplish the transition between the shades of sleep and the lights of day. And it was a lightless day, close and oppressive, like the climate of a harrowing dream. Their driveway was sheltered from the road by some shrubbery, and when she got out of the car and thanked Jack Burden, he followed her up the steps and took advantage of her in the hallway, where they were discovered by Marchand when he came back to get his briefcase.

Marchard left the house then, and Anne never saw him again. He died of a heart attack in a New York hotel ten days later. Her parents-in-law sued for the custody of the only child, and during the trial Anne made the mistake, in her innocence, of blaming her malfeasance on the humidity. The tabloids picked this up—"IT WASN'T ME, IT WAS THE HUMIDITY"—and it swept the country. There was a popular song, "Humid Isabella." It seemed that everywhere she went she heard them singing:

Oh, Humid Isabella
Never kissed a fellah
Unless there was moisture in the air,
But when the skies were cloudy,
She got very rowdy . . .

In the middle of the trial she surrendered her claims, put on smoked glasses, and sailed incognito for Genoa, the outcast of a society that seemed to her to modify its invincible censoriousness only with a ribald sense of humor.

Of course, she had a boodle—her sufferings were only spiritual—but she had been burned, and her memories were bitter. From what she knew of life she was entitled to forgiveness, but she had received none, and her own country, remembered across the Atlantic, seemed to have passed on her a moral judgment that was unrealistic and savage. She had been made a scapegoat; she had been pilloried; and because she was genuinely pure-hearted she was deeply incensed. She based her expatriation not on cultural but on moral grounds. By impersonating a European she meant to express her disapproval of what had gone on at home. She drifted all over Europe, but she finally bought a villa in Tavola-Calda, and spent at least half the year there. She not only learned Italian, she learned all the grunting noises and hand signals that accompany the language. In the dentist's chair she would say "*aiiee*" instead of "ouch," and she could wave a hornet away from her wineglass with great finesse. She was proprietary about her expatriation—it was her demesne, achieved through uncommon sorrow—and it irritated her to hear other foreigners speaking the language. Her villa was charming—nightingales sang in the oak trees, fountains played in the garden, and she stood on the highest terrace, her hair dyed the shade of bronze that was fashionable in Rome that year, calling down to her guests, "*Bentornati. Quanto piacere!*" but the image was never quite right. It seemed like a reproduction, with the slight imperfections that you find in an enlargement—the loss of quality. The sense was that she was not so much here in Italy as that she was no longer there in America.

She spent much of her time in the company of people who, like herself, claimed to be the victims of an astringent and repressive moral climate. Their hearts were on the shipping lanes, running away from home. She paid for her mobility with some loneliness. The party of friends she was planning to meet in Wiesbaden moved on without leaving an address. She looked for them in Heidelberg and Munich, but she never found them. Wedding invitations and weather reports ("Snow Blankets the Northeast U.S.") made her terribly homesick. She continued to polish her impersonation of a European, and while her accomplishments were admirable, she remained morbidly sensitive to criticism and detested being taken for a tourist. One day at the end of the season in Venice, she took a train south, reaching Rome late on a hot September afternoon. Most of the people of Rome were asleep, and the only sign of life was the tourist buses, grinding tirelessly through the streets like some basic piece of engineering—like the drains or the light conduits. She gave her luggage check to a porter and described her bags to him in fluent Italian, but he seemed to see through her and he mumbled something about the Americans. Oh, there were so *many*. This irritated her and she snapped at him, "I am not an American."

"Excuse me, signora," he said. "What, then, is your country?"

"I am," she said, "a *Greek*."

The enormity, the tragedy of her lie staggered her. What have I done? she asked herself wildly. Her passport was as green as grass, and she traveled under the protectorate of the Great Seal of the United States. Why had she lied about such an important part of her identity?

She took a cab to a hotel on the Via Veneto, sent her

bags upstairs, and went into the bar for a drink. There was a single American at the bar—a white-haired man wearing a hearing aid. He was alone, he seemed lonely, and finally he turned to the table where she sat and asked most courteously if she was American.

"Yes."

"How come you speak the language?"

"I live here."

"Stebbins," he said, "Charlie Stebbins. Philadelphia."

"How do you do," she said. "Where in Philadelphia?"

"Well, I was born in Philadelphia," he said, "but I haven't been back in forty years. Shoshone, California's my real home. They call it the gateway to Death Valley. My wife came from London. London, Arkansas. Ha ha. My daughter went to school in six states of the Union. California. Washington. Nevada. North and South Dakota, and Louisiana. Mrs. Stebbins passed away last year, and so I thought I'd see a little of the world."

The Stars and Stripes seemed to break out in the air above his head, and she realized that in America the leaves were turning.

"Where have you been?" she asked.

"You know, it's a funny thing, but I'm not sure myself. This agency in California planned the trip for me, and they told me I'd be traveling with a group of Americans, but as soon as I get on the high seas I find that I'm traveling alone. I'll never do it again. Sometimes there's whole days in which I don't hear any decent American spoken. Why, sometimes I just sit up in my room and talk to myself for the pleasure of hearing American. Why, I took a bus from Frankfurt to Munich, and you know there wasn't anybody on that bus who spoke a word of English? Then I took a bus from Munich to Innsbruck, and there wasn't anybody on that bus who spoke English, either. Then I took a bus from Innsbruck to Venice, and there wasn't anybody on that bus who spoke English, either, until some Americans got on at Cortina. But I don't have any complaints about the hotels. They usually speak English in the hotels, and I've stayed in some very nice ones."

Sitting on a bar stool in a Roman basement, the stranger seemed to Anne to redeem her country. He seemed to gleam with shyness and honesty. The radio was tuned to the Armed Forces station in Verona, where they were playing a recording of "Star Dust."

" 'Star Dust,' " the stranger said. "But I guess you know. It was written by a friend of mine. Hoagy Carmichael. He makes six, seven thousand dollars a year on royalties from that song alone. He's a good friend of mine. I've never met him, but I've corresponded with him. I guess it must seem funny to you that I have a friend I've never met, but Hoagy's a real friend of mine."

This statement seemed much more melodic and expressive to Anne than the music. Its juxtaposition, its apparent pointlessness, and the rhythm with which it was spoken seemed to her like the music of her own country, and she remembered walking, as a girl, past the piles of sawdust at the spoon factory to the house of her best friend. If she made the walk in the afternoon, she would sometimes have to wait at the grade crossing for a freight to pass. First there would be a sound in the distance like a cave of winds, and then the iron thunder, the clangor of the wheels. The freights went through there at full speed; they stormed through. But reading the lettering on the cars used to move her; used to remind her not of any glamorous promise at the end of the line but of the breadth and vastness of her own country, as if the states of the Union—wheat states, oil states, coal states, maritime states—were being drawn down the track near where she stood and where she read Southern Pacific, Baltimore & Ohio, Nickel Plate, New York Central, Great Western, Rock Island, Santa Fe, Lackawanna, Pennsylvania, clackety-clack and out of sight.

"Don't cry, lady," Mr. Stebbins said. "Don't cry."

It was time to go home, and she got a plane for Orly that night and another plane for Idlewild the next evening. She was shaking with excitement long before they saw land. She was going home; she was going home. Her heart was in her throat. How dark and fresh the water of the Atlantic looked, after those years away. In the morning light, the low-lying islands with Indian names passed under their starboard wing, and even the houses of Long Island, arranged like the grids on a waffle iron, excited her. They circled the field once and came down. She planned to find a lunch counter in the airport and order a bacon-lettuce-

and-tomato sandwich. She gripped her umbrella (Parisian) and her handbag (Sienese) and waited her turn to leave the plane, but as she was coming down the steps, even before her shoes (Roman) had touched her native earth, she heard a mechanic who was working on a DC-7 at the next gate singing:

Oh, Humid Isabella
Never kissed a fellah . . .

She never left the airport. She took the next plane back to Orly and joined those hundreds, those thousands of Americans who stream through Europe, gay or sad, as if they were a truly homeless people. They round a street corner in Innsbruck, thirty strong, and vanish. They swarm over a bridge in Venice and are gone. They can be heard asking for ketchup in a Gasthaus above the clouds on the great massif, and be seen poking among the sea caves, with masks and snorkels, in the deep waters off Porto San Stefano. She spent the autumn in Paris. Kitzbühel saw her. She was in Rome for the horse show and in Siena for the Palio. She was always on the move, dreaming of bacon-lettuce-and-tomato sandwiches.

THE DEATH OF JUSTINA

SO HELP ME GOD it gets more and more preposterous, it corresponds less and less to what I remember and what I expect as if the force of life were centrifugal and threw one further and further away from one's purest memories and ambitions; and I can barely recall the old house where I was raised, where in midwinter Parma violets bloomed in a cold frame near the kitchen door, and down the long corridor, past the seven views of Rome—up two steps and down three—one entered the library, where all the books were in order, the lamps were bright, where there was a fire and a dozen bottles of good bourbon locked in a cabinet with a veneer like tortoise shell whose silver key my father wore on his watch chain. Fiction is art and art is the triumph over chaos (no less) and we can accomplish this only by the most vigilant exercise of choice, but in a world that changes more swiftly than we can perceive there is always the danger that our powers of selection will be mistaken and that the vision we serve will come to nothing. We admire decency and we despise death but even the mountains seem to shift in the space of a night and perhaps the exhibitionist at the corner of Chestnut and Elm streets is more significant than the lovely woman with a bar of sunlight in her hair, putting a fresh piece of cuttlebone in the nightingale's cage. Just let me give you one example of chaos and if you disbelieve me look honestly into your own past and see if you can't find a comparable experience. . . .

ON SATURDAY the doctor told me to stop smoking and drinking and I did. I won't go into the commonplace symptoms of withdrawal but I would like to point out that, standing at my window in the evening, watching the brilliant afterlight and the spread of darkness, I felt, through the lack of these humble stimulants, the force of some primitive memory in which the coming of night with its stars and its moon was apocalyptic. I thought suddenly of the neglected graves of my three brothers on the mountainside and that death is a loneliness much crueler than any loneliness hinted at in life. The soul (I thought) does not leave the body but lingers with it through every degrading stage of decomposition and neglect, through heat, through cold, through the long winter nights when no one comes with a wreath or a plant and no one says a prayer. This unpleasant premonition was followed by anxiety. We were going out for dinner and I thought that the oil burner would explode in our absence and burn the house. The cook would get drunk and attack my daughter with a carving knife or my wife and I would be killed in a collision on the main highway, leaving our children bewildered orphans with nothing in life to look forward to but sadness. I was able to observe, along with these foolish and terrifying anxieties, a definite impairment of my discretionary poles. I felt as if I were being lowered by ropes into the atmosphere of my childhood. I told my wife—when she passed through the living room—that I had stopped smoking and drinking but she didn't seem to care and who would reward me for my privations? Who cared about the bitter taste in my mouth and that my head seemed to be leaving my shoulders? It seemed to me that men had honored one another with medals, statuary, and cups for much less and that abstinence is a social matter. When I abstain from sin it is more often a fear of scandal than a private resolve to improve on the purity of my heart, but here was a call for abstinence without the worldly enforcement of society, and death is not the threat that scandal is. When it was time for us to go out I was so light-headed that I had to ask my wife to drive the car. On Sunday I sneaked seven cigarettes in various hiding places and drank two Martinis in the downstairs coat closet. At breakfast on Monday my English muffin stared up at me from the plate. I mean I *saw* a face there in the rough, toasted surface. The moment of recognition was fleeting, but it was deep, and I wondered who it had been. Was it a friend, an aunt, a sailor, a ski instructor, a bartender, or a conductor on a train? The smile faded off the muffin but it had been there for a second—the sense of a person, a life, a pure force of gentleness and censure—and I am convinced that the muffin had contained the presence of some spirit. As you can see, I was nervous.

On Monday my wife's old cousin, Justina, came to visit her. Justina was a lively guest although she must have been crowding eighty. On Tuesday my wife gave her a lunch party. The last guest left at three and a few minutes later Cousin Justina, sitting on the living-room sofa with a glass of good brandy, breathed her last. My wife called me at the office and I said that I would be right out. I was clearing my desk when my boss, MacPherson, came in.

"Spare me a minute," he asked. "I've been bird-dogging all over the place, trying to track you down. Pierce had to leave early and I want you to write the last Elixircol commercial."

"Oh, I can't, Mac," I said. "My wife just called. Cousin Justina is dead."

"You write that commercial," he said. His smile was satanic. "Pierce had to leave early because his grandmother fell off a stepladder."

Now, I don't like fictional accounts of office life. It seems to me that if you're going to write fiction you should write about mountain climbing and tempests at sea, and I will go over my predicament with MacPherson briefly, aggravated as it was by his refusal to respect and honor the death of dear old Justina. It was like MacPherson. It was a good example of the way I've been treated. He is, I might say, a tall, splendidly groomed man of about sixty who changes his shirt three times a day, romances his secretary every afternoon between two and two-thirty, and makes the habit of continuously chewing gum seem hygienic and elegant. I write his speeches for him and it has not been a happy arrangement for me. If the speeches are successful MacPherson takes all the credit. I can see that his presence, his tailor, and his fine voice are all a part of the performance but it makes me angry never to be given credit for what was said. On the other hand, if the speeches are unsuccessful—if his presence and his voice can't carry the hour—his threatening and sarcastic manner is surgical and I am obliged to contain myself in the role of a man who can do no good in spite of the piles of congratulatory mail that my eloquence sometimes brings in. I must pretend—I must, like an actor, study and improve on my pretension—to have nothing to do with his triumphs, and I must bow my head gracefully in shame when we have both failed. I am forced to appear grateful for injuries, to lie, to smile falsely, and to play out a role as inane and as unrelated to the facts as a minor prince in an operetta, but if I speak the truth it will be my wife and my children who will pay in hardships for my outspokenness. Now he refused to respect or even to admit the solemn fact of a death in our family and if I couldn't rebel it seemed as if I could at least hint at it.

The commercial he wanted me to write was for a tonic called Elixircol and was to be spoken on television by an actress who was neither young nor beautiful but who had an appearance of ready abandon and who was anyhow the mistress of one of the sponsor's uncles. *Are you growing old?* I wrote. *Are you falling out of love with your image in the looking glass? Does your face in the morning seem rucked and seamed with alcoholic and sexual excesses and does the rest of you appear to be a grayish-pink lump, covered all over with brindle hair? Walking in the autumn woods do you feel that a subtle distance has come between you and the smell of wood smoke? Have you drafted your obituary? Are you easily winded? Do you wear a girdle? Is your sense of smell fading, is your interest in gardening waning, is your fear of heights increasing, and are your sexual drives as ravening and intense as ever and does your wife look more and more to you like a stranger with sunken cheeks who has wandered into your bedroom by mistake? If this or any of this is true you need Elixircol, the true juice of youth. The small economy size (business with the bottle) costs seventy-five dollars and the giant family bottle comes at two hundred and fifty. It's a lot of scratch, God knows, but these are inflationary times and who can put a price on youth? If you don't have the cash borrow it from your neighborhood loan shark or hold up the local bank. The odds are three to one that with a ten-cent water pistol and a slip of paper you can shake ten thousand out of any fainthearted teller. Everybody's doing it. (Music up and out.)* I sent this in to MacPherson via Ralphie, the messenger boy, and took the 4:16 home, traveling through a landscape of utter desolation.

Now, my journey is a digression and has no real connection to Justina's death but what followed could only have happened in my country and in my time and since I was an American traveling across an American landscape the trip may be part of the sum. There are some Americans who, although their fathers emigrated from the Old World three centuries ago, never seem to have quite completed the voyage and I am one of these. I stand, figuratively, with one wet foot on Plymouth Rock, looking with some delicacy, not into a formidable and challenging wilderness but onto a half-finished civilization embracing glass towers, oil derricks, suburban continents, and abandoned movie houses and wondering why, in this most prosperous, equitable, and accomplished world—where even the cleaning women practice the Chopin preludes in their spare time—everyone should seem to be disappointed.

At Proxmire Manor I was the only passenger to get off the random, meandering, and profitless local that carried its shabby lights off into the dusk like some game-legged watchman or beadle making his appointed rounds. I went around to the front of the station to wait for my wife and to enjoy the traveler's fine sense of crisis. Above me on the hill were my home and the homes of my friends, all lighted and smelling of fragrant wood smoke like the temples in a sacred grove, dedicated to monogamy, feckless childhood, and domestic bliss but so like a dream that I felt the lack of viscera with much more than poignance—the absence of that inner dynamism we respond to in some European landscapes. In short, I was disappointed. It was my country, my beloved country, and there have been mornings when I could have kissed the earth that covers its many provinces and states. There was a hint of bliss; romantic and domestic bliss. I seemed to hear the jinglebells of the sleigh that would carry me to Grandmother's house although in fact Grandmother spent the last years of her life working as a hostess on an ocean liner and was lost in the tragic sinking of the S.S. *Lorelei* and I was responding to a memory that I had not experienced. But the hill of light rose like an answer to some primitive dream of homecoming. On one of the highest lawns I saw the remains of a snowman who still smoked a pipe and wore a scarf and a cap but whose form was wasting away and whose anthracite eyes stared out at the view with terrifying bitterness. I sensed some disappointing greenness of spirit in the scene although I knew in my bones, no less, how like yesterday it was that my father left the Old World to found a new; and I thought of the forces that had brought stamina to the image: the cruel towns of Calabria and their cruel princes, the badlands northwest of Dublin, ghettos, despots, whorehouses, bread lines, the graves of children, intolerable hunger, corruption, persecution, and despair had generated these faint and mellow lights and wasn't it all a part of the great migration that is the life of man?

My wife's cheeks were wet with tears when I kissed her. She was distressed, of course, and really quite sad. She had been attached to Justina. She drove me home, where Justina was still sitting on the sofa. I would like to spare you the unpleasant details but I will say that both her mouth and her eyes were wide open. I went into the pantry to telephone Dr. Hunter. His line was busy. I poured myself a drink—the first since Sunday—and lighted a cigarette. When I called the doctor again he answered and I told him what had happened. "Well, I'm awfully sorry to hear about it, Moses," he said. "I can't get over until after six and there isn't much that I can do. This sort of thing has come up before and I'll tell you all I know. You see, you live in Zone B—two-acre lots, no commercial enterprises and so forth. A couple of years ago some stranger bought the old Plewett mansion and it turned out that he was planning to operate it as a funeral home. We didn't have any zoning provision at the time that would protect us and one was rushed through the Village Council at midnight and they overdid it. It seems that you not only can't have a funeral home in Zone B—you can't bury anything there and you can't die there. Of course it's absurd, but we all make mistakes, don't we? Now there are two things you can do. I've had to deal with this before. You can take the old lady and put her into the car and drive her over to Chestnut Street, where Zone C begins. The boundary is just beyond the traffic light by the high school. As soon as you get her over to Zone C, it's all right. You can just say she died in the car. You can do that or if this seems distasteful you can call the Mayor and ask him to make an exception to the zoning laws. But I can't write you out a death certificate until you get her out of that neighborhood and of course no undertaker will touch her until you get a death certificate."

"I don't understand," I said, and I didn't, but then the possibility that there was some truth in what he had just told me broke against me or over me like a wave, exciting mostly indignation. "I've never heard such a lot of damned foolishness in my life," I said. "Do you mean to tell me that I can't die in one neighborhood and that I can't fall in love in another and that I can't eat . . ."

"Listen. Calm down, Moses. I'm not telling you anything but the facts and I have a lot of patients waiting. I don't have the time to listen to you fulminate. If you want to move her, call me as soon as you get her over to the traffic light. Otherwise, I'd advise you to get in touch with the Mayor or someone on the Village Council." He cut the connection. I was outraged but this did not change the fact that Justina was still sitting on the sofa. I poured a fresh drink and lit another cigarette.

Justina seemed to be waiting for me and to be changing from an inert into a demanding figure. I tried to imagine carrying her out to the station wagon but I couldn't complete the task in my imagination and I was sure that I couldn't complete it in fact. I then called the Mayor but this position in our village is mostly honorary and as I might have known he was in his New York law office and was not expected home until seven. I could cover her, I thought, that would be a decent thing to do, and I went up the back stairs to the linen closet and got a sheet. It was getting dark when I came back into the living room but this was no merciful twilight. Dusk seemed to be playing directly into her hands and she gained power and stature with the dark. I covered her with a sheet and turned on a lamp at the other end of the room but the rectitude of the place with its old furniture, flowers, paintings, etc., was demolished by her monumental shape. The next thing to worry about was the children, who would be home in a few minutes. Their knowledge of death, excepting their dreams and intuitions of which I know nothing, is zero and the bold figure in the parlor was bound to be traumatic. When I heard them coming up the walk I went out and told them what had happened and sent them up to their rooms. At seven I drove over to the Mayor's.

He had not come home but he was expected at any minute and I talked with his wife. She gave me a drink. By this time I was chain-smoking. When the Mayor came in we went into a little office or library, where he took up a position behind a desk, putting me in the low chair of a supplicant. "Of course I sympathize with you, Moses," he said, "it's an awful thing to have happened, but the trouble is that we can't give you a zoning exception without a majority vote of the Village Council and all the members of the Council happen to be out of town. Pete's in California and Jack's in Paris and Larry won't be back from Stowe until the end of the week."

I was sarcastic. "Then I suppose Cousin Justina will have to gracefully decompose in my parlor until Jack comes back from Paris."

"Oh no," he said, "oh *no*. Jack won't be back from Paris for another month but I think you might wait until Larry comes from Stowe. Then we'd have a majority, assuming of course that they would agree to your appeal."

"For Christ's sake," I snarled.

"Yes, yes," he said, "it is difficult, but after all you must realize that this is the world you live in and the importance of zoning can't be overestimated. Why, if a single member of the Council could give out zoning exceptions, I could give you permission right now to open a saloon in your garage, put up neon lights, hire an orchestra, and destroy the neighborhood and all the human and commercial values we've worked so hard to protect."

"I don't want to open a saloon in my garage," I howled. "I don't want to hire an orchestra. I just want to bury Justina."

"I know, Moses, I know," he said. "I understand that. But it's just that it happened in the wrong zone and if I make an exception for you I'll have to make an exception for everyone and this kind of morbidity, when it gets out of hand, can be very depressing. People don't like to live in a neighborhood where this sort of thing goes on all the time."

"Listen to me," I said. "You give me an exception and you give it to me now or I'm going home and dig a hole in my garden and bury Justina myself."

"But you can't do that, Moses. You can't bury anything in Zone B. You can't even bury a cat."

"You're mistaken," I said. "I can and I will. I can't function as a doctor and I can't function as an undertaker, but I can dig a hole in the ground and if you don't give me my exception, that's what I'm going to do."

"Come back, Moses, come back," he said. "Please come back. Look, I'll give you an exception if you'll promise not to tell anyone. It's breaking the law, it's a forgery but I'll do it if you promise to keep it a secret."

I promised to keep it a secret, he gave me the documents, and I used his telephone to make the arrangements. Justina was removed a few minutes after I got home but that night I had the strangest dream. I dreamed that I was in a crowded supermarket. It must have been night because the windows were dark. The ceiling was paved with fluorescent light—brilliant, cheerful but, considering our prehistoric memories, a harsh link in the chain of light that binds us to the past. Music was playing and there must have been at least a thousand shoppers pushing their wagons among the long corridors of comestibles and victuals. Now is there—or isn't there—something about the posture we assume when we push a wagon that unsexes us? Can it be done with gallantry? I bring this up because the multitude of shoppers seemed that evening, as they pushed their wagons, penitential and unsexed. There were all kinds, this being my beloved country. There were Italians, Finns, Jews, Negroes, Shropshiremen, Cubans—

anyone who had heeded the voice of liberty—and they were dressed with that sumptuary abandon that European caricaturists record with such bitter disgust. Yes, there were grandmothers in shorts, big-butted women in knitted pants, and men wearing such an assortment of clothing that it looked as if they had dressed hurriedly in a burning building. But this, as I say, is my own country and in my opinion the caricaturist who vilifies the old lady in shorts vilifies himself. I am a native and I was wearing buckskin jump boots, chino pants cut so tight that my sexual organs were discernible, and a rayon-acetate pajama top printed with representations of the *Pinta*, the *Niña*, and the *Santa María* in full sail. The scene was strange—the strangeness of a dream where we see familiar objects in an unfamiliar light—but as I looked more closely I saw that there were some irregularities. Nothing was labeled. Nothing was identified or known. The cans and boxes were all bare. The frozen-food bins were full of brown parcels but they were such odd shapes that you couldn't tell if they contained a frozen turkey or a Chinese dinner. All the goods at the vegetable and the bakery counters were concealed in brown bags and even the books for sale had no titles. In spite of the fact that the contents of nothing was known, my companions of the dream—my thousands of bizarrely dressed compatriots—were deliberating gravely over these mysterious containers as if the choices they made were critical. Like any dreamer, I was omniscient, I was with them and I was withdrawn, and stepping above the scene for a minute I noticed the men at the check-out counters. They were brutes. Now, sometimes in a crowd, in a bar or a street, you will see a face so full-blown in its obdurate resistance to the appeals of love, reason, and decency, so lewd, so brutish and unregenerate, that you turn away. Men like these were stationed at the only way out and as the shoppers approached them they tore their packages open—I still couldn't see what they contained—but in every case the customer, at the sight of what he had chosen, showed all the symptoms of the deepest guilt; that force that brings us to our knees. Once their choice had been opened to their shame they were pushed—in some cases kicked—toward the door and beyond the door I saw dark water and heard a terrible noise of moaning and crying in the air. They waited at the door in groups to be taken away in some conveyance that I couldn't see. As I watched, thousands and thousands pushed their wagons through the market, made their careful and mysterious choices, and were reviled and taken away. What could be the meaning of this?

WE BURIED JUSTINA in the rain the next afternoon. The dead are not, God knows, a minority, but in Proxmire Manor their unexalted kingdom is on the outskirts, rather like a dump, where they are transported furtively as knaves and scoundrels and where they lie in an atmosphere of perfect neglect. Justina's life had been exemplary, but by ending it she seemed to have disgraced us all. The priest was a friend and a cheerful sight, but the undertaker and his helpers, hiding behind their limousines, were not; and aren't they at the root of most of our troubles, with their claim that death is a violet-flavored kiss? How can a people who do not mean to understand death hope to understand love, and who will sound the alarm?

I went from the cemetery back to my office. The commercial was on my desk and MacPherson had written across it in grease pencil: *Very funny, you broken-down bore. Do again.* I was tired but unrepentant and didn't seem able to force myself into a practical posture of usefulness and obedience. I did another commercial. *Don't lose your loved ones,* I wrote, *because of excessive radioactivity. Don't be a wallflower at the dance because of strontium 90 in your bones. Don't be a victim of fallout. When the tart on Thirty-sixth Street gives you the big eye does your body stride off in one direction and your imagination in another? Does your mind follow her up the stairs and taste her wares in revolting detail while your flesh goes off to Brooks Brothers or the foreign exchange desk of the Chase Manhattan Bank? Haven't you noticed the size of the ferns, the lushness of the grass, the bitterness of the string beans, and the brilliant markings on the new breeds of butterflies? You have been inhaling lethal atomic waste for the last twenty-five years and only Elixircol can save you.* I gave this to Ralphie and waited perhaps ten minutes, when it was returned, marked again with grease pencil. *Do,* he wrote, *or you'll be dead.* I felt very tired. I put another piece of paper into the machine and wrote: *The Lord is my shepherd; therefore can I lack nothing. He shall feed me in a green pasture and lead me forth beside the waters of comfort. He shall convert my soul and bring me forth in the paths of righteousness for his Name's sake. Yea, though I walk through the valley of the shadow of death I will fear no evil for thou art with me; thy rod and thy staff comfort me. Thou shalt prepare a table before me in the presence of them that trouble me; thou hast anointed my head with oil and my cup shall be full. Surely thy loving-kindness and mercy shall follow me all the days of my life and I will dwell in the house of the Lord for ever.* I gave this to Ralphie and went home.

CLEMENTINA

SHE WAS BORN and brought up in Nascosta, in the time of the wonders—the miracle of the jewels and the winter of the wolves. She was ten years old when thieves broke into the shrine of the Holy Virgin after the last Mass on San Giovanni and stole the jewels that had been given to the Madonna by a princess who was cured there of a malady of the liver. On the next day, when Uncle Serafino was walking up from the fields, he saw, in the mouth of the cave where the Etruscans had buried their dead, a youth of great radiance, who beckoned to him, but he was afraid and ran away. Then Serafino was stricken with a fever, and he called for the priest and told him what he had seen, and the priest went to the cave and found the jewels of the Madonna there in the dead leaves where the angel had been standing. That same year, on the road below the farm, her cousin Maria saw the devil, with horns, a pointed tail, and a tight red suit, just as in the pictures. She was fourteen at the time of the big snow, and she went that night after dark to the fountain and, turning back toward the tower where they then lived, she saw the wolves. It was a pack of six or seven, trotting up the stairs of the Via Cavour in the snow. She dropped her pitcher and ran into the tower, and her tongue was swollen with terror, but she looked out the cracks in the door and saw them, more churlish than dogs, more ragged, their ribs showing in their mangy coats and the blood of the sheep they had murdered falling from their mouths. She was terrified and she was rapt, as if the sight of the wolves moving over the snow was the spirits of the dead or some other part of the mystery that she knew to lie close to the heart of life, and when they had passed she would not have believed she had seen them if they had not left their tracks in the snow. She was seventeen when she went to work as a *donna di servizio* for the baron of little importance who had a villa on the hill, and it was the same summer that Antonio, in the dark field, called her his dewy rose and made her head swim. She confessed to the priest and did her penance and was absolved, but when this had happened six times the priest said they should become engaged, and so Antonio became her *fidanzato*. The mother of Antonio was not sympathetic, and after three years Clementina was still his rose and he was still her *fidanzato* and whenever the marriage was mentioned the mother of Antonio would hold her head and scream. In the autumn, the baron asked her to come to Rome as a *donna* and how could she say no when she had dreamed all the nights of her life of seeing the Pope with her own eyes and walking on streets that were lighted after dark with electricity?

In Rome she slept on straw and washed in a bucket, but the streets were a spectacle, although she had to work such hours that she was not often able to walk in the city. The baron promised to pay her twelve thousand lire a month, but he paid her nothing at the end of the first month and nothing at the end of the second, and the cook said that he often brought girls in from the country and paid them nothing. Opening the door for him one evening, she asked with great courtesy for her wages, and he said he had given her a room, a change of air, and a visit to Rome and that she was badly educated to ask for more. She had no coat to wear in the street, and there were holes in her shoes, and all she was given to eat was the leftovers from the baron's table. She saw that she would have to find another post, because she didn't have the money to go back to Nascosta. That next week, the cousin of the cook found her a place where she was both seamstress and *donna*, and here she worked even harder, but when the month was over there were no wages. Then she refused to finish a dress the signora had asked her to make for a reception.

She said she would not finish the dress until she had her wages. The signora angered herself and tore her hair, but she paid the wages. Then that night the cousin of the cook said that some Americans needed a *donna*. She put all the dirty dishes in the oven to give a false appearance of cleanliness, said her prayers in San Marcello's, and flew across Rome to where the Americans lived, feeling that every girl on the street that night was looking for the same post. The Americans were a family with two boys—well-educated people, although she could see that they were sad and foolish. They offered her twenty thousand lire in wages and showed her a very commodious room where she would live and said they hoped she would not be uncomfortable, and in the morning she moved her things to the Americans'.

She had heard much about Americans, about how they were generous and ignorant, and some of this was true, for they were very generous and treated her like a guest in the house, always asking her if she had time to do this and that and urging her to take a passage in the streets on Thursdays and Sundays. The signore was meager and tall and worked in the Embassy. His hair was cropped close like a German or a prisoner or someone recovering from an operation of the brain. His hair was black and strong, and if he had let it go and waved it with *frissone* the girls in the street would have admired him, but he went each week to the barber and had himself disfigured. He was very modest in other things and wore at the beach a concealing bathing costume, but he walked through the streets of Rome with the shape of his head naked for everyone to see. The signora was fine, with a skin like marble and many clothes, and it was a commodious and a diverting life, and Clementina prayed at San Marcello's that it would never end. They left all the lights burning as if electricity cost nothing, and they burned wood in the fireplace only to take off the evening chill, and they drank iced gin and vermouth before dinner. They smelled different. It was a pale smell, she thought—a weak smell—and it might have had something to do with the blood of northerners, or it might be because they took so many hot baths. They took so many hot baths that she could not understand why they were not neurasthenics. They ate Italian food and drank wine, and she hoped that if they ate enough pasta and oil they would have a strong and wholesome smell. Sometimes when she waited on table, she smelled them, but it was always a very weak smell and sometimes nothing. They spoiled their children, and sometimes the children spoke sharply or in an ill temper to their *genitori*, for which they should have been whipped, but they never whipped their children, these strangers, or even raised their voices in anger, or did anything else that would explain to the children the importance of their *genitori*, and once when the smallest boy was very badly disposed and should have been whipped, his mother took him instead to a toy store and bought him a sailboat. And sometimes when they were dressing to go out in the evening the signore would fasten his wife's clothes or her pearls, like a *cafone*, instead of ringing for Clementina. And once when there was no water in the flat and she had gone down the stairs to the fountain to get some, he came after her to help, and when she said that it was not possible for him to carry water, he said that it was not possible for him to sit by his fire while a young woman carried a heavy demijohn up and down the stairs. Then he took the demijohn out of her hands and went down to the fountain, where he could be seen getting water by the porter and all the other servants in the palace, and she watched this from the kitchen window and was so angry and ashamed that she had to take some wine for her stomach, for everyone would say that she was lazy and that she worked for a vulgar and badly educated family. And they did not believe in the dead. Once, walking down the *sala* in the dusk, she saw the spirit of a dead man before her so clearly that at first she thought it was the signore, until she saw him standing in the door. Then she screamed and dropped the tray with the glasses and bottles on it, and when the signore asked her why she had screamed and she said it was because she had seen a ghost he was not sympathetic. And once, in the back hall, she saw another ghost, the ghost of a bishop with a miter, and when she screamed and told the signore what she had seen he was not sympathetic.

But the children were sympathetic, and in the evening, when they were in bed, she told them the stories of Nascosta. The story they liked best was of the young farmer in Nascosta who was married to a beautiful woman named

Assunta. When they had been married a year, they had a fine son with dark curls and a golden skin, but from the first he was sickly, and he cried, and they thought there was a spell on him, and they took him to the doctor in Conciliano, riding all the way there on an *asino,* and the doctor said the baby was dying of starvation. But how could this be, they asked, for the breasts of Assunta were so full of milk they stained her blouse. But the doctor said to watch at night, and they went home by *asino* and ate their supper, and Assunta fell asleep, but the husband stayed awake to watch, and then at midnight he saw in the moonlight a great viper come over the threshold of the farmhouse and come into the bed and suck the milk from the breasts of the woman, but the husband could not move, for if he moved, the viper would have put his fangs into her breast and killed her, and when the serpent had sucked her breasts dry he went back across the floor and over the threshold in the moonlight, and then the farmer gave the alarm, and all the farmers from around came, and they found against the wall of the farm a nest of eight great serpents, fat with milk, who were so poisonous that even their breath was mortal, and they beat them to death with clubs, and this was a true story, because she had passed the farm where it happened a hundred times. And the story they preferred after this was of the lady in Conciliano who became the lover of a handsome stranger from America. But one night she noticed on his back a small mark like a leaf and remembered that the son who had been taken away from her many years ago was so marked, and knew then that this lover was her son. She ran then to the church to ask forgiveness in the confessional, but the priest—he was a fat and a haughty man—said there was no forgiveness for her sin and, *subito,* there was in the confessional a loud clatter of bones. Then the people came and opened the confessional and saw that where there had been a proud and a haughty priest there was nothing but bones. And she also told the children about the miracle of the jewels of the Madonna, and the *tempo infame* when she had seen the wolves coming up the Via Cavour, and the time her cousin Maria had seen the devil in his red suit.

She went with this American family to the mountains in

July, and in August to Venice, and, coming back to Rome in the fall, she understood them to say that they were leaving Italy, and they had the trunks brought up from the cellar, and she helped the signora with the packing. Now she had five pairs of shoes and eight dresses and money in the bank, but the thought of looking for another post with a Roman signora who might spit in her eye whenever she felt like it was discouraging, and one day when she was repairing a dress for the signora she became so discouraged that she cried. Then she explained to the signora how hard the life of a *donna* was working for Romans, and the signora said they would take her to the new world if she liked. They would take her for six months on an impermanent visa; it would be diverting for her and a help to them. Then all the arrangements were made, and she went to Nascosta, and the mamma cried and asked her not to go, and everyone in the village said she should not go, but this was jealousy, because they had never had a chance to go anywhere—not even Conciliano. And for once the world where she had lived and been so happy seemed to her truly to be an old world where the customs and the walls were older than the people, and she felt that she would be happier in a world where the walls were all new, even if the people were savage.

When the time came to go, they drove to Naples, stopping whenever the signore felt like it to have a little coffee and cognac, traveling very commodiously like millionaires and staying in a *di lusso* hotel in Naples, where she had a room to herself. But on the morning when they sailed she felt a great sadness, for who can live out a good life but in his own country? Then she told herself that it was only a voyage—she would come home in six months—and what had the good God made the world so strange and various for if it was not to be seen? She had her passport stamped and went aboard the ship feeling very emotional. It was an American ship, as cold as winter, and at lunch there was ice water on the table, and what was not cold was flavorless and badly cooked, and she came back to her deep feeling that, while these people were kind and generous, they were ignorant and the men fastened their wives' pearls and, with all their money, they did not know any better than to eat platefuls of raw steak washed down with coffee that tasted like medicine. They were not beautiful or elegant and they had pale eyes, but what disgusted her most on the ship were the old women, who in her country would be wearing black in memory of their numerous dead and, as suited their time of life, would move slowly and inspire dignity. But here the old ladies spoke in shrill voices and wore bright clothes and as much jewelry, all of it false, as you find on the Madonna of Nascosta, and painted their faces and tinted their hair. But who was deceived, for you could see how haggard under the paint were their cheeks, and that their necks were rucked and seamed like the necks of turtles, and although they smelled like the *campagna* in spring they were as withered and dry as the flowers on a tomb. They were like straw, and this must be a savage country where the old had no wisdom or taste and did not deserve or receive the respect of their children and their grandchildren and had forgotten their dead.

But it would be beautiful, she thought, because she had seen in magazines and newspapers photographs of the towers of the city of New York, towers of gold and silver, against the blue sky, in a city that had never once been touched by the damage of war. But it was raining when they came up the Narrows, and when she looked for the towers they were not to be seen, and when she asked for the towers she was told they were lost in the rain. She was disappointed, for what she could see of this new world seemed ugly, and all the people who dreamed of it were deceived. It was like Naples in the time of the war, and she wished she had not come. The customs man who went through her bags was badly educated. They took a taxi and a train to Washington, the capital of the new world, and then another taxi, and she could see out of the window that all the buildings were copies of the buildings of Imperial Rome, and they looked ghostly to her in the night lights, as if the Forum had risen again from the dust. They drove into the country, where the houses were all of wood and all new and where the washbasins and bathtubs were very commodious, and in the morning her signora showed her the machines and how to work them.

At first she was suspicious of the washing machine, for it used a fortune in soap and hot water and did not clean the clothes, and it reminded her of how happy she had been at the fountain in Nascosta, talking with her friends and making everything as clean as new. But little by little the machine seemed to her more *carina,* for it was after all only a machine, and it filled itself and emptied itself and turned around and around, and it seemed marvelous to her that a machine could remember so much and was always there, ready and waiting to do its work. And then there was the machine for washing the dishes, and you could wash the dishes in a costume for the evening without getting a drop of water on your gloves. When the signora was away and the boys were at school, first she would put some dirty clothes in the washing machine and start that, and then she would put some dirty dishes in the other machine and start that, and then she would put a nice *saltimbocca alla romana* in the electric frying pan and start that, and then she would sit in the *salone* in front of the TV and listen to all the machines around her doing the work, and it delighted her and made her feel powerful. Then there was the *frigidario* in the kitchen, making ice and keeping the butter as hard as stone, and there was the deep freeze full of lamb and beef as fresh as the day when they had been killed, and there was an electric egg beater, and a machine for squeezing the oranges, and a machine for breathing in the dust, and she would have them all going at once, and a machine for making the toast—all bright silver—where you put in the plain bread and turned your back and *allora,* there were two pieces of toast just the color you had asked for, and all done by the machine.

During the day, her signore was away at the office, but her signora, who in Rome had lived like a princess, seemed in the new world to be a secretary, and she thought perhaps that they were poor and the signora must work. She was always talking on the telephone and making computations and writing letters like a secretary. She was always hurried during the day and tired at night, like a secretary. Because they were both tired at night, the house was not as peaceful as it had been in Rome. Finally she asked the signora to explain what she was a secretary for, and the signora said that she was not a secretary but that she was kept busy raising money for the poor and the sick and the mad. This seemed to Clementina very strange. The climate also seemed to her strange and humid, bad for the lungs and the liver, but the trees at that season were very colorful—she had never seen this before; they were gold and red and yellow, and their leaves fell through the air as in some great hall in Rome or Venice where the paint is flaking from the pictures on the ceiling.

There was a *paisano*, an old man they called Joe, from bas-Italia, who delivered the milk. He had sixty years or more and was bent with carrying milk bottles, but she went with him to the movies, where he could explain the story to her in Italian and where he pinched her and asked her to marry him. This was a joke, as far as Clementina was concerned. There were strange *feste* in the new world—one with a turkey and no saints—and then there was the *festa* of the *Natale*, and she herself had never seen anything so discourteous to the Holy Virgin and the sainted baby. First they bought a green tree and then they put it up in the *salone* and hung it with shining necklaces, as if it were a holy saint with the power of curing evil and hearing prayers. *Mamma mia!* A tree! She was confessed by a priest who gave her the tail of the devil for not coming to church every Sunday of her life and who was very rigid. When she went to Mass, they took the collection three times. She thought that when she returned to Rome she would write an article for the paper about the church in this new world where there was not even the wristbone of a saint to kiss and where they made offerings to a green tree and forgot the travail of the Holy Virgin and took the collection three times. And then there was the snow, but it was more *carina* than the snow in Nascosta—there were no wolves, and the signori skied in the mountains, and the children played in the snow and the house was always warm.

She still went with Joe every Sunday to the movies, where he told her the story, asked her to marry him, and pinched her. Once, before the movies, he stopped at a fine house all made of wood and neatly painted, and he unlocked the door and took her upstairs to a nice apartment with paper on the walls, the floor shining with varnish, and five rooms in all, with a modern bathroom, and he said that if she would marry him it would all be hers. He would buy her a machine for washing the dishes and a machine for beating the eggs and a frying pan like the signora had that knew when to turn off the *saltimbocca alla romana*. When she asked him where he would find all the money to do this, he said that he had saved seventeen thousand dollars, and he took a book out of his pocket, a bankbook, and there was stamped in it seventeen thousand two hundred and thirty dollars and seventeen cents. It would all be hers if she would come and be his wife. She said no, but after the movies, when she was in bed, it made her sad to think of all the machinery and she wished that she had never come to the new world. Nothing would ever be the same again. When she went back to Nascosta and told them that a man—not a beautiful man, but one who was honest and gentle—had offered her seventeen thousand dollars and a place with five rooms, they would never believe her. They would think she was crazy, and how could she lie again on straw in a cold room and be contented? Her impermanent visa expired in April and she would have to go home then, but the signore said that he could apply for an extension if she liked, and she begged him to do this. In the kitchen one night, she heard them speaking in low voices and she guessed they were speaking about her affairs, but he did not speak to her until much later when the others had gone up and she came into the room to say good night.

"I'm very sorry, Clementina," he said, "but they won't give me an extension."

"It doesn't matter," she said. "If I am not wanted in this country, I will go home."

"It isn't that, Clementina, it's the law. I'm very sorry. Your visa expires on the twelfth. I'll get your passage on a boat before then."

"Thank you, signore," she said. "Good night."

She would go back, she thought. She would take the boat, she would debark at Naples, she would catch a train at the Mergellina and in Rome a *pullman,* and go out the Tiburtina with the curtains of the bus swaying and the purple clouds of exhaust rolling out behind them when they climbed the hill at Tivoli. Her eyes filled with tears when she thought of kissing Mamma and giving her the silver-framed photograph of Dana Andrews that she had bought at Woolworth's for her present. Then she would sit on the piazza with such a ring of people around her as would form for an accident, speaking in her own tongue and drinking the wine they had made and talking about the new world where there were frying pans with brains and where even the powder for cleaning the *gabinetti* smelled of roses. She saw the scene distinctly, the fountain spray blowing on the wind, but then she saw gathering in the imagined faces of her townsmen a look of disbelief. Who would believe her tales? Who would listen? They would have admired her if she had seen the devil, like Cousin Maria, but she had seen a sort of paradise and no one cared. In leaving one world and coming to another she had lost both.

Then she opened and reread a package of letters written from Nascosta by her Uncle Sebastiano. That night, his letters all seemed dolorous. The autumn had come on quickly, he wrote; and it was cold, even in September, and many of the olives and the grapes were lost, and *la bomba atomica* had ruined the seasons of Italy. Now the shadow of the town fell over the valley earlier, and she remembered herself the beginnings of winter—the sudden hoarfrost lying on the grapes and wild flowers, and the *contadini* coming in at dark on their *asini,* loaded down with roots and other scraps of wood, for wood was hard to find in that country and one would ride ten *kilometri* for a bundle of green olive cuttings, and she could remember the cold in her bones and see the *asini* against the yellow light of evening and hear the lonely noise of stones falling down the steep path, falling away from their hooves. And in December Sebastiano wrote that it was again the time of the wolves. The *tempo infame* had come to Nascosta, and wolves had killed six of the padrone's sheep, and there was no *abbacchio,* and no eggs, either, for pasta, and the piazza was buried in snow up to the edge of the fountain, and they knew hunger and cold, and she could remember both.

The room where she read these letters was warm. The lights were pink. She had a silver ashtray like a signora, and, if she had wanted, in her private bathroom she could have drawn a hot bath up to her neck. Did the Holy Virgin mean for her to live in a wilderness and die of starvation? Was it wrong to take the comforts that were held out to her? The faces of her people appeared to her again, and how dark were their skin, their hair, and their eyes, she thought, as if through living with fair people she had taken on the dispositions and the prejudices of the fair. The faces seemed to regard her with reproach, with earthen patience, with a sweet, dignified, and despairing regard, but why should she be compelled to return and drink sour wine in the darkness of the hills? In this new world they had found the secret of youth, and would the saints in heaven have refused a life of youthfulness if it had been God's will? She remembered how in Nascosta even the most beautiful fell quickly under the darkness of time, like flowers without care; how even the most beautiful became bent and toothless, their dark clothes smelling, as the mamma's did, of smoke and manure. But in this country she could have forever white teeth and color in her hair. Until the day she died she would have shoes with heels and rings on her fingers, and the attention of men, for in this new world one lived ten lifetimes and never felt the pinch of age; no, never. She would marry Joe. She would stay here and live ten lives, with a skin like marble and always the teeth with which to bite the meat.

On the next night, her signore told her when the boats were leaving, and when he had finished she said, "I am not going back."

"I don't understand."

"I will marry Joe."

"But Joe's a great deal older than you, Clementina."

"Joe is sixty-three."

"And you?"

"I am twenty-four."

"Do you love Joe?'

"Oh no, signore. How could I love him, with his big paunch like a sackful of apples and so many wrinkles at the back of his neck you could tell your fortune there? It is not possible."

"Clementina, I admire Joe," the signore said. "He's an honest man. If you marry him, you must care for him."

"Oh, I'll care for him, signore. I'll make his bed and cook his supper, but I will never let him touch me."

He deliberated, looked down at the floor, and finally said, "I will not let you marry Joe, Clementina."

"But why?"

"I won't let you marry him unless you'll be his wife. You must love him."

"But, signore, in Nascosta there would be no sense in marrying a man whose land did not adjoin yours, and does that mean then that your heart will fly out to him?"

"This is not Nascosta."

"But all marriages are like this, signore. If people married for love, the world would not be a place in which to live, it would be a hospital for the mad. Did not the signora marry you because of the money and the conveniences you bring her?" He did not answer, but she saw his face flush dark with blood. "Oh, signore, my signore," she said, "you talk like a boy with stars in your eyes, a thin boy at the fountain, his head full of the *poesia*. I am only trying to unfold to you that I am only marrying Joe so that I can stay in this country, and you are talking like a boy."

"I am not talking like a boy," he said. Then he rose from the chair. "I am not talking like a boy. Who do you think you are? When you came to us in Rome you didn't have shoes or a coat."

"Signore, you do not understand me. Perhaps I will love him, but I am only trying to unfold to you that I am not marrying for love."

"And that's what I'm trying to explain to you. I won't stand for it."

"I will leave your house, signore."

"I'm responsible for you."

"No, signore. Joe is responsible for me now."

"Then get out of my house."

She went upstairs to her room and cried and cried, in anger and pity for this grown fool, but she packed her things. In the morning she cooked the breakfast, but she stayed in the kitchen until the signore had gone to work, and then the signora came down and cried, and the children cried, and at noon Joe came to get her in his car and took her to the Pelluchis', who were *paisani* and with whom she would stay until she and Joe were married. Maria Pelluchi explained to her that in the new world one was married like a princess, and this was so. For three weeks she was in and out of the stores with Maria—first to buy the wedding dress for herself, all white and the latest mode, with a tail of satin to drag along the ground, but economical, too, because the tail could be adjusted, making the dress like a costume for the grand evening. Then there were the costumes for Maria and her sister, who would be the attendants, and these were yellow and lavender and could be used later as costumes for the evening. Then there were the shoes and the flowers and the clothes for traveling and the suitcase, and nothing was rented. And when the day of the wedding arrived she was so tired that she had milk in the knees and walked through it all like a dream, of which she could remember very little. There were many *paisani* at the reception and much wine, food, and music, and then she took with Joe a train to New York, where the buildings were so tall they made her feel homesick and of little importance. In New York, they spent the night in a hotel, and the next day they took a *di lusso* train, only for signori who were going to Atlantic City, with a special chair for each passenger and a waiter to bring things to eat and drink. She hung behind her chair the mink stole that Joe had given her for a present, and everyone saw it and admired it and judged her to be a rich signora. Joe called the waiter over and told him to bring some whiskey and seltz, but the waiter pretended not to understand what Joe was saying and to be so busy waiting on other people that they would have to be the last, and she felt again that shame and anger at discovering that because they could not speak elegantly the language of this new country they would be treated with great discourtesy, as if they were pigs. And that is the way they were treated on the passage, for the waiter did not come near them again, as if their money was not as good as the money of the others. They went first through a great, dark *galleria* and then out into a country that was ugly and potent with fire exploding from many chimneys, and there were trees and rivers and places for boating. She looked out of the window at the country that streamed by as swiftly and gently as water, to see if it was as fair as Italy, but what she saw was that it was not her country, her earth. Near the cities they passed those places where the poor lived and where washing was hung on lines, and she thought that this was the same—that washing on lines must be the same all over the world. And the houses of the poor were the same, too, the way they leaned against one another and had gardens that were not commodious but that were cultivated, you could see, with gentleness and love. It was in the middle of the day or later when they left, and, as they sped through the country and the afternoon, she saw that the schools were closing and that on the streets there were many children carrying books and riding bicycles and playing games, and many of them waved to the train as it rolled along and she waved back to them. She waved to some children who were walking through the high grass in a field, and she waved to two boys on a bridge, and she waved to an old man, and they all waved back to her, and she waved to three girls, and she waved to a lady who was pushing a baby carriage, and she waved to a little boy who was wearing a yellow coat and carrying a valise, and he waved back. They all waved back. Then she could see that they were coming close to the ocean, for there was a bareness in the air and not so many trees and many pictures of hotels painted on wood saying how many hundreds of rooms they had and how many different kinds of places for drinking cocktails, and she was happy to see the name of their hotel on one of these signs and to be sure that it was *di lusso*. Then the train stopped and it was the end of the passage and she felt shy and timid, but Joe said *andiamo*, and the waiter who had been so discourteous to them took their bags away and reached for her mink stole, but she said, "No, thank you," and got it away from him, the pig. And then there was the largest black car she had ever seen in her life, with a sign on it saying the name of their hotel, and they got into this with some other people, but they did not speak to one another on the passage, because she did not want the others to know that she could not speak the language of this country.

The hotel was very *di lusso*, and they ascended in an elevator, and walked down a hall that was covered with thick carpet, into a fine room, also with thick carpet everywhere, and a toilet—only with no bidet—and when the waiter had gone Joe got a bottle of whiskey out of his valise and had a drink and asked her to come and sit in his lap, and she said a little later, later, for it was unlucky in the daylight, and it would be better to wait for the moon to rise, and she would like to go down and see the dining rooms and lounges. She wondered if the salt air would be bad for the mink, and Joe had another drink, and out of the window she could see the ocean and the lines of white waves coming in, and because the windows were closed and she could not hear the sound the waves made when they broke it seemed like something she was dreaming. They went down again, not speaking, because she had distinctly come to feel that it was better not to speak the *bella lingua* in such a luxurious place, and they looked in the bars and dining rooms, which were grand, and they went out onto a broad walk beside the sea and there was salt in the air, like Venice, and it smelled like Venice, and there was also a smell of frying food in the air, which reminded her of the feast of San Giuseppe in Rome. On one side of them was the green, cold sea, which she had crossed to come to this new world, and on the other side of them there were many diverting things. They walked along until they came to the gypsies, where there was in the window a drawing of the human hand and where one's fortune could be told, and when she asked if they could speak Italian they said, *"Si, si, si, non c'è dubbio!"* and Joe gave her a dollar, and she went behind a curtain with the gypsy, who looked at her hand and began to tell her fortune, but it was not Italian she was speaking, it was a bastard language of a little Spanish and a little something that Clementina had never heard before, and she could only understand a word here and there, like "the sea" and "the voyage," but she could not tell if this was a voyage she would make or a voyage she had made, and she became impatient with the gypsy, who had made a lie in saying that she spoke in Italian, and she asked for her money back, but the gypsy said that if the money was given back there would be a curse on it. And, knowing what strong curses the gypsies make, she did not create a further disturbance, and went out where Joe was waiting for her on the wooden walk, and walked along again between the green sea and the diversion of frying food, where people called to them to come in and spend their money, smiling and beckoning wickedly like the angels of hell. And then there was the *tramonto*, and the lights went on gloriously like pearls, and, looking back, she could see the pink windows of the hotel where they were known, where they had a room of their own they could return to when they pleased, and the noise of the sea sounded like distant blasting in the mountains.

She was a good wife to him, and in the morning he was so grateful that he bought her a silver dish for the butter and a cover for the ironing board and a pair of red pants, laced with gold. The mother would give her the tail of the devil, she knew, for wearing pants, and in Rome she herself would spit in the eye of a woman who was so badly educated as to wear pants, but this was a new world and it was no sin, and in the afternoon she wore the mink stole and the red pants and went with Joe up and down the wooden walk above the sea. On Saturday they went home, and on Monday they bought the furniture, and on Tuesday it was delivered, and on Friday she put on the red pants and went to the supermarket with Maria Pelluchi, who explained the labels on the boxes to her, and she looked so much like an American that people were surprised when she could not speak the language.

But if she could not speak the language she could do everything else, and she even learned to drink whiskey without coughing and spitting. In the morning, she would turn on all the machines and watch the TV, learning the words of the songs, and in the afternoons Maria Pelluchi came to her house and they watched the TV together, and in the evening she watched it with Joe. She tried to write the mother about the things she had bought—much finer things than the Pope possessed—but she realized that the letter would only bewilder the mother, and in the end she sent her nothing but postcards. No one could describe how diverting and commodious her life had become. In the summer, in the evenings, Joe took her to the races in Baltimore, and she had never seen anything so *carina*—the little horses and the lights and the flowers and the red coat on the marshal with his bugle. That summer, they went to the races every Friday and sometimes oftener, and it was one night there, when she was wearing her red pants and drinking whiskey, that she saw her signore for the first time since they had quarreled.

She asked him how he was, and how was his family, and he said, "We are not together. We are divorced." Looking into his face then, she saw not the end of his marriage but the end of his happiness. The advantage was hers, because hadn't she explained to him that he was like a boy with stars in his eyes, but some part of his loss seemed to be hers as well. Then he went away, and, although the race was beginning, she saw instead the white snow and the wolves of Nascosta, the pack coming up the Via Cavour and crossing the piazza as if they were bent on some errand of that darkness that she knew to lie at the heart of life, and, remembering the cold on her skin and the whiteness of the snow and the stealth of the wolves, she wondered why the good God had opened up so many choices and made life so strange and diverse.

BOY IN ROME

IT IS RAINING in Rome (the boy wrote) where we live in a palace with a golden ceiling and where the wisteria is in bloom but you can't hear the noise of the rain in Rome. In the beginning we used to spend the summers in Nantucket and the winters in Rome and in Nantucket you can hear the rain and I like to lie in bed at night and listen to it running in the grass like fire because then you can see in what they call the mind's eye the number of different things that grow in the sea pastures there like heather and clover and fern. We used to come down to New York in the fall and sail in October and the best record of those trips would be the pictures the ship's photographer used to take and post in the library after the whoopee: I mean men wearing lady's hats and old people playing musical chairs and the whole thing lit by flashbulbs so that it looked like a thunderstorm in a forest. I used to play Ping-Pong with the old people and I always won the Ping-Pong tournament on the eastward crossing. I won a pigskin wallet on the Italian Line and a pen and pencil set on American Export and three handkerchiefs from the Home Lines, and once we traveled on a Greek ship where I won a cigarette lighter. I gave the cigarette lighter to my father because in those days I didn't drink, smoke, swear, or speak Italian.

My father was kind to me and when I was little he took me to the zoo, and let me ride horseback, and always bought me some pastry and an orangeade at a café, and while I drank my orangeade he always had a vermouth with a double shot of gin or later when there were so many Americans in Rome a Martini but I am not writing a story about a boy who sees his father sneaking drinks. The only time I spoke Italian then was when my father and I would visit the raven in the Borghese Gardens and feed him peanuts. When the raven saw us he would say *buon giorno* and I would say *buon giorno* and then when I gave him the peanuts he would say *grazie* and then when we walked away he would say *ciao*. My father died three years ago and he was buried in the Protestant Cemetery in Rome. There were a lot of people there and at the end of it my mother put an arm around me and she said, "We won't *ever* leave him alone here, will we, Pietro? We won't ever, *ever*, leave him alone here, will we, dear?" So some Americans live in Rome because of the income tax and some Americans live in Rome because they're divorced or oversexed or poetic or have some other reason for feeling that they might be persecuted at home and some Americans live in Rome because they work there, but we live in Rome because my father's bones lie in the Protestant Cemetery.

My grandfather was a tycoon and I think that is why my father liked to live in Rome. My grandfather started life with nothing at all, but he made plenty and he expected everybody else to do what he did, although this was not possible. The only time I ever saw much of my grandfather was when we used to visit him at his summer house in Colorado. The thing I remember mostly is the Sunday-night suppers which my grandfather used to cook when the maids and the cook were off. He always cooked a steak and even before he got the fire started everybody would be so nervous that you lost your appetite. He always had a terrible time getting the fire started and everyone sat around watching him, but you didn't dare say a word. There was no drinking because he didn't approve of drinking, but my parents used to drink plenty in the bathroom. Well, after it took him half an hour to get the fire started, he would put the steak on the grill and we would all go on sitting there. What made everyone nervous was that they knew they were going to be judged. If we had done anything wrong during the week that Grampa disliked, well now we would know about it. He used to practically have a fit just cooking a steak. When the fat caught on fire his face would turn purple and he would jump up and down and run around. When the steak was done we would each get a dinner plate and stand in line and this was the judgment. If Grampa liked you he would give you a nice piece of meat, but if he felt or suspected that you had done something wrong he would give you only a tiny piece of gristle. Well, you'd be surprised how embarrassing it is to find yourself holding this big plate with just a bit of gristle on it. You feel awful.

One week I tried to do everything right so I would not get a piece of gristle. I washed the station wagon and helped Grandma in the garden and brought in wood for the house fires, but all I got on Sunday was a little bit of gristle. So then I said, *Grampa,* I said, *I don't understand why you cook steak for us every Sunday if it makes you so unhappy. Mother knows how to cook and she could at least scramble some eggs and I know how to make sandwiches. I could make sandwiches. I mean if you want to cook for us that would be nice but it looks to me like you don't and I think it would be nicer if instead of going through this torture chamber we just had some scrambled eggs in the kitchen. I mean I don't see why if you ask people to have supper with you it should make you so irritable.* Well, he put down his knife and his fork and I've seen his face get purple when the fat was burning, but I've never seen it get so purple as it did that night. *You Goddamned weak-minded, parasitic ape,* he shouted at me, and then he went into the house and upstairs to his bedroom, slamming about every door he passed, and my mother took me down into the garden and told me I had made an awful mistake, but I couldn't see that I had done anything wrong. But in a little while I could hear my father and my grandfather yelling and swearing at one another and in the morning we went away and we never came back and when he died he left me one dollar.

It was the next year that my father died and I missed him. It is against everything I believe in and not even the kind of thing I am interested in, but I used to think that he would come back from the kingdom of the dead and give me help. I have the head and shoulders to do a man's work, but sometimes I am disappointed in my maturity and my disappointment in myself is deepest when I get off a train at the end of the day in a city that isn't my home like Florence with the *tramontana* blowing and no one in the square in front of the station who doesn't have to be there because of that merciless wind. Then it seems that I am not like myself or the sum of what I have learned but that I am stripped of my emotional savings by the *tramontana* and the hour and the strangeness of the place and I do not know which way to turn except of course to turn away from the wind. It was like that when I went alone on the train to Florence and the *tramontana* was blowing and there was no one in the piazza. I was feeling lonely and then someone touched me on the shoulder and I thought it was my father come back from the kingdom of the dead and that we would all be happy together again and help one another. Who touched me was a ragged old man who was trying to sell me some souvenir key rings and when I saw the sores on his face I felt worse than ever and it seemed to me that there was a big hole torn in my life and that I was never going to get all the loving I needed and that autumn once in Rome I stayed late in school and was coming home on the trolley car and it was after seven and all the stores and offices were closing and everybody was going home and rushed and someone touched me on the shoulder and I thought it was my father come again from the kingdom of the dead. I didn't even look around this time because it could have been anybody—a priest or a tart or an old man who had lost his balance—but I had the same feeling that we would all be happy together again and then I knew that I was never going to get all the loving I needed, no, never.

After my father passed away we gave up the trips to Nantucket and lived all the time in the Palazzo Orvieta. This is a beautiful and a somber building with a famous staircase, although the staircase is only lighted with ten-watt bulbs and is full of shadows in the evening. There is not always enough hot water and it is often drafty, for Rome is sometimes cold and rainy in the winter in spite of all the naked statues. It might make you angry to hear the men in the dark streets singing melodiously about the roses of eternal spring and the sunny Mediterranean skies. You could sing a song, I guess, about the cold *trattorie* and the cold churches, the cold wine shops and the cold bars, about the burst pipes and the backfired toilets and about how the city lies under the snow like an old man with a stroke and everybody coughing in the streets—even the archdukes and cardinals coughing—but it wouldn't make much of a song. I go to the Sant' Angelo di Padova International School for Catholics although I am not a Catholic and take Communion at St. Paul within the Gates every Sunday morning. In the wintertime there are usually only two of us in church, not counting the priest or canon, and the other is a man I don't like to sit beside because he smells of Chinese Temple Incense although it has occurred to me that when I have not had a bath for three or four days because of the shortage of hot water in the palace he may not want to sit beside me. When the tourists come in March there are more people in church.

In the beginning most of my mother's friends were Americans and she used to give a big American party at Christmas each year. There was champagne and cake and my mother's friend Tibi would play the piano and they would all stand around the piano and sing "Silent Night" and "We Three Kings of Orient Are" and "Hark, the Herald Angels Sing" and other carols from home. I never liked these parties because all the divorcées used to cry. There are hundreds of American divorcées in Rome and they are all friends of my mother's and after the second verse of "Silent Night" they would all begin to bawl, but once I was on the street on Christmas Eve, walking down the street in front of our palace, when the windows were open because it was warm or perhaps to let the smoke out from those high windows, and I heard all these people singing "Silent Night" in this foreign city with its ruins and its fountains and it gave me gooseflesh. My mother stopped giving this party when she got to know so many titled Italians. My mother likes the nobility and she doesn't care what they look like. Sometimes the old Princess Tavola-Calda comes to our house for tea. She is either a dwarf or shrunk with age. Her clothes are thin and held together with darns and she always explains that her best clothes, the court dresses and so forth, are in a big trunk but that she has lost the key. She has chin whiskers and a mongrel dog named Zimba on a piece of clothesline. She comes to our house to fill up on tea cakes, but my mother doesn't care because she is a real princess and has the blood of Caesars in her veins.

My mother's best friend is an American writer named Tibi who lives in Rome. There are plenty of these but I don't think they do much writing. Tibi is usually very tired. He wants to go to the opera in Naples but he is too tired to make the trip. Tibi wants to go to the country for a month and finish his novel but all you can get to eat in the country is roast lamb and roast lamb makes Tibi tired.

Tibi has never seen the Castel Sant' Angelo because just the thought of walking across the river makes Tibi tired. Tibi is always going here or going there but he never gets anywhere because he is so tired. At first you might think someone should put him into a cold shower or light a firecracker under his chair and then you realize that Tibi really is tired or that this tiredness gets him what he wants out of life such as my mother's affections and that he lies around our palace with a purpose just as I expect to get what I want out of life by walking around the streets as if I had won a prize fight or a tennis match.

That autumn we were planning to drive down to Naples with Tibi and say goodbye to some friends who were sailing for home, but Tibi came around to the palace that morning and said he was too *tired* to make the trip. My mother doesn't like to go anywhere without Tibi and first she was gentle with him and said we would all go down together on the train but Tibi was too tired even for this. Then they went into another room and I could hear my mother's voice and when she came out I could see she had been crying and she and I went down to Naples alone on the train. We were going to stay two nights there with an old marquesa and see the ship off and go to the opera at San Carlo. We went down that day and the sailing was the next morning, and we said goodbye and watched the lines fall into the water as the ship began to move.

By now the harbor of Naples must be full of tears, so many are wept there whenever a boat pulls out with its load of emigrants, and I wondered what it would feel like to go away once more because you hear so much talk about loving Italy among my mother's friends that you might think the peninsula was shaped more like a naked woman than a boot. Would I miss it, I wondered, or would it all slip away like a house of cards, would it all slip away and be forgotten? Beside me on the wharf was an old Italian lady in black clothes who kept calling across the water, "Blessed are you, blessed are you, you will see the New World," but the man she was shouting to, he was an old, old man, was crying like a baby.

After lunch there was nothing to do so I bought an excursion ticket to Vesuvius. There were some Germans and Swiss on the bus and these two American girls, the one who had dyed her hair in some hotel washbasin a funny shade of red and was wearing a mink stole in spite of the heat and the other who had not dyed her hair at all and at the sight of whom my heart, like a big owl, some night bird anyhow, spread its wings and flew away. She was beautiful. Just looking at her different parts, her nose and her neck and so forth, made her seem more beautiful. She kept poking her fingers into her black hair—patting and poking it—and just watching her do this made me very happy. I was jumping, I was positively jumping just watching her fix her hair. I could see I was making a fool of myself as I looked out of the window at all the smoking chimneys south of Naples and the *Autostrada* there and thought that when I next saw her she would look less beautiful and so I waited until we got to the end of the *Autostrada* and looked again and she was as fair as ever.

They were together and there wasn't any way of getting between them when we lined up for the chair lift but then after we were swung up the mountain to the summit it turned out that the redhead couldn't walk around because she had on sandals and the hot cinders of the volcano burned her feet so I offered to show her friend the sights, what there were to be seen, Sorrento and Capri in the distance and the crater and so forth. Her name was Eva and she was an American making a tour and when I asked her about her friend she said the redhead wasn't her friend at all but that they had just met in the bus and sat down together because they could both speak English but that was all. She told me she was an actress, she was twenty-two years old and did television commercials, mostly advertising ladies' razors, but that she only did the speaking part, some other girl did the shaving, and that she had made enough money doing this to come to Europe.

I sat with Eva on the bus back into Naples and we talked all the time. She said she liked Italian cooking and that her father had not wanted her to come alone to Europe. She had quarreled with her father. I told her everything I could think of, even about my father being buried in the Protestant Cemetery. I thought I would ask her to have supper with me at Santa Lucia and so forth but then somewhere near the Garibaldi Station the bus ran into one of those little Fiats and there was the usual thing that happens in Italy when you have a collision. The driver got out to make a speech and everybody got out to hear him and then when we got back into the bus again, Eva wasn't there. It was late in the day and near the station and very crowded, but I've seen enough movies of men looking for their loved ones in railroad-station crowds to feel sure that this was all going to end happily and I looked for her for an hour on the street, but I never saw her again. I went back to the place where we were staying, but there was no one at home, thank God, and I went up to my room, a furnished room—I forgot to say that the marquesa rented rooms—and lay down on my bed and put my face in my arms and thought again that I was never going to get all the loving I needed, no, never.

Later my mother came in and said that I would get my clothes all rumpled, lying around like that. Then she sat down in a chair by my window and asked wasn't the view *divine* although I knew that all she could see was a lagoon and some hills and some fishermen on a wharf. I was cross at my mother and with some reason too because she has always taught me to respect invisible things and I have been an apt pupil but I could see that night that nothing invisible was going to improve the way I felt. She has always taught me that the most powerful moral forces in life are invisible and I have always gone along with her thinking that starlight and rain are what keep the world from flying to pieces. I went along with her up until that moment when it was revealed to me that all her teaching was wrong—it was fainthearted and revolting like the smell of Chinese Temple Incense that comes off that man in church. What did the starlight have to do with my needs? I have often admired my mother, especially in repose, and she is supposed to be beautiful but that night she seemed to me very misled. I sat on the edge of the bed staring at her and thinking how ignorant she was. Then I had a terrible impulse. What I wanted to do was to give her a boot, a swift kick, and I imagined—I let myself imagine the whole awful scene—the look on her face and the way she would straighten her skirt and say that I was an ungrateful son; that I had never appreciated the advantages of my life: Christmas in Kitzbühel, etc. She said something else about the divine view and the charming fishermen and I went to the window to see what she was talking about.

What was so charming about the fishermen? They were dirty, you could be sure, and dishonest and dumb and one of them was probably drunk because he kept taking swigs out of a wine bottle. While they wasted their time at the wharf their wives and their children were probably waiting for them to bring home some money and what was so charming about that? The sky was golden but this was nothing but an illusion of gas and fire, and the water was blue but the harbor there is full of sewage and the many lights on the hill came from the windows of cold and ugly houses where the rooms would smell of *parmigiano* rinds and washing. The light was golden, but then the golden light changed to another color, deeper and rosier, and I wondered where I had seen the color before and I thought I had seen it on the outer petals of those roses that bloom late on the mountains after the hoarfrost. Then it paled off, it got so pale that you could see the smoke from the city rising into the air and then through the smoke the evening star turned on, burning like a street light, and I began to count the other stars as they appeared, but very soon they were countless. Then suddenly my mother began to cry and I knew she was crying because she was so lonely in the world and I was very sorry that I had ever wanted to kick her. Then she said why didn't we not go to San Carlo and take the night train to Rome which is what we did and she was happy to see Tibi lying on the sofa when we got back.

WHILE LYING in bed that night, thinking about Eva and everything, in that city where you can't hear the rain, I thought I would go home. Nobody in Italy really understood me. If I said good morning to the porter, he wouldn't know what I was saying. If I went out on the balcony and shouted *help* or *fire* or something like that, nobody would understand. I thought I would like to go back to Nantucket where I would be understood and where there would be many girls like Eva walking on the beach. Also it seemed to me that a person should live in his own country; that there is always something a little funny or queer about people who choose to live in another country. Now my mother has many American friends who speak fluent Italian and wear Italian clothes—everything they have is Italian including their husbands sometimes—but to me there always seems to be something a little funny about them as if their stockings were crooked or their underwear showed and I think that is always true about people who choose to live in another country. I wanted to go home. I talked with my mother about it the next day and she said it was out of the question, I couldn't go alone and she didn't know anyone any more. Then I asked if I could go back for the summer and she said she couldn't afford this, she was going to rent a villa at Santa Marinella and then I asked if I could get the money myself could I go and she said of course.

I began to look around then for a part-time job and these are hard to find, but I asked Tibi and he was helpful. He isn't much, but he is always kind. He said he would keep me in mind and then one day when I came home he asked me if I would like to work for Roncari, the sightseeing company, as a guide on Saturdays and Sundays. This was perfect for me and they tried me out the next Saturday on the bus that goes to Hadrian's Villa and Tivoli and the Americans liked me I guess because I reminded them of home and I went to work on Sunday. The money was fair and the hours fitted in with my schoolwork and I also thought that the job might offer me an opportunity to meet some wealthy American industrialist who would want to take me back to the United States and teach me all about the steel business, but I never did. I saw lots of American wanderers though and I saw, in my course of duty, how great is the hunger in many Americans who have comfortable and lovely homes to wander around the world and see its sights. Sometimes on Saturdays and Sundays when I watched them piling into the bus it seemed to me that we are a wandering breed like the nomads. On the trip we first went out to the villa where they had a half hour to see the place and take pictures, and then I counted them off and we drove up the big hill to Tivoli and the Villa d'Este. They took more pictures and I showed them where to buy the cheapest postcards and then we would drive down the Tiburtina past all the new factories here and into Rome. In the wintertime it was dark when we got back to the city and the bus would go around to all the hotels where they were staying or someplace near anyhow. The tourists were always very quiet on the trip back and I think this was because, in their sightseeing bus, they felt the strangeness of Rome swirling around them with its lights and haste and cooking smells, where they had no friends and relations, no business of any kind really but to visit ruins. The last stop was up by the Pincian Gate and it was often windy there in the winter and I would wonder if there was really any substance to life and if it wasn't all like this, really, hungry travelers, some of them with sore feet, looking for dim hotel lights in a city that is not supposed to suffer winter but that suffers plenty, and everybody speaking another language.

I opened a bank account in the Santo Spirito and on Easter vacation I worked full-time on the Rome–Florence run.

In this business there are shirt, bladder, and hair stops. A shirt stop is two days where you can get a shirt washed and a hair stop is three days where the ladies can get their hair fixed. I would pick up the passengers on Monday morning and sitting up in front with the driver would tell them the names of the castles and roads and rivers and villages we went by. We stopped at Avezano and Assisi. Perugia was a bladder stop and we got to Florence about seven in the evening. In the morning I would pick up another group who were coming down from Venice. Venice is a hair stop.

When vacation was over I went back to school but about a week after this they called me from Roncari and said that a guide was sick and could I take the Tivoli bus. Then I did something terrible, I made the worst decision I ever made so far. No one was listening and I said I would. I was thinking about Nantucket and going home to a place where I would be understood. I played hooky the next day and when I came home nobody noticed the difference. I thought I would feel guilty, but I didn't feel guilty at all. What I felt was lonely. Then Roncari called again and I skipped another day and then they offered me a steady job and I never went back to school at all. I was making money, but I felt lonely all the time. I had lost all my friends and my place in the world and it seemed to me that my life was nothing but a lie. Then one of the Italian guides complained because I didn't have a license. They were very strict about this and they had to fire me and then I didn't have any place to go. I couldn't go back to school and I couldn't hang around the palace. I'd get up in the morning and take my books—I always carried my books—and would just bum around the streets or the Forum and eat my sandwiches and sometimes go to the movies in the afternoon. Then when it was time for school and soccer practice to be over I would go home where Tibi was usually sitting around with my mother.

Tibi knew all about my playing hooky and I guess his friends at Roncari had told him but he promised not to tell my mother. We had a long talk together one night when my mother was getting dressed to go out. He was saying first how strange it was that I wanted to go home and he didn't want to go home. Tibi doesn't want to go home because he has a difficult family situation. He doesn't get along with his father who is a businessman and he has a stepmother named Verna and he hates Verna. He doesn't ever want to go home. But then he asked me how much money I had saved and I told him I had enough to get home but not to live on or anything or get back and he said he thought he could do something to help me and I trusted him because after all he had got me the job with Roncari.

The next day was Saturday and my mother told me not to make any plans because we were going to pay a visit to the old Princess Tavola-Calda. I said I didn't much want to go but she said I had to go and that was that. We went over there around four, after the siesta. Her palace is in an old part of Rome where the streets turn in on themselves and a run-down quarter too where like in any other run-down quarter they sell secondhand mattresses and old clothes and powders against fleas and bedbugs and cures for itchiness and other thorns in the flesh of the poor. We could tell which palace was hers because the old Princess had her head out of one of the windows and was having a fight with a fat woman who was sweeping the steps with a broom. We stopped at the corner because my mother thought the Princess would not want us to see her having a fight. The Princess wanted the broom and the fat woman said that if she wanted a broom she could buy a broom. She, the fat woman, had worked for the Princess forty-eight years and was paid so miserably that every night she and her husband sat down to a supper of water and air. The Princess came right back at her in spite of her age and frailty and said she had been robbed by the government and that there was nothing but air in her own stomach and that she needed the broom to sweep the *salone.* Then the fat woman said that if she gave her the broom she would give it to her in the squash. Then the Princess got sarcastic and called the fat woman *cara, cara,* and said she had cared for her like a baby for forty-eight years, bringing her lemons when she was sick, and that yet she did not have the gentleness to loan her a broom for a moment. Then the fat woman looked up at the Princess and took her right hand and bunched her lips together between her thumb and forefinger and made the loudest raspberry I ever heard. Then the Princess said, *Cara, cara, thank you very much my dear, my old and gentle friend,* and went away from the window and came back with a pot of water which she meant to dump on the fat woman, but she missed and only wet the steps. Then the fat woman said, *Thank you, your royal highness, thank you, Princess,* and went on sweeping and the Princess slammed the windows and went away.

During all of this some men were going in and out of the palace carrying old automobile tires and loading them onto a truck and I found out later that the whole palace, excepting where the Princess lived, was rented out as a warehouse. To the right of the big door there was a porter's apartment and the porter stopped us and asked us what we wanted. My mother said we wanted to take tea with the Princess and he said we were wasting our time. The Princess was crazy—*matta*—and if we thought she was going to give us something we were mistaken because everything she had belonged to him and his wife who had worked for the Princess forty-eight years without salary. Then he said he didn't like Americans because we had bombed Frascati and Tivoli and all the rest of it. Finally I pushed him out of the way and we climbed up to the third floor where the Princess had some rooms. Zimba barked when we rang and she opened the door a crack and then she let us in.

I suppose everyone knows what old Rome is like by now but she needed that broom. First she apologized for her ragged clothes but she said that all her best clothes, the court dresses and so forth, were locked up in this trunk and she had lost the key. She has a fancy way of speaking so that you would be sure to know that she is a Princess or at least some kind of a noble in spite of her rags. She is supposed to be a famous miser and I think this is true because although she sometimes sounds crazy you never lose the feeling that she is cunning and greedy. She thanked us for coming, but she said that she could not offer us any tea or coffee or cake or wine because her life was such a misfortune. The land redistribution projects after the war had drawn all the good peasants away from her farms and she could not find anyone to work her lands. The government taxed her so unmercifully that she could not afford to buy a pinch of tea and all that was left to her was her paintings and while these were worth millions the government claimed that they belonged to the nation and would not let her sell them. Then she said she would like to give me a present, a seashell that had been given to her by the Emperor of Germany when he came to Rome in 1912 and called on her dear father, the Prince. She went out of the room and she was gone a long time and when she came back she said alas, she could not give me the shell because it was locked up with her court dresses in the trunk with the lost key. We said goodbye and went out, but the porter was waiting for us to make sure we hadn't gotten anything and we walked back home through the terrible traffic and the dark streets.

Tibi was there when we got back and he had dinner with us and then late that night when I was reading someone knocked on my bedroom door and it was Tibi. He seemed to have gone out because he had his coat on over his shoulders like a cloak the way the Romans do. He also had on his plush hat and his tight pants and his plush shoes with gold buckles and he looked like a messenger. I think he felt like a messenger too because he was very excited and spoke to me in a whisper. He said it was all arranged. The old Princess had a painting that she wanted to sell in the United States and he had convinced her that I could smuggle it in. It was a small painting, a Pinturicchio, not much bigger than a shirt. All I had to do was look like a schoolboy and no one would search my bags. He had given the old woman all of his money as security and he said some other people had bought in and I wondered if he meant my mother, but I didn't think this was possible. When I delivered the painting in New York I would be paid five hundred dollars. He would drive me down to Naples on Saturday morning. There was a little airline that carried passengers and freight between Naples and Madrid and I could take this and catch a plane for New York in Madrid and pick up my five hundred dollars on Monday morning. Then he went away. It was after midnight, but I got out of bed and packed my suitcase. I wouldn't be leaving for a week but I was on my way.

I remember the morning I left, Saturday, that is. I got up around seven and had some coffee and looked into my suitcase again. Later I heard the maid taking in my mother's breakfast tray. There was nothing to do but wait for Tibi and I went out onto the balcony to watch for him in the street. I knew he would have to park the car in the *piazzale* and cross the street in front of the palace. Saturday in Rome is like any other day and the street was crowded with traffic and there were crowds on the sidewalk—Romans and pilgrims and members of religious orders and tourists with cameras. It was a nice day and while it is not my place to say that Rome is the most beautiful city in the world I have often thought that, with its flat-topped pines and the buildings all the colors of ripening, folded in among the hills like bone and paper, and those big round clouds that in Nantucket would mean a thunderstorm before supper but that mean nothing in Rome, only that the sky will turn purple and fill up with stars and all the lighthearted people make it a lively place to be; and at least a thousand travelers before me, at least a thousand must have said that the light and the air are like wine, those yellow wines from the *castelli* that you drink in the fall. Then in the crowd I noticed someone wearing the brown habit that they wear at the Sant' Angelo School and then I saw it was my home-room teacher, Father Antonini. He was looking for our address. The bell rang and the maid answered it and I heard the priest ask for my mother. Then the maid went down to my mother's room and I heard my mother go out to the vestibule and say, "Oh, Father Antonini, how nice to see you."

"Peter has been sick?" he asked.

"What made you think so?"

"He hasn't been in school for six weeks."

"Yes," she said, but you could tell that all of her heart wasn't in the lie. It was very upsetting to hear my mother telling this lie; upsetting because I could see that she didn't care about me or whether or not I got an education or anything, that all she wanted was that I should get Tibi's old picture across the border so that he would have some money. "Yes. He's been very sick."

"Could I see him?"

"Oh, no. I've sent him home to the States."

I left the balcony then and went down the *salone* to the hall and down the hall to my room and waited for her there. "You'd better go down and wait for Tibi," she said. "Kiss me goodbye and go. Quickly. *Quickly.* I *hate* scenes." If she hated scenes I wondered then why she always made such painful scenes but this was the way we had parted ever since I could remember and I got my suitcase and went out and waited for Tibi in the courtyard.

It was half past nine or later before he showed up and even before he spoke I could tell what he was going to say. He was too *tired* to drive me to Naples. He had the Pinturicchio wrapped in brown paper and twine and I opened my suitcase and put it in with my shirts. I didn't say goodbye to him—I made up my mind then that I was never going to speak to him again—and I started for the station.

I have been to Naples many times but that day I felt very strange. The first thing when I went into the railroad station I thought I was being followed by the porter from the Palazzo Tavola-Calda. I looked around twice but this stranger bent his face over a newspaper and I couldn't be sure but I felt so strange anyhow that it seemed I might have imagined him. Then when I was standing in line at the ticket window someone touched me on the shoulder and I had that awful feeling that my father had come back to give me help. It was an old man who wanted a match and I lighted his cigarette but I could still feel the warmth of the touch on my shoulder and that memory that we would all be happy together again and help one another and then the feeling that I would never get all the loving I needed, no, never.

I got into the train and watched the other passengers hurrying along the platform and this time I saw the porter. There was no mistake. I had only seen him once but I could remember his face and I guessed he was looking for me. He didn't seem to see me and went on down to the third-class compartments and I wondered then if this was the Big World, if this was really what it was like—women throwing themselves away over halfwits like Tibi and purloined paintings and pursuers. I wasn't worried about the porter but I was worried about the idea that life was this much of a contest.

(BUT I AM NOT A BOY in Rome but a grown man in the old prison and river town of Ossining, swatting hornets on this autumn afternoon with a rolled-up newspaper. I can see the Hudson River from my window. A dead rat floats downstream and two men in a sinking rowboat come up against the tide. One of them is rowing desperately with a boat seat and I wonder have they escaped from prison or have they just been fishing for perch and why should I exchange this scene for the dark streets around the Pantheon? Why, never having received from my parents anything but affection and understanding, should I invent a grotesque old man, a foreign grave, and a foolish mother? What is the incurable loneliness that makes me want to pose as a fatherless child in a cold wind and wouldn't the imposture make a better story than Tibi and the Pinturicchio? But my father taught me, while we hoed the beans, that I should complete for better or worse whatever I had begun and so we go back to the scene where he leaves the train in Naples.)

IN NAPLES I got off the train at the Mergellina hoping to duck the porter. Only a handful of people got off there and I don't think the porter was one of them although I couldn't be sure. There was a little hotel on a side street near the station and I went there and took a room and left my suitcase with the painting in it under the bed and locked the door. Then I went out to look for the office of the airline where I could buy my ticket and this was way on the other side of Naples. It was a small airline and a very small office and I think the man who sold me my ticket was probably the pilot too. The plane left at eleven that night so then I walked back to the hotel and as soon as I stepped into the lobby the lady at the desk said that my friend was waiting for me and there he was, the porter, with two *carabinieri*. He began to holler and yell—all the same things. I had bombed Frascati and Tivoli and invented the hydrogen bomb and now I was stealing one of the paintings that formed the invaluable heritage of the Italian people. The *carabinieri* were really very nice although I don't like to talk with people who wear swords but when I asked if I could call the Consulate they said yes and I did. It was about four o'clock then and they said they would send an officer over and pretty soon this big nice American came over who kept saying "Yurp." I told him I was carrying a package for a friend and that I didn't know what it contained and he said, "Yurp, yurp." He had on a big double-breasted suit and he seemed to be having some trouble with his belt or his underwear because every so often he would take hold of his waist and give it a big yank. Then everyone agreed that in order to open my package they would have to get a justice and I got my bag and we all got into the car the consular officer had and drove off to some *questura* or courthouse where we had to wait a half hour for the justice to put on his sash of office with the golden fringe. Then I opened my suitcase and he passed the package to an attendant who undid the knots in the twine. Then the justice unwrapped the package and there was nothing in it but a piece of cardboard. The porter let out such a roar of anger and disappointment when he saw this that I don't think he could have been an accomplice and I think the old lady must have thought the whole thing up herself. They would never get back the money they had paid her, any of them, and I could see her, licking her chops like Reddy the Fox. I even felt sorry for Tibi.

In the morning I tried to get a refund on my plane ticket but the office was shut and so then I walked to the Mergellina to get the morning train to Rome. A ship was in. There were twenty-five or thirty tourists waiting on the platform. They were tired and excited, you could see, and were pointing at the espresso machine and asking if they couldn't have a large cup with cream but they didn't seem funny to me that morning—they seemed to be nice and admirable and it seemed to me that there was a lot of seriousness at the bottom of their wandering. I was not as disappointed myself as I have been about less important things and I even felt a little cheerful because I knew that I would go back to Nantucket sometime or if not to Nantucket to someplace where I would be understood. And then I remembered that old lady in Naples, so long ago, shouting across the water, "Blessed are you, blessed are you, you will see America, you will see the New World," and I knew that large cars and frozen food and hot water were not what she meant. "Blessed are you, blessed are you," she kept shouting across the water and I knew that she thought of a place where there are no police with swords and no greedy nobility and no dishonesty and no briberies and no delays and no fear of cold and hunger and war and if all that she imagined was not true, it was a noble idea and that was the main thing.

A MISCELLANY OF CHARACTERS THAT WILL NOT APPEAR

1. The pretty girl at the Princeton-Dartmouth Rugby game. She wandered up and down behind the crowd that was ranged along the foul line. She seemed to have no date, no particular companion but to be known to everyone. Everyone called her name (Florrie), everyone was happy to see her, and, as she stopped to speak with friends, one man put his hand flat on the small of her back, and at this touch (in spite of the fine weather and the green of the playing field) a dark and thoughtful look came over his face, as if he felt immortal longings. Her hair was a fine dark gold, and she pulled a curl down over her eyes and peered through it. Her nose was a little too quick, but the effect was sensual and aristocratic, her arms and legs were round and fine but not at all womanly, and she squinted her violet eyes. It was the first half, there was no score, and Dartmouth kicked the ball offside. It was a muffed kick, and it went directly into her arms. The catch was graceful; she seemed to have been chosen to receive the ball and stood there for a second, smiling, bowing, observed by everyone, before she tossed it charmingly and clumsily back into play. There was some applause. Then everyone turned their attention from Florrie back to the field, and a second later she dropped to her knees, cover-

ing her face with her hands, recoiling violently from the excitement. She seemed very shy. Someone opened a can of beer and passed it to her, and she stood and wandered again along the foul line and out of the pages of my novel because I never saw her again.

2. All parts for Marlon Brando.

3. All scornful descriptions of American landscapes with ruined tenements, automobile dumps, polluted rivers, jerry-built ranch houses, abandoned miniature golf links, cinder deserts, ugly hoardings, unsightly oil derricks, diseased elm trees, eroded farmlands, gaudy and fanciful gas stations, unclean motels, candlelit tearooms, and streams paved with beer cans, for these are not, as they might seem to be, the ruins of our civilization but are the temporary encampments and outposts of the civilization that we—you and I—shall build.

4. All such scenes as the following: "Clarissa stepped into the room and then ________________________________
____."
Out with this and all other explicit descriptions of sexual commerce, for how can we describe the most exalted experience of our physical lives, as if—jack, wrench, hubcap, and nuts—we were describing the changing of a flat tire?

5. All lushes. For example: The curtain rises on the copy office of a Madison Avenue advertising agency, where X, our principal character, is working out the exploitation plans for a new brand of rye whiskey. On a drafting table to the right of his fruitwood desk is a pile of suggestions from the art department. Monarchal and baronial crests and escutcheons have been suggested for the label. For advertising there is a suggested scene of plantation life where the long-gone cotton aristocracy drink whiskey on a magnificent porch. X is not satisfied with this and examines next a watercolor of pioneer America. How fresh, cold, and musical is the stream that pours through the forest. The tongues of the brook speak into the melancholy silence of a lost wilderness, and what is that in the corner of the blue sky but a flight of carrier pigeons. On a rock in the foreground a wiry young man, in rude leather clothing and a coonskin hat, is drinking rye from a stone jug. This prospect seems to sadden X, and he goes on to the next

suggestion, which is that one entertain with rye; that one invite to one's house one exploded literary celebrity, one unemployed actress, the grandniece of a President of the United States, one broken-down bore, and one sullen and wicked literary critic. They stand grouped around an enormous bottle of rye. This picture disgusts X, and he goes on to the last, where a fair young couple in evening dress stand at dusk on a medieval battlement (aren't those the lights and towers of Siena in the distance?) toasting what must be a seduction of indescribable prowess and duration in the rye that is easy on your dollar.

X is not satisfied. He turns away from the drafting table and walks toward his desk. He is a slender man of indiscernible age, although time seems to have seized upon his eye sockets and the scruff of his neck. This last is seamed and scored as wildly as some disjointed geodetic survey. There is a cut as deep as a saber scar running diagonally from the left to the right of his neck with so many deep and numerous branches and tributaries that the effect is discouraging. But it is in his eyes that the recoil of time is most noticeable. Here we see, as on a sandy point we see the working of two tides, how the powers of his exaltation and his misery, his lusts and his aspirations, have stamped a wilderness of wrinkles onto the dark and pouchy skin. He may have tired his eyes looking at Vega through a telescope or reading Keats by a dim light, but his gaze seems hangdog and impure. These details would lead you to believe that he was a man of some age, but suddenly he drops his left shoulder very gracefully and shoots the cuff of his silk shirt as if he were eighteen—nineteen at the most. He glances at his Italian calendar watch. It is ten in the morning. His office is soundproofed and preternaturally still. The voice of the city comes faintly to his high window. He stares at his dispatch case, darkened by the rains of England, France, Italy, and Spain. He is in the throes of a grueling melancholy that makes the painted walls of his office (pale yellow and pale blue) seem like fabrications of paper put up to conceal the volcanos and floodwaters that are the terms of his misery. He seems to be approaching the moment of his death, the moment of his conception, some critical point in time. His head, his shoulders, and his hands begin to tremble. He opens his dispatch case, takes out a bottle of rye, gets to his knees, and thirstily empties the bottle.

He is on the skids, of course, and we will bother with only one more scene. After having been fired from the office where we last saw him he is offered a job in Cleveland, where the rumors of his weakness seem not to have reached. He has gone to Cleveland to settle the arrangements and rent a house for his family. Now they are waiting at the railroad station for him to return with good news. His pretty wife, his three children, and the two dogs have all come down to welcome Daddy. It is dusk in the suburb where they live. They are, by this time, a family that have received more than their share of discouragements, but in having been recently denied the common promises and rewards of their way of life—the new car and the new bicycle—they have discovered a melancholy but steady quality of affection that has nothing to do with acquisitions. They have glimpsed, in their troubled love for Daddy, the thrill of a destiny. The local rattles into view. A soft spray of golden sparks falls from the brake box as the train slows and halts. They all feel, in the intensity of their anticipation, nearly incorporeal. Seven men and two women leave the train, but where is Daddy? It takes two conductors to get him down the stairs. He has lost his hat, his necktie, and his topcoat, and someone has blacked his right eye. He still holds the dispatch case under one arm. No one speaks, no one weeps as they get him into the car and drive him out of our sight, out of our jurisdiction and concern. Out they go, male and female, all the lushes; they throw so little true light on the way we live.

6. And while we are about it, out go all those homosexuals who have taken such a dominating position in recent fiction. Isn't it time that we embraced the indiscretion and inconstancy of the flesh and moved on? The scene this time is Hewitt's Beach on the afternoon of the Fourth of July. Mrs. Ditmar, the wife of the Governor, and her son Randall have carried their picnic lunch up the beach to a deserted cove, although the American flag on the clubhouse can be seen flying beyond the dunes. The boy is sixteen, well formed, his skin the fine gold of youth, and he seems to his lonely mother so beautiful that she admires him with trepidation. For the last ten years her husband, the Governor, has neglected her in favor of his

intelligent and pretty executive secretary. Mrs. Ditmar has absorbed, with the extraordinary commodiousness of human nature, a nearly daily score of wounds. Of course she loves her son. She finds nothing of her husband in his appearance. He has the best qualities of *her* family, she thinks, and she is old enough to think that such things as a slender foot and fine hair are marks of breeding, as indeed they may be. His shoulders are square. His body is compact. As he throws a stone into the sea, it is not the force with which he throws the stone that absorbs her but the fine grace with which his arm completes the circular motion once the stone has left his hand—as if every gesture he made were linked, one to the other. Like any lover, she is immoderate and does not want the afternoon with him to end. She does not dare wish for an eternity, but she wishes the day had more hours than is possible. She fingers her pearls in her worn hands, and admires their sea lights, and wonders how they would look against his golden skin.

He is a little bored. He would rather be with men and girls his own age, but his mother has supported him and defended him so he finds some security in her company. She has been a staunch and formidable protector. She can and has intimidated the headmaster and most of the teachers at his school. Offshore he sees the sails of the racing fleet and wishes briefly that he were with them, but he refused an invitation to crew and has not enough self-confidence to skipper, so in a sense he chose to be alone on the beach with his mother. He is timid about competitive sports, about the whole appearance of organized society, as if it concealed a force that might tear him to pieces; but why is this? Is he a coward, and is there such a thing? Is one born a coward, as one is born dark or fair? Is his mother's surveillance excessive; has she gone so far in protecting him that he has become vulnerable and morbid? But considering how intimately he knows the depth of her unhappiness, how can he forsake her until she has found other friends?

He thinks of his father with pain. He has tried to know and love his father, but all their plans come to nothing. The fishing trip was canceled by the unexpected arrival of the Governor of Massachusetts. At the ball park a messenger brought him a note saying that his father would be unable to come. When he fell out of the pear tree and broke his arm, his father would undoubtedly have visited him in the hospital had he not been in Washington. He learned to cast with a fly rod, feeling that, cast by cast, he might work his way into the terrain of his father's affection and esteem, but his father had never found time to admire him. He can grasp the power of his own disappointment. This emotion surrounds him like a mass of energy, but an energy that has no wheels to drive, no stones to move. These sad thoughts can be seen in his posture. His shoulders droop. He looks childish and forlorn, and his mother calls him to her.

He sits in the sand at her feet, and she runs her fingers through his light hair. Then she does something hideous. One wants to look away but not before we have seen her undo her pearls and fasten them around his golden neck. "See how they shine," says she, doing the clasp as irrevocably as the manacle is welded to the prisoner's shin.

Out they go; out they go; for, like Clarissa and the lush, they shed too little light.

7. In closing—in closing, that is, for this afternoon (I have to go to the dentist and then have my hair cut), I would like to consider the career of my laconic old friend Royden Blake. We can, for reasons of convenience, divide his work into four periods. First there were the bitter moral anecdotes—he must have written a hundred—that proved that most of our deeds are sinful. This was followed, as you will remember, by nearly a decade of snobbism, in which he never wrote of characters who had less than sixty-five thousand dollars a year. He memorized the names of the Groton faculty and the bartenders at "21." All of his characters were waited on hand and foot by punctilious servants, but when you went to his house for dinner you found the chairs held together with picture wire, you ate fried eggs from a cracked plate, the doorknobs came off in your hand, and if you wanted to flush the toilet you had to lift the lid off the water tank, roll up a sleeve, and reach deep into the cold and rusty water to manipulate the valves. When he had finished with snobbism, he made the error I have mentioned in Item 4 and then moved on into his romantic period, where he wrote "The Necklace of Malvio d'Alfi" (with that memorable scene of childbirth on a mountain pass), "The

Wreck of the S.S. *Lorelei*," "The King of the Trojans," and "The Lost Girdle of Venus," to name only a few. He was quite sick at the time, and his incompetence seemed to be increasing. His work was characterized by everything that I have mentioned. In his pages one found alcoholics, scarifying descriptions of the American landscape, and fat parts for Marlon Brando. You might say that he had lost the gift of evoking the perfumes of life: sea water, the smoke of burning hemlock, and the breasts of women. He had damaged, you might say, the ear's innermost chamber, where we hear the heavy noise of the dragon's tail moving over the dead leaves. I never liked him, but he was a colleague and a drinking companion, and when I heard, in my home in Kitzbühel, that he was dying, I drove to Innsbruck and took the express to Venice, where he then lived. It was in the late autumn. Cold and brilliant. The boarded-up palaces of the Grand Canal—gaunt, bedizened, and crowned—looked like the haggard faces of that grade of nobility that shows up for the royal weddings in Hesse. He was living in a *pensione* on a back canal. There was a high tide, the reception hall was flooded, and I got to the staircase over an arrangement of duckboards. I brought him a bottle of Turinese gin and a package of Austrian cigarettes, but he was too far gone for these, I saw when I sat down in a painted chair (broken) beside his bed. "I'm working," he exclaimed. "I'm working. I can see it all. Listen to me!"

"Yes," I said.

"It begins like this," he said, and changed the level of his voice to correspond, I suppose, to the gravity of his narrative. "The Transalpini stops at Kirchbach at midnight," he said, looking in my direction to make sure that I had received the full impact of this poetic fact.

"Yes," I said.

"Here the passengers for Vienna continue on," he said sonorously, "while those for Padua must wait an hour. The station is kept open and heated for their convenience, and there is a bar where one may buy coffee and wine. One snowy night in March, three strangers at this bar fell into a conversation. The first was a tall, bald-headed man, wearing a sable-lined coat that reached to his ankles. The second was a beautiful American woman going to Isvia to attend funeral services for her only son, who had been killed in a mountain-climbing accident. The third was a white-haired, heavy Italian woman in a black shawl, who was treated with great deference by the waiter. He bowed from the waist when he poured her a glass of cheap wine, and addressed her as 'Your Majesty.' Avalanche warnings had been posted earlier in the day . . ." Then he put his head back on the pillow and died—indeed, these were his dying words, and the dying words, it seemed to me, of generations of storytellers, for how could this snowy and trumped-up pass, with its trio of travelers, hope to celebrate a world that lies spread out around us like a bewildering and stupendous dream?

THE CHIMERA

When I was young and used to go to the circus, there was an act called the Treviso Twins—Maria and Rosita. Rosita used to balance herself on the head of Maria, skulltop to skulltop, and be carried around the ring. Maria, as a result of this strenuous exercise, had developed short, muscular legs and a comical walk, and whenever I see my wife walking away from me I remember Maria Treviso. My wife is a big woman. She is one of the five daughters of Colonel Boysen, a Georgia politician, who was a friend of Calvin Coolidge. He went to the White House seven times, and my wife has a heart-shaped pillow embroidered with the word LOVE that was either the work of Mrs. Coolidge or was at one time in her possession. My wife and I are terribly unhappy together, but we have three beautiful children, and we try to keep things going. I do what I have to do, like everyone else, and one of the things I have to do is to serve my wife breakfast in bed. I try to fix her a nice breakfast, because this sometimes improves her disposition, which is generally terrible. One morning not long ago, when I brought her a tray she clapped her hands to her face and began to cry. I looked at the tray to see if there was anything wrong. It was a nice breakfast—two hard-boiled eggs, a piece of Danish, and a Coca-Cola spiked with gin. That's what she likes. I've never learned to cook bacon. The eggs looked all right and the dishes were clean, so I asked her what was the matter. She lifted her hands from her eyes—her face was wet with tears and her eyes were haggard—and said, in the Boysen-family accent, "I cannot any longer endure being served breakfast in bed by a hairy man in his underwear."

I took a shower and dressed and went to work, but when I came home that night I could see that things were no better; she was still offended by my appearance that morning.

I cook most of the dinners on a charcoal grill in the back yard. Zena doesn't like to cook and neither do I, but it's pleasant being out of doors, and I like tending the fire. Our neighbors, Mr. Livermore and Mr. Kovacs, also do a lot of cooking outside. Mr. Livermore wears a chef's hat and an apron that says "Name Your Pizen," and he also has a sign that says DANGER. MEN COOKING. Mr. Kovacs and I don't wear costumes, but I think we're more serious-minded. Mr. Kovacs once cooked a leg of lamb and another time a little turkey. We had hamburger that night, and I noticed that Zena didn't seem to have any appetite. The children ate heartily, but as soon as they were through—perhaps they sensed a quarrel—slipped off into the television room to watch the quarrels there. They were right about the quarrel. Zena began it.

"You're so inconsiderate," she thundered. "You never think of me."

"I'm sorry, darling," I said. "Wasn't the hamburger done?" She was drinking straight gin, and I didn't want a quarrel.

"It wasn't the hamburger—I'm used to the garbage you cook. What I have for dinner is no longer of any importance to me. I've learned to get along with what I'm served. It's just that your whole attitude is so inconsiderate."

"What have I done, darling?" I always call her darling, hoping that she may come around.

"What have you done? What have you done?" Her voice rose, and her face got red, and she got to her feet and, standing above me, she screamed, "You've ruined my life, that's what you've done."

"I don't see how I've ruined your life," I said. "I guess you're disappointed—lots of people are—but I don't think it's fair to blame it all on your marriage. There are lots of things I wanted to do—I wanted to climb the Matterhorn—but I wouldn't blame the fact that I haven't on anyone else."

"You. Climb the Matterhorn. Ha. You couldn't even climb the Washington Monument. At least I've done that. I had important ambitions. I might have been a businesswoman, a TV writer, a politician, an actress. I might have been a congresswoman!"

"I didn't know you wanted to be a congresswoman," I said.

"That's the trouble with you. You never think of me. You never think of what I might have done. You've ruined my life!" Then she went upstairs to her bedroom and locked the door.

Her disappointment was painfully real, I knew, although I thought I had given her everything I had promised. The false promises, the ones whose unfulfillment made her so miserable, must have been made by Colonel Boysen, but he was dead. None of her sisters was happily married, and how disastrously unhappy they had been never struck me until that night. I mean, I had never put it together. Lila, the oldest, had lost her husband while they were taking a stroll on a high cliff above the Hudson. The police had questioned her, and the whole family, including me, had been indignant about their suspiciousness, but mightn't she have given him a little push? Stella, the next oldest, had married an alcoholic, who systematically drank himself out of the picture. But Stella had been capricious and unfaithful, and mightn't her conduct have hastened his death? Jessica's husband had been drowned mysteriously in Lake George when they had stopped at a motel and gone for a night swim. And Laura's husband had been killed in a freak automobile accident while Laura was at the wheel. Were they murderesses, I wondered—had I married into a family of incorrigible murderesses? Was Zena's disappointment at not being a congresswoman powerful enough to bring her to plot my death? I didn't think so. I seemed much less afraid for my life than to need tenderness, love, loving, good cheer—all the splendid and decent things I knew to be possible in the world.

The next day at lunch, a man from the office told me that he had met a girl named Lyle Smythe at a party and that she was a tart. This was not exactly what I wanted, but my need to reacquaint myself with the tenderer members of the sex was excruciating. We said goodbye in front of the restaurant, and then I went back in to look up Lyle Smythe's number in the telephone book and see if I could make a date. One of the light bulbs in the lamp that illuminated the directory was dead and the print seemed faint and blurred to me. I found her name, but it was on the darkest part of the page, where the binding and the clasp drew the book together, and I had trouble reading the number. Was I losing my sight? Did I need glasses or was it only because the light was dim? Was there some irony in the idea of a man who could no longer read a telephone book trying to find a mistress? By moving my head up and down like a duck I found that I could read the exchange, and I struck a match to read the number. The lighted match fell out of my fingers and set fire to the page. I blew on the fire to extinguish it, but this only raised the flames, and I had to beat out the fire with my hands. My first instinct was to turn my head around to see if I had been watched, and I had been, by a tall, thin man wearing a plastic hat cover and a blue transparent raincoat. His figure startled me. He seemed to represent something—conscience, or evil—and I went back to the office and never made the call.

That night, when I was washing the dishes, I heard Zena speak to me from the kitchen door. I turned and saw her standing there, holding my straight razor. (I have a heavy beard and shave with a straight-edged razor.) "You'd better not leave things like this lying around," she shouted. "If you know what's good for you, you'd better not leave things like this lying around. There are plenty of women in the world who would cut you to ribbons for what I've endured . . ." I wasn't afraid. What *did* I feel? I don't know. Bewilderment, crushing bewilderment, and some strange tenderness for poor Zena.

She went upstairs, and I went on washing the dishes and wondering if scenes like this were common on the street where I live. But God, oh, God, how much then I wanted some kind of liveliness, softness, gentleness, humor, sweetness, and kindness. And when the dishes were done, I went out of the house, out of the back door. In the dusk Mr. Livermore was dyeing the brown spots on his lawn with a squirt gun. Mr. Kovacs was cooking two rock hens. I did not invent this world, with all its paradoxes, but it was never my good fortune to travel, and since yards like these are perhaps the most I will see of life, I looked at the scene—even the DANGER. MEN COOKING sign—with intentness and feeling. There was music in the air—there always is—and it heightened my desire to see a beautiful woman. Then a sudden wind sprang up, a rain wind, and the smell of a deep forest—although there are no forests in my part of the world—mushroomed among the yards. The smell excited me, and I remembered what it was like to feel young and happy, wearing a sweater and clean cotton pants, and walking through the cool halls of the house where I was raised and where, in the summer, the leaves hung beyond all the open doors and windows in a thick curtain of green and gold. I didn't remember my youth—I seemed to recapture it. Even more—because, given some self-consciousness by retrospect, I esteemed as well as possessed the bold privileges of being young. There was the music of a waltz from the Livermores' television set. It must have been a commercial for deodorants, girdles, or ladies' razors, the air was so graceful and so somber. Then, as the music faded—the forest smell was still sharp in the air—I saw her walk up the grass, and she stepped into my arms.

Her name was Olga. I can't change her name any more than I can change her other attributes. She was nothing, I know, but an idle reverie. I've never fooled myself about this. I've imagined that I've won the daily double, climbed the Matterhorn, and sailed, first-class, for Europe, and I suppose I imagined Olga out of the same need for escape or tenderness, but, unlike any other reverie I've ever known, she came with a dossier of facts. She was beautiful, of course. Who, under the circumstances, would invent a shrew, a harridan? Her hair was dark, fragrant, and straight. Her face was oval, her skin was olive-colored, although I could hardly make out her features in the dusk. She had just come from California on the train. She had come not to help me but to ask my help. She needed protection from her husband, who was threatening to follow her. She needed love, strength, and counsel. I held her in my arms, basking in the grace and warmth of her presence. She cried when she spoke of her husband, and I knew what he looked like. I can see him now. He was an Army sergeant. There were scars on his thick neck, left from an attack of boils. His face was red. His hair was yellow. He wore a double row of campaign ribbons on a skin-tight uniform. His breath smelled of rye and toothpaste. I was so delighted by her company, her dependence, that I wondered—not at all seriously—if I wasn't missing a stitch. Did Mr. Livermore, dyeing his grass, have a friend as beautiful as mine? Did Mr. Kovacs? Did we share our disappointments this intimately? Was there such hidden balance and clemency in the universe that our needs were always requited? Then it began to rain. It was time for her to go, but we took such a long, sweet hour to say goodbye that when I went back into the kitchen I was wet through to the skin.

ON WEDNESDAY NIGHT I always take my wife to the Chinese restaurant in the village, and then we go to the movies. We order the family dinner for two, but my wife eats most of it. She's a big eater. She reaches right across the table and grabs my eggroll, empties the roast duck onto her plate, takes my fortune cookie away from me, and then when she's done she sighs a deep sigh and says, "Well, you certainly stuffed yourself." On Wednesdays I always eat a big lunch in town, so I won't be hungry. I always have the calves' liver and bacon or something like that, to fill me up.

As soon as I stepped into the restaurant that night, I thought I would see Olga. I hadn't known that she would return—I hadn't thought about it—but since I've seen the summit of the Matterhorn in my dreams much more than once, mightn't she reappear? I felt happy and expectant. I was glad that I had on my new suit and had remembered to get a haircut. I wanted her to see me at my best, and I wanted to see her in a brighter light than she had appeared in that rainy night. Then I noticed that the Muzak was playing the same somber and graceful waltz that I had heard coming from the Livermores' television, and I thought that perhaps this was no more than a deception of the music—some simple turn of memory that had fooled me as I had been fooled by the smell of the rain into thinking that I was young.

There was no Olga. I had no consolation. Then I felt

desperate, desolate, crushed. I noticed how Zena smacked her lips and gave me a challenging glare, as if she was daring me to touch the shrimp foo-yong. But I wanted Olga, and the force of my need seemed to re-establish her reality. How could anything I desired so ardently be unreal? The music was only a coincidence. I straightened up again and looked around the place cheerfully, expecting her to come in at any minute, but she never did.

I didn't think she would be at the movies—I knew she didn't like movies—but I still had the feeling that I would see her that night. I didn't deceive myself—I want to make this clear; I knew she was unreal, and yet she seemed to have some punctuality, some order, some schedule of engagements, and above all I needed her. After my wife went to bed I sat on the edge of the bathtub reading the newspaper. My wife doesn't like me to sit in the kitchen or the living room, so I read in the bathroom, where the light is bright. I was reading when Olga came in. There was no waltz music, no rain, nothing that could account for her presence, excepting my loneliness. "Oh, my darling," I said, "I thought you were going to meet me at the restaurant." She said something about not wanting to be seen by my wife. Then she sat down beside me on the bathtub, I put my arms around her, and we talked about her plans. She was looking for an apartment. She was then living in a cheap hotel, and she was having trouble finding a job. "It's too bad you can't type and take shorthand," I remember telling her. "It might almost be worthwhile going to school. . . . I'll look around and see if I can find anything. Sometimes there's an opening for a receptionist. . . . You could do that, couldn't you? I won't let you be a hat-check girl or a restaurant hostess. No, I won't let you. I'd rather pay your salary until something better comes along. . . ."

My wife threw open the bathroom door. Women's hair curlers, like grass dye and funny signs, only seem to me reminders of the fact that we must find more serious and finer things upon which to comment, and I will only say that my wife wears so many and such bellicose hair curlers that anybody trying to romance her would lose an eye. "You're talking to yourself," she thundered. "You can be heard all over the neighborhood. They'll think you're nuts. And you woke me up. You woke me out of a sound sleep, and you know that if my first sleep is interrupted I can't ever get to sleep again." She went to the medicine cabinet and took a sleeping pill. "If you want to talk to yourself," she said, "go on up to the attic." She went into her bedroom and locked the door.

A FEW NIGHTS LATER, when I was cooking some hamburgers in the back yard, I saw what looked to be some rain clouds rising in the south. I thought this was a good sign. I wanted some news of Olga. After I had washed the dishes I went out onto the back porch and waited. It isn't really a porch—just a little wooden platform with four steps above the garbage pail. Mr. Livermore was on his porch, and Mr. Kovacs was on his, and I wondered were they waiting as I was for a chimera. If I went over, for instance, and asked Mr. Livermore if his was blond or dark-haired, would he understand? For a minute I wanted terribly to confide in someone. Then the waltz began to play, and just as the music faded she ran up the steps.

Oh, she was very happy that night! She had a job. I knew all about this, because I'd found the job for her. She was working as a receptionist in the same building where I worked. What I didn't know was that she had found an apartment—not a real apartment but a furnished room with a kitchen and bath of her own. This was just as well, because all her furniture was in California. Would I come and see the apartment? Would I come now? We could take a late train in and spend the night there. I said that I would, but first I had to go into the house and see that the children were all right. I went upstairs to the children's room. They were asleep. Zena had already locked herself in. I went into the bathroom to wash my hands and found on the basin a note, written by Betty-Ann, my oldest daughter. "Dere Daddy," she had written, "do not leave us."

This convergence of reality and unreality was meaningless. The children wouldn't know anything about my delusion. The back porch, to their clear eyes, would seem empty. The note would only reflect their inescapable knowledge of my unhappiness. But Olga was waiting on the back porch. I seemed to feel her impatience, to see the way she swung her long legs, glanced at her wristwatch (a graduation present), and smoked a cigarette, and yet

I also seemed nailed to the house by the children's plea. I could not move. I remembered a parade in the village I had taken my youngest son to not long ago. It was the annual march of some provincial and fraternal order. There were two costumed bands and half a dozen platoons of the fraternity. The marchers, the brotherhood, seemed mostly to be marginal workmen—post-office clerks and barbers, I guess. The weather couldn't have accounted for my attitude, because I remembered clearly that it was fair and cool, but the effect of the parade upon me was as somber as if I had stood on some gallows hill. In the ranks I saw faces lined by drink, harried by hard work, wasted by worry, and stamped invariably with disappointment, as if the gala procession was meant to prove that life is a force of crushing compromise. The music was boisterous, but the faces and the bodies were the faces and bodies of compromised men, and I remembered getting to my feet and staring into the last of the ranks, looking for someone with clear features that would dispel my sober feelings. There was no one. Sitting in the bathroom, I seemed to join the marchers. I seemed to experience for the first time in my life what they must all have known—racked and torn with the desire to escape and nailed through the heart by a plea. I ran downstairs, but she had gone. No pretty woman waits very long for anyone. She was a fiction, and yet I couldn't bring her back, any more than I could change the fact that her wristwatch was a graduation present and that her name was Olga.

She didn't come back for a week, although Zena was in terrible shape and there seemed to be some ratio, some connection, between her obstreperousness and my ability to produce a phantom. Every night at eight, the Livermores' television played the somber and graceful waltz, and I was out there every night. Ten days passed before she returned. Mr. Kovacs was cooking. Mr. Livermore was dyeing his grass. The music had just begun to fade when she appeared. Something had changed. She held her head down. What was wrong? As she came up the steps, I saw that she had been drinking. She was drunk. She began to cry as soon as I took her in my arms. I stroked her soft, dark hair, perfectly happy to support and hold her, whatever had happened. She told me everything. She had gone out with a man from the office. He had got her drunk and seduced her. She had felt too ashamed of herself to go to work in the morning, and had spent some time in a bar. Then, half drunk, she had gone to the office to confront her seducer, and there had been a disorderly scene, during which she was fired. It was I she had betrayed, she told me. She didn't care about herself. I had given her a chance to lead a new life and she had failed me. I caught myself smiling fatuously at the depth of her dependence, the ardor with which she clung to me. I told her that it would be all right, that I would find her another job and pay her rent in the meantime. I forgave her, and she promised to return the next evening.

I rushed outdoors the next night—I was there long before eight o'clock, but she didn't come. She wasn't thoughtless. I knew that. She wouldn't deliberately disappoint me. She must be in trouble again, but how could I help her? How could I get word to her? I seemed to know the place where she lived. I knew its smells, its lights, the van Gogh reproduction, and the cigarette burns on the end table, but even so, the room didn't exist, and I couldn't look there. I thought of looking for her in the neighborhood bars, but I was not yet this insane. I waited for her again on the following night. I was worried but not angry when she didn't come, since she was, after all, such a defenseless child. The next night, it rained, and I knew she couldn't come, because she didn't have a raincoat. She had told me that. The next day was Saturday, and I thought she might put off her return until Monday, the weekend train and bus schedules being so erratic. This seemed sensible to me, but I was so convinced that she would return on Monday that when she failed me I felt terribly disappointed and lost. She came back on Thursday. It was the same hour of the day; I heard the same graceful waltz. Even down the length of the yard, long before she reached the porch, I could see she was staggering. Her hair was disheveled, her dress was torn, her wristwatch was missing. I asked her, for some reason, about the wristwatch, but she couldn't remember where it was. I took her in my arms, and she told me what had happened. Her seducer had returned. She had let him in; she had let him move in. He stayed three days, and then they gave a party for some friends of his. The party was late and noisy, and the landlady called the police, who raided the place and took Olga off to jail, where she was charged with using the room for immoral purposes. She was in the Women's House of Detention for three days before her case was heard. A kindly judge gave her a suspended sentence. Now she was going back to California, back to her husband. She was no better than he, she kept insisting; they were two of a kind. He had wired her the money, and she was taking the night train. I tried to persuade her to stay and begin a new life. I was willing to go on helping her; I would take her on any terms. I shook her by the shoulders—I remember that. I remember shouting at her, "You can't go! You can't go! You're all I have. If you go, it will only prove that even the most transparent inventions of my imagination are subject to lust and age. You can't go! You can't leave me alone!"

"Stop talking to yourself," my wife shouted from the television room, and at that moment a thought occurred to me: Since I had invented Olga, couldn't I invent others—dark-eyed blondes, vivacious redheads with marbly skin, melancholy brunettes, dancers, women who sang, lonely housewives? Tall women, short women, sad women, women whose burnished hair flowed to their waists, sloe-eyed, squint-eyed, violet-eyed beauties of all kinds and ages could be mine. Mightn't Olga's going only mean that she was making room for someone else?

THE SEASIDE HOUSES

EACH YEAR, we rent a house at the edge of the sea and drive there in the first of the summer—with the dog and cat, the children, and the cook—arriving at a strange place a little before dark. The journey to the sea has its ceremonious excitements, it has gone on for so many years now, and there is the sense that we are, as in our dreams we have always known ourselves to be, migrants and wanderers—travelers, at least, with a traveler's acuteness of feeling. I never investigate the houses that we rent, and so the wooden castle with a tower, the pile, the Staffordshire cottage covered with roses, and the Southern mansion all loom up in the last of the sea light with the enormous appeal of the unknown. You get the sea-rusted keys from the house next door. You unfasten the lock and step into a dark or a light hallway, about to begin a vacation—a month that promises to have no worries of any kind. But as strong as or stronger than this pleasant sense of beginnings is the sense of having stepped into the midst of someone else's life. All my dealings are with agents, and I have never known the people from whom we have rented, but their ability to leave behind them a sense of physical and emotional presences is amazing. Our affairs are certainly not written in air and water, but they do seem to be chronicled in scuffed baseboards, odors, and tastes in furniture and paintings, and the climates we step into in these rented places are as marked as the changes of weather on the beach. Sometimes there is in the long hallway a benignness, a purity and clearness of feeling to which we all respond. Someone was enormously happy here, and we rent their happiness as we rent their beach and their catboat. Sometimes the climate of the place seems mysterious, and remains a mystery until we leave in August. Who, we wonder, is the lady in the portrait in the upstairs hallway? Whose was the Aqualung, the set of Virginia Woolf? Who hid the copy of *Fanny Hill* in the china closet, who played the zither, who slept in the cradle, and who was the woman who painted red enamel on the nails of the claw-footed bathtub? What was this moment in her life?

The dog and the children run down to the beach, and we bring in our things, wandering, it seems, through the dense histories of strangers. Who owned the *Lederhosen*, who spilled ink (or blood) on the carpet, who broke the pantry window? And what do you make of a bedroom bookshelf stocked with *Married Happiness, An Illustrated Guide to Sexual Happiness in Marriage, The Right to Sexual Felicity*, and *A Guide to Sexual Happiness for Married Couples*? But outside the windows we hear the percussive noise of the sea; it shakes the bluff where the house stands, and sends its rhythm up through the plaster and timbers of the place, and in the end we all go down to the beach—it is what we came for, after all—and the rented house on the bluff, burning now with our lights, is one of those images that have preserved their urgency and their fitness. Fishing in the spring woods, you step on a clump of wild mint and the fragrance released is like the essence of that day. Walking on the Palatine, bored with antiquities and life in general, you see an owl fly out of the ruins of the palace of Septimius Severus and suddenly that day, that raffish and noisy city all make sense. Lying in bed, you draw on your cigarette and the red glow lights an arm, a breast, and a thigh around which the world seems to revolve. These images are like the embers of our best feelings, and standing on the beach, for that first hour, it seems as if we could build them into a fire. After dark we shake up a drink, send the children to bed, and make love in a strange room that smells of someone else's soap—all measures taken to exorcise the owners and secure our possession of the place. But in the middle of the night the terrace door flies open with a crash, although there seems to be no wind, and my wife says, half asleep, "Oh, why have they come back? Why have they come back? What have they lost?"

Broadmere is the rented house I remember most clearly, and we got there at the usual time of day. It was a large white house, and it stood on a bluff facing south, which was the open sea on that coast. I got the key from a Southern lady in a house across the garden, and opened the door onto a hallway with a curved staircase. The Greenwoods, the owners, seemed to have left that day, seemed in fact to have left a minute earlier. There were flowers in the vases, cigarette butts in the ashtrays, and a dirty glass on the table. We brought in the suitcases and sent the children down to the beach, and I stood in the living room waiting for my wife to join me. The stir, the discord of the Greenwoods' sudden departure still seemed to be in the air. I felt that they had gone hastily and unwillingly, and that they had not wanted to rent their summer house. The room had a bay window looking out to sea, but in the twilight the place seemed drab, and I found it depressing. I turned on a lamp, but the bulb was dim and I thought that Mr. Greenwood had been a parsimonious and mean man. Whatever he had been, I seemed to feel his presence with uncommon force. On the bookshelf there was a small sailing trophy that he had won ten years before. The books were mostly Literary Guild selections. I took a biography of Queen Victoria off the shelf, but the binding was stiff, and I think no one had read it. Hidden behind the book was an empty whiskey bottle. The furniture seemed substantial and in good taste, but I was not happy or at ease in the room. There was an upright piano in the corner, and I played some scales to see if it was in tune (it wasn't) and opened the piano bench to look for music. There was some sheet music, and two more empty whiskey bottles. Why hadn't he taken out his empties like the rest of us? Had he been a secret drinker? Would this account for the drabness of the room? Had he learned to take the top off the bottle without making a sound, and mastered the more difficult trick of canting the glass and the bottle so that the whiskey wouldn't splash? My wife came in, carrying an empty suitcase, which I took up to the attic. This part of the house was neat and clean. All the tools and the paints were labeled and in their places, and all this neatness, unlike the living room, conveyed an atmosphere of earnestness and probity. He must have spent a good deal of time in the attic, I thought. It was getting dark, and I joined my wife and children on the beach.

The sea was running high and the long white line of the surf reached, like an artery, down the shore for as far as we could see. We stood, my wife and I, with our arms loosely around one another—for don't we all come down to the sea as lovers, the pretty woman in her pregnancy bathing suit with a fair husband, the old couples who bathe their gnarled legs, and the bucks and the girls, looking out to the ocean and its fumes for some riggish and exalted promise of romance? When it was dark and time to go to bed, I told my youngest son a story. He slept in a pleasant room that faced the east, where there was a lighthouse on a point, and the beam swept in through the window. Then I noticed something on the corner baseboard—a thread or a spider, I thought—and knelt down to see what it was. Someone had written there, in a small hand, "My father is a rat. I repeat. My father is a rat." I kissed my son good night and we all went to sleep.

Sunday was a lovely day, and I woke in very high spirits, but, walking around the place before breakfast, I came on another cache of whiskey bottles hidden behind a yew tree, and I felt a return of that drabness—it was nearly like despair—that I had first experienced in the living room. I was worried and curious about Mr. Greenwood. His troubles seemed inescapable. I thought of going into the village and asking about him, but this kind of curiosity seems to me indecent. Later in the day, I found his photograph in a shirt drawer. The glass covering the picture was broken. He was dressed in the uniform of an Air Force major, and had a long and a romantic face. I was pleased with his handsomeness, as I had been pleased with his sailing trophy, but these two possessions were not quite enough to cure the house of its drabness. I did not like the place, and this seemed to affect my temper. Later I tried to teach my oldest son how to surf-cast with a drail, but he kept fouling his line and getting sand in the reel, and we had a quarrel. After lunch we drove to the boatyard where the sailboat that went with the house was stored. When I asked about the boat, the proprietor laughed. It had not been in the water for five years and was falling to pieces. This was a grave disappointment, but I did not think angrily of Mr. Greenwood as a liar, which he was; I thought of him sympathetically as a man forced into those embarrassing expedients that go with a rapidly diminishing income. That night in the living room, reading one of his books, I noticed that the sofa cushions seemed unyielding. Reaching under them, I found three copies of a magazine dealing with sunbathing. They were illustrated with many pictures of men and women wearing nothing but their shoes. I put the magazines into the fireplace and lighted them with a match, but the paper was coated and they burned slowly. Why should I be made so angry, I wondered; why should I seem so absorbed in this image of a lonely and drunken man? In the upstairs hallway there was a bad smell, left perhaps by an unhousebroken cat or a stopped drain, but it seemed to me like the distillate, the essence, of a bitter quarrel. I slept poorly.

On Monday it rained. The children baked cookies in the morning. I walked on the beach. In the afternoon we visited the local museum, where there was one stuffed peacock, one spiked German helmet, an assortment of shrapnel, a collection of butterflies, and some old photographs. You could hear the rain on the museum roof. On Monday night I had a strange dream. I dreamed I was sailing for Naples on the *Christoforo Colombo* and sharing a tourist cabin with an old man. The old man never appeared, but his belongings were heaped on the lower berth. There was a greasy fedora, a battered umbrella, a paperback novel, and a bottle of laxative pills. I wanted a drink. I am not an alcoholic, but in my dream I experienced all the physical and emotional torments of a man who is. I went up to the bar. The bar was closed. The bartender was there, locking up the cash register, and all the bottles were draped in cheesecloth. I begged him to open the bar, but he said he had spent the last ten hours cleaning staterooms and that he was going to bed. I asked if he would sell me a bottle, and he said no. Then—he was an Italian—I explained slyly that the bottle was not for me but for my little daughter. His attitude changed at once. If it was for my little daughter, he would be happy to give me a bottle, but it must be a beautiful bottle, and after searching around the bar he came up with a swan-shaped bottle, full of liqueur. I told him my daughter wouldn't like this at all, that what she wanted was gin, and he finally produced a bottle of gin and charged me ten thousand lire. When I woke, it seemed that I had dreamed one of Mr. Greenwood's dreams.

We had our first caller on Wednesday. This was Mrs. Whiteside, the Southern lady from whom we got the key. She rang our bell at five and presented us with a box of strawberries. Her daughter, Mary-Lee, a girl of about twelve, was with her. Mrs. Whiteside was formidably decorous, but Mary-Lee had gone in heavily for make-up. Her eyebrows were plucked, her eyelids were painted, and the rest of her face was highly colored. I suppose she didn't have anything else to do. I asked Mrs. Whiteside in enthusiastically, because I wanted to cross-question her about the Greenwoods. "Isn't it a beautiful staircase?" she asked when she stepped into the hall. "They had it built for their daughter's wedding. Dolores was only four at the time, but they liked to imagine that she would stand by the window in her white dress and throw her flowers down to her attendants." I bowed Mrs. Whiteside into the living room and gave her a glass of sherry. "We're pleased to have you here, Mr. Ogden," she said. "It's so nice to have children running on the beach again. But it's only fair to say that we all miss the Greenwoods. They were charming people, and they've never rented before. This is their first summer away from the beach. Oh, he loved Broadmere. It was his pride and joy. I can't imagine what he'll do without it." If the Greenwoods were so charming, I wondered who had been the secret drinker. "What does Mr. Greenwood do?" I asked, trying to finesse the directness of my question by crossing the room and filling her glass again. "He's in synthetic yarns," she said. "Although I believe he's on the lookout for something more interesting." This seemed to be a hint, a step perhaps in the right direction. "You mean he's looking for a job?" I asked quickly. "I really can't say," she replied.

She was one of those old women who you might say were as tranquil as the waters under a bridge, but she seemed to me monolithic, to possess some of the community's biting teeth, and perhaps to secrete some of its venom. She seemed by her various and painful disappointments (Mr. Whiteside had passed away, and there was very little money) to have been pushed up out of the stream of life to sit on its banks in unremittent lugubriousness, watching the rest of us speed down to sea. What I mean to say is that I thought I detected beneath her melodious voice a vein of corrosive bitterness. In all, she drank five glasses of sherry.

She was about to go. She sighed and started to get up. "Well, I'm so glad of this chance to welcome you," she said. "It's so nice to have children running on the beach again, and while the Greenwoods were charming, they had their difficulties. I say that I miss them, but I can't say that I miss hearing them quarrel, and they quarreled every single night last summer. Oh, the things he used to say! They were what I suppose you would call incompatible." She rolled her eyes in the direction of Mary-Lee to suggest that she could have told us much more. "I like to work in my garden sometimes after the heat of the day, but when they were quarreling I couldn't step out of the house, and I sometimes had to close the doors and windows. I don't suppose I should tell you all of this, but the truth will out, won't it?" She got to her feet and went into the hall. "As I say, they had the staircase built for the marriage of their daughter, but poor Dolores was married in the Municipal Building eight months pregnant by a garage mechanic. It's nice to have you here. Come along, Mary-Lee."

I had, in a sense, what I wanted. She had authenticated the drabness of the house. But why should I be so moved, as I was, by the poor man's wish to see his daughter happily married? It seemed to me that I could see them standing in the hallway when the staircase was completed. Dolores would be playing on the floor. They would have their arms around each other; they would be smiling up at the arched window and its vision of cheer, propriety, and enduring happiness. But where had they all gone, and why had this simple wish ended in disaster?

In the morning it rained again, and the cook suddenly announced that her sister in New York was dying and that she had to go home. She had not received any letters or telephone calls that I knew of, but I drove her to the airport and let her go. I returned reluctantly to the house. I had got to hate the place. I found a plastic chess set and tried to teach my son to play chess, but this ended in a quarrel. The other children lay in bed, reading comics. I was short-tempered with everyone, and decided that for their own good I should return to New York for a day or two. I lied to my wife about some urgent business, and she took me to the plane the next morning. It felt good to be airborne and away from the drabness of Broadmere. It was hot and sunny in New York—it felt and smelled like midsummer. I stayed at the office until late, and stopped at a bar near Grand Central Station. I had been there a few minutes when Greenwood came in. His romantic looks were ruined, but I recognized him at once from the photograph in the shirt drawer. He ordered a Martini and a glass of water, and drank off the water, as if that was what he had come for.

You could see at a glance that he was one of the legion of wage-earning ghosts who haunt midtown Manhattan, dreaming of a new job in Madrid, Dublin, or Cleveland. His hair was slicked down. His face had the striking ruddiness of a baseball-park or race-track burn, although you could see by the way his hands shook that the flush was alcoholic. The bartender knew him, and they chatted for a while, but then the bartender went over to the cash register to add up his slips and Mr. Greenwood was left alone. He felt this. You could see it in his face. He felt that he had been left alone. It was late, all the express trains would have pulled out, and the rest of them were drifting in—the ghosts, I mean. God knows where they come from or where they go, this host of prosperous and well-dressed hangers-on who, in spite of the atmosphere of a fraternity they generate, would not think of speaking to one another. They all have a bottle hidden behind the Literary Guild selections and another in the piano bench. I thought of introducing myself to Greenwood, and then thought better of it. I had taken his beloved house away from him, and he was bound to be unfriendly. I couldn't guess the incidents in his autobiography, but I could guess its atmosphere and drift. Daddy would have died or absconded when he was young. The absence of a male parent is not so hard to discern among the marks life leaves on our faces. He would have been raised by his mother and his aunt, have gone to the state university and have majored (my guess) in general merchandising. He would have been in charge of PX supplies during the war. Nothing had worked out after the war. He had lost his daughter, his house, the love of his wife, and his interest in business, but none of these losses would account for his pain and bewilderment. The real cause would remain concealed from him, concealed from me, concealed from us all. It is what makes the railroad-station bars at that hour seem so mysterious. "Stupid," he said to the bartender. "Oh, stupid. Do you think you could find the time to sweeten my drink?"

It was the first note of ugliness, but there would be nothing much but ugliness afterward. He would get very mean. Thin, fat, choleric or merry, young or old, all the ghosts do. In the end, they all drift home to accuse the doorman of incivility, to rail at their wives for extravagance, to lecture their bewildered children on ingratitude, and then to fall asleep on the guest-room bed with all their clothes on. But it wasn't this image that troubled me but the image of him standing in the new hallway, imagining that he saw his daughter at the head of the stairs in her wedding dress. We had not spoken, I didn't know him, his losses were not mine, and yet I felt them so strongly that I didn't want to spend the night alone, and so I spent it with a sloppy woman who works in our office. In the morning, I took a plane back to the sea, where it was still raining and where I found my wife washing pots in the kitchen sink. I had a hangover and felt painfully depraved, guilty, and unclean. I thought I might feel better if I went for a swim, and I asked my wife for my bathing trunks.

"They're around here somewhere," she said crossly.

"They're kicking around underfoot somewhere. You left them wet on the bedroom rug and I hung them up in the shower."

"They're not in the shower," I said.

"Well, they're around here somewhere," she said. "Have you looked on the dining-room table?"

"Now, listen," I said. "I don't see why you have to speak of my bathing trunks as if they had been wandering around the house, drinking whiskey, breaking wind, and telling dirty stories to mixed company. I'm just asking for an *innocent* pair of bathing trunks." Then I sneezed, and I waited for her to bless me as she always did but she said nothing. "And another thing I can't find," I said, "is my handkerchiefs."

"Blow your nose on Kleenex," she said.

"I don't want to blow my nose on Kleenex," I said. I must have raised my voice, because I could hear Mrs. Whiteside calling Mary-Lee indoors and shutting a window.

"Oh, God, you bore me this morning," my wife said.

"I've been bored for the last six years," I said.

I took a cab to the airport and an afternoon plane back to the city. We had been married twelve years and had been lovers for two years before our marriage, making a total of fourteen years in all that we had been together, and I never saw her again.

THIS IS being written in another seaside house with another wife. I sit in a chair of no discernible period or inspiration. Its cushions have a musty smell. The ashtray was filched from the Excelsior in Rome. My whiskey glass once held jelly. The table I'm writing on has a bum leg. The lamp is dim. Magda, my wife, is dyeing her hair. She dyes it orange, and this has to be done once a week. It is foggy, we are near a channel marked with buoys, and I can hear as many bells as I would hear in any pious village on a Sunday morning. There are high bells, low bells, and bells that seem to ring from under the sea. When Magda asks me to get her glasses, I step quietly onto the porch. The lights from the cottage, shining into the fog, give an illusion of substance, and it seems as if I might stumble on a beam of light. The shore is curved, and I can see the lights of other haunted cottages where people are building up an accrual of happiness or misery that will be left for the August tenants or the people who come next year. Are we truly this close to one another? Must we impose our burdens on strangers? And is our sense of the universality of suffering so inescapable? "My glasses, my glasses!" Magda shouts. "How many times do I have to ask you to bring them for me?" I get her her glasses, and when she is finished with her hair we go to bed. In the middle of the night, the porch door flies open, but my first, my gentle wife is not there to ask, "Why have they come back? What have they lost?"

THE ANGEL OF THE BRIDGE

You may have seen my mother waltzing on ice skates in Rockefeller Center. She's seventy-eight years old now but very wiry, and she wears a red velvet costume with a short skirt. Her tights are flesh-colored, and she wears spectacles and a red ribbon in her white hair, and she waltzes with one of the rink attendants. I don't know why I should find the fact that she waltzes on ice skates so disconcerting, but I do. I avoid that neighborhood whenever I can during the winter months, and I never lunch in the restaurants on the rink. Once when I was passing that way, a total stranger took me by the arm and, pointing to Mother, said, "Look at that crazy old dame." I was very embarrassed. I suppose I should be grateful for the fact that she amuses herself and is not a burden to me, but I sincerely wish she had hit on some less conspicuous recreation. Whenever I see gracious old ladies arranging chrysanthemums and pouring tea, I think of my own mother, dressed like a hat-check girl, pushing some paid rink attendant around the ice, in the middle of the third-biggest city of the world.

My mother learned to figure-skate in the little New England village of St. Botolphs, where we come from, and her waltzing is an expression of her attachment to the past. The older she grows, the more she longs for the vanishing and provincial world of her youth. She is a hardy woman, as you can imagine, but she does not relish change. I arranged one summer for her to fly to Toledo and visit friends. I drove her to the Newark airport. She seemed troubled by the airport waiting room, with its illuminated advertisements, vaulted ceiling, and touching and painful scenes of separation played out to an uproar of continuous tango music. She did not seem to find it in any way interesting or beautiful, and compared to the railroad station in St. Botolphs it was indeed a strange background against which to take one's departure. The flight was delayed for an hour, and we sat in the waiting room. Mother looked tired and old. When we had been waiting half an hour, she began to have some noticeable difficulty in breathing. She spread a hand over the front of her dress and began to gasp deeply, as if she was in pain. Her face got mottled and red. I pretended not to notice this. When the plane was announced, she got to her feet and exclaimed, "I want to go home! If I have to die suddenly, I don't want to die in a flying machine." I cashed in her ticket and drove her back to her apartment, and I have never mentioned this seizure to her or to anyone, but her capricious, or perhaps neurotic, fear of dying in a plane crash was the first insight I had into how, as she grew older, her way was strewn with invisible rocks and lions and how eccentric were the paths she took, as the world seemed to change its boundaries and become less and less comprehensible.

At the time of which I'm writing, I flew a great deal myself. My business was in Rome, New York, San Francisco, and Los Angeles, and I sometimes traveled as often as once a month between these cities. I liked the flying. I liked the incandescence of the sky at high altitudes. I liked all eastward flights where you can see from the ports the edge of night move over the continent and where, when it is four o'clock by your California watch, the housewives of Garden City are washing up the supper dishes and the stewardess in the plane is passing a second round of drinks. Toward the end of the flight, the air is stale. You are tired. The gold thread in the upholstery scratches your cheek, and there is a momentary feeling of forlornness, a sulky and childish sense of estrangement. You find good companions, of course, and bores, but most of the errands we run at such high altitudes are humble and terrestrial. That old lady, flying over the North Pole, is taking a jar of calf's-foot jelly to her sister in Paris, and the man beside her sells imitation-leather inner soles. Flying westward one dark night—we had crossed the Continental Divide, but we were still an hour out of Los Angeles and had not begun our descent, and were at such an altitude that the sense of houses, cities, and people below us was lost—I saw a formation, a trace of light, like the lights that burn along a shore. There was no shore in that part of the world, and I knew I would never know if the edge of the desert or some bluff or mountain accounted for this hoop of light, but it seemed, in its obscurity—and at that velocity and height—like the emergence of a new world, a gentle hint at my own obsolescence, the lateness of my time of life, and my inability to understand the things I often see. It was a pleasant feeling, completely free of regret, of being caught in some observable mid-passage, the farther reaches of which might be understood by my sons.

I liked to fly, as I say, and had none of my mother's anxieties. It was my older brother—her darling—who was to inherit her resoluteness, her stubbornness, her table silver, and some of her eccentricities. One evening, my brother—I had not seen him for a year or so—called and asked if he could come for dinner. I was happy to invite him. We live on the eleventh floor of an apartment house, and at seven-thirty he telephoned from the lobby and asked me to come down. I thought he must have something to tell me privately, but when we met in the lobby he got into the automatic elevator with me and we started up. As soon as the doors closed, he showed the same symptoms of fear I had seen in my mother. Sweat stood out on his forehead, and he gasped like a runner.

"What in the world is the matter?" I asked.

"I'm afraid of elevators," he said miserably.

"But what are you afraid of?"

"I'm afraid the building will fall down."

I laughed—cruelly, I guess. For it all seemed terribly funny, his vision of the buildings of New York banging against one another like ninepins as they fell to the earth. There has always been a strain of jealousy in our feelings about one another, and I am aware, at some obscure level, that he makes more money and has more of everything than I, and to see him humiliated—crushed—saddened me but at the same time and in spite of myself made me feel that I had taken a stunning lead in the race for honors that is at the bottom of our relationship. He is the oldest, he is the favorite, but watching his misery in the elevator I felt that he was merely my poor old brother, overtaken by his worries. He stopped in the hallway to recover his composure, and explained that he had been suffering from this phobia far over a year. He was going to a psychiatrist, he said. I couldn't see that it had done him any good. He was all right once he got out of the elevator, but I noticed that he stayed away from the windows. When it was time to go, I walked him out to the corridor. I was curious. When the elevator reached our floor, he turned to me and said, "I'm afraid I'll have to take the stairs." I led him to the stairway, and we climbed slowly down the eleven flights. He clung to the railing. We said goodbye in the lobby, and I went up in the elevator, and told my wife about his fear that the building might fall down. It seemed strange and sad to her, and it did to me, too, but it also seemed terribly funny.

It wasn't terribly funny when, a month later, the firm he worked for moved to the fifty-second floor of a new office building and he had to resign. I don't know what reasons he gave. It was another six months before he could find a job in a third-floor office. I once saw him on a winter dusk at the corner of Madison Avenue and Fifty-ninth Street, waiting for the light to change. He appeared to be an intelligent, civilized, and well-dressed man, and I wondered how many of the men waiting with him to cross the street made their way as he did through a ruin of absurd delusions, in which the street might appear to be a torrent and the approaching cab driven by the angel of death.

He was quite all right on the ground. My wife and I went to his house in New Jersey, with the children, for a weekend, and he looked healthy and well. I didn't ask about his phobia. We drove back to New York on Sunday afternoon. As we approached the George Washington Bridge, I saw a thunderstorm over the city. A strong wind struck the car the moment we were on the bridge, and nearly took the wheel out of my hand. It seemed to me that I could feel the huge structure swing. Halfway across the bridge, I thought I felt the roadway begin to give. I could see no signs of a collapse, and yet I was convinced that in another minute the bridge would split in two and hurl the long lines of Sunday traffic into the dark water below us. This imagined disaster was terrifying. My legs got so weak that I was not sure I could brake the car if I needed to. Then it became difficult for me to breathe. Only by opening my mouth and gasping did I seem able to take in any air. My blood pressure was affected and I began to feel a darkening of my vision. Fear has always seemed to me to run a course, and at its climax the body and perhaps the spirit defend themselves by drawing on some new and fresh source of strength. Once over the center of the bridge, my pain and terror began to diminish. My wife and the children were admiring the storm, and they did not seem to have noticed my spasm. I was afraid both that the bridge would fall down and that they might observe my panic.

I thought back over the weekend for some incident that might account for my preposterous fear that the George Washington Bridge would blow away in a thunderstorm, but it had been a pleasant weekend, and even under the most exaggerated scrutiny I couldn't uncover any source of morbid nervousness or anxiety. Later in the week, I had to drive to Albany, and, although the day was clear and windless, the memory of my first attack was too keen; I hugged the east bank of the river as far north as Troy, where I found a small, old-fashioned bridge that I could cross comfortably. This meant going fifteen or twenty miles out of my way, and it is humiliating to have your travels obstructed by barriers that are senseless and invisible. I drove back from Albany by the same route, and next morning I went to the family doctor and told him I was afraid of bridges.

He laughed. "You, of all people," he said scornfully. "You'd better take hold of yourself."

"But Mother is afraid of airplanes," I said. "And Brother hates elevators."

"Your mother is past seventy," he said, "and one of the most remarkable women I've ever known. I wouldn't bring *her* into this. What *you* need is a little more backbone."

This was all he had to say, and I asked him to recommend an analyst. He does not include psychoanalysis in medical science, and told me I would be wasting my time and money, but, yielding to his obligation to be helpful, he gave me the name and address of a psychiatrist, who told me that my fear of bridges was the surface manifestation of a deep-seated anxiety and that I would have to have a full analysis. I didn't have the time, or the money, or, above all, the confidence in the doctor's methods to put myself in his hands, and I said I would try and muddle through.

There are obviously areas of true and false pain, and my pain was meretricious, but how could I convince my lights and vitals of this? My youth and childhood had their deeply troubled and their jubilant years, and could some repercussions from this past account for my fear of heights? The thought of a life determined by hidden obstacles was unacceptable, and I decided to take the advice of the family doctor and ask more of myself. I had to go to Idlewild later in the week, and, rather than take a bus or a taxi, I drove the car myself. I nearly lost consciousness on the Triborough Bridge. When I got to the airport I ordered a cup of coffee, but my hand was shaking so I spilled the coffee on the counter. The man beside me was amused and said that I must have put in quite a night. How could I tell him that I had gone to bed early and sober but that I was afraid of bridges?

I flew to Los Angeles late that afternoon. It was one o'clock by my watch when we landed. It was only ten o'clock in California. I was tired and took a taxi to the hotel where I always stay, but I couldn't sleep. Outside my hotel window was a monumental statue of a young woman, advertising a Las Vegas night club. She revolves slowly in a beam of light. At 2 A.M. the light is extinguished, but she goes on restlessly turning all through the night. I have never seen her cease her turning, and I wondered, that night, when they greased her axle and washed her shoulders. I felt some affection for her, since neither of us could rest, and I wondered if she had a family—a stage mother, perhaps, and a compromised and broken-spirited father who drove a municipal bus on the West Pico line? There was a restaurant across the street, and I watched a drunken woman in a sable cape being led out to a car. She twice nearly fell. The crosslights from the open door, the lateness, her drunkenness, and the solicitude of the man with her made the scene, I thought, worried and lonely. Then two cars that seemed to be racing down Sunset Boulevard pulled up at a traffic light under my window.

Three men piled out of each car and began to slug one another. You could hear the blows land on bone and cartilage. When the light changed, they got back into their cars and raced off. The fight, like the hoop of light I had seen from the plane, seemed like the sign of a new world, but in this case an emergence of brutality and chaos. Then I remembered that I was to go to San Francisco on Thursday, and was expected in Berkeley for lunch. This meant crossing the San Francisco–Oakland Bay Bridge, and I reminded myself to take a cab both ways and leave the car I rented in San Francisco in the hotel garage. I tried again to reason out my fear that the bridge would fall. Was I the victim of some sexual dislocation? My life has been promiscuous, carefree, and a source of immense pleasure, but was there some secret here that would have to be mined by a professional? Were all my pleasures impostures and evasions, and was I really in love with my old mother in her skating costume?

Looking at Sunset Boulevard at three in the morning, I felt that my terror of bridges was an expression of my clumsily concealed horror of what is becoming of the world. I can drive with composure through the outskirts of Cleveland and Toledo—past the birthplace of the Polish Hot Dog, the Buffalo Burger stands, the used-car lots, and the architectural monotony. I claim to enjoy walking down Hollywood Boulevard on a Sunday afternoon. I have cheerfully praised the evening sky hanging beyond the disheveled and expatriated palm trees on Doheny Boulevard, stuck up against the incandescence, like rank upon rank of wet mops. Duluth and East Seneca are charming, and if they aren't, just look away. The hideousness of the road between San Francisco and Palo Alto is nothing more than the search of honest men and women for a decent place to live. The same thing goes for San Pedro and all that coast. But the height of bridges seemed to be one link I could not forge or fasten in this hypocritical chain of acceptances. The truth is, I hate freeways and Buffalo Burgers. Expatriated palm trees and monotonous housing developments depress me. The continuous music on special-fare trains exacerbates my feelings. I detest the destruction of familiar landmarks. I am deeply troubled by the misery and drunkeness I find among my friends, I abhor the dishonest practices I see. And it was at the highest point in the arc of a bridge that I became aware suddenly of the depth and bitterness of my feelings about modern life, and of the profoundness of my yearning for a more vivid, simple, and peaceable world.

But I couldn't reform Sunset Boulevard, and until I could, I couldn't drive across the San Francisco-Oakland Bay Bridge. What *could* I do? Go back to St. Botolphs, wear a Norfolk jacket, and play cribbage in the firehouse? There was only one bridge in the village, and you could throw a stone across the river there.

I GOT HOME from San Francisco on Saturday, and found my daughter back from school for the weekend. On Sunday morning, she asked me to drive her to the convent school in Jersey where she is a student. She had to be back in time for nine-o'clock Mass, and we left our apartment in the city a little after seven. We were talking and laughing, and I had approached and was in fact on the George Washington Bridge without having remembered my weakness. There were no preliminaries this time. The seizure came with a rush. The strength went out of my legs, I gasped for breath, and felt the terrifying loss of sight. I was, at the same time, determined to conceal these symptoms from my daughter. I made the other side of the bridge, but I was violently shaken. My daughter didn't seem to have noticed. I got her to school in time, kissed her goodbye, and started home. There was no question of my crossing the George Washington Bridge again, and I decided to drive north to Nyack and cross on the Tappan Zee Bridge. It seemed, in my memory, more gradual and more securely anchored to its shores. Driving up the parkway on the west shore, I decided that oxygen was what I needed, and I opened all the windows of the car. The fresh air seemed to help, but only momentarily. I could feel my sense of reality ebbing. The roadside and the car itself seemed to have less substance than a dream. I had some friends in the neighborhood, and I thought of stopping and asking them for a drink, but it was only a little after nine in the morning, and I could not face the embarrassment of asking for a drink so early in the day, and of explaining that I was afraid of bridges. I thought I might feel better if I talked to someone, and I stopped at a gas station and bought some gas, but the attendant was laconic and sleepy, and I couldn't explain to him that his conversation might make the difference between life and death. I had got onto the Thruway by then, and I wondered what alternatives I had if I couldn't cross the bridge. I could call my wife and ask her to make some arrangements for removing me, but our relationship involves so much self-esteem and face that to admit openly to this foolishness might damage our married happiness. I could call the garage we use and ask them to send up a man to chauffeur me home. I could park the car and wait until one o'clock, when the bars opened, and fill up on whiskey, but I had spent the last of my money for gasoline. I decided to take a chance, and turned onto the approach to the bridge.

All the symptoms returned, and this time they were much worse than ever. The wind was knocked out of my lungs as by a blow. My equilibrium was so shaken that the car swerved from one lane into another. I drove to the side and pulled on the hand brake. The loneliness of my predicament was harrowing. If I had been miserable with romantic love, racked with sickness, or beastly drunk, it would have seemed more dignified. I remembered my brother's face, sallow and greasy with sweat in the elevator, and my mother in her red skirt, one leg held gracefully aloft as she coasted backward in the arms of a rink attendant, and it seemed to me that we were all three characters in some bitter and sordid tragedy, carrying impossible burdens and separated from the rest of mankind by our misfortunes. My life was over, and it would never come back, everything that I loved—blue-sky courage, lustiness, the natural grasp of things. It would never come back. I would end up in the psychiatric ward of the county hospital, screaming that the bridges, all the bridges in the world, were falling down.

Then a young girl opened the door of the car and got in. "I didn't think anyone would pick me up on the bridge," she said. She carried a cardboard suitcase and—believe me—a small harp in a cracked waterproof. Her straight light-brown hair was brushed and brushed and grained with blondness and spread in a kind of cape over her shoulders. Her face seemed full and merry.

"Are you hitchhiking?" I asked.

"Yes."

"But isn't it dangerous for a girl your age?"

"Not at all."

"Do you travel much?"

"All the time. I sing a little. I play the coffeehouses."

"What do you sing?"

"Oh, folk music, mostly. And some old things—Purcell and Dowland. But mostly folk music. . . . 'I gave my love a cherry that had no stone,' " she sang in a true and pretty voice. " 'I gave my love a chicken that had no bone/ I told my love a story that had no end/ I gave my love a baby with no cryin'.' "

She sang me across a bridge that seemed to be an astonishingly sensible, durable, and even beautiful construction designed by intelligent men to simplify my travels, and the water of the Hudson below us was charming and tranquil. It all came back—blue-sky courage, the high spirits of lustiness, an ecstatic sereneness. Her song ended as we got to the toll station on the east bank, and she thanked me, said goodbye, and got out of the car. I offered to take her wherever she wanted to go, but she shook her head and walked away, and I drove on toward the city through a world that, having been restored to me, seemed marvelous and fair. When I got home, I thought of calling my brother and telling him what had happened, on the chance that there was also an angel of the elevator banks, but the harp—that single detail—threatened to make me seem ridiculous or mad, and I didn't call.

I wish I could say that I am convinced that there will always be some merciful intercession to help me with my worries, but I don't believe in rushing my luck, so I will stay off the George Washington Bridge, although I can cross the Triborough and the Tappan Zee with ease. My brother is still afraid of elevators, and my mother, although she's grown quite stiff, still goes around and around and around on the ice.

THE BRIGADIER AND THE GOLF WIDOW

I WOULD NOT want to be one of those writers who begin each morning by exclaiming, "O Gogol, O Chekhov, O Thackeray and Dickens, what would you have made of a bomb shelter ornamented with four plaster-of-Paris ducks, a birdbath, and three composition gnomes with long beards and red mobcaps?" As I say, I wouldn't want to begin a day like this, but I often wonder what the dead would have done. But the shelter is as much a part of my landscape as the beech and horse-chestnut trees that grow on the ridge. I can see it from this window where I write. It was built by the Pasterns, and stands on the acre of ground that adjoins our property. It bulks under a veil of thin, new grass, like some embarrassing fact of physicalness, and I think Mrs. Pastern set out the statuary to soften its meaning. It would have been like her. She was a pale woman. Sitting on her terrace, sitting in her parlor, sitting anywhere, she ground an ax of self-esteem. Offer her a cup of tea and she would say, "Why, these cups look just like a set I gave to the Salvation Army last year." Show her the new swimming pool and she would say, slapping her ankle, "I suppose this must be where you breed your gigantic mosquitoes." Hand her a chair and she would say, "Why, it's a nice imitation of those Queen Anne chairs I inherited from Grandmother Delancy." These trumps were more touching than they were anything else, and seemed to imply that the nights were long, her children ungrateful, and her marriage bewilderingly threadbare. Twenty years ago, she would have been known as a golf widow, and the sum of her manner was perhaps one of bereavement. She usually wore weeds, and a stranger watching her board a train might have guessed that Mr. Pastern was dead, but Mr. Pastern was far from dead. He was marching up and down the locker room of the Grassy Brae Golf Club shouting, "Bomb Cuba! Bomb Berlin! Let's throw a little nuclear hardware at them and show them who's boss." He was brigadier of the club's locker-room light infantry, and at one time or another declared war on Russia, Czechoslovakia, Yugoslavia, and China.

It all began on an autumn afternoon—and who, after all these centuries, can describe the fineness of an autumn day? One might pretend never to have seen one before, or, to more purpose, that there would never be another like it. The clear and searching sweep of sun on the lawns was like a climax of the year's lights. Leaves were burning somewhere and the smoke smelled, for all its ammoniac acidity, of beginnings. The boundless blue air was stretched over the zenith like the skin of a drum. Leaving her house one late afternoon, Mrs. Pastern stopped to admire the October light. It was the day to canvass for infectious hepatitis. Mrs. Pastern had been given sixteen names, a bundle of literature, and a printed book of receipts. It was her work to go among her neighbors and collect their checks. Her house stood on a rise of ground, and before she got into her car she looked at the houses below. Charity as she knew it was complex and reciprocal, and almost every roof she saw signified charity. Mrs. Balcolm worked for the brain. Mrs. Ten Eyke did mental health. Mrs. Trenchard worked for the blind. Mrs. Horowitz was in charge of diseases of the nose and throat. Mrs. Trempler was tuberculosis, Mrs. Surcliffe was Mothers' March of Dimes, Mrs. Craven was cancer, and Mrs. Gilkson did the kidney. Mrs. Hewlitt led the birth-control league, Mrs. Ryerson was arthritis, and way in the distance could be seen the slate roof of Ethel Littleton's house, a roof that signified gout.

Mrs. Pastern undertook the work of going from house to house with the thoughtless resignation of an honest and traditional laborer. It was her destiny; it was her life. Her mother had done it before her, and even her old grandmother had collected money for smallpox and unwed mothers. Mrs. Pastern had telephoned most of her neighbors in advance, and most of them were ready for her. She experienced none of the suspense of some poor stranger selling encyclopedias. Here and there she stayed to visit and drink a glass of sherry. The contributions were ahead of what she had got the previous year, and while the money, of course, was not hers, it excited her to stuff her kit with big checks. She stopped at the Surcliffes' after dusk, and had a Scotch and soda. She stayed too late, and when she left it was dark and time to go home and cook supper for her husband. "I got a hundred and sixty dollars for the hepatitis fund," she said excitedly when he walked in. "I did everybody on my list but the Blevins and the Flannagans. I want to get my kit in tomorrow morning—would you mind doing them while I cook the dinner?"

"But I don't know the Flannagans," Charlie Pastern said.

"Nobody does,but they gave me ten last year."

He was tired, he had his business worries, and the sight of his wife arranging pork chops in the broiler only seemed like an extension of a boring day. He was happy enough to take the convertible and race up the hill to the Blevins', thinking that they might give him a drink. But the Blevins were away; their maid gave him an envelope with a check in it and shut the door. Turning in at the Flannagans' driveway, he tried to remember if he had ever met them. The name encouraged him, because he always felt that he could *handle* the Irish. There was a glass pane in the front door, and through this he could see into a hallway where a plump woman with red hair was arranging flowers.

"Infectious hepatitis," he shouted heartily.

She took a good look at herself in the mirror before she turned and, walking with very small steps, started toward the door. "Oh, please come in," she said. The girlish voice was nearly a whisper. She was not a girl, he could see. Her hair was dyed, and her bloom was fading, and she must have been crowding forty, but she seemed to be one of those women who cling to the manners and graces of a pretty child of eight. "Your wife just called," she said, separating one word from another, exactly like a child. "And I am not sure that I have any cash—any *money*, that is—but if you will wait just a minute I will write you out a check if I can find my checkbook. Won't you step into the living room, where it's cozier?"

A fire had just been lighted, he saw, and things had been set out for drinks, and, like any stray, his response to these comforts was instantaneous. Where was *Mr.* Flannagan? he wondered. Traveling home on a late train? Changing his clothes upstairs? Taking a shower? At the end of the room there was a desk heaped with papers, and she began to riffle these, making sighs and noises of girlish exasperation. "I am terribly sorry to keep you waiting," she said, "but won't you make yourself a little drink while you wait? Everything's on the table."

"What train does Mr. Flannagan come out on?"

"Mr. Flannagan is away," she said. Her voice dropped. "Mr. Flannagan has been away for six weeks. . . ."

"I'll have a drink, then, if you'll have one with me."

"If you will promise to make it weak."

"Sit down," he said, "and enjoy your drink and look for your checkbook later. The only way to find things is to relax."

All in all, they had six drinks. She described herself and her circumstances unhesitatingly. Mr. Flannagan manufactured plastic tongue depressors. He traveled all over the world. She didn't like to travel. Planes made her feel faint, and in Tokyo, where she had gone that summer, she had been given raw fish for breakfast and so she had come straight home. She and her husband had formerly lived in New York, where she had many friends, but Mr. Flannagan thought the country would be safer in case of war. She would rather live in danger than die of loneliness and boredom. She had no children; she had made no friends. "I've seen you, though, before," she said with enormous coyness, patting his knee. "I've seen you walking your dogs on Sunday and driving by in the convertible. . . ."

The thought of this lonely woman sitting at her window touched him, although he was even more touched by her plumpness. Sheer plumpness, he knew, is not a vital part of the body and has no procreative functions. It serves merely as an excess cushion for the rest of the carcass. And knowing its humble place in the scale of things, why did he, at this time of life, seem almost ready to sell his soul for plumpness? The remarks she made about the sufferings of a lonely woman seemed so broad at first that he didn't know what to make of them, but after the sixth drink he put his arm around her and suggested that they go upstairs and look for her checkbook there.

"I've never done this before," she said later, when he was arranging himself to leave. Her voice shook with feeling, and he thought it lovely. He didn't doubt her truthfulness, although he had heard the words a hundred times. "I've never done this before," they always said, shaking their dresses down over their white shoulders. "I've never done this before," they always said, waiting for the elevator in the hotel corridor. "I've never done this before," they always said, pouring another whiskey. "I've never done this before," they always said, putting on their stockings. On ships at sea, on railroad trains, in summer hotels with mountain views, they always said, "I've never done this before."

"WHERE have you been?" Mrs. Pastern asked sadly, when he came in. "It's after eleven."

"I had a drink with the Flannagans."

"She told me he was in Germany."

"He came home unexpectedly."

Charlie ate some supper in the kitchen and went into the TV room to hear the news. "Bomb them!" he shouted. "Throw a little nuclear hardware at them! Show them who's boss!" But in bed he had trouble sleeping. He thought first of his son and daughter, away at college. He loved them. It was the only meaning of the word that he had ever known. Then he played nine imaginary holes of golf, choosing his handicap, his irons, his stance, his opponents, and his weather in detail, but the green of the links seemed faded in the light of his business worries. His money was tied up in a Nassau hotel, an Ohio pottery works, and a detergent for window washing, and luck had been running against him. His worries harried him up out of bed, and he lighted a cigarette and went to the window. In the starlight he could see the trees stripped of their leaves. During the summer he had tried to repair some of his losses at the track, and the bare trees reminded him that his pari-mutuel tickets would still be lying, like leaves, in the gutters near Belmont and Saratoga. Maple and ash, beech and elm, one hundred to win on Three in the fourth, fifty to win on Six in the third, one hundred to win on Two in the eighth. Children walking home from school would scuff through what seemed to be his foliage. Then, getting back into bed, he thought unashamedly of Mrs. Flannagan, planning where they would next meet and what they would do. There are, he thought, so few true means of forgetfulness in this life that why should he shun the medicine even when the medicine seemed, as it did, a little crude?

A NEW CONQUEST always had a wonderful effect on Charlie. He became overnight generous, understanding, inexhaustibly good-humored, relaxed, kind to cats, dogs, and strangers, expansive, and compassionate. There was, of course, the reproachful figure of Mrs. Pastern waiting for him in the evenings, but he had served her well, he thought, for twenty-five years, and if he were to touch her tenderly these days she would likely say, "Ouch. That's where I bruised myself in the garden." On the evenings that they spent together, she seemed to choose to display the roughest angles of her personality; to grind her ax. "You know," she said, "Mary Quested cheats at cards." Her remarks fell a good deal short of where he sat. If these were indirect expressions of disappointment, it was a disappointment that no longer touched him.

He met Mrs. Flannagan for lunch in the city, and they spent the afternoon together. Leaving the hotel, Mrs. Flannagan stopped at a display of perfume. She said that she liked perfume, worked her shoulders, and called him "Monkey." Considering her girlishness and her claims to fidelity, there was, he thought, a distinct atmosphere of practice about her request, but he bought her a bottle of perfume. The second time they met, she admired a peignoir in a store window and he bought this. On their third meeting, she got a silk umbrella. Waiting for her in the restaurant for their fourth meeting, he hoped that she wasn't going to ask for jewelry, because his reserves of cash were low. She had promised to meet him at one, and he basked in his circumstances and the smells of sauce, gin, and red floor carpets. She was always late, and at half past one he ordered a second drink. At a quarter to two, he saw his waiter whispering to another waiter—whispering, laughing, and nodding his head in Charlie's direction. It was his first intimation of the chance that she might stand him up. But who was she—who did she think she was that she could do this to him? She was nothing but a lonely housewife; she was nothing but that. At two, he ordered his lunch. He was crushed. What had his emotional life been these last years but a series of sometimes shabby one-night stands, but without them his life would be unendurable.

There is something universal about being stood up in a city restaurant between one and two—a spiritual no-man's-land, whose blasted trees, entrenchments, and ratholes we all share, disarmed by the gullibility of our hearts. The waiter knew, and the laughter and lighthearted conversations at the tables around Charlie honed his feelings. He seemed to be helplessly elevated on his disappointment like a flagpole sitter, his aloneness looming larger and larger in the crowded room. Then he saw his own swollen image in a mirror, his gray hair clinging to his pate like the remains of a romantic landscape, his heavy body shaped a little like a firehouse Santa Claus, the paunch enlarged by one or two of Mrs. Kelly's second-best sofa cushions. He pushed his table away and started for a telephone booth in the hall.

"Is there anything wrong with your lunch, monsieur?" the waiter asked.

She answered the phone, and in her most girlish voice said, "We cannot go on like this. I have thought it over, and we cannot go on. It is not because I do not want to, because you are a very virile man, but my conscience will not let me."

"Can I stop by tonight and talk it over?"

"Well . . ." she said.

"I'll come straight up from the station."

"If you'll do me a favor."

"What?"

"I will tell you when I see you tonight. But please park your car behind the house and come in the back door. I do not want to give these old gossips here anything to talk about. You must remember that I have never done this before."

Of course she was right, he thought. She had her self-esteem to maintain. Her pride, he thought, was so childish, so sterling! Sometimes, driving through a New Hampshire mill town late in the day, he thought, you will see in some alley or driveway, down by the river, a child dressed in a tablecloth, sitting on a broken stool, waving her scepter over a kingdom of weeds and cinders and a few skinny chickens. It is the purity and the irony of their pride that touches one; and he felt that way about Mrs. Flannagan.

SHE LET HIM IN at the back door that night, but in the living room the scene was the same. The fire was burning, she made him a drink, and in her company he felt as if he had just worked his shoulders free of a heavy pack. But she was coy, in and out of his arms, tickling him and then tripping across the room to look at herself in the mirror. "I want my favor first," she said.

"What is it?"

"Guess."

"I can't give you money. I'm not rich, you know."

"Oh, I wouldn't think of taking money." She was indignant.

"Then what is it?"

"Something you wear."

"But my watch is worthless, my cuff links are brass."

"Something else."

"But what?"

"I won't tell you unless you promise to give it to me."

He pushed her away from him then, knowing that he could easily be made a fool of. "I can't make a promise unless I know what it is you want."

"It's something very small."

"How small?"

"Tiny. Weeny."

"Please tell me what it is." Then he seized her in his arms, and this was the moment he felt most like himself: solemn, virile, wise, and imperturbable.

"I won't tell you unless you promise."

"But I can't promise."

"Then go away," she said. "Go away and never, never, come back."

She was too childish to give the command much force, and yet it was not wasted on him. Could he go back to his own house, empty but for his wife, who would be grinding her ax? Go there and wait until time and chance turned up another friend?

"Please tell me."

"Promise."

"I promise."

"I want," she said, "a key to your bomb shelter."

The demand struck at him like a sledge-hammer blow, and suddenly he felt in all his parts the enormous weight of chagrin. All his gentle speculations on her person—the mill-town girl ruling her chickens—backfired bitterly. This must have been on her mind from the beginning, when she first lit the fire, lost her checkbook, and gave him a drink. The demand abraded his lust, but only for a moment, for now she was back in his arms, marching her fingers up and down his rib cage, saying, "Creepy, creepy, creepy mouse, come to live in Charlie's house." His need for her was crippling; it seemed like a cruel blow at the back of his knees. And yet in some chamber of his thick head he could see the foolishness and the obsolescence of his hankering skin. But how could he reform his bone and muscle to suit this new world; instruct his meandering and greedy flesh in politics, geography, holocausts, and cataclysms? Her front was round, fragrant, and soft, and he took the key off its ring—a piece of metal one and one-half inches long, warmed by the warmth of his hands, a genuine talisman of salvation, a defense against the end of the world—and dropped it into the neck of her dress.

THE PASTERNS' BOMB SHELTER had been completed that spring. They would have liked to keep it a secret; would have liked at least to soft-pedal its existence; but the trucks and bulldozers going in and out of their driveway had informed everyone. It had cost thirty-two thousand dollars, and it had two chemical toilets, an oxygen supply, and a library, compiled by a Columbia professor, consisting of books meant to inspire hopefulness, humor, and tranquillity. There were stores of survival food to last three months, and several cases of hard liquor. Mrs. Pastern had bought the plaster-of-Paris ducks, the birdbath, and the gnomes in an attempt to give the lump in her garden a look of innocence; to make it acceptable—at least to herself. For, bulking as it did in so pretty and domestic a scene and signifying as it must the death of at least half the world's population, she had found it, with its grassy cover, impossible to reconcile with the blue sky and the white clouds. She liked to keep the curtains drawn at that side of the house, and they were drawn the next afternoon, when she served gin to the bishop.

The bishop had come unexpectedly. Her minister had telephoned and said that the bishop was in the neighborhood and would like to thank her for her services to the church, and could he bring the bishop over now? She threw together some things for tea, changed her dress, and came down into the hall just as they rang the bell.

"How do you do, Your Grace," she said. "Won't you come in, Your Grace? Would you like some tea, Your Grace—or would you sooner have a drink, Your Grace?"

"I would like a Martini," said the bishop.

He had the gift of a clear and carrying voice. He was a well-built man, with hair as black as dye, firm and sallow skin deeply creased around a wide mouth, and eyes as glittering and haggard, she thought, as someone drugged. "If you'll excuse me, Your Grace . . ."

This request for a cocktail confused her; Charlie always mixed the drinks. She dropped ice on the pantry floor, poured a pint or so of gin into the shaker, and tried to correct what appeared to her to be a lethal drink with more vermouth.

"Mr. Ludgate here has been telling me how indispensable you are to the life of the parish," the bishop said, taking his drink.

"I do try," said Mrs. Pastern.

"You have two children."

"Yes. Sally's at Smith. Carkie's at Colgate. The house seems so empty now. They were confirmed by the old bishop. Bishop Tomlinson."

"Ah, yes," the bishop said. "Oh, yes."

The presence of the bishop made her nervous. She wished she could give the call a more natural air; she wished at least to make her presence in her own parlor seem real. She was suffering from an intense discomfort that sometimes attacked her during committee meetings, when the parliamentary atmosphere had a disintegrating effect on her personality. She would, sitting in her folding chair, seem to go around the room on her hands and knees, gathering the fragments of herself and cementing them together with some virtue, such as, I am a Good Mother, or, I am a Patient Wife.

"Are you two old friends?" she asked the bishop.

"No!" the bishop exclaimed.

"The bishop was just driving through," the minister said weakly.

"Could I see your garden?" the bishop asked.

Taking his Martini glass with him, he followed her out

the side door onto the terrace. Mrs. Pastern was an ardent gardener, but the scene was disappointing. The abundant cycle of bloom was nearly over; there was nothing to see but chrysanthemums. "I wish you could see it in the spring, especially in the *late* spring," she said. "The star magnolia is the first to bloom. Then we have the flowering cherries and plums. Just as they finish, we have the azalea, the laurel, and the hybrid rhododendron. I have bronze tulips under the wisteria. The lilac is white."

"I see that you have a shelter," the bishop said.

"Yes." She had been betrayed by her ducks and gnomes. "Yes, we have, but it's really nothing to see. This bed is all lily of the valley, all this bed. I feel that roses make a better cutting than an ornamental garden, so I keep the roses behind the house. The border is *fraises des bois*. So sweet, so winy."

"Have you had the shelter long?"

"We had it built in the spring," said Mrs. Pastern. "That hedge is flowering quince. Over there is our little salad garden. Lettuce and herbs. That sort of thing."

"I would like to see the shelter," the bishop said.

She was hurt—a hurt that seemed to reverberate all the way back to her childhood, when she had been wounded by the discovery that the friends who came to call on rainy days had not come because they liked her but to eat her cookies and hog her toys. She had never been able to put a good countenance on selfishness, and she scowled as they passed the birdbath and the painted ducks. The gnomes with their mobcaps looked down on the three of them as she unlocked the fire door with a key that she wore around her neck.

"Charming," the bishop said. "Charming. Why, I see you even have a library."

"Yes," she said. "The books were chosen for their humor, tranquillity, and hopefulness."

"It is an unfortunate characteristic of ecclesiastical architecture," said the bishop, "that the basement or cellar is confined to a small space under the chancel. This gives us very little room for the salvation of the faithful—a characteristic, I should perhaps add, of our denomination. Some churches have commodious basements. But I shan't take up any more of your time." He strode back across the lawn toward the house, put his cocktail glass on the terrace wall, and gave her his blessing.

She sat down heavily on her terrace steps and watched the car drive off. He had not come to praise her, she knew that. Was it impious of her to suspect that he was traveling around his domain picking and choosing sanctuaries? Was it possible that he meant to exploit his holiness in this way? The burden of modern life, even if it smelled of plastics—as it seemed to—bore down cruelly on the supports of God, and Family, and the Nation. The burden was top-heavy, and she seemed to hear the foundations give. She had believed all her life in the holiness of the priesthood, and if this belief was genuine, why hadn't she offered the bishop the safety of her shelter at once? But if he believed in the resurrection of the dead and the life of the world to come, why was a shelter anything that he might need?

The telephone rang, and she answered its ringing with a forced lightheartedness. It was a woman named Beatrice, who came to clean Mrs. Pastern's house two days a week.

"This is Beatrice, Mrs. Pastern," she said, "and there is something I think you ought to know. As you know, I'm not a gossip. I'm not like that Adele, who goes around from lady to lady telling that the So-and-Sos aren't sleeping together, and that So-and-So had six empty whiskey bottles in his wastebaskets, and that nobody came to So-and-So's cocktail party. I'm not like that Adele. I'm not a gossip, and you know that, Mrs. Pastern. But there is something I think you ought to know. I worked for Mrs. Flannagan today, and she showed me a key, and she said it was a key to your bomb shelter, and that your husband gave it to her. I don't know whether it was the truth or not, but I thought you ought to know."

"Thank you, Beatrice."

He had dragged her good name through a hundred escapades, debauched her excellence, and thrown away her love, but she had never imagined that he would betray her in their plans for the end of the world. She poured what was left of the bishop's cocktail into a glass. She hated the taste of gin, but her accumulated troubles had grown to seem like the pain of an illness, and gin dimmed this, although it inflamed her indignation. Outside, the sky darkened, the wind changed, it began to rain. What could she do? She couldn't go back to Mother. Mother didn't have a shelter. She couldn't pray for guidance. The bishop's apparent worldliness had reduced the comforts of heaven. She couldn't contemplate her husband's foolish profligacy without drinking more gin. And then she remembered the night—the night of judgment—when they had agreed to let Aunt Ida and Uncle Ralph burn, when she had sacrificed her three-year-old niece and he his five-year-old nephew; when they had conspired like murderers and had decided to deny mercy even to his old mother.

She was quite drunk by the time Charlie came in. "I couldn't spend two weeks in any hole in the ground with that Mrs. Flannagan," she said.

"What are you talking about?"

"I took the bishop down to show him the shelter and he—"

"What bishop? What was a bishop doing here?"

"Stop interrupting me and listen to what I have to say. Mrs. Flannagan has a key to our shelter, and you gave it to her."

"Who told you this?"

"Mrs. Flannagan," she said, "has a key to our shelter, and you gave it to her."

He went back out through the rain to the garage and jammed his fingers in the door. In haste and rage he stalled the car, and, waiting for the carburetor to drain, was faced, in the headlights, with the backstage of his wasteful domestic life which had accumulated in the garage. Here was a fortune in broken garden furniture and power tools. When the car started, he slammed out of his driveway and passed a red light at the first intersection, where, for a moment, his life hung by a thread. He didn't care. Slamming up the hill, he clutched the wheel as if he already had his hands on her plump and silly neck. It was his children's honor and peace of mind that she had damaged. It was his children, his beloved children, that she had harmed.

He stopped the car at the door. The house was lighted, and he could smell wood smoke, but the place was quiet and, peering through the glass pane, he couldn't see any signs of life or hear anything but the rain. He tried the door. It was locked. Then he pounded on the frame with his fist. It was a long time before she appeared, from the living room, and he guessed she must have been asleep. She was wearing the peignoir he had bought her. She straightened her hair. As soon as she opened the door, he pushed his way into the hall and shouted, "Why did you do it? Why did you do such a damn fool thing?"

"I do not know what you are talking about."

"Why did you tell my wife you had the key?"

"I did not tell your wife."

"Then who did you tell?"

"I did not tell anyone."

She worked her shoulders and looked down at the tip of her slipper. Like most incurable fibbers, she had an extravagant regard for the truth, which she expressed by sending up signals meant to indicate that she was lying. He saw then that he could not get the truth out of her, that he could not shake it out of her with all the strength in his arms, and that her confession, if he had it, would have done him no good.

"Get me something to drink," he said.

"I think you had better go away and come back later, when you are feeling better," she said.

"I'm tired," he said. "I'm tired. Oh, God, I'm tired. I haven't sat down all day."

He went into the living room and poured himself a whiskey. He saw his hands, blackened by the trains and the banisters, the doorknobs and the papers, of a long day, and in the mirror he saw that his hair was soaked with rain. He went out of the living room and through the library to the downstairs bathroom. She made a little noise, scarcely a cry. When he opened the bathroom door, he found himself face to face with an absolutely naked stranger.

He shut the door, and then there was that nearly metronomic stillness that precedes a howling confrontation. It was she who broke the silence. "I do not know who he is, and I have been trying to make him go away. . . . I know what you are thinking, and I do not care. It is my house, after all, and I did not invite you into it, and I do not have to explain everything that goes on to you."

"Get away from me," he said. "Get away from me or I'll break your neck."

HE DROVE HOME through the rain. When he let himself

in, he noticed the noise and the smell of cooking from the kitchen. He supposed that these signs and odors must have been one of the first signs of life on the planet, and might be one of the last. The evening paper was in the living room, and, giving it a shake, he shouted, "Throw a little nuclear hardware at them! Show them who's boss!" And then, falling into a chair, he asked softly, "Dear Jesus, when will it ever end?"

"I've been waiting for you to say that," said Mrs. Pastern quietly, coming in from the pantry. "I've been waiting nearly three months now to hear just that. I first began to worry when I saw that you'd sold your cuff links and your studs. I wondered what was the matter then. Then, when you signed the contract for the shelter without a penny to pay for it, I began to see your plan. You *want* the world to end, don't you? Don't you, Charlie, don't you? I've known it all along, but I couldn't admit it to myself, it seemed so ruthless—but then one learns something new every day." She walked past him into the hallway and started up the stairs. "There's a hamburger in the frying pan," she said, "and some potatoes in the oven. If you want a green vegetable, you can heat up the leftover broccoli. I'm going to telephone the children."

WE TRAVEL with such velocity these days that the most we can do is to remember a few place names. The freight of metaphysical speculation will have to catch up with us by slow train, if it catches up with us at all. The rest of the story was recounted by my mother, whose letter caught up with me in Kitzbühel, where I sometimes stay. "There have been so many changes in the last six weeks," she wrote, "that I hardly know where to begin. First, the Pasterns are gone and I mean gone. He's in the county jail serving a two-year sentence for grand larceny. Sally's left college and is working at Macy's, and the boy's still looking for a job, I hear. He's living with his mother somewhere in the Bronx. Someone said they were on home relief. It seems that Charlie ran through all of that money his mother left him about a year ago and they were just living on credit. The bank took everything and they moved to a motel in Tansford. Then they moved from motel to motel, traveling in a rented car and never paying their bills. The motel and the car-rental people were the first ones to catch up with them. Some nice people named Willoughby bought the house from the bank. And the Flanagans have divorced. Remember her? She used to walk around her garden with a silk parasol. He didn't have to give her a settlement or anything and someone saw her on Central Park West in a thin coat on a cold night. But she did come back. It was very strange. She came back last Thursday. It had just begun to snow. It was a little while after lunch. What an old fool your mother is but as old as I am I never cease to thrill at the miracle of a snowstorm. I had a lot of work to do but I decided to let it go and stand by the window awhile and watch it snow. The sky was very dark. It was a fine, dry snow and covered everything quickly like a spread of light. Then I saw Mrs. Flanagan walking up the street. She must have come out on the two-thirty-three and walked up from the station. I don't suppose she can have much money if she can't afford a cab, do you? She was not very warmly dressed and she had on high heels and no rubbers. Well, she walked up the street and she walked right across the Pasterns' lawn, I meant what used to be the Pasterns' lawn, to their bomb shelter and just stood there looking at it. I don't know what in the world she was thinking of but the shelter looks a little like a tomb, you know, and she looked like a mourner standing there with the snow falling on her head and shoulders and it made me sad to think she hardly knew the Pasterns. Then Mrs. Willoughby telephoned me and said there was this strange woman standing in front of her bomb shelter and did I know who it was and I said that I did, that it was Mrs. Flannagan who used to live up on the hill, and then she asked what I thought she should do and I said the only thing to do I guessed was to send her away. So then Mrs. Willoughby sent her maid down and I saw the maid telling Mrs. Flannagan to go away and then in a little while Mrs. Flannagan walked back through the snow to the station."

A VISION OF THE WORLD

THIS IS BEING WRITTEN in another seaside cottage on another coast. Gin and whiskey have bitten rings in the table where I sit. The light is dim. On the wall there is a colored lithograph of a kitten wearing a flowered hat, a silk dress, and white gloves. The air is musty, but I think it is a pleasant smell—heartening and carnal, like bilge water or the land wind. The tide is high, and the sea below the bluff slams its bulkheads, its doors, and shakes its chains with such power that it makes the lamp on my table jump. I am here alone to rest up from a chain of events that began one Saturday afternoon when I was spading up my garden. A foot or two below the surface I found a small round can that might have contained shoe polish. I pried the can open with a knife. Inside I found a piece of oilcloth, and within this a note on lined paper. It read, "I, Nils Jugstrum, promise myself that if I am not a member of the Gory Brook Country Club by the time I am twenty-five years old I will hang myself." I knew that twenty years ago the neighborhood where I live had been farmland, and I guessed that some farmer's boy, gazing off to the green fairways of Gory Brook, had made his vow and buried it in the ground. I was moved, as I always am, by these broken lines of communication in which we express our most acute feelings. The note seemed, like some impulse of romantic love, to let me deeper into the afternoon.

The sky was blue. It seemed like music. I had just cut the grass, and the smell of it was in the air. This reminded me of those overtures and promises of love we know when we are young. At the end of a foot race you throw yourself onto the grass by the cinder track, gasping for breath, and the ardor with which you embrace the schoolhouse lawn is a promise you will follow all the days of your life. Thinking then of peaceable things, I noticed that the black ants had conquered the red ants and were taking the corpses off the field. A robin flew by, pursued by two jays. The cat was in the currant hedge, scouting a sparrow. A pair of orioles passed, pecking each other, and then I saw, a foot or so from where I stood, a copperhead working itself out of the last length of its dark winter skin. What I experienced was not fright or dread; it was shock at my unpreparedness for this branch of death. Here was lethal venom, as much a part of the earth as the running water in the brook, but I seemed to have no space for it in my considerations. I went back to the house to get the shotgun, but I had the misfortune then to meet up with the older of my two dogs, a gun-shy bitch. At the sight of the gun she began to bark and whimper, torn unmercifully by her instincts and anxieties. Her barking brought the second dog, a natural hunter, bounding down the stairs, ready to retrieve a rabbit or a bird, and, followed by two dogs, one barking in joy and the other in horror, I returned to the garden in time to see the viper disappear into a stone wall.

After this I drove into the village and bought some grass seed and then went out to the supermarket on Route 27 to get some brioches my wife had ordered. I think you may need a camera these days to record a supermarket on a Saturday afternoon. Our language is traditional, the accrual of centuries of intercourse. Except for the shapes of the pastry, there was nothing traditional to be seen at the bakery counter where I waited. We were six or seven, delayed by an old man with a long list, a scroll of groceries. Looking over his shoulder I read,

6 eggs
hors d'oeuvres

He saw me reading his document, and held it against his chest like a prudent card player. Then suddenly the piped-in music changed from a love song to a cha-cha, and the woman beside me began to move her shoulders shyly and to execute a few steps. "Would you like to dance, madam?" I asked. She was very plain, but when I held out my arms she stepped into them, and we danced for a minute or two. You could see that she loved to dance, but with a face like that she couldn't have had many chances. She then blushed a deep red, stepped out of my arms, and went over to the glass case, where she studied the Boston cream pies. I felt that we had made a step in the right direction, and when I got my brioches and drove home I was elated. A policeman stopped me at the corner of Alewives Lane, to let a parade go by. First to come was a young girl in boots and shorts that emphasized the fineness of her thighs. She had an enormous nose, wore a busby, and pumped an aluminum baton. She was followed by another girl, with finer and more ample thighs, who marched with her pelvis so far in advance of the rest of her that her spine was strangely curved. She wore bifocals and seemed terribly bored by this forwardness of her pelvis. A band of boys, with here and there a gray-haired ringer, brought up the rear, playing "The Caissons Go Rolling Along." They carried no banners, they had no discernible purpose or destination, and it all seemed to me terribly funny. I laughed all the way home.

But my wife was sad.

"What's the matter, darling?" I asked.

"I just have this terrible feeling that I'm a character in a television situation comedy," she said. "I mean, I'm nice-looking, I'm well-dressed, I have humorous and attractive children, but I have this terrible feeling that I'm in black-and-white and that I can be turned off by anybody. I just have this terrible feeling that I can be turned *off*." My wife is often sad because her sadness is not a sad sadness, sorry because her sorrow is not a crushing sorrow. She grieves because her grief is not an acute grief, and when I tell her that this sorrow over the inadequacies of her sorrow may be a new hue in the spectrum of human pain, she is not consoled. Oh, I sometimes think of leaving her. I could conceivably make a life without her and the children, I could get along without the companionship of my friends, but I could not bring myself to leave my lawns and gardens, I could not part from the porch screens that I have repaired and painted, I cannot divorce myself from the serpentine brick walk I have laid between the side door and the rose garden; and so, while my chains are forged of turf and house paint, they will still bind me until I die. But I was grateful to my wife then for what she had said, for stating that the externals of her life had the quality of a dream. The uninhibited energies of the imagination had created the supermarket, the viper, and the note in the shoe-polish can. Compared to these, my wildest reveries had the literalness of double-entry bookkeeping. It pleased me to think that our external life has the quality of a dream and that in our dreams we find the virtues of conservatism. I then went into the house, where I found the cleaning woman smoking a stolen Egyptian cigarette and piecing together the torn letters in the wastebasket.

We went to Gory Brook that night for dinner. I checked the list of members, looking for Nils Jugstrum, but he wasn't there, and I wondered if he had hanged himself. And for what? It was the usual. Gracie Masters, the only daughter of a millionaire funeral director, was dancing with Pinky Townsend. Pinky was out on fifty thousand dollars' bail for stockmarket manipulation. When bail was set, he took the fifty thousand out of his wallet. I danced a set with Millie Surcliffe. The music was "Rain," "Moonlight on the Ganges," "When the Red Red Robin Comes Bob Bob Bobbin' Along," "Five Foot Two, Eyes of Blue," "Carolina in the Morning," and "The Sheik of Araby." We seemed to be dancing on the grave of social coherence. But while the scene was plainly revolutionary, where was the new day, the world to come? The next set was "Lena from Palesteena," "I'm Forever Blowing Bubbles," "Louisville Lou," "Smiles," and "The Red Red Robin" again. That last one really gets us jumping, but when the band blew the spit out of their instruments I saw them shaking their heads in deep moral disapproval of our antics. Millie went back to her table, and I stood by the door, wondering why my heart should heave when I see people leave a dance floor at the end of a set—heave as it heaves when I see a crowd pack up and leave a beach as the shadow of the cliff falls over the water and the sand, heave as if I saw in these gentle departures the energies and the thoughtlessness of life itself.

Time, I thought, strips us rudely of the privileges of the bystander, and in the end that couple chatting loudly in bad French in the lobby of the Grande Bretagne (Athens) turns out to be us. Someone else has got our post behind the potted palms, our quiet corner in the bar, and, exposed, perforce we cast around for other avenues of observation. What I wanted to identify then was not a chain of facts but an essence—something like that indecipherable collision of contingencies that can produce exaltation or despair. What I wanted to do was to grant my dreams, in so incoherent a world, their legitimacy. None of this made me moody, and I danced, drank, and told stories at the bar until about one, when we went home. I turned on the television set to a commercial that, like so much else I had seen that day, seemed terribly funny. A young woman with a boarding-school accent was asking, "Do you offend with wet-fur-coat odor? A fifty-thousand-dollar sable cape caught in a thundershower can smell worse than an old hound dog who's been chasing a fox through a swamp. *Nothing* smells worse than wet mink. Even a light mist can make lamb, opossum, civet, baum marten, and other less costly and serviceable furs as malodorous as a badly ventilated lion house in a zoo. Safeguard yourself from embarrassment and anxiety by light applications of Elixircol before you wear your furs. . . ." She belonged to the dream world, and I told her so before I turned her off. I fell asleep in the moonlight and dreamed of an island.

I was with some other men, and seemed to have reached the place on a sailing boat. I was sunburned, I remember, and touching my jaw, I felt a three- or four-day stubble. The island was in the Pacific. There was a smell of rancid cooking oil in the air—a sign of the China coast. It was in the middle of the afternoon when we landed, and we seemed to have nothing much to do. We wandered through the streets. The place either had been occupied by the Army or had served as a military way station, because many of the signs in the windows were written in an approximation of English. "Crews Cutz," I read on a sign in an Oriental barbershop. Many of the stores had displays of imitation American whiskey. Whiskey was spelled "Whikky." Because we had nothing better to do, we went into a local museum. There were bows, primitive fishhooks, masks, and drums. From the museum we went to a restaurant and ordered a meal. I had a struggle with the local language, but what surprised me was that it seemed to be an informed struggle. I seemed to have studied the language before coming ashore. I distinctly remembered putting together a sentence when the waiter came up to the table. *"Porpozec ciebie nie prosze dorzanin albo zyolpocz ciwego,"* I said. The waiter smiled and complimented me, and, when I woke from the dream, the fact of the language made the island in the sun, its population, and its museum real, vivid, and enduring. I thought with longing of the quiet and friendly natives and the easy pace of their lives.

Sunday passed swiftly and pleasantly in a round of cocktail parties, but that night I had another dream. I dreamed that I was standing at the bedroom window of the cottage in Nantucket that we sometimes rent. I was looking south along the fine curve of the beach. I have seen finer, whiter, and more splendid beaches, but when I look at the yellow of the sand and the arc of the curve, I always have the feeling that if I look at the cove long enough it will reveal something to me. The sky was cloudy. The water was gray. It was Sunday—although I couldn't have said how I knew this. It was late, and from the inn I could hear that most pleasant sound of dishes being handled, while families would be eating their Sunday-night suppers in the old matchboard dining room. Then I saw a single figure coming down the beach. It seemed to be a priest or a bishop. He carried a crozier, and wore the miter, cope, soutane, chasuble, and alb for high votive Mass. His vestments were heavily worked with gold, and now and then they were lifted by the sea wind. His face was clean-shaven. I could not make out his features in the fading light. He saw me at my window, raised his hand, and called. "*Porpozec ciebie nie prosze dorzanin albo zyolpocz ciwego.*" Then he hurried along the sand, striking his crozier down like a walking stick, his stride impeded by the voluminousness of his vestments. He passed the window where I stood and disappeared where the curve of the bluff overtakes the curve of the shore.

I worked on Monday, and on Tuesday morning woke at about four from a dream in which I had been playing touch football. I was on the winning team. The score was six to eighteen. It was a scrub Sunday-afternoon game on somebody's lawn. Our wives and daughters watched from the edge of the grass, where there were chairs and tables and things to drink. The winning play was a long end run, and when the touchdown had been scored a big blonde named Helene Farmer got up and organized the women into a cheering section. "Rah, rah, rah," they said. "*Porpozec ciebie nie prosze dorzanin albo zyolpocz ciwego.* Rah, rah, rah."

I found none of this disconcerting. It was what I had wanted, in a way. Isn't the unconquerable force in man the love of discovery? The repetition of this sentence had the excitement of discovery for me. The fact that I had been on the winning team made me feel happy, and I went cheerfully down to breakfast, but our kitchen, alas, is a part of dreamland. With its pink, washable walls, chilling lights, built-in television (where prayers were being said), and artificial potted plants, it made me nostalgic for my dream, and when my wife passed me the stylus and Magic Tablet on which we write our breakfast orders, I wrote, *"Porpozec ciebie nie prosze dorzanin albo zyolpocz ciwego."* She laughed and asked me what I meant. When I repeated the sentence—it seemed, indeed, to be the only thing I wanted to say—she began to cry, and I saw in the bitterness of her tears that I had better take a rest. Dr. Howland came over to give me a sedative, and I took a plane to Florida that afternoon.

Now it is late. I drink a glass of milk and take a sleeping pill. I dream that I see a pretty woman kneeling in a field of wheat. Her light-brown hair is full and so are the skirts of her dress. Her clothing seems old-fashioned—it seems before my time—and I wonder how I can know and feel so tenderly toward a stranger who is dressed in clothing that my grandmother might have worn. And yet she seems real—more real than the Tamiami Trail four miles to the east, with its Smorgorama and Giganticburger stands, more real than the back streets of Sarasota. I do not ask her who she is. I know what she will say. But then she smiles and starts to speak before I can turn away. *"Porpozec ciebie . . ."* she begins. Then either I awake in despair or am waked by the sound of rain on the palms. I think of some farmer who, hearing the noise of rain, will stretch his lame bones and smile, feeling that the rain is falling into his lettuce and his cabbages, his hay and his oats, his parsnips and his corn. I think of some plumber who, waked by the rain, will smile at a vision of the world in which all the drains are miraculously cleansed and free. Right-angle drains, crooked drains, root-choked and rusty drains all gurgle and discharge their waters into the sea. I think that the rain will wake some old lady, who will wonder if she has left her copy of *Dombey and Son* in the garden. Her shawl? Did she cover the chairs? And I know that the sound of the rain will wake some lovers, and that its sound will seem to be a part of that force that has thrust them into one another's arms. Then I sit up in bed and exclaim aloud to myself, "Valor! Love! Virtue!

Compassion! Splendor! Kindness! Wisdom! Beauty!" The words seem to have the colors of the earth, and as I recite them I feel my hopefulness mount until I am contented and at peace with the night.

REUNION

THE LAST TIME I saw my father was in Grand Central Station. I was going from my grandmother's in the Adirondacks to a cottage on the Cape that my mother had rented, and I wrote my father that I would be in New York between trains for an hour and a half, and asked if we could have lunch together. His secretary wrote to say that he would meet me at the information booth at noon, and at twelve o'clock sharp I saw him coming through the crowd. He was a stranger to me—my mother divorced him three years ago and I hadn't been with him since—but as soon as I saw him I felt that he was my father, my flesh and blood, my future and my doom. I knew that when I was grown I would be something like him; I would have to plan my campaigns within his limitations. He was a big, good-looking man, and I was terribly happy to see him again. He struck me on the back and shook my hand. "Hi, Charlie," he said. "Hi, boy. I'd like to take you up to my club, but it's in the Sixties, and if you have to catch an early train I guess we'd better get something to eat around here." He put his arm around me, and I smelled my father the way my mother sniffs a rose. It was a rich compound of whiskey, after-shave lotion, shoe polish, woolens, and the rankness of a mature male. I hoped that someone would see us together. I wished that we could be photographed. I wanted some record of our having been together.

We went out of the station and up a side street to a restaurant. It was still early, and the place was empty. The bartender was quarreling with a delivery boy, and there was one very old waiter in a red coat down by the kitchen door. We sat down, and my father hailed the waiter in a loud voice. *"Kellner!"* he shouted. *"Garçon! Cameriere! You!"* His boisterousness in the empty restaurant seemed out of place. "Could we have a little service here!" he shouted. "Chop-chop." Then he clapped his hands. This caught the waiter's attention, and he shuffled over to our table.

"Were you clapping your hands at me?" he asked.

"Calm down, calm down, *sommelier*," my father said. "If it isn't too much to ask of you—if it wouldn't be too much above and beyond the call of duty, we would like a couple of Beefeater Gibsons."

"I don't like to be clapped at," the waiter said.

"I should have brought my whistle," my father said. "I have a whistle that is audible only to the ears of old waiters. Now, take out your little pad and your little pencil and see if you can get this straight: two Beefeater Gibsons. Repeat after me: two Beefeater Gibsons."

"I think you'd better go somewhere else," the waiter said quietly.

"That," said my father, "is one of the most brilliant suggestions I have ever heard. Come on, Charlie, let's get the hell out of here."

I followed my father out of that restaurant into another. He was not so boisterous this time. Our drinks came, and he cross-questioned me about the baseball season. He then struck the edge of his empty glass with his knife and began shouting again. "*Garçon! Kellner! Cameriere! You!* Could we trouble you to bring us two more of the same."

"How old is the boy?" the waiter asked.

"That," my father said, "is none of your God-damned business."

"I'm sorry, sir," the waiter said, "but I won't serve the boy another drink."

"Well, I have some news for you," my father said. "I have some very interesting news for you. This doesn't happen to be the only restaurant in New York. They've opened another on the corner. Come on, Charlie."

He paid the bill, and I followed him out of that restaurant into another. Here the waiters wore pink jackets like hunting coats, and there was a lot of horse tack on the walls. We sat down, and my father began to shout again. "Master of the hounds! Tallyhoo and all that sort of thing. We'd like a little something in the way of a stirrup cup. Namely, two Bibson Geefeaters."

"Two Bibson Geefeaters?" the waiter asked, smiling.

"You know damned well what I want," my father said

angrily. "I want two Beefeater Gibsons, and make it snappy. Things have changed in jolly old England. So my friend the duke tells me. Let's see what England can produce in the way of a cocktail."

"This isn't England," the waiter said.

"Don't argue with me," my father said. "Just do as you're told."

"I just thought you might like to know where you are," the waiter said.

"If there is one thing I cannot tolerate," my father said, "it is an impudent domestic. Come on, Charlie."

The fourth place we went to was Italian. *"Buon giorno,"* my father said. *"Per favore, possiamo avere due cocktail americani, forti, forti. Molto gin, poco vermut."*

"I don't understand Italian," the waiter said.

"Oh, come off it," my father said. "You understand Italian, and you know damned well you do. *Vogliamo due cocktail americani. Subito."*

The waiter left us and spoke with the captain, who came over to our table and said, "I'm sorry, sir, but this table is reserved."

"All right," my father said. "Get us another table."

"All the tables are reserved," the captain said.

"I get it," my father said. "You don't desire our patronage. Is that it? Well, the hell with you. *Vada all' inferno.* Let's go, Charlie."

"I have to get my train," I said.

"I'm sorry, sonny," my father said. "I'm terribly sorry." He put his arm around me and pressed me against him. "I'll walk you back to the station. If there had only been time to go up to my club."

"That's all right, Daddy," I said.

"I'll get you a paper," he said. "I'll get you a paper to read on the train."

Then he went up to a newsstand and said, "Kind sir, will you be good enough to favor me with one of your God-damned, no-good, ten-cent afternoon papers?" The clerk turned away from him and stared at a magazine cover. "Is it asking too much, kind sir," my father said, "is it asking too much for you to sell me one of your disgusting specimens of yellow journalism?"

"I have to go, Daddy," I said. "It's late."

"Now, just wait a second, sonny," he said. "Just wait a second. I want to get a rise out of this chap."

"Goodbye, Daddy," I said, and I went down the stairs and got my train, and that was the last time I saw my father.

AN EDUCATED AMERICAN WOMAN

ITEM: "I remain joined in holy matrimony to my unintellectual 190-pound halfback, and keep myself busy chauffeuring my son Bibber to and from a local private school that I helped organize. I seem, at one time or another, to have had the presidency of every civic organization in the community, and last year I ran the local travel agency for nine months. A New York publisher (knock on wood) is interested in my critical biography of Gustave Flaubert, and last year I ran for town supervisor on the Democratic ticket and got the largest Democratic plurality in the history of the village. Polly *Coulter* Mellow's ('42) stayed with us for a week on her way home from Paris to Minneapolis and we talked, ate, drank, and thought in French during her visit. Shades of Mlle. de Grasse! I still find time to band birds and knit Argyle socks."

This report, for her college alumnae magazine, might have suggested an aggressive woman, but she was not that at all. Jill *Chidchester* Madison held her many offices through competence, charm, and intellect, and she was actually quite shy. Her light-brown hair, at the time of which I'm writing, was dressed simply and in a way that recalled precisely how she had looked in boarding school twenty years before. Boarding school may have shaded her taste in clothing; that and the fact that she had a small front and was one of those women who took this deprivation as if it was something more than the loss of a leg. Considering her comprehensive view of life, it seemed strange that such a thing should have bothered her, but it bothered her terribly. She had pretty legs. Her coloring was fresh and high. Her eyes were brown and set much too close together, so that when she was less than vivacious she had a mousy look.

Her mother, Amelia Faxon Chidchester, was a vigorous, stocky woman with splendid white hair, a red face, and an emphatic accent whose roots seemed more temperamental than regional. Mrs. Chidchester's words were shaped to express her untiring vigor, her triumph over pain, her cultural enthusiasm, and her trust in mankind. She was the author of seventeen unpublished books. Jill's father died when she was six days old. She was born in San Francisco, where her father had run a small publishing house and administered a small estate. He left his wife and daughter with enough money to protect them from any sort of hardship and any sort of financial anxiety, but they were a good deal less rich than their relatives. Jill appeared to be precocious, and when she was three her mother took her to Munich, where she was entered in the Gymnasium für Kinder, run by Dr. Stock for the purpose of observing gifted children. The competition was fierce, and her reaction tests were only middling, but she was an amiable and a brilliant girl. When she was five, they shifted to the Scuola Pantola in Florence, a similar institution. They moved from there to England, to the famous Tower Hill School, in Kent. Then Amelia, or Melee, as she was called, decided that the girl should put down some roots, and so she rented a house in Nantucket, where Jill was entered in the public school.

I don't know why it is that expatriate children should seem underfed, but they often do, and Jill, with her mixed clothing, her mixed languages, her bare legs and sandals, gave the impression that the advantages of her education had worked out in her as a kind of pathos. She was the sort of child who skipped a lot. She skipped to school. She skipped home. She was shy. She was not very practical, and her mother encouraged her in this. "*You* shall not wash the dishes, my dear," she said. "A girl of your intelligence is not expected to waste her time washing dishes." They had a devoted servant—all of Melee's servants worshipped the ground she walked on—and Jill's only idea about housework was that it was work she was not expected to do. She did, when she was about ten, learn to knit Argyle socks and was allowed this recreation. She was romantic. Entered in her copybook was the following: "Mrs. Amelia Faxon Chidchester requests the honor of your company at the wedding of her daughter Jill to Viscount Ludley-Huntington, Earl of Ashmead, in Westminster Abbey. White tie. Decorations." The house in Nantucket was pleasant, and Jill learned to sail. It was in Nantucket that her mother spoke to her once about that subject for which we have no vocabulary in English—about love. It was late afternoon. A fire was burning and there were flowers on the table. Jill was reading and her mother was writing. She stopped writing and said, over her shoulder, "I think I should tell you, my dear, that during the war I was in charge of a canteen at the Embarcadero, and I gave myself to many lonely soldiers."

The remark was crushing. It seemed to the girl emotionally and intellectually incomprehensible. She wanted to cry. She could not imagine her mother giving herself, as she put it, to a string of lonely soldiers. Her mother's manner firmly and authoritatively declared her indifference to this side of things. There seemed to be no way of getting around what had been said. It stuck up in the girl's consciousness like a fallen meteor. Perhaps it was all a lie, but her mother had never lied. Then, for once, she faced up to the limitations of her only parent. Her mother was not a liar, but she was a fraud. Her accent was a fraud, her tastes were fraudulent, and the seraphic look she assumed when she listened to music was the look of someone trying to recall an old telephone number. With her indomitable good cheer, her continual aches and pains, her implacable snobbism, her cultural squatter's rights, her lofty friends, and her forceful and meaningless utterances, she seemed, for a moment, to illustrate a supreme lack of discernment in nature. But was Jill meant to fabricate, single-handed, some cord of love and wisdom between this stranger who had given her life and life itself as she could see it, spread out in terms of fields and woods, wondrous and fair, beyond the windows? Could she not instead— But she felt too young, too thin, too undefended to make a life without a parent, and so she decided that her mother had not said what she said, and sealed the denial with a light kiss.

Jill went away to boarding school when she was twelve, and took all the prizes. Her scholastic, social, and athletic record was unprecedented. During her second year in college, she visited her relatives in San Francisco, and met and fell in love with Georgie Madison. He was not, considering her intelligence, the sort of man she would have been expected to choose, but it may have been sensible of her to pick a man whose interests were so different. He was a quiet, large-boned man with black hair and those gentle looks that break the hearts of the fatherless of all ages; and she was, after all, fatherless. He worked as a junior executive in a San Francisco shipyard. He had graduated from Yale, but when Melee once asked him if he liked Thackeray he said sincerely and politely that he had never tasted any. This simmered down to a family joke. They got engaged in her junior year, and were married a week after she graduated from college, where she again took all the prizes. He was transferred to a Brooklyn shipyard, and they moved to New York, where she got a public-relations job in a department store.

In the second or third year of their marriage, she had a son, whom they called Bibber. The birth was difficult, and she would not be able to have more children. When the boy was still young, they moved to Gordenville. She was happier in the country than she had been in town, since the country seemed to present more opportunities for her talents. The presidencies of the civic organizations followed one after the other, and when the widow who ran the local travel agency got sick, Jill took over and ran this successfully. Their only problem in the country was to find someone to stay with Bibber. A stream of unsatisfactory old women drifted through the house, augmented by high-school girls and cleaning women. Georgie loved his son intemperately. The boy was bright enough, but his father found this brightness blinding. He walked with the boy, played with him, gave him his bath at bedtime, and told him his story. Georgie did everything for his son when he was at home, and this was just as well, since Jill often came in later than he.

When Jill put down the reins of the travel agency, she

decided to organize a European tour. She had not been abroad since their marriage, and if she wrote her own ticket she could make the trip at a profit. This, at least, was what she claimed. Georgie's shipyard was doing well, and there was no real reason for her to angle for a free trip, but he could see that the idea of conducting a tour stimulated and challenged her, and in the end he gave her his approval and his encouragement. Twenty-eight customers signed up, and early in July Georgie saw Jill and her lambs, as she called them, take off in a jet for Copenhagen. Their itinerary was to take them as far south as Naples, where Jill would put her dependents aboard a home-bound plane. Then Georgie would meet her in Venice, where they would spend a week. Jill sent her husband postcards each day, and several of her customers were so enthusiastic about her leadership that they wrote Georgie themselves to tell him what a charming, competent, and knowledgeable wife he possessed. His neighbors were friendly, and he mostly dined with them. Bibber, who was not quite four, had been put into a summer camp.

Before Georgie left for Europe, he drove to New Hampshire to check on Bibber. He had missed the little boy painfully and had seen him much oftener in his reveries than he had seen his wife's vivacious face. To put himself to sleep, he imagined some implausible climbing tour through the Dolomites with Bibber when the boy was older. Night after night, he helped his son up from ledge to ledge. Overhead, the thin snow on the peaks sparkled in the summer sunlight. Carrying packs and ropes, they came down into Cortina a little after dark. The bare facts of his trip north contrasted sharply with this Alpine reverie.

The drive took him most of a day. He spent a restless night in a motel and scouted out the camp in the morning. The weather was mixed, and he was in the mountains. There were showers and then pale clearings—an atmosphere not so much of gloom as of bleakness. Most of the farms that he passed were abandoned. As he approached the camp, he felt that it and the surrounding countryside had the authority of a remote creation; or perhaps this was a reprise of his own experience of summers and camps as interludes unconnected with the rest of time. Then, from a rise of ground, he saw the place below him. There was a small lake—a pond, really: one of those round ponds whose tea-colored waters and pine groves leave with you an impression of geological fatigue. His own recollections of camp were sunny and brilliant, and this rueful water hole, with its huddle of rotting matchboard shanties, collided violently with his robust memories. He guessed—he insisted to himself—that things would look very different when the sun shone. Arrows pointed the way to the administration building, where the directress was waiting for him. She was a blue-eyed young woman whose efficiency had not quite eclipsed her good looks. "We've had a bit of trouble with your son," she said. "He's not gotten along terribly well. It's quite unusual. We seldom if ever have cases of homesickness. The exception is when we take children from divided families, and we try never to do this. We can cope with normal problems, but we cannot cope with a child who brings more than his share of misery with him. As a rule, we turn down applications from children of divorce."

"But Mrs. Madison and I are not divorced," Georgie said.

"Oh, I didn't know. You are separated?"

"No," Georgie said, "we are not. Mrs. Madison is traveling in Europe, but I am going to join her tomorrow."

"Oh, I see. Well, in that case, I don't understand why Bibber has been so slow to adjust. But here is Bibber to tell us all about it himself!"

The boy threw off the hand of the woman with him and ran to his father. He was crying.

"There, there," said the directress. "Daddy hasn't come all this way to see a weeper, has he, Bibber?"

Georgie felt his heart heave in love and confusion. He kissed the tears from the boy's face and held him against his chest.

"Perhaps you'd like to take a little walk with Bibber," the directress suggested. "Perhaps Bibber would like to show you the sights."

Georgie, with the boy clinging to his hand, had to face certain responsibilities that transcended the love he felt for his son. His instinct was to take the boy away. His responsibility was to hearten and encourage him to shoulder the burdens of life. "What is your favorite place, Bibber?" he asked enthusiastically, keenly aware of the fatuity in his tone, and convinced of the necessity for it. "I want you to show me your favorite place in the whole camp."

"I don't have any favorite place," Bibber said. He was trying successfully to keep from crying. "That's the mess hall," he said, pointing to a long, ugly shed. Fresh pieces of yellow lumber had replaced those that had rotted.

"Is that where you have your plays?" Georgie asked.

"We don't have any plays," Bibber said. "The lady in charge of plays got sick and she had to go home."

"Is that where you sing?"

"Please take me home, Daddy," Bibber said.

"But I can't, Bibber. Mummy's in Europe, and I'm flying over tomorrow afternoon to join her."

"When *can* I go home?"

"Not until camp closes." Georgie felt some of the weight of this sentence himself. He heard the boy's breathing quicken with pain. Somewhere a bugle sounded. Georgie, struggling to mix his responsibilities with his instincts, knelt and took the boy in his arms. "You see, I can't very well cable Mummy and tell her I'm not coming. She's expecting me there. And anyhow, we don't really have a home when Mummy isn't with us. I have my dinners out, and I'm away all day. There won't be anyone there to take care of you."

"I've participated in everything," the boy said hopefully. It was his last appeal for clemency, and when he saw it fail he said, "I have to go now. It's my third period." He went up a worn path under the pines.

Georgie returned to the administration building reflecting on the fact that he had loved camp, that he had been one of the most popular boys in camp, and that he had never wanted to go home.

"I think things are bound to improve," the directress said. "As soon as he gets over the hump, he'll enjoy himself much more than the others. I would suggest, however, that you don't stay too long. He has a riding period now. Why don't you watch him ride, and leave before the period's ended? He takes pride in his riding, and in that way you'll avoid a painful farewell. This evening we're going to have a big campfire and a good long sing. I'm sure that he's suffering from nothing that won't be cured by a good sing with his mates around a roaring fire."

It all sounded plausible to Georgie, who liked a good campfire sing himself. Were there any sorrows of early life that couldn't be cured by a rousing performance of "The Battle Hymn of the Republic"? He walked over to the riding ring singing, "They have builded him an altar in the evening dews and damps. . . ." It had begun to rain again, and Georgie couldn't tell whether the boy's face was wet with tears or drops of rain. He was on horseback and being led around the ring by a groom. Bibber waved once to his father and nearly lost his seat, and when the boy's back was turned Georgie went away.

He flew to Treviso and took a train into Venice, where Jill waited for him in a Swiss hotel on one of the back canals. Their reunion was ardent, and he loved her no less for noticing that she was tired and thin. Getting her lambs across Europe had been a rigorous and exhausting task. What he wanted to do then was to move from their third-rate hotel to Cipriani's, get a cabana at the Lido, and spend a week on the beach. Jill refused to move to Cipriani's—it would be full of tourists—and on their second day in Venice she got up at seven, made instant coffee in a toothbrush glass, and rushed him off to eight-o'clock Mass at St. Mark's. Georgie knew Venice, and Jill knew—or should have known—that he was not interested in painting or mosaics, but she led him by the nose, so to speak, from monument to monument. He guessed that she had got into the habit of tireless sightseeing, and that the tactful thing to do would be to wait until the habit spent itself. He suggested that they go to Harry's for lunch, and she said, "What in the world are you *thinking* of, Georgie?" They had lunch in a *trattoria,* and toured churches and museums until closing time. In the morning, he suggested that they go to the Lido, but she had already made arrangements to go to Maser and see the villas.

Jill brought all her competence as a tour director to their days in Venice, although Georgie didn't see why. Most of us enjoy displaying our familiarity with the world, but he could not detect a trace of enjoyment in her assault. Some people love painting and architecture, but there was nothing loving in her approach to the treasures of Venice. The worship of beauty was mysterious to Georgie, but was beauty meant to crush one's sense of humor? She stood, one hot afternoon, before the façade of a church, lecturing him from her guidebook. She recited dates, naval engagements, and so on, and sketched the history of the Republic as if she were preparing him for an examination. The light in which she stood was bright and unflattering, and the generally festive air of Venice made her erudition, the sternness of her enthusiasm, seem ungainly. She was trying to impress him with the fact that Venice was to be taken seriously. And was this, he wondered, the meaning, the sum, of these brilliant marbles, this labyrinthine and dilapidated place, suffused with the rank and ancient smell of bilge? He put an arm around her and said, "Come off it, darling." She put him away from her and said, "I have no idea what you're talking about."

Had she lost an address, a child, a pocketbook, a string of beads, or any other valuable, her canvass of Venice couldn't have been more grueling and exhaustive. He spent the rest of their time in Venice accompanying her on this mysterious search. Now and then he thought of Bibber and his camp. They flew home from Treviso, and in the gentler and more familiar light of Gordenville she seemed herself again. They took up their happiness, and welcomed Bibber when he was released from camp.

"ISN'T IT DIVINE, isn't it the most divine period in domestic American architecture?" Jill always asked, showing guests through their large frame house. The house had been built in the 1870s, and had long windows, an oval dining room, and a stable with a cupola. It must have been difficult to maintain, but these difficulties—at parties, anyhow—were never felt. The high-ceilinged rooms were filled with light and had a special grace—austere, gloomy, and finely balanced. The obvious social responsibilities were all hers; his conversation was confined to the shipbuilding industry, but he mixed the drinks, carved the roast, and poured the wine. There was a fire in the fireplace, there were flowers, the furniture and the silver shone, and no one knew and no one would have guessed that it was he who polished the furniture and forks.

"Housework simply isn't my style," she had said, and he

was intelligent enough to see the truth in her remark; intelligent enough not to expect her to recast this image of herself as an educated woman. It was the source of much of her vitality and joy.

One stormy winter, they weren't able to get any servants at all. A fly-by-night cook came in when they had guests, but the rest of the work fell to Georgie. That was the year Jill was studying French literature at Columbia and trying to finish her book on Flaubert. On a typical domestic evening, Jill would be sitting at her desk in their bedroom, working on her book. Bibber would be asleep. Georgie might be in the kitchen, polishing the brass and silver. He wore an apron. He drank whiskey. He was surrounded by cigarette boxes, andirons, bowls, ewers, and a large chest of table silver. He did not like to polish silver, but if he did not do this the silver would turn black. As she had said, it was not her style. It was not his style, either, nor was it any part of his education, but if he was, as she said, unintellectual, he was not so unintellectual as to accept any of the vulgarities and commonplaces associated with the struggle for sexual equality. The struggle was recent, he knew; it was real; it was inexorable; and while she sidestepped her domestic tasks, he could sense that she might do this unwillingly. She had been raised as an intellectual, her emancipation was still challenged in many quarters, and since she seemed to possess more latitude, to hold a stronger traditional position, it was his place to yield on matters like housework. It was not her choice, he knew, that she was raised as an intellectual, but the choice, having been made by others, seemed irrevocable. His restless sexual nature attributed to her softness, warmth, and the utter darkness of love; but why, he wondered as he polished the forks, did there seem to be some contradiction between these attributes and the possession of a clear mind? Intellect, he knew, was not a masculine attribute, although the bulk of tradition had put decisive powers into the hands of men for so many centuries that their ancient supremacy would take some unlearning. But why should his instincts lead him to expect that the woman in whose arms he lay each night would at least conceal her literacy? Why should there seem to be some rub between the enormous love he felt for her and her ability to understand the quantum theory?

She wandered downstairs and stood in the kitchen doorway, watching him at his work. Her feeling was tender. What a kind, gentle, purposeful, and handsome man she had married. What pride he took in their house. But then, as she went on watching him, she suffered a spiritual chill, a paroxysm of doubt. Was he, bent over the kitchen table at a woman's work, really a man? Had she married some half male, some aberration? Did he like to wear an apron? Was he a transvestite? And was she aberrant herself? But this was inadmissible, and equally inadmissible was the reasoning that would bring her to see that he polished silver because he was forced to. Suddenly some vague, brutish stray appeared in the corner of her imagination, some hairy and drunken sailor who would beat her on Saturday nights, debauch her with his gross appetites, and make her scrub the floor on her hands and knees. That was the kind of man she should have married. That had been her destiny. He looked up, smiled gently, and asked her how her work was coming. "*Ça marche, ça marche,*" she said wearily, and went back upstairs to her desk. "Little Gustave didn't get along at all well with his school chums," she wrote. "He was frightfully unpopular . . ."

He came into their room when his work was done. He ran a hand lightly through her hair. "Just let me finish this paragraph," she said. She heard him take a shower, heard his bare feet on the carpet as he crossed the room and bounded happily into bed. Moved equally by duty and desire but still thinking of the glories of Flaubert, she washed, scented herself with perfume, and joined him in their wide bed, which, with its clean and fragrant linen and equal pools of light, seemed indeed a bower. *Bosquet,* she thought, *brume, bruit.* And then, sitting up in his arms, she exclaimed, "*Elle avait lu 'Paul et Virginie' et elle avait rêvé la maisonnette de bambous, le nègre Domingo, le chien Fidèle, mais surtout l'amitié douce de quelque bon petit frère, qui va chercher pour vous des fruits rouges dans des grands arbres plus hauts que des clochers, ou qui court pieds nus sur le sable, vous apportant un nid d'oiseau . . .*"

"God damn it to hell!" he said. He spoke in utter bitterness. He got out of bed, got a blanket from the closet, and made his bed in the living room.

She cried. He was jealous of her intelligence—she saw that. But was she meant to pose as a cretin in order to be attractive? Why should he rage because she had said a few words in French? To assume that intelligence, knowledge, the very benefits of education were male attributes was an attitude that had been obsolete for a century. Then she felt as if the strain put on her heart by this cruelty was too much. She seemed to feel one of its fastenings give, as if this organ was a cask and so heavily laden with sorrow that, like some ruptured treasure chest of childhood, its sides had burst. "Intelligence" was the word she returned to—intelligence was at stake. And yet the word should ring free and clear of the pain she was suffering. Intelligence was the subject up for discussion, but it had the sentience, at that hour, of flesh and blood. What she faced was the bare bones of pain, cleansed in the stewpot and polished by the hound's tooth; this intelligence had the taste of death. She cried herself to sleep.

Later she was awakened by a crash. She was afraid. Might he harm her? Had something gone wrong with the complicated machinery of the old house? Burglars? Fire? The noise had come from their bathroom. She found him naked on his hands and knees on the bathroom floor. His head was under the washbasin. She went to him quickly and helped him to his feet. "I'm all right," he said. "I'm just terribly drunk." She helped him back to their bed, where he fell asleep at once.

THEY HAD a dinner party a few nights later, and all the silver he had polished was used. The party went off without a hitch. One of their guests, a lawyer, described a local scandal. A four-mile link of highway, connecting two parkways in the neighborhood, had been approved by the state and the local governments. The cost was three million dollars, on a bid given by a contractor named Felici. The road was to destroy a large formal garden and park that had been maintained and open to the public for half a century. The owner, an octogenarian, lived in San Francisco and was either helpless, indifferent, or immobilized by indignation. The connecting road was of no use; no study of traffic patterns had proved that there was any need for such a road. A beautiful park and a large slice of tax money were to be handed over to an unscrupulous and avaricious contractor.

It was the kind of story Jill liked. Her eyes were bright, her color was high. Georgie watched her with a mixture of pride and dismay. Her civic zeal had been provoked, and he knew she would pursue the scandal to some conclusion. She was very happy with this challenge, but it was, on that evening, a happiness that embraced her house, her husband, her way of life. On Monday morning she stormed the various commissions that controlled highway construction, and verified the scandal. Then she organized a committee and circulated a petition. An old woman named Mrs. Haney was found to take care of Bibber, and a high-school girl came in to read to him in the afternoons. Jill was absorbed in her work, bright-eyed and excited.

This was in December. Late one afternoon, Georgie left his office in Brooklyn and went into New York to do some shopping. All the high buildings in midtown were hidden in rain clouds, but he felt their presence overhead like the presence of a familiar mountain range. His feet were wet and his throat felt sore. The streets were crowded, and the decorations on the store fronts were mostly at such an angle that their meaning escaped him. While he could see the canopy of light at Lord & Taylor's, he could only see the chins and vestments of the choir plastered across the front of Saks. Blasts of holy music wavered through the rain. He stepped into a puddle. It was as dark as night; it seemed, because of the many lights, the darkest of nights. He went into Saks. Inside, the scene of well-dressed and brightly lighted pillage stopped him. He stood to one side to avoid being savaged by the crowds that were pushing their way in and out. He distinctly felt the symptoms of a cold. A woman standing beside him dropped some parcels. He picked them up. She had a pleasant face, wore a black mink coat, and her feet, he noticed, were wetter than his. She thanked him, and he asked if she was going to storm the counters. "I thought I would," she said, "but now I think I won't. My feet are wet, and I have a terrible feeling that I'm coming down with a cold."

"I feel the same way," he said. "Let's find some quiet place and have a drink."

"Oh, but I couldn't do that," she said.

"Why not?" he asked. "It's a festival, isn't it?"

The dark afternoon seemed to turn on that word. It was meant to be festive. That was the meaning of the singing and the lights.

"I had never thought of it that way," she said.

"Come on," he said. He took her arm and led her down the avenue to a quiet bar. He ordered drinks and sneezed. "You ought to have a hot bath and go to bed," she said. Her concern seemed purely maternal. He introduced himself. Her name was Betty Landers. Her husband was a doctor. Her daughter was married and her son was in his last year at Cornell. She was alone a good deal of the time, but she had recently taken up painting. She went to the Art Students League three times a week, and had a studio in the Village. They had three or four drinks and then took a cab downtown to see her studio.

It was not his idea of a studio. It was a two-room apartment in one of the new buildings near Washington Square and looked a little like the lair of a spinster. She pointed out her treasures. That's what she called them. The desk she had bought in England, the chair she had bought in France, the signed Matisse lithograph. Her hair and her eyebrows were dark, her face was thin, and she might have been a spinster. She made him a drink, and when he asked to see her paintings she modestly refused, although he was to see them later, stacked up in the bathroom, where her easel and her other equipment were neatly stored. Why they became lovers, why in the presence of this stranger he should suddenly find himself divested of all his inhibitions and all his clothing, he never understood. She was not young. Her elbows and knees were lightly gnarled, as if she were some distant cousin of Daphne and would presently be transformed, not into a flowering shrub but into some hardy and common tree.

They met after this two or three times a week. He never discovered much about her beyond the fact that she lived on Park Avenue and was often alone. She was interested in his clothes and kept him posted on department-store sales. It was a large part of her conversation. Sitting in his lap, she told him that there was a sale of neckties at Saks, a sale of shoes at Brooks, a sale of shirts at Altman's. Jill, by this time, was so absorbed in her campaign that she hardly noticed his arrivals and departures, but, sitting one evening in the living room while Jill was busy on the upstairs telephone, he felt that he had behaved shabbily. He felt that it was time that the affair, begun on that dark afternoon before Christmas, was over. He took some notepaper and wrote to Betty: "Darling, I'm leaving for San Francisco this evening and will be gone six weeks. I think it will be better, and I'm sure you'll agree with me, if we don't meet again." He wrote the letter a second time, changing San Francisco to Rome, and addressed the note to her studio in the Village.

Jill was campaigning on the telephone the next night when he returned home. Mathilde, the high-school girl, was reading to Bibber. He spoke to his son and then went down to the pantry to make a drink. While he was there, he heard Jill's heels on the stairs. They seemed to strike a swift and vengeful note, and when she came into the pantry her face was pale and drawn. Her hands were shaking, and in one of them she held the first of the two notes he had written.

"What is the meaning of this?" she asked.

"Where did you find it?"

"In the wastepaper basket."

"Then I will explain," he said. "Please sit down. Sit down for a minute, and I'll explain the whole thing."

"Do I *have* to sit down? I'm terribly busy."

"No, you don't have to sit down, but would you close the door? Mathilde can hear us."

"I can't believe you have anything to say that would necessitate closing a door."

"I have this to say," he said. He closed the door. "In December, just before Christmas, I took a mistress, a lonely woman. I can't explain my choice. It may have been because she had an apartment of her own. She was not young; she was not beautiful. Her children are grown. Her husband is a doctor. They live on Park Avenue."

"Oh, my God," she said. "Park Avenue!" and she laughed. "I adore that part of it. I could have guessed that f you invented a mistress she would live on Park Avenue. You've always been such a hick."

"Do you think this is all an invention?"

"Yes, I do. I think you've made the whole thing up to try and hurt me. You've never had much of an imagination. You might have done better if you'd tasted some Thackeray. Really. A Park Avenue matron. Couldn't you have invented something more delectable? A Vassar senior with blazing red hair? A colored night-club singer? An Italian princess?"

"Do you really think I've made this all up?"

"I do, I do. I think it's all a fabrication and a loathsome one, but tell me more, tell me more about your Park Avenue matron."

"I have nothing more to tell you."

"You have nothing more to tell me because your powers of invention have collapsed. Isn't that it? My advice to you, old chap, is never to embark on anything that counts on a powerful imagination. It isn't your forte."

"You don't believe me."

"I do not, and if I did I wouldn't be jealous. My sort of woman is never jealous. I have more important things to do."

AT THIS POINT in their marriage, Jill's assault on the highway commission served as a sort of suspension bridge over which they could travel, meet, converse, and dine together, elevated safely above the turbulence of their feelings. She was working to have the issue brought to a public hearing, and was to appear before the commission with petitions and documents that would prove the gravity of her case and the number of influential supporters she had been able to enlist. Unluckily, at this time Bibber came down with a bad cold and it was difficult to find anyone to stay with him. Now and then, Mrs. Haney would come to sit beside his bed, and in the afternoons Mathilde read to him. When it was necessary for Jill to go to Albany, George stayed home from his office for a day so that she could make this trip. He stayed home on another day when she had an important appointment and Mrs. Haney couldn't come. She was sincerely grateful to him for these sacrifices, and he had nothing but admiration for her intelligence and tenacity. She was far superior to him as an advocate and as an organizer. She was to appear before the commission on a Friday, and he looked forward to having this much of their struggle behind them. He came home on Friday at around six. He called out, "Jill? Mathilde? Mrs. Haney?" but there was no answer. He threw off his hat and coat and bounded up the stairs to Bibber's room. The room was lighted, but the boy was alone and seemed to be asleep. Pinned to his pillow was this note: "Dear Mrs. Madison my aunt and uncle came to visit with us and I have to go home to help my mother. Bibber's asleep so he won't know the difference. I am sorry. Mathilde." On the pillow next to the note was a dark stain of blood. He touched the boy lightly and felt the searing heat of fever. Then he tried to rouse the child, but Bibber was not sleeping; he was unconscious.

Georgie moistened the boy's lips with some water, and Bibber regained consciousness long enough to throw his arms around his father. The pathos of seeing the burden of grave illness on someone so innocent and so young made Georgie cry. There was a tumultuous power of love in that small room, and he had to subdue his feelings lest he harm the boy with the force of his embrace. They clung to one another. Then Georgie called the doctor. He called ten times, and each time he heard the idiotic and frustrating busy signal. Then he called the hospital and asked for an ambulance. He wrapped the boy in a blanket and carried him down the stairs, enormously grateful to have this much to do. The ambulance was there in a few minutes.

Jill had stopped long enough to have a drink with one of her assistants and came in a half hour later. "Hail the conquering hero!" she called as she stepped into the empty house. "We shall have our hearing, and the scurvy rascals are on the run. Even Felici appeared to be moved by my eloquence, and Carter said that I should have been an advocate. I was simply stupendous."

ITEM: "INTL PD FLORENCE VIA RCA 22 23 9:35 AMELIA FAXON CHIDCHESTER CARE AMEXCO: BIBBER DIED OF PNEUMONIA ON THURSDAY. CAN YOU RETURN OR MAY I COME TO YOU LOVE JILL"

Amelia Faxon Chidchester was staying with her old friend Louisa Trefaldi, in Fiesole. She bicycled down into Florence late in the afternoon of the twenty-third of January. Her bicycle was an old, high-seated Dutheil, and it elevated her a little above the small cars. She bumped imperturbably through some of the worst traffic in the world. Her life was threatened every few minutes by a Vespa or a trolley, but she yielded to no one, and the look on her ruddy face was serene. Elevated, moving with that somnambulistic pace of a cyclist, smiling gently at the death that menaced her at every intersection, she looked a little supernatural, and it may have been that she thought she was. Her smile was sweet, inscrutable, and adamantine, and you felt that, had she been knocked off her bicycle, this expression, as she sailed through the air, would not lose its patience. She pumped over a bridge, dismounted gracefully, and walked along the river to the American Express office. Here she barked out her greetings in Italian, anxious to disassociate herself from the horseless American cowboys and above all from her own kind, the truly lost and unwanted, who move like leaves around the edges of the world, gathering only long enough to wait in line and see if there is any mail. The place was crowded, and she read her tragic cable in the middle of the crowd. You could not, from her expression, have guessed its content. She sighed deeply and raised her face. She seemed ennobled. She wrote her reply at once: "NON POSSO TORNARE TANTI BACI FERVIDI. MELEE."

"Dearest darling," she wrote that evening. "I was frightfully sorry to have your tragic news. I can only thank God that I didn't know him better, but my experience in these matters is rather extensive, and I have come to a time of life when I do not especially like to dwell upon the subject of passing away. There is no street I walk on, no building or painting I see here that doesn't remind me of Berenson, dear Berenson. The last time I saw him, I sat at his feet and asked if he had a magic carpet what picture in the whole wide world would he ask to be transported to. Without a moment's hesitation he chose the Raphael Madonna in The Hermitage. It is not possible for me to return. The truth will out, and the truth is that I don't like my own countrymen. As for your coming over, I am now staying with dear Louisa and, as you know, with her two is company, three is a crowd. Perhaps in the autumn, when your loss is not so painful, we might meet in Paris for a few days and revisit some of our old haunts."

GEORGIE WAS CRUSHED by the death of his son. He blamed Jill, which was cruel and unreasonable, and it seemed, in the end, that he could be both. Jill went to Reno at his request and got a consent decree. It was all made by Georgie to seem like a punishment. Later on she got a job with a textbook publishing firm in Cleveland. Her acumen and her charm were swiftly recognized and she was very successful, but she didn't marry again, or hadn't married when I last had any news. The last I heard was from Georgie, who telephoned one night and said that we *must* get together for lunch. It was about eleven. I think he was drunk. He hadn't married again either, and from the bitterness with which he spoke of women that night I guessed that he never would. He told me about Jill's job in Cleveland and said that Mrs. Chidchester was bicycling across Scotland. I thought then how inferior he was to Jill, how immature. When I agreed to call him about lunch he gave me his telephone number at the shipyard, his extension there, the telephone number of his apartment, the telephone number of a cottage he had in Connecticut, and the telephone number of the club where he lunched and played cards. I wrote all these numbers on a piece of paper and when we said goodbye I dropped the paper into a wastebasket.

METAMORPHOSES

I

LARRY ACTAEON WAS BUILT along classical lines: curly hair, a triangulated nose, and a large and supple body, and he had what might be described as a Periclean interest in innovation. He designed his own sailboat (it had a list to port), ran for mayor (he was defeated), bred a Finnish wolf bitch to a German shepherd dog (the American Kennel Club refused to list the breed), and organized a drag hunt in Bullet Park, where he lived with his charming wife and three children. He was a partner in the investment-banking firm of Lothard and Williams, where he was esteemed for his shrewd and boisterous disposition.

Lothard and Williams was a highly conservative shop with an unmatched reputation for probity, but it was unconventional in one respect. One of the partners was a woman. This was a widow named Mrs. Vuiton. Her husband had been a senior partner, and when he died she had asked to be taken into the firm. In her favor were her intelligence, her beauty, and the fact that, had she withdrawn her husband's interest from the partnership, it would have been missed. Lothard, the most conservative of them all, supported her candidacy, and she was taken in. Her intellect was formidable, and was fortified by her formidable and immaculate beauty. She was a stunning woman, in her middle thirties, and brought more than her share of business to the firm. Larry didn't dislike her—he didn't quite dare to—but that her good looks and her musical voice were more effective in banking than his own shrewd and boisterous manner made him at least uneasy.

The partners in Lothard and Williams—they were seven—had their private offices arranged around the central offices of Mr. Lothard. They had the usual old-fashioned appurtenances—walnut desks, portraits of dead partners, dark walls and carpets. The six male partners all wore watch chains, stickpins, and high-crowned hats. Larry sat one afternoon in this atmosphere of calculated gloom, weighing the problems of a long-term bond issue that was in the house and having a slow sale, and suddenly it crossed his mind that they might unload the entire issue on a pension-fund customer. Moved by his enthusiasm, his boisterousness, he strode through Mr. Lothard's outer office and impetuously opened the inner door. There was Mrs. Vuiton, wearing nothing but a string of beads. Mr. Lothard was at her side wearing a wristwatch. "Oh, I'm terribly sorry!" Larry said, and he closed the door and returned to his own desk.

The image of Mrs. Vuiton seemed incised in his memory, burnt there. He had seen a thousand naked women, but he had never seen one so stunning. Her skin had a luminous and pearly whiteness that he could not forget. The pathos and beauty of the naked woman established itself in his memory like a strain of music. He had beheld something that he should not have seen, and Mrs. Vuiton had glared at him with a look that was wicked and unholy. He could not shake or rationalize away the feeling that his blunder was disastrous; that he had in some way stumbled into a transgression that would demand compensation and revenge. Pure enthusiasm had moved him to open the door without knocking: pure enthusiasm, by his lights, was a blameless impulse. Why should he feel himself surrounded by trouble, misfortune, and disaster? The nature of man was concupiscent; the same thing might be going on in a thousand offices. What he had seen was commonplace, he told himself. But there had been nothing commonplace about the whiteness of her skin or her powerful and collected stare. He repeated to himself that he had done nothing wrong, but underlying all his fancies of good and evil, merits and rewards, was the stubborn and painful nature of things, and he knew that he had seen something that it was not his destiny to see.

He dictated some letters and answered the telephone when it rang, but he did nothing worthwhile for the rest of that afternoon. He spent some time trying to get rid of the litter that his Finnish wolf bitch had whelped. The Bronx Zoo was not interested. The American Kennel Club said that he had not introduced a breed, he had produced a monstrosity. Someone had informed him that jewelers, department stores, and museums were policed by savage dogs, and he telephoned the security departments of Macy's, Cartier's, and the Museum of Modern Art, but they all had dogs. He spent the last of the afternoon at his window, joining that vast population of the blunderers, the bored—the empty-handed barber, the clerk in the antique store nobody ever comes into, the idle insurance salesman, the failing haberdasher—all of those thousands who stand at the windows of the city and watch the afternoon go down. Some nameless doom seemed to threaten his welfare, and he was unable to refresh his boisterousness, his common sense.

He had a directors' dinner meeting on the East Side at seven. He had brought his evening clothes to town in a suit box, and had been invited to bathe and change at his host's. He left his office at five and, to kill time and if possible cheer himself, walked the two or three miles to Fifty-seventh Street. Even so, he was early, and he stopped in a bar for a drink. It was one of those places where the single women of the neighborhood congregate and are made welcome; where, having tippled sherry for most of the day, they gather to observe the cocktail hour. One of the women had a dog. As soon as Larry entered the place, the dog, a dachshund, sprang at him. The leash was attached to a table leg, and he struck at Larry so vigorously that he dragged the table a foot or two and upset a couple of drinks. He missed Larry, but there was a great deal of confusion, and Larry went to the end of the bar farthest from the ladies. The dog was excited, and his harsh, sharp barking filled the place. "What are you thinking of, Smoky?" his mistress asked. "What in the world are you thinking of? What's become of my little doggy? This can't be my little Smoky. This must be another doggy. . . ." The dog went on barking at Larry.

"Dogs don't like you?" the bartender asked.

"I breed dogs," Larry said. "I get along very well with dogs."

"It's a funny thing," the bartender said, "but I never heard that dog bark before. She's in here every afternoon, seven days a week, and that dog's always with her, but this is the first time there's ever been a peep out of him. Maybe if you took your drink into the dining room."

"You mean I'm disturbing Smoky?"

"Well, she's a regular customer. I never saw you before."

"All right," Larry said, putting as much feeling as he could into his consent. He carried his drink through a doorway into the empty dining room and sat at a table. The dog stopped barking as soon as he was gone. He finished his drink and looked around for another way to leave the place, but there was none. Smoky sprang at him again when he went out through the bar, and everyone was glad to see such a troublemaker go.

The apartment house where he was expected was one he had been in many times, but he had forgotten the address. He had counted on recognizing the doorway and the lobby, but when he stepped into the lobby he was faced with the sameness of those places. There was a black-and-white floor, a false fireplace, two English chairs, and a framed landscape. It was all familiar, but he realized that it could have been one of a dozen lobbies, and he asked the elevator man if this was the Fullmers' house. The man said yes, and Larry stepped into the car. Then, instead of ascending to the tenth floor where the Fullmers lived, the car went down. The first idea that crossed Larry's mind was that the Fullmers might be having their vestibule painted and that, for this or for some other inconvenience or change, he would be expected to use the back elevator. The man slid the door open onto a kind of infernal region, crowded with heaped ash cans, broken perambulators, and steampipes covered with ruptured asbestos sleeving. "Go through the door there and get the other elevator," the man said.

"But why do I have to take the back elevator?" Larry asked.

"It's a rule," the man said.

"I don't understand," Larry said.

"Listen," the man said. "Don't argue with me. Just take the back elevator. All you deliverymen always want to go in the front door like you owned the place. Well, this is one building where you can't. The management says all deliveries at the back door, and the management is boss."

"I'm not a deliveryman," Larry said. "I'm a guest."

"What's the box?"

"The box," Larry said, "contains my evening clothes. Now take me up to the tenth floor where the Fullmers live."

"I'm sorry, mister, but you *look* like a deliveryman."

"I am an investment banker," Larry said, "and I am on my way to a directors' meeting, where we are going to discuss the underwriting of a forty-four-million-dollar bond issue. I am worth nine hundred thousand dollars. I have a twenty-two-room house in Bullet Park, a kennel of dogs, two riding horses, three children in college, a twenty-two-foot sailboat, and five automobiles."

"Jesus," the man said.

AFTER LARRY HAD BATHED, he looked at himself in the

nirror to see if he could detect any change in his appearance, but the face in the glass was too familiar; he had shaved and washed it too many times for it to reveal any secrets. He got through dinner and the meeting, and afterward had a whiskey with the other directors. He was still, in a way that he could not have defined, troubled at having been mistaken for a deliveryman, and hoping to shift his unease a little he said to the man beside him, "You know, when I was coming up in the elevator tonight I was mistaken for a deliveryman." His confidant either didn't hear, didn't comprehend, or didn't care. He laughed loudly at something that was being said across the room, and Larry, who was used to commanding attention, felt that he had suffered another loss.

He took a taxi to Grand Central and went home on one of those locals that seem like a roundup of the spiritually wayward, the drunken, and the lost. The conductor was a corpulent man with a pink face and a fresh rose in his buttonhole. He had a few words to say to most of the travelers.

"You working the same place?" he asked Larry.

"Yes."

"You rush beer up in Yorktown, isn't that it?"

"No," Larry said, and he touched his face with his hands to see if he could feel there the welts, lines, and other changes that must have been worked in the last few hours.

"You work in a restaurant, don't you?" the conductor asked.

"No," Larry said quietly.

"That's funny," the conductor said. "When I saw the soup-and-fish I thought you was a waiter."

It was after one o'clock when he got off the train. The station and the cab stand were shut, and only a few cars were left in the parking lot. When he switched on the lights of the small European car he used for the station, he saw that they burned faintly, and as soon as he pressed the starter they faded to nothing with each revolution of the motor. In the space of a few minutes, the battery gave up the ghost. It was only a little less than a mile to his house, and he really didn't mind the walk. He strode briskly along the empty streets and unfastened the gates to his driveway. He was fastening them when he heard the noise of running and panting and saw that the dogs were out.

The noise woke his wife, who, thinking that he had already come home, called to him for help. "Larry! Larry, the dogs are out! The dogs are out! Larry, please come quickly, the dogs are out and I think they're after someone!" He heard her calling him as he fell, and saw the yellow lights go on in the windows, but that was the last he saw.

II

ORVILLE BETMAN SPENT the three summer months alone in New York, as he had done ever since his marriage. He had a large apartment, a good housekeeper, and a host of friends; but he had no wife. Now, some men have a sexual disposition as vigorous, indiscriminate, and demanding as a digestive tract, and to invest these drives with the crosslights of romantic agony would be as tragic as it would be to invent rituals and music for the bronchial tree. These men do not, when they are eating a piece of pie, consider themselves involved in a sacred contract; no more do they in the bounding act of love. This was not Betman. He loved his wife, and he loved no other woman in the world. He loved her voice, her tastes, her face, her grace, her presence, and her memory. He was a good-looking man, and when he was alone other women pursued him. They asked him up to their apartments, they tried to force their way into his apartment, they seized him in corridors and garden paths, and one of them, on the beach in East Hampton, pulled off his bathing trunks, but, thus incommoded, the only love he had was for Victoria.

Betman was a singer. His voice was distinguished not by its rage and beauty but by its persuasiveness. He gave one recital of eighteenth-century music early in his career and was roasted by the critics. He drifted into television and for a while dubbed voices for animated cartoons. Then, by chance, someone asked him to do a cigarette commercial. It was four lines. The result was explosive. Cigarette sales shot up eight hundred per cent, and from this single commercial he made, with residuals, more than fifty thousand dollars. The element of persuasiveness in his voice could not be isolated or imitated, but it was infallible. Whatever he praised in song—shoe polish, toothpaste, floor wax—hundreds and thousands of men and women would find his praise irresistible. Even little children heeded his voice. He was very wealthy, of course, and the work was light.

He first saw his wife on a Fifth Avenue bus on a rainy night. She was then a young and slender woman with yellow hair, and the instant he saw her he felt a singular attraction or passion that he had never felt before and would never, as it happened, feel again. The strenuousness of his feeling made him follow her when she left the bus, somewhere on upper Fifth Avenue. He suffered, as any lover will who, moved by a pure and impetuous heart, well knows that his attentions, whatever they are, will be mistaken for a molestation, and usually a revolting one. She walked toward the door of an apartment house and hesitated under the awning long enough to shake the raindrops out of her umbrella.

"Miss?" he asked.

"Yes?"

"Could I speak with you for a minute?"

"What about?"

"My name is Orville Betman," he said. "I sing television commercials. You may have heard me. I . . ." Her attention wandered from him to the lighted lobby, and then he sang, in a true, sweet, and manly voice, a commercial he had taped that afternoon:

"Gream takes the ish
Out of washing a dish."

His voice touched her as it seemed to have touched the rest of the world, but it touched her glancingly. "I don't look at television," she said. "What is it you want?"

"I want to marry you," he said sincerely.

She laughed and went on into the lobby and the elevator. The doorman, for five dollars, gave him her name and circumstances. She was Victoria Heatherstone and lived with her invalid father in 14-B. In the space of a morning, the research department in the station where he worked reported that she had graduated from Vassar that spring, and was doing volunteer work in an East Side hospital.

One of the apprentice script girls had been in her class and knew her roommate intimately. In a few days, Betman was able to go to a cocktail party where he met her, and he took her out to dinner. His instinct when he first glimpsed her on the bus had been unerring. She was the woman life meant him to have; she was his destiny. She resisted his claims on her for a week or two, and then she succumbed. But there was a problem. Her old father—a Trollope scholar—was indeed an invalid, and she felt that if she left him he would die. She could not, even if it meant constricting her own life, hold the burden of his death upon her conscience. He was not expected to live for long, and she would marry Betman when her father died; she became, to express the genuineness of her promise, his mistress. Betman's happiness was exalted. But the old man did not die.

Betman wanted to marry; wanted to have the union blessed, celebrated, and announced. He was not content to have Victoria come to his apartment two or three times a week as she did. Then the old man had a stroke and was urged by his doctor to leave New York. He moved to a house he owned in Albany, and this then left Victoria free—or free at least for nine months of the year. She married Betman, and they were vastly happy together, although they had no children. However, on the first of June she left for an island in Lake St. Francis, where the dying old man summered, and she did not return to her husband until September. The old man still thought his daughter unmarried, and Betman was forbidden to visit her. He wrote her three times a week to a postoffice box, and she replied much less frequently, since, as she explained, there was nothing to report but her father's blood pressure, temperature, digestion, and night sweats. He always appeared to be dying. Since he had never seen either the island or the old man, the place naturally took on for Betman legendary proportions, and his three months alone each year was agony.

He woke one summer Sunday morning to feel such love for his wife that he called out her name: "Victoria, Victoria!" He went to church, dismissed the housekeeper after lunch, and late in the afternoon went for a walk. It was inhumanly hot, and the high temperature seemed to draw the city closer to the heart of time; the smell of hot pavings seemed to belong to history. From an open car window he heard himself singing a song about peanut butter. Traffic was heavy on the East River Drive, and this respiratory and melancholy sound came up to where he walked. Traffic would be heavy on all the approaches to the city—and the thought of these lines of cars at Sunday's end made it seem as if the day conformed to some rigid script, part of which was the traffic, part the golden light that poured through the city's parallel streets, part a distant rumble of thunder, as if some leaf had been peeled away from the bulk of sound, and part the unendurable spiritual winter of his months alone. He was overwhelmed by the need for his only love. He got his car and started north a little after dark.

He spent the night in Albany and got to the town of Lake St. Francis in the middle of the morning. It was a small and pleasant resort town, neither booming nor dead. He asked at the boat livery how he could get out to Temple Island. "She comes over once a week," the boatman said. "She comes over to get groceries and medicine, but I don't expect she'll be over today." He pointed across the water to where the island lay, a mile or so distant. Betman rented an outboard and started across the lake. He circled the island and found a landing in a cove, where he made the boat fast. The house above him was a preposterous and old-fashioned cottage, highly inflammable, black with creosote and ornamented with outrageous medieval fancies. There was a round tower of shingles and a wooden parapet that wouldn't have withstood the fire of a .22. Tall firs surrounded the wooden castle and covered it in darkness. It was so dark on that bright morning that lights were burning in most of the rooms.

He crossed the porch and saw, through a glass panel in the door, a long hall ending in a staircase with newel posts. Venus stood on one, a lusterless bronze. In one hand she held a branch of two electric candles, lighted against the gloom of the firs. There was no trace of modesty in her stance, and that her legs were apart made her seem utterly defenseless and a little pathetic, as is sometimes the case with Venus. On the other newel post was Hermes; Hermes in flight. He, too, carried a pair of lighted electric candles. The stairs, carpeted in dark green, led up to a stained-glass window. The colors of the glass, even in the gloom, were of astonishing brilliance and discord. After he had rung, an elderly maid came down the stairs, keeping one hand on the banister. She limped. She came up to the door and, looking out at him through the glass panel, simply shook her head.

He opened the door; it opened easily. "I'm Mr. Betman," he said softly. "I want to see my wife."

"You can't see her now. Nobody can. She's with *him.*"

"I must see her."

"You can't. Please go. Please go away." Her pleading seemed frightened.

Beyond the firs he could see the lake, flat as glass, but the wind in the trees made a sound so like the sea that had he been blindfolded he would have guessed that the house stood on a headland. Then he thought or felt that this was that instant where death enters the terrain of love. These were not the bare facts of life but its ancient and invisible storms, and they moved him like the weight of water. Then he sang:

"Wher-e'er you walk,
cool gales shall fan the glade;
Trees, where you sit,
shall crowd in-to a shade . . ."

The elderly maid, too courteous perhaps to interrupt or moved perhaps by Handel's air and the words, said nothing. Upstairs he heard a door close and footsteps on the carpet. She hastened past the brilliant, ugly window down to where he waited. There was nothing in all the world so sweet to him as her kiss.

"Come back with me now," he said.

"I can't, darling, my darling. He's dying."

"How many times have you thought this before?"

"Oh, I know, but now he *is* dying."

"Come with me."

"I can't. He's dying."

"Come."

He took her hand and led her out the door, down over the treacherous, pungent carpet of pine needles, to the landing. They crossed the lake without speaking but in such a somberness of feeling that the air, the hour, and the light seemed solid. He paid for the boat, opened the car door for her, and they started south. He did not look at her until they were on the main highway, and then he turned to bask in her freshness, her radiance. It was because he loved her too well that her white arms, the color of her hair, her smile distracted him. He veered from one lane into another and the car was crushed by a truck.

She died, of course. He was in the hospital eight months, but when he was able to walk again he found that the persuasiveness of his voice had not been injured. You can still hear him singing about table polish, bleaches, and vacuum cleaners. He always sings of inessentials, never about the universality of suffering and love, but thousands of men and women go off to the stores as if he had, as if this was his song.

III

To WATCH MRS. PERANGER enter the club was a little like choosing up sides for a sand-lot ball game; it was exciting. On her way toward the dining room she would give Mrs. Bebe, who had worked with her on the hospital committee, a fleeting and absent-minded smile. She would cut Mrs. Binger, who was waving and calling her name loudly, dead. She would kiss Mrs. Evans lightly on both cheeks, but she would seem to have forgotten poor Mrs. Budd, at whose house she sometimes dined. She would also seem to have forgotten the Wrights, the Hugginses, the Frames, the Logans, and the Halsteads. A white-haired woman, beautifully dressed, she wielded the power of rudeness so adroitly that she was never caught in an exposed position, and when people asked one another how she got away with it they only increased her advantage. She had been a beauty, and had been painted by Paxton in the twenties. She stood in front of a mirror. The wall was luminous, an imitation of Vermeer, and, as in a Vermeer, the light was put on without its source. There were the usual appurtenances—the ginger jar, the gilt chair, and in the farther room, seen in the glass, a harp on a rug. Her hair had been the color of fire. But this static portrait was only half a world. She had introduced the maxixe to Newport, played golf with Bobby Jones, closed speakeasies at dawn, played strip poker at a Baltimore house party, and even now—an old woman—should she hear on the aromatic summer air the music of a Charleston, she would get up from the sofa and begin to dance with a vigorous pivot step, throwing first one leg out in front of her and then the other, cracking her thumbs and singing, "Charleston! Charleston!"

Mr. Peranger and her only son, Patrick, were dead. Of her only daughter, the nymphlike Nerissa, she would say, "Nerissa is giving me a few days of her time. I don't feel that I can ask her for more. She is *so* sought after that I sometimes think she has never married because she has never found the time. She showed her dogs last week in San Francisco, and hopes to take them to Rome for the dog show there. Everyone *loves* Nerissa. Everyone *adores* her. She is *too* attractive for *words*."

Enter Nerissa then, into her mother's drawing room. She is a thin and wasted spinster of thirty. Her hair is gray. Her slip shows. Her shoes are caked with mud. She is plainly one of those children who, without bitterness or rancor, seem burdened with the graceless facts of life. It is their destiny to point out that the elegance and chic of the world their mothers have mastered is not, as it might appear to be, the end of bewilderment and pain. They are a truly pure and innocent breed, and it would never cross their minds or their hearts to upset or contravene the plans, the dreams, the worldly triumphs that their elders hold out for them. It seems indeed to be the hand of God that leads them to take a pratfall during the tableaux at the débutante cotillion. Stepping from a gondola to the water stairs of some palace in Venice where they are expected for dinner, they will lose their balance and fall into the Grand Canal. They spill food and wine, they knock over vases, they step into dog manure, they shake hands with butlers, they have coughing fits during the chamber music, their taste for disreputable friends is unerring, and yet they are like Franciscans in their goodness and simplicity. Thus, enter Nerissa. In the process of being introduced, she savages an end table with her hipbone, tracks mud onto the rug, and drops a lighted cigarette into a chair. By the time the fire is extinguished, she seems to have satisfactorily ruffled the still waters of her mother's creation. But this is not perversity; it is not even awkwardness. It is her nearly sacred call to restate the pathos and clumsiness of mankind.

The nymphlike Nerissa bred Townsend terriers. Her mother's descriptions of the claims upon her time were, of course, transparent and pathetic. Nerissa was a shy and a lonely woman, mostly occupied with her dogs. Her heart was not unsusceptible, but she always fell in love with gardeners, deliverymen, waiters, and janitors. Late one evening, when her best bitch (Ch. Gaines-Clansman) was about to whelp, she asked the help of a new veterinary, who had just opened a dog-and-cat hospital on Route 14. He came to the kennels at once, and had been there only a few minutes when the bitch threw the first of her litter. He opened the sack and put the dog to suck. His touch with animals, Nerissa thought, was quick and natural, and, standing above him as he knelt at the whelping box, Nerissa felt a strong compulsion to touch his dark hair. She asked if he was married, and when he said that he was not she let herself luxuriate in the fact that she was in love again. Now, Nerissa never anticipated her mother's censure. When she announced her engagement to a garage mechanic or a tree surgeon, she was always surprised at her mother's rage. It never occurred to her that her mother might not like her new choice. She beamed at the veterinary, brought him water, towels, whiskey, and sandwiches. The whelping took most of the night, and it was dawn when they were done. The puppies were sucking; the bitch was proud and requited. All of the litter were well favored and well marked. When Nerissa and the veterinary left the kennels, a cold white light was beaming up beyond the dark trees of the estate. "Would you like some coffee?" Nerissa asked, and then, hearing in the distance the sound of running water, she asked, "Or would you like to swim? I sometimes swim in the morning."

"You know, I would," he said. "That's what I'd like. I'd like a swim. I have to go back to the hospital, and a swim would wake me up."

The pool, built by her grandfather, was of marble and had a deep and graceful curb, curved like the frame of a mirror. The water was limpid, and here and there a sunken leaf threw a shadow, edged with the strong colors of the spectrum. It was the place on her mother's estate that had always seemed to Nerissa—more than any room or garden—her home. When she was away, it was the pool she missed, and when she came back it was to the pool—this watery home-sweet-home—that she returned. She found a pair of trunks in the bathhouse, and they took an innocent swim. They dressed and walked back across the lawns to his car. "You know, you're awfully nice," he said. "Did anyone ever tell you that?" Then he kissed her lightly and tenderly and drove away.

Nerissa didn't see her mother until four the next afternoon, when she went down to tea wearing two left shoes, one brown and one black. "Oh, Mother, Mother," she said, "I've found the man I want to marry."

"Really," said Mrs. Peranger. "Who is this paragon?"

"His name is Dr. Johnson," said Nerissa. "He runs the new dog-and-cat hospital on Route 14."

"But you cannot marry a veterinary, sweet love," said Mrs. Peranger.

"He calls himself an animal hygienist," said Nerissa.

"How revolting!" said Mrs. Peranger.

"But I love him, Mother. I love him, and I'm going to marry him."

"Go to hell!" said Mrs. Peranger.

That night, Mrs. Peranger called the Mayor and asked to speak with his wife. "This is Louisa Peranger," she said. "I am going to put someone up for the Tilton Club this fall, and I was thinking of you." There was a sigh of excitement from the wife of the Mayor. Her head would be swimming. But why? But why? The clubrooms were threadbare, the maids were surly, and the food was bad. Why was there a ferocious waiting list of thousands? "I drive a hard bargain," said Mrs. Peranger, "as everyone knows. There is a dog-and-cat hospital on Route 14 that I would like to have shut down. I'm sure your husband can discover that some sort of zoning violation is involved. It must be some sort of nuisance. If you will speak to your husband about the dog-and-cat hospital, I will get the membership list to you so that you can decide on your other sponsors. I will arrange a luncheon party for the middle of September. Goodbye."

Nerissa pined away, died, and was buried in the little Episcopal church whose windows had been given in memory of her grandfather. Mrs. Peranger looked imperious and patrician in her mourning, and as she left the church she was heard to sob loudly. "She was *so* attractive—she was so *frightfully* attractive."

Mrs. Peranger rallied from her loss, and kept up with her work which, at that time of year, consisted of screening candidates for a débutante cotillion. Three weeks after Nerissa's funeral, a Mrs. Pentason and her daughter were shown into the drawing room.

Mrs. Peranger knew how hard Mrs. Pentason had worked for this interview. She had done hospital work; she had organized theatre parties, strawberry festivals, and antique fairs. But Mrs. Peranger looked at her callers harshly. They would have learned their manners from a book. They would have studied the chapter on how to drink tea. They were the sort who dreamed in terms of invitations that would never be received. *Mr. and Mrs. William Paley request the honor* . . . Their mail, instead, would consist of notices of private sales, trial offers from the Book-of-the-Month Club, and embarrassing letters from Aunt Minnie, who lived in Waco, Texas, and used a spittoon. Nora passed the tea and Mrs. Peranger kept a sharp eye on the girl. The noise of water from the swimming pool sounded very loud, and Mrs. Peranger asked Nora to close the window.

"We have so many applicants for the cotillion these days that we expect a little more than we used to," Mrs. Peranger said. "We not only want attractive and well-bred young women, we want interesting young women." Even with the windows shut, she could hear the sound of water. It seemed to put her at a disadvantage. "Do you sing?" she asked.

"No," the girl said.

"Do you play any musical instruments?"

"I play the piano a little."

"How little?"

"I play some of the Chopin. I mean, I used to. And 'Für Elise.' But mostly I play popular music."

"Where do you summer?"

"Dennis Port," the girl said.

"Ah yes," said Mrs. Peranger. "Dennis Port, poor Dennis Port. There really isn't any place left to go, is there? The Adriatic Coast is crowded. Capri, Ischia, and Amalfi are all ruined. The Princess of Holland has spoiled the Argentario. The Riviera is jammed. Brittany is so cold and rainy. I love Skye, but the food is dreadful. Bar Harbor, the Cape, the Islands—they've all gotten to seem so shabby." She heard again the noise of running water from the pool, as if a breeze carried the sound straight up to the shut windows. "Tell me, are you interested in the theatre?" she asked.

"Oh, yes. Very much."

"What plays did you see last season?"

"None."

"You ride, play tennis, and so forth?"

"Yes."

"What in New York is your favorite museum?"

"I don't know."

"What books have you read recently?"

"I read *The Seersucker Plague*. It was on the best-seller list. They bought it for the movies. And *Seven Roads to Heaven*. That was on the best-seller list, too."

"Please take these things away, Nora," Mrs. Peranger said, making a broad gesture of distaste, as if she expected the maid to remove the Pentasons with the dirty cups and the slop jar. The tea was over, and she walked her guests down the length of the room. If she meant to be cruel, it would have been cruelest to let them wait; to prey upon the common weakness of men and women who look for glad tidings in the mail. She drew Mrs. Pentason aside and said, "I'm *terribly* afraid . . ."

"Well, thank you just the same," said Mrs. Pentason, and she began to cry. The daughter put an arm around the stricken mother and led her out the door.

Mrs. Peranger noticed again the sound of water from the pool. Why was it so loud, and why did it seem to say: *Mother, Mother, I've found the man I want to marry.* . . . Why did it sound so true, and make her task of cutting the Pentasons seem so harsh and senseless? She went down the stairs to the lawn and crossed the lawn to the pool. Standing on the curb, she called, "Nerissa! Nerissa! Nerissa!" but all the water said was *Mother, Mother, I've found the man I want to marry.*

Her only daughter had been turned into a swimming pool.

IV

MR. BRADISH WANTED a change. He did not mean at all by this that he wanted to change himself—only his scenery, his pace, and his environment, and that for only a space of eighteen or twenty days. He could leave his office for that long. Bradish was a heavy smoker, and the Surgeon General's report had made him self-conscious about his addiction. It seemed to him that strangers on the street regarded the cigarette in his fingers with disapproval and sometimes with commiseration. This was manifestly absurd, and he needed to get away. He would take a trip. He was divorced at the time, and would go alone.

One day after lunch he stopped in a travel agency on Park Avenue to see what rates were in force. A receptionist directed him to a desk at the back of the office, where a young woman offered him a chair and lit his cigarette from a matchbook flying the ensign of the Corinthian Yacht Club. She had, he noticed, a dazzling smile and a habit of biting it off when it had served its purpose, as a tailor bites off a thread. He had England in mind. He would spend ten days in London and ten in the country with friends. When he mentioned England, the clerk said that she had recently come back from England herself. From Coventry. She flashed her smile, bit it off. He did not want to go to Coventry, but she was a young woman with the determination and single-mindedness of her time of life, and he saw that he would have to hear her out on the beauties of Coventry, where she seemed to have had an aesthetic and spiritual rebirth. She took from her desk drawer an illustrated magazine to show him pictures of the cathedral. What impressed him, as it happened, was a blunt advertisement in the magazine, stating that cigarettes caused lung cancer. He dismissed England from his mind—the clerk was still on Coventry—and thought that he would go to France. He would go to Paris. The French government had not censured smoking, and he could inhale his Gauloise without feeling subversive. However, the memory of a Gauloise stopped him. Gauloises, Bleues and Jaunes. He recalled how their smoke seemed to drop from an altitude into his lungs and double him up with paroxysms of coughing. In his imagination clouds of rank French tobacco smoke seemed to settle like a bitter fog over the City of Light, making it appear to him an unsavory and despondent place. So he would go to the Tyrol, he thought. He was about to ask for information on the Tyrol when he remembered that tobacco was a state monopoly in Austria and that all you could get to smoke there were flavorless ovals that came in fancy boxes and smelled of perfume. Italy, then. He would cross the Brenner and go down to Venice. But he remembered Italian cigarettes—Esportaziones and Giubeks—remembered how the crude tobacco stuck to his tongue and how the smoke, like a winter wind, made him shiver and think of death. He would go on to Greece, then; he would take a cruise through the islands, he thought—until he recalled the taste of that Egyptian tobacco that is all you can get to smoke in Greece. Russia. Turkey. India. Japan. Glancing above the clerk's head to a map of the world, he saw it all as a chain of tobacco stores. There was no escape. "I think I won't go anywhere," he said. The clerk flashed her smile, bit it off like a thread, and watched him go out the door.

THE QUALITY of discipline shines through a man's life and all his works, giving them a probity and a fineness that preclude disorder, or so Bradish thought. The time had come for him to discipline himself. He put out his last cigarette and walked up Park Avenue with the straitened, pleasant, and slightly dancy step of an old athlete who has his shoes and his suits made in England. As a result of his decision, toward the end of the afternoon he began to suffer from something that resembled a mild case of the bends. His circulatory system was disturbed. His capillaries seemed abraded, his lips were swollen, and now and then his right foot would sting. There was a marked unfreshness in his mouth that seemed by its power and variety to enlarge his mouth, giving it, in fact, the dimensions and malodorousness of some ancient burlesque theatre like the

Howard Athenaeum. Fumes seemed to rise from his mouth to his brain, leaving him with an extraordinary sense of light-headedness. Since he felt himself committed to this discipline, he decided to think of these symptoms in the terms of travel. He would observe them as they made themselves felt, as one would observe from the windows of a train the changes in geology and vegetation in a strange country.

As the day changed to night, the country through which he traveled seemed mountainous and barren. He seemed to be on a narrow-gauge railroad traveling through a rocky pass. Nothing but thistles and wire grass grew among the rocks. He reasoned that once they were over the pass they would come onto a fertile plain with trees and water, but when the train rounded a turn on the summit of the mountain, he saw that what lay ahead was an alkali desert scored with dry stream beds. He knew that if he smoked, tobacco would irrigate this uninhabitable place, the fields would bloom with flowers, and water would run in the streams, but since he had chosen to take this particular journey, since it was quite literally an escape from an intolerable condition, he settled down to study the unrelieved aridity. When he made himself a cocktail in his apartment that night, he smiled—he actually smiled—to observe that there was nothing to be seen in the ashtrays but a little dust and a leaf he had picked off his shoe.

He was changing, he was changing, and like most men he had wanted to change, it seemed. In the space of a few hours, he had become more sagacious, more comprehensive, more mature. He seemed to feel the woolly mantle of his time of life come to rest on his shoulders. He felt himself to be gaining some understanding of the poetry of the force of change in life, felt himself involved in one of those intimate, grueling, and unseen contests that make up the story of a man's soul. If he stopped smoking, he might stop drinking. He might even curtail his erotic tastes. Immoderation had been the cause of his divorce. Immoderation had alienated his beloved children. If they could only see him now, see the clean ashtrays in his room, mightn't they invite him to come home? He could charter a schooner and sail up the coast of Maine with them. When he went, later that night, to see his mistress, the smell of tobacco on her breath made her seem to him so depraved and unclean that he didn't bother to take off his clothes and went home early to his bed and his clean ashtrays.

Bradish had never had any occasion to experience self-righteousness other than the self-righteousness of the sinner. His censure had been aimed at people who drank clam juice and cultivated restrained tastes. Walking to work the next morning, he found himself jockeyed rudely onto the side of the angels; found himself perforce an advocate of abstemiousness, and discovered that some part of this condition was an involuntary urge to judge the conduct of others—a sensation so strange to him, so newly found, so unlike his customary point of view that he thought it exciting. He watched with emphatic disapproval a stranger light a cigarette on a street corner. The stranger plainly had no will power. He was injuring his health, trimming his life span, and betraying his dependents, who might suffer hunger and cold as a result of this self-indulgence. What's more, the man's clothing was shabby, his shoes were unshined, and if he could not afford to dress himself decently he could surely not afford the vice of tobacco. Should Bradish take the cigarette out of his hand? Lecture him? Awaken him? It seemed a little early in the game, but the impulse was there and he had never experienced it before. Now he walked up Fifth Avenue with his newly possessed virtuousness, looking neither at the sky nor at the pretty women but instead raking the population like a lieutenant of the vice squad employed to seek out malefactors. Oh, there were so many! A disheveled old lady, colorless but for a greasy smear of crimson lipstick, stood on the corner of Forty-fourth Street, lighting one cigarette from another. Men in doorways, girls on the steps of the library, boys in the park all seemed determined to destroy themselves.

His light-headedness continued through the morning, so that he found it difficult to make business decisions, and there was some definite injury to his eyesight. He felt as if he had taken his eyes through a dust storm. He went to a business lunch where drinks were served, and when someone passed him a cigarette he said, "Not right now, thank you." He blushed with self-righteousness, but he was not going to demean his struggle by confiding in anyone. Having abstained triumphantly for nearly twenty-four hours, he thought he deserved a reward, and he let the waiter keep filling his cocktail glass. In the end he drank too much, and when he got back to his office he was staggering. This, on top of his disturbed circulatory system, his swollen lips, his bleary eyes, the stinging sensation in his right foot, and the feeling that his brain was filled with the fumes and the malodorousness of an old burlesque theatre made it impossible for him to work, and he floundered through the rest of the day. He seldom went to cocktail parties, but he went to one that afternoon, hoping that it would distract him. He definitely felt unlike himself. The damage by this time had reached his equilibrium, and he found crossing streets difficult and hazardous, as if he were maneuvering over a high and narrow bridge.

The party was large, and he kept going to the bar. He thought that gin would quench his craving. It was hardly a craving, he noticed; nothing like hunger or thirst or the need for love. It felt like some sullen and stubborn ebbing in his bloodstream. The lightness in his head had worsened. He laughed, talked, and behaved himself up to a point, but this was merely mechanical. Late in the party, a young woman wearing a light sack or tube-shaped dress, her long hair the color of Virginia tobacco, came in at the door. In his ardor to reach her he knocked over a table and several glasses. It was, or had been up to that point, a decorous party, but the noise of broken glass, followed by the screaming of the stranger when he wrapped his legs around her and buried his nose in her tobacco-colored hair, was barbarous. Two guests pried him loose. He stood there, crouched with ardor, snorting through his distended nostrils. Then he flung away the arms of the men who held him and strode out of the room.

He went down in the elevator with a stranger whose brown suit looked and smelled like a Havana Upmann, but Bradish kept his eyes on the floor of the carriage and contented himself with breathing in the stranger's fragrance. The elevator man smelled of a light, cheap blend that had been popular in the fifties. The doorman, he noticed, looked and smelled like a briar pipe with a Burley mixture. And on Fifty-seventh Street he saw a woman whose hair was the color of his favorite blend and who seemed to trail after her its striking corrupt perfume. Only by grinding his teeth and bracing his muscles did he keep from seizing her, but he realized that his behavior at the party, repeated on the street, would take him to jail, and there were, as far as he knew, no cigarettes in jail. He had changed—he had changed, and so had his world, and watching the population of the city pass him in the dusk, he saw them as Winstons, Chesterfields, Marlboros, Salems, hookahs, meerschaums, cigarillos, Corona-Coronas, Camels, and Players. It was a young woman—really a child—whom he mistook for a Lucky Strike that was his undoing. She screamed when he attacked her, and two strangers knocked him down, striking and kicking him with just moral indignation. A crowd gathered. There was pandemonium, and presently the sirens of the police car that took him away.

MENE, MENE, TEKEL, UPHARSIN

COMING BACK FROM EUROPE that year, I was booked on an old DC-7 that burned out an engine in mid-Atlantic. Most of the passengers seemed either asleep or drugged, and in the forward section of the plane no one saw the flames but a little girl, an old man, and me. When the fire died down, the plane veered violently, throwing open the door to the crew's quarters. There I saw the crew and the two stewardesses, wearing inflated life jackets. One of the stewardesses shut the door, but the captain came out a few minutes later and explained, in a fatherly whisper, that we had lost an engine and were heading either for Iceland or Shannon. Some time later, he came and said we would be landing in London in half an hour. Two hours later, we landed at Orly, to the astonishment of all those who had been asleep. We boarded another DC-7 and started back across the Atlantic, and when we finally landed at Idlewild we had been traveling in cramped conditions for about twenty-seven hours.

I took a bus into New York and a cab to Grand Central Station. It was an off hour—seven-thirty or eight o'clock in the evening. The newsstands were shut, and the few people on the streets were alone and seemed lonely. There was not a train to where I was going for an hour, so I went into a restaurant near the station and ordered the *plat du jour*. The dilemma of an expatriated American eating his first restaurant meal at home has been worked over too often to be repeated here. After paying the check, I went down some stairs to find the amenities. The place I entered had marble partitions—a gesture, I suppose, toward ennobling this realm. The marble was light brown—it might have been a *giallo antico*, but then I noticed Paleozoic fossils beneath the high polish and guessed that the stone was a madrepore. The near side of the polish was covered with writing. The penmanship was legible, although it had no character or symmetry. What was unusual was the copiousness of the writing and the fact that it was organized into panels, like the pages of a book. I had never seen anything like this before. My deepest instinct was to overlook the writing and study the fossils, but isn't the writing of a man more lasting and wonderful than a Paleozoic coral? I read:

> It had been a day of triumph in Capua. Lentulus, returning with victorious eagles, had amused the populace with the sports of the amphitheater to an extent hitherto unknown, even in that luxurious city. The shouts of revelry died away; the roar of the lion had ceased; the last loiterer retired from the banquet, and the lights in the palace of the victor were extinguished. The moon, piercing the tissue of fleecy clouds, silvered the dewdrop on the corselet of the Roman sentinel and tipped the dark waters of Vulturnus with wavy, tremulous light. It was a night of holy calm, when the zephyr sways the young spring leaves and whispers among the hollow reeds its dreamy music. No sound was heard but the last sob of some weary wave, telling its story to the smooth pebbles of the beach, and then all was still as the breast when the spirit has parted. . . .

I read no more, although there was more to read. I was tired and in some way disarmed by the fact that I had not been home for years. The chain of circumstances that could impel a man to copy this gibberish on marble was unimaginable. Was this a sign of some change in the social climate, the result of some new force of repression? Or was it simply an indication of the fact that man's love of florid prose is irresistible? The sonorities of the writing had the tenacity of bad music, and it was difficult to forget them. Had some profound change in the psyche of my people taken place during my absence? Was there some breakdown in the normal lines of communication, some inordinate love of the romantic past?

I SPENT the next week or ten days traveling in the Middle West. I was waiting one afternoon in the Union Station in Indianapolis for a New York train. The train was late. The station there—proportioned like a cathedral and lit by a rose window—is a gloomy and brilliant example of that genre of architecture that means to express the mystery and drama of travel and separation. The colors of the rose windows, limpid as a kaleidoscope, dyed the marble walls and the waiting passengers. A woman with a shopping bag stood in a panel of lavender. An old man slept in a pool of yellow light. Then I saw a sign directing the way to the men's room, and I wondered if I might not find there another example of that curious literature I had discovered in the first hours of my return. I went down some stairs into a cavernous basement, where a shoeshine man slept in a chair. The walls again were marble. This was a common limestone—a silicate of calcium and magnesium, grained with some metalliferous gray ore. My hunch had been right. The stone was covered with writing, and it had, at a glance, a striking fitness, since it served as a reminder of the fact that it was on walls that the earliest writings and prophecies of man appeared. The penmanship was clear and symmetrical, the work of someone gifted with an orderly mind and a steady hand. Please try to imagine the baneful light, the stale air, and the sounds of running water in that place as I read:

> The great manor house of Wallowyck stood on a hill above the smoky mill town of X——burgh, its countless mullioned windows seeming to peer censoriously into the dark and narrow alleys of the slums that reached from the park gates to the smoky mills on the banks of

the river. It was in the fringes of this wooded park that, unknown to Mr. Wallow, I spent the most lighthearted hours of my youth, roaming there with a slingshot and a sack for transporting my geological specimens. The hill and its forbidding ornament stood between the school I attended and the hovel where I lived with my ailing mother and my drunken father. All my friends took the common path around the hill, and it was only I who climbed the walls of Wallow Park and spent my afternoons in this forbidden demesne.

The lawns, the great trees, the sound of fountains, and the solemn atmosphere of a dynasty are dear to me to this day. The Wallows had no arms, of course, but the sculptors they employed had improvised hundreds of escutcheons and crests that seemed baronial at a distance but that, on examination, petered out modestly into geometrical forms. Their chimneys, gates, towers, and garden benches were thus crested. Another task of the sculptors had been to make representations of Mr. Wallow's only daughter, Emily. There was Emily in bronze, Emily in marble, Emily as the Four Seasons, the Four Winds, the Four Times of Day, and the Four Principal Virtues. In a sense, Emily was my only companion. I walked there in the autumn, watching the wealth of color fall from the trees to the lawns. I walked there in the bitter snow. I watched there for the first signs of spring, and smelled the fine perfume of wood smoke from the many crested chimneys of the great house above me. It was while wandering there on a spring day that I heard a girlish voice crying for help. I followed the voice to the banks of a little stream, where I saw Emily. Her lovely feet were naked, and stuck to one, like some manacle of evil, was the writhing form of a viper.

I plucked the viper from her foot, lanced the wound with my pocketknife, and sucked the poison from her bloodstream. Then I took off my humble shirt, stitched together for me by my dear mother from some discarded blueprint linen that she had found, during her daily foraging, in an architect's ash can. When the wound was cleansed and bound, I gathered Emily in my arms and ran up the lawn towards the great doors of

Wallowyck, which rumbled open at my ring. A butler stood there, pallid at the sight.

"What have you done to our Emily?" he cried.

"He has done nothing but save my life," said Emily.

Then from the dusk of the hall emerged the bearded and ruthless Mr. Wallow. "Thank you for saving the life of my daughter," he said gruffly. Then he looked at me more closely, and I saw tears in his eyes. "Someday you will be rewarded," he said. "That day will come."

The ruin of my linen shirt obliged me to tell my parents that evening about my adventure. My father was drunk, as usual. "You will receive no reward from that beast!" he roared. "Neither in this world nor in heaven nor in hell!"

"Please, Ernest," my mother sighed, and I went to her and held her hands, dry with fever.

Drunk as he was, it seemed that my father possessed the truth, for, in the years that followed, no sign of gratitude, no courtesy, no trifling remembrance, no hint of indebtedness came to me from the great house on the hill.

In the stern winter of 19—, the mills were shut down by Mr. Wallow, in a retaliative gesture at my struggle to organize a labor union. The stillness of the mills—those smokeless chimneys—was a blow at the heart of X——burgh. My mother lay dying. My father sat in the kitchen drinking Sterno. Sickness, hunger, cold, and disease dominated every hovel. The snow in the streets, unbesmirched by the mill smoke, had an accusatory whiteness. It was on the day before Christmas that I led the union delegation, many of them scarcely able to walk, up to the great doors of Wallowyck and rang. It was Emily who stood there when the doors were opened. "You!" she cried. "You who saved my life, why are you killing my father?" Then the doors rumbled shut.

I managed that evening to gather a little grain, and made some porridge of this for my mother. I was spooning this into her thin lips when our door opened and in stepped Jeffrey Ashmead, Mr. Wallow's advocate.

"If you have come," I said, "to persecute me for my demonstration at Wallowyck this afternoon, you have come in vain. There is no pain on earth greater than that which I suffer now, as I watch my mother die."

"I have come about other business," he said. "Mr. Wallow is dead."

"Long live Mr. Wallow!" shouted my father from the kitchen.

"Please come with me," said Mr. Ashmead.

"What business can I have with you, sir?"

"You are the heir to Wallowyck—its mines, its mills, its moneys."

"I do not understand."

There was a piercing sob from my mother. She seized my hands in hers and said, "The truth of the past is no harsher than the truth of our sad lives! I have wanted to shelter you all these years from the truth but you are his only son. As a girl, I waited on table at the great house, and was taken advantage of on a summer's night. It has contributed to your father's destruction."

"I will go with you, sir," I said to Mr. Ashmead. "Miss Emily knows of this?"

"Miss Emily," he said, "has fled."

I returned that evening, and entered the great doors of Wallowyck as its master. But there was no Miss Emily. Before the New Year had come, I had buried both of my parents, reopened the mills on a profit-sharing basis, and brought prosperity to X——burgh, but I, living alone in Wallowyck, knew a loneliness that I had never tasted before. . . .

I was appalled, of course, I felt sick. The matter-of-factness of my surroundings made the puerility of this tale nauseating. I hurried back to the noble waiting room, with its limpid panels of colored light, and sat down near a rack of paperback books. Their lurid covers and their promise of graphic descriptions of sexual commerce seemed to tie in with what I had just read. What had happened, I supposed, was that, as pornography moved into the public domain, those marble walls, those immemorial repositories of such sport, had been forced, in self-defense, to take up the more refined task of literature. I found the idea revolutionary and disconcerting, and wondered if in a year or two I would be able to read the poetry of Sara

Teasdale in a public toilet, while the King of Sweden honored some dirty-minded brute. Then my train came in, and I was happy to get out of Indianapolis and leave, as I hoped, my discovery with the Middle West.

I went up to the club car and had a drink. We belted eastward over Indiana, scaring the cows and the chickens, the horses and the pigs. People waved at the train as it passed—a little girl holding a doll upside down, an old man in a wheelchair, a woman standing in a kitchen doorway with her hair in pin curls, a young man sitting on a freight truck. You could feel the train leap forward in the straightaway, the whistle blew, the warning bells at the grade crossings went off like a coronary thrombosis, and the track joints beat out a jazz bass, versatile, exhilarating, and fleet, like some brilliant improvisation on the beating of a heart, and the wind in the brake boxes sounded like the last, hoarse recordings poor Billie Holiday ever made. I had two more drinks. When I opened the door of the lavatory in the next sleeping car and saw that the walls were covered with writing, it seemed to me like a piece of very bad news.

I didn't want to read any more—not then. Wallowyck had been enough for one day. I wanted only to go back to the club car and have another drink and assert my healthy indifference to the fancies of strangers. But the writing was there, and it was irresistible—it seemed to be some part of my destiny—and, although I read it with bitter unwillingness, I read through the first paragraph. The penmanship was the most commanding of all.

> Why does not everyone who can afford it have a geranium in his window? It is very cheap. Its cheapness is next to nothing if you raise it from seed or from a slip. It is a beauty and a companion. It sweetens the air, rejoices the eye, links you with nature and innocence, and is something to love. And if it cannot love you in return, it cannot hate you, it cannot utter a hateful thing even for your neglecting it, for though it is all beauty, it has no vanity, and such being the case, and living as it does purely to do you good and afford pleasure, how will you be able to neglect it? But, pray, if you choose a geranium . . .

Back in the club car, it was getting dark. I was disturbed by these tender sentiments and depressed by the general gloom of the countryside at that time of day. Was what I had read the expression of some irrepressible love of quaintness and innocence? Whatever it was, I felt then a manifest responsibility to declare what I had discovered. Our knowledge of ourselves and of one another, in a historical moment of mercurial change, is groping. To hedge our observation, curiosity, and reflection with indifference would be sheer recklessness. My three chance encounters proved that this kind of literature was widespread. If these fancies were recorded and diagnosed, they might throw a brilliant illumination onto our psyche and bring us closer to the secret world of the truth. My search had its unconventional aspects, but if we are any less than shrewd, courageous, and honest with ourselves we are contemptible. I had six friends who worked for foundations, and I decided to call their attention to the phenomenon of the writing in public toilets. I knew they had financed poetry, research in zoology, studies of the history of stained glass and of the social significance of high heels, and, at that moment, the writing in public toilets appeared to be an avenue of truth that demanded exploration.

When I got back to New York, I arranged a lunch for my friends, in a restaurant in the Sixties that has a private dining room. At the end of the meal, I made my speech. My best friend there was the first to answer. "You've been away too long," he said. "You're out of touch. We don't go for that kind of thing over here. I can only speak for myself, of course, but I think the idea is repulsive." I glanced down and saw that I was wearing a brocade double-breasted vest and pointed yellow shoes, and I suppose I had spoken in the flat and affected accent of most expatriates. His accusation that my thinking was alien, strange, and indecent seemed invincible. I felt then, I feel now, that it was not the impropriety of my discovery but its explosiveness that disconcerted him, and that he had, in my absence, joined the ranks of those new men who feel that the truth is no longer usable in solving our dilemmas. He said goodbye, and one by one the others left, all on the same note—I had been away too long; I was out of touch with decency and common sense.

I RETURNED to Europe a few days later. The plane for Orly was delayed, and I killed some time in the bar and then looked around for the men's room. The message this time was written on tile. "Bright Star!" I read, "would I were steadfast as thou art—Not in lone splendour hung aloft the night . . ." That was all. My flight was announced, and I sailed through the eaves of heaven back to the city of light.

MONTRALDO

THE FIRST TIME I robbed Tiffany's, it was raining. I bought an imitation-diamond ring at a costume-jewelry place in the Forties. Then I walked up to Tiffany's in the rain and asked to look at rings. The clerk had a haughty manner. I looked at six or eight diamond rings. They began at eight hundred and went up to ten thousand. There was one priced at three thousand that looked to me like the paste in my pocket. I was examining this when an elderly woman—an old customer, I guessed—appeared on the other side of the counter. The clerk rushed over to greet her, and I switched rings. Then I called, "Thank you very much. I'll think it over." "Very well," the clerk said haughtily, and I went out of the store. It was as simple as pie. I walked down to the diamond market in the Forties and sold the ring for eighteen hundred. No questions were asked. Then I went to Thomas Cook and found that the *Conte di Salvini* was sailing for Genoa at five. This was in August, and there was plenty of space on the eastbound crossing. I took a cabin in first class and was standing at the bar when she sailed. The bar was not officially open, of course, but the bar Jack gave me a Martini in a tumbler to hold me until we got into international waters. The *Salvini* had an exceptionally percussive whistle, and you may have heard it if you were anywhere near midtown, although who ever is at five o'clock on an August afternoon?

That night I met Mrs. Winwar and her elderly husband at the horse races. He promptly got seasick, and we plunged into the marvelous skulduggery of illicit love. The passed notes, the phony telephone calls, the affected indifference, and what happened when we were behind the closed door of my cabin made my theft of a ring seem guileless. Mr. Winwar recovered in Gibraltar, but this only seemed like a challenge, and we carried on under his nose. We said goodbye in Genoa, where I bought a secondhand Fiat and started down the coast.

I got to Montraldo late one afternoon. I stopped there because I was tired of driving. There was a semicircular bay, set within high stone cliffs, and one of those beaches that are lined with cafés and bathing houses. There were two hotels, a Grand and a National, and I didn't care for either one of them, and a waiter in a café told me I could rent a room in the villa on the cliff. It could be reached, he said, either by a steep and curving road or by a flight of stone steps—one hundred and twenty-seven, I discovered later—that led from the back garden down into the village. I took my car up the curving road. The cliff was covered with rosemary, and the rosemary was covered with the village laundry, drying in the sun. There were signs on the door in five languages, saying that rooms were for rent. I rang, and a thickset, bellicose servant opened the door. I learned that her name was Assunta. I never saw any relaxation of her bellicosity. In church, when she plunged up the aisle to take Holy Communion, she looked as if she were going to knock the priest down and mess up the acolyte. She said I could have a room if I paid a week's rent in advance, and I had to pay her before I was allowed to cross the threshold.

The place was a ruin, but the whitewashed room she showed me into was in a little tower, and through a broken window the room had a broad view of the sea. The one luxury was a gas ring. There was no toilet, and there was no running water; the water I washed in had to be hauled out of a well in a leaky marmalade can. I was obviously the only guest. That first afternoon, while Assunta was praising the healthfulness of the sea air, I heard a querulous and elegant voice calling to us from the courtyard. I went down the stairs ahead of the servant, and introduced myself to an old woman standing by the well. She was short, frail, and animated, and spoke such a flowery Roman that I wondered if this wasn't a sort of cultural or social dust thrown into one's eyes to conceal the fact that her dress was ragged and dirty. "I see you have a gold wristwatch," she said. "I, too, have a gold wristwatch. We will have this in common."

The servant turned to her and said, "Go to the devil!"

"But it is a fact. The gentleman and I do both have gold wristwatches," the old lady said. "It will make us sympathetic."

"Bore," the servant said. "Rot in hell."

"Thank you, thank you, treasure of my house, light of my life," the old lady said, and made her way toward the open door.

The servant put her hands on her hips and screamed, "Witch! Frog! Pig!"

"Thank you, thank you, thank you infinitely," the old lady said, and went in at the door.

THAT NIGHT, at the café, I asked about the signorina and her servant, and the waiter was fully informed. The signorina, he said, came from a noble Roman family, from which she had been expelled because of a romantic and unsuitable love affair. She had lived as a hermit in Montraldo for fifty years. Assunta had been brought here from Rome to her *donna di servizio,* but all she did for the old lady these days was to go into the village and buy her some bread and wine. She had robbed the old woman of all her possessions—she had even taken the bed from her room—and she now kept her a prisoner in the villa. Both the Grand Hotel and the National were luxurious and commodious. Why did I stay in such a place?

I stayed because of the view, because I had paid my rent in advance, and because I was curious about the eccentric old spinster and her cranky servant. They began quarreling early the next morning. Assunta opened up with obscenity and abuse. The signorina countered with elaborate sarcasm. It was a depressing performance. I wondered if the old lady was really a prisoner, and later in the morning, when I saw her alone in the courtyard, I asked her if she would like to drive with me to Tambura, the next village up the coast. She said, in her flowery Roman, that she would be delighted to join me. She wanted to have her watch, her gold watch, repaired. The watch was of great value and beauty and there was only one man she dared entrust it to. He was in Tambura. While we were talking, Assunta joined us.

"Why do you want to go to Tambura?" she asked the old lady.

"I want to have my gold watch repaired," the old lady said.

"You don't have a gold watch," Assunta said.

"That is true," the old lady said. "I no longer have a gold watch, but I used to have a gold watch. I used to have a gold watch, and I used to have a gold pencil."

"You can't go to Tambura to have your watch repaired if you don't have a watch," Assunta said.

"That is true, light of my life, treasure of my house," the old lady said, and she went in at her door.

I SPENT most of my time on the beach and in the cafés. The fortunes of the resort seemed to be middling. The waiters complained about business, but then they always do. The smell of the sea was riggish but unfresh, and I used to think with homesickness of the wild and magnificent beaches of my own country. Gay Head is, I know, sinking into the sea, but the sinkage at Montraldo seemed to be spiritual—as if the waves were eroding the vitality of that place. The sea was incandescent; the light was clear but not brilliant. The flavor of Montraldo, as I remember it, was immutable, intimate, depleted—everything I detest; for shouldn't the soul of man be as limpid and cutting as a diamond? The waves spoke in French or Italian—now and then a word of dialect—but they seemed to speak without force.

One afternoon a remarkably beautiful woman came down the beach, followed by a boy of about eight, I should say, and an Italian woman dressed in black—a maid. They carried sandwich bags from the Grand Hotel, and my guess was that the boy lived mostly in hotels. He was pitiful. The maid took some toys from an assortment she carried in a string bag. They seemed to be all wrong for his age. There was a sand bucket, a shovel, some molds, a whiffle ball, and an old-fashioned pair of water wings. I suspected that the mother, stretched out on a blanket with an American novel, was a divorcée, and that she would presently have a drink with me in the café.

With this in mind, I got to my feet and offered to play whiffle ball with the boy. He was delighted to have some company, but he could neither throw nor catch a ball, and, making a guess at his tastes, I asked, with one eye on the mother, if he would like me to build him a sand castle. He would. I built a water moat, then an escarpment with curved stairs, a dry moat, a crenelated wall with cannon positions, and a cluster of round towers with parapets. I worked as if the impregnability of the place was a reality, and when it was completed I set flags, made of candy wrappers, flying from every tower. I thought naïvely that it was beautiful, and so did the boy, but when I called his mother's attention to my feat she said, "*Andiamo.*" The maid gathered up the toys, and off they went, leaving me, a grown man in a strange country, with a sand castle.

At Montraldo, the high point of the day came at four, when there was a band concert. This was the largesse of the municipality. The bandstand was wooden, Turkish in inspiration, and weathered by sea winds. The musicians sometimes wore uniforms, sometimes bathing suits, and their number varied from day to day, but they always played Dixieland. I don't think they were interested in the history of jazz. I just think they'd found some old arrangements in a trunk and were stuck with them. The music was comical, accelerated—they seemed to be playing for some ancient ballroom team. "Clarinet Marmalade," "China Boy," "Tiger Rag," "Careless Love"—how stirring it was to hear this old, old jazz explode in the salty air. The concert ended at five, when most of the musicians packed up their instruments and went out to sea with the sardine fleet and the bathers returned to the cafés and the village. Men, women, and children on a beach, band music, sea grass, and sandwich hampers remind me much more forcibly than classical landscapes of our legendary ties to paradise. So I would go up with the others to the café, where, one day, I befriended Lord and Lady Rockwell, who asked me for cocktails. You may wonder why I put these titles down so breathlessly, and the reason is that my father was a waiter.

He wasn't an ordinary waiter; he used to work at a dinner-dance spot in one of the big hotels. One night he lost his temper at a drunken brute, pushed his face into a plate of cannelloni, and left the premises. The union suspended him for three months, but he was, in a way, a hero, and when he went back to work they put him on the banquet shift, where he passed mushrooms to Kings and Presidents. He saw a lot of the world, but I sometimes wonder if the world ever saw much more of him than the sleeve of his red coat and his suave and handsome face, a little above the candlelight. It must have been like living in a world divided by a sheet of one-way glass. Sometimes I am reminded of him by those pages and guards in Shakespeare who come in from the left and stand at a door, establishing by their costumes the fact that this is Venice or Arden. You scarcely see their faces, they never speak a line; nor did my father, and when the after-dinner speeches began he would vanish like the pages on stage. I tell people that he was in the administrative end of the hotel business, but actually he was a waiter, a banquet waiter.

The Rockwells' party was large, and I left at about ten. A hot wind was blowing off the sea. I was later told that this was the sirocco. It was a desert wind, and so oppressive that I got up several times during the night to drink some mineral water. A boat offshore was sounding its foghorn. In the morning, it was both foggy and suffocating. While I was making some coffee, Assunta and the signorina began their morning quarrel. Assunta started off with the usual "Pig! Dog! Witch! Dirt of the streets!" Leaning from an open window, the whiskery old woman sent down her flowery replies: "Dear one. Beloved. Blessed one. Thank you, thank you." I stood in the door with my coffee, wishing they would schedule their disputes for some other time of day. The quarrel was suspended while the signorina came down the stairs to get her bread and wine. Then it started up again: "Witch! Frog! Frog of frogs! Witch of witches!" etc. The old lady countered with "Treasure! Light! Treasure of my house! Light of my life!" etc. Then there was a scuffle—a tug-of-war over the loaf of bread. I saw Assunta strike the old woman cruelly with the edge of her hand. She fell on the steps and began to moan "Aiee! Aiee!" Even these cries of pain seemed florid. I ran across the courtyard to where she lay in a disjointed heap. Assunta began to scream at me, "I am not culpable, I am not culpable!" The old lady was in great pain. "Please, signore," she asked, "please find the priest for me!" I picked her up. She weighed no more than a child, and her clothing smelled of soil. I carried her up the stairs into a high-ceilinged room festooned with cobwebs and put her onto a couch. Assunta was on my heels, screaming, "I am not culpable!" Then I started down the one hundred and twenty-seven steps to the village.

The fog streamed through the air, and the African wind felt like a furnace draft. No one answered the door at the priest's house, but I found him in the church, sweeping the floor with a broom made of twigs. I was excited and impatient, and the more excited I became, the more slow-moving was the priest. First, he had to put his broom in a closet. The closet door was warped and wouldn't shut, and he spent an unconscionable amount of time trying to close it. I finally went outside and waited on the porch. It took him half an hour to get collected, and then, instead of starting for the villa, we went down into the village to find an acolyte. Presently a young boy joined us, pulling on a soiled lace soutane, and we started up the stairs. The priest negotiated ten steps and then sat down to rest. I had time to smoke a cigarette. Then ten more steps and another rest, and when we were halfway up the stairs, I began to wonder if he would ever make it. His face had turned from red to purple, and the noises from his respiratory tract were harsh and desperate. We finally arrived at the door of the villa. The acolyte lit his censer. Then we made our way into that ruined place. The windows were open. There was sea fog in the air. The old woman was in great pain, but the notes of her voice remained genteel, as I expect they truly were. "She is my daughter," she said. "Assunta. She is my daughter, my child."

Then Assunta screamed, "Liar! Liar!"

"No, no, no," the old lady said, "you are my child, my only child. That is why I have cared for you all my life."

Assunta began to cry, and stamped down the stairs. From the window, I saw her crossing the courtyard. When the priest began to administer the last rites, I went out.

I kept a sort of vigil in the café. The church bells tolled at three, and a little later news came down from the villa that the signorina was dead. No one in the café seemed to suspect that they were anything but an eccentric old spin-ter and a cranky servant. At four o'clock the band oncert opened up with "Tiger Rag." I moved that night rom the villa to the Hotel National, and left Montraldo in he morning.

THE OCEAN

I AM KEEPING this journal because I believe myself to be in some danger and because I have no other way of ecording my fears. I cannot report them to the police, s you will see, and I cannot confide in my friends. The osses I have recently suffered in self-esteem, reasonbleness, and charity are conspicuous, but there is always ome painful ambiguity about who is to blame. I might be o blame myself. Let me give you an example. Last night I at down to dinner with Cora, my wife, at half past six. Our only daughter has left home, and we eat, these days, n the kitchen, off a table ornamented with a goldfish owl. The meal was cold ham, salad, and potatoes. When I took a mouthful of salad I had to spit it out. "Ah, yes," my wife said. "I was afraid that would happen. You left your ighter fluid in the pantry, and I mistook it for vinegar."

As I say, who was to blame? I have always been careful bout putting things in their places, and had she meant to oison me she wouldn't have done anything so clumsy as o put lighter fluid in the salad dressing. If I had not left he fluid in the pantry, the incident wouldn't have taken lace. But let me go on for a minute. During dinner a hunderstorm came up. The sky got black. Suddenly there was a soaking rain. As soon as dinner was over, Cora dressed herself in a raincoat and a green shower cap and went out to water the lawn. I watched her from the window. She seemed oblivious of the ragged walls of rain in which she stood, and she watered the lawn carefully, lingering over the burnt spots. I was afraid that she would compromise herself in the eyes of our neighbors. The woman in the house next door would telephone the woman on the corner to say that Cora Fry was watering her lawn in a downpour. My wish that she not be ridiculed by gossip took me to her side, although as I approached her, under my umbrella, I realized that I lacked the tact to get through this gracefully. What should I say? Should I say that a friend was on the telephone? She had no friends. "Come in, dear," I said. "You might get struck."

"Oh, I doubt that very much," she said in her most musical voice. She speaks these days in the octave above middle C.

"Won't you wait until the rain is over?" I asked.

"It won't last long," she said sweetly. "Thunderstorms *never* do."

Under my umbrella, I returned to the house and poured myself a drink. She was right. A minute later the storm blew off, and she went on watering the grass. She had some rightness on her side in both of these incidents, but this does not change my feeling that I am in some danger.

Oh, world, world, world, wondrous and bewildering, when did my troubles begin? This is being written in my house in Bullet Park. The time is 10 A.M. The day is Tuesday. You might well ask what I am doing in Bullet Park on a weekday morning. The only other men around are three clergymen, two invalids, and an old codger on Turner Street who has lost his marbles. The neighborhood has the serenity, the stillness of a terrain where all sexual tensions have been suspended—excluding mine, of course, and those of the three clergymen. What is my business? What do I do? Why didn't I catch the train? I am forty-six years old, hale, well-dressed, and have a more thorough knowledge of the manufacture and merchandising of Dynaflex than any other man in the entire field. One of my difficulties is my youthful looks. I have a thirty-inch waistline and jet-black hair, and when I tell people that I used to be vice-president in charge of merchandising and executive assistant to the president of Dynaflex—when I tell this to strangers in bars and on trains—they never believe me, because I look so young.

Mr. Estabrook, the president of Dynaflex and in some ways my protector, was an enthusiastic gardener. While admiring his flowers one afternoon, he was stung by a bumblebee, and he died before they could get him to the hospital. I could have had the presidency, but I wanted to stay in merchandising and manufacture. Then the directors—including myself, of course—voted a merger with Milltonium Ltd., putting Eric Penumbra, Milltonium's chief, at the helm. I voted for the merger with some misgivings, but I concealed these and did the most important part of the groundwork for this change. It was my job to bring in the approval of conservative and reluctant stockholders, and one by one I brought them around. The fact that I had worked for Dynaflex since I had left college, that I had never worked for anyone else, inspired their trust. A few days after the merger was a fact, Penumbra called me into his office. "Well," he said, "you've had it."

"Yes, I have," I said. I thought he was complimenting me on having brought in the approvals. I had traveled all over the United States and made two trips to Europe. No one else could have done it.

"You've had it," Penumbra said harshly. "How long will it take you to get out of here?"

"I don't understand," I said.

"How the hell long will it take you to get out of here!" he shouted. "You're obsolete. We can't afford people like you in the shop. I'm asking how long it will take you to get out of here."

"It will take about an hour," I said.

"Well, I'll give you to the end of the week," he said. "If you want to send your secretary up, I'll fire her. You're really lucky. With your pension, severance pay, and the stock you own, you'll have damned near as much money as I take home, without having to lift a finger." Then he left his desk and came to where I stood. He put an arm around my shoulders. He gave me a hug. "Don't worry," Penumbra said. "Obsolescence is something we all have to face. I hope I'll be as calm about it as you when my time comes."

"I certainly hope you will," I said, and I left the office.

I went to the men's room. I locked myself up in a cubicle and wept. I wept at Penumbra's dishonesty, wept for the destinies of Dynaflex, wept for the fate of my secretary—an intelligent spinster, who writes short stories in her spare time—wept bitterly for my own naïveté, for my own lack of guile, wept that I should be overwhelmed by the plain facts of life. At the end of a half hour I dried my tears and washed my face. I took everything out of my office that was personal, took a train home, and broke the news to Cora. I was angry, of course, and she seemed frightened. She began to cry. She retired to her dressing table, which has served as a wailing wall for all the years of our marriage.

"But there's nothing to cry about," I said. "I mean, we've got plenty of money. We've got loads of money. We can go to Japan. We can go to India. We can see the English cathedrals." She went on crying, and after dinner I called our daughter Flora, who lives in New York. "I'm sorry, Daddy," she said, when I told her the news. "I'm very sorry, I know how you must feel, and I'd like to see you later but not right now. Remember your promise—you promised to leave me alone."

The next character to enter the scene is my mother-in-law, whose name is Minnie. Minnie is a harsh-voiced blonde of about seventy, with four scars on the side of her face, from cosmetic surgery. You may have seen Minnie rattling around Neiman-Marcus or the lobby of practically any Grand Hotel. Minnie uses the word "fashionable" with great versatility. Of her husband's suicide in 1932 Minnie says, "Jumping out of windows was quite *fashionable*." When her only son was fired out of secondary school for improper conduct and went to live in Paris with an older man, Minnie said, "I know it's revolting, but it seems to be *terribly* fashionable." Of her own outrageous plumage she says, "It's hideously uncomfortable but it's divinely *fashionable*." Minnie is cruel and idle, and Cora, who is her only daughter, hates her. Cora has drafted her nature along lines that are the opposite of Minnie's. She is loving, serious-minded, sober, and kind. I think that in order to safeguard her virtues—her hopefulness, really—Cora has been forced to evolve a fantasy in which her mother is not Minnie at all but is instead some sage and gracious lady, working at an embroidery hoop. Everybody knows how persuasive and treacherous fantasies can be.

I spent the day after I was cashiered by Penumbra hanging around the house. With the offices of Dynaflex shut to me, I was surprised to find that I had almost no place else to go. My club is a college adjunct where they serve a cafeteria lunch, and it is not much of a sanctuary. I have always wanted to read good books, and this seemed to be my chance. I took a copy of Chaucer into the garden and read half a page, but it was hard work for a businessman. I spent the rest of the morning hoeing the lettuce, which made the gardener cross. Lunch with Cora was for some reason strained. After lunch Cora took a nap. So did the maid, I discovered, when I stepped into the kitchen to get a glass of water. She was sound asleep with her head on the table. The stillness of the house at that hour gave me a most peculiar feeling. But the world with all its diversions and entertainments was available to me, and I called New York and booked some theatre tickets for that evening. Cora doesn't much enjoy the theatre, but she came with me. After the theatre we went to the St. Regis to get some supper. When we entered the place, the band was knocking out the last number of a set—all horns up, flags flying, and the toothy drummer whacking crazily at everything he could reach. In the middle of the dance floor was Minnie, shaking her backside, stamping her feet, and popping her thumbs. She was with a broken-winded gigolo, who kept looking desperately over his shoulder, as if he expected his trainer to throw in the sponge. Minnie's plumage was exceptionally brilliant, her face seemed exceptionally haggard, and a lot of people were laughing at her. As I say, Cora seems to have invented a dignified parent, and these encounters with Minnie are cruel. We turned and went away. Cora said nothing during the long drive home.

Minnie must have been beautiful many years ago. It was from Minnie that Cora got her large eyes and her fine nose. Minnie comes to visit us two or three times a year. There is no question about the fact that if she announced her arrivals we would lock up the house and go away. Her ability to make her daughter miserable is consummate and voracious, and so, with some cunning, she makes her arrivals at our house a surprise. I spent the next afternoon trying to read Henry James in the garden. At about five I heard a car stop in front of the house. A little while later it began to rain, and I stepped into the living room and saw Minnie standing by a window. It was quite dark, but no one had bothered to turn on a light. "Why, Minnie," I exclaimed, "how *nice* to see you, what a pleasant surprise.

Let me get you a drink . . ." I turned on a lamp and saw that it was Cora.

She turned on me slowly a level and eloquent look of utter misgiving. It might have been a smile had I not known that I had wounded her painfully; had I not felt from her a flow of emotion like the flow of blood from a wound. "Oh, I'm *terribly* sorry, darling," I said. "I'm terribly sorry. I couldn't see." She went out of the room. "It was the dark," I said. "It got so dark all of a sudden, when it began to rain. I'm terribly sorry, but it was just the dark and the rain." I heard her climb the dark stairs and close the door to our room.

When I saw Cora in the morning—and I didn't see her again until morning—I could tell by the pained look on her face that she thought I had wickedly pretended to mistake her for Minnie. I suppose she was as deeply and lastingly hurt as I had been hurt when Penumbra called me obsolete. It was at this point that her voice became an octave higher, and she spoke to me—when she spoke to me at all—in notes that were weary and musical, and her looks were accusing and dark. Now, I might not have noticed any of this had I been absorbed in my work and tired in the evening. To strike a healthy balance between motion and scrutiny was nearly impossible with my opportunities for motion so suddenly curtailed. I went on with my program of serious reading, but more than half my time was spent in observing Cora's sorrows and the disorganized workings of my house. A part-time maid came four times a week, and when I saw her sweeping dust under the rugs and taking catnaps in the kitchen, I got irritable. I said nothing about this, but a vexatious relationship quickly sprang up between us. It was the same with the gardener. If I sat on the terrace to read, he would cut the grass under my chair, and he took a full day, at four dollars an hour, to cut the lawns, although I knew from experience that this could be done in a much shorter time. As for Cora, I saw how empty and friendless her life was. She never went out to lunch. She never played cards. She arranged flowers, went to the hairdresser, gossiped with the maid, and rested. The smallest things began to irritate and offend me, and I was doubly offended by my unreasonable irritability. The sound of Cora's light and innocent footstep as she wandered aimlessly around the house made me cross. I was even offended at her manner of speaking. "I must *try* to arrange the flowers," she would say. "I must *try* to buy a hat. I must *try* to have my hair done. I must *try* to find a yellow pocketbook." Leaving the lunch table she would say, "Now I shall *try* to lie in the sun." But why try? The sun poured from the heavens down onto the terrace, where there was a large assortment of comfortable furniture, and a few minutes after she had stretched herself out in a long chair she was asleep. Rising from her nap she would say, "I must *try* not to get a sunburn," and entering the house she would say, "Now I am going to *try* to take a bath."

I drove down to the station one afternoon to watch the six-thirty-two come in. It was the rain I used to return home on. I stopped my car in a long line of cars driven mostly by housewives. I was terribly excited. I was waiting for no one, and the women around me were merely waiting for their husbands, but it seemed to me that we were all waiting for much more. The stage, it seemed, was set. Pete and Harry, the two cab drivers, stood by their cars. With them was the Bruxtons' Airedale, who wanders. Mr. Winters, the station agent, was talking with Louisa Balcolm, the postmistress, who lives two stops up the line. These, then, were the attendant players, the porters and gossips who would put down the groundwork for the spectacle. I kept an eye on my wristwatch. Then the train pulled in, and a moment later an eruption, a jackpot of humanity, burst through the station doors—so numerous and eager, so like sailors home from the sea, so hurried, so loving, that I laughed with pleasure. There they all were, the short and the tall, the rich and the poor, the sage and the foolish, my enemies and friends, and they all headed out the door with such a light step, so bright an eye, that I knew I must rejoin them. I would simply go back to work. This decision made me feel cheerful and magnanimous and when I came home my cheer seemed for a moment to be infectious. Cora spoke for the first time in days in a voice that was full and warm, but when I replied, she said, musically, "I was *speaking* to the goldfish." She was indeed. The beautiful smile that she had withheld from me was aimed at the goldfish bowl, and I wondered if she had not left the world, its lights, cities, and the clash of things, for this sphere of glass and its foolish castle. Watching her bend lovingly over the goldfish bowl, I got the distinct impression that she looked longingly into this other world.

I WENT TO NEW YORK in the morning and called the friend who has always been most complimentary about my work with Dynaflex. He told me to come to his office at around noon—I guessed for lunch. "I want to go back to work," I told him. "I want your help."

"Well, it isn't simple," he said. "It isn't as simple as it might seem. To begin with, you can't expect much in the way of sympathy. Everybody in the business knows how generous Penumbra was to you. Most of us would be happy to change places. I mean, there's a certain amount of natural envy. People don't like to help a man who's in a more comfortable position than they. And another thing is that Penumbra wants you to stay in retirement. I don't know why this is, but I know it's a fact, and anybody who took you on would be in trouble with Milltonium. And, to get on with the unpleasant facts, you're just too damned old. Our president is twenty-seven. Our biggest competitor has a chief in his early thirties. So why don't you enjoy yourself? Why don't you take it easy? Why don't you go around the world?" Then I asked, very humbly, if I made an investment in his firm—say fifty thousand dollars—could he find me a responsible post. He smiled broadly. It all seemed so easy. "I'll be happy to take your fifty thousand," he said lightly, "but as for finding you anything to do, I'm afraid . . ." Then his secretary came in to say that he was late for lunch.

I stood on a street corner, appearing to wait for the traffic light to change, but I was just waiting. I was staggered. What I wanted to do was to make a sandwich board on which I would list all my grievances. On it I would describe Penumbra's dishonesty, Cora's sorrow, the indignities I had suffered from the maid and gardener, and how cruelly I had been hurled out of the stream of things by a vogue for youth and inexperience. I would hang this sign from my shoulders and march up and down in front of the public library from nine until five, passing out more detailed literature to those who were interested. Throw in a snowstorm, gale winds, and the crash of thunder; I wanted it to be a spectacle.

I then stepped into a side-street restaurant to get a drink and some lunch. It was one of those places where lonely men eat seafood and read the afternoon newspapers and where, in spite of the bath of colored light and distant music, the atmosphere is distinctly contumacious. The headwaiter was a brisk character off the Corso di Roma. He duck-footed, banging down the heels of his Italian shoes, and hunched his shoulders as if his suit jacket bound. He spoke sharply to the bartender, who then whispered to a waiter, "I'll kill him! Someday I'll kill him!" "You and me," whispered the waiter, "we'll kill him together." The hat-check girl joined the whispering. She wanted to kill the manager. The conspirators scattered when the headwaiter returned, but the atmosphere remained mutinous. I drank a cocktail and ordered a salad, and then I overheard the impassioned voice of a man in the booth next to mine. I had nothing better to do than listen. "I go to Minneapolis," he said. "I have to go to Minneapolis, and as soon as I check into the hotel the telephone's ringing. She wants to tell me that the hot-water heater isn't working. There I am in Minneapolis and she's on Long Island and she calls me long distance to say that the hot-water heater isn't working. So then I ask her why doesn't she call the plumber, and then she begins to cry. She cries over long-distance for about fifteen minutes, just because I suggest that she might call the plumber. Well, anyhow, in Minneapolis there's this very good jewelry store, and so I bought her a pair of earrings. Sapphires. Eight hundred dollars. I can't afford this kind of thing, but I can't afford not to buy her presents. I mean, I can make eight hundred dollars in ten minutes, but as the tax lawyer says, I don't take away more than a third of what I make, and so a pair of eight-hundred-dollar earrings cost me around two thousand. Anyway, I get the earrings, and I give them to her when I get home, and we go off to a party at the Barnstables'. When we come home, she's lost one of the earrings. She doesn't know where she lost it. She doesn't care. She won't even call the Barnstables to see if it's lying around on the floor. She doesn't want to disturb them. So then I say it's just like throwing money into the fire, and she begins to cry and says that sapphires are cold stones—that they express my inner coldness toward her. She says there wasn't any love in the present—it wasn't a loving present. All I had to do was to step into a jewelry store and buy them, she says. They didn't cost me anything in thoughtfulness and affection. So then I ask her does she expect me to make her some earrings—does she want me to go to night school and learn how to make one of those crummy silver bracelets they make? Hammered. You know. Every little hammer blow a sign of love and affection. Is that what she wants, for Christ's sake? That's another night when I slept in the guest room. . . ."

I went on eating and listening. I waited for the stranger's companion to enter into the conversation, to make some sound of sympathy or assent, but there was none, and I wondered for a moment if he wasn't talking to himself. I craned my neck around the edge of the booth, but he was too far into the corner for me to see. "She has this money of her own," he went on. "I pay the tax on it, and she spends it all on clothes. She's got hundreds and hundreds of dresses and shoes, and three fur coats, and four wigs. *Four*. But if I buy a suit she tells me I'm being wasteful. I have to buy clothes once in a while. I mean, I can't go to the office looking like a bum. If I buy anything, it's very wasteful. Last year, I bought an umbrella, just so I wouldn't get wet. Wasteful. The year before, I bought a light coat. Wasteful. I can't even buy a phonograph record, because I know I'll catch hell for being so wasteful. On my salary—imagine, on my salary, we can't afford to have bacon for breakfast excepting on Sundays. Bacon is wasteful. But you ought to see her telephone bills. She has this friend, this college roommate. I guess they were very close. She lives in Rome. I don't like her. She was married to this very nice fellow, a good friend of mine, and she just ran him into the ground. She just disposed of him. He's a wreck. Well, now she lives in Rome, and Vera keeps calling her on the telephone. Last month my telephone bills to Rome were over eight hundred dollars. So I said, 'Vera,' I said, 'if you want to talk with your girl chum so much, why don't you just get on a plane and fly to Rome? It would be a lot cheaper.' 'I don't want to go to Rome,' she said. 'I hate Rome. It's noisy and dirty.'

"But you know when I think back over my past, and her past, too, it seems to me that this is a situation with a very long taproot. My grandmother was a very emancipated woman, she was very strong on women's rights. When my mother was thirty-two years old, she went to law school and got her degree. She never practiced. She said she went to law school so she'd have more things in common with Dad, but what she actually did was to destroy, really *destroy* the little tenderness that remained between them. She was almost never at home, and when she was she was always studying for her exams. It was always 'Sh-h-h! Your mother's studying law. . . .' My father was a lonely man, but there's an awful lot of lonely men around. They won't say so, of course. Who tells the truth? You meet an old friend on the street. He looks like hell. It's frightening. His face is gray, and his hair's all falling out, and he's got the shakes. So you say, 'Charlie, Charlie, you're looking *great*.' So then he says, shaking all over, 'I never felt better in my life, *never*.' So then you go your way, and he goes his way.

"I can see that it isn't easy for Vera, but what can I do? Honest to God sometimes I'm afraid she'll hurt me—brain me with a hammer while I'm asleep. Not because it's me, but just because I'm a man. Sometimes I think women today are the most miserable creatures in the history of the world. I mean, they're right in the middle of the ocean. For instance, I caught her smooching with Pete Barnstable in the pantry. That was the night she lost the earring, the night when I came back from Minneapolis. So then when I got home, before I noticed the earring was gone, I said what is this, what is this smooching around with Pete Barnstable? So then she said—*very* emancipated—that no woman could be expected to limit herself to the attentions of one man. So then I said what about me, did that work for me, too? I mean, if she could smooch around with Pete Barnstable, didn't it follow that I could take Mildred Renny out to the parking lot? So then she said I was turning everything she said into filth. She said I had such a dirty mind she couldn't talk with me. After that I noticed she'd lost the earring, and after that we had the scene about how sapphires are such cold stones, and after that . . ."

His voice dropped to a whisper, and at the same time some women in the booth on the other side of me began a noisy and savage attack on a friend they all shared. I was very anxious to see the face of the man behind me, and I called for the check, but when I left the booth he was gone, and I would never know what he looked like.

WHEN I GOT HOME, I put the car in the garage and came into the house by the kitchen door. Cora was at the table, bending over a dish of cutlets. In one hand she held a can of lethal pesticide. I couldn't be sure because I'm so nearsighted, but I think she was sprinkling pesticide on the meat. She was startled when I came in, and by the time I had my glasses on she had put the pesticide on the table. Since I had already made one bad mistake because of my eyesight, I was reluctant to make another, but there was the pesticide on the table beside the dish, and that was not where it belonged. It contained a high percentage of nerve poison. "What in the world are you doing?" I asked.

"What does it look as if I were doing?" she asked, still speaking in the octave above middle C.

"It looks as if you were putting pesticide in the cutlets," I said.

"I know you don't grant me much intelligence," she said, "but please grant me enough intelligence to know better than that."

"But what are you doing with the pesticide?" I asked.

"I have been dusting the roses," she said.

I was routed, in a way, routed and frightened. I guessed that meat heavily dosed with pesticide could be fatal. There was a chance that if I ate the cutlets I might die. The extraordinary fact seemed to be that after twenty years of marriage I didn't know Cora well enough to know whether or not she intended to murder me. I would trust a chance deliveryman or a cleaning woman, but I did not trust Cora. The prevailing winds seemed not to have blown the smoke of battle off our union. I mixed a Martini and went into the living room. I was not in any danger from which I could not readily escape. I could go to the country club for supper. Why I hesitated to do this seems, in retrospect, to have been because of the blue walls of the room in which I stood. It was a handsome room, its long windows looking out onto a lawn, some trees, and the sky. The orderliness of the room seemed to impose some orderliness on my own conduct—as if by absenting myself from the table I would in some way offend the order of things. If I went to the club for supper I would be yielding to my suspicions and damaging my hopefulness, and I was determined to remain hopeful. The blue walls of the room seemed to be some link in the chain of being that I would offend by driving up to the club and eating an open steak sandwich alone in the bar.

I ate one of the cutlets at dinner. It had a peculiar taste, but by this time I couldn't distinguish between my anxieties and the facts involved. I was terribly sick in the night, but this could have been my imagination. I spent an hour in the bathroom with acute indigestion. Cora seemed to be asleep, but when I returned from the bathroom I did notice that her eyes were open. I was worried, and in the morning I made my own breakfast. The maid cooked lunch, and I doubted that she would poison me. I read some more Henry James in the garden, but as the time for dinner approached I found that I was frightened. I went into the pantry to make a drink. Cora had been preparing dinner, and had gone to some other part of the house. There is a broom closet in the kitchen, and I stepped into it and shut the door. Presently I heard Cora's footsteps as she returned. We kept the pesticides for the roses in a cabinet in the kitchen. I heard her open this cabinet. Then she stepped out into the garden, where I heard her dusting the roses. She then returned to the kitchen, but she did not return the pesticide to the closet. My field of vision through the keyhole was limited. Her back was to me as she spiced the meat, and I couldn't tell if she was using salt and pepper or nerve poison. She then went back to the garden, and I stepped out of the broom closet. The pesticide was not on the table. I went into the living room, and entered the dining room from there when dinner was ready. "Isn't it hot," I asked when I sat down.

"Well," said Cora, "we can't expect to be comfortable, can we, if we hide in broom closets?"

I hung on to my chair, picked at my food, made some small talk, and got through the meal. Now and then she gave me a serene and wicked smile. After dinner I went into the garden. I desperately needed help, and thought then of my daughter. I should explain that Flora graduated from the Villa Mimosa in Florence, and left Smith College in the middle of her freshman year to live in a Lower East Side tenement with a sexual freak. I send her an allowance each month and have promised to leave her alone, but, considering the dangerousness of my position, I felt free to break my promise. I felt that if I could see her I could persuade her to come home. I telephoned her then and said that I must see her. She seemed quite friendly and asked me to come to tea.

I had lunch in town the next day, and spent the afternoon at my club, playing cards and drinking whiskey. Flora had given me directions, and I went downtown on the subway for the first time in I don't know how many years. It was all very strange. I've often thought of going to visit my only daughter and her own true love, and now at last I was making this journey. In my reveries the meeting would take place in some club. He would come from a good family. Flora would be happy; she would have the shining face of a young girl first in love. The boy would be serious, but not too serious; intelligent, handsome, and with the winning posture of someone who stands literally at the threshold of a career. I could see the fatuity in these reveries, but had they been so vulgar and idle that I deserved to have them contravened at every point—the scene changed from a club to the city's worst slum and the substitution of a freak with a beard for an earnest young man? I had friends whose daughters married suitable young men from suitable families. Envy struck me in the crowded subway, then petulance. Why had I been singled out for this disaster? I loved my daughter. The power of love I felt for her seemed pure, strong, and natural. Suddenly I felt like crying. Every sort of door had been open for her, she had seen the finest landscapes, she had enjoyed, I thought, the company of those people who were most free to develop their gifts.

It was raining when I left the subway. I followed her directions through a slum to a tenement. I guessed the building to be about eighty years old. Two polished marble columns supported a Romanesque arch. It even had a name. It was called the Eden. I saw the angel with the flaming sword, the naked couple, stooped, their hands over their privates. Masaccio? That was when we went to visit her in Florence. So I entered Eden like an avenging angel, but once under the Romanesque arch I found a corridor as narrow as the companionway in a submarine, and the power of light over my spirits—always considerable—was in this case very depressing, the lights in the hall were so primitive and sorry. Flights of stairs often appear in my dreams, and the stairs I began to climb had a galling look of unreality. I heard Spanish spoken, the roar of water from a toilet, music, and the barking of dogs.

Moved by anger, or perhaps by the drinks I had had at the club, I went up three or four flights at a brisk clip and then found myself suddenly winded; forced to stop short in my cilmb and engage in a humiliating struggle for breath. It was several minutes before I could continue, and I went the rest of the way slowly. Flora had tacked one of her calling cards to the door. I knocked. "Hi, Daddy," she said brightly, and I kissed her on the brow. Oh, this much of it was good, fresh, and strong. I felt a burst of memory, a recollection of all the happiness we had shared. The door opened onto a kitchen and beyond this was another room. "I want you to meet Peter," she said.

"Hi," said Peter.

"How do you do," I said.

"See what we've made," said Flora. "Isn't it divine? We've just finished it. It was Peter's idea."

What they had made, what they had done was to purchase a skeleton with an armature from a medical supply house and glue butterflies here and there to the polished bone. I recognized some of the specimens from my youth and recognized that I would not at that time have been able to afford them. There was a Catagramme Astarte on the shoulder bone, a Sapphira in one eye socket, and a large cluster of Appia Zarinda at the pubis. "Marvelous," I said, "marvelous," trying to conceal my distaste. Compared to the useful tasks of life, the thought of these two grown people gluing expensive butterflies to the polished bones of some poor stranger made me intensely irritable. I sat in a canvas chair and smiled at Flora. "How are you, my dear?"

"Oh, I'm fine, Daddy," she said. "I'm *fine*."

I kept myself from remarking on either her clothing or her hair. She was dressed all in black, and her hair was straight. The purpose of this costume or uniform escaped me. It was not becoming. It did not appeal to the senses. It seemed to reflect on her self-esteem; it seemed like a costume of mourning or penance, a declaration of her indifference to the silks that I enjoy on women; but what were her reasons for despising finery? His costume was much more bewildering. Was its origin Italian? I wondered. The shoes were effeminate, and the jacket was short, but he looked more like a street boy in nineteenth-century London than someone on the Corso. That would be excepting his hair. He had a beard, a mustache, and long dark curls that reminded me of some minor apostle in a third-rate Passion Play. His face was not effeminate, but it was delicate, and seemed to me to convey a marked lack of commitment.

"Would you like some coffee, Daddy?" Flora asked.

"No, thank you, dear," I said. "Is there anything to drink?"

"We don't have anything," she said.

"Would Peter be good enough to go out and get me something?" I asked.

"I guess so," Peter said glumly, and I told myself that he was probably not intentionally rude. I gave him a ten-dollar bill and asked him to get me some bourbon.

"I don't think they have bourbon," he said.

"Well, then, Scotch," I said.

"They drink mostly wine in the neighborhood," Peter said.

Then I settled on him a clear, kindly gaze, thinking that I would have him murdered. From what I know of the world there are still assassins to be hired, and I would pay someone to put a knife in his back or push him off a roof. My smile was broad, clear, and genuinely murderous, and the boy slipped into a green coat—another piece of mummery—and went out.

"You don't like him?" Flora asked.

"I despise him," I said.

"But, Daddy, you don't *know* him," Flora said.

"My dear, if I knew him any better I would wring his neck."

"He's very kind and sensitive—he's very generous."

"I can see that he's very sensitive," I said.

"He's the kindest person I've ever known," Flora said.

"I'm glad to hear that," I said, "but let's talk about you now, shall we? I didn't come here to talk about Peter."

"But we're living together, Daddy."

"So I've been told. But the reason I came here, Flora, is to find out about you—what your plans are and so forth. I won't disapprove of your plans, whatever they are. I simply want to know what they are. You can't spend the rest of your life gluing butterflies to skeletons. All I want to know is what you plan to do with your life."

"I don't know, Daddy." She raised her face. "Nobody my age knows."

"I'm not taking a consensus of your generation. I am asking you. I am asking you what you would like to make of your life. I am asking you what ideas you have, what dreams you have, what hopes you have for yourself."

"I don't know, Daddy. Nobody my age knows."

"I wish you would eliminate the rest of your generation. I am acquainted with at least fifty girls your age who know precisely what they want to do. They want to be historians, editors, doctors, housewives, and mothers. They want to do something useful."

Peter came back with a bottle of bourbon but he did not return any change. Was this cupidity, I wondered, or absent-mindedness? I said nothing. Flora brought me a glass and some water, and I asked if they would join me in a drink.

"We don't drink much," Peter said.

"Well, I'm glad to hear that," I said. "While you were out, I talked with Flora about her plans. That is, I discovered that she doesn't have any plans, and since she doesn't I'm going to take her back to Bullet Park with me until her thinking is a little more decisive."

"I'm going to stay with Peter," Flora said.

"But supposing Peter had to go away?" I asked. "Suppose Peter had some interesting offer, such as six months or a year abroad—what would you do then?"

"Oh, Daddy," she asked, "you wouldn't do that, would you?"

"Oh yes I would, I most certainly would," I said. "I would do anything on heaven or earth that I thought might bring you to your senses. Would you like to go abroad, Peter?"

"I don't know," he said. His face could not be said to have brightened, but for a moment his intelligence seemed engaged. "I'd like to go to East Berlin," he said.

"Why?"

"I'd like to go to East Berlin and give my American passport to some great creative person," he said, "some writer or musician, and let him escape to the free world."

"Why," I asked, "don't you paint Peace on your arse and jump off a twelve-story building?"

This was a mistake, a disaster, a catastrophe, and I poured myself some more bourbon. "I'm sorry," I said. "I'm tired. However, my offer still stands. If you want to go to Europe, Peter, I'll be happy to pay your bills."

"Oh, I don't know," Peter said. "I've been. I mean, I've seen most of it."

"Well, keep it in mind," I said. "And as for you, Flora, I want you to come home with me. Come home for a week or two, anyhow. That's all I ask. Ten years from now you will reproach me for not having guided you out of this mess. Ten years from now you'll ask me, 'Daddy, Daddy, oh, Daddy, why didn't you teach me not to spend the best years of my life in a slum?' I can't bear the thought of you coming to me ten years from now, to blame me for not having forced you to take my advice."

"I won't go home."

"You can't stay here."

"I can if I want."

"I will stop your allowance."

"I can get a job."

"What kind of a job? You can't type, you can't take shorthand, you don't know the first thing about any sort of business procedure, you can't even run a switchboard."

"I can get a job as a filing clerk."

"Oh my God!" I roared. "Oh my God! After the sailing lessons and the skiing lessons, after the get-togethers and the cotillion, after the year in Florence and the long summers at the sea—after all this it turns out that what you really want is to be a spinster filing clerk with a low civil-service rating, whose principal excitement is to go once or twice a year to a fourth-rate Chinese restaurant with a dozen other spinster filing clerks and get tipsy on two sweet Manhattans."

I fell back into my chair and poured myself some more whiskey. There was a sharp pain in my heart, as if that lumpy organ had weathered every abuse, only to be crippled by misery. The pain was piercing, and I thought I would die—not at that moment, in the canvas chair, but a few days later, perhaps in Bullet Park, or in some comfortable hospital bed. The idea did not alarm me; it was a consolation. I would die, and with those areas of tension that I represented finally removed, my only, only daughter would at last take up her life. My sudden disappearance from the scene would sober her with sorrow and misgiving. My death would mature her. She would go back to Smith, join the glee club, edit the newspaper, befriend girls of her own class, and marry some intelligent and visionary young man, who seemed, at the moment, to be wearing spectacles, and raise three or four sturdy children. She would be sorry. That was it, and overnight sorrow would show her the inutility of living in a slum with a stray.

"Go home, Daddy," she said. She was crying. "Go home, Daddy, and leave us alone! Please go home, Daddy."

"I've always tried to understand you," I said. "You used to put four or five records on the player at Bullet Park, and as soon as the music began you'd walk out of the house. I never understood why you did this, but one night I went out of the house to see if I could find you, and, walking down the lawn, with the music coming from all the open windows, I thought I did understand. I mean, I thought you put the records on and left the house because you liked to hear the music pouring out of the windows. I mean, I thought you liked at the end of your walk to come back to a house where music was playing. I was right, wasn't I? I understand that much?"

"Go home, Daddy," she said. "Please go home."

"And it isn't only you, Flora," I said. "I need you. I need you terribly."

"Go home, Daddy," she said, and so I did.

I HAD SOME SUPPER in town and came home at around ten. I could hear Cora drawing a bath upstairs, and I took a shower in the bathroom off the kitchen. When I went upstairs, Cora was sitting at her dressing table, brushing her hair. Now, I have neglected to say that Cora is beautiful, and that I love her. She has ash-blond hair, dark brows, full lips, and eyes that are so astonishingly large, volatile, and engaging, so strikingly set, that I sometimes think she might take them off and put them between the pages of a book; leave them on a table. The white is a light blue and the blue itself is of unusual depth. She is a graceful woman, not tall. She smokes continuously and has for most of her life, but she handles her cigarettes with a charming clumsiness, as if this entrenched habit were something she had just picked up. Her arms, legs, front, everything is beautifully proportioned. I love her, and, loving her, I know that love is not a reasonable process. I had not expected or wanted to fall in love when I first saw her at a wedding in the country. Cora was one of the attendants. The wedding was in a garden. A five-piece orchestra in tuxedos was half hidden in the rhododendrons. From the tent on the hill you could hear the caterer's men icing wine in wash buckets. She was the second to come, and was wearing one of those outlandish costumes that are designed for bridal parties, as if holy matrimony had staked out some unique and mysterious place for itself in sumptuary history. Her dress was blue, as I remember, with things hanging off it, and she wore over her pale hair a broad-brimmed hat that had no crown at all. She wobbled over the lawn in her high-heeled shoes, staring shyly and miserably into a bunch of blue flowers, and when she had reached her position she raised her face and smiled shyly at the guests, and I saw for the first time the complexity and enormousness of her eyes; felt for the first time that she might take them off and put them into a pocket. "Who is she?" I asked aloud. "Who *is* she?" "Sh-h-h," someone said. I was enthralled. My heart and my spirit leaped. I saw absolutely nothing of the rest of the wedding, and when the ceremony was over I raced up the lawn and introduced myself to her. I was not content with anything until she agreed to marry me, a year later.

Now my heart and my spirit leaped as I watched her comb her hair. A few days ago I had thought that she had retreated into the water of a goldfish bowl. I had suspected her of attempted murder. How could I embrace decently and with the full ardor of my body and mind someone I suspected of murder? Was I embracing despair, was this an obscene passion, had I at that wedding so many years ago seen not beauty at all, but cruelty in her large eyes? I had made her, in my imagination, a goldfish, a murderess, and now when I took her in my arms she was a swan, a flight of stairs, a fountain, the unpatrolled, unguarded boundaries to paradise.

But I awoke at three, feeling terribly sad, and feeling rebelliously that I didn't want to study sadness, madness, melancholy, and despair. I wanted to study triumphs, the rediscoveries of love, all that I know in the world to be decent, radiant, and clear. Then the word "love," the impulse to love, welled up in me somewhere above my middle. Love seemed to flow from me in all directions, abundant as water—love for Cora, love for Flora, love for all my friends and neighbors, love for Penumbra. This tremendous flow of vitality could not be contained within its spelling, and I seemed to seize a laundry marker and write "Luve" on the wall. I wrote "luve" on the staircase, "luve" on the pantry, "luve" on the oven, the washing machine, and the coffeepot, and when Cora came down in the morning (I would be nowhere around) everywhere she looked she would read "luve," "luve," "luve." Then I saw a green meadow and a sparkling stream. On the ridge there were thatched-roof cottages and a square church tower, so I knew it must be England. I climbed up from the meadow to the streets of the village, looking for the cottage where Cora and Flora would be waiting for me. There seemed to have been some mistake. No one knew their names. I asked at the post office, but the answer here was the same. Then it occurred to me that they would be at the manor house. How stupid I had been! I left the village and walked up a sloping lawn to a Georgian house, where a butler let me in. The squire was entertaining. There were twenty-five or thirty people in the hall, drinking sherry. I took a glass from a tray and looked through the gathering for Flora and my wife, but they were not there. Then I thanked my host and walked down the broad lawn, back to the meadow and the sparkling brook, where I lay on the grass and fell into a sweet sleep.

MARITO IN CITTÀ

SOME YEARS AGO there was a popular song in Italy called "Marito in Città." The air was as simple and catching as a street song. The words went, *"La moglie ce ne va, marito poverino, solo in cittadina,"* and dealt with the plight of a man alone, in the lighthearted and farcical manner that seems traditional, as if to be alone were an essentially comic situation such as getting tangled up in a trout line. Mr. Estabrook had heard the song while traveling in Europe with his wife (fourteeen days; ten cities) and some capricious tissue of his memory had taken an indelible impression of the words and the music. He had not forgotten it; indeed, it seemed that he could not forget it, although it was in conflict with his regard for the possibilities of aloneness.

The scene, the moment when his wife and four children left for the mountains, had the charm, the air of ordination, and the deceptive simplicity of an old-fashioned magazine cover. One could have guessed at it all—the summer morning, the station wagon, the bags, the clear-eyed children, the filled change rack for toll stations, some ceremonious observation of a change in the season, another ring in the planet's age. He shook hands with his sons and kissed his wife and his daughters and watched the car move along the driveway with a feeling that this instant was momentous, that had he been given the power to scrutinize the forces that were involved he would have arrived at something like a revelation. The women and children of Rome, Paris, London, and New York were, he knew, on their way to the highlands or the sea. It was a weekday, and so he locked Scamper, the dog, into the kitchen and drove to the station singing, *"Marito in città, la moglie ce ne va,"* et cetera, et cetera.

One knows how it will go, of course; it will never quite

transcend the farcical strictures of a street song, but Mr. Estabrook's aspirations were earnest, fresh, and worth observing. He was familiar with the vast and evangelical literature of solitude, and he intended to exploit the weeks of his aloneness. He could clean his telescope and study the stars. He could read. He could practice the Bach two-part variations on the piano. He could—so like an expatriate who claims that the limpidity and sometimes the anguish of his estrangement promises a high degree of self-discovery—learn more about himself. He would observe the migratory habits of birds, the changes in the garden, the clouds in the sky. He had a distinct image of himself, his powers of observation greatly heightened by the adventure of aloneness. When he got home on his first night, he found that Scamper had got out of the kitchen and slept on a sofa in the living room, which he had covered with mud and hair. Scamper was a mongrel, the children's pet. Mr. Estabrook spoke reproachfully to the dog and turned up the sofa cushions. The next problem that he faced was one that is seldom touched on in the literature of solitude—the problem of his rudimentary appetites. This was to sound, in spite of himself, the note of low comedy, O, *marito in città*. He could imagine himself in clean chinos, setting up his telescope in the garden at dusk, but he could not imagine who was going to feed this self-possessed figure.

He fried himself some eggs, but he found that he couldn't eat them. He made an Old-Fashioned cocktail with particular care and drank it. Then he returned to the eggs, but he still found them revolting. He drank another cocktail and approached the eggs from a different direction, but they were still repulsive. He gave the eggs to Scamper and drove out to the state highway, where there was a restaurant. The music, when he entered the place, seemed as loud as parade music, and a waitress was standing on a chair, stringing curtains onto a rod. "I'll be with you in a minute," she said. "Sit down anywheres." He chose a place at one of the forty empty tables. He was not actually disappointed in his situation, he had by design surrounded himself with a large number of men, women, and children, and it was only natural that he should feel then, as he did, not alone but lonely. Considering the physical and spiritual repercussions of this condition, it seemed strange to him that there was only one word for it. He was lonely, and he was in pain. The food was not just bad; it seemed incredible. Here was that total absence of recollection that is the essence of tastelessness. He could eat nothing. He stirred up his stringy pepper steak and ordered some ice cream, to spare the feelings of the waitress. The food reminded him of all those who through clumsiness or bad luck must make their lives alone and eat this fare each night. It was frightening, and he went to a movie.

The long summer dusk still filled the air with a soft light. The wishing star hung above the enormous screen, canted a little toward the audience with a certain air of doom. Faded in the fading light, the figures and animals of a cartoon chased one another across the screen, exploded, danced, sang, pratfell. The fanfare and the credits for the feature he had come to see went on through the last of the twilight, and then, as night fell, a screenplay of incredible asininity began to unfold. His moral indignation at this confluence of hunger, boredom, and loneliness was violent, and he thought sadly of the men who had been obliged to write the movie, and of the hard-working actors who were paid to repeat these crude lines. He could see them at the end of the day, getting out of their convertibles in Beverly Hills, utterly discouraged. Fifteen minutes was all he could stand, and he went home.

Scamper had shifted from the dismantled sofa to a chair, whose light silk covering he had dirtied with hair and mud. "Bad Scamper," Mr. Estabrook said, and then he took those precautions to save the furniture that he was to repeat each night. He upended a footstool on the sofa, upended the silk chairs, put a wastebasket on the love seat in the hallway, and put the upholstered dining-room chairs upside down on the table, as they do in restaurants when the floor is being mopped. With the lights off and everything upside down, the permanence of his house was challenged, and he felt for a moment like a ghost who has come back to see time's ruin.

Lying in bed he thought, quite naturally, of his wife. He had learned, from experience, that it was sensible to make their separations ardent, and on the day but one before they left, he had declared himself; but Mrs. Estabrook was tired. On the next night, he declared himself again. Mrs. Estabrook seemed acquiescent, but what she then did was to go down to the kitchen, put four heavy blankets into the washing machine, blow a fuse, and flood the floor. Standing in the kitchen doorway, utterly unaccommodated, he wondered why she did this. She had merely meant to be elusive! Watching her, a dignified but rather heavy woman, mopping up the kitchen floor, he thought that she had wanted, like any nymph, to run through the bosky—dappled her back, the water flashing at her feet—and being short-winded these days, and there being no bosky, she had been reduced to putting blankets into a washing machine. It had never crossed his mind before that the passion to be elusive was as strong in her sex as the passion to pursue was in his. This glimpse of things moved him; contented him, in a way; but was, as it so happened, the only contentment he had that night.

The image of a cleanly, self-possessed man exploiting his solitude was not easy to come by, but then he had not expected that it would be. On the next night, he practiced the two-part variations until eleven. On the night after that, he got out his telescope. He had been unable to solve the problem of feeding himself, and in the space of a week had lost more than fifteen pounds. His trousers, when he belted them in around his middle, gathered in folds like a shirt. He took three pairs of trousers down to the dry cleaner's in the village. It was past closing time, but the proprietor was still there, a man crushed by life. He had torn Mrs. Hazelton's lace pillowcases and lost Mr. Fitch's silk shirts. His equipment was in hock, the union wanted health insurance, and everything that he ate—even yoghurt—seemed to turn to fire in his esophagus. He spoke despairingly to Mr. Estabrook. "We don't keep a tailor on the premises no more, but there's a woman up on Maple Avenue who does alterations. Mrs. Zagreb. It's at the corner of Maple Avenue and Clinton Street. There's a sign in the window."

It was a dark night and that time of year when there are many fireflies. Maple Avenue was what it claimed to be, and the dense foliage doubled the darkness on the street. The house on the corner was frame, with a porch.

The maples were so thick there that no grass grew on the lawn. There was a sign—ALTERATIONS—in the window. He rang a bell. "Just a minute," someone called. The voice was strong and gay. A woman opened the door with one hand, rubbing a towel in her dark hair with the other. She seemed surprised to see him. "Come in," she said, "come in. I've just washed my hair." There was a small hall, and he followed her through this into a small living room. "I have some trousers that I want taken in," he said. "Do you do that kind of thing?"

"I do everything," she laughed. "But why are you losing weight? Are you on a diet?"

She had put down her towel, but she continued to shake her hair and rough it with her fingers. She moved around the room while she talked, and seemed to fill the room with restlessness—a characteristic that might have annoyed him in someone else but that in her seemed graceful, fascinating, the prompting of some inner urgency.

"I'm not dieting," he said.

"You're not ill?" Her concern was swift and genuine; he might have been her oldest friend.

"Oh, no. It's just that I've been trying to cook for myself."

"Oh, you poor boy," she said. "Do you know your measurements?"

"No."

"Well, we'll have to take them."

Moving, stirring the air and shaking her hair, she crossed the room and got a yellow tape measure from a drawer. In order to measure his waist she had to put her hands under his jacket—a gesture that seemed amorous. When the measure was around his waist, he put his arms around her waist and thrust himself against her. She merely laughed and shook her hair. Then she pushed him away lightly, much more like a promise than a rebuff. "Oh, no," she said, "not tonight, not tonight, my dear." She crossed the room and faced him from there. Her face was tender, and darkened with indecision, but when he came toward her she hung her head, shook it vigorously. "No, no, no," she said. "Not tonight. Please."

"But I can see you again?"

"Of course, but not tonight." She crossed the room and

laid her hand against his cheek. "Now, you go," she said, "and I'll call you. You're very nice, but now you go."

He stumbled out of the door, stunned but feeling wonderfully important. He had been in the room three minutes, four at the most, and what had there been between them, this instantaneous recognition of their fitness as lovers? He had been excited when he first saw her—had been excited by her strong, gay voice. Why had they been able to move so effortlessly, so directly toward one another? And where was his sense of good and evil, his passionate desire to be worthy, manly, and, within his vows, chaste? He was a member of the Church of Christ, he was a member of the vestry, a devout and habitual communicant, sincerely sworn to defend the articles of faith. He had already committed a mortal sin. But driving under the maples and through the summer night, he could not, under the most intense examination, find anything in his instincts but goodness and magnanimity and a much enlarged sense of the world. He struggled with some scrambled eggs, practiced the variations, and tried to sleep. *"O, marito in città!"*

It was the memory of Mrs. Zagreb's front that tormented him. Its softness and fragrance seemed to hang in the air while he waited for sleep, it followed into his dreams, and when he woke his face seemed buried in Mrs. Zagreb's front, glistening like marble and tasting to his thirsty lips as various and soft as the airs of a summer night.

In the morning, he took a cold shower, but Mrs. Zagreb's front seemed merely to wait outside the shower curtain. It rested against his cheek as he drove to the train, read over his shoulder as he rode the eight-thirty-three, jiggled along with him through the shuttle and the downtown train, and haunted him through the business day. He thought he was going mad. As soon as he got home, he looked up her number in the *Social Register* that his wife kept by the telephone. This was a mistake, of course, but he found her number in a local directory and called her. "Your trousers are ready," she said. "You can come and get them whenever you want. Now, if you'd like."

She called for him to come in. He found her in the living room, and she handed him his trousers. Then he was shy and wondered if he hadn't invented the night before. Here, with his shyness, was the truth, and all the rest had been imagining. Here was a widowed seamstress handing some trousers to a lonely man, no longer young, in a frame house that needed paint on Maple Avenue. The world was ruled by common sense, legitimate passions, and articles of faith. She shook her head. This then was a mannerism and had nothing to do with washing her hair. She pushed it off her forehead; ran her fingers through the dark curls. "If you have time for a drink," she said, "there's everything in the kitchen."

"I'd love a drink," he said. "Will you have one with me?"

"I'll have a whiskey and soda," she said.

Feeling sad, heavyhearted, important, caught up on those streams of feeling that never surface, he went into the kitchen and made their drinks. When he came back into the room, she was sitting on a sofa, and he joined her there; seemed immersed in her mouth, as if it was a maelstrom; spun around thrice and sped down the length of some stupendous timelessness. The dialogue of sudden love doesn't seem to change much from country to country. We say across the pillow, in any language, "Hullo, hullo, hullo, hullo, hullo," as if we were involved in some interminable and tender transoceanic telephone conversation, and the adulteress, taking the adulterer into her arms, will cry, "Oh, my love, why are you so bitter?" She praised his hair, his neck, the declivity in his back. She smelled faintly of soap—no perfume—and when he said so she said softly, "But I never wear perfume when I'm going to make love." They went side by side up the narrow stairs to her room—the largest room in a small house, but small at that, and sparsely furnished, like a room in a summer cottage, with old furniture that had been painted white and with a worn white rug. Her suppleness, her wiles, seemed to him like a staggering source of purity. He thought he had never known so pure, gallant, courageous, and easy a spirit. So they kept saying "Hullo, hullo, hullo, hullo" until three, when she made him leave.

He walked in his garden at half past three or four.

There was a quarter moon, the air was soft and the light vaporous, the clouds formed like a beach and the stars were strewn among them like shells and moraine. Some flower that blooms in July—phlox or nicotiana—had scented the air, and the meaning of the vaporous light had not much changed since he was an adolescent; it now, as it had then, seemed to hold out the opportunities of romantic love. But what about the strictures of his faith? He had broken a sacred commandment, broken it repeatedly, joyously, and would break it at every opportunity he was given; therefore, he had committed a mortal sin, and must be denied the sacraments of his church. But he could not alter the feeling that Mrs. Zagreb, in her knowledgeableness, represented uncommon purity and virtue. But if these were his genuine feelings, then he must resign from the vestry, the church, improvise his own schemes of good and evil, and look for a life beyond the articles of faith. Had he known other adulterers to take Communion? He had. Was his church a social convenience, a sign of deliquescence and hypocrisy, a means of getting ahead? Were the stirring words said at weddings and funerals no more than customs and no more religious than the custom of taking off one's hat in the elevator at Brooks Brothers when a woman enters the car? Christened, reared, and drilled in church dogma, the thought of giving up his faith was unimaginable. It was his best sense of the miraculousness of life, the receipt of a vigorous and omniscient love, widespread and incandescent as the light of day. Should he ask the suffragan bishop to reassess the Ten Commandments, to include in their prayers some special reference to the feelings of magnanimity and love that follow sexual engorgements?

He walked in the garden, conscious of the fact that she had at least given him the illusion of playing an important romantic role, a lead, a thrilling improvement over the sundry messengers, porters, and clowns of monogamy, and there was no doubt about the fact that her praise had turned his head. Was her excitement over the declivity in his back cunning, sly, a pitiless exploitation of the enormous and deep-buried vanity in men? The sky had begun to lighten, and undressing for bed he looked at himself in the mirror. Yes, her praise had all been lies. His abdomen had a dismal sag. Or had it? He held it in, distended it, examined it full face and profile, and went to bed.

THE NEXT DAY was Saturday, and he made a schedule for himself. Cut the lawns, clip the hedges, split some firewood, and paint the storm windows. He worked contentedly until five, when he took a shower and made a drink. His plan was to scramble some eggs and, since the sky was clear, set up his telescope, but when he had finished his drink he went humbly to the telephone and called Mrs. Zagreb. He called her at intervals of fifteen minutes until after dark, and then he got into his car and drove over to Maple Avenue. A light was burning in her bedroom. The rest of the house was dark. A large car with a state seal beside the license plate was parked under the maples, and a chauffeur was asleep in the front seat.

He had been asked to take the collection at Holy Communion, and so he did, but, when he got to his knees to make his general confession, he could not admit that what he had done was an offense to divine majesty; the burden of his sins was not intolerable; the memory of them was anything but grievous. He improvised a heretical thanksgiving for the constancy and intelligence of his wife, the clear eyes of his children, and the suppleness of his mistress. He did not take Communion, and when the priest fired a questioning look in his direction, he was tempted to say clearly, "I am unashamedly involved in an adultery." He read the papers until eleven, when he called Mrs. Zagreb and she said he could come whenever he wanted. He was there in ten minutes, and made her bones crack as soon as he entered the house. "I came by last night," he said.

"I thought you might," she said. "I know a lot of men. Do you mind?"

"Not at all," he said.

"Someday," she said, "I'm going to take a piece of paper and write on it everything that I know about men. And then I'll put it into the fireplace and burn it."

"You don't have a fireplace," he said.

"That's so," she said, but they said nothing much else for the rest of the afternoon and half the night but "Hullo, hullo, hullo, hullo."

When he came home the next evening, there was a letter from his wife on the hall table. He seemed to see directly through the envelope into its contents. In it she would explain intelligently and dispassionately that her old lover, Olney Pratt, had returned from Saudi Arabia and asked her to marry him. She wanted her freedom, and she hoped he would understand. She and Olney had never ceased loving one another, and they would be dishonest to their innermost selves if they denied this love another day. She was sure they could reach an agreement on the custody of the children. He had been a good provider and a patient man, but she did not wish ever to see him again.

He held the letter in his hand thinking that his wife's handwriting expressed her femininity, her intelligence, her depth; it was the hand of a woman asking for freedom. He tore the letter open, fully prepared to read about Olney Pratt, but he read instead: "Dear Lover-bear, the nights are *terribly* cold, and I *miss* . . ." On and on it went for two pages. He was still reading when the doorbell rang. It was Doris Hamilton, a neighbor. "I know you don't answer the telephone, and I know you don't like to dine out," she said, "but I'm determined that you should have at least one good dinner this month, and I've come to shanghai you."

"Well," he said.

"Now you march upstairs and take a shower, and I'll make myself a drink," she said. "We're going to have hot boiled lobster. Aunt Molly sent down a bushel this morning, and you'll have to help us eat them. Eddie has to go to the doctor after dinner, and you can go home whenever you like."

He went upstairs and did as he was told. When he had changed and come down, she was in the living room with a drink, and they drove over to her house in separate cars. They dined by candlelight off a table in the garden, and, washed and in a clean duck suit, he found himself contented with the role he had so recently and so passionately abdicated. It was not a romantic lead, but it had some subtle prominence. After dinner, Eddie excused himself and went off to see his psychiatrist, as he did three nights each week. "I don't suppose you've seen anyone," Doris said. "I don't suppose you know the gossip."

"I really haven't seen anyone."

"I know. I've heard you practicing the piano. Well, Lois Spinner is suing Frank, and suing the buttons off him."

"Why?"

"Well, he's been carrying on with this disgusting slut, a perfectly disgusting woman. His older son, Ralph—he's a marvelous boy—saw them together in a restaurant. They were *feeding* each other. None of his children want to see him again."

"Men have had mistresses before," he said tentatively.

"Adultery is a mortal sin," she said gaily, "and was punished in many societies with death."

"Do you feel this strongly about divorce?"

"Oh, he had no intention of marrying the pig. He simply thought he could play his dirty games, humiliate, disgrace, and wound his family and return to their affections when he got bored. The divorce was not his idea. He's begged Lois not to divorce him. I believe he's threatened to kill himself."

"I've known men," he said, "to divide their attentions between a mistress and a wife."

"I daresay you've never known it to be done successfully," she said.

The fell truth in this had never quite appeared to him. "Adultery is a commonplace," he said. "It is the subject of most of our literature, most of our plays, our movies. Popular songs are written about it."

"You wouldn't want to confuse your life with a French farce, would you?"

The authority with which she spoke astonished him. Here was the irresistibility of the lawful world, the varsity team, the best club. Suddenly, the image of Mrs. Zagreb's bedroom, whose bleakness had seemed to him so poignant, returned to him in an unsavory light. He remembered that the window curtains were torn and that those hands that had so praised him were coarse and stubby. The promiscuity that he had thought to be the wellspring of her pureness now seemed to be an incurable illness. The kindnesses she had showed him seemed perverse and disgusting. She had groveled before his nakedness. Sitting in the summer night, in his clean clothes, he thought of Mrs. Estabrook, serene and refreshed, leading her four intelligent and handsome children across some gallery in his head. Adultery was the raw material of farce, popular music, madness, and self-destruction.

"It was terribly nice of you to have had me," he said. "And now I think I'll run along. I'll practice the piano before I go to bed."

"I'll listen," said Doris. "I can hear it quite clearly across the garden."

The telephone was ringing when he came in. "I'm alone," said Mrs. Zagreb, "and I thought you might like a drink." He was there in a few minutes, went once more to the bottom of the sea, into that stupendous timelessness, secured against the pain of living. But, when it was time to go, he said that he could not see her again. "That's perfectly all right," she said. And then, "Did anyone ever fall in love with you?"

"Yes," he said, "once. It was a couple of years ago. I had to go out to Indianapolis to set up a training schedule, and I had to stay with these people—it was part of the job—and there was this terribly nice woman, and every time she saw me she'd start crying. She cried at breakfast. She cried all through cocktails and dinner. It was awful. I had to move to a hotel, and naturally, I couldn't ever tell anyone."

"Good night," she said, "good night and goodbye."

"Good night, my love," he said, "good night and goodbye."

HIS WIFE CALLED the next night while he was setting up the telescope. Oh, what excitement! They were driving down the next day. His daughter was going to announce her engagement to Frank Emmet. They wanted to be married before Christmas. Photographs had to be taken, announcements sent to the papers, a tent must be rented, wine ordered, et cetera. And his son had won the sailboat races on Monday, Tuesday, and Wednesday. "Good night, my darling," his wife said, and he fell into a chair, profoundly gratified at this requital of so many of his aspirations. He loved his daughter, he liked Frank Emmet, he even liked Frank Emmet's parents, who were rich, and the thought of his beloved son at the tiller, bringing his boat down the last tack toward the committee launch, filled him with great cheer. And Mrs. Zagreb? She wouldn't know how to sail. She would get tangled up in the mainsheet, vomit to windward, and pass out in the cabin once they were past the point. She wouldn't know how to play tennis. Why, she wouldn't even know how to ski! Then, watched by Scamper, he dismantled the living room. In the hallway, he put a wastebasket on the love seat. In the dining room, he upended the chairs on the table and turned out the lights. Walking through the dismantled house, he felt again the chill and bewilderment of someone who has come back to see time's ruin. Then he went up to bed, singing. *"Marito in città, la moglie ce ne va, o povero marito!"*

THE GEOMETRY OF LOVE

IT WAS ONE of those rainy late afternoons when the toy department of Woolworth's on Fifth Avenue is full of women who appear to have been taken in adultery and who are now shopping for a present to carry home to their youngest child. On this particular afternoon there were eight or ten of them—comely, fragrant, and well dressed—but with the pained air of women who have recently been undone by some cad in a midtown hotel room and who are now on their way home to the embraces of a tender child. It was Charlie Mallory, walking away from the hardware department, where he had bought a screwdriver, who reached this conclusion. There was no morality involved. He hit on this generalization mostly to give the lassitude of a rainy afternoon some intentness and color. Things were slow at his office. He had spent the time since lunch repairing a filing cabinet. Thus the screwdriver. Having settled on this conjecture, he looked more closely into the faces of the women and seemed to find there some affirmation of his fantasy. What but the engorgments and chagrins of adultery could have left them all looking so spiritual, so tearful? Why should they sigh so deeply as they fingered the playthings of innocence? One of the women wore a fur coat that looked like a coat he had bought his wife, Mathilda, for Christmas. Looking more closely, he saw that it was not only Mathilda's coat, it was Mathilda. "Why, Mathilda," he cried, "what in the world are you doing here?"

She raised her head from the wooden duck she had been studying. Slowly, slowly, the look of chagrin on her face shaded into anger and scorn. "I detest being spied upon," she said. Her voice was strong, and the other women shoppers looked up, ready for anything.

Mallory was at a loss. "But I'm not spying on you, darling," he said. "I only—"

"I can't think of anything more despicable," she said, "than following people through the streets." Her mien and her voice were operatic, and her audience was attentive and rapidly being enlarged by shoppers from the hardware and garden-furniture sections. "To hound an innocent woman through the streets is the lowest, sickest, and most vile of occupations."

"But, darling, I just happened to be here."

Her laughter was pitiless. "You just happened to be hanging around the toy department at Woolworth's? Do you expect me to believe that?"

"I was in the hardware department," he said, "but it doesn't really matter. Why don't we have a drink together and take an early train?"

"I wouldn't drink or travel with a spy," she said. "I am going to leave this store now, and if you follow or harass me in any way, I shall have you arrested by the police and thrown into jail." She picked up and paid for the wooden duck and regally ascended the stairs. Mallory waited a few minutes and then walked back to his office.

MALLORY WAS a free-lance engineer, and his office was empty that afternoon—his secretary had gone to Capri. The telephone-answering service had no messages for him. There was no mail. He was alone. He seemed not so much unhappy as stunned. It was not that he had lost his sense of reality but that the reality he observed had lost its fitness and symmetry. How could he apply reason to the slapstick encounter in Woolworth's, and yet how could he settle for unreason? Forgetfulness was a course of action he had tried before, but he could not forget Mathilda's ringing voice and the bizarre scenery of the toy department. Dramatic misunderstandings with Mathilda were common, and he usually tackled them willingly, trying to decipher the chain of contingencies that had detonated the scene. This afternoon he was discouraged. The encounter seemed to resist diagnosis. What could he do? Should he consult a psychiatrist, a marriage counselor, a minister? Should he jump out of the window? He went to the window with this in mind.

It was still overcast and rainy, but not yet dark. Traffic was slow. He watched below him as a station wagon passed, then a convertible, a moving van, and a small truck advertising EUCLID'S DRY CLEANING AND DYEING. The great name reminded him of the right-angled triangle, the principles of geometric analysis, and the doctrine of proportion for both commensurables and incommensurables. What he needed was a new form of ratiocination, and Euclid might do. If he could make a geometric analysis of his problems, mightn't he solve them, or at least create an atmosphere of solution? He got a slide rule and took the simple theorem that if two sides of a triangle are equal, the angles opposite these sides are equal; and the converse theorem that if two angles of a triangle are equal, the sides opposite them will be equal. He drew a line to represent Mathilda and what he knew about her to be relevant. The base of the triangle would be his two children, Randy and Priscilla. He, of course, would make up the third side. The most critical element in Mathilda's line—that which would threaten to make her angle unequal to Randy and Priscilla's—was the fact that she had recently taken a phantom lover.

This was a common imposture among the housewives of Remsen Park, where they lived. Once or twice a week, Mathilda would dress in her best, put on some French perfume and a fur coat, and take a late-morning train to the city. She sometimes lunched with a friend, but she lunched more often alone in one of those French restaurants in the Sixties that accommodate single women. She usually drank a cocktail or had a half bottle of wine. Her intention was to appear dissipated, mysterious—a victim of love's bitter riddle—but should a stranger give her the eye, she would go into a paroxysm of shyness, recalling, with something like panic, her lovely home, her fresh-faced children, and the begonias in her flower bed. In the afternoon, she went either to a matinee or a foreign movie. She preferred strenuous themes that would leave her emotionally exhausted—or, as she put it to herself, "emptied." Coming home on a late train, she would appear peaceful and sad. She often wept while she cooked the supper, and if Mallory asked what her trouble was, she would merely sigh. He was briefly suspicious, but walking up Madison Avenue one afternoon he saw her, in her furs, eating a sandwich at a lunch counter, and concluded that the pupils of her eyes were dilated not by amorousness but by the darkness of a movie theater. It was a harmless and a common imposture, and might even, with some forced charity, be thought of as useful.

The line formed by these elements, then, made an angle with the line representing his children, and the single fact *here* was that he loved them. He loved them! No amount of ignominy or venom could make parting from them imaginable. As he thought of them, they seemed to be the furniture of his soul, its lintel and rooftree.

The line representing himself, he knew, would be most prone to miscalculations. He thought himself candid, healthy, and knowledgeable (who else could remember so much Euclid?), but waking in the morning, feeling useful and innocent, he had only to speak to Mathilda to find his usefulness and his innocence squandered. Why should his ingenuous commitments to life seem to harass the best of him? Why should he, wandering through the toy department, be calumniated as a Peeping Tom? His triangle might give him the answer, he thought, and in a sense it did. The sides of the triangle, determined by the relevant information, were equal, as were the angles opposite these sides. Suddenly he felt much less bewildered, happier, more hopeful and magnanimous. He thought, as one does two or three times a year, that he was beginning a new life.

Coming home on the train, he wondered if he could make a geometrical analogy for the boredom of a commuters' local, the stupidities in the evening paper, the rush to the parking lot. Mathilda was in the small dining room, setting the table, when he returned. Her opening gun was meant to be disabling. "Pinkerton fink," she said. "Gumshoe." While he heard her words, he heard them without anger, anxiety, or frustration. They seemed to fall short of where he stood. How calm he felt, how happy. Even Mathilda's angularity seemed touching and lovable; this wayward child in the family of man. "Why do you look so happy?" his children asked. "Why do you look so happy, Daddy?" Presently, almost everyone would say the same. "How Mallory has changed. How well Mallory looks. Lucky Mallory!"

The next night, Mallory found a geometry text in the attic and refreshed his knowledge. The study of Euclid put him into a compassionate and tranquil frame of mind, and illuminated, among other things, that his thinking and feeling had recently been crippled by confusion and despair. He knew that what he thought of as his discovery could be an illusion, but the practical advantages remained his. He felt much better. He felt that he had corrected the distance between his reality and those realities that pounded at his spirit. He might not, had he possessed any philosophy or religion, have needed geometry, but the religious observances in his neighborhood seemed to him boring and threadbare, and he had no disposition for philosophy. Geometry served him beautifully for the metaphysics of understood pain. The principal advantage was that he could regard, once he had put them into linear terms, Mathilda's moods and discontents with ardor and compassion. He was not a victor, but he was wonderfully safe from being victimized. As he continued with his study and his practice, he discovered that the rudeness of headwaiters, the damp souls of clerks, and the scurrilities of traffic policemen could not touch his tranquillity, and that these oppressors, in turn, sensing his strength, were less rude, damp, and scurrilous. He was able to carry the conviction of innocence, with which he woke each morning, well into the day. He thought of writing a book about his discovery: *Euclidean Emotion: The Geometry of Sentiment*.

At about this time he had to go to Chicago. It was an overcast day, and he took the train. Waking a little after dawn, all usefulness and innocence, he looked out the window of his bedroom at a coffin factory, used-car dumps, shanties, weedy playing fields, pigs fattening on acorns, and in the distance the monumental gloom of Gary. The tedious and melancholy scene had the power over his spirit of a show of human stupidity. He had never applied his theorem to landscapes, but he discovered that, by translating the components of the moment into a parallelogram, he was able to put the discouraging countryside away from him until it seemed harmless, practical, and even charming. He ate a hearty breakfast and did a good day's work. It was a day that needed no geometry. One of his associates in Chicago asked him to dinner. It was an invitation that he felt he could not refuse, and he showed up at half past six at a little brick house in a part of the city with which he was unfamiliar. Even before the door opened, he felt that he was going to need Euclid.

His hostess, when she opened the door, had been crying. She held a drink in her hand. "He's in the cellar," she sobbed, and went into a small living room without telling Mallory where the cellar was or how to get there. He followed her into the living room. She had dropped to her hands and knees, and was tying a tag to the leg of a chair. Most of the furniture, Mallory noticed, was tagged. The tags were printed: CHICAGO STORAGE WAREHOUSE. Below this she had written: "Property of Helen Fells McGowen." McGowen was his friend's name. "I'm not going to leave the s.o.b. a thing," she sobbed. "Not a stick."

"Hi, Mallory," said McGowen, coming through the kitchen. "Don't pay any attention to her. Once or twice a year she gets sore and puts tags on all the furniture, and claims she's going to put it in storage and take a furnished room and work at Marshall Field's."

"You don't know *anything*," she said.

"What's new?" McGowen asked.

"Lois Mitchell just telephoned. Harry got drunk and put the kitten in the blender."

"Is she coming over?"

"Of course."

The doorbell rang. A disheveled woman with wet cheeks came in. "Oh, it was awful," she said. "The children were watching. It was their little kitten and they loved it. I wouldn't have minded so much if the children hadn't been watching."

"Let's get out of here," McGowen said, turning back to the kitchen. Mallory followed him through the kitchen, where there were no signs of dinner, down some stairs into a cellar furnished with a Ping-Pong table, a television set, and a bar. He got Mallory a drink. "You see, Helen used to be rich," McGowen said. "It's one of her difficulties. She came from very rich people. Her father had a chain of laundromats that reached from here to Denver. He introduced live entertainment in laundromats. Folk singers. Combos. Then the Musicians' Union ganged up on him, and he lost the whole thing overnight. And she knows that I fool around but if I wasn't promiscuous, Mallory, I wouldn't be true to myself. I mean, I used to make out with that Mitchell dame upstairs. The one with the kitten. She's great. You want her, I can fix it up. She'll do anything for me. I usually give her a little something. Ten bucks or a bottle of whiskey. One Christmas I gave her a bracelet. You see, her husband has this suicide thing. He keeps taking sleeping pills, but they always pump him out in time. Once, he tried to hang himself—"

"I've got to go," Mallory said.

"Stick around, stick around," McGowen said. "Let me sweeten your drink."

"I've really got to go," Mallory said. "I've got a lot of work to do."

"But you haven't had anything to eat," McGowen said. "Stick around and I'll heat up some gurry."

"There isn't time," Mallory said. "I've got a lot to do." He went upstairs without saying goodbye. Mrs. Mitchell had gone, but his hostess was still tying tags onto the furniture. He let himself out and took a cab back to his hotel.

He got out his slide rule and, working on the relation between the volume of a cone and that of its circumscribed prism, tried to put Mrs. McGowen's drunkenness and the destiny of the Mitchells' kitten into linear terms. Oh, Euclid, be with me now! What did Mallory want? He wanted radiance, beauty, and order, no less; he wanted to rationalize the image of Mr. Mitchell, hanging by the neck. Was Mallory's passionate detestation of squalor fastidious and unmanly? Was he wrong to look for definitions of good and evil, to believe in the inalienable power of remorse, the beauty of shame? There was a vast number of imponderables in the picture, but he tried to hold his equation to the facts of the evening, and this occupied him until past midnight, when he went to sleep. He slept well.

THE CHICAGO TRIP had been a disaster as far as the McGowens went, but financially it had been profitable, and the Mallorys decided to take a trip, as they usually did whenever they were flush. They flew to Italy and stayed in a small hotel near Sperlonga where they had stayed before. Mallory was very happy and needed no Euclid for the ten days they spent on the coast. They went to Rome before flying home and, on their last day, went to the Piazza del Popolo for lunch. They ordered lobster, and were laughing, drinking, and cracking shells with their teeth when Mathilda became melancholy. She let out a sob, and Mallory realized that he was going to need Euclid.

Now Mathilda was moody, but that afternoon seemed to promise Mallory that he might, by way of groundwork and geometry, isolate the components of her moodiness. The restaurant seemed to present a splendid field for investigation. The place was fragrant and orderly. The other diners were decent Italians, all of them strangers, and he didn't imagine they had it in their power to make her as miserable as she plainly was. She had enjoyed her lobster. The linen was white, the silver polished, the waiter civil. Mallory examined the place—the flowers, the piles of fruit, the traffic in the square outside the window—and he could find in all of this no source for the sorrow and bitterness in her face. "Would you like an ice or some fruit?" he asked.

"If I want anything, I'll order it myself," she said, and she did. She summoned the waiter, ordered an ice and some coffee for herself, throwing Mallory a dark look. When Mallory had paid the check, he asked her if she wanted a cab. "What a stupid idea," she said, frowning with disgust, as if he had suggested squandering their savings account or putting their children on the stage.

They walked back to their hotel, Indian file. The light was brilliant, the heat was intense, and it seemed as if the streets of Rome had always been hot and would always be, world without end. Was it the heat that had changed her humor? "Does the heat bother you, dear?" he asked, and she turned and said, "You make me sick." He left her in the hotel lobby and went to a café.

He worked out his problems with a slide rule on the back of a menu. When he returned to the hotel, she had gone out, but she came in at seven and began to cry as soon as she entered the room. The afternoon's geometry had proved to him that her happiness, as well as his and that of his children, suffered from some capricious, unfathomable, and submarine course of emotion that wound mysteriously through her nature, erupting with turbulence at intervals that had no regularity and no discernible cause. "I'm sorry, my darling," he said. "What is the matter?"

"No one in this city understands English," she said, "absolutely no one. I got lost and I must have asked fifteen people the way back to the hotel, but no one understood me." She went into the bathroom and slammed the door, and he sat at the window—calm and happy—watching the traverse of a cloud shaped exactly like a cloud, and then the appearance of that brassy light that sometimes fills up the skies of Rome just before dark.

MALLORY HAD TO GO back to Chicago a few days after they returned from Italy. He finished his business in a day—he avoided McGowen—and got the four-o'clock train. At about four-thirty he went up to the club car for a drink, and seeing the mass of Gary in the distance, repeated that theorem that had corrected the angle of his relationship to the Indiana landscape. He ordered a drink and looked out of the window at Gary. There was nothing to be seen. He had, through some miscalculation, not only rendered Gary powerless; he had lost Gary. There was no rain, no fog, no sudden dark to account for the fact that, to his eyes, the windows of the club car were vacant. Indiana had disappeared. He turned to a woman on his left and asked, "That's Gary, isn't it?"

"Sure," she said. "What's the matter? Can't you see?"

An isosceles triangle took the sting out of her remark, but there was no trace of any of the other towns that followed. He went back to his bedroom, a lonely and a frightened man. He buried his face in his hands, and, when he raised it, he could clearly see the lights of the grade crossings and the little towns, but he had never applied his geometry to these.

It was perhaps a week later that Mallory was taken sick. His secretary—she had returned from Capri—found him unconscious on the floor of the office. She called an ambulance. He was operated on and listed as in critical condition. It was ten days after his operation before he could have a visitor, and the first, of course, was Mathilda. He had lost ten inches of his intestinal tract, and there were tubes attached to both his arms. "Why, you're looking marvelous," Mathilda exclaimed, turning the look of shock and dismay on her face inward and settling for an expression of absent-mindedness. "And it's such a pleasant room. Those yellow walls. If you have to be sick, I guess it's best to be sick in New York. Remember that awful country hospital where I had the children?" She came to rest, not in a chair, but on the window sill. He reminded himself that he had never known a love that could quite anneal the divisive power of pain; that could bridge the distance between the quick and the infirm. "Everything at the house is fine and dandy," she said. "Nobody seems to miss you."

Never having been gravely ill before, he had no way of anticipating the poverty of her gifts as a nurse. She seemed to resent the fact that he was ill, but her resentment was, he thought, a clumsy expression of love. She had never been adroit at concealment, and she could not conceal the fact that she considered his collapse to be selfish. "You're so lucky," she said. "I mean, you're so lucky it happened in New York. You have the best doctors and the best nurses, and this must be one of the best hospitals in the world. You've nothing to worry about, really. Everything's done for you. I just wish that once in my life I could get into bed for a week or two and be waited on."

It was his Mathilda speaking, his beloved Mathilda, unsparing of herself in displaying that angularity, that legitimate self-interest that no force of love could reason or soften. This was she, and he appreciated the absence of sentimentality with which she appeared. A nurse came in with a bowl of clear soup on a tray. She spread a napkin under his chin and prepared to feed him, since he could not move his arms. "Oh, let me do it, let me do it," Mathilda said. "It's the least I can do." It was the first hint of the fact that she was in any way involved in what was, in spite of the yellow walls, a tragic scene. She took the bowl of soup and the spoon from the nurse. "Oh, how good that smells," she said. "I have half a mind to eat it myself. Hospital food is supposed to be dreadful, but this place seems to be an exception." She held a spoonful of the broth up to his lips and then, through no fault of her own, spilled the bowl of broth over his chest and bedclothes.

She rang for the nurse and then vigorously rubbed at a spot on her skirt. When the nurse began the lengthy and complicated business of changing his bed linen, Mathilda looked at her watch and saw that it was time to go. "I'll stop in tomorrow," she said. "I'll tell the children how well you look."

It was his Mathilda, and this much he understood, but when she had gone he realized that understanding might not get him through another such visit. He definitely felt that the convalescence of his guts had suffered a setback. She might even hasten his death. When the nurse had finished changing him and had fed him a second bowl of soup, he asked her to get the slide rule and notebook out of the pocket of his suit. He worked out a simple, geometrical analogy between his love for Mathilda and his fear of death.

It seemed to work. When Mathilda came at eleven the next day, he could hear her and see her, but she had lost the power to confuse. He had corrected her angle. She was dressed for her phantom lover and she went on about how well he looked and how lucky he was. She did point out that he needed a shave. When she had left, he asked the nurse if he could have a barber. She explained that the barber came only on Wednesdays and Fridays, and that the male nurses were all out on strike. She brought him a mirror, a razor, and some soap, and he saw his face then for the first time since his collapse. His emaciation forced him back to geometry, and he tried to equate the voracity of his appetite, the boundlessness of his hopes, and the frailty of his carcass. He reasoned carefully, since he knew that a miscalculation, such as he had made for Gary, would end those events that had begun when Euclid's Dry

Cleaning and Dyeing truck had passed under his window. Mathilda went from the hospital to a restaurant and then to a movie, and it was the cleaning woman who told her, when she got home, that he had passed away.

THE SWIMMER

IT WAS ONE of those midsummer Sundays when everyone sits around saying, "I *drank* too much last night." You might have heard it whispered by the parishioners leaving church, heard it from the lips of the priest himself, struggling with his cassock in the *vestiarium,* heard it from the golf links and the tennis courts, heard it from the wildlife preserve where the leader of the Audubon group was suffering from a terrible hangover. "I *drank* too much," said Donald Westerhazy. "We all *drank* too much," said Lucinda Merrill. "It must have been the wine," said Helen Westerhazy. "I *drank* too much of that claret."

This was at the edge of the Westerhazys' pool. The pool, fed by an artesian well with a high iron content, was a pale shade of green. It was a fine day. In the west there was a massive stand of cumulus cloud so like a city seen from a distance—from the bow of an approaching ship—that it might have had a name. Lisbon. Hackensack. The sun was hot. Neddy Merrill sat by the green water, one hand in it, one around a glass of gin. He was a slender man—he seemed to have the especial slenderness of youth—and while he was far from young he had slid down his banister that morning and given the bronze backside of Aphrodite on the hall table a smack, as he jogged toward the smell of coffee in his dining room. He might have been compared to a summer's day, particularly the last hours of one, and while he lacked a tennis racket or a sail bag the impression was definitely one of youth, sport, and clement weather. He had been swimming and now he was breathing deeply, stertorously as if he could gulp into his lungs the components of that moment, the heat of the sun, the intenseness of his pleasure. It all seemed to flow into his chest. His own house stood in Bullet Park, eight miles to the south, where his four beautiful daughters would have had their lunch and might be playing tennis. Then it occurred to him that by taking a dogleg to the southwest he could reach his home by water.

His life was not confining and the delight he took in this observation could not be explained by its suggestion of escape. He seemed to see, with a cartographer's eye, that string of swimming pools, that quasi-subterranean stream that curved across the county. He had made a discovery, a contribution to modern geography; he would name the stream Lucinda after his wife. He was not a practical joker nor was he a fool but he was determinedly original and had a vague and modest idea of himself as a legendary figure. The day was beautiful and it seemed to him that a long swim might enlarge and celebrate its beauty.

He took off a sweater that was hung over his shoulders and dove in. He had an inexplicable contempt for men who did not hurl themselves into pools. He swam a choppy crawl, breathing either with every stroke or every fourth stroke and counting somewhere well in the back of his mind the one-two one-two of a flutter kick. It was not a serviceable stroke for long distances but the domestication of swimming had saddled the sport with some customs and in his part of the world a crawl was customary. To be embraced and sustained by the light green water was less a pleasure, it seemed, than the resumption of a natural condition, and he would have liked to swim without trunks, but this was not possible, considering his project. He hoisted himself up on the far curb—he never used the ladder—and started across the lawn. When Lucinda asked where he was going he said he was going to swim home.

The only maps and charts he had to go by were remembered or imaginary but these were clear enough. First there were the Grahams, the Hammers, the Lears, the Howlands, and the Crosscups. He would cross Ditmar Street to the Bunkers and come, after a short portage, to the Levys, the Welchers, and the public pool in Lancaster. Then there were the Hallorans, the Sachses, the Biswangers, Shirley Adams, the Gilmartins, and the Clydes. The day was lovely, and that he lived in a world so generously supplied with water seemed like a clemency, a beneficence. His heart was high and he ran across the grass. Making his way home by an uncommon route gave him the feeling that he was a pilgrim, an explorer, a man with a destiny, and he knew that he would find friends all along the way; friends would line the banks of the Lucinda River.

He went through a hedge that separated the Westerhazys' land from the Grahams', walked under some flowering apple trees, passed the shed that housed their pump and filter, and came out at the Grahams' pool. "Why, Neddy," Mrs. Graham said, "what a marvelous surprise. I've been trying to get you on the phone all morning. Here, let me get you a drink." He saw then, like any explorer, that the hospitable customs and traditions of the natives would have to be handled with diplomacy if he was ever going to reach his destination. He did not want to mystify or seem rude to the Grahams nor did he have the time to linger there. He swam the length of their pool and joined them in the sun and was rescued, a few minutes later, by the arrival of two carloads of friends from Connecticut. During the uproarious reunions he was able to slip away. He went down by the front of the Grahams' house, stepped over a thorny hedge, and crossed a vacant lot to the Hammers'. Mrs. Hammer, looking up from her roses, saw him swim by although she wasn't quite sure who it was. The Lears heard him splashing past the open windows of their living room. The Howlands and the Crosscups were away. After leaving the Howlands' he crossed Ditmar Street and started for the Bunkers', where he could hear, even at that distance, the noise of a party.

The water refracted the sound of voices and laughter and seemed to suspend it in midair. The Bunkers' pool was on a rise and he climbed some stairs to a terrace where twenty-five or thirty men and women were drinking. The only person in the water was Rusty Towers, who floated there on a rubber raft. Oh, how bonny and lush were the banks of the Lucinda River! Prosperous men and women gathered by the sapphire-colored waters while caterer's men in white coats passed them cold gin. Overhead a red de Haviland trainer was circling around and around and around in the sky with something like the glee of a child in a swing. Ned felt a passing affection for the scene, a tenderness for the gathering, as if it was something he might touch. In the distance he heard thunder. As soon as Enid Bunker saw him she began to scream: "Oh, look who's here! What a marvelous surprise! When Lucinda said that you couldn't come I thought I'd *die*." She made her way to him through the crowd, and when they had finished kissing she led him to the bar, a progress that was slowed by the fact that he stopped to kiss eight or ten other women and shake the hands of as many men. A smiling bartender he had seen at a hundred parties gave him a gin and tonic and he stood by the bar for a moment, anxious not to get stuck in any conversation that would delay his voyage. When he seemed about to be surrounded he dove in and swam close to the side to avoid colliding with Rusty's raft. At the far end of the pool he bypassed the Tomlinsons with a broad smile and jogged up the garden path. The gravel cut his feet but this was the only unpleasantness. The party was confined to the pool, and as he went toward the house he heard the brilliant, watery sound of voices fade, heard the noise of a radio from the Bunkers' kitchen, where someone was listening to a ball game. Sunday afternoon. He made his way through the parked cars and down the grassy border of their driveway to Alewives Lane. He did not want to be seen on the road in his bathing trunks but there was no traffic and he made the short distance to the Levys' driveway, marked with a PRIVATE PROPERTY sign and a green tube for *The New York Times*. All the doors and windows of the big house were open but there were no signs of life; not even a dog barked. He went around the side of the house to the pool and saw that the Levys had only recently left. Glasses and bottles and dishes of nuts were on a table at the deep end, where there was a bathhouse or gazebo, hung with Japanese lanterns. After swimming the pool he got himself a glass and poured a drink. It was his fourth or fifth drink and he had swum nearly half the length of the Lucinda River. He felt tired, clean, and pleased at that moment to be alone; pleased with everything.

It would storm. The stand of cumulus cloud—that city—had risen and darkened, and while he sat there he heard the percussiveness of thunder again. The de Haviland trainer was still circling overhead and it seemed to Ned that he could almost hear the pilot laugh with pleasure in the afternoon; but when there was another peal of thunder he took off for home. A train whistle blew and he wondered what time it had gotten to be. Four? Five? He thought of the provincial station at that hour, where a waiter, his tuxedo concealed by a raincoat, a dwarf with some flowers wrapped in newspaper, and a woman who had been crying would be waiting for the local. It was suddenly growing dark; it was that moment when the pin-headed birds seemed to organize their song into some acute and knowledgeable recognition of the storm's approach. Then there was a fine noise of rushing water from the crown of an oak at his back, as if a spigot there had been turned. Then the noise of fountains came from the crowns of all the tall trees. Why did he love storms, what was the meaning of his excitement when the door sprang open and the rain wind fled rudely up the stairs, why had the simple task of shutting the windows of an old house seemed fitting and urgent, why did the first watery notes of a storm wind have for him the unmistakable sound of good news, cheer, glad tidings? Then there was an explosion, a smell of cordite, and rain lashed the Japanese lanterns that Mrs. Levy had bought in Kyoto the year before last, or was it the year before that?

He stayed in the Levys' gazebo until the storm had passed. The rain had cooled the air and he shivered. The force of the wind had stripped a maple of its red and yellow leaves and scattered them over the grass and the water. Since it was midsummer the tree must be blighted, and yet he felt a peculiar sadness at this sign of autumn. He braced his shoulders, emptied his glass, and started for the Welchers' pool. This meant crossing the Lindleys' riding ring and he was surprised to find it overgrown with grass and all the jumps dismantled. He wondered if the Lindleys had sold their horses or gone away for the summer and put them out to board. He seemed to remember having heard something about the Lindleys and their horses but the memory was unclear. On he went, barefoot through the wet grass, to the Welchers', where he found their pool was dry.

This breach in his chain of water disappointed him absurdly, and he felt like some explorer who seeks a torrential headwater and finds a dead stream. He was disappointed and mystified. It was common enough to go away for the summer but no one ever drained his pool. The Welchers had definitely gone away. The pool furniture was folded, stacked, and covered with a tarpaulin. The bathhouse was locked. All the windows of the house were shut, and when he went around to the driveway in front he saw a FOR SALE sign nailed to a tree. When had he last heard from the Welchers—when, that is, had he and Lucinda last regretted an invitation to dine with them? It seemed only a week or so ago. Was his memory failing or had he so disciplined it in the repression of unpleasant facts that he had damaged his sense of the truth? Then in the distance he heard the sound of a tennis game. This cheered him, cleared away all his apprehensions and let him regard the overcast sky and the cold air with indifference. This was the day that Neddy Merrill swam across the county. That was the day! He started off then for his most difficult portage.

HAD YOU GONE for a Sunday afternoon ride that day you might have seen him, close to naked, standing on the shoulders of Route 424, waiting for a chance to cross. You might have wondered if he was the victim of foul play, had his car broken down, or was he merely a fool. Standing barefoot in the deposits of the highway—beer cans, rags, and blowout patches—exposed to all kinds of ridicule, he seemed pitiful. He had known when he started that this was a part of his journey—it had been on his maps—but confronted with the lines of traffic, worming through the summery light, he found himself unprepared. He was laughed at, jeered at, a beer can was thrown at him, and he had no dignity or humor to bring to the situation. He could have gone back, back to the Westerhazys', where Lucinda would still be sitting in the sun. He had signed nothing, vowed nothing, pledged nothing, not even to himself. Why, believing as he did, that all human obduracy was susceptible to common sense, was he unable to turn back? Why was he determined to complete his journey even if it meant putting his life in danger? At what point had this prank, this joke, this piece of horseplay become serious? He could not go back, he could not even recall with any clearness the green water at the Westerhazys', the sense of inhaling the day's components, the friendly and relaxed voices saying that they had *drunk* too much. In the space of an hour, more or less, he had covered a distance that made his return impossible.

An old man, tooling down the highway at fifteen miles an hour, let him get to the middle of the road, where there was a grass divider. Here he was exposed to the ridicule of the northbound traffic, but after ten or fifteen minutes he was able to cross. From here he had only a short walk to the Recreation Center at the edge of the village of Lancaster, where there were some handball courts and a public pool.

The effect of the water on voices, the illusion of brilliance and suspense, was the same here as it had been at the Bunkers' but the sounds here were louder, harsher, and more shrill, and as soon as he entered the crowded enclosure he was confronted with regimentation. "ALL SWIMMERS MUST TAKE A SHOWER BEFORE USING THE POOL. ALL SWIMMERS MUST USE THE FOOTBATH. ALL SWIMMERS MUST WEAR THEIR IDENTIFICATION DISKS." He took a shower, washed his feet in a cloudy and bitter solution, and made his way to the edge of the water. It stank of chlorine and looked to him like a sink. A pair of lifeguards in a pair of towers blew police whistles at what seemed to be regular intervals and abused the swimmers through a public address system. Neddy remembered the sapphire water at the Bunkers' with longing and thought that he might contaminate himself—damage his own prosperousness and charm—by swimming in this murk, but he reminded himself that he was an explorer, a pilgrim, and that this was merely a stagnant bend in the Lucinda River. He dove, scowling with distaste, into the chlorine and had to swim with his head above water to avoid collisions, but even so he was bumped into, splashed, and jostled. When he got to the shallow end both lifeguards were shouting at him: "Hey, you, you without the identification disk, get outa the water." He did, but they had no way of pursuing him and he went through the reek of suntan oil and chlorine out through the hurricane fence and passed the handball courts. By crossing the road he entered the wooded part of the Halloran estate. The woods were not cleared and the footing was treacherous and difficult until he reached the lawn and the clipped beech hedge that encircled their pool.

The Hallorans were friends, an elderly couple of enormous wealth who seemed to bask in the suspicion that they might be Communists. They were zealous reformers but they were not Communists, and yet when they were accused, as they sometimes were, of subversion, it seemed to gratify and excite them. Their beech hedge was yellow and he guessed this had been blighted like the Levys' maple. He called hullo, hullo, to warn the Hallorans of his approach, to palliate his invasion of their privacy. The Hallorans, for reasons that had never been explained to him, did not wear bathing suits. No explanations were in order, really. Their nakedness was a detail in their uncompromising zeal for reform and he stepped politely out of his trunks before he went through the opening in the hedge.

Mrs. Halloran, a stout woman with white hair and a serene face, was reading the *Times*. Mr. Halloran was taking beech leaves out of the water with a scoop. They seemed not surprised or displeased to see him. Their pool was perhaps the oldest in the country, a fieldstone rectangle, fed by a brook. It had no filter or pump and its waters were the opaque gold of the stream.

"I'm swimming across the county," Ned said.

"Why, I didn't know one could," exclaimed Mrs. Halloran.

"Well, I've made it from the Westerhazys'," Ned said. "That must be about four miles."

He left his trunks at the deep end, walked to the shallow end, and swam this stretch. As he was pulling himself out of the water he heard Mrs. Halloran say, "We've been *terribly* sorry to hear about all your misfortunes, Neddy."

"My misfortunes?" Ned asked. "I don't know what you mean."

"Why, we heard that you'd sold the house and that your poor children . . ."

"I don't recall having sold the house," Ned said, "and the girls are at home."

"Yes," Mrs. Halloran sighed. "Yes . . ." Her voice filled the air with an unseasonable melancholy and Ned spoke briskly. "Thank you for the swim."

"Well, have a nice trip," said Mrs. Halloran.

Beyond the hedge he pulled on his trunks and fastened them. They were loose and he wondered if, during the space of an afternoon, he could have lost some weight. He was cold and he was tired and the naked Hallorans and their dark water had depressed him. The swim was too much for his strength but how could he have guessed this, sliding down the banister that morning and sitting in the Westerhazys' sun? His arms were lame. His legs felt rubbery and ached at the joints. The worst of it was the cold in his bones and the feeling that he might never be warm again. Leaves were falling down around him and he smelled wood smoke on the wind. Who would be burning wood at this time of year?

He needed a drink. Whiskey would warm him, pick him up, carry him through the last of his journey, refresh his feeling that it was original and valorous to swim across the county. Channel swimmers took brandy. He needed a stimulant. He crossed the lawn in front of the Hallorans' house and went down a little path to where they had built a house for their only daughter, Helen, and her husband, Eric Sachs. The Sachses' pool was small and he found Helen and her husband there.

"Oh, *Neddy,*" Helen said. "Did you lunch at Mother's?"

"Not *really,*" Ned said. "I *did* stop to see your parents." This seemed to be explanation enough. "I'm terribly sorry to break in on you like this but I've taken a chill and I wonder if you'd give me a drink."

"Why, I'd *love* to," Helen said, "but there hasn't been anything in this house to drink since Eric's operation. That was three years ago."

Was he losing his memory, had his gift for concealing painful facts let him forget that he had sold his house, that his children were in trouble, and that his friend had been ill? His eyes slipped from Eric's face to his abdomen, where he saw three pale, sutured scars, two of them at least a foot long. Gone was his navel, and what, Neddy thought, would the roving hand, bed-checking one's gifts at 3 A.M., make of a belly with no navel, no link to birth, this breach in the succession?

"I'm sure you can get a drink at the Biswangers'," Helen said. "They're having an enormous do. You can hear it from here. Listen!"

She raised her head and from across the road, the lawns, the gardens, the woods, the fields, he heard again the brilliant noise of voices over water. "Well, I'll get wet," he said, still feeling that he had no freedom of choice about his means of travel. He dove into the Sachses' cold water and, gasping, close to drowning, made his way from one end of the pool to the other. "Lucinda and I want *terribly* to see you," he said over his shoulder, his face set toward the Biswangers'. "We're sorry it's been so long and we'll call you *very* soon."

He crossed some fields to the Biswangers' and the sounds of revelry there. They would be honored to give him a drink, they would be happy to give him a drink. The Biswangers invited him and Lucinda for dinner four times a year, six weeks in advance. They were always rebuffed and yet they continued to send out their invitations, unwilling to comprehend the rigid and undemocratic realities of their society. They were the sort of people who discussed the price of things at cocktails, exchanged market tips during dinner, and after dinner told dirty stories to mixed company. They did not belong to Neddy's set—they were not even on Lucinda's Christmas card list. He went toward their pool with feelings of indifference, charity, and some unease, since it seemed to be getting dark and these were the longest days of the year. The party when he joined it was noisy and large. Grace Biswanger was the kind of hostess who asked the optometrist, the veterinarian, the real-estate dealer, and the dentist. No one was swimming and the twilight, reflected on the water of the pool, had a wintry gleam. There was a bar and he started for this. When Grace Biswanger saw him she came toward him, not affectionately as he had every right to expect, but bellicosely.

"Why, this party has everything," she said loudly, "including a gate crasher."

She could not deal him a social blow—there was no question about this and he did not flinch. "As a gate crasher," he asked politely, "do I rate a drink?"

"Suit yourself," she said. "You don't seem to pay much attention to invitations."

She turned her back on him and joined some guests, and he went to the bar and ordered a whiskey. The bartender served him but he served him rudely. His was a world in which the caterer's men kept the social score, and to be rebuffed by a part-time barkeep meant that he had suffered some loss of social esteem. Or perhaps the man was new and uninformed. Then he heard Grace at his back say: "They went for broke overnight—nothing but income—and he showed up drunk one Sunday and asked us to loan him five thousand dollars. . . ." She was always talking about money. It was worse than eating your peas off a knife. He dove into the pool, swam its length and went away.

The next pool on his list, the last but two, belonged to his old mistress, Shirley Adams. If he had suffered any injuries at the Biswangers' they would be cured here. Love—sexual roughhouse in fact—was the supreme elixir, the pain killer, the brightly colored pill that would put the spring back into his step, the joy of life in his heart. They had had an affair last week, last month, last year. He couldn't remember. It was he who had broken it off, his was the upper hand, and he stepped through the gate of the wall that surrounded her pool with nothing so considered as self-confidence. It seemed in a way to be his pool, as the lover, particularly the illicit lover, enjoys the possessions of his mistress with an authority unknown to holy matrimony. She was there, her hair the color of brass, but her figure, at the edge of the lighted, cerulean water, excited in him no profound memories. It had been, he thought, a lighthearted affair, although she had wept when he broke it off. She seemed confused to see him and he wondered if she was still wounded. Would she, God forbid, weep again?

"What do you want?" she asked.

"I'm swimming across the county."

"Good Christ. Will you ever grow up?"

"What's the matter?"

"If you've come here for money," she said, "I won't give you another cent."

"You could give me a drink."

"I could but I won't. I'm not alone."

"Well, I'm on my way."

He dove in and swam the pool, but when he tried to haul himself up onto the curb he found that the strength in his arms and shoulders had gone, and he paddled to the ladder and climbed out. Looking over his shoulder he saw, in the lighted bathhouse, a young man. Going out onto the dark lawn he smelled chrysanthemums or marigolds—some stubborn autumnal fragrance—on the night air, strong as gas. Looking overhead he saw that the stars had come out, but why should he seem to see Andromeda, Cepheus, and Cassiopeia? What had become of the constellations of midsummer? He began to cry.

It was probably the first time in his adult life that he had ever cried, certainly the first time in his life that he had ever felt so miserable, cold, tired, and bewildered. He could not understand the rudeness of the caterer's barkeep or the rudeness of a mistress who had come to him on her knees and showered his trousers with tears. He had swum too long, he had been immersed too long, and his nose and his throat were sore from the water. What he needed then was a drink, some company, and some clean, dry clothes, and while he could have cut directly across the road to his home he went on to the Gilmartins' pool. Here, for the first time in his life, he did not dive but went down the steps into the icy water and swam a hobbled sidestroke that he might have learned as a youth. He staggered with fatigue on his way to the Clydes' and paddled the length of their pool, stopping again and again with his hand on the curb to rest. He climbed up the ladder and wondered if he had the strength to get home. He had done what he wanted, he had swum the county, but he was so stupefied with exhaustion that his triumph seemed vague. Stooped, holding on to the gateposts for support, he turned up the driveway of his own house.

The place was dark. Was it so late that they had all gone to bed? Had Lucinda stayed at the Westerhazys' for supper? Had the girls joined her there or gone someplace else? Hadn't they agreed, as they usually did on Sunday, to regret all their invitations and stay at home? He tried the garage doors to see what cars were in but the doors were locked and rust came off the handles onto his hands. Going toward the house, he saw that the force of the thunderstorm had knocked one of the rain gutters loose. It hung down over the front door like an umbrella rib, but it could be fixed in the morning. The house was locked, and he thought that the stupid cook or the stupid maid must have locked the place up until he remembered that it had been some time since they had employed a maid or a cook. He shouted, pounded on the door, tried to force it with his shoulder, and then, looking in at the windows, saw that the place was empty.

THE WORLD OF APPLES

Asa Bascomb, the old laureate, wandered around his work house or study—he had never been able to settle on a name for a house where one wrote poetry—swatting hornets with a copy of *La Stampa* and wondering why he had never been given the Nobel Prize. He had received nearly every other sign of renown. In a trunk in the corner there were medals, citations, wreaths, sheaves, ribbons, and badges. The stove that heated his study had been given to him by the Oslo P.E.N. Club, his desk was a gift from the Kiev Writer's Union, and the study itself had been built by an international association of his admirers. The presidents of both Italy and the United States had wired their congratulations on the day he was presented with the key to the place. Why no Nobel Prize? Swat, swat. The study was a barny, raftered building with a large northern window that looked off to the Abruzzi. He would sooner have had a much smaller place with smaller windows but he had not been consulted. There seemed to be some clash between the altitude of the mountains and the disciplines of verse. At the time of which I'm writing he was eighty-two years old and lived in a villa below the hill town of Monte Carbone, south of Rome.

He had strong, thick white hair that hung in a lock over his forehead. Two or more cowlicks at the crown were usually disorderly and erect. He wet them down with soap for formal receptions, but they were never supine for more than an hour or two and were usually up in the air again by the time champagne was poured. It was very much a part of the impression he left. As one remembers a man for a long nose, a smile, birthmark, or scar, one remembered Bascomb for his unruly cowlicks. He was known vaguely as the Cézanne of poets. There was some linear preciseness to his work that might be thought to resemble

Cézanne but the vision that underlies Cézanne's paintings was not his. This mistaken comparison might have arisen because the title of his most popular work was *The World of Apples*—poetry in which his admirers found the pungency, diversity, color, and nostalgia of the apples of the northern New England he had not seen for forty years.

Why had he—provincial and famous for his simplicity—chosen to leave Vermont for Italy? Had it been the choice of his beloved Amelia, dead these ten years? She had made many of their decisions. Was he, the son of a farmer, so naïve that he thought living abroad might bring some color to his stern beginnings? Or had it been simply a practical matter, an evasion of the publicity that would, in his own country, have been an annoyance? Admirers found him in Monte Carbone, they came almost daily, but they came in modest numbers. He was photographed once or twice a year for *Match* or *Epoca*—usually on his birthday—but he was in general able to lead a quieter life than would have been possible in the United States. Walking down Fifth Avenue on his last visit home he had been stopped by strangers and asked to autograph scraps of paper. On the streets of Rome no one knew or cared who he was and this was as he wanted it.

Monte Carbone was a Saracen town, built on the summit of a loafshaped butte of sullen granite. At the top of the town were three pure and voluminous springs whose water fell in pools or conduits down the sides of the mountain. His villa was below the town and he had in his garden many fountains, fed by the springs on the summit. The noise of falling water was loud and unmusical—a clapping or clattering sound. The water was stinging cold, even in midsummer, and he kept his gin, wine, and vermouth in a pool on the terrace. He worked in his study in the mornings, took a siesta after lunch, and then climbed the stairs to the village.

The tufa and pepperoni and the bitter colors of the lichen that takes root in the walls and roofs are no part of the consciousness of an American, even if he has lived for years, as Bascomb had, surrounded by this bitterness. The climb up the stairs winded him. He stopped again and again to catch his breath. Everyone spoke to him. *Salve, maestro, salve!* When he saw the bricked-up transept of the twelfth-century church he always mumbled the date to himself as if he were explaining the beauties of the place to some companion. The beauties of the place were various and gloomy. He would always be a stranger there, but his strangeness seemed to him to be some metaphor involving time as if, climbing the strange stairs past the strange walls, he climbed through hours, months, years, and decades. In the piazza he had a glass of wine and got his mail. On any day he received more mail than the entire population of the village. There were letters from admirers, propositions to lecture, read, or simply show his face, and he seemed to be on the invitation list of every honorary society in the Western world excepting, of course, that society formed by the past winners of the Nobel Prize. His mail was kept in a sack, and if it was too heavy for him to carry, Antonio, the *postina*'s son, would walk back with him to the villa. He worked over his mail until five or six. Two or three times a week some pilgrims would find their way to the villa and if he liked their looks he would give them a drink while he autographed their copy of *The World of Apples*. They almost never brought his other books, although he had published a dozen. Two or three evenings a week he played backgammon with Carbone, the local padrone. They both thought that the other cheated and neither of them would leave the board during a game, even if their bladders were killing them. He slept soundly.

Of the four poets with whom Bascomb was customarily grouped one had shot himself, one had drowned himself, one had hanged himself, and the fourth had died of delirium tremens. Bascomb had known them all, loved most of them, and had nursed two of them when they were ill, but the broad implication that he had, by choosing to write poetry, chosen to destroy himself was something he rebelled against vigorously. He knew the temptations of suicide as he knew the temptations of every other form of sinfulness and he carefully kept out of the villa all firearms, suitable lengths of rope, poisons, and sleeping pills. He had seen in Z—the closest of the four—some inalienable link between his prodigious imagination and his prodigious gifts for self-destruction, but Bascomb in his stubborn, countrified way was determined to break or ignore this link—to overthrow Marsyas and Orpheus. Poetry was a lasting glory and he was determined that the final act of a poet's life should not—as had been the case with Z—be played out in a dirty room with twenty-three empty gin bottles. Since he could not deny the connection between brilliance and tragedy he seemed determined to bludgeon it.

Bascomb believed, as Cocteau once said, that the writing of poetry was the exploitation of a substratum of memory that was imperfectly understood. His work seemed to be an act of recollection. He did not, as he worked, charge his memory with any practical tasks but it was definitely his memory that was called into play—his memory of sensation, landscapes, faces, and the immense vocabulary of his own language. He could spend a month or longer on a short poem but discipline and industry were not the words to describe his work. He did not seem to choose his words at all but to recall them from the billions of sounds that he had heard since he first understood speech. Depending on his memory, then, as he did, to give his life usefulness he sometimes wondered if his memory were not failing. Talking with friends and admirers he took great pains not to repeat himself. Waking at two or three in the morning to hear the unmusical clatter of his fountains he would grill himself for an hour on names and dates. Who was Lord Cardigan's adversary at Balaklava? It took a minute for the name of Lord Lucan to struggle up through the murk but it finally appeared. He conjugated the remote past of the verb *esse*, counted to fifty in Russian, recited poems by Donne, Eliot, Thomas, and Wordsworth, described the events of the Risorgimento beginning with the riots in Milan in 1812 up through the coronation of Vittorio Emanuele, listed the ages of prehistory, the number of kilometers in a mile, the planets of the solar system, and the speed of light. There was a definite retard in the responsiveness of his memory but he remained adequate, he thought. The only impairment was anxiety. He had seen time destroy so much that he wondered if an old man's memory could have more strength and longevity than an oak; but the pin oak he had planted on the terrace thirty years ago was dying and he could still remember in detail the cut and color of the dress his beloved Amelia had been wearing when they first met. He taxed his memory to find its way through cities. He imagined walking from the railroad station in Indianapolis to the memorial fountain, from the Hotel Europe in Leningrad to the Winter Palace, from the Eden-Roma up through Trastevere to San Pietro in Montori. Frail, doubting his faculties, it was the solitariness of this inquisition that made it a struggle.

His memory seemed to wake him one night or morning, asking him to produce the first name of Lord Byron. He could not. He decided to disassociate himself momentarily from his memory and surprise it in possession of Lord Byron's name but when he returned, warily, to this receptacle it was still empty. Sidney? Percy? James? He got out of bed—it was cold—put on some shoes and an overcoat and seized a copy of *Manfred* but the author was listed simply as Lord Byron. The same was true of *Childe Harold*. He finally discovered, in the encyclopedia, that his lordship was named George. He granted himself a partial excuse for this lapse of memory and returned to his warm bed. Like most old men he had begun a furtive glossary of food that seemed to put lead in his pencil. Fresh trout. Black olives. Young lamb roasted with thyme. Wild mushrooms, bear, venison, and rabbit. On the other side of the ledger were all frozen foods, cultivated greens, overcooked pasta, and canned soups.

In the spring, a Scandinavian admirer wrote, asking if he might have the honor of taking Bascomb for a day's trip among the hill towns. Bascomb, who had no car of his own at the time, was delighted to accept. The Scandinavian was a pleasant young man and they set off happily for Monte Felici. In the fourteenth and fifteenth centuries the springs that supplied the town with water had gone dry and the population had moved halfway down the mountain. All that remained of the abandoned town on the summit were two churches or cathedrals of uncommon splendor. Bascomb loved these. They stood in fields of flowering weeds, their wall paintings still brilliant, their façades decorated with griffins, swans, and lions with the faces and parts of men and women, skewered dragons, winged serpents, and other marvels of metamorphoses. These vast and fanciful houses of God reminded Bascomb of the boundlessness of the human imagination and he felt lighthearted and enthusiastic. From Monte Felici they went on to San Giorgio, where there were some painted tombs and a little Roman theatre. They stopped in a grove below the town to have a picnic. Bascomb went into the woods to relieve himself and stumbled on a couple who were making love. They had not bothered to undress and the only flesh visible was the stranger's hairy backside. *Tanti, scusi,* mumbled Bascomb and he retreated to another part of the forest but when he rejoined the Scandinavian he was uneasy. The struggling couple seemed to have dimmed his memories of the cathedrals. When he returned to his villa some nuns from a Roman convent were waiting for him to autograph their copies of *The World of Apples*. He did this and asked his housekeeper, Maria, to give them some wine. They paid him the usual compliments—he had created a universe that seemed to welcome man; he had divined the voice of moral beauty in a rain wind—but all that he could think of was the stranger's back. It seemed to have more zeal and meaning than his celebrated search for truth. It seemed to dominate all that he had seen that day—the castles, clouds, cathedrals, mountains, and fields of flowers. When the nuns left he looked up to the mountains to raise his spirits but the mountains looked then like the breasts of women. His mind had become unclean. He seemed to step aside from its recalcitrance and watch the course it took. In the distance he heard a train whistle and what would his wayward mind make of this? The excitements of travel, the *prix fixe* in the dining car, the sort of wine they served on trains? It all seemed innocent enough until he caught his mind sneaking away from the dining car to the venereal stalls of the Wagon-Lit and thence into gross obscenity. He thought he knew what he needed and he spoke to Maria after dinner. She was always happy to accommodate him, although he always insisted that she take a bath. This, with the dishes, involved some delays but when she left him he definitely felt better but he definitely was not cured.

In the night his dreams were obscene and he woke several times trying to shake off his venereal pall or torpor. Things were no better in the light of morning. Obscenity—gross obscenity—seemed to be the only factor in life that possessed color and cheer. After breakfast he climbed up to his study and sat at his desk. The welcoming universe, the rain wind that sounded through the world of apples had vanished. Filth was his destiny, his best self, and he began with relish a long ballad called The Fart That Saved Athens. He finished the ballad that morning and burned it in the stove that had been given to him by the Oslo P.E.N. The ballad was, or had been until he burned it, an exhaustive and revolting exercise in scatology, and going down the stairs to his terrace he felt genuinely remorseful. He spent the afternoon writing a disgusting confession called The Favorite of Tiberio. Two admirers—a young married couple—came at five to praise him. They had met on a train, each of them carrying a copy of his *Apples.* They had fallen in love along the lines of the pure and ardent love he described. Thinking of his day's work, Bascomb hung his head.

On the next day he wrote The Confessions of a Public School Headmaster. He burned the manuscript at noon. As he came sadly down the stairs onto his terrace he found there fourteen students from the University of Rome who, as soon as he appeared, began to chant "The Orchards of Heaven"—the opening sonnet in *The World of Apples.* He shivered. His eyes filled with tears. He asked Maria to bring them some wine while he autographed their copies. They then lined up to shake his impure hand and returned to a bus in the field that had brought them out from Rome. He glanced at the mountains that had no cheering power—looked up at the meaningless blue sky. Where was the strength of decency? Had it any reality at all? Was the gross bestiality that obsessed him a sovereign truth? The most harrowing aspect of obscenity, he was to discover before the end of the week, was its boorishness. While he tackled his indecent projects with ardor he finished them with boredom and shame. The pornographer's course seems inflexible and he found himself repeating that tedious body of work that is circulated by the immature and the obsessed. He wrote The Confessions of a Lady's Maid, The Baseball Player's Honeymoon, and A Night in the Park. At the end of ten days he was at the bottom of the pornographer's barrel; he was writing dirty limericks. He wrote sixty of these and burned them. The next morning he took a bus to Rome.

He checked in at the Minerva, where he always stayed,

and telephoned a long list of friends, but he knew that to arrive unannounced in a large city is to be friendless, and no one was home. He wandered around the streets and, stepping into a public toilet, found himself face to face with a male whore, displaying his wares. He stared at the man with the naïveté or the retard of someone very old. The man's face was idiotic—doped, drugged, and ugly—and yet, standing in his unsavory orisons, he seemed to old Bascomb angelic, armed with a flaming sword that might conquer banality and smash the glass of custom. He hurried away. It was getting dark and that hellish eruption of traffic noise that rings off the walls of Rome at dusk was rising to its climax. He wandered into an art gallery on the Via Sistina where the painter or photographer—he was both—seemed to be suffering from the same infection as Bascomb, only in a more acute form. Back in the streets he wondered if there was a universality to this venereal dusk that had settled over his spirit. Had the world, as well as he, lost its way? He passed a concert hall where a program of songs was advertised and thinking that music might cleanse the thoughts of his heart he bought a ticket and went in. The concert was poorly attended. When the accompanist appeared, only a third of the seats were taken. Then the soprano came on, a splendid ash blonde in a crimson dress, and while she sang *Die Liebhaber der Brücken* old Bascomb began the disgusting and unfortunate habit of imagining that he was disrobing her. Hooks and eyes? he wondered. A zipper? While she sang *Die Feldspar* and went on to *Le Temps des lilas et le temps des roses ne reviendra plus* he settled for a zipper and imagined unfastening her dress at the back and lifting it gently off her shoulders. He got her slip over her head while she sang *L'Amore Nascondere* and undid the hooks and eyes of her brassiere during *Les Rêves de Pierrot*. His reverie was suspended when she stepped into the wings to gargle but as soon as she returned to the piano he got to work on her garter belt and all that it contained. When she took her bow at the intermission he applauded uproariously but not for her knowledge of music or the gifts of her voice. Then shame, limpid and pitiless as any passion, seemed to encompass him and he left the concert hall for the Minerva but his seizure was not over. He sat at his desk in the hotel and wrote a sonnet to the legendary Pope Joan. Technically it was an improvement over the limericks he had been writing but there was no moral improvement. In the morning he took the bus back to Monte Carbone and received some grateful admirers on his terrace. The next day he climbed to his study, wrote a few limericks, and then took some Petronius and Juvenal from the shelves to see what had been accomplished before him in this field of endeavor.

Here were candid and innocent accounts of sexual merriment. There was nowhere that sense of wickedness he experienced when he burned his work in the stove each afternoon. Was it simply that his world was that much older, its social responsibilities that much more grueling, and that lewdness was the only answer to an increase of anxiety? What was it that he had lost? It seemed then to be a sense of pride, an aureole of lightness and valor, a kind of crown. He seemed to hold the crown up to scrutiny and what did he find? Was it merely some ancient fear of Daddy's razor strap and Mummy's scowl, some childish subservience to the bullying world? He well knew his instincts to be rowdy, abundant, and indiscreet and had he allowed the world and all its tongues to impose upon him some structure of transparent values for the convenience of a conservative economy, an established church, and a bellicose army and navy? He seemed to hold the crown, hold it up into the light, it seemed made of light and what it seemed to mean was the genuine and tonic taste of exaltation and grief. The limericks he had just completed were innocent, factual, and merry. They were also obscene, but when had the facts of life become obscene and what were the realities of this virtue he so painfully stripped from himself each morning? They seemed to be the realities of anxiety and love: Amelia standing in the diagonal beam of light, the stormy night his son was born, the day his daughter married. One could disparage them as homely but they were the best he knew of life—anxiety and love—and worlds away from the limerick on his desk that began: "There was a young consul named Caesar/ Who had an enormous fissure." He burned his limerick in the stove and went down the stairs.

The next day was the worst. He simply wrote F--k

again and again covering six or seven sheets of paper. He put this into the stove at noon. At lunch Maria burned her finger, swore lengthily, and then said: "I should visit the sacred angel of Monte Giordano." "What is the sacred angel?" he asked. "The angel can cleanse the thoughts of a man's heart," said Maria. "He is in the old church at Monte Giordano. He is made of olivewood from the Mount of Olives, and was carved by one of the saints himself. If you make a pilgrimage he will cleanse your thoughts." All Bascomb knew of pilgrimages was that you walked and for some reason carried a seashell. When Maria went up to take a siesta he looked among Amelia's relics and found a seashell. The angel would expect a present, he guessed, and from the box in his study he chose the gold medal the Soviet government had given him on Lermontov's Jubilee. He did not wake Maria or leave her a note. This seemed to be a conspicuous piece of senility. He had never before been, as the old often are, mischievously elusive, and he should have told Maria where he was going but he didn't. He started down through the vineyards to the main road at the bottom of the valley.

As he approached the river a little Fiat drew off the main road and parked among some trees. A man, his wife, and three carefully dressed daughters got out of the car and Bascomb stopped to watch them when he saw that the man carried a shotgun. What was he going to do? Commit murder? Suicide? Was Bascomb about to see some human sacrifice? He sat down, concealed by the deep grass, and watched. The mother and the three girls were very excited. The father seemed to be enjoying complete sovereignty. They spoke a dialect and Bascomb understood almost nothing they said. The man took the shotgun from its case and put a single shell in the chamber. Then he arranged his wife and three daughters in a line and put their hands over their ears. They were squealing. When this was all arranged he stood with his back to them, aimed his gun at the sky, and fired. The three children applauded and exclaimed over the loudness of the noise and the bravery of their dear father. The father returned the gun to its case, they all got back into the Fiat and drove, Bascomb supposed, back to their apartment in Rome.

Bascomb stretched out in the grass and fell asleep. He

dreamed that he was back in his own country. What he saw was an old Ford truck with four flat tires, standing in a field of buttercups. A child wearing a paper crown and a bath towel for a mantle hurried around the corner of a white house. An old man took a bone from a paper bag and handed it to a stray dog. Autumn leaves smoldered in a bathtub with lion's feet. Thunder woke him, distant, shaped, he thought, like a gourd. He got down to the main road, where he was joined by a dog. The dog was trembling and he wondered if it was sick, rabid, dangerous, and then he saw that the dog was afraid of thunder. Each peal put the beast into a paroxysm of trembling and Bascomb stroked his head. He had never known an animal to be afraid of nature. Then the wind picked up the branches of the trees and he lifted his old nose to smell the rain, minutes before it fell. It was the smell of damp country churches, the spare rooms of old houses, earth closets, bathing suits put out to dry—so keen an odor of joy that he sniffed noisily. He did not, in spite of these transports, lose sight of his practical need for shelter. Beside the road was a little hut for bus travelers and he and the frightened dog stepped into this. The walls were covered with that sort of uncleanliness from which he hoped to flee and he stepped out again. Up the road was a farmhouse—one of those schizophrenic improvisations one sees so often in Italy. It seemed to have been bombed, spatch-cocked, and put together, not at random but as a deliberate assault on logic. On one side there was a wooden lean-to where an old man sat. Bascomb asked him for the kindness of his shelter and the old man invited him in.

The old man seemed to be about Bascomb's age but he seemed to Bascomb enviably untroubled. His smile was gentle and his face was clear. He had obviously never been harried by the wish to write a dirty limerick. He would never be forced to make a pilgrimage with a seashell in his pocket. He held a book in his lap—a stamp album—and the lean-to was filled with potted plants. He did not ask his soul to clap hands and sing, and yet he seemed to have reached an organic peace of mind that Bascomb coveted. Should Bascomb have collected stamps and potted plants? Anyhow it was too late. Then the rain came, thunder shook the earth, the dog whined and trembled, and Bascomb caressed him. The storm passed in a few minutes and Bascomb thanked his host and started up the road.

He had a nice stride for someone so old and he walked like all the rest of us, in some memory of prowess—love or football, Amelia, or a good dropkick—but after a mile or two he realized that he would not reach Monte Giordano until long after dark and when a car stopped and offered him a ride to the village he accepted it, hoping that this would not put a crimp in his cure. It was still light when he reached Monte Giordano. The village was about the same size as his own, with the same tufa walls and bitter lichen. The old church stood in the center of the square but the door was locked. He asked for the priest and found him in a vineyard, burning prunings. He explained that he wanted to make an offering to the sainted angel and showed the priest his golden medal. The priest wanted to know if it was true gold and Bascomb then regretted his choice. Why hadn't he chosen the medal given him by the French government or the medal from Oxford? The Russians had not hallmarked the gold and he had no way of proving its worth. Then the priest noticed that the citation was written in the Russian alphabet. Not only was it false gold; it was Communist gold and not a fitting present for the sacred angel. At that moment the clouds parted and a single ray of light came into the vineyard, lighting the medal. It was a sign. The priest drew a cross in the air and they started back to the church.

It was an old, small, poor country church. The angel was in a chapel on the left, which the priest lighted. The image, buried in jewelry, stood in an iron cage with a padlocked door. The priest opened this and Bascomb placed his Lermontov medal at the angel's feet. Then he got to his knees and said loudly: "God bless Walt Whitman. God bless Hart Crane. God bless Dylan Thomas. God bless William Faulkner, Scott Fitzgerald, and especially Ernest Hemingway." The priest locked up the sacred relic and they left the church together. There was a café on the square where he got some supper and rented a bed. This was a strange engine of brass with brass angels at the four corners, but they seemed to possess some brassy blessedness since he dreamed of peace and woke in the middle of the night finding in himself that radiance he had known when he was younger. Something seemed to shine in his mind and limbs and lights and vitals and he fell asleep again and slept until morning.

On the next day, walking down from Monte Giordano to the main road, he heard the trumpeting of a waterfall. He went into the woods to find this. It was a natural fall, a shelf of rock and a curtain of green water, and it reminded him of a fall at the edge of the farm in Vermont where he had been raised. He had gone there one Sunday afternoon when he was a boy and sat on a hill above the pool. While he was there he saw an old man, with hair as thick and white as his was now, come through the woods. He had watched the old man unlace his shoes and undress himself with the haste of a lover. First he had wet his hands and arms and shoulders and then he had stepped into the torrent, bellowing with joy. He had then dried himself with his underpants, dressed, and gone back into the woods and it was not until he disappeared that Bascomb had realized that the old man was his father.

Now he did what his father had done—unlaced his shoes, tore at the buttons of his shirt, and knowing that a mossy stone or the force of the water could be the end of him he stepped naked into the torrent, bellowing like his father. He could stand the cold for only a minute but when he stepped away from the water he seemed at last to be himself. He went on down to the main road, where he was picked up by some mounted police, since Maria had sounded the alarm and the whole province was looking for the maestro. His return to Monte Carbone was triumphant and in the morning he began a long poem on the inalienable dignity of light and air that, while it would not get him the Nobel Prize, would grace the last months of his life.

ANOTHER STORY

Paint me a wall in Verona, then, a fresco above a door. There is a flowery field in the foreground, some yellow houses or palaces, and in the distance the towers of the city. A messenger in a crimson mantle is running down some stairs on the right. Through an open door one sees an old woman lying in bed. The bed is surrounded by court attendants. Higher up the stairs two men are dueling. In the center of the field, a princess is crowning a saint or a hero with flowers. A circle of hunting dogs and other animals, including a lion, is watching the ceremony with reverence. On the far left there is a stretch of green water on which a fleet of sailing ships—five—is heading for port. High against the sky two men in court dress hang from a gibbet. My friend was a prince and Verona his home, but commuting trains, white houses planted with yews, the streets and offices of New York were his landscape, and he wore a green plush hat and a shabby, tightly belted raincoat with a cigarette burn on the sleeve.

Marcantonio Parlapiano—or Boobee, as he was called—was a poor prince. He sold sewing machines for a firm in Milan. His father had lost the last of his patrimony at the casino in Venice, and there had been a good deal of it to lose. There was a Parlapiano castle outside Verona, but the only privilege the family retained was the privilege of being buried in the crypt. Boobee loved his father in spite of his senseless loss of a fortune. He took me to tea in Verona with the old man one day, and his manners with the gambler were reverent and serene. One of Boobee's grandmothers was English, and he had light hair and blue eyes. He was a tall, slender man with an immense nose, and he moved as if he wore Renaissance trappings. He pulled on his gloves finger by finger, tightened the belt of his raincoat as if a sword depended from it, and cocked his plush hat as if it were covered with plumes. When I first knew him, he had a mistress—a stunning and intelligent Frenchwoman. He traveled for his firm, and on a trip to Rome he met and fell in love with Grace Osborn, who was working at the American Consulate. She was a beautiful woman. There was in her character a trace of intransigence that someone shrewder would have concealed. Her politics were reactionary, and she was terribly neat. A drunken enemy once said that she was the sort of woman for whom the water glasses and toilet seats of motels and hotels are sealed. Boobee loved her for a variety of reasons, but he particularly loved the fact that she was an American. He loved America, and was the only Italian I have ever known whose favorite restaurant in Rome was the Hilton. They were married on the Campidoglio and spent their honeymoon at the Hilton. Some time later, he was transferred to the United States, and he wrote to ask if I could help find him a place to live. A house was for rent in our neighborhood, and the Parlapianos arranged to take it.

I WAS AWAY when Boobee and Grace arrived from Italy. The setting for our reunion was the station platform at Bullet Park, at seven-forty one Tuesday morning. It was very much a setting. Around a hundred commuters, mostly men, made up the cast. Here were tracks and ties and the sounds of engines, but the sense was much more of a ceremony than of journeys and separations. Our roles seemed fixed in the morning light, and since we would all return before dark, there was no sense of travel. It was the fixedness, the rectitude, of the scene that made Boobee's appearance in his green plush hat and belted raincoat seem very alien. He shouted my name, bent down and gave me a bone-cracking embrace, and kissed me loudly on both cheeks. I could not have imagined how strange, wild, and indecent such a salutation would appear to be on the station platform at seven-forty. It was sensational. I think no one laughed. Several people looked away. One friend turned pale. Our loud conversation in a language other than English caused as much of a sensation. I suppose it was thought to be affected, discourteous, and unpatriotic, but I couldn't tell Boobee to shut up or explain to him that in America if we talked in the morning we aimed at a sort of ritual banality. While my friends and neighbors talked about rotary lawn mowers and chemical fertilizers, Boobee praised the beauty of the landscape, the immaculateness of American women, and the pragmatism of American politics, and spoke of the horrors of a war with China. He kissed me goodbye on Madison Avenue. I think no one I knew was looking.

We had the Parlapianos for dinner soon after this, to introduce them to our friends. Boobee's English was terrible. "May I drop onto you for staying together?" he would ask a woman, intending merely to sit at her side. He was, however, charming, and his spontaneity and his good looks carried him along. We were unable to introduce him to any Italians, since we knew none. In Bullet Park, the bulk of the small Italian population consisted of laborers and domestics. At the top of the heap was the DeCarlo family, who were successful and prosperous contractors, but whether perforce or by chance, they seemed never to have left the confines of the Italian colony. Boobee's position was therefore ambiguous.

One Saturday morning he called to ask if I would help him with some shopping. He wanted to buy some blue jeans. He pronounced them "blugins," and it was some time before I understood what he meant. He stopped at my house a few minutes later and drove me in to the village Army and Navy store. He had a large air-conditioned car covered with chromium, and he drove like a Roman. We were speaking Italian when we entered the store. At the sound of this language the clerk scowled as if he sensed shoplifting or check kiting.

"We want some blue jeans," I said.

"Blugins," said Boobee.

"What size?"

Boobee and I discussed the fact that we did not know his measurement in inches. The clerk took a tape measure from a drawer and passed it to me. "Measure him yourself," he said. I measured Boobee and told the clerk the size. The clerk threw a pair of blue jeans on the counter, but they were not what Boobee had in mind. He explained at length and with gestures that he wanted something softer and paler. Then the proprietor, from the back of the store, shouted down the canyon of boxed work boots and denim shirts to his clerk, "Tell them it's all we got. Where they come from they wear goatskins."

Boobee understood. His nose seemed to get longer, as it did in every emotional crisis. He sighed. It had never occurred to me that in America a sovereign prince might be penalized for his foreignness. I had seen some anti-American feeling in Italy but nothing as crude as this, and anyhow I wasn't a prince. In America, Prince Parlapiano was a wop.

"Thank you very much," I said, and started for the door.

"Where you from, mister?" the clerk asked me.

"I live on Chilmark Lane," I said.

"I don't mean that," he said. "I mean where you from in Italy."

We left the store and found what Boobee wanted in another place, but I saw that his life as an alien was hazardous. He might be Prince Parlapiano at some place like the Hotel Plaza, but struggling with the menu at Chock Full O'Nuts he would be an untouchable.

I DIDN'T SEE the Parlapianos for about a month, and when I did see Boobee again, on the station platform, he seemed to have made a good many friends, although his English showed no improvement. Then Grace called to say that her parents were paying a visit and would we come for cocktails. This was a Saturday afternoon, and when we got there we found perhaps a dozen neighbors sitting around uncomfortably. Boobee had not caught on to the American cocktail hour. He was serving warm Campari and gumdrops. When I asked, in English, if I could have a Scotch, he asked what kind of Scotch I wanted. I said any Scotch would do. "Good!" he exclaimed. "Then I am giving you rye. Rye is the best Scotch, yes?" I only mention this to show that his grasp of our language and our customs was spotty.

Grace's parents were an ungainly middle-aged couple from Indiana. "We come from Indiana," said Mrs. Osborn, "but we are directly descended from the Osborns who settled in Williamsburg, Virginia, in the seventeenth century. My great-grandfather on my mother's side was an officer in the Confederate Army and was decorated by General Lee. We have this club in Florida. We're all scientists."

"Is it Cape Kennedy?" I asked.

"Christian Scientists."

I shifted to Mr. Osborn, who was a retired used-car dealer. He went on about their club. There were many millionaires among the members. The club had an eighteen-hole golf course, a marina, a college-educated dietitian, and an exacting admissions committee. He lowered his voice and shielding his mouth with one hand, said, "We try to keep out the Jews and Italians."

Boobee, standing in front of my wife, asked, "I am dropping down onto you for staying together?"

His mother-in-law, across the room, asked, "What did you say, Anthony?"

Boobee lowered his head. He seemed helpless. "I am asking Mrs. Duclose," he said shyly, "if I could drop onto her."

"If you can't speak English," Mrs. Osborn said, "it's better to keep quiet. You sound like a fruit peddler."

"I am sorry," Boobee said.

"Please sit down," my wife said, and he did, but his nose seemed to get very long. He had been injured. The awkward party lasted not much over an hour.

THEN BOOBEE CALLED me one night, one late-summer night, and said that he had to see me, and I invited him over. He wore his gloves and his green plush hat. My wife was upstairs, and since she didn't especially like Boobee, I didn't call her down. I made some drinks, and we sat in the garden.

"Listen!" Boobee said. He used the imperative *ascolta*. "Listen to me. Grace is insane. . . . Tonight, dinner is late. I was very hungry, and if I do not have my dinner punctually I lose my appetite. Grace knows this well, but when I arrived at the house there is no dinner. There is nothing to eat. She is in the kitchen burning something in a pan. I explain to her with courtesy that I must have a punctual dinner. Then you know what happens?"

I knew, but it seemed tactless to say that I knew. I said, "No."

"You could not imagine," he said. He put a hand to his heart. "Listen," he said. "She *cries*."

"Women cry easily, Boobee," I said.

"Not European women."

"But you didn't marry a European."

"That is not all. The madness now comes. She cries, and when I ask her why she cries, she explains that she is crying because in becoming my wife she has given up a great career as a soprano in opera."

I don't suppose there is much difference between the sounds of a summer night—a late-summer night—in my country and Italy, and yet it seemed so then. All the softness had gone out of the night air—fireflies and murmuring winds—and the insects in the grass around me made a sound as harsh and predatory as the sharpening of burglar's tools. It made the distance he had come from Verona seem immense. "Opera!" he cried. "La Scala! It is because of me that she is not performing tonight in La Scala. She used to take singing lessons, that is so, but she was never invited to perform. Now she is seized with this madness."

"A great many American women, Boobee, feel that in marriage they have given up a career."

"Madness," he said. He wasn't listening. "Complete madness. But what can one do? Will you speak to her?"

"I don't know what good it will do, Boobee, but I'll try."

"Tomorrow. I'll be late. Will you speak to her tomorrow?"

"Yes."

He stood and pulled on his gloves, finger by finger. Then he tossed on his plush hat with its imaginary feathers and asked, "What is the secret of my charm—my incredible ebullience?"

"I don't know, Boobee," I said, but a warm feeling of sympathy for Grace spread through my chest.

"It is because my philosophy of life includes a grasp of consequences and limitations. She has no such philosophy."

He then got into his car and started it up so abruptly that he scattered gravel all over the lawn.

I turned off the lights on the first floor and went up to our bedroom, where my wife was reading. "Boobee was here," I said. "I didn't call you."

"I know. I heard you talking in the garden." Her voice was tremulous, and then I saw there were tears on her cheek.

"What's the matter, darling?"

"Oh, I feel that I've wasted my life," she said. "I have the most terrible feeling of waste. I know it isn't your fault, but I've really given too much of myself to you and the children. I want to go back to the theatre."

I should explain about my wife's theatrical career. Some years ago a company of amateurs in the neighborhood performed Shaw's *Saint Joan*. Margaret had the lead. I was in Cleveland on business, through no choice of my own, and I didn't see the performance, but I am convinced that it was outstanding. There were to be two performances, and when the curtain came down at the end of the first there was a standing ovation. Margaret's performance has been described to me as brilliant, radiant, magnetic, and unforgettable. There was so much excitement that several directors and producers in New York were urged to come out for the second night. Several of them accepted. I was, as I have said, not there, but Margaret has told me what happened. It was a blindingly bright, cold morning. She drove the children to school and then returned and tried to rehearse her lines, but the telephone kept ringing. Everyone felt that a great actress had been discovered. It clouded over at ten, and a north wind began to blow. It began to snow at half past ten, and by noon the storm developed into a blizzard. The schools closed at one and the children were sent home. More than half the roads were closed by four. The trains were running late or not at all. Margaret was unable to get her car out of the garage, so she walked the two miles to the theatre. None of the producers or directors could make it, of course, and only half the cast showed up, so the performance was canceled. Plans were made to repeat the performance later, but the Dauphin had to go to San Francisco, the theatre was booked for other things, and the producers and directors who had agreed to come seemed, on second thought, to be suspicious about going so far afield. Margaret never played Joan again. She had the most natural regrets. The praise that had been poured into her ears rang there for months. A thrilling promise had been broken and, as anyone would, she felt that her disappointment was legitimate and deep.

I CALLED Grace Parlapiano the next day, and went to their house after work. She was pale and seemed unhappy. I said that I had talked with Boobee. "Anthony has been very difficult," she said, "and I am thinking seriously of getting a divorce or at least a legal separation. I happen to have rather a good voice, but he seems to feel that I've produced this fact out of spite and in order to humiliate him. He claims that I'm spoiled and greedy. This is, after all, the only house in the neighborhood that doesn't have wall-to-wall carpeting, but when I had a man come to give me an estimate on carpeting, Anthony lost his temper. He completely lost his temper. I know that Latins are emotional—everyone told me this before I married—but when Boobee loses his temper it's really frightening."

"Boobee loves you," I said.

"Anthony is very narrow-minded," she said. "I sometimes think he married too late in life. For instance I suggested that we join the country club. He could learn to play golf, and you know how important golf is in business. He could make a great many advantageous business connections if we joined the club, but he thinks this is unreasonable of me. He doesn't know how to dance, but when I suggested that he take dancing lessons he thought me unreasonable. I don't complain, I really don't. I don't, for instance, have a fur coat and I've never asked for one, and you know perfectly well that I'm the only woman in the neighborhood who doesn't have a fur coat."

I ended the interview clumsily, and on that note of spiritual humbug we bring to the marital difficulties of our friends. My words were useless, of course, and things got no better. I happened to know, because Boobee kept me informed on the train every morning. He did not understand that men in America do not complain about their wives, and it was a vast and painful misunderstanding. He came up to me at the station one morning and said, "You are wrong. You are very wrong. That night when I told you she had a madness, you told me it was nothing. Now listen! She is buying a grand piano, and she is hiring a singing coach. She is doing this out of spitefulness. Now do you believe that she is mad?"

"Grace is not mad," I said. "There is nothing wrong with the fact that she likes to sing. You've got to understand that her desire for a career is not spiteful. It is shared by almost every woman in the neighborhood. Margaret is working with a dramatic coach in New York three days a week and I don't consider her spiteful or insane."

"American men have no character," he said. "They are commercial and banal."

I would have hit him then, but he turned and walked away. This was evidently the end of our friendship, and I was tremendously relieved, because his accounts of Grace's madness had come to be a harrowing bore and there seemed to be no hope of changing or illuminating his point of view. He left me alone for two weeks or longer, and then he approached me again one morning. His face was dark, his nose was enlarged, his manner was definitely unfriendly. He spoke in English. "Now you will be agreeing with me," he said, "when I am telling you what she is doing. Now you will be seeing that there is no end to her spitefulness." He sighed; he whistled through his teeth. "She is for having a concert!" he exclaimed and turned away.

A FEW DAYS LATER, we received an invitation to hear Grace sing at the Aboleens'. Now, Mrs. Aboleen is the muse of our province. Through her brother, the novelist W. H. Towers, she has some literary connections, and through the bounty of her husband—a successful dental surgeon—she has a large collection of paintings. On her walls you read Dufy, Matisse, Picasso, and Braque, but the pictures on which these signatures appear are very bad, and Mrs. Aboleen is a surprisingly jealous muse. Any other woman in the neighborhood with similar inclinations is thought to be a vulgar usurper. The paintings, of course, are her paintings, but when a poet comes to spend a weekend at the Aboleens' he becomes her poet. She may display him, urge him to perform, and let you shake his hand, but if you come too close to him or talk with him for more than a minute or two she will cut in with an avid possessiveness, a kind of anger, as if she had caught you pocketing the table silver. Grace had become, I suppose, her princess. The concert was on a Sunday afternoon, a lovely day, and I went bitterly. This may have colored my judgment of Grace's performance, but everybody else said it was terrible. She sang a dozen songs, mostly in English, mostly arch and about love. Boobee's despondent sighs could be heard between the songs, and I knew he was thinking that her abysmal spitefulness had invented the whole scene—the folding chairs, the vases of flowers, the maids waiting to pass tea. He was polite enough when the concert ended, but his nose seemed enormous.

I didn't see him again for some time, and then I read one evening in the local paper that Marcantonio Parlapiano had been injured in an automobile accident on Route 67 and was recovering at the Platner Memorial Hospital. I went there at once. When I asked the nurse on his floor where I could find him, she said gaily, "Oh, you want to see Tony? Poor old Tony. Tony no speaka da English."

He was in a room with two other patients. He had broken a leg, he looked dreadful, and there were tears in his eyes. I asked him when he would be allowed to go home. "To Grace?" he asked. "Never. I am never going back. Her father and mother are with her now. They are arranging a legal separation. I am going to Verona. I am taking the *Colombo* on the twenty-seventh." He sobbed. "You know what she is asking me?" he said.

"No, Boobee. What did she ask you?"

"She is asking me to change my name." He began to cry.

I SAW HIM OFF on the *Colombo,* more because I like ships and sailings than because of the depth of our friendship, and I never saw him again. The last of my story has no more relevance than the wall in Verona, but when it happened I was reminded of Boobee, and so I'll put it down. It was a little town called Adrianapolis, about sixty miles from Yalta on the dry side of the Crimean Mountains. I had come over from the coast in a cab and was waiting for a plane to Moscow when I met another American. We were both, naturally, very happy to encounter someone who spoke English, and we went to the dining room and ordered a bottle of vodka. He was working as an engineer in a chemical-fertilizer plant in the mountains and was on his way back to the States for a six weeks' vacation. We had a table by a window overlooking the airfield, where there was very little activity. At home it would have passed for one of those private airfields you find in the suburbs, mostly used by charter flights. There was a public address system, and a young woman with a very pure and musical voice was making announcements in Russian. I couldn't understand what she was saying, but I suppose she was asking Igor Vassilyevitch Kryukov to please report to the Aeroflot ticket counter.

"That reminds me of my wife," my friend said. "The voice. I'm divorced now, but I was married five years to this girl. She was everything you could ask for. Beautiful, sexy, intelligent, loving, a great cook—she even had some money. She had planned to be an actress, but when this didn't work out she wasn't bitter or disappointed or anything. She realized she wasn't up to the competition, and she gave it up, just like that. I mean, she wasn't one of these women who claim to have given up a big career. We had a little apartment in Bayside, and she looked around for a job, and because of her training—I mean, she knew how to use her voice—they took her on at Newark Airport as an announcer. She had a very pretty voice, not affected or anything, very calm and humorous and musical. She worked on a four-hour shift, saying things like 'Will passengers for United's jet flight to Seattle please board at Gate Sixteen? Will Mr. Henry Tavistock please report to the American Airlines ticket counter? Will Mr. Henry Tavistock please report to the American Airlines ticket counter?' I suppose that girl is saying the same sort of thing." He nodded his head toward the loudspeaker. "It was a great job, and just working four hours a day she made more money than I did, and she had plenty of time to shop and cook and be wifely, at which she was very good. Well, when we had about five thousand in the savings account, we began to think about having a child and moving out to the country. She had been announcing at Newark then for about five years. Well, one night before supper, I was drinking whiskey and reading the paper when I heard her say, in the kitchen, 'Will you please come to the table? Supper is ready. Will you please come to the table?' She was speaking to me in that same musical voice she used at the airport, and it made me angry, and so I said, 'Honey, don't speak to me like that—don't speak to me in that voice,' and then she said, 'Will you please come to the table?' just as if she was saying, 'Will Mr. Henry Tavistock please report to the American Airlines ticket counter?' So then I said, 'Honey, you make me feel as if I were waiting for a plane or something. I mean your voice is very pretty, but you sound very impersonal.' So then she said, in this very well-modulated voice, 'I don't suppose that can be helped,' and she gave me one of those forced, sweet smiles like those airplane clerks give you when your flight is four hours late and you've missed the connecting flight and will have to spend a week in Copenhagen. So then we sat down to dinner, and all through dinner she talked to me in this even and musical voice. It was like having dinner with a recording. It was like having dinner with a tape. So then, after dinner, we watched some television, and she went to bed and then she called to me, 'Will you please come to bed now? Will you please come to bed now?' It was just like being told that passengers for San Francisco were boarding at Gate Seven. I went to bed, and thought things would be better in the morning.

"Anyhow, the next night when I came home I shouted, 'Hello, honey!' or something like that, and I heard this very impersonal voice from the kitchen saying, 'Will you please go to the corner drugstore and get me a tube of Pepsodent? Will you please go to the corner drugstore and get me a tube of Pepsodent?' So then I went into the kitchen and gathered her up in my arms and gave her a big, messy kiss and said, 'Come off it, baby, come off it.' Then she began to cry, and I thought this might be a step in the right direction, but she cried and cried and said I was unfeeling and cruel and just imagined things about her voice that weren't true in order to pick a quarrel. Well, we stayed together for another six months, but that was really the end of it. I really loved her. She was a marvelous girl until she began to give me this feeling that I was a dumb passenger, one of hundreds in some waiting room, being directed to the right gate and the right flight. We quarreled all the time then, and I finally left, and she got a consent decree in Reno. She still works at Newark, and naturally I prefer Kennedy, but sometimes I have to use Newark, and I can hear her telling Mr. Henry Tavistock to please report to the American Airlines ticket counter. . . . But it isn't only in Newark that I hear her voice, it's everywhere. Orly, London, Moscow, New Delhi. I have to travel by air, and in every airport in the whole wide world I can hear her voice or a voice just like hers asking Mr. Henry Tavistock to please report to the ticket counter. Nairobi, Leningrad, Tokyo, it's always the same even if I can't understand the language, and it reminds me of how happy I was those five years and what a lovely girl she was, really lovely, and what mysterious things can happen in love. Shall we have another bottle of vodka? I'll pay for it. They give me more rubles than I can spend for the trip, and I have to turn them in at the border."

PERCY

REMINISCENCE, along with the cheeseboards and ugly pottery sometimes given to brides, seems to have a manifest destiny with the sea. Reminiscences are written on such a table as this, corrected, published, read, and then they begin their inevitable journey toward the bookshelves in those houses and cottages one rents for the summer. In the last house we rented, we had beside our bed the *Memories of a Grand Duchess*, the *Recollections of a Yankee Whaler*, and a paperback copy of *Goodbye to All That*, but it is the same all over the world. The only book in my hotel room in Taormina was *Recordi d'un Soldato Garibaldino*, and in my room in Yalta I found «Повесть о Жизни.» Unpopularity is surely some part of this drifting toward salt water, but since the sea is our most universal symbol for memory, might there not be some mysterious affinity between these published recollections and the thunder of waves? So I put down what follows with the happy conviction that these pages will find their way into some bookshelf with a good view of a stormy coast. I can even see the room—see the straw rug, the window glass clouded with salt, and feel the house shake to the ringing of a heavy sea.

Great-uncle Ebenezer was stoned on the streets of Newburyport for his abolitionist opinions. His demure wife, Georgiana (an artiste on the pianoforte), used once or twice a month to braid feathers into her hair, squat on the floor, light a pipe, and, having been given by psychic forces the personality of an Indian squaw, receive messages from the dead. My father's cousin, Anna Boynton, who had taught Greek at Radcliffe, starved herself to death during the Armenian famine. She and her sister Nanny had the copper skin, high cheekbones, and black hair of the Natick Indians. My father liked to recall the night he drank all the champagne on the New York–Boston train. He started drinking splits with some friend before dinner, and when they finished the splits they emptied the quarts and the magnums and were working on a jero-

oam when the train reached Boston. He felt that this guz-
ling was heroic. My Uncle Hamlet—a black-mouthed old
vreck who had starred on the Newburyport Volunteer
ire Department ball team—called me to the side of his
leathbed and shouted, "I've had the best fifty years of this
ountry's history. *You* can have the rest." He seemed to
and it to me on a platter—droughts, depressions, convul-
ions of nature, pestilence, and war. He was wrong, of
ourse, but the idea pleased him. This all took place in the
nvirons of Athenian Boston, but the family seemed much
loser to the hyperbole and rhetoric that stem from Wales,
Dublin, and the various principalities of alcohol than to
he sermons of Phillips Brooks.

One of the most vivid members of my mother's side of
he family was an aunt who called herself Percy, and who
moked cigars. There was no sexual ambiguity involved.
he was lovely, fair, and intensely feminine. We were
ever very close. My father may have disliked her, al-
hough I don't recall this. My maternal grandparents had
migrated from England in the 1890s with their six children. My Grandfather Holinshed was described as a bound-
er—a word that has always evoked for me the image of a
nan leaping over a hedge just ahead of a charge of buck-
hot. I don't know what mistakes he had made in England,
ut his transportation to the New World was financed by
is father-in-law, Sir Percy Devere, and he was paid a
mall remittance so long as he did not return to England.
He detested the United States and died a few years after
is arrival here. On the day of his funeral, Grandmother
nnounced to her children that there would be a family
onference in the evening. They should be prepared to dis-
uss their plans. When the conference was called, Grand-
nother asked the children in turn what they planned to
nake of their lives. Uncle Tom wanted to be a soldier.
Uncle Harry wanted to be a sailor. Uncle Bill wanted to be
a merchant. Aunt Emily wanted to marry. Mother wanted
o be a nurse and heal the sick. Aunt Florence—who later
called herself Percy—exclaimed, "I wish to be a great
painter, like the Masters of the Italian Renaissance!"
Grandmother then said, "Since at least one of you has a
clear idea of her destiny, the rest of you will go to work and
Florence will go to art school." That is what they did, and
so far as I know none of them ever resented this decision.

How smooth it all seems and how different it must have been. The table where they gathered would have been lighted by whale oil or kerosene. They lived in a farmhouse in Dorchester. They would have had lentils or porridge or at best stew for dinner. They were very poor. If it was in the winter, they would be cold, and after the conference the wind would extinguish Grandmother's candle —stately Grandmother—as she went down the back path to the malodorous outhouse. They couldn't have bathed more than once a week, and I suppose they bathed out of pails. The succinctness of Percy's exclamation seems to have obscured the facts of a destitute widow with six children. Someone must have washed all those dishes, and washed them in greasy water, drawn from a pump and heated over a fire.

The threat of gentility in such recollections is Damoclean, but these were people without pretense or affectation, and when Grandmother spoke French at the dinner table, as she often did, she merely meant to put her education to some practical use. It was, of course, a much simpler world. For example, Grandmother read in the paper one day that a drunken butcher, the father of four, had chopped up his wife with a meat cleaver, and she went directly to Boston by horsecar or hansom—whatever transportation was available. There was a crowd around the tenement where the murder had taken place, and two policemen guarded the door. Grandmother got past the policemen and found the butcher's four terrified children in a bloody apartment. She got their clothes together, took the children home with her, and kept them for a month or longer, when other homes were found. Cousin Anna's decision to starve and Percy's wish to become a painter were made with the same directness. It was what Percy thought she could do best—what would make most sense of her life.

She began to call herself Percy in art school, because she felt that there was some prejudice against women in the arts. In her last year in art school she did a six-by-fourteen-foot painting of Orpheus taming the beasts. This won her a gold medal and a trip to Europe, where she studied at the Beaux-Arts for a few months. When she returned, she was given three portrait commissions, but she was much too skeptical to succeed at this. Her portraits were pictorial indictments, and all three of them were unacceptable. She was not an aggressive woman, but she was immoderate and critical.

After her return from France she met a young doctor named Abbott Tracy at some yacht club on the North Shore. I don't mean the Corinthian. I mean some briny huddle of driftwood nailed together by weekend sailors. Moths in the billiard felt. Salvaged furniture. Two earth closets labeled "Ladies" and "Gentlemen," and moorings for a dozen of those wide-waisted catboats that my father used to say sailed like real estate. Percy and Abbott Tracy met in some such place, and she fell in love. He had already begun a formidable and clinical sexual career, and seemed unacquainted in any way with sentiment, although I recall that he liked to watch children saying their prayers. Percy listened for his footsteps, she languished in his absence, his cigar cough sounded to her like music, and she filled a portfolio with pencil sketches of his face, his eyes, his hands, and, after their marriage, the rest of him.

They bought an old house in West Roxbury. The ceilings were low, the rooms were dark, the windows were small, and the fireplaces smoked. Percy liked all of this, and shared with my mother a taste for drafty ruins that seemed odd in such high-minded women. She turned a spare bedroom into a studio and did another large canvas—Prometheus bringing fire to man. This was exhibited in Boston, but no one bought it. She then painted a nymph and centaur. This used to be in the attic, and the centaur looked exactly like Uncle Abbott. Uncle Abbott's practice was not very profitable, and I guess he was lazy. I remember seeing him eating his breakfast in pajamas at one in the afternoon. They must have been poor, and I suppose Percy did the housework, bought the groceries, and hung out the wash. Late one night when I had gone to bed, I overheard my father shouting, "I cannot support that cigar-smoking sister of yours any longer." Percy spent some time copying paintings at Fenway Court. This brought in a little money, but evidently not enough. One of her friends from art school urged her to try painting magazine covers. This went deeply against all of her aspirations and instincts, but it must have seemed to her that she had no choice, and she began to turn out deliberately sentimental pictures for magazines. She got to be quite famous at this.

She was never pretentious, but she couldn't forget that she had not explored to the best of her ability those gifts that she may have had, and her enthusiasm for painting was genuine. When she was able to employ a cook, she gave the cook painting lessons. I remember her saying, toward the end of her life, "Before I die, I must go back to the Boston Museum and see the Sargent watercolors." When I was sixteen or seventeen, I took a walking tour in Germany with my brother and bought Percy some van Gogh reproductions in Munich. She was very excited by these. Painting, she felt, had some organic vitality—it was the exploration of continents of consciousness, and here was a new world. The deliberate puerility of most of her work had damaged her draftsmanship, and at one point she began to hire a model on Saturday mornings and sketch from life. Going there on some simple errand—the return of a book or a newspaper clipping—I stepped into her studio and found, sitting on the floor, a naked young woman. "Nellie Casey," said Percy, "this is my nephew, Ralph Warren." She went on sketching. The model smiled sweetly—it was nearly a social smile and seemed to partially temper her monumental nakedness. Her breasts were very beautiful, and the nipples, relaxed and faintly colored, were bigger than silver dollars. The atmosphere was not erotic or playful, and I soon left. I dreamed for years of Nellie Casey. Percy's covers brought in enough money for her to buy a house on the Cape, a house in Maine, a large automobile, and a small painting by Whistler that used to hang in the living room beside a copy Percy had made of Titian's *Europa.*

Her first son, Lovell, was born in the third year of her marriage. When he was four or five years old, it was decided that he was a musical genius, and he did have unusual manual dexterity. He was great at unsnarling kite lines and fishing tackle. He was taken out of school, educated by tutors, and spent most of his time practicing the piano. I detested him for a number of reasons. He was extremely dirty-minded, and used oil on his hair. My brother and I wouldn't have been more disconcerted if he had crowned himself with flowers. He not only used oil on his hair but when he came to visit us he left the hair-oil bottle in our medicine cabinet. He had his first recital in Steinway Hall when he was eight or nine, and he always played a Beethoven sonata when the family got together.

Percy must have perceived, early in her marriage, that her husband's lechery was compulsive and incurable, but she was determined, like any other lover, to authenticate her suspicion. How could a man that she adored be faithless? She hired a detective agency, which tracked him down to an apartment house near the railroad station called the Orpheus. Percy went there and found him in bed with an unemployed telephone operator. He was smoking a cigar and drinking whiskey. "Now, Percy," he is supposed to have said, "why did you have to go and do this?" She then came to our house and stayed with us for a week or so. She was pregnant, and when her son Beaufort was born his brain or his nervous system was seriously damaged. Abbott always claimed that there was nothing wrong with his son, but when Beaufort was five or six years old he was sent off to some school or institution in Connecticut. He used to come home for the holidays, and had learned to sit through an adult meal, but that was about all. He was an arsonist, and he once exposed himself at an upstairs window while Lovell was playing the "Waldstein." In spite of all this, Percy was never bitter or melancholy, and continued to worship Uncle Abbott.

The family used to gather, as I recall, almost every Sunday. I don't know why they should have spent so much time in one another's company. Perhaps they had few friends or perhaps they held their family ties above friendship. Standing in the rain outside the door of Percy's old house, we seemed bound together not by blood and not by love but by a sense that the world and its works were hostile. The house was dark. It had a liverish smell.

The guests often included Grandmother and old Nanny Boynton, whose sister had starved herself to death. Nanny taught music in the Boston public schools until her retirement, when she moved to a farm on the South Shore. Here she raised bees and mushrooms, and read musical scores—Puccini, Mozart, Debussy, Brahms, etc.—that were mailed to her by a friend in the public library. I remember her very pleasantly. She looked, as I've said, like a Natick Indian. Her nose was beaked, and when she went to the beehives she covered herself with cheesecloth and sang *Vissi d'arte*. I once overheard someone say that she was drunk a good deal of the time, but I don't believe it. She stayed with Percy when the winter weather was bad, and she always traveled with a set of the Britannica, which was set up in the dining room behind her chair to settle disputes.

The meals at Percy's were very heavy. When the wind blew, the fireplaces smoked. Leaves and rain fell outside the windows. By the time we retired to the dark living room, we were all uncomfortable. Lovell would then be asked to play. The first notes of the Beethoven sonata would transform that dark, close, malodorous room into a landscape of extraordinary beauty. A cottage stood in some green fields near a river. A woman with flaxen hair stepped out of the door and dried her hands on an apron. She called her lover. She called and called, but something was wrong. A storm was approaching. The river would flood. The bridge would be washed away. The bass was massive, gloomy, and prophetic. Beware, beware! Traffic casualties were unprecedented. Storms lashed the west coast of Florida. Pittsburgh was paralyzed by a blackout. Famine gripped Philadelphia, and there was no hope for anyone. Then the lyric treble sang a long song about love and beauty. When this was done, down came the bass again, fortified by more bad news reports. The storm was traveling north through Georgia and Virginia. Traffic casualties were mounting. There was cholera in Nebraska. The Mississippi was over its banks. A live volcano had erupted in the Appalachians. Alas, alas! The treble resumed its part of the argument, persuasive, hopeful, purer than any human voice I had ever heard. Then the two voices began their counterpoint, and on it went to the end.

One afternoon, when the music was finished, Lovell, Uncle Abbott, and I got into the car and drove into the Dorchester slums. It was in the early winter, already dark and rainy, and the rains of Boston fell with great authority. He parked the car in front of a frame tenement and said that he was going to see a patient.

"You think he's going to see a patient?" Lovell asked.

"Yes," I said.

"He's going to see his girl friend," Lovell said. Then he began to cry.

I didn't like him. I had no sympathy to give him. I only wished that I had more seemly relations. He dried his tears, and we sat there without speaking until Uncle Abbott returned, whistling, contented, and smelling of perfume. He took us to a drugstore for some ice cream, and then we went back to the house, where Percy was opening the living-room windows to let in some air. She seemed tired but still high-spirited, although I suppose that she and everyone else in the room knew what Abbott had been up to. It was time for us to go home.

LOVELL ENTERED the Eastman Conservatory when he was fifteen, and performed the Beethoven G-Major Concerto with the Boston orchestra the year he graduated. Having been drilled never to mention money, it seems strange that I should recall the financial details of his début. His tails cost one hundred dollars, his coach charged five hundred, and the orchestra paid him three hundred for two performances. The family was scattered throughout the hall, so we were unable to concentrate our excitement, but we were all terribly excited. After the concert we went to the greenroom and drank champagne. Koussevitzky did not appear, but Burgin, the concertmaster, was there. The reviews in the *Herald* and the *Transcript* were fairly complimentary, but they both pointed out that Lovell's playing lacked sentiment. That winter, Lovell and Percy went on a tour that took them as far west as Chicago, and something went wrong. They may, as travelers, have been bad company for one another; he may have had poor notices or small audiences; and while nothing was ever said, I recall that the tour was not triumphant. When they returned, Percy sold a piece of property that adjoined the house and went to Europe for the summer. Lovell could surely have supported himself as a musician, but instead he took a job as a manual laborer for some electrical-instrument company. He came to see us before Percy returned, and told me what had been happening that summer.

"Daddy didn't spend much time around the house after Mother went away," he said, "and I was alone most evenings. I used to get my own supper, and I spent a lot of time at the movies. I used to try and pick up girls, but I'm skinny and I don't have much self-confidence. Well, one

Sunday I drove down to this beach in the old Buick. Daddy let me have the old Buick. I saw this very fat couple with a young daughter. They looked lonely. Mrs. Hirshman is very fat, and she makes herself up like a clown, and she has a little dog. There is a kind of fat woman who always has a little dog. So then I said something about how I loved dogs, and they seemed happy to talk with me, and then I ran into the waves and showed off my crawl and came back and sat with them. They were Germans, and they had a funny accent, and I think their funny English and their fatness made them lonely. Well, their daughter was named Donna-Mae, and she was all wrapped up in a bathrobe, and she had on a hat, and they told me she had such fair skin she had to keep out of the sun. Then they told me she had beautiful hair, and she took off her hat, and I saw her hair for the first time. It *was* beautiful. It was the color of honey and very long, and her skin was pearly. You could see that the sun would burn it. So we talked, and I got some hot dogs and tonic, and took Donna-Mae for a walk up the beach, and I was very happy. Then, when the day was over, I offered to drive them home—they'd come to the beach in a bus—and they said they'd like a ride if I'd promise to have supper with them. They lived in a sort of a slum, and he was a house painter. Their house was behind another house. Mrs. Hirshman said while she cooked supper why didn't I wash Donna-Mae off with the hose? I remember this very clearly, because it's when I fell in love. She put on her bathing suit again, and I put on my bathing suit, and I sprayed her very gently with the hose. She squealed a little, naturally, because the water was cold, and it was getting dark, and in the house next door someone was playing the Chopin C-Sharp-Minor, Opus 28. The piano was out of tune, and the person didn't know how to play, but the music and the hose and Donna-Mae's pearly skin and golden hair and the smells of supper from the kitchen and the twilight all seemed to be a kind of paradise. So I had supper with them and went home, and the next night I took Donna-Mae to the movies. Then I had supper with them again, and when I told Mrs. Hirshman that my mother was away and that I almost never saw my father, she said that they had a spare room and why didn't I stay there? So the next night I packed some clothes and moved into their spare room, and I've been there ever since."

It is unlikely that Percy would have written my mother after her return from Europe, and, had she written, the letter would have been destroyed, since that family had a crusading detestation of souvenirs. Letters, photographs, diplomas—anything that authenticated the past was always thrown into the fire. I think this was not, as they claimed, a dislike of clutter but a fear of death. To glance backward was to die, and they did not mean to leave a trace. There was no such letter, but had there been one it would, in the light of what I was told, have gone like this:

Dear Polly:

Lovell met me at the boat on Thursday. I bought him a Beethoven autograph in Rome, but before I had a chance to give it to him he announced that he was engaged to be married. He can't afford to marry, of course, and when I asked him how he planned to support a family he said that he had a job with some electrical-instrument company. When I asked about his music he said he would keep it up in the evenings. I do not want to run his life and I want him to be happy but I could not forget the amount of money that has been poured into his musical education. I had looked forward to coming home and I was very upset to receive this news as soon as I got off the boat. Then he told me that he no longer lived with his father and me. He lives with his future parents-in-law.

I was kept busy getting settled and I had to go into Boston several times to find work so I wasn't able to entertain his fiancée until I had been back a week or two. I asked her for tea. Lovell asked me not to smoke cigars and I agreed to this. I could see his point. He is very uneasy about what he calls my "bohemianism" and I wanted to make a good impression. They came at four. Her name is Donna-Mae Hirshman. Her parents are German immigrants. She is twenty-one years old and works as a clerk in some insurance office. Her voice is high. She giggles. The one thing that can be said in her favor is that she has a striking head of yellow hair. I suppose Lovell may be attracted by her fairness but this hardly seems reason enough to marry. She giggled when we were introduced. She sat on the red sofa and as soon as she saw *Europa* she giggled again. Lovell could not take his eyes off her. I poured her tea and asked if she wanted lemon or cream. She said she didn't know. Then I asked politely what she usually took in her tea and she said she'd never drunk tea before. Then I asked what she usually drank and she said she drank mostly tonic and sometimes beer. I gave her tea with milk and sugar, and tried to think of something to say. Lovell broke the ice by asking me if I didn't think her hair was beautiful. I said that it was very beautiful. Well, it's a lot of work, she said. I have to wash it twice a week in whites of egg. Oh, there's been plenty of times when I've wanted to cut it off. People don't understand. People think that if God crowns you with a beautiful head of hair you ought to treasure it but it's just as much work as a sinkful of dishes. You have to wash it and dry it and comb it and brush it and put it up at night. I know it's hard to understand but honest to God there's days when I would just like to chop it off but Mummy made me promise on the Bible that I wouldn't. I'll take it down for you if you'd like.

I'm telling you the truth, Polly. I am not exaggerating. She went to the mirror, took a lot of pins out of her hair, and let it down. There was a great deal of it. I suppose she could sit on it although I didn't ask. I said that it was very beautiful several times. Then she said that she had known I would appreciate it because Lovell had told her I was artistic and interested in beautiful things. Well she displayed her hair for some time and then began the arduous business of getting it back into place again. It was hard work. Then she went on to say that some people thought her hair was dyed and that this made her angry because she felt that women who dyed their hair were immoral. I asked her if she would like another cup of tea and she said no. Then I asked her if she had ever heard Lovell play the piano and she said no, they didn't have a piano. Then she looked at Lovell and said that it was time to go. Lovell drove her home and then came back to ask, I suppose, for some words of approval. Of course my heart was broken in two. Here was a great musical career ruined by a head of hair. I told him I never wanted to see her again. He said he was going to marry her and I said I didn't care what he did.

Lovell married Donna-Mae. Uncle Abbott went to the wedding, but Percy kept her word and never saw her daughter-in-law again. Lovell came to the house four times a year to pay a ceremonial call on his mother. He would not go near the piano. He had not only given up his music, he hated music. His simple-minded taste for obsceneness seemed to have transformed itself into simple-minded piety. He had transferred from the Episcopal church to the Hirshmans' Lutheran congregation, which he attended twice on Sundays. They were raising money to build a new church when I last spoke with him. He spoke intimately of the Divinity. "He has helped us in our struggles, again and again. When everything seemed hopeless, He has given us encouragement and strength. I wish I could get you to understand how wonderful He is, what a blessing it is to love Him. . . ." Lovell died before he was thirty, and since everything must have been burned, I don't suppose there was a trace left of his musical career.

But the darkness in the old house seemed, each time we went there, to deepen. Abbott continued his philandering, but when he went fishing in the spring or hunting in the fall Percy was desperately unhappy without him. Less than a year after Lovell's death, Percy was afflicted with some cardiovascular disease. I remember one attack during Sunday dinner. The color drained out of her face, and her breathing became harsh and quick. She excused herself and was mannered enough to say that she had forgotten something. She went into the living room and shut the door, but her accelerated breathing and her groans of pain could be heard. When she returned, there were large splotches of red up the side of her face. "If you don't see a doctor, you will die," Uncle Abbott said.

"You are my husband and you are my doctor," she said.

"I have told you repeatedly that I will not have you as a patient."

"You are my doctor."

"If you don't come to your senses, you will die."

He was right, of course, and she knew it. Now, as she saw the leaves fall, the snow fall, as she said goodbye to friends in railroad stations and vestibules, it was always with a sense that she would not do this again. She died at three in the morning, in the dining room, where she had gone to get a glass of gin, and the family gathered for the last time at her funeral.

There is one more incident. I was taking a plane at Logan Airport. As I was crossing the waiting room, a man who was sweeping the floor stopped me.

"Know you," he said thickly. "I know who you are."

"I don't remember," I said.

"I'm Cousin Beaufort," he said. "I'm your cousin Beaufort."

I reached for my wallet and took out a ten-dollar bill.

"I don't want any money," he said. "I'm your cousin. I'm your cousin Beaufort. I have a job. I don't want any money."

"How are you, Beaufort?" I asked.

"Lovell and Percy are dead," he said. "They buried them in the earth."

"I'm late, Beaufort," I said. "I'll miss my plane. It was nice to see you. Goodbye." And so off to the sea.

THE FOURTH ALARM

I SIT IN THE SUN drinking gin. It is ten in the morning. Sunday. Mrs. Uxbridge is off somewhere with the children. Mrs. Uxbridge is the housekeeper. She does the cooking and takes care of Peter and Louise.

It is autumn. The leaves have turned. The morning is windless, but the leaves fall by the hundreds. In order to see anything—a leaf or a blade of grass—you have, I think, to know the keenness of love. Mrs. Uxbridge is sixty-three, my wife is away, and Mrs. Smithsonian (who lives on the other side of town) is seldom in the mood these days, so I seem to miss some part of the morning as if the hour had a threshold or a series of thresholds that I cannot cross. Passing a football might do it but Peter is too young and my only football-playing neighbor goes to church.

My wife, Bertha, is expected on Monday. She comes out from the city on Monday and returns on Tuesday. Bertha is a good-looking young woman with a splendid figure. Her eyes, I think, are a little close together and she is sometimes peevish. When the children were young she had a peevish way of disciplining them. "If you don't eat the nice breakfast Mummy has cooked for you before I count three," she would say, "I will send you back to bed. One. Two. *Three. . . .*" I heard it again at dinner. "If you don't eat the nice dinner Mummy has cooked for you before I count three I will send you to bed without any supper. One. Two. Three. . . ." I heard it again. "If you don't pick up your toys before Mummy counts three Mummy will throw them all away. One. Two. Three. . . ." So it went on through the bath and bedtime and one two three was their lullaby. I sometimes thought she must have learned to count when she was an infant and that when the end came she would call a countdown for the Angel of Death. If you'll excuse me I'll get another glass of gin.

When the children were old enough to go to school, Bertha got a job teaching social studies in the sixth grade. This kept her occupied and happy and she said she had always wanted to be a teacher. She had a reputation for strictness. She wore dark clothes, dressed her hair simply, and expected contrition and obedience from her pupils. To vary her life she joined an amateur theatrical group. She played the maid in *Angel Street* and the old crone in *Desmonds Acres*. The friends she made in the theatre were all pleasant people and I enjoyed taking her to their parties. It is important to know that Bertha does not drink. She will take a Dubonnet politely but she does not enjoy drinking.

Through her theatrical friends, she learned that a nude show called *Ozamanides II* was being cast. She told me this and everything that followed. Her teaching contract gave her ten days' sick leave, and claiming to be sick one day she went into New York. *Ozamanides* was being cast at a producer's office in midtown, where she found a line of a hundred or more men and women waiting to be interviewed. She took an unpaid bill out of her pocketbook, and waving this as if it were a letter she bucked the line saying, "Excuse me please, excuse me, I have an appointment. . . ." No one protested and she got quickly to the head of the line, where a secretary took her name, Social Security number, etc. She was told to go into a cubicle and undress. She was then shown into an office where there were four men. The interview, considering the circumstances, was very circumspect. She was told that she would be nude throughout the performance. She would be expected to simulate or perform copulation twice during the performance and participate in a love pile that involved the audience.

I remember the night when she told me all of this. It was in our living room. The children had been put to bed. She was very happy. There was no question about that. "There I was naked," she said, "but I wasn't in the least embarrassed. The only thing that worried me was that my feet might get dirty. It was an old-fashioned kind of place with framed theatre programs on the wall and a big photograph of Ethel Barrymore. There I sat naked in front of these strangers and I felt for the first time in my life that I'd found myself. I found myself in nakedness. I felt like a new woman, a better woman. To be naked and unashamed in front of strangers was one of the most exciting experiences I've ever had. . . ."

I didn't know what to do. I still don't know, on this Sunday morning, what I should have done. I guess I should have hit her. I said she couldn't do it. She said I couldn't stop her. I mentioned the children and she said this experience would make her a better mother. "When I took off my clothes," she said, "I felt as if I had rid myself of everything mean and small." Then I said she'd never get the job because of her appendicitis scar. A few minutes later the phone rang. It was the producer offering her a part. "Oh, I'm so happy," she said. "Oh, how wonderful and rich and strange life can be when you stop playing out the roles that your parents and their friends wrote out for you. I feel like an explorer."

THE FITNESS of what I did then or rather left undone still confuses me. She broke her teaching contract, joined Equity, and began rehearsals. As soon as *Ozamanides* opened she hired Mrs. Uxbridge and took a hotel apartment near the theatre. I asked for a divorce. She said she saw no reason for a divorce. Adultery and cruelty have well-marked courses of action but what can a man do when his wife wants to appear naked on the stage? When I was younger I had known some burlesque girls and some of them were married and had children. However, they did what Bertha was going to do only on the midnight Saturday show, and as I remember their husbands were third-string comedians and the kids always looked hungry.

A day or so later I went to a divorce lawyer. He said a consent decree was my only hope. There are no precedents for simulated carnality in public as grounds for divorce in New York State and no lawyer will take a divorce case without a precedent. Most of my friends were tactful about Bertha's new life. I suppose most of them went to see her, but I put it off for a month or more. Tickets were expensive and hard to get. It was snowing the night I went to the theatre, or what had been a theatre. The proscenium arch had been demolished, the set was a collection of used tires, and the only familiar features were the seats and the aisles. Theatre audiences have always confused me. I suppose this is because you find an incomprehensible variety of types thrust into what was an essentially domestic and terribly ornate interior. There were all kinds there that night. Rock music was playing when I came in. It was that deafening old-fashioned kind of rock they used to play in places like Arthur. At eight-thirty the houselights dimmed, and the cast—there were fourteen—came down the aisles. Sure enough, they were all naked excepting Ozamanides, who wore a crown.

I can't describe the performance. Ozamanides had two sons, and I think he murdered them, but I'm not sure. The sex was general. Men and women embraced one another and Ozamanides embraced several men. At one point a stranger, sitting in the seat on my right, put his hand on my knee. I didn't want to reproach him for a human condition, nor did I want to encourage him. I removed his hand and experienced a deep nostalgia for the innocent movie theatres of my youth. In the little town where I was raised there was one—the Alhambra. My favorite movie was called *The Fourth Alarm*. I saw it first one Tuesday after school and stayed on for the evening show. My parents worried when I didn't come home for supper and I was scolded. On Wednesday I played hooky and was able to see the show twice and get home in time for supper. I went to school on Thursday but I went to the theatre as soon as school closed and sat partway through the evening show. My parents must have called the police, because a patrolman came into the theatre and made me go home. I was forbidden to go to the theatre on Friday, but I spent all Saturday there, and on Saturday the picture ended its run. The picture was about the substitution of automobiles for horse-drawn fire engines. Four fire companies were involved. Three of the teams had been replaced by engines and the miserable horses had been sold to brutes. One team remained, but its days were numbered. The men and the horses were sad. Then suddenly there was a great fire. One saw the first engine, the second, and the third race off to the conflagration. Back at the horse-drawn company, things were very gloomy. Then the fourth alarm rang—it was their summons—and they sprang into action, harnessed the team, and galloped across the city. They put out the fire, saved the city, and were given an amnesty by the Mayor. Now on the stage Ozamanides was writing something obscene on my wife's buttocks.

Had nakedness—its thrill—annihilated her sense of nostalgia? Nostalgia—in spite of her close-set eyes—was one of her principal charms. It was her gift gracefully to carry the memory of some experience into another tense. Did she, mounted in public by a naked stranger, remember any of the places where we had made love—the rented houses close to the sea, where one heard in the sounds of a summer rain the prehistoric promises of love, peacefulness, and beauty? Should I stand up in the theatre and shout for her to return, return, return in the name of love, humor, and serenity? It was nice driving home after parties in the snow, I thought. The snow flew into the headlights and made it seem as if we were going a hundred miles an hour. It was nice driving home in the snow after parties. Then the cast lined up and urged us—commanded us in fact—to undress and join them.

This seemed to be my duty. How else could I approach understanding Bertha? I've always been very quick to get out of my clothes. I did. However, there was a problem. What should I do with my wallet, wristwatch, and car keys? I couldn't safely leave them in my clothes. So, naked, I started down the aisle with my valuables in my right hand. As I came up to the action a naked young man stopped me and shouted—sang—"Put down your lendings. Lendings are impure."

"But it's my wallet and my watch and the car keys," I said.

"Put down your lendings," he sang.

"But I have to drive home from the station," I said, "and I have sixty or seventy dollars in cash."

"Put down your lendings."

"I can't, I really can't. I have to eat and drink and get home."

"Put down your lendings."

Then one by one they all, including Bertha, picked up the incantation. The whole cast began to chant: "Put down your lendings, put down your lendings."

The sense of being unwanted has always been for me acutely painful. I suppose some clinician would have an explanation. The sensation is reverberative and seems to attach itself as the last link in a chain made up of all similar experience. The voices of the cast were loud and scornful, and there I was, buck naked, somewhere in the middle of the city and unwanted, remembering missed football tackles, lost fights, the contempt of strangers, the sound of laughter from behind shut doors. I held my valuables in my right hand, my literal identification. None of it was irreplaceable, but to cast it off would seem to threaten my essence, the shadow of myself that I could see on the floor, my name.

I went back to my seat and got dressed. This was difficult in such a cramped space. The cast was still shouting. Walking up the sloping aisle of the ruined theatre was powerfully reminiscent. I had made the same gentle ascent after *King Lear* and *The Cherry Orchard*. I went outside.

It was still snowing. It looked like a blizzard. A cab was stuck in front of the theatre and I remembered then that I had snow tires. This gave me a sense of security and accomplishment that would have disgusted Ozamanides and his naked court; but I seemed not to have exposed my inhibitions but to have hit on some marvelously practical and obdurate part of myself. The wind flung the snow into my face and so, singing and jingling the car keys, I walked to the train.

ARTEMIS, THE HONEST WELL DIGGER

ARTEMIS LOVED the healing sound of rain—the sound of all running water—brooks, gutters, spouts, falls, and taps. In the spring he would drive one hundred miles to hear the cataract at the Wakusha Reservoir. This was not so surprising, since he was a well driller and water was his profession, his livelihood as well as his passion. Water, he thought, was at the root of civilizations. He had seen photographs of a city in Umbria that had been abandoned when the wells went dry. Cathedrals, palaces, farmhouses had all been evacuated by drought—a greater power than pestilence, famine, or war. Men sought water as water sought its level. The pursuit of water accounted for epochal migrations. Man was largely water. Water was man. Water was love. Water was water.

To get the facts out of the way: Artemis drilled with an old Smith & Mathewson chain-concussion rig that struck the planet sixty blows a minute. It made a terrible racket and there had been two complaints. One was from a very nervous housewife and the other from a homosexual poet who said that the concussion was ruining his meter. Artemis rather liked the noise. He lived with his widowed mother at the edge of town in one of those little conclaves of white houses that are distinguished by their displays of the American flag. You find them on outlying roads—six or seven small houses gathered together for no particular reason. There is no store, no church, nothing central. The lawns on which dogs sleep are well trimmed and everything is neat, but every house flies its Old Glory. This patriotic zeal cannot be traced back to the fact that these people have received an abundance of their country's riches. They haven't. These are hard-working people who lead frugal lives and worry about money. People who have profited splendidly from our economy seem to have no such passion for the Stars and Stripes. Artemis' mother, for example—a hard-working woman—had a flagpole, five little flags stuck into a window box, and a seventh flag hanging from the porch.

His father had chosen his name, thinking that it referred to artesian wells. It wasn't until Artemis was a grown man that he discovered he had been named for the chaste goddess of the hunt. He didn't seem to mind and, anyhow, everybody called him Art. He wore work clothes and in the winter a seaman's knitted cap. His manner with strangers was rustic and shy and something of an affectation, since he read a good deal and had an alert and inquisitive intelligence. His father had learned his trade as an apprentice and had not graduated from high school. He regretted not having an education and was very anxious that his son should go to college. Artemis went to a small college called Laketon in the north of the state and got an engineering degree. He was also exposed to literature through an unusually inspiring professor named Lytle. Physically, there was nothing remarkable about Lytle, but he was the sort of teacher in whose presence students had for many years felt an irresistible desire to read books, write themes, and discuss their most intimate feelings about the history of mankind. Lytle singled out Artemis and encouraged him to read Swift, Donne, and Conrad. He wrote four themes for this course, which Lytle charitably graded A. His ear for prose was damaged by an incurable fascination for words like "cacophony," "percussion," "throbbingly," and "thumpingly." This may have had something to do with his profession.

Lytle suggested that he get an editorial job on an engineering journal and he seriously thought about this, but he chose instead to be a well driller. He made his decision one Saturday when he and his father took their rig to the south of the county, where a large house—an estate—had been built. There was a swimming pool and seven baths and the well produced three gallons a minute. Artemis contracted to go down another hundred feet, but even then the take was only six gallons a minute. The enormous, costly, and useless house impressed him with the importance of his trade. Water, water. (What happened in the end was that the owner demolished six upstairs bedrooms to make room for a storage tank, which the local fire department filled twice a week.)

Artemis' knowledge of ecology was confined to water.

Going fishing on the first of April, he found the falls of the South Branch foaming with soapsuds. Some of this was bound to leach down to where he worked. Later in the month, he caught a five-pound trout in the stream at Lakeside. This was a phenomenal fish for that part of the world and he stopped to show his catch to the game warden and ask him how it should be cooked. "Don't bother to cook that fish," said the warden. "It's got enough DDT to put you in the hospital. You can't eat these fish any more. The government sprayed the banks with DDT about four years ago and the stuff all washed into the brook." Artemis had once dug a well and found DDT, and another had traces of fuel oil. His sense of a declining environment was keen and intensely practical. He contracted to find potable water and if he failed he lost his shirt. A polluted environment meant for him both sadness at human stupidity and rapaciousness and also a hole in his pocket. He had failed only twice, but the odds were running against him and everybody else.

Another thing: Artemis distrusted dowsers. A few men and two women in the county made their living by divining the presence of subterranean water with forked fruit twigs. The fruit had to have a pit. An apple twig, for example, was no good. When the fruit twig and the diviner's psyche had settled on a site, Artemis would be hired to drill a well. In his experience, the dowsers' average was low and they seldom divined an adequate supply of water, but the fact that some magic was involved seemed to make them irresistible. In the search for water, some people preferred a magician to an engineer. If magic bested knowledge, how simple everything would be: water, water.

Artemis was the sort of man who frequently proposed marriage, but at thirty he still had no wife. He went around for a year or so with the Macklin girl. They were lovers, but when he proposed marriage, she ditched him to marry Jack Bascomb because he was rich. That's what she said. Artemis was melancholy for a month or so, and then he began going around with a divorcée named Maria Petroni who lived on Maple Avenue and was a bank teller. He didn't know, but he had the feeling that Maria was older than he. His ideas about marriage were romantic and a little puerile and he expected his wife to be a fresh-faced virgin. Maria was not. She was a lusty, hard-drinking woman and they spent most of their time together in bed. One night or early morning, he woke at her side and thought over his life. He was thirty and he still had no bride. He had been dating Maria for nearly two years. Before he moved toward her to wake her, he thought of how humorous, kind, passionate, and yielding she had always been. He thought, while he stroked her backside, that he loved her. Her backside seemed almost too good to be true. The image of a pure, fresh girl like the girl on the oleomargarine package still lingered in some part of his head, but where was she and when would she appear? Was he kidding himself? Was he making a mistake to downgrade Maria for someone he had never seen? When she woke, he asked her to marry him.

"I can't marry you, darling," she said.

"Why not? Do you want a younger man?"

"Yes, darling, but not one. I want seven, one right after the other."

"Oh," he said.

"I must tell you. I've done it. This was before I met you. I asked seven of the best-looking men around to come for dinner. None of them were married. Two of them were divorced. I cooked veal scaloppine. There was a lot to drink and then we all got undressed. It was what I wanted. When they were finished, I didn't feel dirty or depraved or shameful. I didn't feel anything bad at all. Does that disgust you?"

"Not really. You're one of the cleanest people I've ever known. That's the way I think of you."

"You're crazy, darling," she said.

He got up and dressed and kissed her good night, but that was about it. He went on seeing her for a while, but her period of faithfulness seemed to have passed and he guessed that she was seeing other men. He went on looking for a girl as pure and fresh as the girl on the oleomargarine package.

This was in the early fall and he was digging a well for an old house on Olmstead Road. The first well was running dry. The people were named Filler and they were paying him thirty dollars a foot, which was the rate at that time. He was confident of finding water from what he knew of the lay of the land. When he got the rig going, he settled down in the cab of his truck to read a book. Mrs.

Filler came out to the truck and asked if he didn't want a cup of coffee. He refused as politely as he could. She wasn't bad-looking at all, but he had decided, early in the game, to keep his hands off the housewives. He wanted to marry the girl on the oleomargarine package. At noon he opened his lunch pail and was halfway through a sandwich when Mrs. Filler came back to the cab. "I've just cooked a nice hamburger for you," she said.

"Oh, no, thank you, ma'am," he said. "I've got three sandwiches here." He actually said "ma'am" and he sometimes said "shucks," although the book he was reading, and reading with interest, was by Aldous Huxley.

"You've got to come in now," she said. "I won't take no for an answer." She opened the cab door and he climbed down and followed at her side to the back door.

She had a big butt and a big front and a jolly face and hair that must have been dyed, because it was a mixture of grays and blues. She had set a place for him at the kitchen table and she sat opposite him while he ate his hamburger. She told him directly the story of her life, as was the custom in the United States at that time. She was born in Evansville, Indiana, had graduated from the Evansville North High School, and had been elected apple-blossom queen in her senior year. She then went on to the university in Bloomington, where Mr. Filler, who was older than she, had been a professor. They moved from Bloomington to Syracuse and then to Paris, where he became famous.

"What's he famous for?" asked Artemis.

"You mean you've never heard of my husband?" she said. "J. P. Filler. He's a famous author."

"What did he write?" asked Artemis.

"Well, he wrote a lot of things," she said, "but he's best known for *Shit*."

Artemis laughed, Artemis blushed. "What's the name of the book?" he asked.

"*Shit*," she said. "That's the name of it. I'm surprised you never heard of it. It sold about half a million copies."

"You're kidding," Artemis said.

"No, I'm not," she said. "Come with me. I'll show you."

He followed her out of the kitchen through several rooms, much richer and more comfortable than anything he was familiar with. She took from a shelf a book whose title was *Shit*. "My God," said Artemis, "how did he come to write a book like that?"

"Well," she said, "when he was at Syracuse, he got a foundation grant to investigate literary anarchy. He took a year off. That's when we went to Paris. He wanted to write a book about something that concerned everybody, like sex, only by the time he got his grant, everything you could write about sex had been written. Then he got this other idea. After all, it was universal. That's what he said. It concerned everybody. Kings and Presidents and sailors at sea. It was just as important as fire, water, earth, and air. Some people might think it was not a very delicate subject to write about, but he hates delicacy, and anyhow, considering the books you can buy these days, *Shit* is practically pure. I'm surprised you never heard about it. It was translated into twelve languages. See." She gestured toward a bookcase, where Artemis read *Merde*, *Kaka*, くそ and говно. "I can give you a paperback, if you'd like."

"I'd like to read it," said Artemis.

She got a paperback from a closet. "It's too bad he isn't here. He would be glad to autograph it for you, but he's in England. He travels a lot."

"Well, thank you, ma'am," said Artemis. "Thank you for the lunch and the book. I have to get back to work."

He checked the rig, climbed into the cab, and put down Huxley for J. P. Filler. He read the book with a certain amount of interest, but his incredulity was stubborn. Except to go to and from college, Artemis had never traveled, and yet he often felt himself to be a traveler, to be among strangers. Walking down a street in China, he would have felt no more alien than he felt at that moment, trying to comprehend the fact that he lived in a world where a man was wealthy and esteemed for having written a book about turds.

That's what it was about: turds. There were all shapes, sizes, and colors, along with a great many descriptions of toilets. Filler had traveled widely. There were the toilets of New Delhi and the toilets of Cairo and he had either imagined or visited the Pope's chambers in the Vatican and the facilities of the Imperial Palace in Tokyo. There were quite a few lyrical descriptions of nature—loose bowels in a lemon grove in Spain, constipation in a mountain pass in Nepal, dysentery on the Greek islands. It was not really a dull book and it had, as she had said, a distinct universality, although Artemis continued to feel that he had strayed into some country like China. He was not a prude, but he used a prudent vocabulary. When a well came too close to a septic tank, he referred to the danger as "fecal matter." He had been "down on" (his vocabulary) Maria many times, but to count these performances and to recall in detail the techniques seemed to diminish the experience. There was, he thought, a height of sexual ecstasy that by its immensity and profoundness seemed to transcend observation. He finished the book a little after five. It looked like rain. He killed the rig, covered it with a tarpaulin, and drove home. Passing a bog, he tossed away his copy of *Shit*. He didn't want to hide it and he would have had trouble describing it to his mother and, anyhow, he didn't want to read it again.

The next day it rained and Artemis got very wet. The rig worked loose and he spent most of the morning making it secure. Mrs. Filler was worried about his health. First she brought him a towel. "You'll catch your death of cold, you darling boy," she said. "Oh, look how curly your hair is." Later, carrying an umbrella, she brought him a cup of tea. She urged him to come into the house and change into dry clothes. He said that he couldn't leave the rig.

"Anyhow," he said, "I never catch cold." As soon as he said this, he began to sneeze. Mrs. Filler insisted that he either come into her house or go home. He was uncomfortable and he gave up around two. Mrs. Filler had been right. By suppertime, his throat was sore. His head was unclear. He took two aspirins and went to bed around nine. He woke after midnight in the hot-and-cold spasms of a high fever. The effect of this was strangely to reduce him to the emotional attitudes of a child. He curled up in an embryonic position, his hands between his knees, alternately sweating and shivering. He felt himself lonely but well protected, irresponsible, and cozy. His father seemed to live again and would bring him, when he came home from work, a new switch for his electric train or a lure for his tackle box. His mother brought him some breakfast and took his temperature. He had a fever of 103 and dozed for most of the morning.

At noon his mother came in to say that there was a lady downstairs to see him. She had brought some soup. He said that he didn't want to see anyone, but his mother seemed doubtful. The lady was a customer. Her intentions were kind. It would be rude to turn her away. He felt too feeble to show any resistance, and a few minutes later Mrs. Filler stood in the doorway with a preserve jar full of broth. "I told him he'd be sick, I told him that yesterday."

"I'll go next door and see if they have any aspirin," said his mother. "We've used ours all up." She left the room and Mrs. Filler closed the door.

"Oh, you poor boy," she said. "You poor boy."

"It's only a cold," he said. "I never get sick."

"But you are sick," she said. "You are sick and I told you you would be sick, you silly boy." Her voice was tremulous and she sat on the edge of his bed and began to stroke his brow. "If you'd only come into my house, you'd be out there today, swinging your sledge hammer." She extended her caresses to his chest and shoulders and then, reaching under the bedclothes, hit, since Artemis never wore pajamas, pay dirt. "Oh, you lovely boy," said Mrs. Filler. "Do you always get hard this quickly? It's so hard." Artemis groaned and Mrs. Filler went to work. Then he arched his back and let out a muffled yell. The trajectory of his discharge was a little like the fireballs from a Roman candle and may explain our fascination with these pyrotechnics. Then they heard the front door open and Mrs. Filler left his bed for a chair by the window. Her face was very red and she was breathing heavily.

"All the aspirin they have is baby aspirin," said his mother. "It's pink, but I guess if you take enough of it, it works all right."

"Why don't you go to the drugstore and buy some aspirin?" said Mrs. Filler. "I'll stay with him while you're gone."

"I don't know how to drive," said Artemis' mother. "Isn't that funny? In this day and age. I've never learned how to drive a car." Mrs. Filler was about to suggest that she walk to the drugstore, but she realized that this might expose her position. "I'll telephone the drugstore and see if they deliver," his mother said, and left the room with the door open. The telephone was in the hallway and Mrs. Filler remained in her chair. She stayed a few minutes longer and parted on a note of false cheerfulness.

"Now, you get better," she said, "and come back and dig me a nice well."

He was back at work three days later. Mrs. Filler was not there, but she returned around eleven with a load of groceries. At noon, when he was opening his lunch pail, she came out of the house carrying a small tray on which there were two brown, steaming drinks. "I've brought you a toddy," she said. He opened the cab door and she climbed in and sat beside him.

"Is there whiskey in it?" asked Artemis.

"Just a drop," she said. "It's mostly tea and lemon. It will help you get better." Artemis tasted his toddy and thought he had never tasted anything so strong. "Did you read my husband's book?" she asked.

"I looked at it," Artemis said slyly. "I didn't understand it. I mean, I didn't understand why he had to write about that. I don't read very much, but I suppose it's better than some books. The kind of books I really hate are the kind of books where people just walk around and light cigarettes and say things like 'good morning.' They just walk around. When I read a book, I want to read about earthquakes and exploring and tidal waves. I don't want to read about people walking around and opening doors."

"Oh, you silly boy," she said. "You don't know anything."

"I'm thirty years old," said Artemis, "and I know how to drill a well."

"But you don't know what I want," she said.

"You want a well, I guess," he said. "A hundred gallons a minute. Good drinking water."

"I don't mean that. I mean what I want now."

He slumped a little in the seat and unfastened his trousers. She dipped her head, a singular gesture rather like a bird going after seed or water. "Hey, that's great," said Artemis, "that's really great. You want me to tell you when I'm going to come?" She simply shook her head. "Big load's on its way," said Artemis. "Big load's coming down the line. You want me to hold it?" She shook her head. "Ouch," yelled Artemis. "Ouch." One of his limitations as a lover was that, at the most sublime moment, he usually shouted, "Ouch, ouch, ouch." Maria had often complained about this. "Ouch," roared Artemis. "Ouch, ouch, ouch," as he was racked by a large orgasm. "Hey, that was great," he said, "that was really great but I'll bet it's unhealthy. I mean, I'll bet if you do that all the time, you'd get to be round-shouldered."

She kissed him tenderly and said, "You're crazy." That made two. He gave her one of his sandwiches.

The rig was then down to three hundred feet. The next day, Artemis hauled up the hammer and lowered the cylinder that measured water. The water was muddy but not soapy and he guessed the take to be about twenty gallons a minute. When Mrs. Filler came out of the house, he told her the news. She didn't seem pleased. Her face was swollen and her eyes were red. "I'll go down another fifteen or twenty feet," Artemis said. "I think you'll have a nice well."

"And then you'll go away," she said, "and never come back." She began to cry.

"Don't cry," said Artemis. "Please don't cry, Mrs. Filler. I hate to see women crying."

"I'm in love," she sobbed loudly.

"Well, I guess a nice woman like you must fall in love pretty often," Artemis said.

"I'm in love with you," she sobbed. "It's never happened to me before. I wake up at five in the morning and start waiting for you to come. Six o'clock, seven o'clock, eight o'clock. It's agony. I can't live without you."

"What about your husband?" asked Artemis cheerfully.

"He knows," she sobbed. "He's in London. I called him last night. I told him. It didn't seem fair to have him come home expecting a loving wife when his wife is in love with someone else."

"What did he say?"

"He didn't say anything. He hung up. He's scheduled to come back tonight. I have to meet the plane at five. I love you. I love you. I love you."

"Well, have to get back to work, ma'am," said Artemis at his most rustic. "You go back to the house now and get some rest." She turned and started for the house. He would have liked to console her—sorrow of any sort distressed him—but he knew that any gesture on his part would be hazardous. He reset the rig and went down another twenty feet, where he estimated the take to be about thirty gallons a minute. At three-thirty, Mrs. Filler left. She scowled at him as she drove past. As soon as she had gone, he moved hastily. He capped the well, got his rig onto the truck, and drove home. About nine that night, the phone rang. He thought of not answering or of asking his mother to take it, but his mother was watching television and he had his responsibilities as a well driller. "You've got around thirty-five gallons a minute," he said. "Haversham will install the pump. I don't know whether or not you'll need another storage tank. Ask Haversham. Goodbye."

The next day, he took his shotgun and a package of sandwiches and walked the woods north of the town. He was not much of a wing shot and there weren't many birds, but it pleased him to walk through the woods and pastures and climb the stone walls. When he got home, his mother said, "She was here. That lady. She brought you a present." She passed him a box in which there were three silk shirts and a love letter. Later that evening, when the telephone rang, he asked his mother to say that he was out. It was, of course, Mrs. Filler. Artemis had not taken a vacation in several years and he could see that the time to travel had arrived. In the morning, he went to a travel agency in the village.

The agency was in a dark, narrow room on a dark street, its walls blazing with posters of beaches, cathedrals, and couples in love. The agent was a gray-haired woman. Above her desk was a sign that said: YOU HAVE TO BE CRAZY TO BE A TRAVEL AGENT. She seemed harassed and her voice was cracked with age, whiskey, or tobacco. She chain-smoked. She twice lighted cigarettes when there was a cigarette smoking in the ashtray. Artemis said that he had five hundred to spend and would like to be away for about two weeks. "Well, I suppose you've seen Paris, London, and Disneyland," she said. "Everyone has. There's Tokyo, of course, but they tell me it's a very tiring flight. Seventeen hours in a 707, with a utility stop in Fairbanks. My most satisfied customers these days are the ones who go to Russia. There's a package." She flashed a folder at him. "For three hundred and twenty-eight dollars, you get economy round-trip air fare to Moscow, twelve days in a first-class hotel with all your meals, free tickets to hockey, ballet, opera, theatre, and a pass to the public swimming pool. Side trips to Leningrad and Kiev are optional." He asked what else she might suggest. "Well, there's Ireland," she said, "but it's rainy now. A plane hasn't landed in London for nearly ten days. They stack up at Liverpool and then you take a train down. Rome is cold. So is Paris. It takes three days to get to Egypt. For a two-week trip the Pacific is out, but you could go to the Caribbean, although reservations are very hard to get. I suppose you'll want to buy souvenirs and there isn't much to buy in Russia."

"I don't want to buy anything," Artemis said. "I just want to travel."

"Take my advice," she said, "and go to Russia."

It seemed the maximum distance that he could place between himself and Mr. and Mrs. Filler. His mother was imperturbable. Most women who owned seven American flags would have protested, but she said nothing but "Go where you want, Sonny. You deserve a change." His visa and passport took a week, and one pleasant evening he boarded the eight-o'clock Aeroflot from Kennedy to Moscow. Most of the other passengers were Japanese and couldn't speak English and it was a long and a lonely trip.

It was raining in Moscow, so Artemis heard what he liked—the sound of rain. The Japanese spoke Russian and he trailed along behind them across the tarmac to the main building, where they formed a line. The line moved slowly and he had been waiting for an hour or longer when a good-looking woman approached him and asked, "Are you Mr. Artemis Bucklin? I have very good news for you. Come with me." She found his bag and bucked the lines for customs and immigration. A large black car was waiting for them. "We will go first to your hotel," she said. She had a marked English accent. "Then we will go to the Bolshoi Theatre, where our great Premier, Nikita Sergeevich Khrushchev, wants to welcome you as a member of the American proletariat. People of many occupations come to visit our beautiful country, but you are the first well driller." Her voice was lilting and she seemed very happy with her news. Artemis was confused, tired, and dirty. Looking out of the car window, he saw an enormous portrait of the Premier nailed to a tree. He was frightened.

Why should he be frightened? He had dug wells for rich and powerful people and had met them without fear or shyness. Khrushchev was merely a peasant who, through cunning, vitality, and luck, had made himself the master of a population of over two hundred million. That was the rub; and as the car approached the city, portraits of Khrushchev looked in at Artemis from bakeries, department stores, and lampposts. Khrushchev banners flapped in the wind on a bridge across the Moskva River. In Mayakovsky Square, a large, lighted portrait of Khrushchev beamed down upon his children as they rushed for the subway entrance.

Artemis was taken to a hotel called the Ukraine. "We are already late," the young woman said.

"I can't go anywhere until I've taken a bath and shaved," said Artemis. "I can't go anywhere looking like this. And I would like something to eat."

"You go up and change," she said, "and I'll meet you in the dining room. Do you like chicken?"

Artemis went up to his room and turned on the hot water in his tub. As anyone could guess, nothing happened. He shaved in cold water and was beginning to dress when the hot-water spout made a Vesuvian racket and began to ejaculate rusty and scalding water. He bathed in this, dressed, and went down. She was sitting at a table in the dining room, where his dinner had been served. She had kindly ordered a carafe of vodka, which he drank off before he ate his chicken. "I do not want to hasten you," she said, "but we will be late. I will try to explain. Today is the jubilee of the Battle of Stavitsky. We will go to the Bolshoi Theatre and you will sit on the presidium. I won't be able to sit with you, so you will understand very little of what is said. There will be speeches. Then, after the speeches are over, there will be a reception at the rear of the stage, where our great Premier, Nikita Sergeevich Khrushchev, will welcome you as a member of the American proletariat to the Union of Soviet Socialist Republics. I think we should go."

The same car and driver waited for them and, on the trip from the Ukraine to the Bolshoi, Artemis counted seventy portraits of the man he was about to meet. They entered the Bolshoi by a back door. He was taken onto the stage, where the speeches had begun. The jubilee was being televised and the lights for this made the stage as hot as a desert, an illusion that was extended by the fact that the stage was flanked with plastic palm trees. Artemis could understand nothing that was said, but he looked around for the Premier. He was not in the principal box. This was occupied by two very old women. At the end of an hour of speeches, his anguish turned to boredom and the unease of a full bladder. At the end of another hour, he was merely sleepy. Then the ceremony ended. There was a buffet backstage and he went there as he had been directed, expecting Khrushchev to make his terrifying appearance, but the Premier was not around and when Artemis asked if he was expected, he was given no answer. He ate a sandwich and drank a glass of wine. No one spoke to him. He decided to walk home from the Bolshoi in order to stretch his legs. As soon as he left the theatre a policeman stopped him. He kept repeating the name of his hotel and pointing to his shoes, and when the policeman understood, he gave him directions. Off went Artemis. It seemed to be the same route he had taken in the car, but all the portraits of Khrushchev had vanished. All those pictures that had beamed down on him from bakeries, lampposts, and walls were gone. He thought he was lost, until he crossed a bridge over the Moskva River that he remembered for its banners. They no longer flew. When he reached the hotel, he looked for a large portrait of Khrushchev that had hung in the lobby. Gone. So, like many other travelers before him, he went upstairs to a strange room in a strange country humming the unreality blues. How could he have guessed that Khrushchev had been deposed?

He had breakfast in the dining room with an Englishman who told him the facts. He also suggested that if Artemis needed an interpreter, he should go to the Central Government Agency and not Intourist. He wrote, in the Cyrillic alphabet, an address on a card. He ordered the waiters around officiously in Russian and Artemis was impressed with his fluency; but he was, in fact, one of those travelers who can order fried eggs and hard liquor in seven languages but who can't count to ten in more than one.

There were cabs in front of the hotel and Artemis gave the address to a driver. They took the same route they had taken to the Bolshoi and Artemis was able to recheck the fact that all the portraits of Khrushchev had been removed in two hours or three at the most. It must have taken hundreds of men. The address was a dingy office building with a sign in English as well as Russian. Artemis climbed some shabby stairs to a door that was padded. Why padded? Silence? Madness? He opened the door onto a brightly lighted office and told a striking young woman that he wanted an interpreter to take him around Moscow.

The Russians don't seem to have gotten the bugs out of illumination. There is either too much light or too little and the light the young woman stood in was seedy. She had, however, or so he thought, enough beauty to conquer the situation. If a thousand portraits of Khrushchev could vanish in three hours, couldn't he fall in love in three minutes? He seemed to. She was about five foot five. He was six feet, which meant that she was the right size, a consideration he had learned to respect. Her brow and the shape of her head were splendid and she stood with her head raised a little, as if she were accustomed to speaking to people taller than herself. She wore a tight sweater that showed her fine breasts and her skirt was also tight. She seemed to be in charge of the office, but in spite of her manifest executive responsibilities, there was not a trace of aggressiveness in her manner. Her femininity was intense. Her essence seemed to lie in two things: a sense of girlishness and the quickness with which she moved her head. She seemed capable of the changeableness, the moodiness of someone much younger. (She was, he discovered later, thirty-two.) She moved her head as if her vision were narrow, as if it moved from object to object, rather than to take in the panorama. Her vision was not narrow, but that was the impression he got. There was some nostalgia in her appearance, some charming feminine sense of the past. "Mrs. Kosiev will take you around," she said. "Without taxi fares, that will be twenty-three rubles." She spoke with exactly the same accent as the woman who had met him at the airport. (He would never know, but they had both learned their English off a tape made at the university in Leningrad by an English governess turned Communist.)

He knew none of the customs of this strange country, but he decided to take a chance. "Will you have dinner with me?" he asked.

She gave him an appraising and pleasant look. "I'm going to a poetry reading," she said.

"Can I come with you?" he asked.

"Why, yes," she said. "Of course. Meet me here at six." Then she called for Mrs. Kosiev. This was a broad-shouldered woman who gave him a manly handshake but no smile. "Will you please give our guest from the United States the twenty-three-ruble tour of Moscow?" He counted out twenty-three rubles and put them on the desk of the woman with whom he had just fallen in love.

Going down the stairs, Mrs. Kosiev said, "That was Natasha Funaroff. She is the daughter of Marshal Funaroff. They have lived in Siberia. . . ."

After this piece of information, Mrs. Kosiev began to praise the Union of Soviet Socialist Republics and continued this for the rest of the day. They walked a short distance from the office to the Kremlin, where she first took him to the Armory. A long line was waiting at the door, but they bucked this. Inside, they put felt bags over their shoes and Artemis was shown the crown jewels, the royal horse tack, and some of the royal wardrobe. Artemis was bored and had begun to feel terribly tired. They toured three churches in the Kremlin. These seemed to him rich, lofty, and completely mysterious. They then took a cab to the Tretyakov Gallery. Artemis had begun to notice that the smell of Moscow—so far from any tilled land—was the smell of soil, sour curds, sour whey, and earth-stained overalls. It lingered in the massive lobby of the Ukraine. The golden churches of the Kremlin, scoured of their incense, smelled like barns, and in the gallery, the smell of curds and whey was augmented by a mysterious but distinct smell of cow manure. At one, Artemis said he was hungry and they had some lunch. They then went to the Lenin Library and, after that, to a deconsecrated monastery that had been turned into a folk museum. Artemis had seen more than enough, and after the monastery he said that he wanted to return to the hotel. Mrs. Kosiev said that the tour was not completed and that there would be no rebate. He said he didn't care and took a cab back to the Ukraine.

He returned to the office at six. She was waiting in the street, waiting by the door. "Did you have a nice tour?" she asked.

"Oh, yes," said Artemis. "Oh, yes. I don't seem to like museums, but then, I've never been in any and perhaps it's something I could learn."

"I detest museums," she said. She took his arm lightly, lightly touched his shoulder with hers. Her hair was a very light brown—not really blond—but it shone in the street lights. It was straight and dressed simply with a short queue in the back, secured with an elastic band. The air was damp and cold and smelled of diesel exhaust. "We are going to hear Luncharvsky," she said. "It isn't far. We can walk."

Oh, Moscow, Moscow, that most anonymous of all anonymous cities! There were some dead flowers on the bust of Chaliapin, but they seemed to be the only flowers in town. Part of the clash of a truly great city on an autumn night is the smell of roasting coffee and (in Rome) wine and new bread and men and women carrying flowers home to a lover, a spouse, or nobody in particular, nobody at all. As it grew darker and the lights went on, Artemis seemed to find none of the excitement of a day's ending. Through a window he saw a child reading a book, a woman frying potatoes. Was it because with all the princes gone and all the palaces still standing one felt, for better or for worse, that a critical spectrum of the city's life had been extinguished? They passed a man carrying three loaves of new bread in a string basket. The man was singing. This made Artemis happy. "I love you, Natasha Funaroff," he said.

"How did you know my name?"

"Mrs. Kosiev told me all about you."

They saw ahead of them the statue of Mayakovsky, although Artemis didn't (doesn't today) know anything about the poet. It was gigantic and tasteless, a relic of the Stalin era that reshaped the whole pantheon of Russian literature to resemble the sons of Lenin. (Even poor Chekhov was given posthumously heroic shoulders and a massive brow.) It grew darker and darker and more lights went on. Then, as they saw the crowd, Artemis saw that the smoke from their cigarettes had formed, thirty or forty feet in the air, a flat, substantial, and unnatural cloud. He supposed this was some process of inversion. Before they reached the square, he could hear Luncharvsky's voice. Russian is a more percussive language than English, less musical but more diverse, and this may account for its carrying power. The voice was powerful, not only in volume but in its emotional force. It seemed melancholy and exalted. Artemis understood nothing beyond the noise. Luncharvsky stood on a platform below the statue of Mayakovsky, declaiming love lyrics to an audience of one thousand or two thousand, who stood under their bizarre cloud or canopy of smoke. He was not singing, but the force of his voice was the force of singing. Natasha made a gesture as if she had brought him to see one of the wonders of the world and he thought that perhaps she had.

He was a traveler, a stranger, and he had traveled this far to see strange things. The dusk was cold, but Luncharvsky was in his shirt sleeves. His shoulders were broad—broad-boned, that is. His arms were long. His hands were large and when he closed them into a fist, as he did every few minutes, the fist seemed massive. He was a tall man. His hair was yellow, not cut and not combed. His eyes had the startling and compelling cast of a man unremittently on the up and up. Artemis had the feeling that not only did he command the attention of the crowd but had anyone there been momentarily inattentive, he would have known it. At the end of the recitation, someone passed him a bouquet of dying chrysanthemums and his suit coat. "I'm hungry," said Artemis.

"We will go to a Georgian restaurant," she said. "A Georgian kitchen is our best kitchen."

They went to a very noisy place where Artemis had chicken for the third time. Leaving the restaurant, she took his arm again, pressed her shoulder against his, and led him down a street. He wondered if she would take him home and if she did, what would he find? Old parents, brothers, sisters, or perhaps a roommate? "Where are we going?" he asked.

"To the park. Is that all right?"

"That's fine," said Artemis. The park, when they reached it, was like any other. There were trees, losing their leaves at that time of year, benches, and concrete walks. There was a concrete statue of a man holding a child on his shoulders. The child held a bird. Artemis supposed they were meant to represent progress or hope. They sat on a bench, he put an arm around her and kissed her. She responded tenderly and expertly and for the next half hour they kissed each other. Artemis felt relaxed, loving, close to sappy. When he stood to straighten the protuberance in his trousers, she took his hand and led him to an apartment house a block or so away. An armed policeman stood by the door. She took what Artemis guessed was an identity card out of her purse. The policeman scrutinized this in a way that was meant to be offensive. He seemed openly bellicose. He sneered, glowered, pointed several times to Artemis, and spoke to her as if she were contemptible. In different circumstances—in a different country—Artemis would have hit him. Finally, they were allowed to pass and they took an elevator—a sort of cage—to another floor. Even the apartment house smelled to Artemis like a farm. She unlocked a door with two keys and led him into a dingy room. There was a bed in one corner. Clothes hung to dry from a string. On a table, there was half a loaf of bread and some scraps of meat. Artemis quickly got out of his clothes, as did she, and they (his choice of words) made love. She cleaned up the mess with a cloth, put a lighted cigarette between his lips, and poured him a glass of vodka. "I don't ever want this to end," Artemis said. "I don't ever want this to end." Lying with her in his arms, he felt a thrilling and galvanic sense of their indivisibility, although they were utter strangers. He was thinking idly about a well he had drilled two years ago and God knows what she was thinking about. "What was it like in Siberia?" he asked.

"Wonderful," she said.

"What was your father like?"

"He liked cucumbers," she said. "He was a marshal until we were sent to Siberia. When we came back, they gave him an office in the Ministry of Defense. It was a little office. There was no chair, no table, no desk, no telephone, nothing. He used to go there in the morning and sit on the floor. Then he died. Now you'll have to go."

"Why?"

"Because it's late and I'll worry about you."

"Can I see you tomorrow?"

"Of course."

"Can you come to my hotel?"

"No, I couldn't do that. It wouldn't be safe for me to be seen in a tourist hotel and, anyhow, I hate them. We can meet in the park. I'll write the address." She left the bed and walked across the room. Her figure was astonishing—it seemed in its perfection to be almost freakish. Her breasts were large, her waist was very slender and her backside was voluminous. She carried it with a little swag, as if it were filled with buckshot. Artemis dressed, kissed her good night, and went down. The policeman stopped him but finally let him go, since neither understood anything the other said. When Artemis asked for his key at the hotel, there was some delay. Then a man in uniform appeared, holding Artemis' passport, and extracted the visa.

"You will leave Moscow tomorrow morning," he said. "You will take SAS flight 769 to Copenhagen and change for New York."

"But I want to see your great country," Artemis said. "I want to see Leningrad and Kiev."

"The airport bus leaves at half past nine."

In the morning, Artemis had the Intourist agent in the lobby telephone the interpreters' bureau. When he asked for Natasha Funaroff, he was told there was no such person there; there never had been. Forty-eight hours after his arrival, he was winging his way home. The other passengers on the plane were American tourists and he was able to talk and make friends and pass the time.

ARTEMIS WENT to work a few days later drilling in hardpan outside the village of Brewster. The site had been chosen by a dowser and he was dubious, but he was wrong. At four hundred feet he hit limestone and a stream of sweet water that came in at one hundred gallons a minute. It was sixteen days after his return from Moscow that he got his first letter from Natasha. His address on the envelope was in English, but there was a lot of Cyrillic writing and the stamps were brilliantly colored. The letter disconcerted his mother and had, she told him, alarmed the postman. To go to Russia was one thing, but to receive letters from that strange and distant country was something else. "My darling," Natasha had written. "I dreamed last night that you and I were a wave on the Black Sea at Yalta. I know you haven't seen that part of my country, but if one were a wave, moving toward shore, one would be able to see the Crimean Mountains covered with snow. In Yalta sometimes when there are roses in bloom, you can see snow falling on the mountains. When I woke from the dream, I felt elevated and relaxed and I definitely had the taste of salt in my mouth. I must sign this letter Fifi, since nothing so irrational could have been written by your loving Natasha."

He answered her letter that night. "Dearest Natasha, I love you. If you will come to this country, I will marry you. I think of you all the time and I would like to show you how we live—the roads and trees and the lights of the cities. It is very different from the way you live. I am serious about all of this, and if you need money for the plane trip, I will send it. If you decided that you didn't want to marry me, you could go home again. Tonight is Halloween. I don't suppose you have that in Russia. It is the night when the dead are supposed to arise, although they don't, of course, but children wander around the streets disguised as ghosts and skeletons and devils and you give them candy and pennies. Please come to my country and marry me."

This much was simple, but to copy her address in the Russian alphabet took him much longer. He went through ten envelopes before he had what he thought was a satisfactory copy. In the morning, before he went to work, he took his letter to the post office. The clerk was a friend. "What in hell are you doing, Art, writing this scribble-scrabble to Communists?"

Artemis got rustic. "Well, you see, Sam, I was there for a day or so and there was this girl." The letter took a twenty-five-cent stamp, a dismal gray engraving of Abraham Lincoln. When Artemis, thinking of the brilliant stamps on her letter, asked if there weren't something livelier, his friend said no.

He got her reply in ten days. "I like to think that our letters cross and I like to think of them flapping their wings at each other somewhere over the Atlantic. I would love to come to your country and marry you or have you marry me here, but we cannot do this until there is peace in the world. I wish we didn't have to depend upon peace for love. I went to the country on Saturday and the birds and the birches and pines were soothing. I wish you had been with me. A Unitarian doctor of divinity came to the office yesterday looking for an interpreter. He seemed intelligent and I took him around Moscow myself. He told me I didn't have to believe in God to be a Unitarian. God, he told me, is the progress from chaos to order to human responsibility. I always thought God sat on the clouds, surrounded by troops of angels, but perhaps He lives in a submarine, surrounded by divisions of mermaids. Please send me a snapshot and write again. Your letters make me very happy."

"I'm enclosing a snapshot," he wrote. "It's three years old. It was taken at the Wakusha Reservoir. This is the center of the Northeast watershed. I think of you all the time. I woke at three this morning thinking of you. It was a nice feeling. I like the dark. The dark seems to me like a house with many rooms. Sixty or seventy. At night now after work I go skating. I suppose everybody in Russia must know how to skate. I know that Russians play hockey, because they usually beat the Americans in the Olympics. Three to two, seven to two, eight to one. It is beginning to snow. Love, Artemis." He had another struggle with the address.

"Your last letter took eighteen days," she wrote. "I find myself answering your letters before they come, but there's nothing mystical about this, really, for there's an immense clock at the post office with one side black and the other white showing what time it is in different parts of the world. By the time dawn breaks where you are, we are halfway through the day. They have just painted my stairs. The colors are the colors favored by all municipal painters—light brown with a dark-brown border. While they were about it, they splashed a little white paint on the bottom of my mailbox. Now when the lift carries me down, the white paint gives me the illusion that there is a letter from you. I cannot cure myself of this. My heart beats and I run to the box, only to find white paint. Now I ride the lift with my back turned, the drop of paint is so painful."

As he returned from work one night, his mother told him that someone had called from the county seat and said that the call was urgent. Artemis guessed that it must be the Internal Revenue Service. He had had difficulty trying to describe to them the profit and loss in looking for water. He was a conscientious citizen and he called the number. A stranger identified himself as Mr. Cooper and he didn't sound like the Internal Revenue Service. Cooper wanted to see Artemis at once. "Well, you see," Artemis said, "it's my bowling night. Our team is tied for first place and I'd hate to miss the games if we could meet some other time." Cooper was agreeable and Artemis told him where he was working and how to get there. Cooper said he would be there at ten and Artemis went bowling.

In the morning, it began to snow. It looked like a heavy storm. Cooper showed up at ten. He did not get out of his car, but he was so very pleasant that Artemis guessed he was a salesman. Insurance.

"I understand that you've been in Russia."

"Well, I was only there for forty-eight hours. They canceled my visa. I don't know why."

"But you've been corresponding with Russia."

"Yes, there's this girl. I went out with her once. We write each other."

"The State Department is very much interested in your experience. Undersecretary Hurlow would like to talk with you."

"But I didn't really have any experience. I saw some churches and had three chicken dinners and then they sent me home."

"Well, the Undersecretary is interested. He called yesterday and again this morning. Would you mind going to Washington?"

"I'm working."

"It would only take a day. You can take the shuttle in the morning and come back in the afternoon. It won't take long. I think they'll pay your expenses, although this hasn't been decided. I have the information here." He handed the well digger a State Department letterhead that requested the presence of Artemis Bucklin at the new State Department building at 9 A.M. on the following day. "If you can make it," Cooper said, "your Government will be very grateful. I wouldn't worry too much about the 9 A.M. Nobody much gets to work before ten. It was nice to have met you. If you have any questions, call me at this number." Then he was gone and gone very quickly, because the snow was dense. The well site was in some backwoods where the roads wouldn't be plowed and Artemis drove home before lunch.

Some provincialism—some attachment to the not unpleasant routines of his life—made Artemis feel resistant to the trip to Washington. He didn't want to go, but could he be forced to? The only force involved was in the phrase that his Government would be grateful. With the exception of the Internal Revenue Service, he had no particular quarrel with his Government and he would have liked—childishly, perhaps—to deserve its gratitude. That night he packed a bag and checked the airline schedules and he was at the new State Department building at nine the next morning.

Cooper had been right about time. Artemis cooled his heels in a waiting room until after ten. He was then taken up two floors, not to see the Undersecretary but to see a man named Serge Belinsky. Belinsky's office was small and bare and his secretary was a peevish Southern woman who wore bedroom slippers. Belinsky asked Artemis to fill out some simple bureaucratic forms. When had he arrived in Moscow? when had he left Moscow? where had he stayed? etc. When these were finished, Belinsky had them duplicated and took Artemis up another floor to the office of a man named Moss. Here things were very different. The secretary was pretty and flirtatious and wore shoes. The furniture was not luxurious, but it was a cut above Belinsky's. There were flowers on the desk and a painting on the wall. Artemis repeated the little he remembered, the little there was to remember. When he described the arrangement for his meeting with Khrushchev, Moss laughed; Moss whooped. He was a very elegant young man, so beautifully dressed and polished that Artemis felt himself uncouth, unwashed, and shabby. He was clean enough and mannerly, but his clothes bound at the shoulders and the crotch. "I think the Undersecretary would like to see us now," said Moss, and they went up another flight.

This was an altogether different creation. The floors were carpeted, the walls were paneled, and the secretary wore boots that were buckled with brass and reached up past her skirts, ending God knows where. How far they had come, in such a short distance, from the peevish secretary in bedroom slippers. How Artemis longed for his rig, his work clothes, and his lunch pail. They were served coffee and then the secretary—the one with the boots—dismissed Moss and took him in to the Undersecretary.

Except for a very small desk, there was nothing businesslike about the office. There were colored rugs, sofas, pictures, and flowers. Mr. Hurlow was a very tall man who seemed tired or perhaps unwell. "It was good of you to come, Mr. Bucklin. I'll go straight to the point. I have to go to the Hill at eleven. You know Natasha Funaroff."

"I took her out once. We had dinner and sat in a park."

"You correspond with her."

"Yes."

"Of course, we've monitored your letters. Their Government does the same. Our intelligence feels that your letters contain some sort of information. She, as the daughter of a marshal, is close to the Government. The rest of her family were shot. She wrote that God might sit in a submarine surrounded by divisions of mermaids. That same day was the date of our last submarine crisis. I understand that she is an intelligent woman and I can't believe that she would write anything so foolish without its having a second meaning. Earlier she wrote that you and she were a wave on the Black Sea. The date corresponds precisely to the Black Sea maneuvers. You sent her a photograph of yourself beside the Wakusha Reservoir, pointing out that this was the center of the Northeast watershed. This, of course, is not classified information, but it all helps. Later you write that the dark seems to you like a house divided into seventy rooms. This was written ten days before we activated the Seventieth Division. Would you care to explain any of this?"

"There's nothing to explain. I love her."

"That's absurd. You said yourself that you only saw her once. How can you fall in love with a woman you've only seen once? I can't at the moment threaten you, Mr. Bucklin. I can bring you before a committee, but unless you're willing to be more cooperative, this would be a waste of our time. We feel quite sure that you and your friend have worked out a cipher. I can't forbid you to write, of course, but we can stop your letters. What I would like is your patriotic cooperation. Mr. Cooper, whom I believe you've met, will call on you once a week or so and give you the information or rather the misinformation that we would like you to send to Russia, couched, of course, in your cipher, your descriptions of the dark as a house."

"I couldn't do that, Mr. Hurlow. It would be dishonest to you and to Natasha."

The Undersecretary laughed and gave a little girlish tilt to his shoulders. "Well, think it over and call Cooper when you've made up your mind. Of course, the destiny of the nation doesn't depend on your decision. I'm late." He didn't rise, he didn't offer his hand. Artemis, feeling worse than he had felt in Moscow and singing the unreality blues, went past the secretary with the boots and took an elevator down past the secretary with the shoes and the one in bedroom slippers. He got home in time for supper.

He never heard again from the State Department. Had they made a mistake? Were they fools or idle? He would never know. He wrote Natasha four very circumspect letters, omitting his hockey and his bowling scores. There was no reply. He looked for letters from her for a month or so. He thought often of the spot of paint on her mailbox. When it got warmer, there was the healing sound of rain to hear, at least there was that. Water, water.

THREE STORIES

I

THE SUBJECT TODAY will be the metaphysics of obesity, and I am the belly of a man named Lawrence Farnsworth. I am the body cavity between his diaphragm and his pelvic floor and I possess his viscera. I know you won't believe me, but if you'll buy a *cri de coeur* why not a *cri de ventre*? I play as large a part in his affairs as any other lights and vitals, and while I can't act independently he too is at the mercy of such disparate forces in his environment as money and starlight. We were born in the Middle West and he was educated in Chicago. He was on the track team (pole vault) and later on the diving team, two sports that made my existence dangerous and obscure. I did not discover myself until he was in his forties, when I was recognized by his doctor and his tailor. He stubbornly refused to grant me my rights and continued for almost a year to wear clothes that confined me harshly and caused me much soreness and pain. My one compensatio was that I could unzip his fly at will.

I've often heard him say that, having spent the first hal of his life running around behind an unruly bowsprit, h seemed damned to spend the rest of his life going aroun behind a belly that was as independent and capricious a his genitals. I have been, of course, in a position to ob serve his carnal sport, but I think I won't describe th thousands—or millions—of performances in which I hav participated. I am, in spite of my reputation for grossness truly visionary, and I would like to look past his gymnas tics to their consequences, which, from what I hear, ar often ecstatic. He seems to feel that his erotic life is an en try permit into what is truly beautiful in the world. Ballin in a thunderstorm—any rain will do—is his idea of a tota relationship. There have been complaints. I once heard woman ask, "Will you never understand that there is mor to life than sex and nature worship?" Once, when he ex claimed over the beauty of the stars his *belle amie* giggled My open knowledge of the world is confined to the limitec incidence of nakedness: bedrooms, showers, beaches, swim ming pools, trysts, and sunbathing in the Antilles. The rest of my life is spent in a sort of purdah between his trousers and his shirts.

Having refused to admit my existence for a year or more, he finally had his trousers enlarged from thirty to thirty-four. When I had reached thirty-four inches and was striving for thirty-six his feelings about my existence became obsessive. The clash between what he had been and wanted to be and what he had become was serious. When people poked me with their fingers and made jokes about his Bay Window his forced laughter could not conceal his rage. He ceased to judge his friends on their wit and intelligence and began to judge them on their waistbands. Why was X so flat and why was Z, with a paunch of at least forty inches, contented with this state of affairs? When his friends stood his eye dropped swiftly from their smiles to their middles. We went one night to Yankee Stadium to see a ball game. He had begun to enjoy himself when he noticed that the right fielder had a good thirty-six inches. The other fielders and the basemen passed but the pitcher—an older man—had a definite bulge—and two of the umpires—when they took off their guards—were disgusting. So was the catcher. When he realized that he was not watching a ball game—that because of my influence he was unable to watch a ball game—we left. This was at the top of the fourth. A day or two later he began what was to be a year or a year and a half of hell.

We started with a diet that emphasized water and hard-boiled eggs. He lost ten pounds in a week but he lost it all in the wrong places, and while my existence was imperiled I survived. The diet set up some metabolic disturbance that damaged his teeth, and he gave this up at his doctor's suggestion and joined a health club. Three times a week I was tormented on an electric bicycle and a rowing machine and then a masseur would knead me and strike me loudly and cruelly with the flat of his hand. He then bought a variety of elastic underpants or girdles that meant to disguise or dismiss me, and while they gave me great pain they only challenged my invincibility. When they were removed in the evening I reinstated myself amply in the world I so much love. Soon after this he bought a contraption that was guaranteed to destroy me. This was a pair of gold-colored plastic shorts that could be inflated by a hand pump. The acidity of the secretions I had to refine informed me of how painful and ridiculous he felt. When the shorts were inflated he read from a book of directions and performed some gymnastics. This was the worst pain to be inflicted on me so far, and when the exercises were finished my various parts were so abnormally cramped and knotted that we spent a sleepless night.

By this time I had come to recognize two facts that guaranteed my survival. The first was his detestation of solitary exercise. He liked games well enough but he did not like gymnastics. Each morning he would go to the bathroom and touch his toes ten times. His buttocks (there's another story) scraped the washbasin and his forehead grazed the toilet seat. I knew from the secretions that came my way that this experience was spiritually crushing. Later he moved to the country for the summer and took up jogging and weight lifting. While lifting weights he learned to count in Japanese and Russian, hoping to give this performance some dignity, but he was not successful. Both jogging and weight lifting embarrassed him intensely. The second factor in my favor was his conviction that we lead a simple life. "I really lead a very simple life," he often said. If this were so I would have no chance for prominence, but there is, I think, no first-class restaurant in Europe, Asia, Africa, or the British Isles to which I have not been taken and asked to perform. He often says so. Going after a dish of crickets in Tokyo he gave me a friendly pat and said: "Do your best, man." So long as he considers this to be a simple life my place in the world is secure. When I fail him it is not through malice or intent. After a Homeric dinner with fourteen entrées in southern Russia we spent a night together in the bathroom. This was in Tbilisi. I seemed to be threatening his life. It was three in the morning. He was crying with pain. He was weeping, and perhaps I know more than any other part of his physique about the true loneliness of this man. "Go away," he shouted at me, "go away." What could be more pitiful and absurd than a naked man at the dog hour in a strange country casting out his vitals. We went to the window to hear the wind in the trees. "Oh, I should have paid more attention to spiritual things," he shouted.

If I were the belly of a secret agent or a reigning prince my role in the clash of time wouldn't have been any different. I represent time more succinctly than any scarecrow with a scythe. Why should so simple a force as time—told accurately by the clocks in his house—cause him to groan and swear? Did he feel that some specious youthfulness was his principal, his only lure? I know that I reminded him of the pain he suffered in his relationship to his father. His father retired at fifty-five and spent the rest of his life polishing stones, gardening, and trying to learn conversational French from records. He had been a limber and an athletic man, but like his son he had been overtaken in the middle of the way by an independent abdomen. He seemed, like his son, to have no capacity to age and fatten gracefully. His paunch, his abdomen seemed to break his spirit. His abdomen led him to stoop, to walk clumsily, to sigh, and to have his trousers enlarged. His abdomen seemed like some precursor of the Angel of Death, and was Farnsworth, touching his toes in the bathroom each morning, struggling with the same angel?

Then there was the year we traveled. I don't know what drove him, but we went around the world three times in twelve months. He may have thought that travel would heighten his metabolism and diminish my importance. I won't go into the hardships of safety belts and a chaotic eating schedule. We saw all the usual places as well as Nairobi, Malagasy, Mauritius, Bali, New Guinea, New Caledonia, and New Zealand. We saw Madang, Goroka, Lee, Rabaul, Fiji, Reykjavík, Thingvellir, Akureyri, Narsarssuak, Kagsiarauk, Bukhara, Irkutsk, Ulan Bator, and the Gobi Desert. Then there were the Galápagos, Patagonia, the Mato Grosso jungle, and of course the Seychelles and the Amirantes.

It ended or was resolved one night at Passetto's. He began the meal with figs and Parma ham and with this he ate two rolls and butter. After this he had spaghetti carbonara, a steak with fried potatoes, a serving of frogs' legs, a whole spigola roasted in paper, some chicken breasts, a salad with an oil dressing, three kinds of cheese, and a thick zabaglione. Halfway through the meal he had to give me some leeway, but he was not resentful and I felt that victory might be in sight. When he ordered the zabaglione I knew that I had won or that we had arrived at a sensible truce. He was not trying to conceal, dismiss, or forget me and his secretions were bland. Leaving the table he had to give me another two inches, so that walking across the piazza I could feel the night wind and hear the fountains, and we've lived happily together ever since.

II

MARGE LITTLETON would, in the long-gone days of Freudian jargon, have been thought maternal, although she was no more maternal than you or you. What would have been meant was a charming softness in her voice and her manner and she smelled like a summer's day, or perhaps it is a summer's day that smells like such a woman. She was a regular churchgoer, and I always felt that her devotions were more profound than most, although it is impossible to speculate on anything so intimate. She was on the liturgical side, hewing to the Book of Common Prayer and avoiding sermons whenever possible. She was not a native, of course—the last native along with the last cow died twenty years ago—and I don't remember where she or her husband came from. He was bald. They had three children and lived a scrupulously unexceptional life until one morning in the fall.

It was after Labor Day, a little windy. Leaves could be seen falling outside the windows. The family had breakfast in the kitchen. Marge had baked johnnycake. "Good morning, Mrs. Littleton," her husband said, kissing her on the brow and patting her backside. His voice, his gesture seemed to have the perfect equilibrium of love. I don't know what virulent critics of the family would say about the scene. Were the Littletons making for themselves, by contorting their passions into an acceptable social image, a sort of prison, or did they chance to be a man and woman whose pleasure in one another was tender, robust, and invincible? From what I know it was an exceptional marriage. Never having been married myself I may be unduly susceptible to the element of buffoonery in holy matrimony, but isn't it true that when some couple celebrates their tenth or fifteenth anniversary they seem far from triumphant? In fact they seem duped while dirty Uncle Harry, the rake, seems to wear the laurels. But with the Littletons one felt that they might live together with intelligence and ardor—giving and taking until death did them part.

On that particular Saturday morning he planned to go shopping. After breakfast he made a list of what they needed from the hardware store. A gallon of white acrylic paint, a four-inch brush, picture hooks, a spading fork, oil for the lawn mower. The children went along with him. They went, not to the village, which, like so many others, lay dying, but to a crowded and fairly festive shopping center on Route 64. He gave the children money for Cokes. When they returned the southbound traffic was heavy. It was as I say after Labor Day, and many of the cars were towing portable houses, campers, sailboats, motorboats, and trailers. This long procession of vehicles and domestic portables seemed not the spectacle of a people returning from their vacations but rather like a tragic evacuation of some great city or state. A car carrier, trying to pass an exceptionally bulky mobile home, crashed into the Littletons and killed them all. I didn't go to the funeral but one of our neighbors described it to me. "There she stood at the edge of the grave. She didn't cry. She looked very beautiful and serene. She had to watch four coffins, one after the other, lowered into the ground. Four."

She didn't go away. People asked her to dinner, of course, but in such an intensely domesticated community the single are inevitably neglected. A month or so after the accident the local paper announced that the State Highway Commission would widen Route 64 from a four-lane to an eight-lane highway. We organized a committee for the preservation of the community and raised ten thousand dollars for legal fees. Marge Littleton was very active. We had meetings nearly every week. We met in parish houses, courtrooms, high schools, and houses. In the beginning these meetings were very emotional. Mrs. Pinkham once cried. She wept. "I've worked sixteen years on my pink room and now they're going to tear it down." She was led out of the meeting, a truly bereaved woman. We chartered a bus and went to the state capital. We marched down 64 one rainy Sunday with a motorcycle escort. I don't suppose we were more than thirty and we straggled. We carried picket signs. I remember Marge. Some people seem born with a congenital gift for protest and a talent for carrying picket signs, but this was not Marge. She carried a large sign that said: STOP GASOLINE ALLEY. She seemed very embarrassed. When the march disbanded I said goodbye to her on a knoll above the highway. I remember the level gaze she gave to the line of traffic, rather, I guess, as the widows of Nantucket must have regarded the sea.

When we had spent our ten thousand dollars without any results our meetings were less and less frequent and very poorly attended. Only three people, including the speaker, showed up for the last. The highway was widened, demolishing six houses and making two uninhabitable, although the owners got no compensation. Several wells were destroyed by the blasting. After our committee was disbanded I saw very little of Marge. Someone told me she had gone abroad. When she returned she was followed by a charming young Roman named Pietro Montani. They were married.

Marge displayed her gifts for married happiness with Pietro although he was very unlike her first husband. He was handsome, witty, and substantial—he represented a firm that manufactured innersoles—but he spoke the worst English I have ever heard. You could talk with him and drink with him and laugh with him but other than that it was almost impossible to communicate with him. It didn't really matter. She seemed very happy and it was a pleasant house to visit. They had been married no more than two months when Pietro, driving a convertible down 64, was decapitated by a crane.

She buried Pietro with the others but she stayed on in the house on Twin-Rock Road, where one could hear the battlefield noises of industrial traffic. I think she got a job. One saw her on the trains. Three weeks after Pietro's death a twenty-four-wheel, eighty-ton truck, northbound on Route 64 for reasons that were never ascertained, veered into the southbound lane demolishing two cars and killing their four passengers. The truck then rammed into a granite abutment there, fell on its side, and caught fire. The police and the fire department were there at once, but the freight was combustible and the fire was not extinguished until three in the morning. All traffic on Route 64 was rerouted. The women's auxiliary of the fire department served coffee.

Two weeks later at 8 P.M. another twenty-four-wheel truck with a load of cement blocks went out of control at the same place, crossed the southbound lane, and felled four full-grown trees before it collided with the abutment. The impact of the collision was so violent that two feet of granite was sheared off the wall. There was no fire, but the two drivers were so badly crushed by the collision that they had to be identified by their dental work.

On November third at 8:30 P.M. Lt. Dominic DeSisto reported that a man in work clothes ran into the front office. He seemed hysterical, drugged, or drunk and claimed to have been shot. He was, according to Lieutenant DeSisto, so incoherent that it was some time before he could explain what had happened. Driving north on 64, at about the same place where the other trucks had gone out of control, a rifle bullet had smashed the left window of his cab, missed the driver, and smashed the right window. The intended victim was Joe Langston of Baldwin, South Carolina. The lieutenant examined the truck and verified the broken windows. He and Langston drove in a squad car back to where the shot had been fired. On the right side of the road there was a little hill of granite with some soil covering. When the highway had been widened the hill had been blasted in two and the knoll on the right corresponded to the abutment that had killed the other drivers. DeSisto examined the hill. The grass on the knoll was trampled and there were two cigarette butts on the ground. Langston was taken to the hospital, suffering from shock. The hill was put under surveillance for the next month, but the police force was understaffed and it was a boring beat to sit alone on the hill from dusk until midnight. As soon as surveillance was stopped a fourth oversized truck went out of control. This time the truck veered to the right, took down a dozen trees, and drove into a narrow but precipitous valley. The driver, when the police got to him, was dead. He had been shot.

In December Marge married a rich widower and moved to North Salem, where there is only one two-lane highway and where the sound of traffic is as faint as the roaring of a shell.

III

He took his aisle seat—32—in the 707 for Rome. The plane was not quite full and there was an empty seat between him and the occupant of the port seat. This was taken, he was pleased to see, by an exceptionally good-looking woman—not young, but neither was he. She was wearing perfume, a dark dress, and jewelry and she seemed to belong to that part of the world in which he moved most easily. "Good evening," he said, settling himself. She didn't reply. She made a discouraging humming noise and raised a paperback book to the front of her face. He looked for the title but this she concealed with her hands. He had met shy women on planes before—infrequently, but he had met them. He supposed they were understandably wary of lushes, mashers, and bores. He shook out a copy of *The Manchester Guardian*. He had noticed that conservative newspapers sometimes inspired confidence in the shy. If one read the editorials, the sports page, and especially the financial section shy strangers would sometimes be ready for a conversation. The plane took off, the smoking sign went dark, and he took out a gold cigarette case and a gold lighter. They were not flashy, but they were gold. "Do you mind if I smoke?" he asked. "Why should I?" she asked. She did not look in his direction. "Some people do," he said, lighting his cigarette. She was nearly as beautiful as she was unfriendly, but why should she be so cold? They would be side by side for nine hours, and it was only sensible to count on at least a little conversation. Did he remind her of someone she disliked, someone who had wounded her? He was bathed, shaved, correctly dressed, and accustomed to making friends. Perhaps she was an unhappy woman who disliked the world, but when the stewardess came by to take their drink orders the smile she gave the young stranger was dazzling and open. This so cheered him that he smiled himself, but when she saw that he was trespassing on a communication that was aimed at someone else she turned on him, scowled, and went back to her book. The stewardess brought him a double Martini and his companion a sherry. He supposed that his strong drink might increase her uneasiness, but he had to take that chance. She went on reading. If he could only find the title of the book, he thought, he would have a foot in the door. Harold Robbins, Dostoevsky, Philip Roth, Emily Dickinson—anything would help. "May I ask what you're reading?" he said politely. "No," she said.

When the stewardess brought their dinners he passed her tray across the empty seat. She did not thank him. He settled down to eat, to feed, to enjoy this simple habit. The meal was unusually bad and he said so. "One can't be too particular under the circumstances," she said. He thought he heard a trace of warmth in her voice. "Salt might help," she said, "but they neglected to give me any salt. Could I trouble you for yours?" "Oh, certainly," he said. Things were definitely looking up. He opened his salt container and in passing it to her a little salt spilled on the rug. "I'm afraid the bad luck will be yours," she said. This was not said at all lightly. She salted her cutlet and ate everything on her tray. Then she went on reading the book with the concealed title. She would sooner or later have to use the toilet, he knew, and then he could read the title of the book, but when she did go to the stern of the plane she carried the book with her.

The screen for the film was lowered. Unless a picture was exceptionally interesting he never rented sound equipment. He had found that lipreading and guesswork gave the picture an added dimension, and anyhow the dialogue was usually offensively banal. His neighbor rented equipment and seemed to enjoy herself heartily. She had a lovely musical laugh and communicated with the actors on the screen as she had communicated with the stewardess and as she had refused to communicate with her neighbor. The sun rose as they approached the Alps, although the film was not over. Here and there the brightness of an Alpine morning could be seen through the cracks in the drawn shades, but while they sailed over Mont Blanc and the Matterhorn the characters on the screen relentlessly pursued their script. There was a parade, a chase, a reconciliation, an ending. His companion, still carrying her mysterious book, retired to the stern again and returned wearing a sort of mobcap, her face heavily covered with some white unguent. She adjusted her pillow and blanket and arranged herself for sleep. "Sweet dreams," he said, daringly. She sighed.

He never slept on planes. He went up to the galley and had a whiskey. The stewardess was pretty and talkative and she told him about her origins, her schedule, her fiancé, and her problems with passengers who suffered from flight fear. Beyond the Alps they began to lose altitude and he saw the Mediterranean from the port and had another whiskey. He saw Elba, Giglio, and the yachts in the harbor at Porto Ercole, where he could see the villas of his friends. He could remember coming into Nantucket so many years ago. They used to line the port railing and shout, "Oh, the Perrys are here and the Saltons and the Greenoughs." It was partly genuine, partly show. When he returned to his seat his companion had removed her mobcap and her unguent. Her beauty in the light of morning was powerful. He could not diagnose what he found so compelling—nostalgia, perhaps—but her features, her pallor, the set of her eyes, all corresponded to his sense of beauty. "Good morning," he said, "did you sleep well?" She frowned, she seemed to find this impertinent. "Does one ever?" she asked on a rising note. She put her mysterious book into a handbag with a zipper and gathered her things. When they landed at Fiumicino he stood aside to let her pass and followed her down the aisle. He went behind her through the passport, emigrant, and health check and joined her at the place where you claim your bags.

But look, look. Why does he point out her bag to the porter and why, when they both have their bags, does he follow her out to the cab stand, where he bargains with a driver for the trip into Rome? Why does he join her in the cab? Is he the undiscourageable masher that she dreaded? No, no. He is her husband, she is his wife, the mother of his children, and a woman he has worshipped passionately for nearly thirty years.

THE JEWELS OF THE CABOTS

FUNERAL SERVICES for the murdered man were held in the Unitarian church in the little village of St. Botolphs. The architecture of the church was Bullfinch with columns and one of those ethereal spires that must have dominated the landscape a century ago. The service was a random collection of Biblical quotations closing with a verse. "Amos Cabot, rest in peace/Now your mortal trials have ceased. . . ." The church was full. Mr. Cabot had been an outstanding member of the community. He had once run for Governor. For a month or so, during his campaign, one saw his picture on barns, walls, buildings, and telephone poles. I don't suppose the sense of walking through a shifting mirror—he found himself at every turn—unsettled him as it would have unsettled me. (Once, for example, when I was in an elevator in Paris I noticed a woman carrying a book of mine. There was a photograph on the jacket and one image of me looked over her arm at another. I wanted the picture, wanted I suppose to destroy it. That she should walk away with my face under her arm seemed to threaten my self-esteem. She left the elevator at the fourth floor and the parting of these two images was confusing. I wanted to follow her, but how could I explain in French—or in any other language—what I felt.) Amos Cabot was not at all like this. He seemed to enjoy seeing himself, and when he lost the election and his face vanished (excepting for a few barns in the back country where it peeled for a month or so) he seemed not perturbed.

There are, of course, the wrong Lowells, the wrong Hallowells, the wrong Eliots, Cheevers, Codmans, and Englishes, but today we will deal with the wrong Cabots. Amos came from the South Shore and may never have heard of the North Shore branch of the family. His father had been an auctioneer, which meant in those days an entertainer, horse trader, and sometimes crook. Amos owned real estate, the hardware store, the public utilities, and was a director of the bank. He had an office in the Cartwright Block, opposite the green. His wife came from Connecticut, which was, for us at that time, a distant wilderness on whose eastern borders stood the City of New York. New York was populated by harried, nervous, avaricious foreigners who lacked the character to bathe in cold water at six in the morning and to live, with composure, lives of grueling boredom. Mrs. Cabot, when I knew her, was probably in her early forties. She was a short woman with the bright-red face of an alcoholic although she was a vigorous temperance worker. Her hair was as white as snow. Her back and her front were prominent and there was a memorable curve to her spine that could have been a cruel corset or the beginnings of lordosis. No one quite knew why Mr. Cabot had married this eccentric from faraway Connecticut—it was, after all, no one's business—but she did own most of the frame tenements on the East Bank of the river where the workers in the table-silver factory lived. Her tenements were profitable but it would have been an unwarranted simplification to conclude that he had married for real estate. She collected the rents herself. I expect that she did her own housework, and she dressed simply, but she wore on her right hand seven large diamond rings. She had evidently read somewhere that diamonds were a sound investment and the blazing stones were about as glamorous as a passbook. There were round diamonds, square diamonds, rectangular diamonds, and some of those diamonds that are set in prongs. On Thursday morning she would wash her diamonds in some jewelers' solution and hang them out to dry in the clothesyard. She never explained this, but the incidence of eccentricity in the village ran so high that her conduct was not thought unusual.

Mrs. Cabot spoke once or twice a year at the St. Botolphs Academy, where many of us went to school. She had three subjects: My Trip to Alaska (slides), The Evils of Drink, and The Evils of Tobacco. Drink was for her so unthinkable a vice that she could not attack it with much vehemence, but the thought of tobacco made her choleric. Could one imagine Christ on the Cross smoking a cigarette? she would ask us. Could one imagine the Virgin Mary *smoking?* A drop of nicotine fed to a pig by trained laboratory technicians had killed the beast. Etc. She made smoking irresistible, and if I die of lung cancer I shall blame Mrs. Cabot. These performances took place in what we called the Great Study Hall. This was a large room on the second floor that could hold us all. The academy had been built in the 1850s and had the lofty, spacious, and beautiful windows of that period in American architecture. In the spring and in the autumn the building seemed gracefully suspended in its grounds but in the winter a glacial cold fell off the large window lights. In the Great Study Hall we were allowed to wear coats, hats, and gloves. This situation was heightened by the fact that my Great-aunt Anna had bought in Athens a large collection of plaster casts, so that we shivered and memorized the conative verbs in the company of at least a dozen buck-naked gods and goddesses. So it was to Hermes and Venus as well as to us that Mrs. Cabot railed against the poisons of tobacco. She was a woman of vehement and ugly prejudice, and I suppose she would have been happy to include the blacks and the Jews but there was only one black and one Jewish family in the village and they were exemplary. The possibility of intolerance in the village did not occur to me until much later, when my mother came to our house in Westchester for Thanksgiving.

This was some years ago, when the New England highways had not been completed and the trip from New York or Westchester took over four hours. I left quite early in the morning and drove first to Haverhill, where I stopped at Miss Peacock's School and picked up my niece. I then went on to St. Botolphs, where I found Mother sitting in the hallway in an acolyte's chair. The chair had a steepled back, topped with a wooden fleur-de-lis. From what rain-damp church had this object been stolen? She wore a coat and her bag was at her feet. "I'm ready," she said. She must have been ready for a week. She seemed terribly lonely. "Would you like a drink?" she asked. I knew enough not to take this bait. Had I said yes she would have gone into the pantry and returned, smiling sadly, to say: "Your brother has drunk all the whiskey." So we started back for Westchester. It was a cold, overcast day and I found the drive tiring, although I think fatigue had nothing to do with what followed. I left my niece at my brother's house in Connecticut and drove on to my place. It was after dark when the trip ended. My wife had made all the preparations that were customary for Mother's arrival. There was an open fire, a vase of roses on the piano, and tea with anchovy-paste sandwiches. "How lovely to have flowers," said Mother. "I so love flowers. I can't live without them. Should I suffer some financial reverses and have to choose between flowers and groceries I believe I would choose flowers. . . ."

I do not want to give the impression of an elegant old lady because there were lapses in her performance. I bring up, with powerful unwillingness, a fact that was told to me by her sister after Mother's death. It seems that at one time she applied for a position with the Boston Police Force. She had plenty of money at the time and I have no idea of why she did this. I suppose that she wanted to be a policewoman. I don't know what branch of the force she planned to join, but I've always imagined her in a dark-blue uniform with a ring of keys at her waist and a billy club in her right hand. My grandmother dissuaded her from this course, but the image of a policewoman was some part of the figure she cut, sipping tea by our fire. She meant this evening to be what she called Aristocratic. In this connection she often said, "There must be at least a drop of plebeian blood in the family. How else can one account for your taste in torn and shabby clothing. You've always had plenty of clothes but you've always chosen rags."

I mixed a drink and said how much I had enjoyed seeing my niece.

"Miss Peacock's has changed," Mother said sadly.

"I didn't know," I said. "What do you mean?"

"They've let down the bars."

"I don't understand."

"They're letting in Jews," she said. She fired out the last word.

"Can we change the subject?" I asked.

"I don't see why," she said. "You brought it up."

"My wife is Jewish, Mother," I said. My wife was in the kitchen.

"That is not possible," my mother said. "Her father is Italian."

"Her father," I said, "is a Polish Jew."

"Well," Mother said, "I come from old Massachusetts stock and I'm not ashamed of it although I don't like being called a Yankee."

"There's a difference."

"Your father said that the only good Jew was a dead Jew although I did think Justice Brandeis charming."

"I think it's going to rain," I said. It was one of our staple conversational switch-offs, used to express anger, hunger, love, and the fear of death. My wife joined us and Mother picked up the routine. "It's nearly cold enough for snow," she said. "When you were a boy you used to pray for snow or ice. It depended upon whether you wanted to skate or ski. You were very particular. You would kneel by your bed and loudly ask God to manipulate the elements. You never prayed for anything else. I never once heard you ask for a blessing on your parents. In the summer you didn't pray at all."

THE CABOTS had two daughters—Geneva and Molly. Geneva was the older and thought to be the more beautiful. Molly was my girl for a year or so. She was a lovely young woman with a sleepy look that was quickly dispelled by a brilliant smile. Her hair was pale brown and held the light. When she was tired or excited sweat formed on her upper lip. In the evenings I would walk to their house and sit with her in the parlor under the most intense surveillance. Mrs. Cabot, of course, regarded sex with utter panic. She watched us from the dining room. From upstairs there were loud and regular thumping sounds. This was Amos Cabot's rowing machine. We were sometimes allowed to take walks together if we kept to the main streets, and when I was old enough to drive I took her to the dances at the club. I was intensely—morbidly—jealous and when she seemed to be enjoying herself with someone else I would stand in the corner, thinking of suicide. I remember driving her back one night to the house on Shore Road.

At the turn of the century someone decided that St. Botolphs might have a future as a resort, and five mansions, or follies, were built at the end of Shore Road. The Cabots lived in one of these. All the mansions had towers. These were round with conical roofs, rising a story or so above the rest of the frame buildings. The towers were strikingly unmilitary, and so I suppose they were meant to express romance. What did they contain? Dens, I guess, maid's rooms, broken furniture, trunks, and they must have been the favorite of hornets. I parked my car in front of the Cabots' and turned off the lights. The house above us was dark.

It was long ago, so long ago that the foliage of elm trees was part of the summer night. (It was so long ago that when you wanted to make a left turn you cranked down the car window and *pointed* in that direction. Otherwise you were not allowed to point. Don't point, you were told. I can't imagine why, unless the gesture was thought to be erotic.) The dances—the Assemblies—were formal and I would be wearing a tuxedo handed down from my father to my brother and from my brother to me like some escutcheon or sumptuary torch. I took Molly in my arms. She was completely responsive. I am not a tall man (I am sometimes inclined to stoop), but the conviction that I am loved and loving affects me like a military bracing. Up goes my head. My back is straight. I am six foot seven and sustained by some clamorous emotional uproar. Sometimes my ears ring. It can happen anywhere—in a ginseng house in Seoul, for example—but it happened that night in front of the Cabots' house on Shore Road. Molly said then that she had to go. Her mother would be watching from a window. She asked me not to come up to the house. I mustn't have heard. I went with her up the walk and the stairs to the porch, where she tried the door and found it locked. She asked me again to go, but I couldn't abandon her there, could I? Then a light went on and the door was opened by a dwarf. He was exhaustively misshapen. The head was hydrocephalic, the features were swollen, the legs were thick and cruelly bowed. I thought of the circus. The lovely young woman began to cry. She stepped into the house and closed the door and I was left with the summer night, the elms, the taste of an east wind. After this she avoided me for a week or so and I was told the facts by Maggie, our old cook.

But more facts first. It was in the summer, and in the summer most of us went to a camp on the Cape run by the headmaster of the St. Botolphs Academy. The months were so feckless, so blue, that I can't remember them at all. I slept next to a boy named DeVarennes whom I had known all my life. We were together most of the time. We played marbles together, slept together, played together on the same backfield, and once together took a ten-day canoe trip during which we nearly drowned together. My brother claimed that we had begun to look alike. It was the most gratifying and unself-conscious relationship I had known. (He still calls me once or twice a year from San Francisco, where he lives unhappily with his wife and three unmarried daughters. He sounds drunk. "We were happy, weren't we?" he asks.) One day another boy, a stranger named Wallace, asked if I wanted to swim across the lake. I might claim that I knew nothing about Wallace, and I knew very little, but I did know or sense that he was lonely. It was as conspicuous as—or more conspicuous than—any of his features. He did what was expected of him. He played ball, made his bed, took sailing lessons, and got his life-saving certificate, but this seemed more like a careful imposture than any sort of participation. He was miserable, he was lonely, and sooner or later, rain or shine, he would say so and, in the act of confession, make an impossible claim on one's loyalty. One knew all of this but one pretended not to. We got permission from the swimming instructor and swam across the lake. We used a clumsy side-stroke that still seems to me more serviceable than the overhand that is obligatory these days in those swimming pools where I spend most of my time. The sidestroke is Lower Class. I've seen it once in a swimming pool, and when I asked who the swimmer was I was told he was the butler. When the ship sinks, when the plane ditches I will try to reach the life raft with an overhand and drown stylishly, whereas if I had used a Lower-Class sidestroke I would have lived forever.

We swam the lake, rested in the sun—no confidences—and swam home. When I came up to our cabin DeVarennes took me aside. "Don't ever let me see you with Wallace again," he said. I asked why. He told me. "Wallace is Amos Cabot's bastard. His mother is a whore. They live in one of the tenements across the river."

The next day was hot and brilliant and Wallace asked if I wanted to swim the lake again. I said sure, sure and we did. When we came back to camp DeVarennes wouldn't speak to me. That night a northeaster blew up and it rained for three days. DeVarennes seems to have forgiven me and I don't recall having crossed the lake with Wallace again. As for the dwarf, Maggie told me he was a son of Mrs. Cabot from an earlier marriage. He worked at the table-silver factory but he went to work early in the morning and didn't return until after dark. His existence was meant to be kept a secret. This was unusual but not—at the time of which I'm writing—unprecedented. The Trumbulls kept Mrs. Trumbull's crazy sister hidden in the attic and Uncle Peepee Marshmallow—an exhibitionist—was often hidden for months.

It was a winter afternoon, an early-winter afternoon. Mrs. Cabot washed her diamonds and hung them out to dry. She then went upstairs to take a nap. She claimed that she had never taken a nap in her life, and the sounder she slept, the more vehement were her claims that she didn't sleep. This was not so much an eccentricity on her part as it was a crabwise way of presenting the facts that was prevalent in that part of the world. She woke at four and went down to gather her stones. They were gone. She called Geneva, but there was no answer. She got a rake and scored the stubble under the clothesline. There was nothing. She called the police.

As I say, it was a winter afternoon and the winters there were very cold. We counted for heat—sometimes for survival—on wood fires and large coal-burning furnaces that sometimes got out of hand. A winter night was a threatening fact, and this may have partly accounted for the sentiment with which we watched—in late November and December—the light burn out in the west. (My father's journals, for example, were full of descriptions of winter twilights, not because he was at all crepuscular but because the coming of the night might mean danger and pain.) Geneva had packed a bag, gathered the diamonds, and taken the last train out of town: the 4:37. How thrilling it must have been. The diamonds were meant to be stolen. They were a flagrant snare and she did what she was meant to do. She took a train to New York that night and sailed three days later for Alexandria on a Cunarder—the S.S. *Serapis*. She took a boat from Alexandria to Luxor, where, in the space of two months, she joined the Moslem faith and married an Egyptian noble.

I read about the theft next day in the evening paper. I delivered papers. I had begun my route on foot, moved on to a bicycle, and was assigned, when I was sixteen, to an old Ford truck. I was a truck driver! I hung around the linotype room until the papers were printed and then drove around to the neighboring villages, tossing out bundles at the doors of the candy and stationery stores. During the World Series a second edition with box scores was brought out, and after dark I would make the trip again to Travertine and the other places along the shore. The roads were dark, there was very little traffic, and leaf burning had not been forbidden, so that the air was tannic, melancholy, and exciting. One can attach a mysterious and inordinate amount of importance to some simple journey, and this second trip with the box scores made me very happy. I dreaded the end of the World Series as one dreads the end of any pleasure, and had I been younger I would have prayed. CABOT JEWELS STOLEN was the headline and the incident was never again mentioned in the paper. It was not mentioned at all in our house, but this was not unusual. When Mr. Abbott hung himself from the pear tree next door this was never mentioned.

Molly and I took a walk on the beach at Travertine that Sunday afternoon. I was troubled, but Molly's troubles were much graver. It did not disturb her that Geneva had stolen the diamonds. She only wanted to know what had become of her sister, and she was not to find out for another six weeks. However, something had happened at the house that night. There had been a scene between her parents and her father had left. She described this to me. We were walking barefoot. She was crying. I would like to have forgotten the scene as soon as she finished her description.

Children drown, beautiful women are mangled in automobile accidents, cruise ships founder, and men die lingering deaths in mines and submarines, but you will find none of this in my accounts. In the last chapter the ship comes home to port, the children are saved, the miners will be rescued. Is this an infirmity of the genteel or a conviction that there are discernible moral truths? Mr. X defecated in his wife's top drawer. This is a fact, but I claim that it is not truth. In describing St. Botolphs I would sooner stay on the West Bank of the river where the houses were white and where the church bells rang, but over the bridge there was the table-silver factory, the tenements (owned by Mrs. Cabot), and the Commercial Hotel. At low tide one could smell the sea gas from the inlets at Travertine. The headlines in the afternoon paper dealt with a trunk murder. The women on the streets were ugly. Even the dummies in the one store window seemed stooped, depressed, and dressed in clothing that neither fitted nor became them. Even the bride in her splendor seemed to have got some bad news. The politics were neo-fascist, the factory was nonunion, the food was unpalatable, and the night wind was bitter. This was a provincial and a traditional world enjoying few of the rewards of smallness and traditionalism, and when I speak of the blessedness of all small places I speak of the West Bank. On the East Bank was the Commercial Hotel, the demesne of Doris, a male prostitute who worked as a supervisor in the factory during the day and hustled the bar at night, exploiting the extraordinary moral lassitude of the place. Everybody knew Doris, and many of the customers had used him at one time or another. There was no scandal and no delight involved. Doris would charge a traveling salesman whatever he could get but he did it with the regulars for nothing. This seemed less like tolerance than hapless indifference, the absence of vision, moral stamina, the splendid Ambitiousness of romantic love. On fight night Doris drifts down the bar. Buy him a drink and he'll put his hand on your arm, your shoulder, your waist, and move a fraction of an inch in his direction and he'll reach for the cake. The steam fitter buys him a drink, the high-school dropout, the watch repairman. (Once a stranger shouted to the bartender, "Tell that son of a bitch to take his tongue out of my ear"—but he was a stranger.) This is not a transient world, these are not drifters, more than half of these men will never live in any other place, and yet this seems to be the essence of spiritual nomadism. The telephone rings and the bartender beckons to Doris. There's a customer in room 8. Why would I sooner be on the West Bank where my parents are playing bridge with Mr. and Mrs. Eliot Pinkham in the golden light of a great gas chandelier?

I'll blame it on the roast, the roast, the Sunday roast bought from a butcher who wore a straw boater with a pheasant wing in the hat band. I suppose the roast entered our house, wrapped in bloody paper, on Thursday or Friday, traveling on the back of a bicycle. It would be a gross exaggeration to say that the meat had the detonative force of a land mine that could savage your eyes and your genitals but its powers were disproportionate. We sat down to dinner after church. (My brother was living in Omaha so we were only three.) My father would hone the carving knife and make a cut in the meat. My father was very adroit with an ax and a crosscut saw and could bring down a large tree with dispatch, but the Sunday roast was something else. After he had made the first cut my mother would sigh. This was an extraordinary performance, so loud, so profound, that it seemed as if her life were in danger. It seemed as if her very soul might come unhinged and drift out of her open mouth. "Will you never learn, Leander, that lamb must be carved against the grain?" she would ask. Once the battle of the roast had begun the exchanges were so swift, predictable, and tedious that there would be no point in reporting them. After five or six wounding remarks my father would wave the carving knife in the air and shout, "Will you kindly mind your own business, will you kindly shut up?" She would sigh once more and put her hand to her heart. Surely this was her last breath. Then, studying the air above the table, she would say, "Feel that refreshing breeze."

There was, of course, seldom a breeze. It could be airless, midwinter, rainy, anything. The remark was one for all seasons. Was it a commendable metaphor for hope, for the serenity of love (which I think she had never experienced), was it nostalgia for some summer evening when, loving and understanding, we sat contentedly on the lawn above the river? Was it no better or no worse than the sort of smile thrown at the evening star by a man who is in utter despair? Was it a prophecy of that generation to come who would be so drilled in evasiveness that they would be denied forever the splendors of a passionate confrontation?

The scene changes to Rome. It is spring, when the canny swallows flock into the city to avoid the wing shots in Ostia. The noise the birds make seems like light as the light of day loses its brilliance. Then one hears, across the courtyard, the voice of an American woman. She is screaming. "You're a God-damned fucked-up no-good insane piece of shit. You can't make a nickel, you don't have a friend in the world, and in bed you stink. . . ." There is no reply, and one wonders if she is railing at the dark. Then you hear a man cough. That's all you will hear from him. "Oh, I know I've lived with you for eight years, but if you ever thought I liked it, any of it, it's only because you're such a chump you wouldn't know the real thing if you had it. When I really come the pictures *fall* off the walls. With you it's always an act. . . ." The high-low bells that ring in Rome at that time of day have begun to chime. I smile at this sound although it has no bearing on my life, my faith, no true harmony, nothing like the revelations in the voice across the court. Why would I sooner describe church bells and flocks of swallows? Is this puerile, a sort of greeting-card mentality, a whimsical and effeminate refusal to look at facts? On and on she goes but I will follow her no longer. She attacks his hair, his brain, and his spirit while I observe that a light rain has begun to fall and that the effect of this is to louden the noise of traffic on the Corso. Now she is hysterical—her voice is breaking—and I think perhaps that at the height of her malediction she will begin to cry and ask his forgiveness. She will not, of course. She will go after him with a carving knife and he will end up in the emergency ward of the Policlinico, claiming to have wounded himself, but as I go out for dinner, smiling at beggars, fountains, children, and the first stars of evening, I assure myself that everything will work out for the best. Feel that refreshing breeze.

My recollections of the Cabots are only a footnote to my principal work and I go to work early these winter mornings. It is still dark. Here and there, standing on street corners, waiting for buses, are women dressed in white. They wear white shoes, white stockings, and white uniforms can be seen below their winter coats. Are they nurses, beauty-parlor operators, dentist's helpers? I'll never know. They usually carry a brown paper bag holding, I guess, a ham on rye and a thermos of buttermilk. Traffic is light at this time of day. A laundry truck delivers uniforms to the Fried Chicken Shack and in Asburn Place there is a milk truck—the last of that generation. It will be half an hour before the yellow school buses start their rounds.

I work in an apartment house called the Prestwick. It is seven stories high and dates, I guess, from the late twenties. It is of a Tudor persuasion. The bricks are irregular, there is a parapet on the roof, and the sign advertising vacancies is literally a shingle that hangs from iron chains and creaks romantically in the wind. On the right of the door there is a list of perhaps twenty-five doctors' names, but these are not gentle healers with stethoscopes and rubber hammers, these are psychiatrists, and this is the country of the plastic chair and the full ashtray. I don't know why they should have chosen this place, but they outnumber the other tenants. Now and then you see, waiting for the elevator, a woman with a grocery wagon and a child, but you mostly see the sometimes harried faces of men and women with trouble. They sometimes smile; they sometimes talk to themselves. Business seems slow these days, and the doctor whose office is next to mine often stands in the hallway, staring out of the window. What does a psychiatrist think? Does he wonder what has become of those patients who gave up, who refused Group Therapy, who disregarded his warnings and admonitions? He will know their secrets. I tried to murder my husband. I tried to murder my wife. Three years ago I took an overdose of sleeping pills. The year before that I cut my wrists. My mother wanted me to be a girl. My mother wanted me to be a boy. My mother wanted me to be a homosexual. Where had they gone, what were they doing? Were they still married, quarreling at the dinner table, decorating the Christmas tree? Had they divorced, remarried, jumped off bridges, taken Seconal, struck some kind of truce, turned homosexual, or moved to a farm in Vermont where they planned to raise strawberries and lead a simple life? The doctor sometimes stands by the window for an hour.

My real work these days is to write an edition of *The New York Times* that will bring gladness to the hearts of men. How better could I occupy myself? The *Times* is a critical if rusty link in my ties to reality, but in these last years its tidings have been monotonous. The prophets of doom are out of work. All one can do is to pick up the pieces. The lead story is this: PRESIDENT'S HEART TRANSPLANT DEEMED SUCCESSFUL. There is this box on the lower left: COST OF J. EDGAR HOOVER MEMORIAL CHALLENGED. "The subcommittee on memorials threatened to halve the seven million dollars appropriated to commemorate the late J. Edgar Hoover with a Temple of Justice. . . ." Column three: CONTROVERSIAL LEGISLATION REPEALED BY SENATE. "The recently enacted bill, making it a felony to have wicked thoughts about the administration, was repealed this afternoon by a standup vote of forty-three to seven." On and on it goes. There are robust and heartening editorials, thrilling sports news, and the weather of course is always sunny and warm unless we need rain. Then we have rain. The air-pollutant gradient is zero, and even in Tokyo fewer and fewer people are wearing surgical masks. All highways, throughways, and expressways will be closed for the holiday weekend. Joy to the World!

BUT TO GET BACK to the Cabots. The scene that I would like to overlook or forget took place the night after Geneva had stolen the diamonds. It involves plumbing. Most of the houses in the village had relatively little plumbing. There was usually a water closet in the basement for the cook and the ash man and a single bathroom on the second floor for the rest of the household. Some of these rooms were quite large, and the Endicotts had a fireplace in their bathroom. Somewhere along the line Mrs. Cabot decided that the bathroom was her demesne. She had a locksmith come and secure the door. Mr. Cabot was allowed to take his sponge bath every morning, but after this the bathroom door was locked and Mrs. Cabot kept the key in her pocket. Mr. Cabot was obliged to use a chamber pot, but since he came from the South Shore I don't suppose this was much of a hardship. It may even have been nostalgic. He was using the chamber pot late that night when Mrs. Cabot came to the door of his room. (They slept in separate rooms.) "Will you close the door?" she screamed. "Will you close the door? Do I have to listen to that horrible noise for the rest of my life?" They would both be in nightgowns, her snow-white hair in braids. She picked up the chamber pot and threw its contents at him. He kicked down the door of the locked bathroom, washed, dressed, packed a bag, and walked over the bridge to Mrs. Wallace's place on the East Bank.

He stayed there for three days and then returned. He was worried about Molly, and in such a small place there were appearances to be considered—Mrs. Wallace's as well as his own. He divided his time between the East and the West banks of the river until a week or so later, when he was taken ill. He felt languid. He stayed in bed until noon. When he dressed and went to his office he returned after an hour or so. The doctor examined him and found nothing wrong.

One evening Mrs. Wallace saw Mrs. Cabot coming out of the drugstore on the East Bank. She watched her rival cross the bridge and then went into the drugstore and asked the clerk if Mrs. Cabot was a regular customer. "I've been wondering about that myself," the clerk said. "Of course she comes over here to collect her rents, but I always thought she used the other drugstore. She comes in here to buy ant poison—arsenic, that is. She says they have these terrible ants in the house on Shore Road and arsenic is the only way of getting rid of them. From the way she buys arsenic the ants must be terrible." Mrs. Wallace might have warned Mr. Cabot but she never saw him again.

She went after the funeral to Judge Simmons and said that she wanted to charge Mrs. Cabot with murder. The drug clerk would have a record of her purchases of arsenic that would be incriminating. "He may have them," the judge said, "but he won't give them to you. What you are asking for is an exhumation of the body and a long trial in Barnstable, and you have neither the money nor the reputation to support this. You were his friend, I know, for sixteen years. He was a splendid man and why don't you console yourself with the thought of how many years it was that you knew him? And another thing. He's left you and Wallace a substantial legacy. If Mrs. Cabot were provoked to contest the will you could lose this."

I WENT OUT to Luxor to see Geneva. I flew to London in a 747. There were only three passengers; but as I say the prophets of doom are out of work. I went from Cairo up the Nile in a low-flying two-motor prop. The sameness of wind erosion and water erosion makes the Sahara there seem to have been gutted by floods, rivers, courses, streams, and brooks, the thrust of a natural search. The scorings are watery and arboreal, and as a false stream bed spreads out it takes the shape of a tree, striving for light. It was freezing in Cairo when we left before dawn. Luxor, where Geneva met me at the airport, was hot.

I was very happy to see her, so happy I was unobservant, but I did notice that she had gotten fat. I don't mean that she was heavy; I mean that she weighed about three hundred pounds. She was a fat woman. Her hair, once a coarse yellow, was now golden but her Massachusetts accent was as strong as ever. It sounded like music to me on the Upper Nile. Her husband—now a colonel—was a slender, middle-aged man, a relative of the last king. He owned a restaurant at the edge of the city and they lived in a pleasant apartment over the dining room. The colonel was humorous, intelligent—a rake, I guess—and a heavy drinker. When we went to the temple at Karnak our dragoman carried ice, tonic, and gin. I spent a week with them, mostly in temples and graves. We spent the evenings in his bar. War was threatening—the air was full of Russian planes—and the only other tourist was an Englishman who sat at the bar, reading his passport. On the last day I swam in the Nile—overhand—and they drove me to the airport, where I kissed Geneva—and the Cabots—goodbye.